Shadow Over Shandahar
Child of Prophecy

T.R. CHOWDHURY
& T.M. CRIM

SHADOW OVER SHANDAHAR
Child of Prophecy

A NOVEL

2005

Shadow Over Shandahar
Child of Prophecy

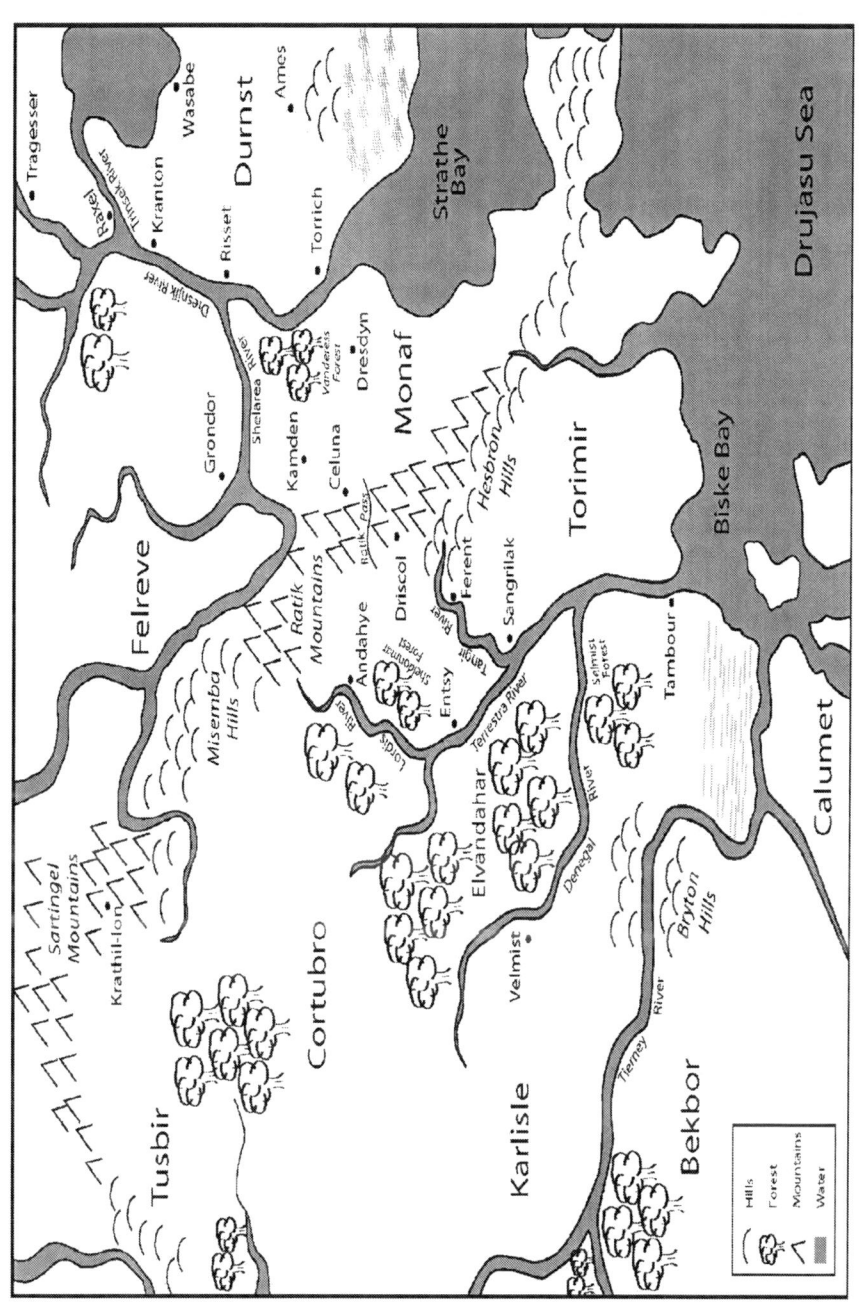

Child of prophecy; Warrior of Destiny
Into the world a child will come
Born into darkness, she will bring light
Where once there was none
To her cause people will rally
And they will fight the Good Fight
For the birth of a new era
And she will wield great power
That can be harnessed only by the One
Man who has sworn his soul to her
But the undead master will rise
And into abominable life bring an army
Such as the world has never seen
And that may only be stopped by the magic
Of the Warrior and the sworn Protector

* Excerpt from the Chardelis Prophecies

PROLOGUE

7 Enaren CY570

H e slowly walked towards the small house. It was dark and candlelight shone through the windows of every room, but he instinctively knew to which window he needed to go. He walked around to the side of the house, and up to the window through which he wanted to look. The Historian took in the scene before him, and he prepared himself to document the events about to unfold.

Upon the bed situated on the left side of the room lay a woman. She writhed as though in great pain, her distended abdomen rippling with the muscle spasms associated with immenent birth. Sweat beaded her brow, and another woman who was seated next to the bed placed a cloth there. As though he was inside the room, the Historian began to hear the sounds within. He heard the labored breathing of the woman on the bed, as well as her agonized moans. The woman sitting beside her whispered words of comfort and continued to pat her brow.

At the far side of the room opposite the window a door opened. Yet another woman entered the chamber. In her arms were a stack of clean cloths, and she deposited them near the washstand on the right side of the room before making her way back to the bed. She positioned herself at the foot of the bed, and then leaned over the laboring woman upon it. The woman cried out as the midwife examined her. The midwife shook her head as she righted herself once more, an expression of concern on her face. "The child has not made progress. I fear the worst for it."

The woman sitting next to the bed regarded the midwife for a moment. "I fear more for my sister. I don't know how much longer Gemma will be able to endure this. Please, is there nothing that you can do?"

Sadly, the midwife shook her head. "No. I have tried everything, but the child will not come. I am afraid that it has died by now."

The woman looked back down at her sister as Gemma moaned once more. Sharra could tell that she was weak, and becoming more so by the moment. The contractions leached every erg of energy from Gemma, and she still bled from the birth of the first child. The poor infant lay untended in the basket on the far side of the room. Sharra felt the instinctive urge to go to the baby and hold her in her arms, but she dared not disturb the sleeping infant. A tear fell down her cheek and onto the pale hand held within hers. Gemma had been so happy when she first knew that her babies were coming. But so many hours had passed since then, and only one had been born.

Suddenly there was a knock on the door. The midwife walked over and opened it. At the entrance stood Thane. Behind him stood a young boy no older than seven or eight years of age. "How is she? How is my wife?"

Sharra regarded the man from her place beside the bed. His face was pale, and dark shadows rested beneath his eyes. His expression was haunted, his fear for Gemma manifest. Even though nothing had been said to him, he knew that something was wrong. His son's birth had been an easy one compared to this, and he saw the lines of strain upon the face of the distraught midwife.

From behind Thane approached another woman. Mairi glanced inside the chamber only a moment before turning to the boy. "Come Gareth. I have something for you. I prepared your favorite meal . . ." Mairi took the boy's hand, leading him away from the doorway, and the possibility of hearing his mother's desperate cries.

"My Lord, your wife still labors to bring forth your second child. It is proving to be rather difficult, but these things take time," replied the midwife.

Thane nodded and then began to turn away from the doorway. At that moment, there was a tiny cry from the infant lying in the basket across the room. Thane turned around, and Sharra was able to see the pain written upon his usually stoic countenance. She saw him swallow convulsively, struggling to keep his emotions in check. She saw the fear reflected in his light brown eyes and her heart went out to him. She had never seen a man who loved his wife more than Thane.

"Mairi, could you please come to care for the baby? She needs you." Sharra could hear his voice crack as he turned from the doorway once more. Within moments Mairi was there, and was passing him to enter the room. The midwife shut the door behind her and Sharra could hear his footfalls as he moved away from the door.

The hours crept by. It wasn't until the last moon had risen before Gemma's second daughter finally began to make her way into the world. With all of the energy that Gemma had left in her tortured body, she pushed the child out in a huge gush of blood. The midwife quickly scooped the baby up from the sodden bed-linens, cutting the umbilical cord, and rubbing the tiny body with a rough towel. The child was blue, and hung limply from the midwife's hands. The midwife slapped the infant's feet, first once, and then again. Suddenly there was a cry, the tiniest cry that Sharra had ever heard, emerging from the baby.

The midwife turned to Sharra, smiling. "She lives! The child lives!"

Sharra looked down at her sister and grinned. Gemma, your daughters are beautiful."

Gemma slowly opened her eyes and looked at Sharra. "I knew they would be. Please, let me hold my youngest daughter."

The midwife laid the baby within her mother's arms, and then beagn to tend to Gemma. The blood continued to flow heavily and unchecked, staining the linens and the towels that the midwife brought to the bed. Gemma held the baby close to her, murmuring soft and tender words, while the midwife and Mairi desperately worked to stop the bleeding. As the moments continued to pass by, Gemma became weaker and paler. Sharra took the baby while the midwife pressed upon Gemma's abdomen, trying to get the muscles to contract and stop the bleeding.

But nothing worked. As Gemma began to fade, Sharra rushed to the door, opened it, and called for Thane. Gemma was dying, and he deserved every chance to tell her goodbye. Within moments Thane was at Germma's side, holding her hand within his. He brought his face close to hers, and his tears fell onto her pale cheeks. "Please, Gemma. Don't leave me. I need you so much . . ."

But it was too late. Gemma took her last breath and the room was suddenly silent. Thane laid his head upon Gemma's chest, his tears wetting the white nightgown she wore. Sharra stood against the far wall, next the two baskets holding the tiny babies. She looked down at them and felt a pang of sorrow. They would never know their mother. They would never feel her gentle kiss, her soft voice, or her strong embrace. They would never know how wonderful she had been, and that she loved them very much.

Suddenly Sharra caught movement at the doorway. It was her young nephew, Gareth. With wide eyes he looked into the room, saw his mother on the bed, the blood soaked into the linens all around her legs. "Father?"

The small voice was hesitant, fearful. Thane did not move from his position next to Gemma. Mairi went to to boy, wrapping him within a maternal embrace. "Come Gareth. Your father needs to spend some time with you mother for a while . . ." Mairi led Gareth from the doorway and down the hall.

The Historian stepped away from the window. He was saddened by what he had seen, but it was like that many times when he had to document an event. Of course, he enjoyed the happier events the most, those where he got the chance to document some type of victory, the birth of an important person, or the coronation of a great king. Despite this being a birth, it was also the death of someone who had been greatly loved.

The Historian shook his head. Sometimes, he did not entirely understand the meaning of an assignment, did not realize the true import of an event until several years later. Something about this event was important, and would change the destiny of the world. This was the Fifth Cycle. The Historian had seen many events, many of them in duplicate or triplicate. However, he did not remember seeing this one. Perhaps this would be the one that made the difference, and would stop the curse that controlled the world.

The Historian walked in the darkness away from the house. Soon he would be teleported to his next assignment. He hoped that it would be happier than this one, as well as one that he had not seen before. The duplicates were the hardest to document, he having a preconceived notion of them already in his mind, thus making it more difficult to pick up any obscure differences. Suddenly, there was a small flash of light. When it disappeared, the Historian was gone.

CHAPTER 1

Adrianna awoke from a deep sleep. She stretched languorously as her mind emerged from the recesses of her dreams. Once again, she could not remember her dreams, only that they were about a man whose face she could never recall and a voice that was always familiar to her. Those dreams were always good ones, and she was happy when she had them because they would give her reprieve from her other dreams, those borne upon hooves of flame and manes of darkness . . . Nightmares . . . Nyxlarian. Slowly, Adrianna sat up in her bed, rubbing the sleep from her eyes. She rose and placed her feet within the slippers next to her bed. She then went to the washbasin where she splashed the cold water upon her face and neck. She ran a comb through her pale tresses, pausing only at the snarls, and then rapidly plaited the unruly mass into a braid that she coiled upon the crown of her head. Adrianna donned tunic and trousers. The tunic was simple, embroidered only at the sleeves and hem. It reached down to her knees. The trousers were loose about her thighs and tightened only about her ankles and lower legs. Adrianna wrapped a silken cord about her torso and waist, upon which she hung her pouches of spell components and other such things. She then put a white gold belt about her hips, its adornments tinkling softly.

Adrianna swiftly snatched her cloak from the bedpost on her way to the door. Upon opening it, a piece of folded parchment caught her attention as it glided to the floor. She stooped to pick up the note and unfolded it as she straightened herself. It was from the Master.

Adrianna,

Early this morn, I found that I have pressing business of utmost importance. I will not be home until dusk. Take this day for yourself; you have worked hard for it. Do not wait for me.

Master Tallek

Adrianna frowned slightly as she read her master's fine, precise handwriting. This was quite out of the ordinary. He had never left so suddenly like this before. However, Master Tallek had recently mentioned to her that her apprenticeship with him was nearly over and that she was free to leave him in the near future. Was this what Tallek's message implied? Did he intend for her to leave and never come back? She quickly went back into her room to slip on her soft leather boots and then made her way to the spiraling staircase. Within moments she had descended the tower and was striding through the house proper. She went first to the master's rooms. She knocked on the door, and when there was no answer, she cracked open the door and peeked inside. He was not there. However, it was obvious to her that he had left in haste. Many parchments were strewn about the desk, and his cabinets were in disarray. In a quick look throughout the rest of his chambers and the house she found no trace of her master, but Tallek's spellbook continued to rest upon its customary pedestal in the laboratory, ensconced within a magical envelope. His traveling spellbook was gone. Once more Adrianna frowned. It was unlike Master Tallek to up and leave so suddenly. She wondered what type of business it was and if he was safe. A tingle shot up her spine and her flesh broke out into goosepimples. She had a bad feeling.

Adrianna wandered into the kitchens. As usual, Cook had left her breakfast on the countertop . . . cooked grains with sweetened goats'milk, toast, and jam. She took the tray to the dining table and ate. She felt strange eating alone, especially when she was so accustomed to breaking her fast with Master Tallek every morning. Once again Adrianna felt a disturbance in the pit of her stomach . . . something just wasn't quite right.

Suddenly there was a ring at the front door. Adrianna jumped involuntarily, and with a hand upon her chest to quiet her rapidly beating heart, she padded over to the front of the house. Upon opening the door, she found a small, skinny brown boy upon her steps. He handed her a message. She took the parchment from the boy's hand and upon unfolding it saw that it was from the Temple of Corellian. With trepidation, she read the words written upon the yellowed page.

Mistress,

We regret to inform you that we have in our possession the remains of what appears to be one Magician Master Tallek Alestrande. We ask that you come to verify our opinion upon this matter as promptly as possible. Upon your arrival we will also discuss with you your legal rights and privileges. We are deeply sorry about your loss, but your action at this time is greatly needed. Thank you.

Father Rankin

In a state of shock and disbelief, she looked up from the message. Startled, she saw the small boy still standing before her. Numbly, she dug into her coin pouch and pulled out all that lay within. She dropped the coins into the boy's outstretched hand and turned in the doorway. The boy gave her a look of disgust as he hopped down the steps. "Cheap . . ." he mumbled aloud as he ran off. He kicked up the gravel in the street as he left, reminding himself never to deliver to this house again, no matter what the priests at the temple said about getting money for work well done. Adrianna softly closed the door behind her, clenching the message in nerveless fingers. She then turned and pressed her back into the door, arms at her sides, and slid downward until her behind reached the floor. How long she sat there she did not know, but it wasn't until the sun was high in the sky that she stirred herself once more.

Adrianna donned her fur-lined cloak, collected her spellbook and a few other belongings and left the house, which was now hers by law, since she was the only current apprentice of the deceased owner. For some reason that she could not begin to explain, she did not doubt that the priests at the temple were correct about the identity of the body they had obtained. She wished it could be otherwise, prayed that it could be, but in her heart she knew that Master Tallek was gone.

Adrianna slowly walked the city streets, taking no interest in the activity to be found there. It was cold, and she numbly wrapped her dark maroon cloak tightly about her. Mindlessly she walked up to the Temple of Corellian. Unlike many of the temples dedicated to other deities, this temple was very utilitarian in its design. Corellian's followers wore simple garments, and the décor of the place was unembellished.

Once inside the temple, the priests led her down a series of hallways and doors that she would not remember passing through later. Finally they brought her into a room that smelled of medicines and preservatives. Beneath these odors, her faelin nose picked up the scent of death, and her throat constricted. She had to force the passage open in order to breathe, but her breath came in ragged gasps thereafter. If the priests heard, they gave no sign. She felt a hand upon her arm, a gentle hand, but she did not realize it until she had recoiled and the hand was gone. She turned her head to see a priest standing beside her, compassion in his brown eyes. She turned once more to look in front of her. It was then that she saw it, the table upon which a body lay beneath a white fabric cover. Slowly she went over to the table, every step as though she bore weights upon the soles of her boots. Beneath the blanket she found the mutilated body of her master. Thankfully, his eyes were closed. Had she seen his blue eyes open as they had been in life, she may have fallen to the floor right there on the spot. But just to see him at all was almost enough to drop her anyway.

The look upon her face must have told the priests what they had already known. They returned the covering to rest upon the body of Master Tallek and handed her a box containing what remained of his belongings. She took nothing from the box; all of the articles within were now useless. It appeared as though they had been scorched by wizard fire. Adrianna gently inquired about the proper burial of the body of her master. The clerics did not ask for money for their labor, but she gave them all that she had: twenty gold coins. It was the least she could do for a man whose home now belonged to her, a man that had accepted her when many others had not, and one that had given her the ability to make her own way in the world.

After leaving the temple, Adrianna wandered the streets of Andahye. She wandered aimlessly, without direction or intention. She passed the school and wondered if anyone else knew about Tallek's death. They probably did not, it being her duty to spread the unpleasant news. Not even Tallek's journeyman, Tannin, would know. Adrianna shook her head numbly. She had no desire to seek out the man. He had disliked her right from the start, and would probably think of some way to make her life more difficult now that the master was gone. But Adrianna knew her rights, and she would abide by them, as Tallek would want her to do.

Adrianna returned to her house. She walked through the dark halls, searching. She knew not what she sought, only that she wished that Master Tallek were sitting within his laboratory, at the dinner table, or in his reading room, waiting for her to join him in whatever activity they had chosen to undertake. Upon entering the laboratory, she saw the previous day's lesson resting upon the table. She crossed the room and was about to pick up the series of parchments when she stopped herself.

She remembered Master Tallek laying the lesson parchments down upon the table the evening before, a smile set upon his mouth, laughter in his eyes as she had finished telling him a most ridiculous answer to a question she had learned long ago. He had dismissed her from her studies then, as she always gave him answers such as those when she was tired of her studies, fatigued from the rigors of the day, or just simply lazy. He had always catered to her desires, and had not pushed her with such things because he knew that she did not abuse his generosity. She had left him then, remembering the tender smile set upon his features as she took the winding staircase to her room. It was the last time she saw him . . .

Adrianna came to, just to see her hand poised above the lesson parchments. She slowly drew her hand away. She would leave them where her master had left them. She did not want to disturb his touch . . . Adrianna crumpled to her knees upon the stone floor, her hands to her face, as the sobs came. She cried there within the laboratory, her mind running through all of the years she and the master had spent there. He was all around her . . . his spirit floating through the halls, down the stairs. And then Adrianna remembered seeing him beneath the covering at the temple: his throat ripped out, deep lacerations in his chest, much of his flesh burned from his bones. It was as if he had been mauled by a great creature with claws larger than her torso, and then burned as though to hide what had been done. She shook her head, trying to rid herself of the memory. He was all she had within this city, and now he was gone. She felt so alone, confused and afraid. What would she do with herself? What was this gift that Master Tallek had given her? This magic? She could feel the energies about her respond to her desires already, and she had not even begun to concentrate upon them. He had said she had a Talent, a gift from the gods, and that what he gave her was simply the knowledge about how use what had already been bestowed. And she had cared about him. She had cared about that man who had taught her these things, despite what had happened in her past. She would later find that she had loved him, even though she had promised herself she would never care about a man so much, and that he had been to her what no man had ever been before . . . the vision of what a man should be.

Many hours later, Adrianna stumbled from the laboratory and to her bedchamber. She slept a fitful sleep, a sleep that was not quite sleep but that place between reality and dreams. She rose in the morning, unrefreshed. But she knew what she must do. She must take what Master Tallek had given her and leave the city of Andahye. He had given her the means with which to survive, and she would use that as she had always been meant to. She would go to a place she had not seen for many years.

Adrianna mechanically went about her morning ritual and then focused her attention upon gathering all that she would need to take with her upon her journey. She would have space in her pack for only two changes of clothing. The rest of the space she needed for her spell book, the ingredients for many of her spell components, and a healing kit containing common medicinal herbs, bandages and salves. Then Adrianna sat down behind her desk and composed the message she would send to the Vanderlinde Academy. She would at least conduct this formality on behalf of Master Tallek. She would not bother attempting to contact Tannin. He was a massive thorn in her side and she did not wish to aggravate the wound.

On her way out of the chamber, Adrianna turned to take a look around. She saw her oak staff against the wall near her bed. She considered not taking it with her. She was not good with it, quite clumsy to be truthful. But she knew that she could not just leave it there. It had been a gift from Master Tallek. She walked across the room and took the smooth wood into her hands. She remembered the day he had presented it to her, looking intently at her as she accepted it from him, his eyes giving away the hope that it would please her. And it had. His gifts were always pleasing to her.

Once prepared, she walked through the corridors of her home one last time. She looked all about her, setting the place into her memory forever; she knew not when she would return and she would miss it. She took in the beautifully patterned rugs set upon a polished stone floor, lush tapestries upon the walls, chandeliers from the ceilings, carved wooden furnishings. She went to the little desk in the front hall and removed from it the deed to the house. She would take it with her. She had not a copper to her name, but she always had a home to which she may return. At the doorway, she turned around one last time. Then she closed the door and shut away the past. She turned the key in the lock, making sure the past was safe within. Adrianna then walked down the street towards the city proper. She would find a means with which to travel, and go to the city of Sangrilak. She would go home.

***

Once out of the city, the shroud that had sheltered her fell away. Perhaps her master had placed it there, to save her from the cruelty of her dreams, to give her the reprieve that she needed from them in order to succeed. But spells only last for so long, and for only so far, if it had indeed been a spell at all. And so it slipped away from her as she slumbered in the wagon, laying bare her mind once more. The dreams came back to her ten-fold . . .

Adrianna sat bolt upright, the shout at the tip of her tongue. Her tunic was plastered to her sweat-soaked body and she could smell her fear. She pulled her legs up to her chest and began to rock back and forth, her face on her knees. She had forgotten how vivid they could be, as though she was there again, reliving her childhood. It had all come rushing back to her so fast, cutting her like a knife. They came to her in chronological order, starting from when she could first remember the pain of her father's hatred.

She remembered it all so well, like it had been just yesterday that she had experienced it. He had been unable to stand the sight of her, the creature who had killed his beloved Gemma. And in a way, she had. Adrianna's birth had ended her mother's life. The labor had been so difficult; it was as though Gemma had given her own life so that her daughter could live. The pain had been more than he could bear, and so he had cast his infant daughter from him, while keeping the first-born twin at his side. So thus had been created a sister of light and one of dark. While Sheridana was all sunshine and happiness, garrulous, and inquisitive, Adrianna was dull and lackluster, shy, and withdrawn.

Mairi, she who had been Gemma's good friend, had raised the girls. Mairi had loved her and Sheri deeply, and had given them all that they could ever want. But Mairi could not give Adrianna what she truly needed, which was acceptance from her father. While Sheri spent the days after school with him,

Adrianna came home to Mairi. It was not such a bad thing in and of itself. But Mairi's husband, Hafgan, embittered by the fact that he had been unable to sire any living children with his wife, was a harsh man with which to live. Luckily for Adrianna, Mairi withstood the brunt of his ire, constantly reminding both herself and Adrianna that he had once been a good man, before an accident had taken one of his legs. So Hafgan did not hit Adrianna often, although she knew he wanted, needed, to take his anger out on someone. Although, the mental abuse was much worse . . .

Adrianna breathed deeply, calming herself. Why was it that she was returning to Sangrilak? What could that place possibly hold for her? All that she could remember was heartsickness, and an all-encompassing loss. But then she remembered Sheridana, remembered the reason why she wished to return to the city of her birth. In her early childhood, her sister had been her only ray of sunshine. Despite the extenuating circumstances, they had been everything to one another, forging a bond that could never be broken, even after eight years.

15 Jicaren CY593

Sirion sauntered slowly into the city of Sangrilak. Travel-weary and tired, he made his way towards the Inn of the Hapless Cenloryan, Dramati bumping against his side as he walked. Irritably, Sirion brushed a lock of copper brown hair out of his eyes and then buried his fingers into the thick ruff about the corubis' neck. It was almost evening. Anyanka would catch up with him in a few moments and the rest of the group would follow about an hour behind her. He turned up his nose in distaste. His hair was greasy and he was sure that he stank of his travels, he who rarely bathed while on the run. His grooming habits had made a precipitous drop in recent years, as he was not feeling the desire or the need, to make himself presentable in any way. Yet, upon entering the world of civilization, he realized how he must seem to the people he passed: a dirty bum from the wilds.

Their travels had been difficult. After being accused of committing a crime they did not perpetrate, the Wildrunners had gone after those who had, seeking to clear their good name. However, the Wildrunners had done just what the others had known they would do. After the ambush, all they could do was seek shelter and tend to their wounds. Everyone was downtrodden and dispirited, but at least the others had not gotten away unscathed. Sorn had nearly killed his double before the rest of the other group had been able to intervene and take him from harm's way.

And that was what the other group was made up of . . . their duplicates.

There was one for every member of the Wildrunners except for Breesa and Dinim, who had joined the group after the doubles had been created. And that had been Gaknar's doing. When the Wildrunners had stepped through that mirror in the temple in Nampoor, the group had been re-created. Before them had stood their counterparts, evil in every way that they themselves were good.

Sirion sighed heavily. That was one advantage that Gaknar had over the group. He could not have created a better weapon against them than their own selves. For the men and women that had been created not only looked like the Wildrunners, but they possessed all of the physical and mental attributes of them as well. The ambush had been the second skirmish they had had since their creation. Sirion knew when next they met, that only one group or the other would prevail.

Sirion looked up. He found himself standing before the Inn of the Hapless Cenloryan. It would be good to rest within this safe haven. The gods knew that he needed a break. He began to walk up the steps that led to the veranda. In Hinterlic, he uttered a command to Dramati, and pointed behind the establishment. Without complaint, the large canine went to his place in the back of the inn, where Volstagg would be sure to give him the scraps from the meals that were being prepared that day. Sirion opened the door that led into the building.

***

Adrianna slowly walked through the city gates. Her journey had been a featureless one, much different from the journey that had brought her to Andahye in the first place. But she struck that thought from her mind as she looked all about her. Many things were as she remembered, but many more things were not. The city of Sangrilak had definitely grown. She continued to look around as she walked. Before she knew it, she was at the entrance to the Inn of the Hapless Cenloryan. She smiled to herself. It would be good to see her old friend Volstagg again. Adrianna pushed open the doors to the Inn and stepped through the opening. The place was much as she remembered it. Some things never changed. She smiled once more. She was glad of that. She made her way up to the bar, past tables seating all kinds of people, humans, faelin, and halfen alike. She even saw a few individuals who could have been like herself . . . half-faelin. Sangrilak was one of the few places that allowed such diversity. She was glad that this fact at least had not changed. As she made her way through, some people cast a few glances her way. She was one who did not quite fit the ordinary and was deserving of such glances, but she paid them no notice. Adrianna had all of her attention focused upon the bar. Upon reaching it, she seated herself there, waiting for her friend to take notice of her after . .

. eight years! Momentarily, her eyes grew wide. It had been quite some time since she had been home. She hadn't bothered to send but perhaps a handful of letters, and those to Mairi, just to let the woman know that she still lived. Mairi would definitely be surprised to see her as well. Adrianna could hardly wait to see the woman who had raised her.

Volstagg emerged from the kitchens. He was an interesting creature, the only one of his kind Adrianna had ever seen. He had the head, torso and arms of a human man, and the rest of him was the form of a large lloryk. He carried a large pitcher of ale in one hand and a platter of steaming stew in another. He handed the food and drink off to a serving girl and then began to head in Adrianna's direction, his massive cloven hooves thudding against the stone floor as he moved over it. It was then that he saw her. Volstagg stopped. He stared at her for a few moments, knowing it was she, but not knowing . . . And then he was rushing towards her, and she was standing up from her seat. Just as she had done as a child, she climbed over the counter-top to the other side. Then the cenloryan was upon her. He picked her up, the muscles in his forearms flexing as he held her above his head. He smiled hugely and then brought her to him, holding her body close to him in a massive hug of the type that only Volstagg could give. She wrapped her arms about his neck, remembering that she had done so as a child. Finally he set her down.

Volstagg was breathless. "My dear Adrianna! How have you been all of these years? It is so good to set these old eyes upon a good friend after so long! Come. Break your fast. By the look of you, you have been traveling for quite a long while. Rest and I will bring you good food and drink."

Without allowing her to reply, Volstagg lifted her and set her upon her seat on the other side of the bar. He looked at her once more, as if to make sure she was really there, and then went back into the kitchens. After watching him trot through the swinging oak doors leading to the kitchens, she heard him roar to his staff to hurry the preparation of a plate of fresh vegetables, grains, and fruits for a special guest. A few moments later he emerged to bring her a tall glass of honeyed mead. He then leaned his elbows upon the counter and assessed her. She regarded him in return, smiling. He was the same as she had always remembered, with only a few exceptions. The aging process had not left him behind; his chestnut-colored hair and coat were peppered with gray, and the lines about his eyes were more pronounced. But his smile was the same. His body had lost none of its tone, and he had lifted her with ease over the counter. His gray eyes were just as bright and mischievous as they had always been, since that first day she had met him more than a score ago.

"So, my dear friend, what has been happening here since my departure eight years hence?" Unnerved by Volstagg's ponderous gaze, Adrianna felt compelled to ask what had been upon her mind since she had made the decision to come home.

"Ah, now that is quite a bit to tell, but I will try to make some short work of it." And he did. He told her of the expansion of the city and the rise of the merchant class at the expense of farmers, who were beginning to live only at the city outskirts. He told her of the influx of peoples from other cities, hoping to make their fortune in Sangrilak, and of the increase of traveling folk who made their way through on their way to other destinations. He also told her of the most recent set of appalling events: that the advisor to the Prince of Ristran had been murdered, and that a well-known party of individuals, the Wildrunners, had been pinned with the crime. They were currently within the city, working to clear their good name of the false accusation. However, he did not mention her sister.

Suddenly, a serving girl carrying a plate of food rushed up to Volstagg. He very quickly excused himself as he set the plate down in front of Adrianna, telling her he would return shortly. She watched him go back into the kitchens to mend whatever mishap had occurred in his absence, and then went deep into thought. She was dispirited that he had not mentioned her sister. It meant that Sheridana had probably not returned to Sangrilak. But despite the disappointment her mind was drawn to something else Volstagg had said. The Wildrunners! She had heard a lot about them during her childhood and years of study in Andahye. It was said that they traveled in the company of a half-orog and a faelin woman whose skill with the bow was unsurpassed. She took a few bites of her meal. The food was delicious.

Finally, Volstagg returned to her, moaning about the trials and tribulations of innkeeping. It was then that a very unappealing odor wafted through the air. Volstagg got a huge grin upon his face and he looked past Adrianna. Adrianna was about to turn about to see what had caught Volstagg's attention, when she saw a deeply tanned faelin man who stood just a little taller than herself approaching the bar. The thick, tangled mass of his brownish-red hair was long and tied back with a piece of leather. He was dirty and disheveled, and appeared to be very tired. It was obvious that he had traveled from afar, for it was to him that the stench clung. He seated himself to her left at the bar, speaking to Volstagg in Hinterlic, a language which she had learned long ago as the young girl who had wanted to know how to speak virtually every known faelinish language. As he spoke, she quickly turned to look at him, surprised. The Hinterlean rarely emerged from their forest kingdom. Volstagg responded to the faelin in the same tongue, smiling at him all the while. They were obviously friends.

Sirion sat stiffly in his seat. He couldn't believe that *she* was here. He had not seen her about the city in nearly a decade. At first he had not realized that she was gone. But when he did, it took him nearly a year to ask Volstagg about her, knowing that the two had been friends. He had tried to ask him as though in passing, as though her absence was just a little thing that he had noticed. But Volstagg knew better. He always knew better, knew Sirion better than he knew himself sometimes. Sirion had wondered about her for all of those years, even those before she had left Sangrilak. He had never met her, not really. They had just passed a few times in the street, and she had never noticed him. However, despite what he had shared with Joselyn, he had definitely noticed the woman they called Adrianna, saw how much people liked her, how much Volstagg had come to love her. And he had not been able to keep himself from being attracted to her ethereal beauty, her quiet strength, and the way she made the people around her happy.

But here she was, sitting next to him in Volstagg's inn. His superior sense of smell had not picked up her scent. He must be more tired than he thought, although her scent was muted and she did not use the same bath oils as she did all of those years ago. And that was not the only thing about her that had changed. Out of the corner of his eye, while he continued his conversation with Volstagg, he had seen that she was even more beautiful than she had been almost a decade ago. He also saw that she was watching him. Volstagg trotted away to get him a tankard of ale. Sirion slowly inhaled and turned to her. He caught her gaze and held it, noticing the widening of her dark brown eyes.

She looked more faelin than human with her slightly canted eyes, delicately pounted ears, high cheekbones, small nose, and small but full mouth. Her long hair cascaded down her back like a moonlight waterfall. An intricately crafted clasp swept the sides of the hair back from her face, the ends having a tendancy to spiral and curl. He raised an eyebrow as he speculated about her, wondered what she saw when she looked at him. He was more than just a few years her senior. Perhaps she saw a dirty old man who stank of the road, himself, and the dried blood of his double, whom he had fought about a week ago.

Suddenly affronted, Sirion took his eyes from her face and allowed his gaze to take in the rest of her. He had never viewed her quite this close before. Her maroon winter cloak spilled behind, and he saw that she wore a finely made tunic, vest, and trousers, the stitching at the shoulders, sleeves and hem of excellent quality. The clothes were not form fitting, but he could see the shape of her beneath them. Her breasts and hips were small, similar to those of most faelin women, but her human heritage gave her womanly curves just the slightest bit of roundness. Her face was also not as angular, and her ears not as long and pointed at the upper tips. Sirion began to notice the rise and fall of her chest; that her breathing had accelerated slightly. Anger rose within him, anger towards himself. He treated her badly; she was undeserving of his censure when it was he who chose not to make himself more presentable. He looked back up into her face, saw the slight flush to her cheeks, and abruptly turned away from her.

Before she could turn away, in fear that she was being rude, the faelin man had caught Adrianna's gaze. His amber eyes captured hers and she felt her heart skip a beat. He raised an eyebrow at her and allowed his gaze to slide over her for a few moments before returning to her face. Then he abruptly turned away. Adrianna also turned away, discomfited. Her body was tense and her mind whirled with confusion. Volstagg had left to get something for the Hinterlean, but had returned within a few moments. Adrianna watched the faelin out of the corner of her eye as he received his tankard of drink from Volstagg, handed the cenloryan a large sack, and left.

For a few moments, Adrianna sat there and said nothing. Volstagg placed the sack beneath the bar and busied himself wiping off the countertop near her. When he set it down, Adrianna heard the unmistakable tinkle of coins moving against one another. The bag obviously contained a lot of money. She then turned back to the cenloryan and asked, "Volstagg, who is that man? How do you know him so well?"

"Well now, my Lady, that is a story all in itself, and not easily told within a mere sentence or two, but he is Sirion Timberlyn, a member of the Wildrunners, the group of individuals I was telling you about earlier. I met him long ago, when he was but a boy trying to make a path for himself in the world. And what a road did he cut for himself!" Volstagg said the last with pride in his voice; his eyes alight with his happiness for the man Sirion. "There was a time when I wanted the two of you to meet, but that was when you had begun to study with old Nahum, and, well, you never came by as often, and Sirion was working a lot. At the time, he was a hired tracker." Volstagg looked up from his countertop and smiled at her. She smiled back at him, remembering the time he spoke about . . . and Nahum . . .. Once more, Volstagg was called away, and Adrianna pondered his words.

As she sat and continued to eat her meal, another faelin seated himself next to her. She saw that he was rather tall for a Terralean faelin, standing almost six feet. He had shoulder-length raven black hair, and canted startling green eyes, an unusual combination. Adrianna surmised that he must be a faelin half-blood, possibly a mixture of Terralean and Savanlean faelin lines. He wore dark tunic and trousers, as well as two long swords, one at each hip. He glanced momentarily at her before he spied Volstagg and gestured him over. The man asked the cenloryan about opportunities for employment in and about the city, anyone who was looking for a sword to hire. Volstagg thought upon it for a moment and then trotted over to the other end of the bar and spoke to a serving girl who then took herself to the table seating the faelin Adrianna now knew as Sirion. Within moments Volstagg returned and told the tall young faelin next to her that if he wanted some work, he needed to meet Sirion in the back of the tavern.

Volstagg abruptly turned to Adrianna. "You, too, should go to Sirion, my friend. He can tell you more about the goings-on around here than I can." Adrianna raised an eyebrow, and was about to ask Volstagg what Sirion would know that he did not, when she suddenly felt something hit her hard across her backside. She grunted, quickly turned on her barstool, and met the gaze of the faelin with black hair and green eyes.

"Sorry. They sometimes have a mind of their own." The man spoke to her in Common, his eyes sparkling as she glared up at him. He winked at her and indicated the swords at his hips. That he was flirting with her escaped her notice, but Volstagg was quick to realize the ploy and grinned as he shook his head and went back into the kitchens. Adrianna rose from her seat and began to step towards the back of the tavern where Sirion waited. Just maybe Volstagg was right, and he would be able to inform her about the state of the Kingdom.

CHAPTER 2

As Adrianna made her way to the back of the tavern, she noticed a human man join the tall faelin who walked in front of her. He stood very tall, even for a human, and was very muscular. His sandy brown hair was cropped short, and his blue eyes lazily took in all the activity around him. Adrianna assumed him to be Recondian. She took her gaze from him and focused it upon her destination. She saw three other individuals seated with Sirion at the table. The first to catch her attention was the woman. Her copper hair gleamed brightly in the torchlight. She was very beautiful, in her warrior's way, and it was then that Adrianna knew that this was the lady archer that she had heard so much about. The next to catch Adrianna's eye was the halfen. He was tall for a halfen, standing almost four and a half feet tall. He would have been quite ordinary, but for the fact that he wore his brown hair in a pattern of spikes upon the crown of his head. Next to the halfen was seated another faelin. He appeared to be of both Savanlean and Terralean descent. His light brown hair just brushed the top of his shoulders and his blue eyes were slightly canted. He wore simple tunic and trousers and over the back of his chair hung a longbow.

The three faelin and the halfen made room for them at the table. The others glanced at her speculatively as she seated herself. Adrianna ignored the hooded glances, quite accustomed to them by now. She did not know, or understand, why people regarded her so, but had come to accept it. She had learned to realize that there was something strange about her that people found fascinating, but as of yet, she had not discovered exactly what it was, and had been unable to ask anyone else about it. Perhaps it was that she was afraid to know the answer and thus ignored what, to everyone else, seemed so fascinating.

Sirion was more than a little surprised when he saw Adrianna walk over to his table. As his heartrate increased, he schooled his expression into one of nonchalance. What she could possibly want that would bring her to him he could not fathom. He glanced at her as she pulled up a chair, along with a large human man and a man that appeared to be of mixed faelin descent. Still incensed with himself over his earlier behavior, Sirion did not favor her with even a nod as everyone was seated. He noticed the hooded glances of appreciation from the other men at the table. He was glad that they were decent men, for if they had not been, he would have found himself forced to confront them. He was glad when all they did was look at her beautiful countenance for a few moments and then look away. But it was to be expected. Her beauty was rare and overpowering. If they had not noticed her, they would not have been men at all.

Adrianna quickly determined that the four men at the table, with, of course, the exception of Sirion, were looking for the same thing, employment. Introductions were made, and Sirion's lady companion was used as an interpreter, as Sirion could not speak Common. Adrianna learned that the woman was not only the well-known archer, but Sirion's sister as well, and went by the name of Anya. The tall faelin introduced himself as Armond and the big Recondian warrior with him as Zorg. The mixed race Terralean introduced himself as Dartanyen and the halfen as Bussimot. Anya turned to Sirion and told him all of the introductions as they were made.

Adrianna sensed Sirion's slight tension, despite his efforts to hide it. Thinking that the language barrier was the cause of his unease, she thought to bridge it. When the time came, Adrianna introduced herself first in Hinterlic and then in Common. "Greetings. I was born here, within the city of Sangrilak, but have been away for several years studying in the city of Andahye. Just today I have returned, and wish to learn of the goings-on here since my departure so many years ago."

Adrianna found herself being awarded with another arched eyebrow from Sirion. He ignored her efforts to put him at ease with the language barrier and went on, in Common no less, to say that there had been a recent upheaval in Sangrilak. Anya awarded her brother with a sidelong glance but said nothing as he spoke. "As you all probably know already, the advisor to Ristran, prince of Torimir has been murdered. Another thing you may possibly know is that my companions and I have been blamed for the crime. We are currently trying to absolve ourselves of any wrongdoing. We know the identity of the perpetrators of the crime, and it is just a matter of time before we catch up to them."

Sirion paused and turned to look at his sister. She had her head down, but then turned to him as well. The two passed a significant glance before Sirion turned back to them. "We may be able to use your help in this matter. Our enemy isn't so much the persons who committed the crime, but the individual for whom they committed it. The real enemy is a creature by the name of Gaknar."

Sirion lowered his voice as he mentioned the name. He knew that he was taking a chance by telling these people the Wildrunners' problem with Gaknar. He could be placing the Wildrunners and these young people at risk. For all he knew, one of these people was a spy for the enemy, although he much doubted it. Besides, he trusted the young woman Adrianna without even knowing her, only because Volstagg trusted her. Not only that, but he knew where she had been studying. Andahye. City of mystery and power, it was the seat of magic in all of the known realms. It was the place where the greatest of mages were trained and tested. And she had passed, for she was sitting here before him, alive. Whether she knew it or not, she would be a great asset to someone someday. If trouble came her way, he had no doubt that she would find some way to diffuse it.

Adrianna regarded Sirion pensively. She knew of the man about whom he spoke. Gaknar was one of the greatest magic-users that the world has ever seen. However, as his power increased, so did his greed. It was rumored that he was the head of a secret sect of daemon worshippers bent on ending the world as it was known. In recent years there had been little known of his whereabouts, and hearing Sirion speak his name was a surprise to her. In her circles, those of a magic-user, Gaknar continued to be a man of magnificent and awesome powers, whose influence has been succeeded by only a few.

Sirion continued. "My companions and I have been doing a little bit of research. When Gaknar became the leader of a secret sect decades ago, in order to remain hidden, he created a series of underground temples. It is thought that one of them may be near this city. We would ask that you research this possibility for us, and even try to find it if your research tells you what ours has told us. We cannot guarantee payment for this service, but if there is indeed a temple dedicated by Gaknar near this city, the kingdom will consider paying you handsomely for your efforts towards bringing about its downfall, which is simply discovering that it is there in the first place. We do not expect you to do anything more than to contact us when you have sound evidence of the location of the temple."

"And exactly how would we contact you?" asked Dartanyen.

"Leave a message with Volstagg. For the most part, he knows where we are and how to contact us."

Sirion and Anya rose from the table, the others following suit. Slowly, Adrianna also arose, pensive. She felt foolish and out of place. She should never have tried to meet Sirion on his terms. It had been silly of her to think that she could even begin to guess what was making Sirion so tense. Adrianna sighed. She knew little more than what she had already known before she met Sirion, and his divulgence about his groups' involvement with Gaknar only made her apprehensive. The Wildrunners had probably chosen the worst individual to be at odds with.

Adrianna followed slowly behind the others, her head lowered in thought. Upon noticing a commotion at the entrance to the establishment, Adrianna looked up to find that everyone had made their way out onto the veranda.

Through the open door she saw the most beautiful corubis she had ever seen. Upon arriving on the scene, it was soon apparent to her that the animal looked to Sirion. The animal was large, at least six feet tall at the shoulder. He was tawny in color, dappled with dark brown spots. His thickly furred tail arced over his back. The beast listened to Sirion as he spoke to him in Hinterlic, his large ears rotating at the sound of the man's voice. The creature had begun to investigate the other individuals in the group with his nose. The faelin were accustomed to animals such as these and were not alarmed, but the halfen and the human kept their distance. When Adrianna stepped out onto the veranda, the huge canine looked over and padded up to her. Adrianna was delighted, for she loved animals. She looked over to where Sirion stood, with his back leaning against one of the support columns. He was watching her intently, his face impassive.

Sirion slightly inclined his head to her, letting her know that it was safe to touch the corubis. Adrianna couldn't help but smile as she ran her fingers through the soft tawny fur. The creature leaned in to her touch and she could feel the warmth of his breath upon her neck. "His name is Dramati. He doesn't take to people very often, but he likes you." Adrianna looked up and was startled to find Sirion standing next to her. The corners of his mouth turned up slightly into a hesitant smile. Adrianna smiled back. It was such a drastic change from the man she had encountered only minutes before. He was almost handsome beneath the dirt on his face. Their eyes met and locked, and she was delving into a pool of molten amber. She felt a tingle rise up her spine and her heart began to beat faster.

Adrianna struggled to tear her eyes away from him. Nonplussed, she turned back to the animal that was rubbing his large head against her torso, hoping that she would take the hint and scratch behind his ears. Adrianna obliged him and then looked around the porch. She saw Dartanyen speaking to Anya on the top of the stairs. Armond and Zorg had taken two chairs and Bussi was busy lighting a pipe.

Adrianna's attention snapped back to herself when she felt Sirion's arm and hand brush hers. He rubbed the corubis' neck and back with both hands, and the beast began to lean his full weight upon them. Adrianna could feel the animal's muscles ripple beneath her palms. The animal made a noise deep in his throat, telling them that he derived pleasure from their ministrations. Despite her efforts to keep herself upright, however, Adrianna began to topple backwards with Dramati's weight against her. She felt herself falling . . . and then being caught about the waist.

Sirion and Adrianna stumbled back. Sirion was able to regain his footing with the help of the inn wall at his side. He could not keep the grin from his lips as he steadied Adrianna and looked into her face to be sure that she was all right. He was relieved to find her smiling as well, and began to chuckle, releasing her. They shared a hearty laugh as Dramati cocked his head at them and yelped in his throat. He served only to make them laugh all the more.

Once she had herself under control, Adrianna seated herself upon the wooden flooring. She gestured for the corubis to join her, and he was more than willing to lie next to her, his large head in her lap. Sirion watched them as she caressed the animal's head and face gently. A mixture of emotions swept through him. He had never seen Dramati behave in such a manner with anyone with the exception of himself. It appeared that he had chosen her as a companion, as a corubis was wont to do. He was touched to find that Adrianna liked Dramati just as much as he liked her, and that she would go out of her way to make the animal happy. Sirion found himself sitting next to her on the floor of the veranda, looking out into the approaching night.

Adrianna was filled with a mixture of emotions. She was very aware of Sirion sitting next to her. She felt comfortable having him there, safe. He exuded an aura of power and security that made her feel that she need not have any worries. So she allowed her body to relax against the outer wall of Volstagg's inn and stroked the beast in lap, crooning to him in Hinterlic. She glanced at Sirion a couple of times, once to find him regarding her intently, and another to see him staring out into the night.

Before too long, the rest of the Wildrunners finally made it to the inn. They were obviously tired, shoulders slumped and feet dragging. Triath, Sorn, Naemmious, Arn, Laura, and Breesa nodded at Sirion and Anya as they filed into the inn. From her position beside him on the floor Adrianna rose. Bussi, Dartanyen, Zorg, and Armond entered the inn behind the Wildrunners. Sirion stood as well, stretching his weary muscles. He told Dramati to return to his place, and the corubis acquiesced, loping away into the darkness alongside the inn.

Sirion followed Adrianna into the building. Volstagg was busy at the bar, handing out keys to the Wildrunners. Armond, Zorg, Dartanyen, and Bussi must have had their keys already, for they made their way up the stairs to their rooms right away. Adrianna touched his arm gently and he turned to face her. She smiled and nodded a "good evening" to him and began to make her way past his companions. She seated herself at the bar, patiently waiting for Volstagg to finish his business.

Sirion slowly began to make his way towards his room. Adrianna had looked tired as she bade him goodnight. He had forgotten that she had been traveling for a very long time, all the way from Andahye, which was located almost a month's journey to the north. The rest of the Wildrunners would end up sharing rooms with one another, all but him. Volstagg had a room for him on the first floor behind the kitchens. It had been his room for years, and Volstagg never lent it out to any of his customers. Sirion stopped and was about to turn around, thinking to see how Sorn was doing, wondering if the trek back to Sangrilak had overtaxed him. But then he thought better of it, his body once more realizing its fatigue. He knew that Sorn must be just as tired, if not even more so.

Sirion stepped up to the door to his room when he saw Adrianna coming down the hall towards him. She smiled as she stopped at the door of the room next to his. Sirion was surprised. In all of the years he had known Volstagg, he had never known that Adrianna had a room in the inn. He found himself returning the smile. "May your sleep be restful and your dreams peaceful."

"May you have a good night as well," she replied. She opened her door and stepped into her room. She then closed the door behind her. She heard Sirion close his door a moment later. She was so tired, all she could think to do was remove her belt, pouches, and boots before she climbed into bed. She sighed deeply as she settled herself beneath the covers. Her thoughts were of Sirion as she nodded off. Her sleep was restful and she dreamed no dreams.

***

Adrianna awoke the next morning, sunlight beaming through her window. Quickly, she hopped out of bed; she had awoken late. She smoothed her hands over her rumpled clothes and then, with a sigh of exasperation, began shucking them. She went over to her pack and pulled out a fresh tunic and trousers. Once dressed, she washed her face at the basin. She re-plaited her hair, all the while wishing that she had at least stayed awake long enough to take a bath the night before. She folded the rumpled clothing and placed it in the pack to be washed later. She then donned her belt and pouches and pulled on her boots. She picked up her pack and left the chamber.

Upon entering the common room, Adrianna looked around. The inn was empty but for Dartanyen, Bussi, Armond, and Zorg sitting at one of the tables. It appeared that they had just finished breaking their fast. At least she wasn't the only late-riser this day. Dartanyen saw her enter and gestured for her to join them at the table. Adrianna smiled, happy that he wished to include her, and made her way over to them. Armond made room for her to pull up a chair. A serving girl came to ask her if she wanted anything to eat and drink. She asked for a cup of tea and a biscuit. The group was silent for a few moments as Adrianna awaited her meal.

"So, are we willing to do this? I mean, are we going to take the Wildrunners up on their offer?" Armond asked. He looked about the table as he spoke.

"I think we should. There is the risk that we won't get anything out of it, but at least we will have tried to help ourselves get into a position where we could make a little bit of money. And who knows? Perhaps, if we do a good job, we will begin to get a reputation, and it will make it easier for any one of us to find employment later."

A deep voice spoke up. "I'm all for gettin' a good reputation and all, but I'm not quite so sure about the possibility of not gettin' paid for what we are about to do. I mean, I don't want people thinkin' that they can get somethin' without payin' for it," said Zorg.

"I don't think that will be the case," said Dartanyen. "Most people won't even know that we aren't getting paid. Not only that, but we will be getting in good with the Wildrunners by doing them this favor. Maybe they will spread the word about us to others. They do have more than a little influence in these parts."

The serving girl returned with Adrianna's biscuit and tea. The table was silent as she ate and drank. She was just about finished when Sirion walked into the inn. He must have been up early. He too, it seemed, had not bothered to get a bath, although he had washed his face and arms. He had donned fresh tunic and trousers, but his studded leather vest was still covered with dirt and grime.

Sirion raised his hand in greeting and Dartanyen gestured for him to join them. Sirion began to make his way over to their table when a man burst through the front door. He dashed into the common room and quickly surveyed the area, his chest heaving as he sought to catch his breath. "Something's . . . happened." He struggled to speak and he held his sides. He had obviously been running as fast as he could. Sirion stepped up to the man and grasped his elbow.

"What is it? What has happened?" asked Sirion, concern shadowing his voice.

"At the library . . . people killed . . ."

Sirion looked towards the table. Adrianna and her companions had already risen and began to make their way towards the door. Adrianna made sure to grab her pack as she left. The group ran through the city streets towards the library. Sangrilak sported a rather large one, built just before she had left to study in Andahye. Adrianna looked to find Sirion and Armond running on either side of her, Dramati having taken the lead.

Adrianna was out of breath when they reached the library. The city guard had arrived on the scene and had already begun to question a few individuals, probably those who had discovered what was inside. Sirion began to walk up the steps. A few of the city guard came up to him, but when his name was given, they stepped aside. Sirion gestured for the rest of them to follow.

The front doors were open, and upon entering the building Adrianna paused. The place reeked of death. Slowly, she followed the group into the library proper, and what met her eyes when she entered was a sight she hoped never to see again. She swallowed down the bile that rose from her stomach at the horrible sight. Blood covered the floor, along with the bodies of what had once been two men. The bodies had been mutilated. The walls were splattered with blood and gore, gruesome testimony that the men had not died a quick death. Adrianna vaguely heard someone heaving outside the entrance to the library. Her stomach stirred momentarily, but she would not allow herself to be sick. For once, she was glad that she had an iron constitution.

Adrianna saw that the back door of the library had been broken down. Dramati immediately went over to it and began to sniff around. Within moments he was barking loudly, beckoning Sirion to come to him. Sirion turned away from the bodies that he was about to investigate and instead answered Dramati's call. He joined the corubis at the mangled door leaning crazily on its hinges. Dartanyen began to search what remained of the bodies. They appeared to be human. He found a letter on one of them. Dartanyen read the letter first to himself and then out loud as Bussi, Armond, and Zorg began to gather around. Adrianna was not paying much attention, as she was still engrossed in the horror around her. She could not help but wonder how two people could have so much blood. Dartanyen's voice was a monotone and barely even entered her consciousness until she heard a familiar name. THANE.

"What? What was that?" Adrianna's head snapped towards Dartanyen, her eyes wide and her nostrils flaring. Dartanyen began to read the letter again, but Adrianna stopped him by reaching out her hand toward the parchment. Dartanyen handed the crumpled message to her. She read it with some trepidation, having already heard the name at the end of the letter.

Kyrin,

Since I am unable to come to collect him myself, you must bring the wizard Dinim Coabra to me. Make haste in this matter for the Master wishes for him to be ready when the time comes. Remember, I am watching you. Do not fail me again.

Lord Thane

As Adrianna read the name at the bottom of the page, her face became pale and she began to shake. Her palms became sweaty and she was suddenly cold. Thane. What did her father have to do with the man that lay dead at her feet, his heart ripped out of his chest, his throat gone? Who was the man, Dinim, whom Thane told the man to collect for him? But no. It couldn't be her father who had signed the bottom of the page. But it had to be. The handwriting was familiar to her, as every father's handwriting is familiar to his child, even if the father had rejected that child. Adrianna clutched the paper in clenched white fists. "Sheridana," she murmured. Her sister. Where was she?

Abruptly, Adrianna realized that Dartanyen was speaking to her, demanding her to tell him what she knew of the man Thane. "Nothing," she replied stiffly. But Dartanyen would not be easily deterred and told her once more to tell him what she knew. Adrianna snapped out of her trance and growled at the Savanlean, "Just please leave me alone, and stop invading my privacy!"

Adrianna stalked from Dartanyen's immediate vicinity, making her way to the far end of the room where the remnants of the massacre had not intruded. She walked amongst the tall bookcases, thinking. She shook her head. She should never have spoken to Dartanyen like that. It was wrong of her to keep information to herself, but by the gods, the man was her father! Damnation! She just *had* to find this man Dinim, the man written about in the message. Maybe he had answers that she did not. Was Dinim here, in the library? It was possible, since the man, Kyrin, had been looking for him.

Sirion returned to the others after his cursory inspection of the door. He knew what had broken through it. The creature had left its scent behind, a scent with which he was all too familiar. He had suspected it the moment he had seen the bodies of the two mutilated men. As he approached, he saw Adrianna stalk away from the others, obviously very upset. He strode up to Dartanyen, who had not moved, continuing to stare at her retreating back as she walked to the other side of the large room.

"What bothers her?" Sirion asked.

"She knows something. It disturbs her greatly. I pressed her to tell me. I found out the hard way that she is not ready." Dartanyen smiled wanly.

Sirion clapped Dartanyen on the back. "Such is often the case with women. Do not worry about it. She will get over it. Be assured that she will tell you in time. I don't feel that she is one who would put others in jeopardy just to keep some information to herself."

Suddenly, there was a commotion at the entrance. The rest of the Wildrunners had finally arrived upon the scene. Adrianna made her way back over to Zorg and Armond as the other group began searching the place. There were six. First entered the lady-archer Anya, followed by a hulk of a man that could only be a half-oroc. Next was a handsome young Recondian man with a patch over one eye and a man who appeared to be a cross-race faelin. Then there was a human/faelin woman like herself, dressed in traditional clerical robes and a large Recondian man with a massive, two-handed sword strapped to his back. Sirion walked up to the cross-race faelin man. He was taller, much like Armond, with a pale skin tone, straight dark brown hair, and canted violet eyes. He was beautiful. Adrianna couldn't help but watch the two as they made their way to the wrecked door. She heard Sirion call his companion by the name of Sorn. The handsome, finely clothed Recondian man met them there and the three conferred for several moments.

Adrianna cast a sidelong glance at the half-oroc. He was frightening to behold, a creature out of her darkest dreams. He was large, bigger than any other man in the room. He was at least eight feet tall. His flesh was slightly greyish, his hair so dark it was almost black. His lower jaw jutted out, his bottom canines so long that they emerged from his mouth to rest on top of his upper lip. But, despite his monstrous appearance, there was a more human-like side to him as well. His canines were shorter than that of full-blooded orocs, his flesh paler, and his pointed ears smaller. And then there were his eyes. His eyes did not have a reddish cast, but were a deep medium brown. Adrianna had never seen his like ever before, the orocs being the mortal enemies of all of the faelin races.

Adrianna returned her attention to Sirion and his companion. The cross-race faelin man was an enigma to her. Suddenly she knew what he was. Cimmerean. Known also as 'dark' faelin, they were inhabitants of vast labyrinths beneath the surface of the eastern world. She had never heard of a faelin of any other race who would chose a Cimmerean as his or her mate, they considering the Cimmereans as outcasts. Although, it was rumored that Adrianna's mother's sister had married a Cimmerean faelin. She had never quite believed the stories, but now, looking at this man, she suddenly found herself imagining that it just may have been true. But then again, maybe not. It was said that not only their hair was dark but their souls as well, they who lived in the Underdark practicing the black arts. She could not imagine any sister of her mother's ever yoking herself to one such as that.

Adrianna snapped out of her thoughts as the Wildrunners approached them. The finely clad man with the eye-patch, Triath, appeared somewhat agitated. Sirion spoke. "I have assessed some of the damages and I am led to believe that a Shirwemic played some part in the terror that occurred here last night. We have decided that we need to go after it, while the trail is still fresh." Sirion paused, allowing his companions to digest his words. "However, we would have it that you all stay here, assess the situation further, to possibly discover what exactly went on here. We will return when we can. We will meet you at Volstagg's inn." Then he nodded. "Good luck."

The Wildrunners began to file out of the library, nodding to them as they left. Sirion was the last to depart, Dramati at his side. He lifted his hand in farewell as he followed his companions from the library. Adrianna watched Sirion as he walked away. A feeling of foreboding washed over her, a portent that things would be different when next they met. She so much wanted to call out to the Hinterlean, but chose not to do so. Not once did he turn back, and she did not call his name.

Regaining her senses after the departure of the Wildrunners, Adrianna turned back to her companions. They just stood there, seemingly not knowing where to begin. Adrianna once more began to consider her situation. Her father had written a disturbing letter to a man who lay mangled upon the floor. He wished to have a man by the name of Dinim Coabra within his possession. The last time she had seen him, he had been in the company of her sister and uncle on the way to the eastern continent. She felt compelled to find the man about whom he spoke about in the letter. She could not help but think that he may be a source of information.

"Hey. I was thinking. Maybe we should search the other rooms in this building, see what these men had in their possession. Maybe we will find something that will give us a clue as to why this happened," said Adrianna. Privately, she thought that perhaps she could find out if the man Dinim had been at the library, and if he had, why he had been there.

Dartanyen nodded, regarding her intently. "That's a good idea. Perhaps we will discover some information that lies unfound." They first searched through the bedchamber of the head-librarian, Corellan. They found nothing there but the furniture in the room and the clothes he had worn. Adrianna's flagging spirits began to lift when they entered the second bedroom. It was obviously the dwelling of one who dealt in magic. Upon the desk were several scrolls, parchments and vials of unfamiliar material. Within a locked drawer, which Bussi conveniently smashed open with his battle-axe, Adrianna discovered a notebook and an obsidian stone hanging from a silver chain. Dartanyen took the neckchain into his possession while Adrianna pocketed the notebook and scrolls, as well as a personal diary she found on the worktable. She flipped rapidly through the diary and found that it was written in a language that she could not read. Finding nothing else of interest in the room, the group left it, moving into the third bedroom. Upon finding nothing of interest in it, they went back into the main room of the library.

Pensively, Adrianna began looking about the ravaged room once more. They had found nothing in the other rooms to allude to the reason behind the attack. It was obvious that only two men stayed at the library. Adrianna suspected that the man Dinim was one of them. She also knew that Dinim was not one of the dead men on the floor. None of those had been a wizard. That meant that the third man on the floor had been a visitor. Did he have something to do with the attack? Adrianna sighed, becoming frustrated. They were getting nowhere.

Adrianna squinted her eyes and began to focus. She concentrated upon *seeing* what she had been unable to perceive before. It was a special ability she had acquired from the faelin aspect of her bloodline. It allowed her to look past the obvious and to see that which was not. She, Dartanyen, Bussimot, and Armond arrived upon the same place, a carefully concealed door behind one of the many bookcases within the library. Adrianna got her bearings and found that they were in the historical section. All of the names of well-known historians stared at her from their bindings. Her eyes began to scour over the bookcases, trying to find anything that would give them a clue as to how they were to possibly move the massive bookshelf without laying siege to it. After a few moments her eyes caught sight of a slender book with an elegant binding. Adrianna stepped closer to it, craning her neck to catch sight of the title. It looked different than the other books, and bore a title that seemed out of place, *Mineff's Composition, 2nd Edition*. Upon turning, she saw Armond standing next to her, Zorg just behind him, both looking at the same book. Armond turned to her and grinned slightly, shrugging his shoulders. Zorg reached out and began to pull the book from its position. Upon his doing so, the bookcase slid backwards and then to the left, behind the bookcase next to it. For a moment everyone just stood there looking at one another bewilderingly, and then down into the staircase that had been discovered.

Without a second thought, the group walked down the musty, ancient stairwell, bearing torches that Zorg had given to them from his backpack. At the bottom of the stairs stretched a long corridor. Adrianna walked alongside Zorg, behind Dartanyen and Armond, with the halfen bringing up the rear. She felt vaguely out of place. What was she doing here with these people? She had never met them before yesterday, and here she was traipsing down an old forgotten corridor with them as though she had known them for years. She shook her head, trying to determine how this had all come about, how she had gotten herself into the interesting situation she appeared to be in. Without warning, Armond and Dartanyen stopped. She almost ran into Armond, but stopped herself just as she was about to stumble into his backside. Bringing herself up short, she looked up to find that they had come to a dead end. All that existed was the wall in front of them and an old, dusty pipe organ.

The group formed a semi-circle around the dilapidated instrument. They eyed it askance, not knowing what to make of an organ in a subterranean tunnel behind a library. "Humpf," mumbled Zorg. "What in the Hells . . ." Adrianna and Armond went to the tunnel wall. They felt around and were unable to find anything that would indicate that the wall would open. The halfen had begun to busy himself with the organ, and, upon his investigation, Bussi found an ancient parchment lying beneath the instrument. He brought it up for all to see, cracked and dust-ridden as it was. He then carefully unfolded it and placed it on the spot upon the organ that was obviously meant to hold a page or book of music. What lay before them was almost illegible, the notes of music upon the page having faded over time. Dartanyen began to inspect the organ's numerous yellowed keys for clues that would show them precisely which of the keys they needed to press in order to play what had once been written upon the page.

"Are ye sure we should touch the thing?" Bussi eyed Dartanyen warily.

Dartanyen looked at Bussi and then at the rest of the group. "Well, what else should we do? We are at a dead end. There is a pipe organ just . . . sitting here."

Armond joined Dartanyen and Bussi at the organ. He cleared his throat. "I . . . I have a little bit of experience with this type of thing."

Adrianna noticed that he said it in such a way that it seemed that he had not really wanted to say it at all, and had only done so out of the sheer necessity of it. Dartanyen and Bussi stepped out of the way and Armond placed himself before the instrument. He stood there regarding it and the parchment for several moments. Dartanyen and Bussi looked at each other and then back at the dark-haired faelin standing before the organ. Finally Armond placed his hands above the keys. He depressed a key and Adrianna jumped as a loud sound, accompanied by a billow of dust, emitted from one of the pipes. Adrianna held her breath, waiting. All was silent. Armond pressed another key. They heard another loud, discordant noise from another pipe, also accompanied by a stream of dust. All of a sudden, they heard a loud *crack* from above. All looked upward to see a series of long iron spears racing towards them from above. Adrianna fell to the stone floor, pressing herself flat. Alongside her, Zorg did the same as well as Dartanyen, Armond, and Bussi. She next heard a resounding *clang*. Then there was silence.

Adrianna opened her eyes to find herself looking into the crystal clear blue gaze of Zorg. Together, they slowly looked up to the ceiling to see the iron spikes only a few feet above them. It appeared as though the trap mechanism had rusted and caught upon itself, not allowing the spears to fall upon them. Very quickly, Dartanyen and Armond were up again and standing before the organ. "I thought you said that you had experience," said Dartanyen, a harried expression on his face.

Armond glared intently at Dartanyen for a moment before returning his focus to the task. He rubbed his hands together. It was very obvious to Adrianna that he was nervous. He then poised his hands above the organ keys once more. He paused, indecisive about which key to press. He was about to press a key when he changed his mind at the last moment and pressed a different one. Once more they experienced the noise and the dust. They group waited, and nothing happened. All they heard was the creaking of the iron spikes hanging above them.

Armond pressed yet another key upon the pipe organ. After the noise and dust receded, everyone began to hear a slight rumbling. The rumbling grew louder and louder. The walls around them began to shake and bits of dirt began to fall from the vaulted ceiling. The iron spikes dangling from above began to creak and moan with the desire to fall to the floor. "Gods, the place is falling in upon us," whispered Zorg. The group pressed together towards the tall faelin hovering above the organ keyboard. Armond's eyes darted from the ceiling to the keys, beads of sweat beginning to form upon his brow.

"Armond . . . the spikes' mechanism will give at any moment. *Just do it!*" hissed Dartanyen. The faelin pressed the last key. There was a large crash, and suddenly the floor fell from beneath the group. Everyone jumped back just in time to avoid falling into the yawning pit that lay before them, all except Armond. He was the only one who was unable to regain his footing and he fell into the hole that encompassed a large portion of the floor. The rumbling continued to echo through the corridor, and the falling debris began to get larger. From within the dark hole they heard Armond shout that he was all right and that all he could see was a stairway leading downward. From above, the creaking iron spears became ever louder.

"Time to go," Dartanyen raised his voice above the sound of the tunnel collapsing all about them. Zorg gave Adrianna a gentle push towards the hole and Dartanyen took her arm as she made towards him. He pointed downward and she saw a steep stairwell leading into the pit.

In single file the rest of the group hastily descended to the landing upon which Armond had fallen. Just as Zorg's head cleared the floor of the tunnel above, the iron spikes loosened from their rusty prison and crashed down. "Damnation," he shouted.

Dirt and other debris fell upon Zorg as he continued downward, and once standing upon the landing with them, his hair and shoulders were covered with it. Adrianna assessed the group. Armond was scuffed and bruised, but appeared to be all right. Zorg appeared to be a little shaken but he too seemed to be hale and whole. The landing upon which they were standing was merely that. The staircase upon which they had been walking continued downwards. The group continued. Finally they reached the end of the stairwell and began to tread on soil. Bussi was confused, mumbling about the nature of subterranean tunnels. They appeared to be at ground level. However, many feet above, within the tunnel that had almost caved in upon them, they had also been at ground level. Adrianna began to ponder upon this phenomenon. Some time within the long ago past had an earthquake caused this portion of the ground to cave in? Or was it made by magical means?

The group walked onward into darkness, further away from the beacon that Dartanyen had lit at the base of the stairwell in order to find their way back. They walked through the wide tunnel in virtual darkness, a couple of the torches having been left behind when the tunnel began to cave in upon them so many feet above them. Only Zorg and Armond carried them now, Zorg near the front of the small procession, and Armond in the rear with Dartanyen, who had his longbow ready in case of any trouble.

It seemed like they walked for days, although Adrianna was sure it was just a few hours. The group finally reached the end of the tunnel. Before them stretched a huge cavern. Slowly they walked into it. Adrianna felt a slight chill ripple up her spine. There was something about the place, something that made her feel nervous and on edge. Then, from out of the darkness before them emerged what appeared to be a cemetery. They walked around the place, the paranoid Bussi looking over his shoulder every few minutes. The headstones were eerie in the flickering torchlight, and the shadows seemed to jump out at them at every step. Adrianna shivered. It was cold beneath the surface, and it was creepy in the cemetery, where she felt that they trespassed. A large mausoleum stood within the center of the cemetery and the group made their way over to it. Bussi looked once more into the darkness from which they had come. His eyes widened. His paranoia had paid off. "By the gods," he croaked. Then Adrianna heard a sound that seemed to reach within and stop her beating heart. It was an eerie moan emanating from multiple throats in the close distance.

In amazement, Adrianna watched as Bussi broke from the protective numbers of the group and ran towards the movement. Suddenly he stopped short. Zorg began to step towards the halfen, when within the dim light cast by his torch, creatures of nightmarish proportions were illuminated in sharp relief, seeming to ooze out of the darkness from which they had come. Zombie-like, they shuffled their feet as they walked and seemed to stoop over themselves, their arms hanging loosely at their sides. Decaying flesh hung from white bones and many of them wore the remains of dark robes. The stench of rot began to permeate the air.

Bussi shouted and ran back towards the group. Everyone just stood there, not knowing what to do, the mausoleum at their backs and the route from which they had come flooding with the undead. While deciding whether to stay and try to make a stand or to flee and make a wide berth about the progressing horde, the undead priests advanced until there was no choice. Their rather small escape route was blocked. Fear gripped the group of young people, all knowing very well that they were severely outnumbered. The men, to Adrianna's intense relief and gratitude, formed a barrier between herself and the advancing menace. Then the undead were upon them.

Armond swung at the enemy but did not have a chance. He was struck down almost immediately by the horde, and belatedly all realized that he had been in worse shape than he had let on after his fall into the stairwell. In horror, Adrianna watched as Zorg, Dartanyen, and Bussi battled the seemingly mindless undead. She forced herself to close her mind to what was happening. She needed to concentrate. She began to incant the words to her spell and made the motions necessary for its casting. She held her hands out before her, thumbs touching, fingers spread. Suddenly, a wide arc of flame was emitted from her fingertips. It swept between Dartanyen and Bussi and hit one of the creatures. It erupted into flame. It made no sound as it was burned to a crisp.

Adrianna saw her companions recoil when they saw the magic. It was to be expected. Most people reacted thusly when finding out a person was a magic-user. It was probably a shock to them, as she had hardly given them any indication of her profession. She had told them that she had studied in Andahye, but many people did not know what went on in that city, and many more did not even know that it existed. She felt guilty about being unable to protect herself against the foe any further. The magic she had summoned had drained her. Wavering on her feet, she berated herself fiercely for her inadequacy . . . she was unable to help more when her aid was so greatly needed.

The horde pressed into the group. Dartanyen pulled Armond out of reach of the creatures and leapt back into the fray. In fascination, Adrianna saw the undead priests hacked to pieces. *No blood*, she thought to herself. Then she saw Zorg waver, and he fell upon the ground some distance from her. Fear gripped her anew. Now, only Bussi and Dartanyen were in the position to keep harm away from her. They increased their efforts as desperation overcame them.

Adrianna once more considered her options. The horde crowded ever nearer to her as they pressed Dartanyen and Bussi back. For a moment she considered running, hiding behind the mausoleum at her back. But then she saw Zorg in the distance, his life's blood pumping onto the ground beneath him. She could see it from the distance that she maintained. Her mind whirled and she steeled herself. She ran from the mausoleum towards Zorg. Out from behind the protection of Dartanyen and Bussi, she placed a wide berth between herself and the ensuing battle, making her way towards the unmoving body of Zorg on the ground. The monsters had left him and Armond behind as they sought to destroy the two remaining combatants.

Upon reaching Zorg, she dropped to her knees. Looking about her to be sure that none of the enemy approached, she unsheathed her dagger and quickly cut strips of cloth from his tunic and began to bind the wound at his shoulder. She then moved to his thigh. The wound was deep. Her breath caught in her throat as she desperately placed her hand on top of the gaping wound. She felt the warmth of his blood as it spilled from between her fingertips. She cut another strip of cloth from his tunic and wrapped it tightly about the gash.

Finally, Adrianna looked up from her work. She frowned. It was her first field dressing, and she saw that it was sorely lacking. She turned to the battle and saw that Dartanyen and Bussi continued to fight. It was evident that they were quickly tiring. Her companions had seen that she had removed herself beyond their protection and had renewed their efforts yet again, trying to keep the battle away from her and the injured men to which she tended. However, it was not to be. The undead had seen her and recognized her attempts to revive her fallen comrades. The battle slowly moved in her direction.

Adrianna stood and ran to Armond's side. He had lain for quite some time with no attention. His face was deathly pale, the wound in his side caked with drying blood. She cut through the length of his tunic, fully exposing the wound. It was a long gash in his side, although not as deep as Zorg's wounds. She cut away the clothing and tore thick strips from it as quickly as possible. She began to wrap the lengths of fabric about Armond's ribs. The blood flowed anew from his wound as she moved his body to complete her work. She hissed when she saw the damage she had wrought. Yet she continued and bound him tightly, knowing intuitively that the ribs were broken. She felt the battle coming ever nearer to her, yet dared not take the time to look up from her task.

Finally she was finished. She looked up just in time to see that one of the creatures had made it through the defenses and was bearing upon her. She tried to block herself from the blow and braced herself as the monster slashed at her. Shock rippled through her body as she felt something sharp slicing the flesh of her right forearm. Then Dartanyen was standing over her and was dispatching the gruesome creature. The blood ran warm and thick down to her elbow, the frayed edges of her sleeve absorbing some of it as it flowed. Then she saw another monster appear behind Dartanyen and he went down, the force of the creature's blow too much for his weary body. Desperately, Adrianna looked around her. The number of undead priests had decreased drastically, but it was not enough . . . one against six, and the one already with battle wounds. Suddenly something changed. Bussimot seemed to explode into a frenzy of movement. He hacked and slashed with no apparent direction, at a speed that was phenomenal. He seemed larger than life, wild with the rage that was upon him. It was then that Adrianna realized that she too was in danger, for berserkers slashed at anything while in their rage, friend or foe. Adrianna heard a shout in the distance to her left, but then out of the shadows the dark figure that had felled Dartanyen swept at her. She felt something hard connecting with the top of her head and the halfen was the last thing she saw as oblivion took her.

Sirion and Anya rushed towards the group. Sirion watched in horror as an undead abomination lunged for the woman kneeling at the side of her fallen comrade. "Lady, ware behind you!" he shouted at the top of his lungs. He increased his speed in desperation, passing Anya as he saw the creature strike Adrianna down. Fear gripped his innards as the monster stooped by her prone form lying on the bloody ground. It slashed downward and he saw its dagger red with her blood as it straightened again.

Sirion careened past the monster, lopping its head off as he swept by with his quarterstaff. Out of the corner of his eye, he saw the halfen fell another of the undead. He knew that the man was working only on energy reserves, that he would need serious medical attention when the rage ended. He was covered with splatters of blood, some from his comrades, but most from himself. Then Sirion saw his sister as she entered the fray. She was effective and efficient as she began to methodically dispatch the enemy.

Sirion knelt before Adrianna. He cursed to himself as he placed his hand over the deep cut in the flesh below her ribs. The blood flowed dark and free from the gaping wound. The lower-most bone must have waylaid the dagger; the wound could have been much deeper than what it was. He tore open the fabric of her tunic and upon feeling around the area, Sirion discovered that the rib was indeed broken. He tore off a piece of the blue sash about his waist and pressed it over the hole, hoping to stop the flow.

Within moments the battle was over. The halfen fell as the last undead priest toppled to the ground. Anya kicked at the bodies of the grotesque creatures as she made her way over to Sirion. He felt her hand grip his shoulder. "Come. We must find them aid as soon as possible."

He sighed. He knew that she was right. He was loath to leave Adrianna and the rest of the group, but he knew that he must in order to find help. He could not expect Anya to travel through the tunnel alone, not with the dangers they now knew to be present. He quickly bound the wound tightly, hoping that it would be enough. Then he rose and began to run back through the tunnel, Anya just behind.

CHAPTER 3

The priestess slowly walked up the stairs to her chambers. The morning devotional had just finished and she had a small amount of time to herself before the day's work was to begin. Today she would be in the kitchen. Tianna crinkled her nose. Cooking was not her favorite past time. Although she did not really mind it, and even seemed to be pretty good at it, preparing meals was boring business. Besides, she much preferred to be in the garden tending to her herbs. Herbal lore was quickly becoming her area of expertise, and many of her Brothers and Sisters came to her for the answers to questions pertaining to the healing properties of this herb or that one.

Once reaching her quarters, Tianna went over to the window and opened it. It was a beautiful day, and she wanted to let the fresh air circulate the room. The room was simple in its décor, having only a bed, a desk, an armoire, and a washstand. The desk was the nicest piece of furniture, large enough to keep several of her books upon it. Many of the volumes contained scriptures about her goddess, Beory. Others had information about the medicinal properties of the local flora, and there were even a few about common healing techniques and methods, including the basics of humanoid anatomy and physiology.

Tianna leaned out the window, allowing the wind to sift through her chestnut hair. What a beautiful day . . . and what a shame to have to spend it indoors. Suddenly she heard a knock. Startled, Tianna spun from the window, her hand to her chest. She was relieved to find that it was only her young Brother, Razlul. The boy smiled impishly when he saw that he had alarmed her. Tianna frowned in mock disapproval. "Razlul, you scamp! I almost jumped out of my skin. What do you want?" Tianna put her hands on her hips and glared at him.

Razlul simply continued to smile. "Only to bring you a message from Sirion, Sister, but if you are busy I can bring it to you some other time." The boy began to back out of her room and into the hallway.

Tianna's blue eyes widened. "Raz, you are such a rascal! Give the message to me at once lest I come to tackle it from you."

"Are you sure you want it now, Sister? It is obvious that I have disturbed you. I offer you many apologies. Allow me to come back later when you are not so occupied."

The boy stood in the doorway, regarding Tianna mischievously. Razlul knew that she wanted the letter, especially since it was from Sirion. He knew that she had feelings for the handsome ranger, and he was using this knowledge to his advantage, daring her to chase him down the hallway like she did when she was an acolyte. But that was the hitch. No longer was she an acolyte, but a priestess of Beory, and with that title came responsibility, and more than a small degree of standard decorum. And it definitely would not be very decorous of her to chase her Brother through the halls of the temple.

Tianna could not help the smile from lighting her face. It was difficult to retain any semblance of seriousness when Razlul was about. When they were children, he had been one of her fondest companions, but now that they were older, things had changed. She was not a child anymore, and within but one more year, Razlul would not be a child anymore either, but a fully functioning member of the priesthood. Looking at him, Tianna could easily see that he would be a handsome man. His hair was blond, and his eyes pale blue. His complexion was so fair that the sun in the summer time easily burned him. Currently he sported a slender build, but Tianna could see the changes in his body, the muscle developing in his arms and chest. After he completed his growth in height, he would begin to fill out. He would not stay a slender boy for much longer.

"Come on, Raz. You know that I don't have much time. Let me have the message so that I have time to read it and make a response before I have to tend to my duties."

Razlul re-entered the room. "Here, Sirion just brought it. He told me to give it directly to you."

Tianna concealed a frown. Why didn't Sirion just bring it to her himself? It was not like she had seen him anytime recently. It had been several weeks since she had last seen him. She took the message from Razlul. "Thank you."

"I suppose I had better be going. Brother Wayne is probably looking for me."

Tianna nodded and watched the boy leave her room, closing the door behind him. Not only was he beautiful to look at on the outside, but he was beautiful inside as well. His heart was good and his soul pure. He would make an excellent priest someday, as well as a wonderful husband and father. She had never met anyone as devoted to people as Razlul, and his kindness was unsurpassed. It was these qualities that had always drawn her to him, the young boy who had approached an orphan girl from Elvandahar.

An orphan himself, Razlul had been raised by the Priesthood of Beory. When Tianna had first arrived with Sirion from Elvandahar, she was downtrodden and scathing. But, somehow the boy had raised her up and put spirit back into her young withered soul. For three years Tianna knew Razlul as a playmate, but when it came time for her to say her vows and take her place within the priesthood, her childhood had to be placed in the past. It was difficult for Razlul, but he came to accept the change with time. For over two years now Tianna had been a priestess of the fold, and soon Razlul would be joining the ranks. Finally he would become a man and they would be equals once more.

Tianna sat down on the edge of her bed and opened the letter. It was a short message, written in fine print. Right away she could see that it was Sirion's handwriting, his being easy to distinguish from most others.

Sister Tianna,

As you read this message, I am on my way to re-join the Wildrunners. I am a few days behind them, having stayed behind in Sangrilak to see to the welfare of some friends. Currently they are staying within the Temple of Hermod, and are slowly recuperating from a mission upon which the Wildrunners had bid them undertake. To our dismay, the group was brutally attacked. They had no field medic, and someone could have easily died before we were able to bring them to the temple.

By now you have probably figured out what I am going to ask you to do. It would be as a great favor to me if you were to accompany the group on another excursion into an underground temple we think is connected to Gaknar. We asked the group that they investigate the area and determine if it is, indeed, a temple dedicated to his worship. They will need someone who is fluent in the healing arts. I hope that you can help.

Thank you so much. I hope I will be seeing you soon. May the sun shine upon you, and your goddess bless you.

Sirion Timberlyn

Tianna refolded the parchment. How exciting! She had always wanted to accompany Sirion and the Wildrunners on one of their 'adventures'. Now she would be having one of her own. She would show Brother Rashid the message. She was sure that he would give her his blessing. Tianna placed the parchment in her belt-pouch. She would speak with him later in the day, after the completion of her duties. Despite her excitement, she would just have to wait until she presented the message to her elder and he had given her his approval. Then she would pack her bags and go across the city to the Temple of Hermod. There she would meet this mysterious group of stangers and begin an adventure.

2 Enaren CY593

Adrianna slowly awoke. She knew that she was alive because she felt the pain. Her body refused to move. Disoriented, she saw Zorg lying on a pallet next to her. A woman's face floated into her field of view. "Greetings. I am called Elainia. I am glad to see that you are doing well." Her hair fell in soft brown ringlets about her shoulders. "Rest, go back to sleep . . ."

Adrianna closed her eyes and when next she awoke, the pain was nearly gone. As she slowly rose from the pallet, the woman was there once more. Elainia checked her healing wounds. One was a large slash that ran the length of her forearm. The other was a gash in her midsection. Adrianna stared at it. It was an addition to the thin vertical scar that ran the length of her torso, between her breasts down to her navel. Adrianna cast a quick glance at Elainia, knowing that the other woman had seen the older scar, but she tended to Zorg, who was also rising from his sleep. Once Adrianna had donned her clothes, which had obviously been cleaned for her, Elainia led her out of the room. Upon entering the hallway she began to smell the tempting aroma of freshly prepared food. She found that she was ravenous. How long had she been asleep? The woman led her through the temple into a room that Adrianna saw was a dining hall. Platters of food lay on a large table. Her companions sat at the table, obviously just finishing their meal. Adrianna seated herself into the nearest chair and Zorg, behind her, followed suit. Dartanyen, Armond, and Bussi each nodded to them as Adrianna and Zorg began to help themselves to the food. Elainia left the dining hall.

The mess upon the table attested to the mass gorging that had occurred during her sleep. Men had absolutely no table manners. However, Adrianna found herself eating with the same voracious appetite that had obviously gripped her companions earlier. She had never been so hungry. However, she was full before she had finished her plate. Her stomach complained to her, growling unpleasantly. It seemed to have shrunk, unable to contain the amounts of food that she was accustomed to eating. Beside her, Zorg continued to eat ravenously, as if he had no intention of ever stopping.

Movement at the entrance of the dining hall caught her attention. The woman Elainia had returned and a man stood beside her. Adrianna couldn't help but stare at him. He was a full-blooded Cimmerean, one of the finest looking men she had ever seen. His skin was pale and he had black eyebrows over eyes the color of deepest lavender. His short black hair stood upright on the top of his head and extended in a thick stripe down to the nape of his neck. The sides of his head were shaved. He wore a sleeveless russet tunic and billowy trousers. About his narrow waist he wore a short-sword sheathed in a silver embossed black scabbard. Elainia spoke to the group, saying that it was to this man and his comrades that they all owed their lives. Then the Cimmerean spoke and all other sounds were obliterated from Adrianna's mind. Her heart began to beat rapidly, pounding against her ribcage. She couldn't hear anything but his name, " . . . Dinim".

Adrianna stared at the man before her. She couldn't believe her good fortune. Suddenly, Adrianna realized that she was holding her breath; the sound of it exploding through her parted lips startled her. *I've found him. I've found him . . .*Adrianna's mind chanted to her as she stood up from her seat. Breathlessly she said, "Wizard Dinim, I have found you!" Her voice sounded strange to her ears. Dinim's gaze rested upon her, surprised. Once again her breath caught in her throat. Deep purple eyes showed a hint of amusement and the corners of his mouth turned up slightly.

"Well, you can have me if you want," the man replied suavely, his eyes twinkling with suppressed laughter. Adrianna felt the blood rise to her face, and she was about to reply when Armond began to speak. That the tall faelin was angry was readily apparent, and his gaze upon the Cimmerean was depreciating.

"I don't believe this. It must be a joke." Armond's green eyes flashed with anger. "Why would *you*, a Cimmerean, want to salvage a group of amateurs whom you know can give you nothing in return? Or can we? What is it you want from us Cimmerean?" Armond threw his arm wide, encompassing all who were sitting at the table.

Dinim calmly regarded the angry young man at the other end of the table, but to Adrianna, his eyes portrayed all. He was angry. "Well, this is a fine way to repay me for my efforts." Dinim spoke calmly, collectedly.

"I repeat . . . what do you want, warlock?" Armond shouted, his face suffused with blood, his fists clenched at his sides. "All of you Dark faelin want something, evil bastards that you are." Armond leaned forward over the table. "What . . . do . . . you . . . want . . ."

Adrianna's gaze flickered between the two faelin. She became nervous, knowing that the impetuous Armond may destroy any hopes of her finding the answers to her dilemma. "From you I want nothing." Dinim shouted, his eyes blazing with suppressed rage. "We followed the path you had taken and found you defeated at the mausoleum. We called others in, and we brought you here. But it was Sirion who got the money to . . . ." Dinim abruptly stopped speaking, his lips pressed together into a thin line.

"Sirion was here?" Adrianna whispered out loud. No one heard her as Armond spoke yet again.

"Yeah, whatever. I know all about you people. All you do is *take*. I have yet to see a Cimmerean *give* . . ." Armond threw his arm out again, encompassing the group once more. "If you want to believe him, fine. But don't expect me to give in to him so easily."

"Ballocks, I've no problem depositing you back where we found you," Dinim replied hotly, stepping towards Armond menacingly.

"Curse you, daemon. Touch me and you will find my sword up your backside." Armond stepped towards Dinim as well, closing the distance. Adrianna inhaled deeply, hoping that this scenario was not playing out to be what she feared it would be. Armond's hatred for the Cimmerean race was turning out to be a liability, and she would be the first to pay the consequences of his prejudice. Out of the corner of her eye, Adrianna noticed that the woman Elainia had returned to the hall, followed by her fellow clerics. With them were everyone's belongings. Adrianna hadn't even known the woman had left the dining room.

Dinim's forceful words then broke through her thoughts. ". . . my room ravaged . . . important items missing . . . ." With shame, Adrianna looked up at Dinim and found his eyes riveted upon her. Dartanyen, backpack in hand, reached within and pulled out the neck-chain. He gave the item to Dinim, who thanked Dartanyen for its return. Adrianna went to her own pouch and pulled out the diary and notebook. She now knew for certain to whom the items belonged. She had hoped that they belonged to the man who now stood before her. At the time, desperately hoping that he may want the books back, she had taken them in the belief that he may come for them. Adrianna approached the Cimmerean. His gaze seemed to scathe her as she came to him, and she flinched inwardly. She knew that he was angry, but why was he turning it towards her? She was returning what she had taken, willingly and without regret or prejudice.

Adrianna sighed deeply, her emotions having been stirred by the argument between Dinim and Armond. What was Dinim's problem? What more did he want from her? She was returning what rightfully belonged to him. She proffered the items to him and he took them from her, saying nothing. Disappointed, she turned from him. Excellent. Armond had just alienated the only man who could have helped her to find her father.

Suddenly, Adrianna felt a hand on her shoulder. She slowly turned round. "Thank-you," Dinim said. "I . . ."

He was about to say something further when Armond's voice cleaved through the air. "Don't you touch her!" Tension knotted Dinim's features as he faced Armond once more and the verbal battle began anew. The two faelin became menacing in their fervor. Adrianna was about ready to step between the two, in hopes of ending the conflict, when she saw Dartanyen pick up a chair. Dartanyen raised the chair above his head and began to make his way to

Armond. Fear of the repercussions of Dartanyen's action prompted Adrianna to rush over to Armond as well. Priests and group members alike urged Dartanyen to put down the chair, and to everyone's relief, Armond quit the room with a wave of his hand, dismissing them as though they meant nothing to him at all.

With Armond's exit, the tension seemed to leave the room and everyone began to relax. Dinim turned back toward Adrianna. Before his attention could be distracted from her again, she quickly pulled out the letter with Thane's signature at the bottom and extended it out to him.

Dinim put out his hand towards the letter, but before taking it he regarded her intently. "I apologize for my rude behavior when you returned to me my diary and spell-book. It was unmannerly and unnecessary. Please forgive me."

Adrianna was surprised. She had not expected an apology from him. He seemed almost tense as he searched her face, perhaps even anxious. His gaze was so sincere that she could not help but feel her apprehensive feelings concerning him abate.

The woman Elainia chose that moment to approach them. She smiled warmly at Adrianna. "My dear, how do you fare? You had us worried for a while, you and your big friend." She turned to glance at Zorg, who continued to eat ravenously at the table. She then turned to Dinim. "The cleric that Sirion sent for should be arriving shortly."

Adrianna's thoughts turned inwards once more. *Sirion . . . he has been here. He has made it possible for us to escape what surely would have been . . .* She didn't want to contemplate it. It was enough to know that he had been there. The thought gave her a feeling of security somehow.

Adrianna's mind returned to the present, and as she listened to Dinim and Elainia converse, Adrianna began to get the feeling that quite a length of time had passed while she and her companions had slept. Her suspicions continued to grow as the conversation wore on. Adrianna cleared her throat, "Excuse me, but exactly how long have we been asleep?"

Dinim and Elainia exchanged glances of amusement. "My dear, almost two weeks have passed since your ordeal within the Temple of Gaknar!" she replied.

"Two weeks! I've been asleep for two weeks!" Adrianna nearly shouted at them. Dinim started to become distressed and quickly told her that Sirion and Anya had found them at the completion of the battle, that they were only able to do so much for their grave wounds before trekking back through the cavern and back to the surface for help.

When Dinim mentioned Sirion and the Wildrunners and what the imam priestess Laura and the Hermodian clerics within the temple had done to remove herself, Dartanyen, Armond, Zorg, and Bussi from their places upon the battleground of the cemetery, shame flooded Adrianna. How ungrateful she must sound! She stopped Dinim from explaining any more. She held out a conciliatory hand to him and said, "Please, I wish to thank you for what help you did give us, and to tell you how appreciative I am." She then smiled at him, hoping that he did not think her an ungrateful wretch.

Adrianna watched Dinim as his body relaxed and thought that it would be a good time to show him the letter. She held out the letter once again to him and motioned for Dinim to read it. He did so. "My, I have been popular recently. Everyone seems to want to see me for one thing or another." He arched an eyebrow, his tone amused and sarcastic at the same time. Dinim regarded her. "So what do you know of this man?"

Adrianna was shocked. How could he know that she knew the man who had written the letter? For all Dinim knew, she had only wanted to show him the parchment because Dinim's name was on it. He must have seen the question in her eyes because he began to explain himself. "I can only help you if you can tell me what you know about the man and I can see that you know something of him by the expression on your face."

"He . . . he is just someone I met once," she replied lamely.

Once again, she must have given herself away because Dinim said, "That's all right. We can talk about it some other time . . . when you are ready. A time when there are not so many people around and you know me better."

"What do you mean?" Adrianna felt her hands become clammy. *Was this man some kind of mind reader? Or was she so readable that even a stranger could fathom her most intimate thoughts?*

As if sensing her panic, Dinim soothed her. "Don't worry. We will talk later. I can sense that there is more to this than what you are saying."

Adrianna was about to reply when she noticed that someone was entering the room. Elainia, the Captain of the City Guard, and a woman she had never seen before stood at the doorway.

Elainia brought the woman to Dinim. "The Lady Tianna has arrived in answer to Sirion's message, and the Captain of the City Guard is also here to speak with you." Elainia gestured to the man who continued to stand at the doorway. With that, Elainia left, motioning the man towards the table and the food as she passed him.

Tianna stepped forward and Dinim held out his hands to her. "I am glad you were able to come." Tianna smiled. She was a very beautiful woman. She moved with natural grace, seeming to glide effortlessly across the space to where Adrianna and Dinim stood. She had long light chestnut colored hair and large, sparkling blue-gray eyes. She had a small waist, rounded hips, and ample bosom. Standing half a foot above Adrianna, at about Dinim's height, she seemed to be a perfect model of the way a woman should be.

Adrianna followed Dinim, Tianna, and the Captain back to the table with the rest of the group. The other woman introduced herself to everyone. Her voice was beautiful, having a musical quality that was slightly soothing. "I am Tianna, cleric to the Goddess Beory. I have been sent to help you in your mission in any way that I can. I am most proficient as a healer and I have dedicated my life to the arts surrounding medical herbalism."

Dartanyen nodded and rose from his seat. "It is good to have you with us, Lady. We owe Sirion a favor for bringing you to us. Thank you for accepting the summons to aid us. Your skills will be invaluable."

Tianna smiled and nodded to him. Dartanyen took his seat and the Captain of the City Guard began to speak. He explained that he wished to hire them. He wanted the group to go back to the mausoleum in order to discover what was being guarded there. He offered the group ten thousand gold pieces for their service. The room was silent. Adrianna was about to say something when Dinim spoke. He seemed slightly agitated with the Captain. "So you want us to go do the work that others can not? You say that thirty of your men have gone down there and not returned, and you want us to do this service for only ten thousand gold? And you say that you and yours protect this city? You want us to do your dirty work . . ."

Dinim became more flustered and the Captain started to become defensive. In the end, with the help of Tianna's charm, Dinim ended up weaseling free room and board for the duration of the excursion as well as free weapons and provisions in exchange for a portion of the ten thousand. When the Captain left, grumbling and cursing to himself, Dinim turned to the group. "How about us all getting a drink somewhere to help us think about this list of weapons and provisions we need to come up with? It's on me." Everyone nodded, agreeing to Dinim's suggestion and began to file out of the room, into the hall, and out the front doors of the Temple of Hermod. It was mid-day and Dartanyen and Bussi were eager to eat again. Adrianna hung behind, for some reason feeling fatigued. She had been sleeping for two entire weeks and she was tired! It was hard to believe but true. She tried to shake herself out of it and hastened to catch up with the others.

Ahead of her she saw Dinim and Tianna walking close together and making conversation, the woman's long white clerical robes a sharp contrast to his dark trousers. The woman laughed at something Dinim said, brushing her arm against his . . . almost seductively. "If you come any closer I'll have to dance with you," Adrianna heard Dinim say as she caught up to them.

"I don't do that when I first meet a man. I have to get to know him better," Tianna replied, her voice husky and alluring. Adrianna felt her cheeks burn. Tianna definitely knew how to use her body to her advantage. It also seemed that the woman liked to be flirtacious. Adrianna had walked up at the tail end of their conversation, but she had heard the hidden message in their exchange, or was she just imagining Dinim's sexual invitation? Once again she felt the mild sensation of being out of place, but this time it was also couched with feelings of self-consciousness.

Adrianna glanced sharply at Tianna. *How can she stand there so inviting and enticing and come away unscathed, when I, merely walking down a road, dragging my feet tiredly and covered in dust, could not?* Adrianna shuddered at the memory. Not by any means did Adrianna wish misfortune upon the other woman, but she felt sincerely confused and disheartened, and wished she had never heard the exchange.

The group was just starting down the road towards The Inn of the Hapless Cenloryan when Armond appeared. Soot smeared his face and clothing. He seemed a little out of breath, and very weary. He looked at Tianna inquiringly before he turned to the sound of Dinim's voice addressing him. "We are going to the Inn of the Hapless Cenloryan for drink and a place to compile a list of needs for our mission. You are welcome to join us. I am sure that there are some things that you need for the excursion."

"Well, I have some work to finish. Maybe I will join you later."

Seeing the uncertain look on Armond's face, Adrianna stepped up next to him and lightly put her hand on his arm. "Yes, you should come with us." She surprised herself when she did so, as she was usually not quite so bold.

"Well, I would, but I've really got to get this done. It is essential that I return to work as quickly as possible. I left the forge burning. I'll join you all when I can." Adrianna looked into his face and saw that he was being truthful. She let it go, but Dinim did not see what she did and began to protest that he sincerely had no problem with Armond accompanying them.

"That's all right," she said. "We will see you later then." By cutting in, Adrianna hoped to waylay the possibility of any confrontation. Armond quickly took his leave of them, walking back the way he had come.

Once there, the group walked into the inn. Adrianna immediately went up to the bar where Volstagg stood. An expression of relief washed over him. "My dear Adria! I had heard that you had been injured at the temple. How are you?" Without waiting for an answer, Volstagg came around the bar and held her to him. Finally he released her.

"I am well." Adrianna flashed him a big smile, happy to see him.

"Sirion came to me and told me what had become of you. I wanted to come to see you, but the priests said that it would be best if I waited. They said that you were injured badly."

"Perhaps so, but I am fine now . . . we all are." Adrianna paused. "So how is Sirion?"

"He waited for a few days to be sure of your recovery, and then he left." Volstagg then lowered his voice. "Supposedly the Wildrunners have some business in Grondor."

Adrianna nodded. The whereabouts of the Wildrunners was not supposed to be common knowledge. That Volstagg told her of their location meant that he trusted her. The Captain of the City Guard had mentioned that their excursion back into the temple was not public knowledge either, that most of his force did not know about the goings on beneath the city. She was sure that, in part, it was because the Wildrunners were involved.

When Adrianna returned to the group, everyone was sitting at a large circular table beginning to order food and drink. When all were served, everyone began to tell Dinim what should be included on the list of provisions. Somehow, Adrianna found the opportunity to tell Dinim what she needed as well, although she wasn't sure he heard her over the conversations going on around the table. Adrianna listened attentively for a while, sometimes making a few comments about this issue or that one, all the while looking about the common room. Adrianna relaxed in her seat, taking note of the people that came and went. She noticed a young woman enter. Adrianna could tell that she was a Denedrian. She was small and pretty. Her skin tone was bronzed and her black hair cropped short, the ends of it curling around the back of her ears.

The place soon became busy and there were a lot of people coming in and out for their mid-day meal. It was during this period of observation that she noticed a Hinterlean making his way amongst the crowd towards their table. For the most part, he was quite non-descript, although large in stature for a Hinterlean faelin. She noticed that he had thick dark hair and eyebrows, the eyebrows coming together above his nose to form a mono-brow. As he got closer, other members of the table began to notice him making his way towards them. He smiled and greeted everyone in Common as he reached the table. He then grabbed the empty chair beside Adrianna and sat down. It was Tianna's seat, but she had excused herself a few moments before, and Adrianna did not see her anywhere.

"I do not intend to intrude upon your privacy, but the inn-keep told me that you all know a friend of mine by the name of Sirion Timberlyn. I was wondering if you would give him a message from me." He paused and then continued. "You see, we haven't seen one another for several years, and I am anxious to see him again after so long. I will be staying in town for a while and the message tells him where I will be."

He held out the message and when no one else took it, Adrianna reached out and accepted the parchment from the faelin. A chill crept up her spine as he passed the message to her. He smiled a small smile, almost as though to himself. "May I ask your name at least, sir?" Adrianna asked.

"Sydonnia. Thank you for your aid. He will be happy to hear that I am back. Have a good day and may the gods smile upon you." The faelin then rose from the chair and left. Adrianna looked at the parchment in her hand for a moment before putting it in her pouch. Everyone at the table began to resume their interrupted conversations. Adrianna watched as the faelin made his way out of the inn. At the entrance, Armond and the Hinterlean almost ran into one another. Each man excused himself and Armond came over and seated himself with the group. Adrianna looked around at the group. No one inquired about the letter. She thought it more than a little strange. She was naturally very suspicious about the contents of a message that a stranger had left in her hands, for a man she hardly knew. She resolved that she would open the letter later, if, of course, no one asked her about it sooner.

Adrianna began to look about the inn once more, her gaze passing over the young woman she had seen enter earlier. She was sitting by herself at a small table next to one that seated two Savanlean faelin. Still feeling tired, Adrianna's mind became detached from the activity around her and she allowed herself to relax. She vaguely noticed when Tianna returned to the table and took her seat. She started to close her eyes, letting herself get comfortable.

Suddenly, there was a commotion on the other side of the room. Adrianna opened her eyes and saw that the room was full of people. Her gaze was drawn to the two Savanlean she had noticed before. One was complaining about a stolen belt-pouch. He held the young, black-haired woman by the front of her blouse, shaking her as he emphasized his words. "I know you stole my money pouch. It was with me before you bumped me and gone after you left."

Out of the corner of her eye Adrianna noticed movement. Dinim had risen from his seat and begun to walk over to the scene. "Is there something wrong here?"

"Yeah. This girl stole my money and I would like to have it back." He shook her again, her head snapping back on her neck. She said nothing, remaining calm and silent throughout the accusation.

Dinim looked at the young girl, for indeed that is what she was. From a distance she had appeared older than what she really was. Adrianna and the rest of the group arrived at the scene upon Dinim's heels. "Do you have this man's money?" She shook her head. "Release this girl. She claims not to have it . . ."

The Savanlean became even angrier and interrupted, "I know she has it. She is a thief and a liar. I have seen her kind before." The faelin's face was red with suppressed rage, and he shook her again menacingly.

The girl's face paled visibly. Dinim held up his hands. "Well now, it's your word against hers. Let her prove that she does not have it and search her."

Dinim looked at the girl for the answer to an unspoken question and received a nod.

The Savanlean glared at Dinim. "Well, I don't see as you have a say in the matter, *friend*. So why don't you just step away and let me finish my business with this little imp." He turned back towards the girl.

Adrianna looked at her companions on either side of her. Armond seemed slightly amused while Dartanyen appeared tense, his gaze intent upon the situation. Beside her, Adrianna felt a flurry of movement. She turned her head just in time to see a mug fly from Tianna's hand. It struck a man in the head a couple of tables away. The man shouted and stood from his seat, his hand at the back of his head. Tianna grasped Adrianna's arm and gave her a look as she spoke up. "What in damnation is that?" Her eyes were wide and she was pointing towards the front of the inn. Everyone, including the angry faelin and his companion, looked towards the front entrance. What they saw was an angry man gripping the back of his head, looking around the common room in order to ascertain who had thrown the mug.

The faelin glanced scathingly at Tianna and then returned his focus to the young girl. He growled in his throat. But the man who had been struck by Tianna's mug was suspiciously looking in their direction. He began to make his way over to the scene. Adrianna felt Tianna's hand tighten about her arm. This really was not a good situation. The Savanlean was angrily shaking the girl once more, and Dinim was beginning to raise his voice. Mug man had made it to the scene and was asking who had hit him in the head. Everyone except Tianna, who seemed to be trying to hide behind Adrianna, ignored him.

At that moment, Volstagg appeared at the scene, consternation written upon his rough features. "What is this going on here? I will have no trouble in here. If you have something to settle, do it outside." When he heard the stories from Dinim, the angry Savanlean, and Mug man, Volstagg quickly remedied the situation. With the flick of a wrist and an upraised forefinger, Volstagg's burly cook made his way over to the table. The man then led the outraged faelin and his companion out of the establishment. Volstagg apologized to Mug man and told him his next ale would be on the house. He then turned back towards the group. "I don't know exactly what's going on here, and I don't want to know. What I *do* know is that I don't want any trouble in here. I think it's time for you all to leave." With these words, Adrianna's spirits dropped. She knew that the girl had stolen the faelin's money pouch, having noticed the unspoken exchange between her and Dinim. Not only that, but more trouble had been created when Tianna had tried to take everyone's attention off of the situation by throwing a mug at another patron. Dispiritedly, Adrianna followed the group out of the inn.

For the next several minutes, the group stood about at the entrance to The

Inn of the Hapless Cenloryan. In general, everyone was quiet and withdrawn. Even Tianna seemed thus, and Adrianna began to believe that she felt truly regretful for having had such a strong hand in the group's expulsion from the inn. The girl stood amongst them, her dark head bowed. Finally she spoke. "Why did you do that?"

Adrianna abandoned her brooding and looked up. The girl's brown eyes searched Dinim's face.

"What?" asked Dinim.

"Why did you help me?" she asked again.

Dinim just shrugged his shoulders. "You looked in need of helping, so I obliged."

"But I stole the money. You know that I stole it, so why did you help me?" The girl's voice was both imploring and accusing, and her expression one of confusion and suspicion.

"I feel that you have skills that may be invaluable to us."

The girl's eyes narrowed slightly, and her expression became ever more suspicious. She had realized the obvious. He had helped her only to place her within his debt.

"I owe you nothing," she retorted ardently.

Dinim's gaze became coldly calculating. "Oh, I believe you do."

The girl's gaze wavered before his. It was apparent to Adrianna that the girl was afraid that he would call the City Guard upon her if she did not cede to his wish for her to join them. Adrianna lowered her eyes to her feet. For some reason, despite what had just occurred, she felt sorry for the young girl. It was a terrible feeling to be indebted to someone, especially one you did not know. She felt Dartanyen shift beside her. He did not seem comfortable with the turn of events.

Dinim turned to them and began to discuss the few remaining items that were needed for their trip back down to the temple, and their imminent meeting with the Captain. Because Adrianna didn't know if Dinim had added her own needs to the list, she asked him to be sure. "Don't worry," he said with a smile. "I have us covered." He winked at her conspiratorially, as if they shared something together that no one else knew about. He turned to the girl and asked her what types of things she would need, adding that all would be paid for. She told him that she needed a new set of lock picks and he informed her that she would also get a set of silver daggers. Agreeable to this, she seemed to loosen up, her body losing its rigid stance.

"By the way, what shall we call you?" asked Dinim.

She seemed to ponder the question for a moment. "Amethyst."

"Welcome to the group, Amethyst." Dinim smiled amiably and she slowly returned it.

When the time for the appointment arrived, the group walked over to the Captain's office. There, Dinim handed over the rather long list and the Captain looked over it. As they stood there, he crossed out several items, one of which Adrianna was sure was the larian she had jokingly mentioned while in the Inn. The Captain then said that he would give the list to his secretary, who would be the one in charge of appropriating the provisions. On their way down the street from the office building, the group met a man who introduced himself as Vincent, the very secretary who would be taking care of getting their provisions. He said that he would look over the list shortly, and not to worry, that he would get for everyone all that had been asked for, including any items that had been crossed off. Vincent smiled. "I do the books. The Captain is a miser and I take every opportunity that I can to counteract him. I enjoy it. Do you have a place that you are staying at? So that I can add the room and board charges to your account?"

Everyone was delighted. "You mean that you will take care of that expense as well?" asked Zorg.

Once again Vincent smiled. "I do the books." Everyone agreed that they owed their loyalty to Volstagg at the Inn of the Hapless Cenloryan, if he would accept them of course. So Vincent and the group went back to Volstagg's inn.

Upon their entrance into the inn, the group was met by a frown from Volstagg. The cenloryan refrained from saying anything when he also saw Vincent. The Captain's secretary explained to Volstagg about the group's situation. After thinking it over for a moment, Volstagg half-heartedly agreed to have them all stay at his inn and to have the charges billed to the group's account with the City Guard. After these arrangements were made, Vincent asked that they meet again later that evening and he left. Adrianna had noticed that Volstagg was still upset by what had happened earlier that day. When Vincent was gone, she went over to her old friend. His reception of her was the same as it was towards any other of the group's members. He was very cold and distant towards her. It was obvious that he truly wished that he had not been placed in a situation where he felt it would have been disrespectful of him to have not accepted the group at his establishment.

Adrianna stated the obvious. "You are still upset over this afternoon." He barely glanced up at her as he continued drying a mug with a clean rag he used solely for that purpose. He grunted in response. "Volstagg." Her gentle tone commanded his attention and he looked at her. "Don't judge us all by the actions of a single individual."

Volstagg looked at the girl in front of him and he considered her words. He looked into her dark eyes and saw regret and sadness there. He saw sincerity and warmth there as well, things he had always seen there before. His heart melted before her gaze and he finally smiled. "You are right." *Such wise words for one so young,* he thought. Her eyes brightened then, and for a moment the sadness seemed to disappear. She smiled at him in return and for the first time in many long years she touched him, putting her hand on his arm and squeezing momentarily.

Then she walked away, but not before he saw a hint of sadness return to her eyes, the same he had seen on the first night he had seen her after her eight years' sabbatical in Andahye. What had hurt her so? It couldn't just be her negligent father, or the abusive Hafgan. She had never had such an air of sorrowfulness before, not like this.

Volstagg watched Adrianna move towards the rest of the group. He smiled to himself as the memories came to him, memories of a small girl coming to his inn many, many turns ago. At first she came because he was a cenloryan, and as such, very interesting to her. But as she grew older, she came to him for someone who would talk to her, and to listen to her as well. She came to him in the name of friendship. He knew, deep within his heart, he would always be that friend.

Adrianna rejoined the group. They had only a few moments to wait while Volstagg came up with a room arrangement for them. Within a few minutes, Volstagg called everyone back over to the bar and gave them their room numbers. For the most part, everyone's rooms were relatively close together on the second level of the inn. Adrianna walked to the rear of the establishment through the corridor behind the kitchens that led to her room. She wondered why Volstagg had bothered to keep it for her all of those years during her absence. For all he knew, she may never have returned. Nevertheless, he had never given it out to any other persons. It was solely hers, ever since she was a child. Adrianna smiled. She knew that Volstagg loved her. No other had been so kind to her. *Except for maybe two others*, Adrianna thought. Nahum and Mairi. Nahum had died for her, and Mairi had been the only mother she had ever known.

Adrianna paused at the door, looking over to the door that led into Sirion's room. She sighed and opened her own door. She found it as she had two weeks ago, as it had always been, as she had last left it. It was a very nice but simple room. It had a bed with a sturdy oak frame, a desk and chair, and a small wooden table with a basin and clean washcloth on it. She dipped the cloth into the water within the basin and washed her face and neck. She then stripped off the delicately worked silver belt that her master had given to her as a gift for the hard work she had given to him. She then took off her cloak and hung it on the bedpost. She was tired. She would rest until it was time to meet with Vincent later on in the evening. She was so tired that she didn't even remember to examine the note that the strange faelin had given to her earlier in the day. She dreamed no dreams.

***

As dusk approached, everyone filtered out of their rooms and down the stairs. As the sun set on the horizon, Vincent strode into the inn. He was smiling as he walked up to the group. He explained that he had been able to make arrangements for the group to appropriate virtually every item on their list. However, some of the items would not be able to be made in time before the group was to go back down to the mausoleum, especially those weapons which were to be made of a silver/steel alloy. Dinim had suggested having them made in order to effectively fend off any lycanthrope that were possibly within the area. The group decided that they would go to the weaponsmith early the next day. Vincent wished everyone good fortune and asked them to come to him for any needs they may have. Then he left. Adrianna acquired a mug of honeyed mead and a bowl of nuts and fruits, wished everyone a good evening, and went to her room. She planned on studying for a couple of hours and then going to bed so that she may get an early start in the morning. She was just settling down to her book when she remembered the message for Sirion. She fumbled about in her belt-pouch for the folded parchment.

Adrianna had just drawn out the message when a knock sounded at her door. It startled her and momentary fear tingled down her spine. She heard thunder in the distance and she could smell rain in the air that entered her room through her open window.

"It's Volstagg, Adria."

Adrianna quickly got up and answered the door. She motioned Volstagg inside her room and shut the door behind him. He asked after her welfare and if she needed anything. She responded that she was well and that she needed nothing else that evening. However, Volstagg noticed some hesitancy in her voice. He raised an eyebrow at her.

"Well, I have this message for Sirion. It's from a faelin that I have never seen before and who knew none of us within the group. He gave me the message to give to Sirion the next time I see him," Adrianna said.

Volstagg waited for a moment. "Then what is the problem?"

"Don't you think it is strange? Why would he put his message into the hands of a person he doesn't know? He must not care overmuch if it is opened, for it is not sealed." Adrianna's voice trailed off. She did not mention the mixed feelings that she had concerning the large Hinterlean.

Volstagg squinted his eyes and looked at her closely. "Now, I can have naught to do with what you ask, Adria. I cannot take the risk that persons could become upset over such an infraction as for me to read a message that is not meant for my eyes. I cannot stand to lose what I have worked so hard to have. You understand?"

Adrianna did understand and could not blame Volstagg for his caution. But she could not ignore the strange and disquieting feelings she had about the letter. She smiled at him, and he knew she was not disturbed by his words. He invited her to help herself to anything in the kitchen if she needed it. She wished him a good night and he departed her room.

Once again, she settled herself on the edge of her bed. It began to rain outside. She looked at the folded parchment and all of a sudden she found that she was both anxious to read it and dreading it as well. It began to rain harder and lightening flashed outside her window. She slowly unfolded the letter. She read the words. Thunder crashed and a gust of wind blew into her room. One of the candles blew out.

Sirion,

I have you in my sights. It will not be long before I catch up to you. I will crush you and drink the blood from your pulsating heart. You are but a dead man walking . . .

Sydonnia

Adrianna trembled with fear of what would come. The words had been written in blood, she knew. Her hands were clammy as she refolded the disturbing letter and put it back into her pouch. *Sirion, who is this man who desires the taking of your life?* At that moment Adrianna was afraid, afraid for a man she hardly knew. She thought of telling Volstagg about it, but quickly discarded that notion. He had already told her he wanted nothing to do with the letter. She mentally went through the people within the group, but she felt she knew none of them well enough to tell them about the message. But what did that really matter? She hardly knew Sirion herself. However, for some reason, she felt she could only confide in someone she knew. She lay down on her bed and tried to study, but found she could not. Concentration would not come to her this night. The storm had quieted. It had been almost a momentary thing, lasting only about fifteen minutes. She didn't know how long she had lain there, only that she had had time to calm herself and her thoughts. Another knock rapped at her door, this one softer than the last. "Who is it?"

"It is I, Tianna."

As Adrianna went to open the door, she wondered why Tianna was coming to her room. Adrianna opened the door, and out of courtesy, motioned for Tianna to enter. Adrianna motioned towards the bed and Tianna sat on it. For a moment there was silence before Tianna spoke. "Listen, I don't really know anyone in the group and I was hoping on acquainting myself with you first. You know, as one woman to another."

"All right," replied Adrianna, although she really did not know, and did not think that she *wanted* to know.

Tianna smiled then, a pretty smile that not only turned up the corners of her mouth, but shone in her misty blue eyes. Tianna situated herself on the bed and regarded Adrianna a moment before speaking once more. It was as though Tianna was trying to determine just the right way to approach her. "Well, I was wondering . . ." she paused for a moment and licked her lips nervously, looking down at her hands folded neatly in her lap. "What exactly happened down there the last time . . . in the cemetery . . .?" Her voice trailed off as she looked back up at Adrianna. "And why were you all down there in the first place?" Her expression was despondent, bearing an almost haunted look, as though she dreaded what Adrianna would say.

Adrianna looked at the young woman perched upon her bed. She felt a little uncomfortable talking to someone she hardly knew, sharing a negative experience with a virtual stranger. She sighed as she went to the desk and retrieved the chair sitting before it. She brought the chair to rest near the bed, in front of Tianna. She seated herself on it backwards, folding her hands upon the chair back and resting her chin upon them. Hesitantly, Adrianna began to speak. She spoke as though she told a story, almost as though it had not happened to her at all, but to someone else entirely. "We searched the library as a favor to the Wildrunners. They had not the time to do it themselves, although I wish they had for all of this would never have taken place."

Adrianna imparted to Tianna most of what she knew about the situation, as well as what she knew about the other members of the group, which was not much. Adrianna forbore to mention the letter that Dartanyen had found upon one of the mutilated corpses, not wanting to speak about it with this woman, although Tianna seemed to be a very friendly person and sincere in her desire to know Adrianna. However, as Adrianna neared the ending of her story, Tianna seemed to become restless, shifting her position upon the bed and picking at the fabric of the quilt with her fingertips. "And that was when they came. From out of the darkness they advanced upon us, moaning eerily . . ."

"Ugh!" exclaimed Tianna, covering her face with her hands, her body shuddering convulsively.

Adrianna stopped. She watched as Tianna composed herself, but her face was a bit pale, and her hands shook as she placed them back in her lap. The haunted look in her eyes had returned. Adrianna was surprised to discover that Tianna was afraid. In a flare of sympathy, Adrianna quickly started speaking about waking up in the temple where Tianna had met them. After Adrianna had finished, the room was quiet.

"I don't like to hear about the undead." Tianna breathed in deeply, her eyes shifting about the room until they finally rested once more upon Adrianna.

"Something of a similar sort raided my childhood home . . . something frightful . . . something *dead* . . . " Tianna's voice trailed away and her eyes got a sad, faraway look to them. After a moment she shook herself out of the memory. She smiled wanly, trying to make light of the situation. Tianna tried to make small conversation, but Adrianna's answers were short and she herself did not speak to Tianna until the other woman spoke first. It was apparent to Adrianna when Tianna had tired of it all. In haste, Tianna finally wished Adrianna a good night and left.

Adrianna felt a momentary pang of loss, as though she had had a chance to acquire a possible confidante in Tianna and let it go. However, staying aloof and distant from others had become so second nature to her, Adrianna genuinely did not realize that she used these tactics as part of her everyday dealings with people. She sighed heavily to herself, lying down upon the softness of the bed.

Adrianna's thoughts returned to Sirion and the message she had read prior to Tianna's arrival. What in the Nine Hells was going on? What should she do? Then it hit her. She had to warn him. Somehow she had to get a message to Sirion warning him of the intentions of the man Sydonnia. Adrianna jumped up out of the bed and went over to the small desk. She opened the drawer and pulled out a small sheet of parchment. She then opened the jar of ink on the desktop and picked out a quill. She began to write a message to Sirion, and the first words that came to her mind found themselves on the parchment.

Sirion,

I write to offer thanks for your aid in taking us from the temple. It seems we had walked into a situation that seeped over our heads without our knowing it. Once more we will walk in the Underdark, but at least this time we hope to gain access to the temple proper. However, there is something more that I need share with you. I have told no one else about it, not really knowing who to tell, but it is here, sealed to the bottom of this page. The message has concerned me, and although we do not really know one another very well, I find myself concerned for your welfare.

Take care and give Dramati a neck rub for me. May you transcend all obstacles and the sun shine upon you.

Yours truly,
Adrianna Serine Darnesse

Adrianna stared at the message she had written. It would have to do. She would give it to Volstagg come morning. Adrianna went back over to her bed and lay herself within it, blowing out her light on the way. Despite feelings of foreboding, Adrianna finally fell into a restless sleep, her dreams troubled.

CHAPTER 4

Adrianna woke the next morning, unrefreshed. She knew that the nightmares had returned, but thankfully she did not remember them. It was just as well, because if she had remembered them, she would have spent a large portion of the day pondering them, thus putting her in a bad mood and a weak state of mind. She had awoken early, and was able to speak to Volstagg before he got busy. He took the message from her and told her that he would get the letter to Sirion. He would take it to his friend, who would send it to Grondor via his best hawk. She smiled at him gratefully and he gave her a quick hug before returning to his duties.

Adrianna wandered out into the common room and found that she was the first one to breakfast. As she ate the meal that was brought to her, she thought about the next few days. She was more than a little glad that they had a few days to rest before they entered what had to be a pit from one of the Hells again.

Finally the rest of the group made it to the common room. Everyone ate their breakfast, and soon all were ready to begin the day. Dinim told them that he had some business to take care of and would see them that evening back at the inn. Without any further explanation, he left. Everyone else spent most of the day with the weaponsmith and the armorer, haggling with them over how soon appropriate weapons and protective covering could be made for their use. Finally it was agreed that the items could be ready in four days, although for a handsome price. The group agreed to the increased cost of the items, knowing that it would all be covered by the city. The smiths would be at their forges day and night, preparing the weapons and armor needed by the group to face the enemy.

The rest of their day was spent on a farm at the outskirts of the city. It was owned by a man who bred and sold beasts of burden: larian, lloryk, and umberhulks. His stock had come highly recommended by several informants. What they had heard was true. The man was knowledgeable and friendly. His stock was of excellent quality, all of the animals healthy and strong. Everyone picked out a beast that they favored. Adrianna chose a dark, steel grey lloryk with paler markings. Everyone else chose from the variety of tawny colored larian, those animals being smaller and more of the appropriate size for riding.

All except for Zorg, who found that the larger lloryk more easily carried his larger frame. He chose a white animal, with only the merest hint of grey shading in the mane and tail.

After the purchase, everyone led their respective animals back into the city. Beneath the light cast by the fading sunlight, the shimmering iridescent scales shone beneath the soft fur, and the twice and thrice cloven hooves thudded lightly upon the cobbled streets. Once reaching the inn, the stable boys rushed out to take the animals. Adrianna and Dartanyen, knowing much about larian and lloryk and remembering all that the breeder had told them about the animals, gave the boys instructions for the feeding of each beast.

Once finished tending to the animals, Adrianna and Dartanyen followed the rest of the group into the inn. Dinim was already there, sitting at a table in the back. Adrianna studied him as she, Tianna, and Amethyst approached, the others having separated from them and gone up to the bar to make their orders to Volstagg. Dinim appeared upset, his dark brows pulled together into a frown. Upon realizing their presence, his countenance changed. Adrianna watched as he schooled his features into an expression of pleasant welcome that did not quite seem to reach his eyes. He stood as they made it to the table and began to seat themselves. Adrianna wondered what could have put him in such a mood.

Dartanyen, Bussi, Armond, and Zorg returned with some mugs and a tankard of ale, and after a while their food was brought out to them. Throughout the meal Dinim remained distant and aloof. Not once did he try to join in the conversation. Adrianna cast surreptitious glances in his direction, noting how different he seemed from the animated and free-spirited person she had met just yesterday. She had meant to speak with Dinim this evening about her father, tell him that she needed his help in discovering what had become of Thane after he, Ian, and Sheridana had left Sangrilak all of those years ago. But in light of his aura of indifference she was now loathe to do so. He seemed unapproachable to her. Remote.

The food platters were removed from the table, and the men had retrieved another tankard of ale. They were well on their way to becoming intoxicated. Tianna joined them, but the girl Amethyst seemed out of place, her dark eyes taking in everything all around her. She excused herself from the table. Dartanyen asked her where she was going. A slight look of irritation passed over her features before she answered that she wished to take a walk in the cool night air. Adrianna surmised that the girl had never before had someone in which to answer, and thus found it annoying. Adrianna smiled to herself, knowing that feeling. But she also knew that Dartanyen only asked because he cared, so that if something were to happen, he would know where to go looking for her.

It was then that Adrianna realized exactly who would be leading this group of individuals in which she had found herself a part. It was the way he spoke to Dinim, the way he wanted to know everything on their list of purchases. It was the way he had insisted that she tell him what she knew about the man Thane. It was the way he asked the whereabouts of the group members, even if someone was just going to the outhouse. It was even in the way he walked, a self-assured saunter.

Adrianna watched as Amethyst made her way past the tables and to the front door of the inn. Once she was at the door, Adrianna turned back toward the table. Her eyes were drawn to Dinim, whose gaze was locked on Amethyst as she left the establishment. A chill walked up Adrianna's spine. His brows were once more drawn together in a frown above cold, dark eyes. Abruptly his gaze shifted and he was looking at her. He stared into her eyes and she suddenly felt trapped. A tingling sensation arose upon her flesh and her breath slowed . . . almost as though her body sought to still itself. Then he smiled and his expression was changed. Once again he was the handsome, dynamic individual she had met the day before.

Released, Adrianna looked away from him. All of a sudden, she too, felt the need to get out. She rose from the table and looked about it. "I'm going out for a ride. I will see you all in a couple of hours." Dartanyen nodded to her as she stepped away from her seat. It was then that Bussi announced that he wanted a smoke. He asked if anyone else wanted to join him. "Wouldn't mind if I do." Adrianna heard Dinim reply as she walked away from the table.

Adrianna left the inn and walked quickly to the stables. She would go to visit Mairi. It had been too long, much too long since she had last seen her. Adrianna went to the stall that housed the lloryk that had been purchased for her that day. The dark shape inside moved and the animal approached the door. He was a fine animal with a thick arched neck, a sturdy chest, well-muscled legs, and friendly eyes. He was a large creature, larger than what she needed to carry her. From out of the corral this afternoon, he seemed to have called out to her, wanting her to choose him. She could not help but do so, and now, looking at him, she was pleased that she had followed her instincts.

The lloryk was quickly and efficiently saddled, and once out of the stables she was on his back. She felt his muscles ripple as he expressed his happiness to be out of his stall. He pranced about joyfully, head held high, nostrils flared. He awaited her commands and then began to trot. His stride was excellent and his footing sure. She took him to the front of the Hapless Cenloryan. She saw the group out on the porch, Dinim seated between Bussi and Dartanyen on the steps, Tianna seated in a rocking chair, and Armond leaning against a support column. Everyone seemed to be enjoying some light-hearted banter. She felt a momentary twinge of . . . something. She put the inexplicable feeling into the back of her mind as she urged the lloryk into a canter, and ran past the inn and into the darkness.

Adrianna rode through the city to the far northeastern edge of Sangrilak, out onto the plains. It was a good ride. She hadn't realized how much she had missed riding upon the back of a lloryk. She deliberated to herself as she rode, thinking of a good name to give to the beast that she rode. She liked the name Sethanon, and settled on it before she reached the first mile out of the city. Thoughts continued through her mind and once more she remembered the message to Sirion came to her mind. She had not told anyone about it, and no one had asked her. She felt so uncertain about it, wondering if she should tell anyone, and whom it was that she should tell.

She was so deep in thought that she was there before she knew it. She came to an area that was familiar and she slowed her mount. Out of the darkness appeared the house in which she had spent her childhood. It looked the same as it had eight years ago. Adrianna dismounted and looped Sethanon's reins around a pole in front of the house. It felt strange to walk up the porch steps, the very ones she had run up and down as a young girl. She knocked on the door. Adrianna had only to wait but a moment before the familiar figure appeared. Mairi opened the door and gasped when she saw Adrianna, her brown eyes lighting up with joy as the older woman grasped Adrianna in her arms. "My dear, sweet Adria . . ."

"Oh Mairi, I have missed you so much." Adrianna felt guilty for having not written to Mairi more often, but then she was enveloped within the warm embrace of the woman she had called 'mother' as a child. Adrianna instinctively held Mairi, and found that the close embrace was the same as she had always remembered.

The two women held one another for long moments, each one reveling in the presence of the other. When they finally parted, Mairi had tears in her eyes. Mairi bade Adrianna enter and led her into the sitting room, where she offered her some biscuits and tea. Once all had been prepared and set before them, Mairi sighed and smiled sadly. "It is so good to have you here, Adria. There has been so much I have wanted to share with you, and when you stayed away so long, I wished we had spoken more before you left."

Adrianna rose and went to the older woman, kneeling on the floor at her feet. She then lay her head in Mairi's lap. "I am here now." Adrianna swallowed heavily and closed her eyes, feeling the tears seeking to be freed. She sniffed and straightened, knowing she needed to ask the question although she wished not to. "How is Hafgan?"

"Ah, my husband sleeps. He is old and tired." Mairi smiled her sad smile once more. "Such is the price I pay . . ." Her voice trailed off, but to Adrianna, the older woman need not have said more. A half-faelin had married a human, and for that Mairi would spend many a long year without her mate. Adrianna shivered momentarily, struggled to take her mind off of Hafgan, the old memories resurfacing. She had resolved to forget the abuse she had suffered at his hand, refused to allow it to affect her life any longer. He had rarely touched her, except in the name of punishment, and his harsh words had left their scar upon her soul. But she would not allow his past treatment of her ruin her reunion with Mairi, who had never known the full extent of her husband's unkindness towards Adrianna.

The two women spoke well into the night, remembering the past, speaking of Adrianna's studies in Andahye, and dreaming of what the future may hold for her. Adrianna balked when it came time that she should leave. There was a part of her that wanted to stay, but the voice of reason within her knew that Hafgan would be angry that she had returned. It would be best if she were gone before he knew that she had ever been there. Adrianna rose. "Mairi, I should go know. I am weary, and I have much ahead of me on the morrow."

Mairi stood as well, and placed a hand on Adrianna's arm. "Adria, wait. There is something I want to tell you."

Adrianna regarded the other woman, and noted the tone in her voice. "What is it?"

"Actually, we should have spoken more about her years ago, when you were yet still a girl. But I could scarcely bring myself to do so, knowing how much it could hurt you to hear about her, especially the way your father treated you. But now I feel that, in some way, it could have helped you to have heard about her, to have known how wonderful she was, and especially how much she loved you."

"My mother."

"Oh, yes. I so much wish that you had known her. She was a special kind of person, so genuine and so caring. It is frightening to know just how fragile life is, and that it can be taken away in just the space of a heartbeat."

Adrianna felt her voice crack. "Mairi, please . . ."

"A long time ago, before you were born, I knew your mother. We were the best of friends." Mairi smiled with the memory, a sad smile that seemed to touch Adrianna's soul. "Your father was gone much of the time, so we got to know one another quite well. She was so vibrant, and full of life. After she became pregnant with you and your sister, she could not wait to show you the world. But it was not meant to be. When the labor went on for so long, and she became weaker and weaker, she seemed to know that she would die. After you finally came, she held you close. She spoke softly to you, and I could hardly hear. She said, 'You will be the child of my heart. You have a part of me that will always be with you. You will have knowledge of those things that have passed and of those that will come to be. Listen to your heart, and you will always be free.' She named you and then she died.

"But your mother, she seemed to know things. She knew things that would happen in the future. And she knew part of the circumstances into which you would be born. While she yet carried you and your sister in her belly, she showed something to me. She told me that she would give it not to the child born in the light, but the one who would be born in darkness. When the time came, your sister was born during the light of the day, and the sun shone upon her as she emerged from your mother's body. You were born in the middle of the night. Not even the light of the moon touched you. I knew it was to you that your mother meant for this gift to be given."

Mairi sighed. "You have grown into such a lovely woman Adrianna. Your mother was right. You definitely are the child of her heart. You look just like her." Mairi shook her head. "I hid the gift that your mother left for you, knowing that it had been special to her. I was afraid that Thane would find it and keep it from you. I will find it for you, and when next you come I will give it to you."

Adrianna took Mairi within her arms and held her close. "Thank you so much . . . for everything. You are the only mother I have ever known. I love you so much."

"And I love you. I have always loved you, just as I would have loved a daughter of my own."

Adrianna released Mairi. "I will come back as soon as I can. Take care until then."

Mairi led Adrianna to the door. Adrianna stepped out into the cool night. She mounted Sethanon and waved as she trotted away into the darkness. After a few moments, she turned her head to look back at the house. In the distance she could still see Mairi framed by the light in the doorway.

Under the light of the moons Sethanon carried Adrianna safely back to The Hapless Cenloryan Inn. She watered him and gave him two handfuls of grain for his work. Just then, she heard movement behind her. She whirled around to see a brown-haired boy standing at the entrance to the stall behind her. "My, you startled me." Adrianna held a hand to her chest, calming herself.

The boy looked to the ground. "I apologize to you, milady. I just wanted to see if you had need of me. I am Joral, the stable-hand here."

Adrianna smiled slightly. The boy could not be more than thirteen years old. He was skinny, wearing brown tunic and trousers, and he had clear blue eyes. "Thank you Joral, but I think all is well."

"Goodnight then, milady." The boy nodded to her, and then left.

Adrianna patted the animal for a moment before she walked back into the inn. As she came to the front entrance, she found Dinim and Bussi still sitting and smoking his pipe. Dinim looked up as she walked up the porch stairs. His startling purple eyes searched her face, and once again it was as if he could read her mind. "It is good to see old friends".

Adrianna startled. "Yes, it is." she said slowly. Disconcerted, she swept past the men and into the inn. As she passed through the wall of smoke she noticed that it made her feel relaxed and a little lethargic. "Bussi." Frowning, Adrianna turned toward the halfen. "Did you know that the leaf you are smoking has certain . . . properties to it?"

"Oh yes, I know." The halfen smiled and nodded his head emphatically. Adrianna smiled, shrugged her shoulders, and went to her room. She ordered a tub of warm water for a bath and then prepared herself for bed. As she slipped beneath the furs she once more thought of Dinim and the strange feelings she had about him. She sighed. She could not help but like him. She hoped he would help her to discover the truth about her father, and she wanted to trust him. But there was that small part of herself that was wary of people . . . of every man she met. And it would not let her put her guard down. Adrianna slept a restless sleep.

***

Sirion scouted ahead of the group. Every sense was alert to any change in the environment. His body was attuned to his surroundings, and he would know if anything were out of place. That was a part of his profession. As a ranger of Elvandahar, he made it his business to know everything there was to know about his terrain of choice, that being the forests on this side of the continent. But even if he were out of his territory, he would continue to see, hear, taste, smell, and feel the world around him.

Atop of Dramati, Sirion moved between the trees. This time, as it was most times, he was glad for the solitariness of his existence. His profession required it and his personality demanded it. It allowed him to think without the interference that being social brings. But this day, his thoughts were not upon his work, but rested upon the memory of what he had seen almost two weeks before.

Sirion's mind still recoiled at the sight of the monster's bloody dagger as it rose from its victim. In slow motion, he remembered sweeping by the creature, seeing its grotesque head fly through the air and land a few feet away. He remembered the fear as he knelt beside her body, placing his hand over the wound, the warmth of her blood pumping against his palm. He remembered the paleness of her face, the way she lay beside her fallen companion, her head in the crook of his arm. He saw the strips of fabric, knew she had been trying to help the man Armond. Sirion had pressed into the cut, heard her moan momentarily as she slipped into certain oblivion as her blood spilled upon the already blood-soaked ground. He had bound her wounds then, hoping to staunch the flow, hoping to get back in time to save her life. And then he had run, run like had had never run before, back to the surface to find the only people he knew would be able to save her and the rest.

Now, on his way to the city of Grondor, he wondered about the woman Adrianna, hoped that she fared well. He had not left until he knew that she would live. He had run for three days and nights to catch up with the rest of the Wildrunners, and then it was as though he was there with her still. She never quite seemed to leave his mind, but remained a constant companion to him. To his surprise, he found that he did not mind, and discovered that he never tired of thinking about her and wondering about her welfare.

Sirion smiled to himself. Such a change from what he had always known before, even when he had been with Joselyn. Despite the feelings he had borne for the druidess, she had never been able to take him away from his work. But now, a mere slip of a girl did more than just that. Adrianna consumed more than just his thoughts as he traveled through the thick Vanderess Forest.

Joselyn. It had been a long time since he had last thought of her. Whatever had become of her? What had she accomplished? It was for their professions that each one of them had decided to end their rather steamy acquaintanceship. And he could not refer to it as more than that, because that was all it had been, a meeting of their bodies and nothing more. All he knew of her dreams and goals in life was that she wished to rise in the clerical ranks, to be known as a master. And that was all she really knew of him, that he strove to be the best in his own chosen vocation.

For quite a while, with the exception of his profession, Joselyn Quemirren had consumed his mind . . . and his body. He had been a tracker, and after each job he would come to see her in the encampment. They would share a few days with one another before his next assignment. In a way, he had honestly cared for her, maybe even loved her. But the feelings he had for her had never transcended his desires to be a successful ranger, and neither would she give up her own endeavors to be with him. Thus, it had ended. A few times, he had thought that he might regret it, but in all honesty he never did. But now, as he thought of the young woman Adrianna, he thought that he just may give it all up . . . just to be with her.

***

Adrianna joined Dartanyen at the table in the farthest corner of the large common room. He was an early riser, earlier than anyone else. Soon after, Dinim, Armond, Zorg, Tianna, Bussi, and finally Amethyst arrived at the table. The girl was the last to come to the table, and was obviously still tired. Either she had spent half of her night awake, or she just simply was not a morning person. The sour expression on her pretty face told all at the table that she was not in a sociable mood, and no one spoke to her. Finally, when everyone had broken their fast, it was suggested that they go to bazaar to purchase those things that they would need to make life easier while on the road. "For all we know, this may not be the last of our assignment. I mean, lets think about this. Sirion sent for Tianna to come to us, knowing that she is a healer of some renown," said Dartanyen. He then turned to the lady he was discussing. "Am I correct in saying this?"

Tianna smiled. "Perhaps. I am a healer. That much is true. But the well-known part . . . well . . ."

Dartanyen chuckled. "Hmm, a modest healer. But don't you see what I am saying?" Dartanyen turned to the rest of the group. "Sirion sent for her, knowing that we would need her skills. Would he have done that if it were just going to be for one more excursion into the temple?"

Armond nodded. "You do have a point."

Dartanyen then turned to Dinim. "You know him better than any of us. What do you think?"

Dinim seemed to consider it for a moment. "I think that you are probably right. I would dare to guess that the Wildrunners, after this assignment, are considering asking us to help them further."

Adrianna considered it as well. She wasn't quite so sure. She felt that Sirion would possibly have sent for Tianna just to help them with this mission, especially if he found it important enough. However, it was indeed possible that what Dartanyen was saying could be true. Though, Adrianna was not so sure that she liked that idea. She had her own concerns to focus upon. She needed to find her sister and her uncle, discover how the dead man in the library had come to know her father, and why her father was looking for Dinim.

Despite these thoughts, Adrianna remained silent throughout the rest of the exchange. It was decided that items for use in travel would be bought. She had no money of her own, having given most of it to the priests that had taken care of the body of her master. The rest she had spent on her journey to Sangrilak in the form of food, lodging, and protection.

Adrianna rose with the others as they left the inn and made their way to bazaar. It was a beautiful spring day, mild and seasonably warm. It was a good day for a walk through the marketplace. The merchants had opened their doors at the crack of dawn. It was a day of rest, so the street vendors had set up their booths early as well, setting out their wares for the coming day. The group wandered in and among the shops and booths, the merchants smiling at them warmly, hoping that one of them would stop long enough for him or her to come over and begin preaching upon the virtues of this length of fabric, or that pair of boots. And finally they did stop, Bussi having become fascinated first by a carved wooden pipe, and then by the varieties of dried herbs and leaves offered by the merchant. The big man lumbered over to the halfen and Bussi began to barrage the merchant with questions. The rotund man answered them all with good-natured patience, and even seemed to be sincerely pleased that someone was as interested in the varieties as he was.

The group stood by for a few moments as Bussi and the cigar merchant conversed. They then began to disperse to nearby booths. Adrianna found herself wandering over to the beautiful stall of a fabric merchant. The many colored and textured lengths of cloth waved in the mid-morning breeze. She walked among the billowing waves of color, silently choosing those shades that she liked best, although she knew that she did not have the money to purchase any. "This one would look best on you, I think."

Startled, Adrianna turned to find a woman holding out a silken length of fabric. It was indeed beautiful, a soft shade of brown, that, when held this way and that, shifted from light to dark. Adrianna shook her head. "Oh no. I can't. I was just looking. You have so many beautiful pieces."

Adrianna turned away from the woman and began to continue her perusal when suddenly she found Dinim standing in front of her. "She is right, you know. With just the right touch, it would be most becoming on you." Dinim held out a strip of textured red cloth.

Adrianna began to feel her cheeks flush. Slightly embarrassed, she glanced first at Dinim and then at the stall owner, who continued to hold the brown silk. "Really, I can't. It must cost a fortune." She declined once again, silently wishing that Dinim had never come upon her, wishing that she had never decided to have a look in the fabric booth in the first place. It was true that she needed a new cloak. The one she wore would soon be too thick and heavy for her to carry in the summer-time heat. But she did not know how it would be possible to acquire one, unless she were to borrow money from Volstagg. And that was something she did not wish to do, not because he would not give her the money, but because he would give her more money than she would need, and would not allow her to pay him back.

Dinim raised a dark eyebrow. "Do you like it?"

Dinim's question caught her off-guard. She looked up into his face to find him regarding her solemnly. Adrianna shrugged her shoulders. "Sure. I like it. But that's not the point."

"You're right. That is not the point . . . precisely. More like, you need the fabric, and you may as well like the thing that you need to have."

Adrianna sighed heavily and put her hands on her hips. "Dinim, what in the Nine Hells are you talking about?"

He smiled a broad smile, and his eyes glinted mischievously. "Just what I said. You need the fabric. You may as well like it, and it may as well look good on you."

Adrianna rolled her eyes. "Dinim, you don't understand." She pointed to the fabric. "That length of fabric will cost a fortune! I am not in any position to be purchasing clothing of any such kind, especially one so costly."

"No, my dear. It is *you* who does not understand. *I* am in a position to purchase such an item, and I will. Knowing that you like it makes it only that much easier."

Adrianna felt her eyes widen. "You will do no such thing! I have not the means to repay you for such an item!"

"I did not ask you for repayment, nor would I ever expect it of you. You are supposed to consider it a gift and accept it as such." With that, Dinim took the strip of red fabric up to the merchant, who wore a satisfied smile on her face. Dinim did not even bother to haggle with the woman over the price of the brown silk and red piece, she knowing that he would buy it anyway. The woman gently placed the fabric in a cloth sack and gave it to Dinim, who then gave it to Adrianna.

Numbly, Adrianna took the sack. Smirking to himself, Dinim took her by the elbow and lead her from the booth. The rest of the group continued to wander around in the near vicinity. Zorg was found in a leather-workers shop, being sized for a new pair of boots. Tianna was found in yet another fabric shop, haggling with the merchant over the cost of a shock of deep green fabric. Dartanyen and Bussi lounged against the wall of the fabric store. Amethyst was nowhere to be seen.

***

Adrianna sat in the rocking chair on the porch of the Inn of the Hapless Cenloryan. Sighing, she leaned back into it and began to rock. She closed her eyes, remembering the last time she had spent out there. Sirion had been there, and Dramati. She looked back on that memory fondly, it being one of the only good memories she had experienced since coming home. That, and seeing Volstagg again, visiting Mairi, and meeting Dinim. Dinim. She found that she liked him very much, her wariness having given way to an easy camaraderie. It had been so thoughtful of him to purchase the cloth for her. She had immediately taken it to a tailor who would shape the fabric into a fine summer cloak for her, trimmed with the red satin that Dinim had chosen.

Adrianna had then returned to the inn to spend the rest of her day with her studies. She had slacked off since her master's death. She shamed his memory by letting her studies slide. She knew what he would have said had he been alive to say it. She could see him now, sitting at the lesson table in the laboratory. "A mind unused is a vessel for mischief. A mind without intellect is a waste, a repository for the useless garbage that it takes in on a common day. A mind without something to learn will go stagnant, rot like the thousands of other minds in this world of monotony. It is up to you to use the Talent bestowed upon you, to extend your mind to reach the farthest of horizons. It is my job merely to guide you on your way." He would smile then, his clear blue eyes crinkling at the corners. And then, having been rightly chastised, she would meekly return to her lesson, ashamed that she had not met up to his expectations of her all because she had not kept up her studies.

Adrianna sighed again. How she missed him. She wondered how Journeyman Tannin had taken his death. Now, looking back, she realized that she should not have left Andahye so hastily. Master Tallek's previous apprentices deserved to have had her presence, despite their dislike of her, especially Tannin. But what was done was done. She would have been sorely put out to have to wait for him to return to Andahye, and Master Jancet had been similarly out of town.

After several hours of study, Adrianna had gone to the common room, where she discovered that Amethyst had finally returned. The young girl had been away all day, without a word to anyone. Adrianna remembered Dartanyen's silence as the group returned to the Inn after visiting the tailor. She could tell that he was angry by the set of his lower jaw; the muscles clenched there, the sparkle in his blue eyes. Adrianna was just in time to see the verbal battle that ensued upon Amethyst's return.

"It's about time you decided to walk in here," Adrianna heard Dartanyen say icily from his chair.

Amethyst shrugged her shoulders noncommittally, her expression impassive. "I was just out and about."

"Just 'out and about', hunh? Well, next time why don't you consider telling someone you are going to be 'out and about' before you just go traipsing off to gods know where."

Amethyst sneered disdainfully. "I'll do whatever I damn well please. I don't recall anyone naming you my keeper. So just bother off, will ya?"

Dartanyen rose from his chair. His next words were loud, louder than Adrianna thought they would be. He was angry, his blue eyes flashing dangerously. "For your information little miss, I named *myself* your warden, and as such, you will come to me when you plan on going anywhere. That includes 'out and about', inside out, and sideways. Do you understand?"

Amethyst's brown eyes narrowed angrily. "Piss off," she hissed. She then turned on her heel and began to walk away.

Quick as lightening, before Amethyst could even go two paces, Dartanyen was upon her. He took her arm and spun Amethyst around to face him. The girl's eyes widened. They stood face to face, she being as tall as he. But that did not diminish him, his anger fueling his body, making him appear larger than she by far. "Do not turn your back to me in an argument. You may one day come to regret it," he said softly.

Amethyst's voice held none of its previous hauteur as she replied, "Don't threaten me."

"Oh, it's no threat." Dartanyen leaned in closer to her. "It's a promise."

Amethyst was silent for a moment as she regarded him, her wide brown eyes taking in his face, judging his sincerity. Then she stiffened. "Let me go," she said as she began to struggle.

Dartanyen released her arm forcefully and she stumbled back. Amethyst blinked with surprise, but said nothing as she rubbed the area where he had held her.

"You will agree to tell one of us when you are going next time. It is not my job to be your baby-sitter. You made me and everyone else here worry needlessly over your absence. Another hour or so and we would have begun to search for you." Dartanyen paused and then continued. "I know that you are not accustomed to this, but I can not have the integrity of this group threatened by the impetuous nature of a child. It's time that you began to grow up and take responsibility for your actions. Dinim will not always be there to save your silly hide."

Amethyst's gaze went to where the mage was seated. He had not stirred from his position in his seat, lazily taking in the scene before him. Her eyes swept over the rest of the group, who were silently watching the scene that had been created. She then returned to Dartanyen, whose temper seemed to have cooled. Then, saying nothing, she turned and walked slowly up the stairs to her room.

Adrianna had stared after the girl for a moment before going to the bar and asking for some cooked grains and tea. In a way, she felt sorry for Amethyst. But at the same time, she did not, disliking the lack of respect the girl had shown for Dartanyen. But the Terralean had quickly remedied that, his harsh treatment of her instilling the respect that he required from her.

As she waited for her meal, Adrianna wondered why Dartanyen had not shown his anger to her when she had refused to tell him what she knew about Thane's letter. She had spouted off to him, raised her voice and turned her back on him the same as Amethyst had just done. But perhaps the difference was that he had seen the disbelief mirrored in her eyes, the helplessness. Perhaps he had seen that it was anger and fear that spoke, rather than arrogance and lack of respect. Perhaps Dartanyen was more perceptive than she gave him credit.

Adrianna walked back to her room with her bowl of grains and mug of steaming tea. After eating, she went to bed. She thought of the group of people with which she had found herself and the road that lay ahead of them.

***

The next day, Adrianna once again sat on the veranda outside of the inn. She had focused on her studies for most of the morning and early afternoon, and within only a few hours the day would be coming to a close. Adrianna watched as Armond walked wearily towards the inn. It was only a couple hours after mid-day, but he had been at the smithy since early morning. He had told Dartanyen that he was a pretty good weaponsmith himself, and that he would be sure they were getting quality weapons from four days of good hard work. And it was obvious that he had worked hard. His face and clothing were covered with the dark grime that came with working at the forges. His hands were black with the material, and she was sure that there were numerous cuts and abrasions beneath the layer of soil.

Adrianna stood from her chair, went to the door, and opened it for him. Armond smiled wearily and nodded gratefully to her as he entered. She heard him call for a bath on his way up the stairs to the room he shared with Zorg. Adrianna glanced around the common room and spied Tianna sitting at the bar. The other woman caught her gaze and stepped down. Adrianna waited until she had joined her at the entrance. "How do you feel about a post mid-day walk?"

Adrianna shrugged her shoulders and then smiled. "Sure. I suppose my body could handle a little physical stimulation." Inwardly, she cringed at her offhand comment. It was such an understatement. While apprenticed under Master Tallek, her body had been accustomed to so much more. Within the first week of her apprentice-ship, he had taken her to Lady Wilhelmina, who had taught her to control the movements of her body through the art of dance. And much to her disbelief, Adrianna had excelled at the exercises. But it wasn't just the body control, or the physical stimulation. It was the release . . . that little piece of something that her mind and body could devour without the need for intellectual challenge.

Adrianna and Tianna stepped into the busy street. An umberhulk cart loaded with lumber rumbled by them, followed by a group of boys chasing a mangy dog, the nearly hairless canine yapping as it sped down the street. Adrianna glanced after the boys as they passed by. She had been much like them once. She had never chased dogs through the streets, but she had definitely spent most of her time there, wandering about and meeting people. That was how she had finally met Volstagg. Hot after spending the day in the sun, she had stepped into the inn.

Adrianna remembered it like it was yesterday. The inside of the building had been cool against the bare flesh of her arms and legs. It was dark and it took her eyes a few moments to adjust to the dim lighting. She registered movement in the back of the establishment behind the bar. She followed the movement as her eyes adjusted. The form emerged from behind the bar and began to wipe off some tables nearby. She could hear the clap of hard shoes against the wooden floor, much like the sound of a larian's hooves. And then the form took shape. Her eyes had widened with something akin to awe as she beheld him for the first time. She had seen her very first cenloryan.

Adrianna felt herself jolted out of her memory. "Effin Calotebas", she heard Tianna mumble as the other woman caught herself from falling, clutching Adria's arm as she did so. Tianna glanced back at the offending passerby, a tall man with a dark cloak. She then turned back to Adrianna. "Sorry," she said. "I had forgotten how rude most people can be."

Adrianna smiled. "That's all right. I probably remember enough for the both of us."

The two women continued to walk, enjoying the late afternoon sun. Adrianna became introspective, recalling the letter she had received for Sirion. It disturbed her greatly to know that someone desired his death. She thought about telling Tianna about it, so much wanting to share it with someone. Despite her initial thoughts about the other woman, Tianna seemed to be a kind person, someone who would be easy to talk to and get along with. Not only that, but she had known Sirion. She would probably want to know about the letter, Tianna obviously being a friend of his. Sirion evidently thought well of her, having sent for her to join them in their efforts at the temple.

Finally, Adrianna decided that she would tell Tianna about the letter. She would tell her later, in the privacy of her bedchamber. Just as Adrianna reached her decision, she began to hear a commotion in the distance. Adrianna and Tianna glanced momentarily at each other before rushing in the direction of the sounds of a fight.

The two women entered upon the scene. Between themselves and the combatants was a quickly growing mass of spectators. They were able to squeeze between a couple of burly men and a group of gaping women on their way to the front line. Upon reaching it they stopped suddenly, both having seen the same thing. It was Dinim. He held a glowing silver short-sword in his right hand. His face was contorted with rage as he leapt at his opponent, a human man wielding a short sword. The other man parried Dinim's blow. Both of them carried wounds, Dinim with a slash to his arm and shoulder, and the other man a nasty gash at his side. Adrianna saw the man put his hand to the wound a couple of times, almost as though to be sure nothing was emerging from it.

Amid the noise from the growing crowd, Adrianna could hear the two men shouting at one another but was unable to make out their words. She could see Dinim getting angrier. She knew that he wanted to use his magic. Any sorcerer would. But she knew that he could not. In the presence of such a large number of onlookers, it would be sheer stupidity to use magic.

The Talent to harness magic was a rare one. Master Tallek had taught her that only the most gifted of the Talented could learn to use their innate ability to harness and tame the energies that flowed between and among all living things. The ability to harness magic was an awesome ability, and to the common masses, nothing less than frightening. Those who knew how to use magic were a mysterious lot and much under the scrutiny of those who did not posses the Talent. If Dinim were to use magic here, he would inflict much fear and prejudice. He could not afford to do that, and thus used his sword, albeit a magical one. Most of the people gathered would not even notice it as such, seeing it only as an item of quality and beauty.

The men lunged at one another again, the magic of the sword offering Dinim more power and finesse than he would have had ere he not held it. But the other man was a more practiced swordsman, and despite the magical nature of Dinim's blade, turned the tables of the fight in his favor. With a quick twist of his wrist, the man sent Dinim's weapon flying from his hand.

The crowd gasped. Adrianna saw Tianna put her hand to her mouth. Returning her attention to the fight, Adrianna caught a glimpse of a big man making his way through the crowd on the other side of the combatants. After another moment she saw that it was Zorg. In shock, Dinim cursed at his opponent as the other man spun past him. But Dinim did not turn to follow the man. Instead he kept his back to him. The human saw his opportunity and took it. He leapt at Dinim. At the last moment before impact, Dinim spun around. He sheathed his dagger deep into the man's belly, using the force of the man's leap to aid him. That same force made Dinim stagger backwards and fall, the weight of the dying man on top of him.

Adrianna heard herself and all of those around her exhale. She watched as Zorg succeeded in pushing past the front line of the crowd on the other side. He rushed towards the fallen men and pulled the dead man off Dinim. Worried, Adrianna watched for any signs of movement from their companion. For a few moments she saw none, and then, finally, she saw him begin to try to lift himself from the ground. The big warrior was instantly at his side, and after a few words were exchanged, Dinim was picked up by Zorg and carried from the scene.

Adrianna and Tianna were pushed from behind as the crowd began to surge forward. They quickly got out of its way and followed Zorg en route back to the inn. Up ahead they could see Dartanyen and Bussi had joined him. They too must have seen the fight.

Adrianna and Tianna were right behind as the three men and their burden were hurried into the inn. "Volstagg, come quick. Dinim has been injured," shouted Dartanyen as the front door was swung open. Volstagg came bursting out of the kitchens. He was up and over the bar within a single moment, his massive hooves striking sparks on the stone as he landed on the other side.

Dartanyen ran to the nearest table and swept all that was on it onto the floor. Zorg followed quickly behind with the limp body of Dinim in his arms. Upon the cleared table he lay the semi-conscious Cimmerean. Bussi stood near the entrance to the inn, wanting to stay out of everyone's way. In his hands was Dinim's magical blade. Amethyst had entered the inn as well. Adrianna took up her stance between Bussi and Amethyst, also wishing to keep herself out from underfoot. Tianna advanced upon the injured man, a look of intense concentration already having formed across her brow.

By the time Tianna reached the table, Dinim's clothing had already been removed from the wound sites. "Bring another table and move it up against this one," she ordered. This table is too high to work on him effectively." Zorg was quick to do her bidding, he and Dartanyen bringing another table so that it abutted the one upon which Dinim lay.

The moment that Tianna was climbing up onto the second table so that she may work upon Dinim, Armond came down the stairs. With a look of concern on his face, Armond walked up to Dartanyen and Zorg, who began to fill him in on what had occurred. Tianna leaned over her patient, her left hand clutched at an amulet around her neck. Feeling that it may be all right to approach the table, Adrianna did so. She stood silently on the side of Dinim across from the healer and simply watched, fascinated.

Within her mind, Tianna prayed. Her eyes were closed and her lips moved only slightly with her words as she continued to clutch the talisman in her grip. Then, opening her eyes and removing her hand from the symbol of Beory, Tianna leaned over Dinim and placed her hands near his wounds. He stirred for a moment beneath her touch and then subsided. She frowned. There was something amiss, something not quite right about this man. She sensed something from his bodily vibrations that she had never encountered before.

Tianna continued her ministrations. With her gifts and skills as a healer, she analyzed the wounds. They were not bad ones and easily mended. Dinim would not suffer adversely in the future from these wounds. Tianna took up the wet cloth that Volstagg had had the presence of mind to set beside her. He had even known enough to boil it so that it would not be the cause of any infection that may enter the wounds. The water was hot, very hot, but she kept her focus upon the task before her.

Tianna lay the hot cloth upon the wounds on Dinim's upper arm and shoulder. She cleansed the areas thoroughly. She would not know for sure if there would be any infection, but in her professional opinion there would be none. She planned to apply an herbal salve to help to keep infection away. She had prepared it herself, gathered the dark bark from the khaobab tree, pulverized it and steeped it with water over flame. She had then added leonine to it, not only to make it soothing as it was applied, but to make it thick and oily. It had a medicinal smell, but it was worth it to reek of plants for a few days in order to avoid the massive infections that so often took the limbs and lives of many a good warrior.

Finally Tianna was finished. She lay her hand upon Dinim's brow and felt no fever. But, once again, she could not keep the frown from creasing her forehead. It was that strange sensation she had received earlier, the feeling that there was something strange about this man, something not right. However, unable to put her finger on it, Tianna was forced to dismiss the feeling yet again, although she was somewhat loathe to do so.

That evening the group sat around the dinner table. Zorg and Armond ordered a large tankard of ale. Most decided to partake of the flavorful beverage, knowing that it was the last night they could before their excursion back to the temple. Adrianna liked the taste of the ale, it being one of Volstagg's best. However, she decided not to drink any of it, disliking the feelings that imbibing such beverages brings. She noticed that Dinim was unusually quiet, to be expected considering the events of the day.

Inevitably, the conversation went to those events that had taken place earlier. Dartanyen was the first to bring it up. Adrianna had been wondering when he would. "So Dinim, what happened this afternoon? What was all of the commotion about? You know that the City Guard came while you were sleeping, wanting to ask you some questions. I told them that you had been injured and were resting." Dartanyen stopped and looked at Dinim.

Dinim shrugged nonchalantly. Adrianna noticed a slight frown of irritation before he quickly covered it up. "I really don't know. The man bumped into me as we were passing in the street. He stopped and gave me an attitude. Of course I said words back to him. The man became angry and unsheathed his sword. In order to protect myself I was forced to do the same." Dinim stopped. Adrianna saw him cast a glance around the table. Adrianna followed his gaze and stopped at Amethyst. She was looking at Dinim with a strange expression on her face. Then she looked down into her lap.

Adrianna brought her attention back to Dinim. Zorg whistled. "That was it? You was fightin' because you bumped each other in the street? Gads, it sounds like somethin' I would do." Zorg guffawed loudly, the drink beginning to take a hold of him. Armond and Bussi snickered as well.

Dartanyen smiled. "Well, won't that be a story for the City Guard tomorrow. I think they were looking for something a little more . . . well . . . interesting." Then he began to laugh as well. Even Adrianna could not help a smile from creeping onto her face, imagining the looks on the faces of the City Guard the next day.

After a few more jokes were thrown about the City Guard, Bussi took control of the conversation, telling them a tale about his earlier days. After a couple more rounds of drink, Amethyst rose from the table. The girl nodded to the group and left. Not even Dartanyen stirred from his seat, as it was now common knowledge that Amethyst took a walk every night before retiring to bed.

Dinim watched as Amethyst went out the front door. After about fifteen minutes, he also rose from the table. "I think I am going to get some rest. I'm more tired than I thought I was."

Tianna stood as well. "Are you feeling all right? Is there anything I can get for you?"

Dinim grinned and raised his hands. "No, no. I'm fine. I just need some sleep is all. You have done more than enough to help me. Thank you. See you all in the morning." Dinim stepped away from the table and walked up the stairs to his room.

Well into the night the men talked. Adrianna and Tianna just sat and listened, entertained by the stories the men told about their lives and the lives of those they knew. Finally, with bellies full of drink, the men stumbled up the stairs with the help of the two women. They giggled as they tucked the men tightly in their beds. Adrianna remembered that she wanted to tell Tianna about the letter, but she was so tired she decided to tell her in the morning. Adrianna fell into bed and slept a restless sleep.

***

The group waited. Everyone had eaten breakfast and was ready for the day. They had decided that they would all go together to get their weapons from the smithy. They would each need to check the weapons to be sure of their quality. Armond was certain of their caliber and had practically guaranteed them himself. But there was one person missing. Amethyst still had not emerged from her room.

Adrianna sighed. No one showed any inclination of going upstairs to get her. Adrianna rose from the table at the same time as Tianna. They nodded to one another and left the rest of the group sitting there talking about the political situation between Torimir and Karlisle. They made their way up to Amethyst's room. Upon reaching it Adrianna knocked on the door. There was no answer. "Amethyst. Amethyst, everyone is waiting for you downstairs," said Adrianna.

There was no reply. Adrianna frowned. She put her hand on the doorknob and turned it, expecting it to be locked. To her surprise, the door opened. Adrianna glanced at Tianna. The other woman nodded and they entered the room. They looked around in consternation. It was empty of an occupant. All that attested that someone was staying there was a back-sack sitting on the nicely prepared bed.

"Adrianna, it looks like she didn't come back last night."

"I know." An uneasy feeling swept through her. "I wonder if something happened."

"You mean, you wonder if she got caught?" Tianna cast her an apathetic glance.

Adrianna rolled her eyes. "Of course."

"But don't you think she would have found a way to get a message to us?"

"From prison . . . no."

Tianna huffed. "It probably serves her right. This was bound to happen. I mean, look at the circumstances that brought her to us in the first place."

"I know, I know. But before we speculate any further, let us first find out if she is indeed imprisoned for a crime. Let's go tell the others."

The two women went downstairs. "She is not in her room."

Dartanyen looked up at Adrianna. His brows drew together into a scowl. "What do you mean?

"Exactly what I said. Amethyst is not in her room. In fact, it appears that she never came back last night at all."

Dartanyen's lips drew into a thin line. "All right." He stood from his seat. "We go without her then."

Adrianna continued. "Well, Tianna and I feel that she may have gotten herself into trouble. We were thinking of looking around for her a little. You know, check out the local jail to see if she is there."

"Forget it." Adrianna turned in the direction of Dinim's voice. He wore a frown of irritation across his face. "Let her deal with the consequences of her actions. We can't always be here to get her out of trouble."

Adrianna frowned. "You see that's just it. We weren't here. Think of all the years she has been living on the streets. She obviously has always been able to elude trouble before we came along."

"Yeah. Maybe with the help of the local thieves' guild," said Armond.

"But how do we know that?" interjected Tianna. "We have to give her the benefit of the doubt. I mean, she is a member of this group, isn't she?"

"At least let's check out the jail. Just to be sure that she isn't there. We have to know for sure," said Adrianna.

Dartanyen sighed. "All right. We'll go."

The group began to file out of the inn. Adrianna noticed Dinim shaking his head. Zorg, Armond, and Bussi just shrugged and followed behind. In silence they walked to the city jailhouse located on the north side. Upon reaching it, they entered the establishment. Dartanyen asked the guard at the front desk if anyone had been brought in the night before. The man replied that no one had been brought in for several days. Dartanyen thanked the guard and they left.

For a few moments everyone just stood outside the jailhouse. Finally Dartanyen spoke. "All right. She's not here. Maybe she has no intention of coming back. I mean, she acts like she doesn't want to be a part of our mission anyway."

"No. I don't think that is the case. Tianna and I saw her backpack still in her room when we went to check on her. I feel that she has every intention of coming back," said Adrianna.

"Well where in the Hells is she then?" asked Armond.

"Listen, I don't have time for this," said Dinim petulantly. "I have a lot to do before we go back down to the temple tomorrow."

Dartanyen planted his fists at his hips and sighed heavily. "I know. We all have a lot to do before tomorrow. Let's just go and complete our business for the day. Maybe she will have shown up back at the inn by the time we get back."

"But what if something's happened to her and she needs our help? Maybe we should search for her," said Tianna.

Adrianna had just been thinking the same thing. A feeling of foreboding began to creep up her spine. "Well, it seems that she did not return from her nightly walk. Perhaps we should just search around some of the main streets. Maybe someone has seen her,"she said.

"Well, you all can spend the rest of the day standing here talking about it. I have a lot of business to take care of. I'll see you later." With that said, Dinim walked away. Adrianna watched him leave. He was acting like he didn't even care if something had happened to Amethyst. Her eyebrows furrowed in thought. It was as though he wanted nothing to do with any kind of a search for her.

Dartanyen sighed again. "All right. Why don't we do this: Armond, Zorg, Bussi and I will go to the smithy. We have to at least do that. In the mean time, you and Tianna begin searching. After the rest of us are done we will join you. We will meet back at the inn at quarter past mid-day."

"Agreed," piped Tianna. "Let's go, Adria."

Tianna took a surprised Adrianna's arm in her own and began leading her down the street. Tianna had used the name that Sheri had always called her when they were children. Strangely, it made her feel good. She grinned to herself for a moment. Perhaps she would make a place for herself with this group after all.

For two hours Adrianna and Tianna searched for Amethyst to no avail. No one had seen her. They searched all of the main streets, and even some of the side streets. "Tianna, we have to go back to the inn now. Who knows, maybe Dartanyen and the others were able to find her. Or maybe Dartanyen was right and she went back to the inn on her own."

Tianna cast her a withering glance. "And you really believe that?"

"Well, no. But we still have to be getting back. I don't want to find out later that they sent out a search party for us too. Besides, I think we are in over our heads and we need to ask some professional assistance."

"You mean you think we should ask the City Guard to help us? Don't you think that we have made ourselves high profile enough already?"

"Yeah, but one more thing won't hurt us any more than we are already."

Tianna nodded. "True. All right then. Let's go back. But you know, I think that if we just look a little longer . . . "

"I know. Let's go. Maybe the others have found out something."

When the women returned to the inn, they found Dartanyen, Bussi, Zorg, and Armond waiting for them. Dartanyen stepped towards them. "So, did you find her?"

Adrianna frowned. She had been nursing the secret hope that despite her feelings that something was terribly amiss, Amethyst either would have returned to the inn, or that the others would have found her. "No. We searched everywhere. What should we do?"

Dartanyen shook his head. "We'll have to go to the City Guard. They have professionals who do this type of thing all the time. Every city usually has at least one on duty. They are called Streetsliders. They are the ones that discover those who are missing and probably murdered."

"How are we going to get one of those people to search for us?" asked Tianna. "Amethyst hasn't even been missing for an entire day. Not only that, the possibility still remains that she decided not to return, back-sack or no."

"My dear," began Dartanyen, "it is always possible to get others to do the work one wishes of them. One needs only to use a bit of style." Dartanyen regarded her seriously.

"You mean lie," replied Tianna, her eyes narrowing.

Dartanyen spread his arms. "It is merely a matter of viewpoint. I see it differently."

"Come on," said Armond. "Let's go and get this over with. I am not beyond a bit of manipulation myself."

"I knew someone would see it my way." Dartanyen grinned mischievously.

"Yeah, well I just want to get a full night's rest tonight. I don't relish the idea of being awake all night long searching for children who should be at home in their beds."

"Hear, hear," mumbled Zorg as he followed Dartanyen and Armond out the door.

"Whatever gets the job done," whispered Adrianna to herself.

***

The Captain of the City Guard eyed them speculatively. "How long did you say that she has been missing?"

"Almost three days," said Dartanyen.

"And she was one of the ones hired to contribute to our efforts in the temple?"

Dartanyen lifted his arms from his sides. "Of course."

"And you have reason to believe that something may have happened to her?"

"Yes. Just being in contact with us could cause anyone to be endangered. For all we know, Gaknar has infiltrated this city with his spies. They could have caught her unawares."

The Captain leaned back in his chair. "You know, you people are ending up being a pain in my backside. Do you know what kind of money you have cost me already?"

"And I am sure it is worth every penny to keep the citizens of this province safe from the machinations of one such as Gaknar," said Dartanyen.

The Captain glared at him. "Fine. I will call in Harris. Maybe he will find your friend for you. Just you bring me back the proof that it is indeed Gaknar's temple when you go down there tomorrow." The Captain then waved them out of his office.

It seemed they waited forever outside of the Guards' Headquarters. Just when Dartanyen was about ready to go back inside to ask if they had been forgotten, a man called to them as he emerged from the side of the building. Behind him followed two other men. They were armed with crossbows and each had a long-sword that hung from his hip.

The men approached the group. "Good evening. The name's Harris. This is Darric," he indicated to his right, "and Burke. We will be working on your case. The Captain gave us a description of your companion. We had better hurry though before we lose our light. Where can we reach you?"

"The Inn of the Hapless Cenloryan," replied Dartanyen.

"All right. See you there when we are done." Harris turned on his heel and the two others followed him down the street.

Dartanyen turned back to the group. "Now we wait."

The group went back to the inn. They found Dinim there waiting for them. Dartanyen filled him in on the events of the day, ending with their hire of the Streetsliders to find the girl Amethyst.

"I tell you that it's all a waste of time. She's gone. You should have let it be." The Cimmerean shook his head and sat at a table, slouching down in the chair and crossing his arms at his chest.

"Perhaps, but Tianna and Adrianna seem to feel otherwise. At least now no one can say that we didn't try."

Dinim said nothing, a dark brooding expression on his face. Adrianna regarded him out of the corner of her eye. He seemed so uncaring and abrasive, very unlike the way he had been before his skirmish in the city streets. She felt Tianna step up beside her. Adrianna glanced at the other woman and noticed her watching Dinim strangely. Perhaps she too sensed the duality of Dinim's attitudes.

Hours passed and it began to get late. But no one, including Dinim, was willing to climb the stairs to his or her bedchamber for the night. All waited expectantly for the arrival of the street rangers. Finally it came. The front doors swung open suddenly, causing Adrianna to lurch up from her seat. The three men strode into the room, Harris carrying a limp body in his arms. "Hurry, she needs medical attention as soon as possible."

Tianna jumped up from her chair and ran towards the stairs. "We will take her up to my room so that I may help her as I can."

Harris followed Tianna up the stairs, the rest of the group following behind. Once in her room, Harris laid the body down on the bed. He pulled aside the tangled mass of dark hair to reveal a battered face. It was Amethyst. She had been beaten badly, and had probably been left for dead.

Adrianna had already collected the washbasin and cloth, bringing it to Tianna. The healer had her eyes closed, her talisman gripped firmly in her hand. Adrianna dipped the cloth in the water and began to wipe the blood off of Amethyst's face. The girl did not move, did not even perceptibly breathe. Adrianna feared for her, feared that she would not live. Her clothes were torn and covered with blood. Her flesh was pale, almost like she was a ghost, and cold, like the warmth of life had left her already.

Tianna lay her hands upon Amethyst's face. Adrianna caught the whispers of her prayers, but could not make out the words. Tianna released the remaining buttons of the blouse and pulled it open. Adrianna heard the intake of breath from around the room. Adrianna looked upon the bruised and beaten body of the girl on the bed. Unbidden, tears sprung to her eyes. *That was me, once.* Adrianna shook her head, willing the memories away. Adrianna examined the rest of the girl's clothes. Her trousers were still intact. At least whoever had done this had not violated her.

Tianna looked around the room. "Please, leave us in privacy." She than began to remove the rest of the girl's clothing. Dartanyen nodded and went out the door, the others following suit.

"I hope we found her in time, milady," said Harris as he and his men left the room behind Dartanyen, Armond, Zorg, Bussi, and Dinim. Adrianna placed the cloth in the red waters in the washbasin and rose to leave with the others.

"No. Adrianna, wait." Tianna put her hand out toward her. "Please stay.

I could use your help. It's just that I didn't feel comfortable having the men here. Besides, they weren't doing any good just standing there anyway. I want to afford the poor girl as much privacy as I can. It's the least I can do."

Adrianna smiled at Tianna warmly. "I am glad. I would be happy to help. Here, let me get a fresh basin of water." Adrianna went downstairs and retrieved some warm water and fresh cloths. When she returned she found Tianna praying over Amethyst again, her delicate hands resting upon the bruises on her ribs and abdomen. Adrianna sat beside the bed and once more began to cleanse the girl's face and head. She was careful not to wash away the blood that had clotted at some of the cuts and abrasions on her scalp. She then began to wash the matted hair, knowing that in its filth it could carry infection to the wounds.

Finally Tianna looked up from her work. Her shoulders sagged and she had hollows beneath her eyes. "She has been beaten badly. Her right wrist is broken, several of her ribs are cracked or broken, and she is bleeding inside. I have done all I can to help her. She needs more than I have the strength to give. Obviously she will not be going to the temple beneath the city tomorrow, so I feel that we should take her to the Temple of Hermod to heal and rest until our return."

Adrianna regarded Tianna with open concern. She looked haggard, like she hadn't slept in days. Her hands shook as she took them through her hair. It was obvious to Adrianna that she had spent every last vestige of her energy upon the girl lying between them. Such was the price that Tianna paid for her prayers to her goddess, much like the price that magic exacted from Adrianna when she opted for its use. "Come then. Let us take her there now. We need to get as much rest as possible before tomorrow morn."

Tianna nodded. Adrianna went downstairs and told the others about their decision. Zorg followed her back to the room. Gently, the big man picked Amethyst up from the bed and carried her back down the stairs. Only Dartanyen accompanied them to the temple, for Armond, Dinim, and Bussi had each gone to their beds. The priests and clerics at the Temple of Hermod had no problem keeping the girl with them until the group returned from their mission. Dartanyen gave them gold for the ministrations that would be given to their comrade. Then they left, hoping that the girl would be well when they returned.

CHAPTER 5

He walked in darkness, seemingly at one with it. His tattered dark robes swished about his ankles as he moved. From within the crevices he could hear the skittering of tiny feet. Rats. Although he was accustomed to them, had lived his entire childhood near them, he hated rats. They were vermin, scavengers, not even worth eating.

Dinim stopped. The dark tunnel seemed to continue, but in actuality it ended. Two feet away was a barrier, the invisible walls of his prison. Slowly he made his way forward. Before the ward he stopped, knowing exactly where it lay. Very quickly he had learned the confines of his prison cell. For the first few days of captivity, he had done nothing but attempt to find a way out, find some way to breach the magical barriers that confined him.

Dinim put his hand out, felt the hum of the magic behind the barrier, and withdrew. If he touched it, he would be pulsed with electrical energy. He knew from personal experience. He had touched it several times, trying in vain to escape. But it was to no avail. So he had rotted within the dungeons of Gaknar's temple, an angry spirit that roamed the halls and corridors. Not many entered there, the guards thinking it haunted. Several he had maimed and a few he had killed. It had been in the beginning when they did not know any better. But now hardly anyone came.

Deep within him the anger stirred. Dinim turned and moved away from the ward. He thought of the creature that had stolen his identity, taken his life away from him. Shapeshifter . . . doppelganger. Ixitchitl had used the magic of Aasarak to capture him, defeat him, and then assume his form. With sickening clarity he remembered the invasion of his mind, how the creature had scoured his memories, learned his strengths and his weaknesses, acquired his skills, incorporated them unto itself. And then the creature had left him, picked clean of everything he had ever been.

Dinim made his way to the next ward. He checked them all every day in the hope that he would find a weakness and discover a way out. But deep in his mind he always knew that Ixitchitl would return. Aasarak would come to claim his prize and the creature would be with him. Dinim would be ready.

***

The next morning everyone awoke early in order to prepare themselves for their journey. Dawn was quite some time away, but they had felt it important to get as early a start as possible. It did not take them long, for they were eager to go. They walked through the quiet streets to the library. The clouds rested low to the ground and Adrianna could feel the moisture in the air. They approached the newly replaced front doors of the library and opened them with the key placed in their care. The mess that they had seen the last time they were there had been cleaned up. The group went over to what was once a secret passageway. The bookcase had been propped open and the corridor had been well lit with a multitude of torches set in sconces along the walls.

The group progressed in silence. Bussi and Dartanyen led them; Adrianna, Dinim, and Tianna comprised the center of the procession, while Zorg and Armond brought up the rear. When they reached the area that had collapsed, they saw that the tunnel had been cleared of large debris. They had to step over a few bits of the walls and ceiling lying upon the floor to get to the staircase they knew to be located at the very end of the corridor. When they reached it, they saw that it too had been well lit by torches mounted upon the walls. One by one they progressed down the steep winding staircase, not stopping until it ended.

When they finally reached ground level, the group arrayed themselves in a diamond formation. Once again, Adrianna and Dinim were in the center, while Bussi stayed in the front. Zorg and Armond were on the sides of the diamond formation, while Dartanyen moved to the rear, his bow cocked and ready to let loose arrows over their heads if need be. The group walked in silence for a moment before Armond spoke. "I wonder . . . there must be another way to get down to this temple. I mean, it's quite obvious that no one had come the way we did for a long time. And this passage has only been disturbed by ourselves and the Wildrunners."

"Yeah. I was thinking about that myself," said Dartanyen. "We must have found the one that they would use if for some reason they were unable to access the main entrance. But, I am sure that one was just as hidden." Dartanyen sighed. "Oh well. This one will have to do for us."

They continued towards the mausoleum and reached the place with no interference. Adrianna shuddered as she remembered what had happened at this very spot where they now stood unmolested. The cemetery was eerie in its silence, as if the dead themselves waited for something to happen. As a unit, the group moved towards the massive double doors of the mausoleum, and the warriors began to arrange themselves strategically about them. Each door bore the head of a lion with a ring in its mouth. Suddenly, the lion on the left spoke with a deep voice, "Entrance can be gained you will see. Answer correctly; it will set the locks free." Adrianna jumped when she heard the voice emanating from the lion head. It was strange; the jaws of the bronze object had moved when it had spoken.

The lion on the right spoke the riddle. "Round they are, yet flat as boards, the altars of the lupine lords. Jewels of black velvet, pearls of the sea, unchanged, yet changing eternally."

For a moment the group was silent. Adrianna spoke the answer to the riddle just as Dartanyen did the same. "The moons: Steralion, Hestim, and Meriliam." They both glanced quickly at one another as they heard the click of a mechanism behind the lions heads. The sound of the doors opening sounded like thunder in the stillness of the cemetery and everyone looked quickly about to see if anything had come to the noise. Nothing emerged out of the dark stillness.

The group filed into the mausoleum. Zorg lit two torches and handed one to Armond. The bones of humanoid skeletons littered the floor. She could not be certain, but Adrianna thought that most of them appeared human. Everyone tried not to step on them as they walked through the corridor, as if they were afraid they would inadvertently disturb the spirits of men long gone. For a moment, the group walked through, unchecked. But their luck was too good to be true for long. While they made their way through the remains of the dead, the dead began to rise.

Bussi shouted as he drew his battleaxe. He wasted no time and rushed towards the nearest skeletal form rising from the floor. His face was florid with excitement as he raised his axe. The skeleton burst apart as he swept through it, the bones splintering with the impact, slamming against the stone walls. Then he made to the next one. Zorg and Armond tossed away their torches and quickly joined the fray that ensued. The threesome began hacking and slashing at their adversaries before many of them even had time to stand upright. These skeletons were quicker than the zombie-like undead priests they had encountered during their last visit into the Underdark, but they were no match against Bussi, Zorg, Armond, and Dartanyen. Adrianna thought of holding back her spell when she saw how well they were doing against the opponent. But she remembered the last time, when she had had very little recourse to her magic and had been unable to help them when they had so badly needed it. So she began to speak her spell, her delicate fingers weaving intricate patterns in the air. She held out her hand, palm out, and a missile of magical energy burst from it, scorching the skeletal monster closest to her. To Adrianna's surprise, Tianna finished off the creature with her scimitar. Adrianna then watched her as she rushed to help the others. The battle was shortly over. Tianna used her skills as a healer to treat as many wounds as she could, everyone thanking her for her aid. Then the group moved on.

They made their way down into the bowels of Shandahar beneath the mausoleum. The passageways were long and narrow, having a tendency to turn back upon themselves. It was a virtual maze. After the second time of realizing that they were back-tracking, Armond took a lump of coal out of his satchel and began to leave marks on the walls that told them from whence they had come. Adrianna sighed. They would have a merry time trying to find their way back out again.

After getting turned around a few more times, the group found the appropriate passages to take to the temple proper. Slowly and quietly they walked through the rooms of the ancient pagoda. It was obvious that what had once been a place teeming with activity was now nothing more than a hollow shell. In their wanderings they saw no one. Adrianna thought it more than a little strange. She began to realize that Dartanyen did as well, his tension mounting with each step they took deeper into the temple. Adrianna looked around at the rest of the group. She noticed the signs of strain on their features. Except, possibly, for Dinim. The stress of the situation seemed not to have taken a toll on him at all.

Finally they stopped. The men placed their packs against the wall opposite the entranceway and settled down beside them. With the exception of a few large empty chests, the room was empty. Adrianna sat and leaned against an adjacent wall. She opened her pack and removed the loaf of bread and the cheese she had packed that morning. She was starving. She felt as though she had not eaten all day. Well, for all she knew, an entire day had indeed passed; it was so difficult to keep track of the time when one had not the resources to do so, being underground and all.

Tianna settled herself next to Adrianna and opened her own pack. She took out two cannis fruits and held one out to Adrianna. Smiling appreciatively, Adrianna took the hard yellow sphere. She tore a piece from her loaf and offered it to Tianna, who accepted it graciously. Adrianna looked around to see that everyone else had decided to take a meal as well. The men passed their food around, all having packed something a little different from his comrade.

When everyone was finished, the remainder of the food was packed carefully away. Dartanyen announced that they should rest here for a time. They did not know when they would get their next opportunity. The group began to lay out their bedrolls and blankets. Adrianna watched them for a moment and then took out her spellbook. She did not have the space in her pack for anything besides her clothing, food, and books. Not only that, but she could not be encumbered with the weight and bulk of such items. They may interfere with her spell-casting abilities. She leaned against the wall and opened her book. She had to study so that she would be prepared on the morrow.

Adrianna jumped when she felt a touch on her arm. She looked up to find Tianna standing above her with a woolen blanket. "You know, you should at least pack one of these. It will keep people from feeling so sorry for you."

"But I . . ." Adrianna halted when she saw the twinkle in Tianna's eye. "Don't worry. I have another."

Adrianna accepted the blanket. "Thank you. This means a lot to me."

"You are welcome." Tianna then moved a few feet away to her bedroll. The other woman sat upon it, folding and crossing her legs beneath her. She then closed her eyes. Adrianna looked away. Tianna was praying to her goddess. That was a private act and she did not wish to be intrusive or rude.

Adrianna looked around the room one more. Dartanyen, Armond, and Bussi lay on their bedrolls, their blankets wrapped around them. It was cold in the Underdark, and the edges of the blankets were tucked securely around each body. Zorg leaned against the wall adjacent to the one Adrianna and Tianna occupied. He was the first to take watch. Next was Armond, and then Dartanyen. Adrianna glanced at Dinim leaning against the wall opposite to hers. He had a book in his lap upon which he appeared to be concentrating. Earlier, he had offered to take one of the watches. When the others stopped to consider it, Adrianna found herself interjecting, reminding him that as a magic-user, he needed as much rest as possible for the upcoming day, asking him to let the other men do what they knew best.

She had surprised the group, Dinim, and especially herself. Normally, she held the conviction that if one felt he needed to do something, then he should do it. But when it came to Dinim, it had been found lacking. Despite what the rest of the group felt about the Cimmerean, she had come to feel wary of him. She did not know why, but he had begun to make her edgy. She did not want their lives in his hands.

Dinim objected, saying that he was more than capable of helping the group in any way he could, but Dartanyen agreed with Adrianna, taking the last watch for himself. Dartanyen left then, nodding almost imperceptibly at her as he passed. Somehow he knew how she felt, perhaps even had felt a little of it himself. She glanced back at Dinim to find him glaring at her intensely. He then turned abruptly from her, his stance rigid. She could not help a chill from crawling up her spine. His momentary glare of undisguised malice only made her wariness towards him increase.

***

The group moved cautiously. It was a part of the temple they had not yet explored. The corridors were dark and musty. The torchlight cast strange shadows upon the walls and ceiling as they moved through. It seemed that they had entered the more habitable portion of the temple. Many of the corridors contained a series of closed doors. These doors were summarily opened and the rooms apprised of recent habitation. It came as no surprise that the chambers had indeed been recently lived in. Strangely however, the rooms seemed to have been left in chaos. It almost seemed as though the inhabitants had been quick to leave, or that the rooms had been searched for any valuables. Many of them had pieces of parchment, articles of clothing, bed linens and pieces of furniture strewn all over the floor. They eventually came upon a laboratory, which also seemed to have been hastily abandoned.

The place was in shambles. They quickly made their way through it, picking up things here and there, and then discarding them again. Adrianna found an open scroll beneath an overturned chair. Sensing no magic surrounding the scroll, she unrolled it and scrutinized the writing within. She could not read it, but she knew enough to realize that it was a spell scroll, probably one belonging to a priest. She placed the scroll within her belt pouch and continued on towards the rear of the room.

She smelled it before she saw it. Her senses immediately became alert. There was death here. Proceeding cautiously, she stepped behind a large table to find the body of a priest lying on the stone floor. He was dead, had obviously been dead for at least a few days. She covered her nose and mouth with her hand and looked back towards the rest of the group, who were circulating the large laboratory. Dartanyen had noticed her and was making his way over, Bussi right behind him. Adrianna moved aside to allow them access.

Dartanyen knelt beside the body. "It's been a while." He then plucked at the black fabric of the man's tunic. "Died of a chest wound . . . sword."

"What in the Hells is going on here? We haven't encountered a soul. Not to mention that all of the rooms we have been in are deserted," grouched Bussi.

Dartanyen shook his head. "I don't know, but it makes me really nervous. We have to stay on constant guard. Whoever killed this man could still be around."

"Not too much of a loss if you ask me."

Adrianna turned at the sound of Tianna's voice at her side.

"And why in the Hells not?" asked Bussi, raising an eyebrow.

Tianna shrugged. "He's on the dark side. I can tell just by the color of his robes. No priest of the light arts would wear a dark colored tunic."

Adrianna sighed to herself. She had thought as much. She knew at least that much about the priest-hood.

Dartanyen began to search the dead man. All he had on him was a talisman. He pulled it out from beneath the tunic. It was attached to a thick silver chain about the man's neck. Tianna knelt next to Dartanyen. "That is a symbol of Gaknar."

Dartanyen frowned. "I don't understand. This is supposed to be a Temple dedicated by Gaknar. Why would one of his followers have been killed like this?"

"Maybe he did something he shouldn't have," said Armond testily. "Come on. Let's get out of here. We are kyerrean-bait standing around here like this. Just because we haven't seen anyone does not mean that someone doesn't know we are here."

"You're right. Let's go," said Dartanyen, rising from the floor.

They left the laboratory the same way they had entered and continued through the maze of corridors, Armond continuing to mark where they had been with his chunk of coal. No one was unduly surprised when they came upon more bodies of dead priests, all bearing the symbol of Gaknar. However, tensions continued to escalate as they proceeded quietly, questions remaining unasked and unanswered.

The group went back up a flight of stairs, past another series of rooms and through a hallway that led into a large audience chamber. The room was dimly lit, and was virtually empty, which made it appear all the larger. Quietly they walked across the room towards the double doors at the other side, knowing that they were getting closer. Closer to what, they did not know, but the fact that the lanterns hanging on the walls were lit told them all they needed to know. They were about to open the doors when Bussi called out a warning. As a unit the group turned toward the halfen just in time to see a dark figure slowly walking toward them from across the room. They held their ground until the figure was distinguishable. It was a Cimmerean faelin. He was hooded, but his eerie eyes shone crimson red in the lanternlight. He wore dark trousers, a tunic and a long cloak that swept the floor as he moved. He carried a knarled black staff in his left hand.

The Cimmerean continued towards them, his eyes glittering menacingly. As he neared, Adrianna could tell that he was concentrating on something, his lips moving silently. It took her less than a moment to realize he was in the middle of casting a spell. Just as she was about to divulge to the group the faelin's intentions, Dartanyen raised his longbow, arrow already knocked, and let loose the projectile. In fascination and horror, the group watched as the faelin caught the speeding arrow just as it penetrated his chest. He proceeded to pull the half-embedded arrow from his flesh and throw it aside. His lips pressed into a thin line, the only indication of his increasing anger.

The ring of steel echoed throughout the room and Armond, Zorg and Bussi began to sprint towards the Dark faelin, weapons drawn. They had run only a few paces when the Cimmerean uttered a few words and swept the staff in an arc before him. The room was blanketed in blackness. Adrianna's breath caught in her throat. She heard muttered curses from the men as they groped about in the darkness. Adrianna began to hear Tianna's soft voice, and a few moments later the room once again had light. The Cimmerean had moved and a quick scan of the area revealed his location near a large support pillar on the other side of the room. The men hurled more oaths, they having found themselves further away from the mage now than they had been when they started. Adrianna sensed a shift in energy in the distance to her right and turned to see Dinim cast his spell. Having been swept up in the moment, she had forgotten him. The set of his shoulders was rigid, and she could tell by the downward turn of his mouth and the gleam in his eyes that he was angry. Fire burst from his fingertips and raced towards the dark-cloaked faelin. In shock, Adrianna saw the fire begin to diminish as it neared the Cimmerean, and it sputtered away completely before touching him.

Adrianna returned her gaze to Dinim but he was turned away from her, his hands balled in fists at his sides. He was obviously upset, his spell having failed. The Dark faelin had either cast a protective shell around himself, or he was naturally immune to the magic that had been cast. This man was powerful, very powerful indeed to have been able to find the means to enhance his reflexes, thus enabling him to catch the lightning-quick arrow. And then to have in his possession an object like the staff he carried, one with the ability to create darkness. The possibility that he had immunity to magic told Adrianna that he was an experienced magic-user. She had been about to cast her own spell, but was beginning to think better of it. Uncertainty and fear had begun to batter her mind and she had unconsciously begun to back away from the group, away from the threat of the Cimmerean mage.

Adrianna continued to back towards the door, feeling utterly defenseless. For a moment the room was silent, the enemy having riveted his gaze upon Dinim. Then, with lightening quick speed, she watched as Dartanyen knocked another arrow in his bow and let it fly. This time it caught the Cimmerean unawares and hit him full in the chest. The shaft went in deep and the Cimmerean stumbled backwards, his hand above his heart where the arrow protruded. He then fell back. For a few moments his body twitched on the stone floor, his throat gurgling as he tried to take a breath. Finally he was still.

It took a few moments for Adrianna to begin to breathe normally. She looked around and found her backside pressed firmly into the door. As she began to realize that the threat had been taken away, she unclenched her bloodless hands and began to relax her muscles, stepping gingerly away from the door.

Silently, the group went over to the body of the fallen mage. Dinim reached him first, having broken out of the shock that had encompassed them more quickely than everyone else. When the rest of the group arrived they found him searching through the folds of the fallen man's robes and cloak. The dark hood had fallen away to reveal long ebony hair that shone in the dim light. He had been young, younger than Adrianna would have thought him to be.

And he had been handsome. Adrianna was coming to realize that, despite the darkness of their nature, the Cimmereans were a physically handsome race.

Finally, with the dead man's staff in hand, Dinim rose. "There is nothing else on him. Any spell-book or other valuables he may have had are probably located somewhere in this temple." Dinim indicated the staff. "I would like to keep this, if no one objects."

Dinim looked around the group. "Keep it," said Dartanyen. "'Tis a wizards' thing and fit for you to have. That is, if the Lady does not mind." Dartanyen turned to indicate Adrianna.

For a brief moment, Adrianna was surprised. It was the first time anyone in the group had made mention of her profession. She had wondered about it, wondered what they thought of her, now knowing where her skill lay. She found that she was relieved that they seemed to think nothing of it at all, at least, not anymore. Any reservations that they may have had about her when they first discovered her Talent had been set aside and dealt with.

"No, I do not mind." Adrianna said the words, although she was not quite so sure that she meant them. The staff would give a man that she did not trust even more power. But she did not know quite what else to say, and did not wish to openly repudiate him. So she remained quiet as the group followed Dartanyen through the doors that led out of the room.

Uneventfully, the group passed through more corridors and rooms. But after a while, they realized that they had to rest again, fatigue overcoming them despite the stress of their situation. By this time no one really knew what time of day it was, or *which* day it was, for that matter. Such things just did not matter in the Underdark. All they knew was that they pushed themselves to the acceptable limits of their endurance, and then stopped to eat and rest.

Half-heartedly, Adrianna settled herself against one of the walls of the room they had chosen to inhabit. The rest of the group seated themselves as well, situating travel gear around them. Food was removed from bags and passed around. Adrianna ate slowly of her portion, her thoughts returning to the skirmish with the Cimmerean. She was pleased with the outcome, at the ease and rapidity with which the group was able to dispatch the enemy. However, she was very unhappy about the fact that she had not borne a contribution to that outcome. She hadn't even tried.

Adrianna sighed, rubbed her hands on her trousers. She felt like a fool. She remembered the role she had played during the fight . . . that of a coward. Even now she could feel the press of the doors against her backside, the erratic beating of her heart, the sweat gathering beneath the pits of her arms. For a moment the group had faltered. There had been a pause . . . that brief moment in time when she could have cast her spell and made a difference. But she had hesitated. Dartanyen had taken up the slack, had acted when she could not.

She should have cast her spell. Just because Dinim's spell had failed did not mean that hers would have failed as well. Had she not learned a thing from Master Tallek? Maybe, just maybe, her spell would have broken through the enemy's resistance. She hadn't even given it a chance, and now she felt like a dismal failure. But that wasn't all. It was more than the fact that she had not acted when needed. It was her fear. It had consumed her, eaten up all rational thought. While the rest of the group sought to dispose of the threat, all she could think of doing was escaping.

Adrianna looked around the room. No one had said anything to her. No one had brought up the fact that she had failed to contribute to the defeat of the enemy. Her gaze paused on Dinim. He had his spell book open and on his lap. He, also, had said nothing to her, but she had caught him watching her a couple of times as they had walked, his gaze calculating. He undoubtedly considered her a weak Talent, one not worthy of her master's praise, one that would be a hindrance to the group.

But Dinim would definitely not hamper the group in any way. He had well proven his worth with the spell he cast today. *Flamesphere* . . . a deadly weapon. It had been known to incinerate entire villages. And now he studied, dedicated to the welfare of the group in a way in which she was not. Adrianna was about to turn away and then stopped. As unobtrusively as possible, she gazed at Dinim more keenly. Perhaps he did not study at all. She could see that his attention was focused upon something else, perhaps a dirty fingernail. Maybe he did not deserve such a high pedestal after all.

Finally Adrianna finished her meal. Tianna stopped next to her and offered her the use of her blanket. Adrianna thanked her and once more focused on Dinim out of the corner of her eye. Still she could see that he did not truly study. He merely dabbled about, looking at this, that, or the other, all the while appearing to study. Then, after the rest of the group had settled beneath their blankets, he closed the book and lay down himself.

Adrianna thought it more than a little strange. Perhaps Dinim had not really needed to study. After all, he had cast only one spell today. Why the subterfuge, then? Why bother to appear to be studying when one really was not? Adrianna shook her head to herself. Was she just being overly critical, looking for faults in others so that she could make less of her own? She did not know, and so turned away, disgusted with the fact that she did not even seem to know herself anymore.

***

Dinim pressed himself up against the cold stone wall, blending with the dark shadows. The priests hurried past him, intent upon their destination, unheedful of the warnings given them by their peers that a creature resided within these walls, a monster who would maim and kill. Silently, Dinim slipped behind the priests, wondering how he would kill them. They were Aasarak's priests, having come here after the slaughter of Gaknar's followers. He did not know much about the situation, only what Aasarak's assassins had spoken to one another as they bragged about their exploits. Somehow, Gaknar had angered Aasarak, resulting in him sending his minions to take over this temple. Probably, just to piss off Gaknar. Maybe Aasarak hoped for a good fight; or was it the fact that Gaknar had won the last fight that Aasarak had attacked the temple?

Dinim did not know, nor did he really care. What he did find himself caring about, however, was the subject of the conversation between the two priests he now followed. They were human, and spoke in Common. The syntax of their speech was a little strange, but easy enough to follow.

"I tell you they are here, have been for a few days. They have been traveling through the northern quadrant. *They killed Minos.*"

The short priest glanced at his taller companion. "Humph. How come I haven't heard about this before now?"

"You don't pay enough attention. You wouldn't know it if a *Flamesphere* swept through."

"So how did they kill him?"

"It was an arrow . . . through the heart."

"Humph. Minos always was a fool."

"One of us travels with them."

"Then why did Minos meet such unfortunate demise? Did not our man try to stop it?"

"Who knows?" There was a pause. "They say that Lord Thane will be here soon."

"That man gives me the shivers. He is chaos incarnate. I wonder how the master keeps him?"

"Are you sure that he does?"

The shorter man almost stopped in the passageway. "I am sure that you jest Theron. The master has powers that we can not even begin to imagine."

The other man chuckled. "Believe what you will, but I feel that Lord Thane is seriously underestimated . . . has become something more than what the master planned for."

There was another pause. "So what are they doing about the intruders?"

"We have begun to block the way they have come. It is the only way they know. Once they seek a means of escape, they will find themselves trapped."

"Why toy with them? Why not just kill them and be done with it?"

The taller man chuckled again. "But where is the fun in that? They will be an interesting diversion from the monotony of our lives down in this stinking pit."

Dinim stopped in the passageway. The two priests continued on, not knowing that they had been followed and overheard. Someone was here, or, more precisely, a group of someones. They had created unease among Aasarak's priests. Perhaps they were a group to be reckoned with. Not only that, but Lord Thane was coming. That meant that the creature that had stolen his identity would not be far behind. Ixitchitl's time was coming, Dinim would be sure of that. He turned in the passageway and began to make his way back. He would go towards the northern quadrant. Perhaps these people would stumble into his prison. Maybe he would be able to use them to his benefit.

***

Volstagg swept the last of the refuse into the dustpan. He then took it to the nearest trash bin and disposed of it. He sighed heavily. Finally there was quiet. It had been a long day. He had let the inn wardens go just a few moments before and the only ones that remained were Mia, one of his serving girls, and Nolan, his cook. All of a sudden, Volstagg felt a chill touch him. He paused, listening. Then he frowned and shook his head. It was nothing. He was just being paranoid. He continued with his work, hoping he would be resting soon.

Volstagg was instantly on alert when he heard the noise outside. Quickly and quietly he went behind the bar and grasped his battle-axe. Volstagg felt the hairs on his arms begin to rise. Something felt very wrong. Suddenly, the front doors burst open. A tall dark figure strode into the inn. His platemail armor was black as pitch, as was the cloak that swirled behind him. His horned helmet concealed his face and he wore a long-sword at his right hip. The man reeked of death and decay. The dark warrior looked all about the inn assessively. "We are closed for the evening," said Volstagg, his grip on the axe tightening.

The mailed warrior turned toward Volstagg. The cenloryan tried not to cringe. The warrior did not move for a few moments, but then put his hand to his left hip. He took a flanged mace from his belt. Volstagg stiffened and began to prepare himself for a fight. He noticed the arrival of two more dark robed figures, but he did not take his eyes off of the one that stood before him. Just as he remembered that Mia and Nolan were in the back and was wishing them to stay there, he heard the doors leading back into the kitchens open.

Mia and Nolan burst into the dining room. Each held an old sword in his or her grip, the ones that Volstagg always kept in the back for situations such as these. But this was an extremely bad situation. There was something very amiss with these men, and Volstagg knew that Mia and Nolan should have remained hidden in the back. Before Volstagg knew what was happening, the two men standing at the entrance had cocked their crossbows and let fly. Volstagg heard the bolts strike their targets, heard them enter flesh. He heard one body hit the floor, but when he did not hear the second one, he turned back and saw Mia standing there, her dark eyes wide with fear and shock, the bolt protruding from her belly. Her small hands grasped the shaft, red with her blood.

"Master Volstagg . . . Nolan . . ." Volstagg saw the tears in her eyes. He knew that she knew she was going to die. Her body rocked back as another bolt struck her in the chest. She fell, her hands clutching the wood shaft in her belly, her eyes echoing her fear, even in death.

Volstagg turned back to the dark warrior before him. The man had not moved to strike him; he very easily could have. "Get out of my inn . . . now." Volstagg spoke with grief and barely suppressed rage, despite his fear. The warrior raised his mace. Volstagg raised his own weapon just as the mace came crashing down. Volstagg staggered with the force of the blow. He was stunned. Volstagg was a large creature, and having some physical power of his own, he was surprised at the strength behind the dark warrior's blow. The warrior took advantage of the cenloryan's weakness and struck again. This time there was no axe to parry his attack and the mace struck Volstagg in the right shoulder. The cenloryan clutched at the shoulder, and regarded the warrior with slitted eyes. "Who are you?"

Volstagg could feel that the warrior smiled from behind the helmet. He spoke in a low, deep voice, almost otherworldly in quality. "Hmf. I suppose I do not expect you to remember me. It has been quite some time since we last saw one another."

Volstagg could not suppress his feelings of dread. He knew he would have remembered had he met one such as the warrior standing before him now. Volstagg pursed his lips. "What do you want?"

The warrior chuckled, the sound causing a chill to race up Volstagg's spine. The warrior raised his hands to his helmet and lifted it from his head. Volstagg felt his heart stop in his chest. The man that stood before him was no longer a man. The flesh was pale, pale as death. The eyes were sunken, the irises consumed by blackness. The reek of decay intensified. The creature standing before him was once Thane Darnesse.

"Ah, so you *do* remember me. Then you will also know my daughters, Sheridana and Adrianna . . ."

The words tumbled out of Volstagg's mouth before he could control them. "Strange, this is the first time that I have heard you refer to Adrianna as your daughter. Death has changed you, Thane."

Thane's eyes narrowed. Before Volstagg could react, Thane swung his mace once more. It struck Volstagg in the side. He staggered, felt the cracking of his ribs. Thane kicked him in the abdomen, once, and then three more times in quick succession. Then Volstagg felt a gauntleted fist strike him on the side of the head. He fell to his knees, his hand covering the gash at his temple. He felt the blood flow between his fingers, saw it drip onto the stone floor. Slowly he looked up, saw the warrior looking down at him from cold, emotionless eyes.

"Let's start again, shall we? My offspring, yes we were talking about my daughters. Where is Adrianna? I know that you were her good friend."

Volstagg's body thrummed with fear. He knew that if this man knew where Adrianna was he would surely kill her. He was certain of it. "I . . . I don't know what you mean. I haven't seen her in years."

Thane's eyes narrowed once more. He kicked Volstagg in the belly once more. "Lie! You lie!" he shrieked. "I have not the patience for your lies . . . your stupid, insignificant desire to protect her from me. My sources tell me that she was seen here!" Thane pointed his finger downward, indicating the inn.

"I swear, I really don't know where she is. She left days ago"

"And if you did know her whereabouts?" Thane leaned over Volstagg, his black eyes piercing into him, into his soul.

With effort, Volstagg looked back at him. Despite his fear, he refused to back down, refused to play the coward. He would keep his pride, at least some measure of it, as well as his honor. Adrianna's life would depend on it, even if his own life was forfeit. "I still would not tell you."

Thane paused for a moment and then laughed. His laugh was like none Volstagg had ever heard before. It seemed to grope for his heart within his chest and to wither his soul. The sound of it was fearsome, with undertones of evil in its purest form. "Still protecting my weak little Adrianna, hoping that I never find her. Such an endearing human quality. I am touched . . . really. You are indeed her good friend, aren't you?" Thane paused for a moment, regarded Volstagg intently. "Listen up. My other daughter is on her way to this town. She will most likely stay at this inn. You will tell me when she arrives here."

"What makes you think that I would do that?"

Thane smiled. "You have seen how effortlessly I killed your cook and serving wench. I will kill your precious Adrianna the same way if you do not accede to my wishes."

"Why are you looking for your daughter?"

Thane studied the fallen cenloryan once more. It would not matter if he knew or not. It would not save her, neither of them. "Her bastard child must die and I will be the one to do it."

Volstagg swallowed heavily. "How will I contact you?"

"With this." From within the folds of his black cloak, Thane pulled out a small horn. "You need blow on it for a moment and I will know that Sheridana is here. It will make no audible sound to your ears but I will hear it, no matter where in Shandahar I may be."

Volstagg took the horn. Thane placed the helmet back over his head, and then motioned to the other robed figures standing at the entrance to the inn. Volstagg had forgotten that they were there. "Remember my promise, innkeeper. I do not make idle threats. I will kill Adrianna if you do not deliver." With that, the warrior turned on his heel and strode from the inn, the others following.

Volstagg heard the sound of receding hoof-beats and then all was silent. He looked around his inn, and saw the fallen bodies of Mia and Nolan. Tears streamed down his face. Somehow, he knew that it was not the last bloodshed that he would see.

***

Adrianna stumbled. She cursed inwardly as she caught herself against the wall. She would be happy when this was over, when she could see the sky above her head, the sun shining down. The stone walls of the temple made her feel closed in, trapped. Truth be told, she hated it. All of her life, she had much preferred the open sky to the confines of life behind wood, stone, or brick walls. However, in more recent years she had not really had a choice in the matter, and so had settled for the stone walls of her master's tower, but the wilderness had continued to call for her. Now, so far beneath the surface of the world, she felt no such call. It was as though there was nothingness and it frightened her. She wanted so much to be out of the Underdark, but not as much as she wanted to discover the truth behind what her father had been doing for the last ten years.

Adrianna sighed heavily and looked up to find Dinim watching her yet again. He quickly averted his gaze, making it seem as though he had not seen her at all, but had merely been glancing in her direction. It made her nervous, this watching, this sneaking around to make it appear otherwise. She had caught him at it several times that day already, and she got the distinct impression that his thoughts were not savory ones. But what was she to do? Go to Dartanyen and say, "Excuse me, but can you make Dinim stop watching me? He is scary when he does that."

Adrianna rubbed wearily at her temples. She had a horrible headache. It was just as well that they walked in silence, with no one saying a word. Everyone was sullen and withdrawn. The silence was not companionable; the situation was too tense and weary for that. She was sure that everyone had thought the same thing she had at least once . . . *what in blazes am I doing here?* They were even quiet during their rest times, when they ate, before and after sleeping. It was odd, and she had never met a stranger group of people. She had to admit that Tianna had said a few words to her, that Zorg had made some comment or other to Armond, and that Bussi had grumbled a couple of times. Dinim had tried to initiate polite conversation with her after they had rested.

At first she had felt herself responding to him as she always had before, drawn to him like a moth to a lantern. But she halted it when she realized what it was, turned away from him after a hasty acknowledgement.

Adrianna looked behind her once again, past the taller forms of Armond and Zorg. She saw nothing in the darkness through which they had just passed. Yet, she could not escape the sensation that someone watched them, followed them. She knew that this would be the day, knew that they could not go on much longer, that they had to be close to the end of this maze. The rest of the group knew it as well, sensed the same thing she did. The hallways they walked through had been recently traversed. They were in the inhabited portion of the temple.

Suddenly, in the distance ahead, they began to hear the sounds of someone speaking. Dartanyen and Bussi stopped, then hurried forward, the rest of the group quickly following. They ducked into an unlit side corridor. The voices became louder. They scurried into the darkness and then pressed themselves up against the walls on either side of the corridor. The voices passed their hallway and continued on down the corridor they had abandoned. There were several persons, the sounds of the footfalls that passed told them so.

After a few moments more, they detached themselves from the walls and gathered together. Adrianna could see the sheen of sweat on Dartanyen's brow. Without saying a word, he beckoned them back out into the corridor. Slowly and quietly they walked. At the end of the corridor they found a downward-leading staircase. They took it and emerged into another corridor. At its end was a door. Beyond it they heard the sound of someone speaking.

Slowly they approached the door and when they stood a few feet from it they stopped. Dinim made his way to the front of the group and held up his hand. He then motioned that he would be the one to quietly open the door and look beyond. The door made no noise as he slowly opened it. He did not open it much, but as everyone stepped up to it, they could see that no light came from the opening. It appeared that a curtain hung a few feet beyond the door. There was only a narrow space between the door and the curtain. Dinim disappeared within the space.

Everyone waited in tense anticipation. Suddenly, a voice behind them spoke. "Who are you and what are you doing here?" Almost in unison, they turned around. Tianna was limp within the grasp of a Cimmerean faelin, and two others flanked him. The Cimmerean put his wickedly curved dagger to Tianna's pale throat. "Keep your arms to your sides and step back into the worship hall."

The group hesitated, glancing at one another. "Back up into the worship hall . . . *now,*" said the Cimmerean. He pressed the dagger into the flesh of Tianna's neck. A thin trickle of blood began to flow from the cut. The two other

Cimmereans, their swords drawn, moved forward and the group pressed back into the curtained chamber behind them. Adrianna felt herself in the middle of the press of bodies, Zorg, Armond, and Dartanyen surrounding her. Behind them there was an exclamation of surprise and she knew it to be Dinim.

The group pressed back and into the curtain. As it shrouded them, Dartanyen leaned into her and whispered, "Be ready." But she had already begun to incant the words to her spell. She would be able to cast it when she stepped beyond the curtain. She moved slowly, and once she was within the thick folds of the curtain she paused to give herself more time. The warriors attempted to keep their circle around her, knowing that she may be their most valuable weapon.

The Cimmereans pressed forward. "Move it," one of them growled. Slowly, Adrianna began to move back again. Then they emerged from the curtain. Her spell completed, she whirled around and let it fly. Dartanyen stepped aside just in time. A vivid fan of rainbow color sprang from her hands and struck the six priests closest to them in the foremost pew of the worship hall. All but one of them dropped to the ground. The other placed his hands to his eyes and yelled out, "I can't see . . . can't see."

The Cimmerean holding Tianna emerged from behind the curtain as pandemonium broke out. "Damn bitch," he muttered. He began to press the dagger into her throat just to find a hand stilling his arm. Armond drove his fist into the Cimmerean's face. Tianna's captor released her as he fell back from the blow. Tianna fell onto the floor, still unconscious. Armond knelt to find her pulse. It was slow but steady.

Zorg had drawn his sword, and stood above Armond. The other two Cimmereans rushed back to them, their long-swords arcing towards him. Zorg blocked one while parrying the other. By the time they were attacking again, Armond was ready. Zorg chose one of them as his opponent while Armond took the other.

After casting her spell, Adrianna glanced quickly around her. They stood upon a raised dais. To her right was an elaborately robed high priest. He stood before a pulpit. To his right there was an altar. Adrianna sidled to her left, hoping to remove herself from the thick of the fight. Adrianna noticed that the old priest did the same.

Adrianna then turned her attention to the hall below. The room was split down the middle, rows of pews on either side. The priests were shouting and many were beginning to jump over the pews to get to them. Five priests lay upon the floor among the rows of pews on the left side of the hall. She wondered how long they would remain unconscious. The one that had been blinded by her spell had fallen over one of his unconscious companions. He crawled about on the floor, cursing and moaning to himself. Beside her, Dartanyen cocked his bow and let his arrows fly. He shot the arrows one right after the other, both hitting the same target. The last standing priest fell like a stone, the arrows protruding from his chest. He crumpled over the blinded priest, who shrieked when he felt the weight of the dying man.

Adrianna felt her eyes widen as the clerical priests from the right side of the hall began to step up onto the dais, their angry shouts and curses preceding them. She began to retreat back as they advanced. Dartanyen dropped his bow and unsheathed his sword. He and Bussi met them and they began to fight. A few others remained where they were, concentrating on their spells. They were the imam priests, specializing in magic while the clerical ones specialized in weapons.

Adrianna began to concentrate on her next spell. She felt drained from her last spell, but knew that she had the energy, the *power*, to cast another. She would use it upon one of the imam priests. They would be dangerous to her comrades, many of their spells having the ability to exact some type of control over others, either by causing them to feel fear, to render them stationary, or to attempt to command their actions. Suddenly, Adrianna felt a hand upon her shoulder, and then a strange sensation overcame her. As she turned to face her adversary, she began to feel the pain of wounds being inflicted onto her body. They just simply appeared of their own accord, no weapon having put them there.

The imam priest slipped away from her, he having caused the wounds to appear so as to weaken her. And indeed they did, her blood flowing freely from them. Involuntarily, Adrianna began to sink to the floor. She felt weak, drained. She would rest . . . for just a moment. She looked about, saw the men engaged in the fight, saw Tianna lying on the floor. But Dinim, she could not find him anywhere. Curse that man. Where was he?

From behind the curtain, Dinim watched the battle unfold. All morning he had been trailing the group. Just as he had hoped, they had wandered into the confines of his prison. They were a tired lot, obviously sick of the maze of Gaknar's Temple. They were quite a mixture . . . two humans, a halfen, and three faelin. Ixitchitl he did not count. The creature would be dead within the hour. Dinim had retained a certain distance behind the group throughout, not wanting the doppelganger to sense his presence. However, the creature definitely had Dinim on its mind, its furtive backward glances making Dinim smile to himself.

The members of the group seemed common enough, all but one. She had a presence about her, one that intrigued him immensely. He had watched her carefully: the way she moved, the way she spoke. She distrusted the one who called himself Dinim, was always seeking to place distance between them. Yet the creature was drawn to her, like a moth to a flame. Her beauty was extraordinary; Dinim had never seen a woman quite as lovely as this one.

Dinim watched as the young woman sank to the floor. The dark imam priest had touched her, caused gashes and bruises to appear upon her body. Some of the wounds bled profusely and she tried to staunch the flow with the hem of her tunic. Something within him made him want to go to her, but he restrained himself. He did not wish to give himself away, not yet.

Dinim turned back to the place where Ixitchitl had hidden itself. The coward had found a place out of harm's way. It hid behind the same curtain as Dinim, only at the end closest to the high priest. Dinim stood at the end of the curtain nearest the wounded woman. The creature would wait until the battle was almost over before it would emerge once more, offering one excuse or another for its inability to help the group.

Adrianna cleared her head, removed the pain from her mind. She took in the battle scene. The clerical priest opposing Dartanyen swung his Flameblade. It sliced into Dartanyen's side. The faelin screamed in pain, his flesh cauterizing even after it had just been parted. The stench of burning flesh filled the hall. Two opponents had beset Zorg. He handled his enemies marvelously, although his injuries appeared more quickly than they would have had he been against only a single opponent.

Beyond Zorg, the high priest caught Adrianna's attention. He had raised his staff and had aimed it at the big warrior. Before she could utter a cry, a spurt of flame emerged from the top of the staff. It struck Zorg in the back. His tunic ignited and began to burn. Zorg bellowed a series of curses and then dropped to the ground. He rolled around for a few moments while his opponents sought to pierce him with their scimitars.

Adrianna forced herself to close her eyes, to concentrate upon her spell. She spoke the words and scribed the runes into the air before her. Adrianna raised her hand and a bolt of magical energy left her fingertips to race towards the high priest. He made as if to ward it off, but it slammed into his chest. The high priest stumbled backwards, barely regaining his balance as he righted himself.

Bussi swung his mighty battleaxe. It severed the leg of the cleric before him. The man dropped and another took his place. Armond faced yet another cleric. Adrianna watched Armond for a moment as he fought. The man was skilled, very skilled. His movements were fluid and graceful. His handsome face bore an intense look of concentration as he fought his opponent but his mouth moved, as though he was speaking. Then something began to happen.

Adrianna blinked her eyes, not quite sure what she was seeing. Armond's movements accelerated, his swords beginning to move more and more quickly. A few moments longer and the head rolled off of the priest's shoulders, striking the ground at Armond's feet. The body crumpled after it.

Adrianna crawled away from her spot near the curtain. She sought to make her way to the wounded Dartanyen. He had been able to vanquish his fiery enemy before he succumbed to his injuries, and he lay humped on top of the priest. She hoped that he was all right, hoped that the fiery blade had not touched one of Dartanyen's organs. It would have cauterized any of them as well, possibly causing obstruction in the intestines, or extensive scarring of the liver.

Tianna opened her eyes to the sound of battle all around her. Groggily, she lifted her head from the floor. A massive pair of boots stood right in front of her face. Her eyes widened. The boots stepped closer, and just as she thought that she surely would be trampled, she rolled out of the way. She jumped to her feet and drew her scimitar. The owner of the boots had been burned, and he also sported numerous other injuries. Rivulets of sweat poured from Zorg's head and into his eyes. He shook his head and she felt the spray across her face.

Tianna stepped away from Zorg and his opponent, and saw Adrianna kneeling next to a fallen Dartanyen. Just beyond her was Bussi, wildly swinging his battleaxe. Beyond the halfen there was a drop, and a small group of three imam priests nestled among the pews. They had cast their spells, the effects wreaking havoc among the group. Bussi bellowed with rage, and Tianna could see the heat emanating from his chain mail, saw it beginning to burn through his leather tunic. Dartanyen suffered the same, his semi-conscious mind registering the pain that the metal studs embedded within his leather vest caused.

Adrianna tried to soothe Dartanyen as he cried out in pain. She attempted to take the vest off of him. She burned her hands on the searing hot studs. The pain brought tears to her eyes. Damn, she felt so weak. She saw the imam priests, knew that they wanted to harm her. She knew that one of them had tried to affect her with his spell already. He had scowled at her when he realized that it was not taking effect. She had felt it probing at her, the strange magic so different from her own. He concentrated upon the casting of yet another spell, as did the others. But Adrianna paid them no mind. She continued to aid Dartanyen to the best of her ability. Finally the vest came off and she tossed it away from them.

Praying to her goddess, Tianna touched the ground and brought forth her spell. The *Darkness* enveloped the three imam priests. They would not be casting their evil spells now. At least, not until the *Darkness* was lifted. Tianna then scurried to Adrianna and Dartanyen. She heard Bussi howl again, and knew that he was close to the end of his endurance. Tianna knelt next to Adrianna, taking in her pale face, and her body, covered with wounds. Hells, they had gotten her too. Tianna began to examine Dartanyen, realized the extent of his injuries, and shook her head. She placed her hands over the cauterized wound across his belly, closed her eyes and began to pray.

Adrianna was relieved when she saw Tianna making her way over to them. She did not know what to do for Dartanyen; his wounds were so extensive. She glanced back at the imam priests and instead saw a vague area of *Darkness*. Thank the gods. Finally Dinim had put the staff to good use.

"Adrianna." She turned when she heard her name, saw Bussi stumble towards her and then fall. She scrambled over to him and then put her hands on him, hoping to drag him back to Tianna and Dartanyen. Her hands touched his metal armor. It took a moment for the pain to register, but by then her flesh had begun to sizzle upon the searing metal. She screamed and tore her hands away, portions of her flesh left behind upon the chain mail.

Tianna snapped out of prayer, her mind having registered the cry of agony that was emitting from her friend. She saw Adrianna on her knees next to a fallen Bussimot. Adrianna held her hands cradled to her chest and with sickening clarity, Tianna knew what had happened. Adrianna had touched Bussi's armor. "By the Goddess," she exclaimed. Tianna rushed over to Adrianna and Bussi. Being careful not to touch his armor, Tianna dragged Bussi over to where Dartanyen lay. Adrianna slowly followed, but collapsed onto her knees when she reached her comrades. She moaned against her hands, the pain stripping away what energy she had left. She felt nauseous, and when she felt the urge come to her, she turned her head and vomited.

Dinim knew when the time had come. He cast a *Darkness* spell of his own within the area in which he knew Ixitchitl to be. Then he left the sanctuary of the curtain. The group had been greatly outnumbered by the priests, and they had suffered for it. Two of them had fallen, and the others were barely standing. He felt he should give them a hand, at least some measure of thanks for their having brought Ixitchitl to him.

His sword drawn, Dinim slunk between the rows of pews on the left side of the hall. No one noticed him scurry across the way to the right side of the hall. Dinim passed silently towards the imam priests, saw them ensconced within the *Darkness*. He waited. After only a moment, the spell was diffused and there was light in the area once more. Dinim moved once again, slipping into the row of pews behind the priests. He saw them take stock of the situation; saw them realize that the battle could be won, and that the enemy had been greatly reduced. Then the priests began to concentrate upon their spells once more.

Dinim took his chance. He placed his dagger to the throat of one of the priests while he impaled another upon his blade. Then he slit the first priest's throat. Blood sprayed into his face but he paid it no heed as he stared the third priest in the eyes. Dinim saw the fear in the man's eyes, saw him attempt to reach for his own weapon. Dinim ran him through with his sword, felt the blade catch upon the man's ribs as it passed through him. Dinim pulled the blade back and watched the man fall next to his companions.

Dinim looked back up onto the dais. He saw the large human and the tall faelin dispatch their opponents. He knew that one of the priests was missing, that he had fled the scene with the intention of bringing others to the fight. He saw that Ixitchitl had diffused the spell and emerged from his spot behind the curtain. He watched the creature interacting with the rest of the group; saw it making excuses for itself.

At first, no one noticed him standing there among the pews. Then he sensed her. The sorceress's eyes were upon him, boring into him. She said nothing, just merely stared at him. The other woman they called Tianna was too busy to notice her friend's preoccupation. But one other did begin to notice, and that was when Dinim began to move from between the pews.

Adrianna's breath caught in her throat. How could this be? Her gaze darted between the two Cimmerean faelin that had begun to dominate the room. Armond and Zorg had joined them near the edge of the dais. They also watched, not knowing what to think or what to do. Everyone looked from one figure to the next, wondering which one was the "real" Dinim, if one even existed. The two Cimmerean looked almost exactly alike. The only difference was the clothes each one wore. The newly arrived Dinim wore tattered dark robes of many layers. The Dinim that had been with them for the past few days wore a freshly laundered single robe over tunic and trousers. The two Cimmerean moved to stand a few feet in front of each other to the right of the dais. Upon the "new" Dinim's arrival, the "old" Dinim's eyes had first widened in shock, and he had then grown rather pale. He now stood before a magnificent visage of himself, and it seemed that it was something he had thought was not possible.

Ixitchitl silently watched as the sorcerer strode towards him. Damnation! This should not be possible. Aasarak's spell should have kept him properly imprisoned. How had he reached this far within the temple? The confines of the prison should have kept him within the dungeons. Or had Ixitchitl underestimated the wizard? It was indeed possible, for the stronger the creature being imprisoned, the larger the prison. He knew that the power of the prisoner would automatically oppose the wards of the spell, possibly causing them to widen the distance between each other. But if master Dinim was powerful enough for the wards to have expanded this much, Ixitchitl was in great danger, for Ixitchitl was only able to mimic the power of the magic-user up to a certain point.

The creature readied itself. It would attempt to put the wizard back in his place, where he belonged. But first, it would attempt to place the battle in its own favor. Once out of the wizard's range, Ixitchitl would find a spell that would incapacitate the wizard. Then Lord Thane would dispose of him as he saw fit.

Dinim strode towards Ixitchitl, the creature who had stolen his life from him. For several weeks now, he had been dreaming of this moment. Nothing could take it from him. He could see the fear mirrored in its eyes. Then it bolted. It darted past the rows of pews to the rear of the worship hall. Dinim turned and began to follow. He must not let the creature step out of the bounds of the prison. Dinim heard the shouts from the group, heard them beginning to follow. He slowed down, began to cast the Force Projection. They could not interfere in this. It was his only chance to escape. When the spell was complete he stopped and turned around. He hoped that there was enough space between himself and them . . . that no one would be crushed. Dinim raised his right hand. A ray of energy sprang from his palm to strike the ceiling between him and the rest of the group. The ceiling came crumbling down with a thunderous crash. He turned and ran out of the worship hall as debris rained down upon the group. He would try to determine where the creature was going, and then take a shortcut to that location. He knew these corridors better than anyone. Dinim grinned wickedly. Now he had the creature all to himself, and that was all that mattered to him.

CHAPTER 6

Adrianna slowly tried to lift herself from the floor, coughing. The air was filled with dust, and it coated her throat and nostrils as she breathed. It got in her eyes and they began to tear up as she tried to look about the room. She kept her hands cradled to her chest, afraid that the dirt would get into the extensive wounds that now covered the palms. She heard the coughing and shuffling of the others as they roused themselves. She heard a thump and then a curse. She turned toward the source of the noise and saw Zorg stumbling over Armond. "Is everyone all right?"

"I was," said Armond irritably.

"Dartanyen and Bussi seem to be all right for now, but they need help. There is only so much I can do for them here," said Tianna. By the tone of her voice, Adrianna could tell that she was tired and probably had wounds of her own.

Adrianna put the back of her hand on Tianna's arm comfortingly. "We will do the best we can," she said.

Armond limped over to them and then sat next to Tianna. Zorg sat next to Adrianna. "Let's just try to do what we can for now. Who knows when they will be back to finish us off." Armond looked around at them as he spoke.

Zorg looked over at the felled ceiling. The wreckage was a barricade, keeping them from the possibility of escaping beyond the worship hall. It would be easy for Aasarak's priests to pick them off now, especially in their condition. "Maybe we should try to make a way through the debris," said Zorg.

"Yes, I was just thinking the same thing," replied Armond.

The two men rose from the floor and made their way to the piles of stone and shards of wood and glass. The dust was beginning to clear, making it easier for Adrianna to see them as they methodically began to clear a way through the rubble. After a few moments they stumbled past with a large stone. They climbed on top of the dais and behind the curtain. Adrianna knew that they would place it at the entrance, hoping to keep the priests from them as long as possible. The two men placed several more such stones there before returning to the arduous task before them.

Tianna took one of Adrianna's hands and looked at it. She hissed when she saw the extent of the damage. She knew that they had to get out soon, for there was very little water to wash Adrianna's wounds, which had been coated with a layer of dust when the ceiling fell. Tianna feared that they would become infected.

But Tianna said nothing of this, merely pulled a vial of water from her pouch and tried to rinse the hands as best she could without using all of the liquid. She then pulled a jar of salve from the pouch and began to apply it to the raw flesh. Adrianna cried out piteously but did not take her hands away, knowing that they needed the medicine that Tianna offered. Tianna felt like crying herself, knowing how painful it must be. After applying as much of the salve as she could, Tianna wrapped the hands in clean cloths, hoping to keep the wounds from acquiring even more of the dust that now characterized the room.

Tianna turned her attentions back to Dartanyen and Bussi. Their wounds were even more extensive, and she would need to pray to her goddess to heal them. But Tianna knew that it would not be enough. There were basic needs that could not be met here, and her ability to heal her comrades depended on those necessities, water being the primary one.

Adrianna lay down upon the floor next to Dartanyen. She felt drained, and the throbbing of her hands made her feel queasy. She hoped that Tianna would be able to help Dartanyen and Bussi, who moaned in their unconscious states, their burns much more extensive than hers. And Dartanyen. She hoped that he would live, his injuries being the worst of all. Finally Adrianna was able to fall into a semi sleep, the sound of Tianna's voice lulling her, as well as the thumping sounds of moving rock as Armond and Zorg worked to clear the debris in the distance.

***

"Adrianna . . . Adrianna. You have to wake up now." Groggily, Adrianna awoke to feel Tianna shaking her. She looked around the darkened room. Most of the torches had expired, and those that remained were in the vicinity of Zorg and Armond. From this distance, she could see that they had been able to clear at least some of the rubble away, although they had quite a bit more to do before they would reach the doorway. But it seemed that time was of the essence, for she heard sounds coming from behind the curtain. Finally, the temple inhabitants had decided to come and finish what they had started.

Adrianna sat up and looked at Tianna. The woman was hurriedly packing away her ointments and salves. She had taken the armor and other accoutrements off of Dartanyen and Bussi, leaving them only in their trousers. She had treated their wounds the best she could. Much of Bussi's chest was covered in wet cloths. Adrianna could smell the medicinal odor emanating from them and wrinkled her nose. The cloths covered the flesh that had been in contact with the searing hot armor. The chain mail lay in a heap beside him, much of it scorched and darkened. The integrity of the armor had been compromised and it would probably never be useful again. The studs on Dartanyen's armor were similarly blackened and the leather around the studs was crispy. It also would never be of use again. Adrianna looked at Dartanyen. He was very pale. "Will he live?" Adrianna looked back to Tianna.

The other woman paused and regarded Adrianna for a moment. "Yes. None of his organs appear to have been hit by the *Flameblade*. He is lucky." Tianna looked away and continued to pack her bags. Adrianna stood from the floor. She felt slightly woozy, and rocked a bit on her heels. The pain of her hands had diminished, probably as a result of Tianna's salve. She looked toward the men, hard at work trying to move as much of the debris as they could. Their bare chests were shiny with sweat. Zorg was definitely a bastion of brute strength. The muscles in his chest and arms were well defined and rippled as he moved. But, where Zorg was large, Armond's build was slender. He sported the lean muscle of a warrior. His belly was concave, and she could see the rows of abdominal muscles on either side of his midline. The men worked diligently upon their task, unwavering despite the various cuts and bruises on their bodies.

There was a loud crack behind the curtain. Adrianna jumped. The enemy was breaking through. "Zorg . . . Armond . . ." Tianna called out, a note of desperation to her usually calm voice. The men stopped their labors and jogged over to them. "They are coming." Zorg stooped to Dartanyen and looped the man's arm about his broad shoulders. Dartanyen stirred and moaned as Zorg stood with him. His eyes fluttered open. Adrianna heard Bussi curse as Armond did the same. The men helped their comrades toward the mound of rubble. Tianna shoved some packs towards Adrianna. She hissed as she caught them, her palms aching with the pressure of holding them. Tianna glanced at her in sympathy before picking up her own load of bags and proceeding after the men. Adrianna followed close behind.

When they made it over to the debris of the felled ceiling, Zorg and Armond went to an empty area to the right of it. There was a relatively secluded spot there, one that was more defensible than any other. They gently deposited their companions on the floor and then began to don their tunics and armor. Tianna stood over Bussi and Dartanyen, clutching her amulet. The sounds of destruction from behind the curtain became louder. They were breaking the door down, despite the presence of the boulders on the other side of it. The enemy would eventually overcome the obstacle and infiltrate their resting place. Adrianna felt her fear course through her like a river, her heart responding by increasing its tempo. The men readied their weapons and walked several feet in front of them. It would be a last stand.

***

Dinim ran through the passageway in the direction of the worship hall. His imprisonment was finally over, the spell broken. The creature lay dead several passages away, decapitated and dismembered. Dinim had not realized that such savagery existed within him, and he was almost remorseful of what he had done, afraid of accepting that it was indeed he who had committed those acts. Almost. But he was most definitely fearful of what he may have done to the people he had left behind in the worship hall. What had become of them? Had anyone been harmed when the ceiling fell?

Dinim turned a corner. The worship hall was just ahead. The door was open, and beyond it all that he could see was a pile of large stones. Damn! He would have to use his last spell to clear through the rubble. But did anyone stand on the other side? Would someone be hit by the flying rock when he cast his *Project Force* spell? He wracked his brain, trying to decide what he should do. If only he could tell them, somehow communicate to them that they should move away from the debris. But he was not a telepath. Dinim stopped at the blocked doorway. He could hear a loud crashing sound, and then some shouts on the other side. Dinim made his decision. At least they had been able to clear away some of the rock on the other side, otherwise he would not be able to hear what was going on so well. It also meant that there would be fewer projectiles when he cast the spell. Dinim completed the incantation and then directed the energy. It blasted through the barricade. He stepped into the pass that he had created, hoping that he had not done more harm than good. Finally, when some of the dust subsided, he was able to view what he had wrought.

Adrianna watched with horror as the priests advanced. She was sure that there were some necromancers in their midst and they were flanked by Cimmerean warriors. She felt that there were at least twelve priests and six Cimmereans. They were far outnumbered. Any hope of their living to see the end of this day fled her. The enemy glared at them wickedly and grinned, knowing that they would be the winners of this battle. Zorg and Armond stood at combat readiness. Tianna stood next to her, scimitar in hand. They would fight any who broke through Zorg and Armond. Adrianna had not been able to rest well enough to regain sufficient energy to cast any of her spells, so she wielded her dagger. She knew it would not be enough, but she would die with a weapon in her hand.

Suddenly there was an explosion of sound. Adrianna sensed the vibration of the stone beneath her feet and then felt the rain of debris for the second time that day. But instead of pelting her from overhead, it hit her right side. She choked and coughed on the thick dust. She felt Tianna's hand on her arm, heard the other woman coughing as well. She struggled to see through the cloud of particulate debris, and when it finally started to settle, what met her questing gaze was nothing short of a godsend.

Most of the enemy lay, unmoving, on the floor. Those that stirred were rising slowly, looking around themselves, bewildered. Zorg and Armond also rose from the floor, their eyes fixed upon something in the field before them. Adrianna focused her gaze past them and saw none other than the form of Dinim. She could only imagine that the explosion was of his doing. But wait. This was not the Dinim with which they had been traveling. It was the other one, the one she had seen in the worship hall after the first battle, the one who had caused the ceiling to collapse.

Dinim strode towards the group, saw the weary expressions on the faces of the two men standing in the fore. But he did not have time for the questions he knew they would want to ask of him, as he knew that more priests and necromancers would come. He had to get them out of the temple before it was too late. "I will help you get your men. We have to leave as quickly as possible."

The tall faelin man nodded. "We will hold them off while you pass through." Armond turned back to the two women standing over Bussi and Dartanyen. "Get them out of here," he shouted. He then turned back to Zorg. The two men began to advance upon the few enemy that were left. Dinim rushed over to them. Tianna and Adrianna struggled to get Bussi while Dinim helped Dartanyen. Bussi grumbled at them as they began to make towards the rubble. Adrianna felt like boxing his ears. Her hands throbbed with the pain and it felt like any healing that they had accomplished was quickly being undone.

Adrianna began to hear the sounds of battle. She turned her head to see Zorg and Armond had engaged the Cimmerean warriors that had survived the spell Dinim had cast. Most of the priests continued to lie on the floor. Those that still lived were severely injured and Adrianna knew that few of them would survive the day.

The foursome stumbled into the pass that Dinim had created. Zorg and Armond followed slowly, continuing to hold off those who would pursue them. Adrianna moaned inwardly, wishing that Bussi were not quite so heavy. What flesh remained on her palms felt as though it was being stripped away. Then they were on the other side and making their way down the passageway. Adrianna heard an agonizing cry behind them and cringed. She worried about the men, hoped that they would not come to harm.

"Over here . . . this way." Adrianna saw Dinim gesturing them down a side passage. She and Tianna struggled to maintain their grip on Bussi; Adrianna knew that she would not be able to last much longer. One of the bags she carried slipped off of her shoulder and she stumbled. Bussi fell to the floor, but he said nothing, he having passed out not long after being dragged through the passage. She held her hands to her chest, felt a wetness on her cheeks. Tianna patted her shoulder. Then she felt a presence on her other side and looked up to find Dinim standing over her. Adrianna saw Tianna turn quickly. Adrianna turned in the same direction and saw Zorg and Armond jogging toward them. Zorg stooped to pick up Bussi, and Armond stepped over to help Dinim with Dartanyen. Armond looked a little worse for wear, and by the way that he walked, Adrianna knew that he had been hurt.

Tianna helped her to stand. They leaned on one another as they began to make their way down the passageway once more. They had only walked for a few more yards before the sounds of shouting could be heard behind them. "Hurry . . . we must hurry. They are coming for us. This way." Dinim gestured down yet another passageway. The group followed him, no one even bothering to ask him why he bothered to help them. They knew that Dinim could be leading them into a trap, yet they knew it would be no different from what they left behind. So out of desperation they followed him, hoping that he would lead them to salvation.

11 Enaren CY593

The group shuffled down the main road through Sangrilak. In the darkness they made their way slowly to the Inn of the Hapless Cenloryan. No one else was about and so no one witnessed the weary group of half-beaten individuals walking down the street. As they finally stumbled up to the front steps, Adrianna sighed, looking forward to finally falling into bed.

The man Dinim had led them out of the temple. They had scurried through the passageways like animals, skulking about in the shadows and behind the corners the best they could. Their fallen comrades dragged at them and their pursuers dogged their footsteps. Yet they had escaped. They emerged from the bowels of the temple; up up up they climbed, and once they reached the top, Zorg and Armond were able to pull Bussi and Dartanyen to the surface by ropes. They found themselves at what looked like a deserted well; yet another hidden entrance to the damned temple.

They had then stood there for a moment, regarding each other, wondering. "It wasn't me, you know, but a doppelganger. The man who had settled within your midst was no man at all, but an intruder. I do not know if you believe me, neither do I care. But I wanted to at least say it . . ." Dinim had paused for a moment, then turned and began to walk away.

Armond had called after him, thanking him for his aid. Dinim had paused and nodded his head without looking back. Then he continued away from them. Adrianna stared after him. It was strange; she felt that she should know him, yet she obviously could not. She shook her head, remembering how she had warred with herself. It was as though there was a part of her that had known, known that something was wrong . . . terribly amiss. And the creature would have killed them, had it been given the chance.

Adrianna had found herself calling out to him, somehow unwilling to just let him walk away, not when she felt that there was some type of connection between them. Her father. For some reason, Thane wanted this man dead, and Adrianna felt that it was a piece of the puzzle, that Dinim could offer her some insight, help her to discover the truth. And he had told her that he would find her, that when his business was complete, he would come to the Inn of the Hapless Cenloryan.

They stepped up onto the veranda. Zorg knocked heavily on the door and pulled the rope that hung beside it. It would ring a bell that was suspended within Volstagg's chambers and alert him of visitors that came in the wee hours of the morning, like they did now. After only a few moments Volstagg threw open the doors to the inn. He stood quickly aside as the group filed inside. Without saying a word, he took in their tattered condition. He then relieved Adrianna and Tianna of Dartanyen's weight. He led them to the rear of the establishment and into an empty room. He lay the faelin on a bed while Zorg and Armond did the same with Bussi. Tianna busied herself getting some clean water. Suddenly Adrianna found herself being swept into Volstagg's embrace. "Dear Adria, thank the gods you are safe!" Volstagg then held her at arms' length from him, his dark brown eyes scrutinizing her from head to toe, making sure she was hale and whole. Adrianna regarded him in return, noticing that one side of his face was red and swollen, his eye half-closed. His ribs had been bound and he moved with the stiffness of one who had suffered broken bones. He had obviously been beaten.

Adrianna frowned, her eyebrows coming together. "Aye, Volstagg. But what has happened to you?" Her expression deepened and became solemn and distressed. "Who did this? Who. . ."

"Adria, listen." Volstagg tightened his hands upon her upper arms, led her out of the room away from the group. His voice was deep with anger and worry and his eyes shone with fear. "Someone was here. A man was here looking for you. He overpowered me . . ."

Adrianna's world began to spin. She stiffened in Volstagg's embrace and she felt him release her. "Who . . . who was it?"

"Adrianna, it was your father. Thane was here. He is looking for you, and means you harm."

"No . . ." She stepped away from Volstagg, reeling. Before she was about to fall to the floor, she reached out and steadied herself upon the nearby wall. She made herself breathe deeply, in and out, despite the tightness of her locked jaws. The man had been here, seeking her. What would her want with her, after

T.R. CHOWDHURY & T.M. CRIM

so many years? After so many years of repudiating her, wanting to believe that she did not exist?

"Adrianna." Volstagg stood beside her. He lay his hand upon her shoulder. "All will be well. I am here, and no harm will come to you while I yet live." She looked at him, and into his eyes. She searched their depths and found what she had known already. He would die for her. "Come. You must hide. He searches for you still, and I would not have him find you."

Adrianna paused. Inadvertently, she had put her friend in danger, and as long as the rest of the band was with her, they too, would be in danger. Adrianna looked back inside the room. Armond stood in the center of the room, hands on his hips. He regarded her intently, a frown upon a face framed by long dark hair. By his side stood Zorg. The two had obviously overheard portions of the conversation. Tianna sat on the bed next to Dartanyen, worry and confusion written upon her features as she looked back and forth from Adrianna and Volstagg to Zorg and Armond.

Silence reigned. Everyone was waiting for her, knowing there was a decision that she needed to make, and that she was the only one who could make it. But they also knew she must make it now. She looked back to Volstagg and nodded.

***

Tallachienan sat alone in his dark tower. He sat in a massive cushioned oak chair, brooding. He had his hands clasped in front of him, the knuckles touching his chin, and one leg crossed over the other. He thought about what had just recently transpired. He had known that it would have to happen soon, he just didn't realize *how* soon. His student, Dinim, had finally contacted him via the Travel Notebook. The man had told him of the young Talent that he had found, that she had potential, great potential. He had described the woman to him . . . described her as "the most beautiful mortal woman he had ever seen".

TC remembered her, saw her in his mind's eye as though it was yesterday, saw her looking at him from dark eyes that could look into his heart and the very depths of his soul. A cool breeze whispered through the room, brushing his shoulder.

> *"I do swear, that I'll always be there.*
> *I'd give you anything, and everything,*
> *And I will always care.*
> *Through weakness and strength, and happiness and sorrow,*
> *Through all space, and all time*
> *I will love you*
> *With every beat of my heart."*

Remembering her words, spoken so long ago, he grimaced in pain, undiminished over the centuries, and put his head in his hands. His heart cried out in agony, and it echoed throughout the world, all of its dimensions, and the very fabric of time . . .

Adrianna was jolted awake. She did not know exactly what it was that had awakened her, but it had been full of pain and loneliness. She looked about her room in the citadel, seeking it within the shadows, but found nothing. She reached out next to her even though she knew that Tallachienan would not be there. He had told her that he had a lot of work to do in his laboratory before he could even think about sleeping. But he had told Adrianna to sleep, and to sleep well, because she would need all of her strength and all of her wits about her for the upcoming battle with Aasarak. But she knew that she would not be able to go back to sleep. The things that had awakened her had been only feelings and emotions, but they had seemed so real, and they made her feel upset. To think . . . someone, somewhere in the world was feeling that miserable. She got out of bed and sought out Tallachienan, drawn to do so although she knew not why. She found him in his library, poring over a thick volume. She stepped up behind him and put her hands upon his shoulders and began to knead the taut flesh beneath his velvet tunic. Her unbound hair fell, golden, in stark contrast against the dark fabric. Tallachienan brought his head back and looked up at her, a smile curving the fullness of his lips. She came around the chair to face him, and he moved the large oak chair back so that she could settle herself onto his lap. When she did so, Adrianna wrapped her arms around Tallachienan's neck, and put her head on his broad shoulder. For a few moments he held her there, but then began to gently massage her skin through the thin nightgown. She slowly brought her head up, and looked deep into his eyes. They smoldered with his desire for her, but not just that of the lustful type. It was something more . . . something like need, or maybe it was love *. . . She cupped his face in her hands and gently kissed his lips. His arms wrapped around her and she was enfolded within his warm, strong embrace. She held on to him in return, never wanting to let him go. "I do swear . . ."*

TC came back to himself. Despite everything, he would have to face her again, and he would have to go to her, to aid her in her mission. It was her destiny now, just as it had been then. He would have to train her, and make her the best at what it was she would be. But not now. He would wait, wait and see. And he did not want to give up his most promising apprentice just yet. There were a few things he would have Dinim do for him before the young man dedicated himself to a series of missions that had failed six times before. Tallachienan slumped deep into the recesses of the chair, thought about the upcoming future, and remembered the long ago past.

***

Dinim quickly opened one of the doors to the inn, slipped inside, and then closed it behind him. He took in the room, the positioning of the bar, the tables. There were no other people in the room. It was empty, save for himself and the cenloryan coming through the doors leading into the kitchens. Volstagg saw him and stopped. Dinim saw a multitude of emotions pass over the man's face, and then he spoke. "Dinim, I wondered about you when you did not return with the group."

Dinim blinked. Then he remembered. The creature, Ixitchitl, had been with the group. Volstagg would have encountered it . . . thought it to be him, just as everyone else had thought it was him. "Volstagg, I do not have time to explain. There is someone following me".

Volstagg was instantly on alert. ""Who is it?"

"I'm not sure, but it may be someone who has had me imprisoned for the last few months."

Volstagg frowned. He opened his mouth, a question poised upon his lips, but Dinim raised a hand, forestalling him. "Please, I will answer all of your questions, but tell me . . . is the Lady Adrianna here?"

Volstagg stiffened, his eyebrows coming together into a frown. "Why? Don't you know?"

Dinim sighed heavily. This was proving to be rather difficult. "Please Volstagg, just tell me. Is she here?"

Volstagg inhaled, his chest puffing out. "Yes."

"All right. Good." Dinim paused. "Volstagg, I need a place to hide for a day or two. How about it?"

Volstagg frowned once more. Where had the man been? What did he mean by 'imprisoned'? Volstagg had just seen him several days past, when the group had left to go into the temple. Not only that, but he acted as though he did not know the whereabouts of the group. Then he asked to be hidden in the same place as they were. Yet, Volstagg could not deny him. Dinim was a member of the Wildrunners, and Volstagg had sworn to support and aid the Wildrunners in any way possible.

Volstagg eyed Dinim warily. "I suppose." He paused. "Follow me."

Dinim followed Volstagg into the back of the establishment. He knew that Volstagg was confused, and that he wondered about him. He would explain it all when a few days had passed . . . when Lord Thane was no longer in the vicinity. He had taken pains to avoid being followed, but he could not be sure that he had not been, or that the spies knew where the Lady Adrianna was located. Volstagg could be in great danger, but Dinim did not really know what to do about it. He was nothing against the Azmathous, and the group would most probably die if they were to meet them. It was best if they all remained hidden for now, at least until the immediate threat had dissipated.

114

Finally Volstagg stopped. He pulled away the massive rug in the center of the floor. Beneath it was a heavy wooden door. Volstagg looked at Dinim. "This is it."

Dinim nodded. "Volstagg, where is the Lady Adrianna? I have reason to believe that she is in danger. She needs to be in hiding as well."

Volstagg regarded Dinim intensely. Then he nodded towards the door. "You had better get yourself inside. You will find your companion within."

Dinim nodded. Volstagg had already hidden her. That was good. Her safety was of paramount importance, not only to himself, but to Master Tallachienan as well. The Master had taken a rather undisguised interest in the potential that lay within this girl.

"Thank you, Volstagg. I am in your debt."

"You have already been in my debt," replied the cenloryan, lifting the heavy door. It moaned upon its hinges as it opened.

"Nevertheless . . . I thank you," replied Dinim.

"You are welcome."

Dinim climbed down into the darkness and the door was cast down behind him. "Praise the gods for those such as Volstagg," he whispered to himself.

***

Adrianna closed her book. She could not study anymore. It was just too much to ask. She was withering away with boredom. She flung herself back upon the bed. Volstagg had a great place down here beneath the inn. He had a series of rooms, each with its own place to sleep. The rooms were small but cozy. It was a safe place. She was sure that wards had been placed upon the area, for she had sensed the magic as she passed them by on her way down.

Everyone had begun to heal from the wounds they had suffered in the temple. Dartanyen and Bussi were still bed-ridden, but Tianna was sure that they would be up and about in another day or two. Adrianna's hands were healing nicely. Much of the pain had receded and new flesh had begun to cover the areas that had been scorched. Just this morning, Tianna had removed the bandages in which she had been covering Adrianna's hands. She told Adrianna that at this stage in the healing process, the wounds needed the air to touch them.

Adrianna stretched and then paused. Someone was watching her. She looked toward the entrance to her room. There in the doorway stood Dinim. Adrianna sat upright on the bed. The Cimmerean continued to watch her from the doorway. She regarded him solemnly. He was different. His black hair was grown out, the hair on top longer than that on the sides. He wore new tunic and trousers, the dark colors accenting his pale complexion, dark hair, and lavender eyes. Now that he sported more hair, Adrianna could see a streak of silver that characterized him. It sprang from the peak at his forehead and fell to the left.

Adrianna stood from the bed. She walked across the room to the doorway. Then she stopped. There was something magnetic about the man, something about him that she could not resist, for he was indeed quite handsome. His face was finely chiseled, the planes delicate yet pronounced. The one who had mimicked him had been the same. Yet, there was something different about this man, something . . .

"Hello Lady."

Adrianna smiled to herself. He was so formal, it was almost endearing. She nodded to him. "My Lord."

Dinim shook his head. "No. Please call me Dinim."

"Only if you call me Adrianna."

Dinim paused and then smiled. "As you wish."

"I do." Adrianna smiled in return. "Please, come in."

Dinim entered the room. He looked around. "Cozy."

"That's just what I thought."

Dinim smiled for a moment, but then his countenance became serious. "Adrianna, I think that someone is hunting you."

"I *know* that someone is hunting me."

Dinim regarded her solemnly. "Do you know who it is?"

Adrianna swallowed heavily and then cast her eyes to the floor. She could not look him in the face. "Yes."

Dinim waited, clearly wanting her to elaborate. Adrianna suddenly found herself afraid. She had never had to speak it aloud before . . . that her father wanted to kill her. What father wanted to kill his own daughter? "One by the name of Thane."

"Why does he want you? Besides being a Talent, what are you to him?"

"He . . . I am his daughter."

Silence. Adrianna slowly looked up. She saw Dinim watching at her. He bore an expression of sad understanding. Yet it also seemed that he was bewildered.

Dinim looked at Adrianna, took in her calm submission. He did not understand. He had not known that the other faelin races also rejected their children. Yet, Adrianna was a female. If she had been born Cimmerean, she would have been prized, unlike himself. Having been born a male, he had been considered weak, not worthy of the opportunities offered the females of his race. Yet, Master Tallachienan had changed that for him.

"Does the rest of your group know about this?"

"Somewhat. I think that Dartanyen is suspicious. He knows that Thane means something to me, just not what. I was more than a little shocked to find my father's name on a message belonging to a dead man we found at the library."

"Ah, Kyrin. The bastard tricked me. He was a governing force in my capture by the creature Ixitchitl."

Dinim spoke the name, yet Adrianna knew that she would never be able to replicate the pronunciation, despite her proclivity for languages. His features had remained expressionless, yet Adrianna knew that he must feel at least *something*.

"Well, let us hope that Thane does not find us here."

Adrianna regarded Dinim. "Yes. But what is he to you?"

"Merely my jailer." Dinim forbore to mention that his association with the man was nothing compared to hers, for she knew it already. Dinim somehow knew that Adrianna's death meant more to Thane than Dinim's own, despite Dinim's power as a ripened Talent.

Adrianna nodded. "We wait then."

"Yes."

"But I cannot wait forever. I refuse to hide indefinitely."

Dinim heard the hauteur in her voice, the desire to feel confident, even though she did not.

Dinim nodded. "I, also, can not stay here forever."

"Perhaps we can help one another."

Dinim got the impression that the girl did not know what she was up against . . . did not know that her father was Azmathous. It was unlikely that she even knew that such a person existed, that her father had sold his soul to the DeathMaster. "Perhaps."

Adrianna continued to look him in the eye. "Tell me what you know."

Dinim found himself taken aback. She was more perceptive than he had given her credit for. Dinim nodded.

***

Adrianna walked down the hallway to the common area. She had been surprised to find that there was one, especially since this was a place of hiding. Volstagg and the Wildrunners had obviously gone all out to produce this place. Perhaps they thought that they would need to use it often. She sighed, her thoughts turning to Dinim once again. Over the last couple of days she had been able to learn a lot from him. He seemed to know about a great many things, especially for one who was as young as he was. Perhaps it was because he had been forced to learn. She knew that he had known great adversity in his life, and hardship tended to cause one to want to learn about as much as one could, hoping that the knowledge could somehow help.

One of the things that Dinim described to her was the doppelganger who had impersonated him. "In their natural form, doppelgangers are thin humanoids with gray flesh. They have no hair, nor any real distinguishing features. They are templates for what they wish to become. When they choose a victim and touch him or her, their shape shifts into the form of that particular individual. They then enter the mind of their victim, learning all they can about the person: their personality, temperament, skills, and interests. They replicate that person in almost every way. Most people would never be able to tell that the doppelganger was an imposter."

Adrianna remembered listening to Dinim with rapt attention. The things he told her were disturbing, but she felt so isolated down there, in the secret place beneath Volstagg's inn, that she felt somehow far removed from all of the things that Dinim described to her. He also told her about the Wildrunners' involvement with Gaknar. She mentioned the dead priest that they had discovered in the temple, and that the man had been a follower of Gaknar. Dinim nodded and explained to her that Aasarak had taken over the temple, and that the two mages were at war with one another. "But right now, Gaknar doesn't have the time to deal with his nemesis. He has his mind focused on bringing the daemon, Tharizdune, from his world into ours."

Adrianna had looked at Dinim in shock. Surely he could not possibly be talking about Tharizdune of Malchur, the one daemon god who had the most influence on this world. Dinim nodded at her stunned expression, verifying that her thoughts were accurate. "The Wildrunners and I are trying to stop Gaknar from reaching his goal. And if he does succeed in bringing Tharizdune here, we need to know how to stop the daemon from wreaking havoc on the world."

Adrianna nodded. "But where does my father fit in all this?"

Dinim regarded her intently for a moment. "I am not sure. When I find out I will let you know."

Adrianna had accepted this. She knew that Dinim had a lot on his mind, but she felt that he was keeping something from her. Perhaps he felt that he was protecting her, but he did her a disservice by not giving her all of the information that she needed in order to survive against Thane. But she did not argue. Maybe he had a good reason for not telling her everything that he knew.

Adrianna entered the room to find Dartanyen, Tianna, Bussi, Zorg, and Armond sitting around on the various sofas and chairs. The conversation slowed as she sat down, but quickly picked up again. "What I'm trying to say is that I don't think that the Wildrunners are even thinking about us right now. They have their own concerns that don't involve us. I don't think that they were ever considering us to help them after our excursion into the temple. Actually, they were lucky to have happened upon us. They were able to foist the temple off on us while they went to pursue bigger, better and probably more dangerous things."

"You are probably right, Armond" said Dartanyen. "Sirion did not mention us coming to join them in his message. So I guess we all need to think about where we will be going from here."

For a few moments the room was quiet. Tianna motioned her over to the sofa, and patted the space beside her. Adrianna seated herself and then looked from one person to the next. Armond leaned with his shoulder against the wall. In many ways, he seemed to be a voice of reason for the group, a reality check. He had the ability to state facts in such a way that the truth could be found amongst them. His statement about the Wildrunners was most likely correct. Adrianna had thought so right from the start. But she had been so consumed with her own worries that she had not bothered to voice her opinion.

Zorg sat slumped upon a chair, his feet crossed and propped up on the table before him. He was a quiet man, not very good with words. But he was a good fighter, and he and Armond made a good team. With Armond's speed, and his brute strength, they could conquer many an enemy. Adrianna then turned to Bussi. He also was a good fighter. Yet, he frightened her. His maniac display in the mausoleum did not repeat itself in the temple, but she knew that it was there, crouching like a kyerrean, waiting to be set free. And then there was Dartanyen. Adrianna turned her gaze to him to find him watching her.

For a moment they regarded one another. She was glad that he was doing so well for one who had been injured so extensively. From the look in his eyes, Adrianna knew that he was wondering about her, wishing that he knew what she was about. The others had obviously told him what had transpired between herself and Volstagg upon the night of their return. Adrianna knew that she should tell him . . . it was time. His blue eyes bore into her, but she did not look away. Finally he spoke again, continuing to look at her. "A part of me feels that something remains unfinished. Sure, we brought proof from the temple that it was dedicated to Gaknar, that it has been taken over by another power, and that that power now has control there. But there are so many parts to the puzzle that we do not yet understand." Dartanyen raised an eyebrow before glancing around at the rest of the group. His attentions had not gone unnoticed however, as Armond and Tianna looked back and forth from her to Dartanyen.

Adrianna glanced down at her hands, folded in her lap. Where did she begin? What exactly did she say? Suddenly she was nervous, as she was now the focus of attention. How would it sound to these people, that yes, she was indeed being sought after by a father who wished to kill her? However, there was that part of him that was no longer truly her father. That man had withered away when he had allowed himself to become the monster that Volstagg said was hunting her.

"Good afternoon." Adrianna sighed with relief as Dinim sauntered into the room. Everyone turned to him and greeted him as he entered. With his appearance, the focus had left her. The group was most assuredly more interested in him, and what exactly had happened down in the temple after the collapse.

Dinim went to the pitcher and poured himself a mug of water. Then he took a chunk from the bread loaf and sat down at the table across from Zorg. The other man removed his feet from the tabletop and instead placed them upon another chair nearby. Dinim glanced around at the group of people seated around the room. Before entering, he had paused at the doorway. Upon feeling the tension in the room, and seeing Adrianna's nervousness begin to heighten, he had chosen to proceed within, even though he knew that he would soon be the focus of attention. But that was all right. He would give her a little more time to collect her thoughts, decide what she would say.

"So, who are you? I mean . . . never mind." Tianna stammered sheepishly and then looked away, not really knowing what to say, and then realizing that she may sound rude. Adrianna raised an eyebrow, looked at Tianna, and then back at Dinim. He wore a slight grin on his face.

"That's all right. I understand. It must be difficult for you to have known the creature, thought it to be who I now claim to be. You must also feel daft and embarrassed, having placed your trust in it. Well, try not to feel that way. The creature fooled everyone, including the Wildrunners.

"My name is Dinim Dimitri Coabra. The creature that you had known was a doppelganger, Ixitchitl. By someone's order, it was bid to take my form, my memories, and everything else about me and walk as me, live my life. In the meantime, I was to remain a prisoner within the temple. One by the name of Thane was sent to collect me to take me to the one who had ordered me imprisoned in the first place. However, it seems that Thane had other matters to see to in addition to bringing me to his master." Dinim glanced at Adrianna and then continued.

"The creature was surprised to see me when I emerged from the pews in the worship hall. It must have thought that I would not have been able to extend my prison that far. But it was wrong, and it died from its mistake. In the battle, the staff it carried was incinerated. That is why it is not with me. I had heard about the death of the man whom you all had defeated while wandering the maze. With the power that Ixitchitl had obtained from me, it could have dispatched that man with ease. But I heard that the man was killed with an arrow." Dinim glanced at Dartanyen.

"Is it possible that the creature had made its spell look like it had failed, when in fact it had diffused the spell itself?" asked Dartanyen.

Adrianna knew the answer before Dinim replied. "In all probability that is exactly what it did. The creature probably wanted you to think that the man had a magical resistance, so that all future magical attacks would be futile. It is apparent that it did not realize the extent of your skill." The guilt that Adrianna had felt about that battle resurfaced. She had behaved like such a coward. If only she had gone ahead with her own spell instead of being influenced by someone else.

Then Tianna spoke. "The creature . . . it seemed so temperamental, so unpredictable. Is . . . is that who you truly are? I mean, did the creature replicate you in *every* way?"

Adrianna turned to look at Tianna. The woman seemed a little disturbed and upset. Adrianna remembered the rapport that had been shared between Tianna and Dinim when they had left the Temple of Hermod. There had been an attraction there; she had sensed it. Adrianna glanced at Dinim to find him also regarding Tianna intently.

"In many ways the creature replicated me in every detail," Dinim began. "But it can only go so far before the environment and its own natural bent begin to influence the creature. In some ways, I am temperamental and unpredictable, but not to the extent in which you found the creature to be. Doppelgangers tend to be that way, and the natural inclination of the creature was beginning to show through its disguise."

Tianna nodded, her eyes downcast. Her hands plucked at her skirt and she played with the ring about her middle finger. Suddenly she rose from the sofa and began to walk towards the platter of food that had been brought to them from Volstagg earlier in the day. Dinim's eyes followed her for a moment before returning to the group.

"I've been wondering about the details of your skirmish with the doppelganger," said Armond intently, a slight grin upon his lips.

"I was just thinking about that myself," said Dartanyen, leaning forward in his chair.

Dinim smiled.

CHAPTER 7

Volstagg opened the secret door beneath the rug. The group filed out and entered the building proper. The sight that met their eyes was shocking to behold. The place was in shambles. Tables and chairs lay overturned upon the floor, many of them broken. An assortment of plates, bowls, and cups also lay scattered about the floor. Adrianna's eyes were lugubrious as she turned to him. "Volstagg, what happened here?"

Volstagg watched as the group made their way through the devastation. Adrianna had insisted upon leaving hiding, stating that they could not stay there forever and that she would have to face her father eventually. Unhappily, Volstagg had acquiesced, indeed wishing that she would stay in hiding until she was hunted no longer. But he realized that it was a silly intention. He could not expect her to hide herself away indefinitely.

The group had remained in hiding for six days. Within that time, Thane had returned. Volstagg spoke about the experience, his eyes haunted. "He asked about you, Adrianna. Of course, I told him I had not seen you since the last I had spoken to him but a mere six days past. In his anger, he threatened me, telling me that I had better tell him of your whereabouts or that he would kill me. I asked him why he wanted you . . ."

Volstagg paused in his recitation. He did not want to tell Adrianna what the monster had said. He never wanted her to know. A part of him knew that he should tell her, but he could not bring himself to tell her what her father had said . . . that he had always hated the child that had killed his beloved Gemma, and that he would kill her with his own two hands. He would kill Sheridana's bastard child as well, but he had made Adrianna his ultimate priority. Volstagg continued. "I would tell him nothing. At that moment, I feared for your life more than ever before. One of his informants had told him they had seen the lot of you walking through the streets upon your return from the temple. Another informant had told him that you all came here. As he put his sword to my throat, he ordered his minions to search the place. They demolished the inn, but they did not find the hidden door. When they reported to Thane, he released me angrily, slashing at me with his sword and slicing my chest. His eyes narrowed and he spoke angrily in an unfamiliar tongue. His minions left the inn. He told me to 'ware, and that, no matter where you were, he would always find you, for your blood had stained his hands already and he would have you . . ."

Volstagg stopped speaking, caught Adrianna's gaze. His eyes were haunted, echoing his fear . . . fear for her. "He called the last of his minions to him, and he preceded them out my front door. He has not returned."

Volstagg stopped speaking, his eyes wide as he regarded Adrianna and the rest of the group. Everyone was silent. Adrianna sat there, motionless. "Do you know where he went?" Dartanyen asked, breaking the silence.

Volstagg shook his head. "I have no idea. But I fear that his informants continue to watch my establishment." Then he seemed to remember something. "I have something for you. Wait just a moment while I get them." Volstagg went to the back of the inn and into another room.

Adrianna thought about her predicament. It seemed that her father would stop at nothing to have her. Why he wanted her she could not fathom, for he had never cared to have anything to do with her before. Adrianna began to have a strange feeling in the back of her mind, as though she was forgetting something. For a moment she tried to capture what it was, but it eluded her. She then gave up, thinking that it would come to her sooner or later.

Volstagg returned to them, two folded parchments in his hands. One he gave to Dartanyen. The other he gave to Adrianna. Confused, she looked up at him as he gave her the parchment. "'Tis for you Adrianna . . . from Sirion. They arrived to me just two days ago."

"Sirion" she breathed his name softly as she held the parchment. Where was he? How did he fare? How went his mission these days past? Slowly she opened the sealed page, strangely pleased that he had chosen to respond to her message personally. She then began to read.

Lady Adrianna,

I received your message. Thank you so much for taking the time to warn me. It means so much to me that you consider my welfare as something of import to yourself. In light of this new situation, please be careful. Sydonnia is a very dangerous man and could ultimately mean you harm. I will have to deal with him myself when I am finished here. I am sorry we were unable to stay in Sangrilak to help you and the rest of the group, but urgent business called us away. I hope you understand. Good luck with your endeavors. Be sure to take care and keep safe. Danger is afoot and I fear that the Powers That Be may have caught wind of you all.

Sincerely,
Sirion Timberlyn

Adrianna read over the letter once more, her mind slowly processing what she had read. She was surprised at the tone he had taken, one of mild wonderment as well as brief concern. She folded the parchment and looked toward Dartanyen as he told the rest of the group that Sirion thanked them for their gratitude and words of encouragement. Adrianna caught a glimpse of Tianna watching her for a moment before the other woman turned away, making it seem that she had not been watching Adrianna at all.

Adrianna moved away from the group and sat down on one of the chairs that remained intact. Finding that she was weary, Adrianna bowed over herself, placing a hand to her forehead and her elbow on her thigh. She wished that Sirion could be here, somehow sure that he would know how to help her with the situation in which she currently found herself. Suddenly she felt a hand on her shoulder. She looked up into the friendly face of Volstagg. She placed her hand over his, and then brought her cheek to rest upon it. Silent tears sprang to her eyes and ran down her face. "This is all my fault. "Oh Volstagg, I am so sorry . . ."

Adrianna put her hands to her face and began to cry. For a moment, all Volstagg could do was stand there. Sorry? She was *sorry*? For what? For something beyond her control . . . for something that she could not do anything about? Volstagg pulled her close to him and put his arms around her. "Silly girl. You did not know this would happen. There is nothing to feel sorry about. Besides, I have plenty of money. I can replace what has been lost."

Adrianna shook her head. "But nothing can replace your life, Volstagg. He could have killed you. Your friendship . . . it means so much to me."

Volstagg stroked her hair. "As does yours to me. Adria, I would protect you always. I value your life much more than my own."

"No. I do not want that . . ."

"But that is what you have, and nothing you say or do will change it."

Adrianna quieted herself, not wishing to make any more of a scene that she already had. But she could not escape her feelings of guilt aboutplacing her friend in danger not once, but two times. She thought of the group, knew that the longer they were in association with her, the more endangered they became as well. And then she thought of someone else. A wave of fear rushed over her. That was it, the thing she had not thought of! It was something she should have thought about when Volstagg first told her that Lord Thane had come seeking her out at the inn. If the daemon had known to look for her at the inn, he would also have traced her . . . home. Her heart began to race.

Volstagg felt Adrianna's body stiffen within his embrace. Then she pulled back from him. "Where did he go after he left here?"

"I . . . I don't know."

Adrianna began to make her way to the front doors.

Volstagg followed behind her. "Adria, wait. Where are you going?"

"If my father tracked me here, knew that I had been here, he must have also known that I had gone home."

Volstagg stopped. With sickening clarity he knew that she was right. He felt his chest constrict, felt the bile rise into his throat.

"Someone should go with you, just in case," said Armond.

"I also will come with you," stated Dinim.

Adrianna nodded to them as she continued toward the entrance.

"Adrianna, at least use the doors in the back of the kitchens. I do not know about the rear exit, but I know that the front entrance is being watched," said Volstagg.

She paused, and then turned around and began to make her way to the rear of the inn. Adrianna quickly made her way through the kitchens and out the back doors. She ran down the steps, Dinim, Armond, and Dartanyen following closely behind. They raced to the stables. Upon entering, Adrianna went straight to Sethanon's stall. The animal raised his head as she entered. She slowed as she approached the lloryk. He whickered a greeting to her. She placed her hands on him, murmured to him in Hinterlic. Then she stepped a few paces away from the lloryk. Adrianna turned back and sprang towards him. She vaulted onto the animal's back, gripping his mane in her hands.

Dinim followed Adrianna to the stall where her animal was housed. Truth be told, he had never ridden a lloryk before. The animal was large, colored a pale dappled grey. Astonished, Dinim watched as the woman vaulted onto the animal's back. The lloryk pranced about for a moment before settling. But then they were out of the stall and into the barn proper. Dinim turned to find Dartanyen and Armond leading their smaller larian out of the stalls.

Dinim turned back when he heard the sound of cloven hooves on stone. At a trot, Adrianna began to leave the barn. "Adrianna, hold up," called Dartanyen.

"Adrianna . . ." Dinim called out to her and she turned her mount. The large animal pranced about nervously, having felt the tension of his rider. Dinim saw the lines of worry around her mouth and eyes. He began to hurry over to her. "I do not have a mount . . . have never ridden . . ."

Before he could finish, she was reaching down to him. He quickened his pace, and when he reached her, he took her hand and propelled himself upward. Much to his surprise, Dinim made it onto the back of the lloryk. He clutched Adrianna around the waist and then they were running, cantering through the city of Sangrilak, Armond and Dartanyen close behind.

They rode through the city and out into the surrounding farmlands. For a while they rode around the outskirts of the city, slowing the lloryk and larian to a trot as they neared Adrianna's home. They then slowed to a walk. Adrianna frowned. She should have seen the house by now. They walked onward, her feelings of panic getting stronger. Then she saw it, a scarred place on the landscape, a blackened heap of rubble in the distance.

"No . . . no. This can't be . . ."

Dinim felt the muscles in Adrianna's legs tighten. Sethanon stretched out his neck and increased his speed. Adrianna lowered herself closer to the lloryk. Dinim clutched at the woman before him, leaning forward with her. Then Dinim saw it, saw the smoldering remains of what had once been a rather large house. Upon reaching the area, Adrianna sat back up. Sethanon began to slow, but even before the animal could come to a halt Adrianna was off of his back.

The foundation was all that remained of the house, the rest of it having, somehow, been burned down. The stones crumbled all about the low, flame-blackened walls that stood from the ground. Adrianna stumbled away from Sethanon towards the wreckage. Armond jumped down from his own lloryk, following. Dinim also dismounted, although not quite so gracefully. He picked himself up from the grass, and made his way to Adrianna, knowing what had happened. It had been wizard's fire that had downed the structure. Thane had a sorcerer with him.

Adrianna walked among the ruins of her childhood home. She was afraid, so afraid of what she would find. But she had to know, could not live without knowing. She saw very few items that were distinguishable among the blackened stones, although she was sure that most of it was just simply lying beneath. Then she saw them. It was the remains of two humanoids lying a few feet away. In anguish, Adrianna quickly made her way over to the bones.

Dinim just reached Adrianna as she fell to the ground, sobbing hysterically. Dinim fell with her as he sought to cushion her fall, the sharp shards of many fractured stones and glass biting into his flesh. He too, saw the remains. A part of him had hoped that she would never find them, although he had known they were there the moment they had come upon the ruins. Caught up in her pain and loss, Adrianna struck out at Dinim, beating her fists into his chest, screaming at him in the tongue of the Savanlean faelin. He was eventually able to capture her fists in his hands, and, having done so, he pulled her to him, comforting her the best that he knew how. He mumbled to her in a soothing tone, rocking her back and forth within his firm embrace.

Finally, Adrianna controlled her emotions. She pulled herself away from Dinim, let her gaze travel over the skeletal bodies of Mairi and Hafgan. She could easily distinguish between the two, Mairi having had a much more slender build. She hovered over the remains of Mairi, wishing that she could hold her just one last time, tell her how much she loved her. Then she saw it, hidden beneath the remains of the woman who had raised her.

Adrianna reached down and gently moved aside the skeletal arm. Beneath it, almost completely hidden within the ashes, was a small box. She slowly pulled it free, the debris falling away from it to reveal an object of beauty. It had been unharmed by the inferno that had destroyed the house, it appearing as though it had never had contact with fire at all. It was made of the finest wood, probably from one of the silver oak trees of Elvandahar. The engravings were exquisite, made by the finest of artisans. The delicate flowers seemed to dance across the wood, and tiny inlaid gems made them sparkle. Adrianna ran her hands over the silky smooth wood, caressingly. She sensed the magic of the object, knowing that it was why the fire had been unable to harm it. She also knew that this was the gift her mother had left for her; the gift that Mairi spoke of the last time Adrianna had seen her.

Adrianna looked up from the box. She saw Dinim regarding her, an expression of sorrow mixed with interest on his face. Dusk was falling and the winds were beginning to pick up. It was going to rain; she could smell it in the air. Behind them, in the close distance, she saw Armond and Dartanyen. They stood next to their larian, unobtrusively watching.

Adrianna looked back down at the box. On the front of it there was a small metal hook that fit into a metal loop. She pulled the hook free. She was surprised that it opened so easily for her, thinking that the magic of the box would surely have kept it locked. But then she remembered that the box was meant for her. Adrianna slowly opened the lid to the box. Inside, sitting on a bed of scarlet satin, was a tightly coiled golden serpent. The creature was beautiful, its scales glistening in what was left of the light. The object was artfully designed, perfect in every detail. Its eyes were tiny rubies, looking at her from a delicately sculpted head.

Amazed by the beauty of the object, Adrianna put her index finger on the serpent, caressing it lovingly. Suddenly, the serpent moved. Adrianna jerked her finger back, but the serpent was quicker. Like lightening it shot up her hand and slithered around her arm until it reached the top. There it settled, wrapping its small body around her, just above the crook of her arm. In shock, Adrianna and Dinim stared at the creature, who stared balefully back at them from its ruby eyes. Adrianna touched the serpent once more, but it did not move from its place about her arm. Adrianna exerted pressure upon it, thinking perhaps to remove it. Adrianna felt the creature coil more tightly about her arm. Adrianna stopped and looked up at Dinim.

It began to drizzle, and thunder sounded in the distance. Dinim frowned at the serpent, wondering. What was it? He had never seen anything quite like it before. However, it did not seem to be harmful, and seemed to feel that it had found its place. And perhaps it had, being made as an item of protection. Dinim reached out and touched it. The serpent did not move. The creature had slightly flattened itself, and molded itself to fit upon Adrianna's arm perfectly.

Dinim then reached down to take Adrianna's hand. The rain was becoming to fall more heavily. The storm was upon them. "Come, there is nothing more that we can do here."

Adrianna balked. She did not want to leave Mairi, but she did not have much choice. She was dead, and there was nothing that Adrianna could do that would change that. Slowly Adrianna rose from the ground, the box cradled within the crook of her arm. The tears began to fall once more, mixing with the water that now began to stream down her face and neck. "Goodbye, dearest Mairi," she whispered. "I will always love you." Then she went with Dinim, following him away from her past toward a strange and unknown future.

***

"Okay, this is it. This is the time. I deserve to know; we all deserve to know . . . what in the Nine Hells is going on?" Dartanyen propped his booted foot up onto a chair. He glared at Volstagg and then at Dinim. The group had just watched as a sodden and dispirited Adrianna walked across the common room and back into the rear of the establishment to her chamber. Any offerings of sympathy were waved away, and her only words to them were that she needed to be alone. Tianna had wanted to go to her, but chose to respect Adrianna's wishes, at least for now.

Tianna looked back and forth from Dartanyen to Volstagg and Dinim. The rest of the group sat quietly in their seats. The room was tense with expectancy. The time of reckoning had come. "People are dying . . . you need to tell us what we are up against."

Volstagg cleared his throat. "You are right. You do deserve to know. Adrianna should be the one to tell you, but she is clearly not in a state of mind that she can do so at this time. So I will tell you." Volstagg paused and looked around at the group. Dinim sat down in the chair nearest him and leaned back in it.

"It has become obvious to most of you that the man you have come to know as Lord Thane is someone that Adrianna knows. Dartanyen, you saw her shock when she read his name on the message found on the dead man in the library. Armond, you saw how upset she was when she discovered that he had accosted me while you were in hiding. However, as it turns out, he is much more than someone that she just knows in passing. He is the man who sired her. He is her father."

The room was silent. Tianna's mind reeled with the shock. Her father? The bastard was Adrianna's father? No wonder she had been so loathe in telling anyone about her connection with him. Tianna looked over to Dartanyen to see that he was shaken about the revelation, as well as everyone else in the room. Except for Dinim. It seemed that he had known already what Thane meant to Adrianna.

Volstagg continued. "As you know, Thane has been behind much of the trouble in which you have recently found yourselves. He is evil . . . and no longer quite mortal. Something has happened to him in the years he has been away. Something has transformed him into some kind of monster. He is an animal, a predator hunting his prey. And that prey happens to be Adrianna."

Dinim heard a quick intake of breath at the table nearest to his. He saw Tianna's shocked expression, as well as those of all of the others around him. "Are you trying to say that Thane wants to kill his own daughter?" Dartanyen asked the question incredulously, not believing the words that Volstagg had spoken.

It was unheard of for a faelin to want to kill his or her offspring. Homicide was virtually unknown within most faelin cultures. In general, faelin had the utmost respect for life, and did not believe in the act of killing another. However, it was different for the Cimmereans, who lived their lives by progressing up the social ladder and stepping upon the bones of those who got in their way. Many Cimmerean mothers committed infanticide, not wanting to bother with the male children they bore. Dinim had been lucky; his mother had not killed him at birth, but he remembered some points in his life when he wished that she had.

"That is exactly what I am trying to say." Volstagg sighed heavily. "If Thane finds her, he will surely kill her. Adrianna is in great jeopardy while she stays here. She must leave Sangrilak as soon as possible. For all I know, Thane's spies have discovered her whereabouts and will be coming for her."

"But why? Why does he hate her so much?" asked Tianna.

"Thane loved his wife very much. When she died giving birth to Adrianna, he went into despair. He would never accept the child that killed his beloved Gemma. It is said that he loved his wife so desperately that he could not bear the sight of the daughter who caused her death."

"But it could not possibly be Adrianna's fault. Many women die in childbirth," exclaimed Tianna.

"Yes, that is true. But Thane needed someone to blame, and he lay that blame upon his infant daughter."

Once more the room was quiet. The tension was gone only to be replaced by sorrow. Armond rose from his table. "I am going to bed. We have to meet with the Captain of the City Guard tomorrow."

"Yes, it will be a big day for us all," said Dartanyen thoughtfully.

Everyone left, each person going to his or her own room. Dartanyen remained behind, quietly looking at the floor. Finally he looked up to find Volstagg regarding him intently. "We are all in danger as well. If she leaves, and he is unable to find her, he will hunt the rest of us down. He will demand that we tell him where she is. If we do not know, he will kill us." Dartanyen made his statement in a monotone. He did not ask Volstagg if his reasoning was correct; he knew the answer already. Dartanyen nodded to himself and then turned away. He walked slowly out of the room, deep in thought. Dinim and Volstagg glanced at one another before they too left to find their beds for the night.

***

It was late. Dinim sat within his room. He tapped his fingers upon the desk, thinking . . . deciding what he should do. He thought about the young woman Adrianna and the chain of events that had been played out that day. She had discovered that her childhood guardians had met uncertain demise. Not only that, but it had been her own father who had killed them. It was such an evil twist of fate that would make one woman suffer so much all at once.

Dinim leaned back in his chair, stretching out his legs beneath the desk. Almost instinctively he had reacted to her. Upon seeing her pain he had run to her, thinking she may harm herself, or that she was in need of someone. Him. Dinim sighed heavily. He had sought to comfort her. All he could think to do was to hold her to him, despite her initial protestations. His chest bore testimony of her emotion; the bruises were faintly there, but there nonetheless. After her initial shock, she had sought the comfort that he offered. He could still feel her wrapping her arms around his neck, pulling his head down to her. He had crooned to her in Cimmerean, nonsense phrases that he came with on the spur of the moment . . . because no phrases of sympathy, friendship, or love existed in his native tongue.

Dinim's thoughts began to whirl. They spiraled back into the past . . . during his life spent in the Underdark. It was a matriarchal society, a realm ruled by priestesses of Tholana, Queen of Darkness. From the very beginning, life for him was a game of survival, as it was for most of the other males born within the dark recesses below the surface of the world. Very quickly he learned how to tread quietly, to hide within the shadows, and to use a dagger proficiently, for someone was always out to use someone else as a stepping-stone to their own advancement. The death of the unfortunate individual who had been thus used was of no consequence, for it was just one less Cimmerean to impede future advancement. Many of the priestesses used their males badly, threatening them if they did not obey their wishes. Most of the time, not even one's family could be trusted; the treatment he had received from his own mother had been appalling to say the least, and his brother had used treachery of the worst kind against him.

Dinim shook his head smartly, ridding himself of the memories. He refocused his eyes on his hands upon the desk. He smiled faintly. But there had been a light at the end of his tunnel. A man by the name of Tallachienan

Chroalthone had saved his life. The man had taken the young Dinim to his citadel in the sky and trained him in the ways of a sorcerer. And now here he sat within the comfort of a well-kept inn, with thoughts of a lovely lady . . .

Dinim sighed again. He wished that he had more time. He knew that he needed to go to the Wildrunners. They had a big fight ahead of them and he knew that they would need him more than ever before. But there was a part of him that wanted to stay with Adrianna and the rest of this group of individuals. He wanted to help her discover the truth of her father. He knew there was more to Thane than met the eye. He had power, and Dinim wanted to know how he had obtained it.

But it would have to wait. Not only did he need to join up with the Wildrunners, but Master Tallachienan had given him the task of discovering why the Talents of Shandahar were being hunted down and killed. Someone was behind the assassinations, and Dinim himself had been one of the next to go. Lord Thane definitely had something to do with the murders, so Dinim knew that he would be working on the same cause as Adrianna, but it wasn't the same as actually traveling with the group.

Dinim had much to learn about the assassinations. TC had reason to believe that a secret cult was behind the murders. Dinim felt that the cult may be working with one by the name of Aasarak, for Thane was one of Aasarak's minions. But he still could not be sure. It was possible that Aasarak had singled out Dinim because of his skills as a Dimensionalist, that his capture had nothing to do with the deaths of the other Talents.

Dinim stood from the desk and blew out the candles. He was tired, and he needed as much rest as he could get. It had been a long day, and he knew that he needed to leave as soon as he could on the morrow.

***

Adrianna tiredly awoke. It was still dark, the sun not having yet begun to rise in the sky. Reluctantly, she lifted herself from the bed. The events of the previous day weighed heavily on her mind. Sleep had not come easily to her, her last conversation with Mairi replaying itself over and over in her mind, thoughts of the woman's agonizing death haunting her dreams, and memories of times long gone echoing through her head.

They had ridden back to the inn in the middle of a downpour. Armond had helped her upon Sethanon's back, she having been unable to do it herself. Then Dinim had mounted behind her, placing his arms around her to be sure she would not fall. Upon reaching the inn, she had gone straight to her room and collapsed upon the bed. She did not know how long she lay there before she felt hands on her shoulders, rolling her over. Tianna pulled off her soaked clothing, wrapped her within the blankets and smoothed back her hair before leaving her alone once more.

Adrianna went to the washbasin and splashed the water on her face, feeling it dribble down her neck and then down between her breasts. She took up the comb and began to work on the tangled mass of her hair. She hissed at the snarls and cursed when she had to pull to get them out. Finally, her hair was respectable once again and she tied it back with a clip, rolling it into a coil atop her head. The ruby gaze of the serpent was speculative as it assessed her from her bare upper arm. She caressed it with a thumb, wondering about it. She pulled fresh tunic and trousers out of her pack, donning them slowly. She then sat back down on the bed and took up the small box within which she had found the serpent.

Adrianna opened the box once more. She touched the softness of the satin bed upon which the serpent had lay. She knew that the serpent was not a living creature, yet it had moved just like any other snake would move. It regarded her as though intelligent, watching her benignly with its jeweled eyes. Adrianna lifted the satin pillow from the box. Beneath it she found a folded parchment. She removed the parchment and replaced the pillow. Slowly she opened the parchment, almost afraid of what she would find written there. The message was written in the most beautiful script, and it swept across the page artfully.

Dearest Child,

Once more the nights are becoming shorter and the days warmer. Spring approaches and my belly swells ever larger. I can feel you and your sister moving within me. I am filled with joy, knowing that the life that I carry within me will endure even when I am gone. I know that you have Talent. I have been able to feel it, even though you yet reside within my womb. And Power. You will inherit my ability to see what was and what will be. I do not know from whence this Power comes; only that I have it, you have it and your daughter will have it.

I can't wait to meet you. I will show you everything: all of the wonderful things that life has to offer. We will be good friends, you, your sister and I. Your father and brother wait expectantly of your birth. They speak to you through the wall of my belly. I am sure that you will know their voices when you are born. What a wonderful family we will make.

I have set aside this gift for you. I will present it to you when you go to make your own place in the world. My mother gave it to me, and thus I will pass it down to you. It will protect you wherever you are and will continue to do so until you choose to pass it on to your own offspring. Always remember that I love you, and I will be with you forever. Never forget your destiny. Sometimes it is all that we have.

Love Always,
Gemma

Something wet dropped onto the parchment and Adrianna hurriedly rubbed it off. It was then that she realized that her tears were falling into her lap, precariously close to the precious parchment. She folded the message her mother had written so long ago. Gemma had not realized that she would not be there when Adrianna received her gift, had not known that her daughters would live their lives without her, that she would never see their first footsteps, or hear their first words. Adrianna brought the parchment to her chest and bent herself over it. She sobbed pitifully, wishing so much that she had known her mother, met her even just once. And her mother had spoken so well of her father, saying that Thane awaited her birth, as though he would love her when she came. Adrianna keened from deep within her throat, so deep she felt that it emanated from her chest. Her heart ached with the pain of loss, and she felt as though it would burst. She hoped that her children would never have to feel the way she felt now, and knew that if Gemma was there, she would be crying too.

***

Dinim pulled the maroon tunic over his head. He snatched up the navy sash and wrapped it about his lean waist. He secured his pouches of most commonly used spell components on it, arranging them near his right hip. At his left hip he secured his short sword. He pulled the weapon from its sheath and examined the blade. It felt so good to have the weapon in his hand again. Since he had taken it back from the doppelganger he had spent many an hour with the weapon, sharpening the blade and polishing the grip.

Dinim looked from the blade towards the door. A moment later, there was a soft knock. Dinim sheathed his weapon and went to the door. He opened it to find Volstagg standing in the hallway. Dinim stood aside to allow the cenloryan to enter. Volstagg entered the room and Dinim closed the door behind him. Volstagg turned to regard the young Cimmerean standing before him. He had noticed a big difference in Dinim since he had returned from the temple. The man who had left with the group had seemed more arrogant, anxious, and ambiguous. Volstagg had thought it odd behavior since he had never known Dinim to be those things before. Now, he saw Dinim as the young man he had known several months ago as a member of the Wildrunners.

Dinim smiled slightly, the emotion not quite reaching his eyes. Suddenly, he seemed tired, the lines beneath the man's eyes telling a story of their own. Volstagg felt his heart go out to him. "I know you are wondering about me, why I have been behaving so strangely recently. Let's just say that I wasn't myself." Dinim's grin widened as he made the last statement, almost as though he was telling a joke.

"Well, I have been wondering. But we have more important things to discuss than your weird antics as of late. Tell me, what are your plans? Will you run to catch up with the Wildrunners or will you be staying here?"

Dinim's smile widened once more. Volstagg was always one to get right to the point. Then he sighed. He knew what he *wanted* to do, but it did not coincide with what he *needed* to do. However, he had a duty and he would live by it, at least for now. When the menace of Tharizdune's release was dissipated, he would live by his own will. "I will be leaving to join the Wildrunners tomorrow morning. I need to get a few supplies, and I would like to have one more night of good rest before I depart."

"Good, I am glad to hear it. Just a couple of days ago I received a message from them, asking for your whereabouts. Although it wasn't stated in the message, I know that they need you." Volstagg paused and cocked his head to the side. "I also know that you feel torn. Just so you know, I am going to try to convince Adrianna to return to Andahye. There, she will have at least some measure of protection."

"Hmph, good luck."

"What do you mean by that?"

"I mean that you will have a difficult time with that endeavor. I get the feeling that she will not be wanting to go back there."

"And why is that?"

"Don't you know?"

"Stop being so cryptic, Dinim. It gets on my nerves, not to mention that I don't have the time for guessing games."

Dinim sighed explosively and frowned. "And your warm personality has always been one of your better qualities, Volstagg."

Volstagg frowned in return. "So, tell me. Why won't Adria want to go back to Andahye?"

"Because of the reason why she left there in the first place. The master under whom she was apprenticed was murdered. She has nothing there now, no one to turn to."

Volstagg's eyes widened with incredulity. "Why didn't she say anything to me?"

"Why would she? She hardly got a chance to realize that she had finally come home when everything started happening. She didn't even have the chance to see her foster mother but one time since she has been back."

Volstagg nodded slowly. "You are right. She would not have had the chance. But how do you know all of this?"

"We got a chance to talk while we were in hiding. You can learn a lot from a person if you just take the time."

Volstagg had the decency to look chagrined. He shook his head and looked down at the floor. "I was so focused on her safety that I was not a very good friend to her. I didn't even come down to ask her how she was doing . . ."

Dinim sighed and put a hand on the cenloryan's arm. "Listen Volstagg, you are a good friend. It wasn't my intention to make you feel otherwise. You are a good man. Few others would have done what you have for Adrianna. She is lucky to have a champion like you."

Volstagg raised his head. "Thanks. That means a lot to me."

"So, did the Wildrunners happen to mention where they were located?"

"The message originated from Grondor. I am assuming they are still there."

"Then that is where I will be heading." Dinim turned away from Volstagg and walked over to his travel-sack. He carried the sack over to the desk and placed his journal, ink, and stylus into it.

"There was something else I wanted to discuss with you. It has to do with Thane."

Dinim turned back around to face Volstagg. He regarded the cenloryan, quietly waiting for him to elaborate.

"From speaking with Adrianna you probably know that she has a sister."

"Yes, I do seem to remember her mentioning that."

"Well, Adrianna is not the only one on Thane's hit list. Her sister has a child. That child is also in danger. Thane wants the child destroyed."

Dinim frowned. "I understand why Thane wants to kill Adrianna, but why the child?"

"The child is a bastard. That is all that I know. It does not seem to warrant that Thane should want to kill the child because its parents were not wed-locked when it was born, but Thane ceased to be sane years ago."

Dinim frowned. "I will have to look into this. Perhaps I will be able to find something out when I go to Grondor. You know how information seems to find its way there. It just takes a little bit of skill to find that information."

Volstagg grinned slightly. "I knew that I would be able to count on you."

"So, tell me a little bit more about this sister of Adrianna's . . ."

***

Finally Adrianna stood up from the bed. She placed the parchment back into the box and then put the box into her bag. She dried her eyes with the cloth next to the washbasin. Adrianna sighed heavily. She was in no hurry to face her comrades. They would look upon her with pity and concern. They would worry about her mental well-being. Hesitantly she left her room and walked down the hallway towards the front of the inn. Once there, she walked through the empty kitchens and through the double doors. There, seated at a large table, were Dartanyen, Bussi, Armond, Zorg, and Tianna.

The quiet conversation stopped as Adrianna entered the room. For a moment everyone was silent. Then Dartanyen stood up and beckoned her over to them. He offered her his seat as she approached the table. He pulled over another chair as she took the proffered seat.

Everyone remained quiet, not knowing what to say. Adrianna supposed that she could not blame them. She would not know what to say either. It wasn't every day that one found out that one's companion had a father who killed people for sport. Then Dartanyen spoke. It was only natural that he would be the first, he who had taken a leadership role. "Adrianna, I know this must be a difficult time for you. I will not pretend to understand what you are feeling, but I want you to know that we are here for you."

Adrianna heard agreement from around the table. She appreciated the gesture, but disliked the fact that her comrades pitied her. She did not need their pity. Adrianna heard him before he entered. Volstagg came through the front door from the porch outside. Adrianna looked in his direction and saw Dinim enter behind him.

Dinim. He was the one from whom she had sought comfort the evening before. And it had felt good, so good to have him wrap his arms around her and hold her tight. She regarded him for a moment as he entered the establishment. His long black hair was tied at the nape of his neck. The silver streak that started at his hairline lay to the left side and was a stark contrast to the rest of his appearance. He wore darkly colored tunic, trousers, and cloak . . . all of which offset his pale complexion.

Dinim walked to the table and pulled up a seat. He turned the chair around and straddled the back. For a moment he looked around the table. "I just wanted to let you know that I will be leaving soon. It probably isn't a good idea, considering that I am still being hunted, but I can't remain here indefinitely." Dinim glanced at Adrianna as he said the last, remembering the conversation they had had only a few days before.

Everyone nodded in understanding. Adrianna was taken aback. He had not mentioned his leaving during the six days he had been in hiding with them. When she had shared her dilemma with him, she had assumed that he would be staying to help her learn more about Thane. She looked up at him to find him catching her gaze.

"I have some business that I must see to, but I hope that I can meet up with you all later," said Dinim, finally looking away from Adrianna to glance around at the rest of the group. "Do you know where you will be in a few weeks?"

Dartanyen shrugged. "We may not even be together in a few weeks. Employment is paramount on everyone's minds right now. We will be paid handsomely for our services here, but that money won't last very long."

"I have been entertaining thoughts of going to Karlisle," said Armond. The nobles there are always looking for a sword to hire."

"Before I answered Sirion's summons to help you, I had heard that Elvandahar has been suffering from lycanthrope infiltration," said Tianna. "My family lives there, so I was going to go see exactly what is going on. I was going to ask if you all might consider accompanying me there; I don't know how dangerous the situation is and I was loathe to go alone."

Dartanyen nodded to her. "Sure, I'll go with you. I know that the Hinterleans don't take well to strangers, but maybe I will be able to get a position as one of the palace guards. I'm good with the bow. Perhaps they will not want to turn me away once they see my skill."

"Hey, Armond. Maybe you will want a companion with you to Karlisle?" asked Zorg.

"I would appreciate the company," Armond replied.

Dinim just looked from one person to the next. He had not intended for the conversation to take this turn, but they were right in wanting to think about what they were going to do next. Once more he glanced at Adrianna to find her looking down at the table. Her shoulders were slightly slumped. For a moment, he considered taking her with him, and then discarded the notion. He would be taking her into a very dangerous situation. He knew that she was in the middle of one already, but he did not know if he was willing to take responsibility for her life if something were to happen to her when he and the rest of the Wildrunners met up with Gaknar.

"Well, I am going to see about some of my preparations. I will see you later this afternoon," said Dinim, rising from the table.

"Yes, we will have dinner this evening and see you off in the morning," said Dartanyen.

Adrianna watched as Dinim left the establishment. She felt at a loss. She did not know what to do. She knew that she could not stay in one place for too long. Her father would find her. She knew also that she needed to find her sister. Perhaps Sheridana could help her. But if she was on her father's death list, then it was also possible that Sheri was on it as well. Sheri could also be in grave danger. However, Adrianna did not even know the first place to begin searching for her.

Adrianna stood from the table. Dartanyen looked up at her as she began to make towards the door. "We will be leaving soon to collect payment for our services in the temple."

Adrianna shook her head. "Please, go ahead without me. I will meet up with you all later." Adrianna turned and walked out of the establishment. It was still early in the morning and not many people were yet wandering the streets. She hoped that there were no spies about, for her sake as well as that of Dinim. She looked back and forth down the street. She spotted him in the distance to her left and hastened to catch up to him. "Dinim," she called out as she neared him.

Dinim turned around when he heard her call his name. He knew it was Adrianna by the sound of her voice. Her cheeks were slightly flushed from her mild exertion, and the color made her look lovelier than ever before. He felt himself smiling as she caught up to him. "Dinim, I was not aware that you had plans to leave."

"Yes. The Wildrunners are expecting me to join them as soon as possible. Volstagg and I sent the message just this morning."

Adrianna looked down at the ground, hoping to hide her expression of disappointment. "I see."

Dinim regarded her intently. His heart went out to her. Once more he had the urge to take her with him, but he knew that the Wildrunners, and Triath in particular, would be upset by that decision. It was too dangerous for her, but Dinim wondered if it was any more dangerous than what she faced already. "Listen, I will return to you as soon as I can. I promise."

Adrianna looked up at him once more. "You promise?"

"You have my word." Dinim noticed a smile tugging at the corner of her mouth and he immediately began to relax.

Adrianna's eyes sparkled with mirth. "You know what they say about Cimmereans, though."

Dinim grinned in return. "No, what would that be?"

"Only a fool would trust one."

"Well, what do *you* say?"

"That I must be a fool."

Dinim's smile widened. He could scarcely understand the emotions that swept through him at that moment, there were so many. He was happy that she would even think to trust him, especially after what had happened. And he was attracted to her. Her large eyes were slightly canted, and her lashes so long that when she looked up at him as she did now, they reached her brows. The color was that of the darkest mead, a warm rich brown. It was a striking feature with her pale golden complexion, and her hair was so light that it was like a golden halo.

"Come. I will accompany you while you collect your supplies for your journey." Adrianna took his arm and began to lead him down the street. Then suddenly she stopped. "That is, if you want some company."

"Always. I would be honored to have your company while I shop for my supplies."

"Oh, good. I had hoped so." Her face bore an expression of relief. Dinim got the impression that she must prefer his company to that of the others. This pleased him and his stride was light as they began to make their way down the street.

After a moment they heard a voice in the distance behind them. "Excuse me. Please, excuse me."

Dinim and Adrianna turned in the street and looked back in the direction of the inn. A man walked towards them. He was travel-stained and dusty. He was weary, and had obviously been on the road for quite some time.

When he caught up to them the man stopped. He was a faelin of medium build, with dark hair and dark eyes. His skin was also rather dark, colored a deep bronze. Adrianna deducted that he must be a Terralean, those faelin that live on the steppes and lightly forested borderlands in the more southerly parts of the continent. "Please, could you show me the way to the closest smithy?"

"Of course. You will go up this street. When you pass the apothecary, you will turn left down another street. The smithy is located at the end of that street," said Dinim, pointing the way out to the man.

"Thank you. I appreciate you stopping." Then the man paused and regarded Dinim intently. "Hey, do I know you?"

Dinim shook his head. "I do not think so."

The man nodded. "Yes, I am sure of it. We have met before. My name is Sabian Makonnen. I apprenticed under Master Tregorn."

Dinim's eyes widened. "Yes, I remember you now. Whatever happened to the old man? It just seemed that, suddenly, he was gone . . . disappeared. Master Tallachienan wondered where he had gone."

Sabian smiled. "Master Tregorn is doing well. Whenever he begins talking about Master TC, you can't get him to stop."

Dinim smiled in return. "So, what brings you to Sangrilak?"

Sabian's smile faded and his expression became serious. "No good reason actually, except for the fact that I am being followed. Someone means to do me harm, and I honestly don't know why. I was hoping on finding refuge here for a night or two before heading north. I heard that Grondor was a good place to get lost if you don't want to be found."

"I have heard the same thing. Perhaps you would like to travel together? I will be leaving tomorrow morning however. Is this too soon for you?"

"Not at all. The sooner the better, and I must say, a companion would be good to have on the journey. But are you sure that you want to hitch yourself with me? You may be putting yourself at risk."

"No, it will not be a problem. I, too, am being hunted. It may even be the same people who have been pursuing you. Perhaps I will be able to discover more about them if we travel together."

Sabian nodded and then glanced at Adrianna. Dinim noticed and put his palm to his head. "Oh, excuse me. I am sorry I did not introduce you. Sabian, this is Adrianna. Adrianna, this is Sabian. I met him in Andahye a few years ago while I was still an apprentice to Master TC. Master Albus Tregorn, Sabian's mentor, is a good friend of Master TC. They knew one another in their younger days, and even had a few adventures together."

"Yes, Master Tregorn told me about some of those. I must say, those were some reckless days." Sabian laughed and Dinim joined him. "Well, I had best get myself to the smithy. Where are you staying? Perhaps I can join you there later."

"Yes, I am staying at the Inn of the Hapless Cenloryan. When you are ready, go ahead and get a room there. I will return to the inn when I have finished some business of my own. I will see you for the mid-day meal?"

"Yes, I will see you then. It is so good that we have run into one another."

Dinim nodded and Sabian walked away in the direction that Dinim had indicated before. Dinim stared after him for a moment before turning back to Adrianna. "It is good to see an old face. Master TC will be happy to know that Master Tregorn is well. Come let us collect some supplies. Perhaps there is something you need as well?"

"Yes. I will be able to repay you as soon as I get my share of the monies Dartanyen and the others will be collecting from the city today."

"Aha. So you were able to escape that onerous task. You are a smart one."

"I like to think so."

***

It was late afternoon. Dartanyen, Armond, Bussi, Zorg, and Tianna sat in the common room of Volstagg's inn. He had closed the establishment to any other patrons, the damage to the place too extensive to have other persons occupying the premises. Amethyst had rejoined them at last. Her extensive wounds had healed nicely. The priests at the Temple of Hermod had taken care of her, bandaging her wounds night and day until they closed. A few days after having arrived there, while the rest of the group yet made their way through the maze within the belly of the world, Amethyst was finally able to move around. She wanted to leave, to return to her life on the streets, but the priests bade her stay. They told her that the group would be back for her when they returned from their task.

But Amethyst found that she was guilt ridden. She was supposed to be with them, aiding them with this task that they now faced without her. She knew that she had little to offer them, but the skills that she did have were valuable. Perhaps, just perhaps, she would have been able to make a difference. And it meant so much to her, that she make a difference to someone. She did not really yet know the group, but she felt an affinity towards them, and that had to mean something.

The days passed. Amethyst wondered how the group fared. She became restless within what she came to call her self-imposed prison, for she knew that she was free to leave, yet chose no to do so. When she finally received word from Volstagg that the group had returned, she was enervated. But when she realized that the message told her to stay at the temple, she became disheartened once more. The group had returned, but they were being pursued. Many of them had been injured and needed to recover. Volstagg said that he had hidden them and that he would let her know when she should return to the inn, that it was too dangerous for her to go there until he gave the word.

So Amethyst waited. For seven more days she waited, and when the next message from Volstagg arrived telling her that the group was out of hiding, she was ecstatic. She packed her few belongings into a pack that the priests gave to her. They had also given her nice clothes: tunic and trousers as well as a warm cloak. Amethyst thanked the priests, and they told her that she was always welcome if she ever needed aid.

Amethyst sat back in a chair at one of the tables that had not been destroyed. The woman Tianna had tried to fill her in on what had been going on since she had been gone, but there was so much to tell and so many interruptions by other members of the group, that Amethyst knew she did not get the whole story. But the group was more interested in *her* story, and Dartanyen asked her to tell them about what she remembered from the night that she was attacked.

Amethyst paused, aware of all of their eyes on her. She felt slightly intimidated, unaccustomed to having so much attention upon herself. She looked around at the group and Tianna caught her gaze. The woman nodded at her encouragingly and Amethyst found that she felt a little better. "Well, I guess I should start with what I noticed earlier that day."

Dartanyen nodded. "What happened? Tell us everything that you remember."

Amethyst continued. "I remember walking through the streets, minding my own business. Then I saw Dinim. He was talking with another man. They were in an alleyway, out of the way of the general populace walking through the streets. Most people would not have even noticed them, but it is my *job* to notice these things." Amethyst caught Dartanyen's gaze, hoping that he understood what she was saying. She had made it her vocation to know when people were trying to be inconspicuous. It usually meant that they were up to no good, and in her world, this could come to her benefit.

Dartanyen nodded his understanding, his expression remaining neutral. "I got closer, being sure that they did not see me. I got close enough that I could hear portions of their conversation. Dinim became angry. He and the man argued. Dinim said something about disposing of something when he got to the temple." Amethyst paused again, furrowing her brow. "I remember that someone bumped into me. The person got angry and yelled at me. Dinim and the other man turned, and before I could get out of his line of sight, Dinim had seen me.

"Suddenly I was afraid. The expression on his face was murderous. Dinim kept staring at me. The other man was trying to get his attention. He started to yell at Dinim and pushed him. Dinim turned back to the man and pushed him back. Suddenly they were brawling and everyone on the street was getting out of their way. They drew their swords and the rest you remember."

Dartanyen nodded. "We brought him back to the inn and Tianna used her skills as a healer to help him."

"Yes, I remember sensing something strange about him as I called upon the goddess to help me heal him. Something was not quite right about him," said Tianna.

"So what happened when you left the inn that night, while the rest of us were drinking?" asked Dartanyen.

"I remember walking through the streets as I usually do, keeping to the shadows, and watching for anything out of the ordinary. I walked for quite some time. Then I began to realize that I was being followed. I stopped and tried to determine who it was and where they were coming from. But he was good. He came at me, seemingly from out of nowhere. He threw me to the ground, and before I could utter a cry, a cloth was stuffed into my mouth. When I saw Dinim's face hovering above me, I was terrified. By his expression I knew that he wanted to kill me. And I knew it was because I had heard what he said . . ."

Amethyst stopped her recitation. She found that she was shaking and that she was no longer looking at the group, but at the minute cracks in the stone floor. Suddenly she felt a hand on her shoulder. Instinctively, Amethyst cringed away from the hand. She looked up to find Tianna standing beside her, a despondent expression on her face. She felt wretched for having reacted that way, showing everyone her weakness.

"Amethyst, you are safe now. None of us will let this happen again."

A part of her wanted to accept Tianna's kind intentions, to surrender to the comfort that she offered. But the other part of her knew that she should not, that any sign of weakness could be used against her later. So Amethyst stood up and walked over to the bar, where she poured herself a mug of mead. By the time she had seated herself once more, Tianna had returned to her seat, and Dartanyen was addressing the group once more.

"Listen, I know that everyone has begun to make plans for where they will be going when they leave here. I was tempted to make my own plans . . ." Dartanyen paused and looked at Tianna. Then he continued. "But I know that I can not."

Zorg grunted. "An' why not? You're just as free to do as you please as the rest of us."

Dartanyen shook his head. "I wish that were so. But that is just not the case . . . for any of us." Dartanyen looked around the room. Armond wore a ponderous expression on his face. Tianna looked confused. Bussi and Zorg were mutinous.

"Now see here, Dartanyen. What are ya tryin' ta say?" asked Bussi.

"I thought you were planning on coming with me to Elvandahar," said Tianna.

Dartanyen swung his gaze back to Armond. The other man regarded him intently. His expression was now one of enlightenment. Dartanyen knew that the tall faelin would be the first to figure things out. "I think that we need to all stay together for now. By association, we are currently in a dangerous situation."

"Dartanyen, what in the Hells are you talking about?" asked Tianna.

Dartanyen opened his mouth to reply, only to be cut off by Armond.

"Because we have been in Adrianna's company, Lord Thane will not think twice to hunt us all down and slaughter us," said Armond. "Our association with her has put every single one of us at great risk. You saw how Thane came for Volstagg. If he had been a weaker man, he would not have survived Thane's visit."

The room was silent. Even Tianna understood what Armond was saying. "So what are we going to do?" asked Amethyst hesitantly.

"That has yet to be decided," replied Dartanyen.

Just then the front door opened. Adrianna and Dinim walked into the inn. "Good afternoon everyone," said Dinim affably as he joined them. Tianna noticed the widening of Amethyst's eyes when she saw Dinim, as well as her hands clutching the edge of the tabletop. Despite the fact that Amethyst knew that the man who had beaten her had been a monster, and that the real Dinim did not even know her, the girl understandably remained afraid of him. Tianna's heart went out to her, but she made no move towards the girl. Amethyst needed was the type of person who needed to deal with her fears her own way, in her own time.

Adrianna followed slowly behind Dinim to the table where everyone was seated. She noticed the tension hanging around the room and wondered what it was from. Then she noticed that the girl Amethyst had rejoined them. She looked slightly pale, but well considering the beating she had suffered several days ago. Adrianna and Dinim seated themselves at an adjacent table and started to open the packages that they carried. Everyone heard him before they could see him, and their attention was already focused on the kitchen doors before Volstagg walked through them. "Hello. It is good to see that everyone is well. How about a meal? I have some leftovers heating over the fire."

"That would be wonderful, Volstagg," said Adrianna.

Volstagg made his way over to her table. "Great. It should be ready soon." Volstagg paused and then cleared his throat. He wondered how he should proceed, Dinim's warning echoing through his mind. Adrianna and Dinim were busy sorting through the things they had purchased that day. They discussed each item quietly among themselves and then placed a portion of each into his or her personal arsenal.

Adrianna noticed that Volstagg continued to loom over the table and she looked back up at him. "Adrianna, I think that perhaps you should return to Andahye," said Volstagg.

Adrianna frowned. "Why?"

"I know that you will be safer there than anywhere else. Thane may think to look for you there, but there are many there who would be able to offer you some measure of protection. Besides, you have a home there . . ."

Adrianna's frown deepened. "I may have a house there, but I do not have a home. Home is where one's family lives. I have no family in Andahye."

"But Adria, surely you must have friends. They will be able to offer you protection that no one else will be able to match."

"No. I have no one." Adrianna's tone was clipped. "There is no reason for me to go to Andahye. I will not go there." Adrianna's firm tone brooked no argument. Volstagg pressed his lips together into a thin line. "I have decided that I will search for my sister. I want . . . need to know how she fares."

"So, there is nothing that I can say that will change your mind?"

Adrianna regarded him intently. "No, nothing."

The tension in the room had intensified over the course of the discussion. The rest of the group sat quietly all around them. Dinim looked around the room and noticed that everyone seemed to be waiting for something.

"Fine. Be stubborn then." Volstagg grumbled to himself as he walked away. "Supper will be ready shortly," he added as he went back into the kitchens.

For a few moments the room continued to stay quiet. Then Dartanyen spoke. "So, you plan to look for your sister?"

Adrianna swung her gaze over to Dartanyen. "Yes. It has been a long time. Besides, she is the only family that I have left. We need each other." Then she looked away. Despite her words, Adrianna was unsure about finding her sister. It was Sheri who had left Adrianna behind all of those years ago, not even bothering to look back. Perhaps Sheridana felt differently, that she did not need Adrianna. Besides, she at least had Ian with her, and perhaps he was enough family for her.

Dartanyen nodded. "It is a harsh road to travel alone."

Adrianna sighed and loked back up at Dartanyen. "Yes, I suppose it is. But I don't really feel that I have a choice."

"Do you even know where to begin looking for her?"

"Not really. I thought that I would begin to think about it tomorrow. I will see you all off on your respectable paths and then sit down and decide what to do."

"But do you really think that you can do this all alone?"

"Dartanyen, I don't know," said Adrianna irritably. "Why are you asking me all this?"

"I was just thinking that you should hire someone to accompany you, that's all. You should hire someone who can protect you while you are on the road, someone you can trust."

"Oh, and I suppose you know someone? I hope that he comes cheap because its not like I am swimming in gold or anything." Adrianna's tone had become sarcastic and defensive. Dartanyen was making her feel like a fool for thinking that she could find her sister.

Dartanyen raised a placating hand. "Actually, I do know someone, and he will work for free, for a little while, anyway."

Adrianna raised an eyebrow. "Really. Who is this gentleman?"

Dartanyen stepped forward, walked to her table, placed his arm at his middle, and then bowed. "Dartanyen Hildranis at your service, my Lady. I will aid you as long as I may. My sword and bow will protect you as you set forth upon your endeavor."

Adrianna sat in her seat, stunned. She could not believe that Dartanyen was offering her his services. It was too good to be true. He was exactly what she needed in order to succeed. She would be unable to pay him right away, but one day she would give him the gold that he deserved. Adrianna rose from her seat. She placed her hand on his arm. "Dartanyen, you will never know what this means to me."

Dartanyen smiled. The expression on her lovely face told him more than any words she could have spoken. Suddenly, he felt a presence behind him. Dartanyen turned to find Armond and Zorg had stepped up behind him. They, too, bowed. "We also would like to extend our services to you."

Then the whole group was there, standing behind him. "Yes Adrianna. We will all come with you to help you find your sister," said Tianna. Despite the need she felt to go to Elvandahar, she knew that it would have to wait. Dartanyen and Armond were correct in their assessment of the situation. They would all need to stick together in order to survive.

Adrianna looked at all of the faces before her. Tears sprang to her eyes and she hurriedly wiped them away with the back of her hand. "Dear gods. You are all so good to me. I don't know what to say . . ."

"Just say that you will have us with you," said Armond.

"Yes, yes. I would be honored to have you all at my side . . ." Then she was rushing towards them, her arms outstretched. Dartanyen reached out to her and he hugged her to him. She cried onto his chest for a moment before moving on to Armond, Zorg, Bussi, Tianna, and Amethyst. Then she realized that Volstagg was there, and she hugged him too. Finally she stepped back from them all.

"I am glad that you all have decided to stay together. I was so worried about you, Adria. But now, I have no need to worry so much," said Volstagg, smiling. "Here, I have brought food for you all to eat. I will bring out some ale and mead."

Adrianna felt a hand on her shoulder. She turned to find Dinim standing behind her. She smiled happily up at him. She still couldn't believe her good fortune.

"Come, let us sort out the rest of these things. Then we can focus on food and drink," he said.

Adrianna nodded and sat back down at the table. The rest of the group helped themselves to the food. Everyone seemed to be in high spirits. It only took a short while for them to complete their task, and then Dinim and Adrianna were joining their comrades. The stew was delicious and the mead flowed easily. Adrianna rose to get herself another serving and then noticed someone entering the establishment. It was the faelin man that she and Dinim had met in the street that morning. Adrianna got Dinim's attention and gestured toward the entrance. Dinim looked in the direction that she indicated and then stood from his seat. He went over to Sabian and led him back to the tables.

"Everyone. I have someone I would like to introduce to you." The rest of the group looked up towards Dinim and the new arrival. "This is Sabian Makonnen. He is someone that I met a few years ago. I invited him to join us all here this evening. He will be leaving with me in the morning."

There were nods all around, and an invitation to join them at their meal. Sabian graciously accepted and helped himself to a bowl of stew and a mug of ale. The banter went on well into the evening, but after a couple of hours Dinim declared that he would have to turn in for the night. "I have a very long road ahead of me," he said as he rose from the table. Sabian rose as well, thanking them for the meal and the camaraderie.

Adrianna watched as the two men left the common room to return to their chambers for the night. Dinim was right. He had a long road ahead of him, and she did as well. Adrianna rose from her seat and bid everyone goodnight. She slowly made her way to her bedchamber. Tomorrow morning she would have to see Dinim off. That would be difficult for her. She had so much hoped that he would remain with the group. But at least she had the others. They had all pledged themselves to her and her cause. Just as easily, they all could have chosen to all go their separate ways. She knew that they were placing themselves in grave danger by staying with her. But she also knew that they still would have been in danger had they not chosen this path. No matter what, they would have had trouble following behind them, and it was probably for the best that they all stayed together to help Adrianna find her sister and to fight the menace as a unit. At least she hoped so. All she could do was have faith in herself . . . and in the people who followed her.

CHAPTER 8

It was early. Dawn had not yet begun to paint the horizon. Adrianna, Dartanyen, Armond, Zorg, Bussi, and Tianna sat around a table, the largest one left in the inn. Tianna had tried to rouse Amethyst, but to no avail. The young girl simply refused to awaken, and Tianna's efforts had been rewarded only by muffled curses and threats to her well-being. It wasn't long before Dinim and his companion walked into the common room. Both men were garbed for travel. Each wore loosely fitting trousers and cotton tunics. Their packs were loaded with all of their belongings as well as several days' worth of food pouches.

The group rose from their seats as the two men stopped by the table. Dartanyen put out a hand. "Thank you for all that you have done. I don't think we could have escaped the temple without you. I hope you have a safe journey."

Dinim grasped Dartanyen's arm and nodded. "The best of luck to you all. I hope that you can all help Adrianna find what she is looking for." Dinim glanced at Adrianna as he said the last. "However, I have spoken to my companion and he has agreed to accompany you all."

Sabian stepped up next to Dinim. "I hope that you will accept me into your ranks. I have much that I can offer the group. My Talent is strong and I have had many years to hone my skills. I know the areas in and around the Central Kingdoms and the Free Cities rather well. Dinim feels that I could be an excellent addition to your group."

"My friend, this is not necessary. I assure you and Dinim, that Adrianna will be safe with us," said Dartanyen. Then his gaze swung to Dinim. "You have nothing to worry about."

"Please, for my own peace of mind, take Sabian with you. It can't hurt to have another person around, willing to lend a helping hand."

Dartanyen stared fixedly at Dinim for a moment. Adrianna looked from one man to the next. Finally Dartanyen took in a deep breath. "Fine. I suppose he could accompany us."

Dinim smiled. "Good. It is settled then." Dinim clapped Sabian on the shoulder and Sabian returned the gesture. "Thank you, Sabian. This means a lot to me."

Sabian nodded. "Take care on your journey."

"I will." Dinim turned to Adrianna. "Walk with me to the wall."

Adrianna nodded. The group followed the two out of the establishment. Dinim waved at them as he and Adrianna made their way down the street. Adrianna was quiet as they walked, her eyes downcast. After a few moments Dinim spoke. "Adrianna, be sure that you do not stay here too much longer. I am sure that Thane has caught wind of your whereabouts."

Adrianna nodded and looked up at him. He was regarding her intently, his lavender eyes scrutinizing her. Suddenly he stopped. He turned to her and took her shoulders in his hands. "Adrianna, I *will* return to you."

Adrianna smiled then, a small smile. "I know."

Dinim smiled back and then brought her to him. It felt good to hold her, and even better when she wrapped her arms around his neck to bring him closer. "I will miss you," she whispered.

"And I, you," he replied.

They stepped apart and regarded one another for a moment. Dinim raised his hand in farewell and Adrianna returned the gesture. She watched him as he walked away, out of the city, towards the people who awaited him. Sirion. He would be going to Sirion. There was a part of her that wished that she were going too. But she knew that she had her own responsibilities, and they did not include the Wildrunners and their problems.

Adrianna turned and made her way back to the inn. Yes, she knew that her time in Sangrilak was running out. She had all of today to find out all what she could about her sister and her possible whereabouts. After that, she would have to go from city to city and town to town, everywhere and anywhere that she could think of where anyone would know anything about Sheridana.

***

The caravan pulled out of the city of Tragesser. Their wagon was one of several that comprised the large caravan of merchants and wanderers. It was a dangerous land through which they traveled, and there was safety in numbers. One wagon carried a few bards, each playing his instrument of choice. Actually, the one with the harp annoyed Sheridana to no end. It seemed that he did not like to take 'no' for an answer, and was constantly finding new reasons to be near her. He had asked her for her company several times, and her answer was always the same. Unfortunately, his wagon happened to be the one directly in front of hers, placing her within his vicinity far longer than she deemed bearable.

Sheridana mounted her larian and rode up to the front of the caravan, escaping before the bard with the harp could even think about speaking with her. He would have found something, she knew, to discuss with her. And it was always something quirky, trivial or mundane that he sought her out to discuss. What was his name again? She could scarcely remember, although she thought that it must be Kling . . . or perhaps Klon . . . whatever. Sheri waved as she passed the other caravan drivers. Most of them were friendly and unobtrusive.

Sheridana spotted another rider up ahead. Besides the drivers, she was not the only one up and about at this early hour of the morning. But of course Fitanni was awake. The baby always awakened early, appearing to enjoy the discomfort she caused her mother and nanny. Sheri smiled at the thought of her daughter, the baby cooing with delight when Sheri picked her up from the furs in the morning to give her milk. The baby would watch Sheri as she nursed, her eyes exploring every contour of Sheri's face. The baby would tap Sheri with her tiny hands, and try to grab the errant strands of dark hair that came loose from her long braid. The baby gave Sheridana more happiness than she would have ever thought possible, especially before her birth. But Fitanni had brought a joy to her life that never existed before.

But something was missing. Sheridana regretted many things in her life, and the one thing that she regretted the most was leaving her sister behind. While she, Ian and her father sought fortune on the open road, Adrianna was left alone in Sangrilak. Sure, Adria had Mairi, and even her friend Volstagg there, but it was not the same. Sheridana would never forget the expression on Adrianna's face when Sheri and the others rode away that fateful day.

Sheridana shook herself, freeing herself from the memories. Several years had passed since she had seen her sister last. She wondered how Adria fared, if she had changed, if she had ever left Sangrilak. Sheri had written to Adrianna several times when she first left, determined to still keep in contact with her sister. But Adria had never replied to the letters. Finally, Sheri stopped sending them. For a time, she allowed herself to be angry, telling herself that Adria was being selfish and mean-spirited. But after a while, she could hold up the façade no longer, knowing that it was she who was the selfish one. Sheri had been the one to leave, not Adria. Her sister had every right to be upset.

Sheridana turned her larian and rode back in the direction of her wagon. Carli and Fitanni would be waiting for her. Carli enjoyed preparing their meals and probably had breakfast awaiting her. Once more Sheri counted her blessings. Carli was a wonderful companion, and an excellent caregiver for Fitanni. Sheri did not allow motherhood to interfere with her duties, and Carli would care for the child while Sheri was unable to do so.

Carli had left her family behind to travel with Sheridana. After having the baby, Sheri had been ill for quite some time. She had lost a lot of blood during the birth, and her depression over Ian's loss had impeded her ability to become well. Carli's family had taken Sheri into their home, had helped care for her and her baby until she was well again. Carli had been given most of the responsibility of caring for the baby, and Fitanni had grown rather attached to the young woman.

When Carli announced to her parents that she wished to journey with Sheridana to her home, they were upset. They did not want to lose their daughter. But Carli insisted that she would leave anyway, that she was old enough to make her own decisions about her life. She had hoped to have their blessing, but its absence would not change her decision to leave. Finally, they realized that their daughter was right. At twenty and two years of age, she was indeed old enough to make her own life's decisions. So they blessed her, and two mornings later, she left with Sheri and Fitanni.

Several weeks later, here they were, slowly but surely making their way towards Sangrilak. Riding with the caravans made it an even slower process, but she would not place Carli and Fitanni at risk by travelling alone. There was safety in numbers, and although there was still a chance that they could be robbed, the risk was smaller with herself and the other caravan guards-men taking care of everyone. Eventually she would make it home, and finally she would see her sister once more. She couldn't wait for Adrianna to see her baby, and they would finally be a family again, after so many years of being apart.

***

Adrianna slowly walked up the steps to the veranda of the Inn of the Hapless Cenloryan. She had been all over the city, asking if anyone had any idea of the whereabouts of one Sheridana Darnesse. Most of the people she spoke to were merchants, as they were often privy to information that came in from the outside. They were the ones most likely to hear about anything happening in another city or town, even one in another Kingdom. She also spoke to some caravan drivers and a couple of wandering bards. But none of them had any information about her sister or the group with which she had been travelling.

The front door to the building opened and Dartanyen and Armond came out onto the veranda. By the expressions on their faces Adrianna knew that they had not met success. Adrianna slumped into one of the rocking chairs, dismally contemplating the route she would take on the morrow. She knew that they had to leave the city. Her father would be coming for her. She knew that she could not run from him forever, but she preferred to have her sister at her side when they did finally meet. It would be best if they left in a few hours, in the darkness of the night. She knew that the others would not complain much, they wanting to get out of the city as much as she. Besides, most of the group had been resting throughout the day anyway, with the exception of Dartanyen and Armond. Three bodies searching the city would be much better than just one, and they had definitely covered more places that way.

Adrianna looked out toward the street in the direction of the wall. Only this morning Dinim had left, yet she missed him abominably. He was traveling north, and within a couple of days he would reach the town of Ferent. He would then cross the Tangir River, a tributary of the Terrestra River, and travel to the city of Driscol, the last city he would see before he had to cross the Ratik Mountains. He would take the Ratik Pass through the mountains and go to the city of Celuna. There, he would prepare for his several days' journey to Grondor. Adrianna wondered if she should go in the same direction in her search for Sheri. Or perhaps she should travel more towards the west. Within a day they would be able to make it to the Terrestra River. They would take a ferry to cross it and then be on the outskirts of Elvandahar. They would probably skirt the forest, she not being familiar with the inhabitants there, although she did seem to remember Tianna saying that she lived within Elvandahar as a child. Once passing through Elvandahar, they would cross the Denegal River and then enter the realm of Karlisle. Adrianna would not be surprised if they had gone there, it being a place rich with opportunities.

As Adrianna ruminated upon her choices, she noticed a small group of individuals walking up the street from the direction of the city wall. However, she did not pay them much heed until she realized that they were making their way towards the inn. Dartanyen and Armond focused their attention on the group as they approached the establishment. There were three men and two women. They were obviously very weary, their packs seeming to weigh heavily upon them. They began to make their way up the steps when Armond called out, "The inn is closed. You will need to find other accommodations for the night."

The travelers eyed them skeptically. "I see. I suppose you are just hanging around here for the view then," one of the men replied sarcastically.

Dartanyen shook his head. "We are friends of the proprietor. He has allowed us to stay, but we will be leaving on the morrow anyway. Many repairs have to be made to this place before it will be ready to accommodate travelers again."

The man nodded and his shoulders slumped. "I hope you can direct us to the closest inn."

Dartanyen pointed down the street. "Macey's Tavern and Inn is just down the road. You can't miss it."

The man raised a hand in farewell and the group turned to leave. Adrianna felt sorry for them, hated for them to have to walk even further just so they could take a rest. She noticed that their clothes were not only dusty from the road, but bloodstained as well, as though they had seen some trouble. One of the women seemed weaker than the rest, and she leaned against one of her companions. "Wait," Adrianna called out. "Do you happen to know anyone by the name of Sheridana Darnesse?"

The man stopped and turned toward her. His expression was ponderous as he regarded her for a moment. "Darnesse. That name sounds familiar to me."

Excitedly, Adrianna stood from her chair and approached the man. "Please, try to remember. How long ago have you heard that name?"

"Several months ago." The man paused. "Wait. I remember now. It was a man. He bore that name. He traveled with a group called Thritean's Pride. The last time I saw them was out near Kranton, a city in the northern province of Durnst."

"Do you remember what the man looked like?"

"Can't say as I do, but I think I heard his lady companion call him Ian. It is an uncommon enough name that I remembered it."

"Do you remember what *she* looked like?"

"As a matter of fact, I do. Her hair was dark, almost black, and her eyes were blue. Her features were out of the ordinary, but she was a beautiful woman. She looked like her blood-lines were crossed . . . you know, a half-faelin." The man looked closely at her then. "Perhaps like you, lady."

Adrianna smiled. The man had described her sister. Inside, she was brimming with joy. It was her first lead, the first step towards Sheri.

"Well, we had best be off. We have some beds somewhere that are calling our names." The man turned away once more. He stepped down from the veranda, and the group began to make their way down the street.

"Wait." Adrianna heard herself calling out to them once more. She wanted to do something for them, a favor in return for the one they had done her. Adrianna hurried down the steps and approached the group. The man turned to her once more. "I am sure that Volstagg could keep you for the night. He owes me a favor. Please, come inside and share a meal with us."

The man regarded her speculatively for a moment before turning to the rest of his group. The others nodded. He turned back to her and held out his hand. "My name is Vornec. Thank you for the offer. This means a lot to us. As you can probably tell, we have had a rough journey."

Adrianna grasped his arm in welcome. "I am Adrianna. Please come inside and make yourselves comfortable . . ."

***

The threesome walked down the main street of Sangrilak, enjoying the early evening. They spoke of the route that they would be traveling, how long it would take, and what supplies that they would need. No attention was paid to the hour, and they did not realize that it was getting late. The activity of the day had died down, and the shadows that usually existed only in the alleyways began to encroach upon the street.

This was Dartanyen's first chance to talk with Adrianna. He felt that it would be a good idea to get to know her a little better before their journey. Through the course of the conversation that he shared with her as they walked, he found her to be as much of a mystery as ever. Honestly, he could not entirely figure her out. She was an intelligent person, and her understanding of the things he spoke to her about was complete. She was knowledgeable and charismatic as well. However, he noticed that she seemed to lack in confidence, and she seemed to have a desire to melt into the background. In a way, this was just right with Dartanyen, who was accustomed to being in a leadership position. He knew that, technically, Adrianna was the leader of the group, and that he was merely a hired hand. However, he got the impression that she was going to leave much of the decision-making up to him. He was strong-minded and opinionated, and it was just as well. Although, he did note that Adrianna was a woman who knew what she wanted. She did not hesitate when she told him the route she wished to take in search of her sister. It seemed, however, that she was going to leave the rest up to him.

Dartanyen, Adrianna and Tianna walked for some time, discussing their options, making plans and even making a few jokes. Before he knew it, Dartanyen realized that they had come to a rather run-down section of the city. Many of the buildings were in disrepair. There was a filthy smell to the place, and the streets were testament as to why. It was then that Dartanyen took in the state of his person. He had very little upon him, no leathers and very few weapons. All he wore was his dagger, and he was sure that it was the same for Tianna and Adrianna. His gaze darted about as he began to get nervous. He placed a hand on Adrianna's shoulder, about to tell her that they should head back to the inn, when they heard a scuffling sound accompanied by another strange noise in an alleyway up ahead.

Instantly the group slowed to a halt. The noise continued for a moment and then stopped. It had been an odd gargling sound, like someone was struggling to breathe through water. They heard the scuffling sounds again, as well as a groaning sound. The group instinctively pressed together. The sun was beginning to set over the horizon and the fading light was casting wickedly eerie shadows from the side streets and alleyways. Dartanyen remembered the fate they had recently endured. He felt his heart pick up in tempo and he realized he was afraid, an emotion that he did not feel very often. It was too soon. He was just finished healing from the wounds he had suffered in the temple.

The group quickly took stock of their surroundings. They were in the middle of the street, which was deserted. There was a side street they had just passed. Dartanyen figured that they could reach it in a few strides if they ran. But he was not sure that was the best course of action, and was unwilling to make the mistake of their footfalls being heard by whoever was up ahead.

At that moment laughter could be heard as well as the voices of multiple individuals. They were close . . . coming from the alley closest to them.

"Just stay quiet. Parley is our only option. Let me do the talking," whispered Dartanyen. The women nodded mutely. Dartanyen pressed them back slowly, hoping on making it to the side street they had passed before the men made it around the corner. Instinctively, Dartanyen knew the men were trouble, their mocking laughter and the way they spoke to one another telling him that they had just overcome some poor, unfortunate individual. Dartanyen, Adrianna, and Tianna were lucky. They made it to the side street and slipped into it just as three men emerged into the main road.

Adrianna was nervous. She could sense that Dartanyen was apprehensive and this bothered her greatly. She had never seen him this way before. He slowly pressed her and Tianna back until they reached a side street that they had passed just moments before. They slipped behind a building just as the men they had heard from up ahead came around a corner. From her vantage point, Adrianna could see the men in the dimming light. One of the men caused a shiver to rise up her spine. She remembered him! It was the faelin man who had given her a message to send to Sirion . . . the man who wanted him dead.

Adrianna began to tremble. The men were all very muscular, wearing leather vests with fur at the collar. The one who had given her the message for Sirion was obviously the leader. He radiated an aura of power that made her heart palpitate. She remembered his name . . . Sydonnia. Sirion had warned her about him, had told her that he was dangerous. She wanted to warn her comrades, tell them that they needed to leave . . . now. "It's him. By the gods we have to leave. Please . . ."

Dartanyen heard Adrianna's whispers and frowned. They could not afford to be discovered. He motioned to Tianna to hush the other woman, keeping his eyes fixed upon the men in the close distance. One of them carried a mean cross-bow, one he had never seen the likes of ever before. It appeared that it could discharge six bolts at a time. Another man carried a broadsword strapped over his right shoulder. He appeared to be the leader.

Tianna turned to her friend. "Adrianna, you have got to be quiet." Then she paused, noticing the fearful expression on Adrianna's face. "What's wrong?"

"That man, Sydonnia. He wants to kill Sirion."

Tianna's eyes widened with incredulity. "What . . . what are you talking about? Why?"

"I don't know. He gave me this message and . . ."

"What message? Why didn't *I* know about this?"

Dartanyen tried to still Tianna with a hand on her arm. Her whispers had attracted the men in the street and they were heading in their direction. Damnation! Women were such garrulous creatures.

Adrianna lunged for Tianna, tried to grab her as she broke away from the wall. Tianna defiantly strode towards the men, whom she found to be walking in their direction. Dartanyen whispered a curse and pulled himself and Adrianna further back into the lane. They could hear the guffaws of the men as Tianna neared them.

"Hey Sy, it looks like we have a wench to take advantage of." The man chuckled and nudged his companion with the crossbow.

Tianna stopped in front of the leader. She knew this man to be Sydonnia, for she had met him once before. She had always felt him to be the shady type, and couldn't believe he was a blood relative to Sirion, his uncle as a matter of fact. Sirion had always told her to steer clear of the man, but she refused to lie low this time. He had threatened Sirion, and he would pay.

"I have your wench right here, you bastard." Tianna slammed her fist into Sydonnia's smirking face. For a moment, the street was silent. The men all looked at one another and then began to laugh. Tianna regarded them indignantly. "You think this is funny? Well maybe I should give you another . . ."

Tianna's words were cut short as Sydonnia caught her flying fist. With his other hand he grabbed Tianna's face beneath her jaw and brought it close to him. "Now listen here, bitch. I don't take kindly to wenches offering me this kind of treatment . . . unless it is in the bed, of course." The other men laughed raucously at the remark and Tianna stiffened. Fear began to course through her, for she felt the power within the man's grip, saw the evil in his eyes as he gazed on her.

Dartanyen and Adrianna heard the exchange from within their hiding place. Adrianna heard Dartanyen sigh heavily. He then took her arm and pulled her out into the street with him.

"Now, you had best answer me quickly . . . *why* are you here and *what* is the meaning of this?" Sydonnia's grip on Tianna's jaw tightened as he asked the questions. The pain was enough to make her want to cry out . . . except she was too afraid to even make a mew. However, he expected an answer from her, and she feared his wrath if she did not cooperate.

"I . . . I heard that you are looking for a friend of mine." Tianna could barely get the words out through her fear, and the pain of Sydonnia's grip intensified as she spoke.

Sydonnia's eyes narrowed into slits. "Well now, I am looking for a lot of people. Who might this person be?"

Suddenly there was another voice. "Hey now. How about letting her go. She has had too much to drink and she doesn't know what she is talking about," said Dartanyen.

Sydonnia looked up from Tianna's face for a moment to look at Dartanyen. He glanced at Adrianna, merely taking note of her presence, and then returned his gaze to Tianna. "You know if there is one thing in this world that I hate the most, it is a terrible liar. I don't mind a good liar, or even a halfway decent one. And one can always tell who are his enemies by the way they lie. My dear, your friend is definitely a bad liar, is he not? I don't smell the least bit of alcohol on your breath, and let me tell you, I would definitely be able to smell it if you had had anything to drink today." Sydonnia grinned at her evilly, the smile not quite making it to his eyes.

Just then, from out of the alley in which the three men had come, stumbled a man. He was covered in blood. His clothes appeared as though a gigantic claw had shred them and he sported several deep lacerations to his face, arms and chest. He held one arm across his abdomen while with the other he sought to hold himself up against the nearest building. Momentarily, the man caught Sydonnia's attention. Sydonnia turned to his companion with the crossbow and nodded to him. The man cocked the weapon, aimed and fired. Three bolts struck the injured man in the chest. The unfortunate man slid down the side of the wall that had been holding him up until he lay in a crumpled heap on the ground.

Sydonnia returned his attention to Tianna, releasing her jaw. "So my dear, what were you saying? Oh yes, you were about to tell me about this person that I am looking for."

The moment Sydonnia released her, Tianna took a step back from him. Dartanyen couldn't believe what he had just witnessed, the murder of a man in cold blood, out in the open. The man was arrogant, and it was obvious that he felt he could do whatever he wished to whomever he wanted to do it to.

Tianna was silent, not knowing how to answer. She didn't want to say Sirion's name, afraid of what Sydonnia's response would be if she did. Dartanyen and Adrianna stood a few feet behind her, but this fact offered her little comfort. She now knew that this man could do whatever he wanted with them in the blink of an eye. Sydonnia watched her like a predator inspects its prey. She knew that he knew that she was afraid. She could see it in his eyes. And something else lurked there in his eyes, waiting.

The corner of Sydonnia's mouth curved up in mild amusement. "Tsk, tsk. So closed-mouthed we have become. Well, at least tell me where he is from." Sydonnia put his hands on his hips, waiting for her to respond.

Tianna swallowed, her mouth and throat dry. "El . . . Elvandahar. He is from Elvandahar."

Sydonnia's gaze suddenly became intense. He glanced at Adrianna once more and then a wave of realization passed over his face. Pure, undisguised malice shone in his eyes as he spoke. "Ah, my wayward nephew. I have been wondering . . . how does he fare? You are right, my dear, I *have* been looking for Sirion. Now I know why you look so familiar to me. We met once, a few years ago while I was passing through. You are the girl that liked to tag along on Sirion's heels like a corubis cub."

Adrianna heard the mocking tone in Sydonnia's voice as he spoke. It was almost as though he was goading Tianna . . . urging her to react. And react she did, her hands clenching into fists at her sides. "You bastard," she hissed. "I knew that you were a pile of pig droppings when I first laid eyes on you. You are nothing but a wretched snake who gets his kicks by intimidating people."

Within but a moment Dartanyen was at Tianna's side, taking her upper arm in his grip. He jerked her backward into his body and held her there. Adrianna saw her expression of surprise intermingled with pain. "Shut up, Tianna. What is your problem?"

Sydonnia's eyes were slitted once more, and his voice was low as he spoke. "Yes, you are indeed a rude little wench. You would do well to watch your tongue, my dear, lest you find it down your throat."

Adrianna stepped forward to stand next to Dartanyen. As she regarded Sydonnia, she felt a chill crawl up her spine. There was something there, in the man's eyes, crouching . . . waiting. It made her want to run, to flee for her life. And then Sydonnia was speaking again, saying something that she could not quite understand. His voice sounded garbled and she felt herself beginning to panic. Then she felt Dartanyen's hand on her arm, and he was pulling her back, back, back with him.

Dartanyen found himself moving backward and excusing himself to Sydonnia, mentioning that they needed to return to the inn. He then pulled Tianna and Adrianna with him, hurrying them down the street. As the threesome made good their escape, they heard laughter behind them, tauntingly wicked. Dartanyen felt the evil that they left behind. He found himself whispering and then realized that he was talking to himself . . . speaking words of thankfulness. And then he realized exactly how afraid he had been. He had been more than just simply intimidated; he had been reduced to nothing more than a mere whelp. There was something about that man, something predatory. Dartanyen knew that Sydonnia would have derived much pleasure from killing them all, and he wondered why the man hadn't.

***

The sun was beginning to set. It was his favorite time of the day, a time in which his powers, many of which were dormant during the daylight hours, began to strengthen. There was just something about the lowering of the sun, and the feel of power rushing through his veins. It was excruciating and invigorating at the same time, making him feel like an addict taking his first hit after several hours of having had none.

He stood upon the open plain, the sky wide and open before him. The setting sun bathed the sky in hues of blue and lavender. Soon, the first moon, Steralion, would become visible, soon followed by her sisters, Hestim and Meriliam. It was at this time, when all three of the moons were bright in the night sky, that his powers were greatest. And when he was strong, his followers were strong. Thane looked back towards his band. Within the small copse of trees they waited. He frowned. He hated waiting.

But the waiting was nearly over. In the distance he could see a small speck. As it got closer, the speck turned into a blob, and then finally into the form of a larian and rider. As the twosome thundered into camp, Thane frowned once more. The man had been riding hard. His animal was lathered in a sheet of sweat, its breathing labored. The rider himself was in a state of weariness, obviously having ridden without stopping. He slid from the back of the larian, and immediately went to Thane, bending in obeisance.

Thane tapped the man on the shoulder and he straightened. "So, what news do you bring me? I assume it is of some importance." Thane paused and regarded the poor larian, whose head was hanging close to the ground. "Especially since you have nearly killed your larian to bring it to me."

The man looked at Thane. "My Lord, we have located the group for which you have been searching. They are in Sangrilak; have been there the entire time. I came as quickly as I could . . ."

Thane's wrapped his hand around the man's throat. The man gasped and brought his hands up to his neck, clawing at Thane's hand as it began to tighten. "You fool!" Thane said. "Why did you not contact me through Grimwell? I would have known immediately that they were there, and I would have been in Sangrilak by now!"

The man continued to gasp, and opened his mouth as though he wanted to say something. Thane suddenly released his grip on the man, who fell back, holding his neck with his hands. "My Lord, I tried to find him, but was unable to do so. I don't know where he is."

Thane clenched his hands into fists. Why . . . why was he surrounded by idiots? Poor fools who had not a brain among them all? He was angry . . . extremely angry. They had gotten away once, in the temple, when his master's priests were supposed to have been able to keep them there until he arrived. When he reached the temple, he had found the worship hall in a shambles. The doppelganger, Ixitchitl, was dead, as were several of the master's priests. The wizard, Dinim, had escaped, as had his daughter and the group of individuals with which she had allied herself.

And then he had gone into a fit of rage. He had murdered several more of the priests before he finally controlled himself. He did not care about the loss of Dinim, had not really cared to capture him in the first place. He had only done it because the master wished it, saying something about having something that his nemesis, Gaknar, wanted. But really, who gave a damn about Gaknar anyway? That man was down a bad path; consorting with daemons was a risky business at best.

But the loss of his daughter was something that he did care about. He wanted her dead, wanted her to be gone from this world, gone the way Gemma was gone. He hated her with a passion that he did not understand, did not care to understand. And then there was her twin, the daughter that had betrayed him . . . sleeping with his brother and then conceiving his child. The whore. He thought about killing her, but then he realized that the revenge would be sweeter if she had to see her child die. He would kill the bastard with his own two hands.

Thane grabbed the man again, hoisting him to his feet. Somewhere in his mind he knew that the man was not at fault, but he did not care. He needed an outlet, and the man was there, so pathetic, so vulnerable. Thane took the man's head between his hands and twisted it savagely. He felt the pop of the skull separating from the spinal column, felt the body go limp before him. The dead man fell to the ground. Thane spun away and strode towards the trees. He felt only marginally better, but better nonetheless. He walked amongst the foliage and saw his band waiting for him, standing with the lloryk. He grabbed his lloryk's reins from one of his knights, swinging himself up into the saddle effortlessly. "We ride to Sangrilak." He raised a fist into the air and ground his heels into the lloryk's sides. The animal trumpeted and then sprung forward. The others followed behind.

***

Shrouded by the darkness of the night, the group traveled northeast, leaving the city of Sangrilak behind them. It was with a light heart that Adrianna left, knowing that when she returned, her sister would be with her. A lloryk pulled the small wagon that they had decided to purchase with the money they had received from the city. Everyone was able to load many of their possessions within it and it made the burdens for the animals they rode much lighter. The only ones who did not ride astride were Amethyst, who did not know how, and Bussimot, who refused. "It jus' isn't meant to be . . . halfen riding on these animals. We needs to be having our feet on the ground. Can't know what the land is tellin' ye if you aren't walkin' on it."

The group traveled with ease into the morning. The land was flat and easy to traverse, the long prairie grasses sweeping beneath the larian's bellies as they walked alongside the road. For most of the night they traveled in silence, Dartanyen's mood serious and contemplating. Tianna was sullen and withdrawn, her thoughts, too, focused inwards. After only a few hours of riding

Adrianna found that she was tired, as she had been busy most of the day trying to find a lead about where her sister may be located. She noticed that Armond seemed to be similarly afflicted, his shoulders slumped and his chin to his chest. Adrianna wished that she could rest as well, but found herself unable to do so. She thought about going into the wagon for a rest, but then decided against it. She would wait to sleep until they stopped for the night.

As they rode, the group formed a procession. Bussi had grudgingly accepted the task of driving the wagon, despite his intentions of 'keeping his feet on the ground'. Dartanyen rode up ahead of the wagon, scouting the terrain before they rolled over it. Tianna rode alongside the wagon. Since the encounter with Sydonnia, Tianna had been quiet and withdrawn. Adrianna couldn't blame her. It had been an eye-popping experience for all, and one not easily forgotten. When they had returned to the inn, Tianna had asked Adrianna about the message that Sydonnia had given to her several weeks ago. Adrianna told her what it said, and that she had sent it to Sirion. Tianna asked why Adrianna had not told her about the message sooner. The only reason that Adria could give was simply that, at the time, she had not known Tianna very well, and that she did not know in whom to confide. With a wounded expression on her face, Tianna had merely nodded and left to go pack her bags for the journey. Adrianna felt sorry that she had hurt the other woman's feelings, for they had become rather close in the last several weeks. She hoped that Tianna would come to realize that Adrianna had not meant any harm.

Zorg and Armond rode together, their mounts stark contrast to one another. Where the lloryk were large, strong, and pale in coloration, their larian cousins were smaller, faster, and more colorful. Most lloryk were some shade of medium grey, with darker or lighter dapples at the hindquarters. Some few were white or maybe even blue in color. The larian varied in color from pale blond to deep bronze. They tended to be more docile and were the preferred species for riding purposes. Luckily, they had found a docile lloryk female to pull the wagon. She was a strong animal, and preferable to have over an umberhulk, which was a cumbersome creature, oftentimes slow, and not very intelligent.

Next in the procession came Adrianna, and Sabian brought up the rear. Amethyst rode in the wagon, her feet dangling from the back. Oftentimes, Adrianna would glance over to see an expression upon her face that asked, "What in the Hells am I doing here, with these strange people?" The girl's shoulders were often slumped forward, boredom overcoming her usually sharp senses. She would mutter curses to herself, seeming to rue the day that she met this band of odd folk.

They traveled well into the day, taking their meals as they rode. After mid-day, Dartanyen announced that they would soon be finding a place where they would rest for the night. "I know that it is a little early to be stopping for the day, but considering that we have been riding all night, I feel that we need the extra rest." Everyone nodded in agreement, ready to stop for the day. Finally they found a place hidden within a small stand of trees several feet away from the road. Everyone laid out their sleeping rolls for the night. No fire was lit; they did not want to bring any unwanted attention to themselves. They ate pack rations: some bread, dried meat, cheese, and figs that Volstagg packed for them before they left. For a time there was silence, everyone too busy eating to say much. And then, after the meal was packed away, they were too tired. The watch was set. First Zorg would sit, then Sabian, Tianna, and finally Amethyst. Adrianna, Armond, and Dartanyen were left out because they had not had a chance to rest the day before. Adrianna was grateful for the reprieve and fell asleep the moment her head hit the blankets.

The next morning Adrianna awoke to the sound of shouting. Groggily she opened her eyes and saw that the sun had barely begun to rise over the distant horizon. She sat up and looked around the camp. Her focus was soon riveted upon the scene at the far side of the space the group had occupied throughout the night. Amethyst stood there, her hands on her hips, a disgruntled expression on her face. Dartanyen was shouting at her angrily. "What if someone . . . or some*thing* had happened upon us while you were dozing? We could be murdered in our sleep. You know that it is very possible that we are being followed; yet you allowed yourself to become derelict in your duty. Everyone's lives are in you hands while you are on watch!"

Amethyst rolled her eyes skyward. "Dartanyen, I already told you that I was sorry. I didn't mean to fall asleep."

"Well 'sorry' is not good enough. Not when it is as important as something like this. Our lives are at stake out here, and we need everyone to be trustworthy. If you can't handle something as simple as the nightly watch, then maybe you should just go back home."

Amethyst narrowed her eyes, hiding the hurt that lurked there. Despite her golden complexion, Adrianna could see the color that suffused her cheeks. "Fine, I will do just that." The girl then proceeded to stomp over to her bedroll and begin stuffing things away into her pack.

Suddenly a new voice spoke up, cutting through the air like a knife. "Dartanyen! Just who do you think you are? I didn't know that we had voted you master and commander here. Lay off of the girl. She apologized for her mistake. What more do you want from her?" Tianna stalked up to Dartanyen, her chestnut hair flying about her shoulders as she berated him. Dartanyen's expression turned from anger to surprise. "What really is the issue here? The fact that Amethyst made a mistake, or the fact that she is young, younger than you feel that she should be in order to participate fully as a functioning member of this group?"

Dartanyen's expression turned to bewilderment and then to chagrin. He regarded Tianna intently for a moment and then looked back to Amethyst, the girl continuing to prepare her pack for her trip back to Sangrilak. He sighed and then walked over to her. "Amethyst, wait. I was a little too harsh on you. Tianna is right, I do feel that you are too young to be traveling with us. But, here you are . . ." Dartanyen paused. "I will try to remember that all of this is very new to you, if you try a little harder not take some things too lightly."

Amethyst looked up at Dartanyen. Her lips were pressed obstinately into a thin line. For a moment, Adrianna thought that the girl would reject his apology. Then Amethyst shrugged. "All right. I can do that."

Dartanyen nodded and then turned away to put his own bedroll away. He walked by Tianna on the way over to his belongings, patting her on the shoulder and nodding as he passed. Adrianna saw Tianna's mouth curve into a small smile before she, too, began to pack up. Adrianna watched the silent exchange, realizing that Dartanyen harbored no ill feelings towards Tianna, had even seemed to appreciate her input about the situation. Adrianna's respect for the faelin archer grew. It was a good leader who took the opinions of his group members to heart. And only a man who had the utmost confidence in himself would take the censure of another, and go so far as to amend his behaviors.

All day they rode. Unfortunately for Adrianna, she was extremely sore from the ride of the day before, her muscles unaccustomed to being in the saddle for so many hours at a time. But they did not want to stop, the possibility of being followed too much of a probability, the repercussions they would suffer if they were discovered too hideous to contemplate. And so they continued, despite the discomfort. That morning, Tianna had rubbed Adrianna's sore leg muscles with an ointment that suffused the areas with warmth, helping her to be able to deal with the upcoming ride. The two women rode together for most of their day after that, Tianna keeping Adrianna's mind busy with natural lore. Tianna would point out a particular tree, bush, or flower, and tell her the name of the plant, its characteristics, and healing properties, if any. Adrianna liked to hear Tianna speak, the other woman's voice soothing and relaxing, and she liked to learn everything that Tianna taught her, sucking up the knowledge like a sponge. Adrianna was glad that Tianna seemed to have recovered from the shock of meeting Sydonnia, and finding out about the message that had been sent to Sirion. Their easygoing friendship seemed to be back to normal.

The group rode until dusk, and then quickly found a place away from the road to set up camp. Once again they lit no fire, eating only the pack rations that had been provided to them. At the end of the next day, they would reach the town of Ferent. There, they would replenish their supplies and rest for the night. Then they would journey to the Tangir River. They would take a ferry across the river and then continue northeast to the city of Driscol. There, they would re-supply themselves once more, and rest up for the journey through the Ratik Mountain Pass. It was the easiest route through the mountains, but that did not mean that it would be an effortless journey. They would spend at least four days in the pass before emerging on the other side. Adrianna took it all in good stride, despite her aches. Everything was all so new to her, she never having journeyed to the mountains before. And each step they took northward took her closer to her sister.

***

The wagon went over yet another bump. Dinim cursed eloquently in Cimmerean and slammed the book shut. It was useless. He couldn't concentrate with the bumpy terrain rocking him about within the wagon. It was to the point where he needed to constantly catch himself lest he risk falling over, despite his seated position. Dinim berated the wagon, but actually felt lucky to have found it. He met the owner in Ferent, and was happy that the man was willing to take a passenger with him to his destination, which happened to be the same place that Dinim needed to go. Grondor. The Wildrunners awaited him there. He did not look forward to this meeting. He knew that they were angry with him for his behavior in the recent past. Although it had not really been his behavior but that of the doppelganger, he would have a jolly time trying to tell them that story.

Sirion would be the most skeptical. To this day, even after all of the months they had fought beside one another, Dinim had yet to win that man's trust. There was no love lost between them, for Dinim disliked Sirion almost as much as Sirion disliked him. Dinim was surprised to discover that it was Sirion who had made the decision to have him stay behind with Adrianna's group after they were rescued from the temple. But it had not really been him. Dinim sighed. He hated to contemplate what could have happened. Ixitchitl would have killed the group had he been given the proper chance. If they had been any less cautious, they probably would never have left that temple alive.

Dinim was sure that the doppelganger received instructions to catch up with the rest of the Wildrunners as soon as the group recovered from the wounds they sustained during their first foray into the temple. He was sure that the doppelganger was not supposed to return to the temple the second time. Dinim hoped that it was not too late. Before he had been captured and imprisoned by Thane and the doppelganger, he had made an important discovery that could potentially increase his powers of spell-casting ten-fold.

Spell reversal was something that was a common practice among most spell-casters. It was something that could be achieved rather easily, if one knew how. With only a slight modification of the incantation, one could accomplish the opposite effect of what the original spell had intended. One day, while doing some research in the library in Sangrilak, Dinim found an old text. It was a strange book that Dinim thought mostly to be full of nonsense. However, as he read on, he began to see the power behind what was being stated. Dinim secreted the book within his robes and took the book back to his chambers. It was there that he read the volume to completion. The most interesting thing he had read was the practice of casting a spell backwards. At first, Dinim thought that the words had been erroneously scribed. Surely the writer was talking about spell reversal. But as he continued to read, Dinim realized that he was wrong. The author was most definitely speaking of casting a spell backwards, speaking the words of an incantation in the reverse order. Dinim was flabbergasted. He had never heard of such a thing.

That evening, Dinim was captured and brought before Lord Thane. He was imprisoned, and his identity stolen by the creature Ixitchitl. During his several weeks of incarceration, Dinim had a lot of time to think. He wondered about what he had learned from the book. As he worked to slowly increase the size of his prison, he was finally able to come across some scrolls and books. He practiced reading the passages backwards, and after a few days, was able to read backwards at a rather decent rate.

Finally, when Dinim was able to defeat Ixitchitl, he took the scroll that imprisoned him and destroyed it. He helped the group to escape from the temple, and then left them to return to the library. He found the book still resting upon the shelf in the room he had inhabited there. He took the book and left the library. In the middle of the night, Dinim walked through the streets towards the Inn of the Hapless Cenloryan, the place where Adrianna said she would be. He kept to the shadows, not wanting to bring any attention to himself. He knew that someone would come in search of him, Thane would not give him up easily. As he continued to walk, he started to hear whispers in the alley ahead of him. Very cautiously he crept closer, and when he was close enough to hear what was being said he stopped.

What Dinim heard surprised him. Adrianna . . . they were looking for Adrianna. Someone wanted her, and Dinim quickly discovered that it was Lord Thane. The young woman was in grave danger to be wanted by Thane. He was the epitome of evil and cruelty. He was no longer human, Aasarak having made him into something more . . . Azmathous.

Despite his extensive knowledge of things arcane, even Dinim knew very little about the Azmathous. He knew he should have told Adrianna what little that he knew, but he did not have the heart to tell her that her father was Undead . . . a death-knight. What humanity he had once possessed was gone forever. Whoever had made Thane as such was indeed powerful, and Dinim knew that it was paramount that he discover the identity of Thane's master as soon as he was able. He suspected Aasarak, but could not be entirely certain. However, Dinim had learned that Thane was 'Lord' to several others like him, undead monsters that were in search of revenge. But they were all connected to the Azmathous Death-Master, he who brought them to 'life' after a hideous and tormented death.

Dinim sighed to himself. Her father's true identity was not the only secret he kept from her. He did not even know himself why he never told her about her sister's child. He knew that he should have, but he had not quite been able to bring himself to do so. Perhaps it was the pleasure he derived from knowing things that others did not, or perhaps he was jealous, knowing that Adrianna had a connection to her sister that he could not fathom, could never understand. If she ever found out that he knew and never told her, she would undoubtedly be upset. And he could not blame her.

The wagon went over yet another bump. Dinim cursed and rubbed his backside. It was going to be a long trip.

***

Tallachienan strode purposefully through the northwestern quandrant of his citadel. His mind was full of the preparations that he needed to make for his students' arrival. A couple of them had arrived already, two young men whom he had been tracking for quite some time. Their Talent had been difficult to determine, but that probably had much to do with the circumstances surrounding each one's upbringing. But they had potential. All of his students had potential, and that was why he chose them. Out of all of the Talents of Shandahar, TC always chose those with the brightest aura. Only they would have enough Talent to succeed at what he would teach them.

TC opened the door to his laboratory and swept within. He made his way to the rear of the study and walked into the next room. There, sitting upon a pedestal, was a large orb. When he approached it, the orb began to glow softly green. TC splayed his hands over the surface of the orb, bringing to the forefront of his mind the person that he wished to see. The dense mist within the orb began to move, the colors varying from blue and green to pale yellow. Then, within the center of the orb appeared the face of a man.

The man was a Cimmerean. His hair was black, his eyes lavender, and his complexion pale. He appeared to be riding in a wagon, his image moving about rhythmically within the orb. The man appeared strained, but TC could not tell if it was just the fact that he was forced to endure a wagon ride, or if he was overly tired. TC shook his head. It was obvious that Dinim had not yet reached the Ratik Pass. TC had hoped that Dinim would be well into the mountains by now, but he had a tendency to forget that most people had to use common modes of travel. It had been decades since TC had even considered riding in a wagon to reach a desired destination. As it was, Dinim would not reach the Wildrunners until it was too late. Damn Aasarak! If the mage had not put his nose into business that was not his own, Dinim would have been with the rest of his companions by now.

Tallachienan turned from the orb. It was time for him to pay Dinim a visit. He would go to his apprentice within the darkness of the night in order to minimize the possibility of anyone seeing him. Without Dinim, the Wildrunners would be hard-pressed to achieve victory over Gaknar. Without question, the man had to be destroyed. With the information he had obtained, Gaknar had become more than just one of the greatest sorcerers who had ever lived. He had become a threat to Shandahar. With his power and knowledge, he would be able to bring greater daemons into the world. The Wildrunners would need to get to Gaknar before he could make any such attempt. And if Gaknar happened to succeed, then the Wildrunners would need all of the help they could get.

TC sighed heavily. The Wildrunners and their upcoming trial was not the only thing on his mind. The preparations that he had been making had been primarily for one person. Adrianna Darnesse. Her training would soon begin. A part of him longed to see her, to have her here with him once more, but another part wanted nothing to do with her. But he had a duty to perform. First and foremost, he was her master, and always would be. Only he could teach her the things she would need to know in order to meet her destiny. As of yet, he still had not sought her out within the orb, had not wanted to deal with his emotions concerning her just yet. He would have too much of that soon enough.

TC left the laboratory. He needed to complete a few things before he went to visit Dinim. He would write a message to him in the Travel Notebook, telling Dinim to be expecting him. Once there, TC would ask Dinim about the Lady Adrianna. TC would be able to determine how much she had changed since the last cycle, if at all. Damn, he so much hoped that she had changed, that she would not be so desirable to him this time. Was that really so much to ask? Did he not deserve to be freed from this torment, this eternal guilt?

***

Stealthily, Sirion crept through the undergrowth. Every sense was alert and focused upon his quarry. They were a small group, but extremely conspicuous and they made no effort to conceal their passage. There were eight of them, four men and four women. Three of them were faelin, and four of them were human. One of them was large, about the size of a small oorg. There was also a large corubis. Everything about this group was an anathema to him, and one person in particular was his antithesis in every nuance of the word. Sirion was a ranger, one who knew the natural world in a way in which few others could. When he worked, he was one with nature; every cell in his body was attuned to the environment around him. It was not so with his antagonist. The natural world shunned him. In this way, his double was easy to trail, nature falling away from him, exposing him like a merchant displays his wares in the market place.

For quite some time, Sirion trailed the group, Dramati at his side. In many ways they were very similar to the Wildrunners. They had the same faces, the same bodily physique, wore the same type of clothing, and even carried the same type of weapons as their counterparts. It was frustrating, knowing that many people would think this group to be the real Wildrunners. And when trouble came knocking, as it always did when this group was in town, the Wildrunners were blamed for the crime. This group was ruining the Wildrunners' reputation, and they had to be stopped before any more innocent people could be hurt.

Sirion remembered the day that the group had been created. It had been a bad situation, a battle between themselves and several of Gaknar's priests. They had no fire power, Dinim not having joined the group yet. But they had a lot of muscle. Naemmious could break down a solid oak door with a single shove, and Arn was lethal with a broadsword. Anya and Sirion were the naturalists of the group, Laura the healer, and Sorn was good with picking locks and other such secretive skills.

But then there was the mirror. It appeared to be some type of doorway. The priests retreated into it, as though they were falling back from the Wildrunners. They found themselves pushing forward, and the priests continued to pass into the mirror and onto the other side. Sirion could see them in the mirror, walking around. It looked harmless enough. Triath had even put his hand out and touched the mirror. Nothing happened except that his hand passed into it, disappearing the way the priests had disappeared. But the priests had re-appeared, into that place on the other side of the mirror. And so in they went . . . following the priests to the other side.

That was one of the biggest mistakes that Sirion felt they had ever made. He was sure that if they had had a spell-caster with them, it would never have happened. Dinim wore an expression of shock on his face when they related the story to him later, telling him how the 'evil' Wildrunners had come about. When the Wildrunners walked through the mirror and emerged on the other side, the magic of the object created the alignment opposite of them. The two groups squared off in the temple, while the priests made good their escape. However, the skirmish came to a rapid ending, neither group willing to suffer the damage they knew would be inflicted. So they parted, each one promising to the other that, one day, they would finish the fight and be victorious.

And so here he was, tracking them down. Sirion took stock of his location, and suddenly realized that, in his engrossed state, he had not realized that he was traveling in the same direction in which he had initially come. He had made a 180o turn. The group was heading towards the Wildrunners! He cursed silently to himself and vaulted onto Dramati's back. He had to reach the Wildrunners before the other group.

They sprinted through the shrubs and tall grasses. Mentally he berated himself, knowing that he should have been paying better attention. Hopefully the Wildrunners had not been too far behind him and were not that much farther away. Within minutes Sirion was sighing in relief. He had reached them just in time. He made a call as he approached, one that Triath would realize was a distress call. Instantly, the rest of the group was on guard, and dispersing into the foliage all around. But it was too late. Sirion could smell them before he saw them. The other group emerged all around the Wildrunners from out of the grasses and shrubs within which they were about to conceal themselves.

Dinim hid within the tall bushes, watching the scene unfold. He had rejoined the Wildrunners just a couple of days ago, Master Tallachienan having facilitated his arrival into Grondor. Actually, without the master, he would have spent at least another two or three weeks on the road. Dinim never got the chance to find out why TC had come to him in the first place, but his visit had been propitious and had saved him and the Wildrunners some much needed time.

He was faced with an unusual situation to say the least. With some degree of astonishment, Dinim saw the similarities between the individuals. Nothing that the Wildrunners had told him about this renegade group prepared him for this, despite what he had just gone through with the doppelganger. Many of them wore the same clothes, armor, and weapons as their duplicates. Dinim could hear Dramati growling deep in his throat. The large corubis was eyeing his twin menacingly. The other animal reciprocated the gesture and the two beasts began to circle one another. Suddenly there was a flurry of activity. As the two corubi leapt at one another, the antithesis of Sorn rushed Sirion, slicing his scimitars across the left side of Sirion's back and arm. Sirion spun around, but before he could retaliate, Sorn was there, and he had captured the attention of anti-Sorn. Anti-Arn rushed at Laura, but found himself being lifted into the air and slammed into the nearest treetrunk. Dinim knew that to be Triath's work. It had appeared that a giant invisible hand had attacked anti-Arn. However, in actuality, it was Triath's psionic ability . . . the ability to manipulate the world with his mind. Anti-Arn rose from the ground where he had fallen and found himself face-to-face with Arn. The two warriors began to attack one another with their swords. Anya let loose a couple of arrows at anti-Triath, only to find them freezing in mid-air before him. They then dropped to the ground. Anya suddenly found herself being struck by an arrow, and spun around to find that it had been fired by her double. Frowning in pain, she pulled the arrow free from her arm and then sprinted towards the other woman. It was then that Dinim realized that the members of each of the groups had located one another and paired off. Dinim was not sure if this was done deliberately, or if each person bore an inexplicable hatred for his 'twin' that caused him or her to automatically hunt the other down.

After another few moments, Dinim started to become confused. Sirion was fighting anti-Sirion, one of the Sorns had the other backed against a tree, and Naemmious was beating Naemmious into a bloody pulp. Triath was using his mental energy to attack his nemesis, who held his head in his hands, screaming from the mental lashing. Breesa seemed to be trying to create some kind of illusion, but she was having a difficult time of it. Arn was at a stalemate with Arn, neither man getting in a successful attack. At the edge of the battle scene, Laura was grappling with Laura, each woman clawing wildly at the other.

Dinim began to perspire profusely. He was dumbfounded; uncertain of what action he should take. Suddenly a thick fog rolled in. Right away Dinim could tell that it was magic-made. Damn! He had to act quickly! He no longer knew who was who, and he was afraid that he would do more harm than good. Perhaps he should break Breesa's concentration?

By the time Dinim decided upon what action to take, the fog was thick all around them. But he was not concerned. Dinim began to incant the words to his spell and when he was finally about to cast it, the fog cloud suddenly lifted. To his consternation, the only ones standing before him were the Wildrunners. Despite the similarities, Dinim was able to tell this group from the group of evil doubles that were, somehow, no longer there. Immediately Dinim diffused his spell. He emerged from behind the shrubbery and approached the group. They were bloodstained, weary and confused. Where the other group had gone, they did not know.

***

He slowly drifted into consciousness. It was a strange sensation, like something kept trying to pull him back into the thick blackness from which he had emerged. Sluggishly, he made an attempt to move his limbs. The sound of the moan escaping his lips startled him into further wakefulness, as well as the pain that seemed to ache in every joint of his body. As his mind freed itself from the drug-induced sleep, it became more alert. He felt the coolness of the environment on his bare limbs, the hardness of the substrate beneath his prone body, and the abominable dryness of his parched throat.

Slowly he began to open his eyes. All he could perceive was darkness, inky blackness all around. Once more he tried to move and he realized that his arms were bound behind his back. His muscles, sore from the abuse, wailed at him to free them from their torment. Once more he heard himself moan involuntarily, heard it echo within the enclosed space. He could smell the damp and the mold, could feel the dirt shift beneath him as he tried to move.

The boy moved his head, trying to see something, anything, in the darkness. By the goddess, where was he? Was this some kind of dream? If it was, it was so real . . . He should be at home, at the temple, in his bed. Like a river, the fear began to course through him, giving him the impetus to struggle against his bonds. The ropes sawed into his wrists, making him want to struggle all the more, the fear of being unable to escape urging him. His body protested as he made it onto his knees. Suddenly nauseous, he heaved, but all that emerged was a spattering of foul smelling fluid. It burned his throat as it passed through, causing him to groan yet again.

For how long he knelt there, he did not know. After a while he stopped working at the ropes that bound his wrists. He could feel the stickiness of the blood that had dribbled down to his palms, and the wounds stung horribly. Dejectedly, his head hung until his chin touched his chest. For some reason someone had drugged him, taken him from his bed in the night, and brought him to this place. Would they ever return for him? Or would he stay here until he died of thirst?

Suddenly there was a loud noise, a grating sound that made him cringe. From within the darkness directly in front of him the sound emanated. There was a click, and then there was light, a light so bright that he clenched his eyes tightly shut when it entered the room. He heard the sound of approaching footsteps, heard them pause before him, but the pain would not allow him to open his eyes. There was silence. The visitor waited. He struggled to open his eyes, and when the lids finally parted, he saw a robed figure standing before him. The visitor had muted the light cast by a lantern that he carried at his side. The boy had yet to hear the figure speak, or to see his face, but he knew that the visitor was a man.

The dark-robed figure stared down at him, a hood pulled over his head, concealing his face. The boy could feel the weight of the stare, despite being unable to see the eyes. But then the figure was placing the lantern at his feet, and pulling the hood down from his head. The boy felt his eyes widen when he saw the face of his visitor. But then again, it wasn't so much the face, but the eyes . . . bright red eyes that bore slits for pupils. The cheekbones were prominent, as was the ridge over the eyes. The nose was long, and had a downward curve to the tip. The lips were a reddish purple, and were thin within the long face.

"So, you have finally awakened."

The boy startled when he heard the voice of the figure before him. He was so accustomed to the silence that the sound was loud to his ears. It was a normal man's voice, bearing no hint of maliciousness or condemnation. The strange man knelt before him, a bowl of water in his hands.

"Drink this. It will make you stronger."

The man put the bowl to the boy's mouth and he drank greedily. The liquid was cool, and slightly sweet. It cascaded down his parched throat, bringing life back to his bruised body. After several swallows, the man took back the bowl. "Not too much," he warned. "It could make you ill if you drink too much all at once. I will give you more later."

He watched the man place the half-emptied bowl next to the lantern. Then the man sat on the floor in front of him and removed a dagger from his belt. The boy felt his breath catch in his throat. The man leaned forward, took the rope that bound the boy's feet, and swiftly cut it. He then sat back and placed the weapon back into its sheath. For a moment the boy just knelt there, regaining his equilibrium. Then he painfully maneuvered himself into a seated position. His mind whirled. He sensed that the man before him was a creature of great evil, someone who had conducted many acts of terror upon many people. Yet, the man had shown him nothing but kindness. The fear began to resurface. What did this man want him for? What purpose could he possibly have for a young acolyte?

"Why have you brought me here?" He asked the question despite his fear, needed to have some answers.

"I have some special plans for you. You are a very important young man, deserving of great honor. I would be the one who would bestow upon you that honor."

"Then . . . then why am I tied up? Why did you steal me from my home in the middle of the night?"

"You are bound because I was afraid you would try to get away before I could explain things to you. Now that you know, and are a willing recipient, I can remove them. And my people took you in the middle of the night, well, because your priesthood would not understand. They have such a limited outlook on things. But soon, you will have knowledge and power that you can not even begin to imagine."

"But why me? How am I so special?"

"It took my people a long time to find you. Of all of the many young men we came across, only you have the traits we are looking for."

"And what would those be?"

"Goodness of heart and purity of soul." The man paused. "You also have a peacefulness of spirit that very few possess. You will be the perfect recipient."

"What is it that I will be receiving?"

"Now, that is something we will have to discuss at a later time. Come, food awaits us outside." Once again the man took his dagger and sliced through the bonds. The ropes fell away from his torn wrists. "Tsk, tsk. Look what you have gone and done. This is just not acceptable. We will have to treat these wounds before we partake of the evening meal."

The boy nodded and slowly rose to his feet. The man was beside him, just in case he should fall. He began to follow the man out of the small, dungeon-like room. His stomach rumbled. Indeed he was hungry. His fears had been eased somewhat, but had not been alleviated. There was something that the man was not telling him.

"By the way, what is your name?" asked the man, turning just before they reached the stairs.

"My name is Razlul."

CHAPTER 9

Upon the sixth day out of Sangrilak, the group reached the foothills of the Ratik Mountain Range. In the distance, the mountains could be seen rising from amongst the hills, large and imposing. Adrianna and Amethyst stared at them in awe, for they had never been to the mountains before, much less traveled through them. Dartanyen, Zorg, Armond, Bussi, and Tianna ignored them, having traversed them before. They would continue to travel north, skirting the foothills, until they reached the city of Driscol. Once there, they would equip themselves for mountain travel, for it was the last city they would see until they had traversed the Ratik Pass, the safest path through the mountains.

Thus, once reaching the foothills, the group veered true north, keeping the foothills to their right. The land was now littered with various bushes and scrub of all types, offering a break in the monotony of the steppe grasslands. As the days passed, Tianna had begun to regain more of her former spirit. Much to Adrianna's happiness, the other woman sought her out the most. They would ride side-by-side next to the wagon, often near the rear. Adrianna caught Amethyst listening in to their conversations a time or two, but her interaction with the group tended to be minimal. It was the same with Sabian. Adrianna thought him to be a rather strange sort, keeping to himself most of the time. He seemed friendly enough, and participated in basic group functions. However, Sabian held an air of mystery about him, and Adrianna was left wondering what exactly he was about.

For a day more they traveled, stopping only for the mid-day meal. It began to rain, and cloaks were donned, hoods up over their heads, although the rain soaked through. For the remainder of the day it rained. The animals walked with heads lowered, their cloven feet tromping through mud puddles that splattered onto their fur, turning their undersides into a dirty brown. The riders also had their heads down in misery, the rain seeping through all their layers of clothing. Nothing was dry. The rain even soaked clothing items that had been tucked away deep within their packs. That night, they slept upon wet bedrolls, and no fire could be lighted for lack of dry kindling.

Finally the rain let up and the sun shone in the sky once more. Spirits began to lift and clothing dried out. It was the next day when Dartanyen noticed something. He raised his hand for Bussi to halt the wagon. He jumped down from atop his bronze larian and knelt at the ground near the animal's feet. He then straightened. "Trolag sign. They are not far from us."

Tianna dismounted as well. Surprisingly, she boasted tracking abilities she had learned from her days spent with Sirion. "Yes, there is a rather large group of them, about seven or eight; probably a family group. The males will be excessively protective. The trail continues down there." Tianna pointed straight and a little to the left down the hill.

They sat there for a moment, deciding upon what course of action to take. "Let us skirt around the beasts, say, about a half mile berth around them, avoiding them completely." Armond suggested. Dartanyen nodded and Zorg grunted his approval. The group moved off the trail and into the tall grasses and scrub. For most of the day they moved at a rapid pace, arcing about the main trail so as to avoid the trolags. After several miles, they finally made their way back to the road. It was near nightfall when Dartanyen and Tianna searched the other side for signs of trolag passage. They found none.

The group decided to continue traveling until they reached Driscol. It would be late when they got there, but they would have warm beds to sleep in, with a shelter over their heads. They ate their evening meal as they rode, rations that they purchased in Ferent. Since leaving that city, Dartanyen had hunted. The game had presented itself as an easy catch; colorful little scrub ptarmigans were abundant in the area they currently passed through. Thus, everyone had eaten well and Dartanyen deserved a good rest, as well as Tianna, who had been the one to prepare the meat, and who provided them with tea every morning when they broke their fast.

Some time after sundown the weary group passed into the city of Driscol. They entered the first inn that they noticed, and were glad when there were rooms available for the night. Dartanyen paid the innkeeper for three rooms. Tianna, Amethyst, and Adrianna would share one room, while the men split up into pairs to occupy the others. Once reaching the room, Adrianna was happy to slump down upon one of the two beds. She would share it with Tianna. The two women had discovered that Amethyst was not a good sleeping companion; she was too restless and kicked out in the night. Adrianna shucked her outer garments and crawled beneath the blankets. Sleep was quick to come to her and she was so tired that she dreamed no dreams.

***

Early the next morning, the group awoke later than usual. They had agreed to the strategy the evening before, wanting to be well rested for their foray into the Ratik Pass. Quickly and efficiently they purchased the supplies that they would need while they traveled through the mountains. They had to sell the wagon because it would be too difficult to take it through the pass. They would buy another one when they reached Celuna.

A little before mid-day the group left Driscol, traveling north through the foothills that would lead them to the pass. Before them, the mountains rose precipitously. Adrianna regarded them with awe, their majesty touching her profoundly. There was something about those mountains, an aura of power and mystery that she could not help but appreciate. A few hours after mid-day, the pass lay before them, twining ever upwards. The riders dismounted from their animals, and they evenly distributed their belongings to each of the lloryk and larian. The group started their ascent. The way was slow, the animals having to take the time to find the proper purchase for their cloven hooves. For the rest of that day they moved, and as dusk approached they camped amongst trees so large that Adrianna was amazed. Adrianna felt comforted by the huge trees, their beauty and grandeur wonderful to behold. Tianna, Dartanyen, and Armond also seemed to find solace in the presence of the magnificent trees. However, Amethyst, Zorg, and Bussi just passed as though they had not a care in the world. To them, the trees were just like any others, except bigger.

The band awoke early the next day, hoping to use as much sunlight as possible since the going was slower than it had been across the plains. As they traveled, the journey became ever more laborious, the air beginning to thin as they moved ever upwards and the climate becoming cooler so as they had to don warmer clothing. The terrain became ever more rocky as they traveled and the tree cover became sparse with the change in soil constitution. Everyone plodded devoutly onward. The grass grew less plentifully as the group climbed in altitude, so they were awarded extra handfuls of grain at the end of each day. Dartanyen and Bussi walked in the front of the group with Tianna and Adrianna close behind, Tianna constantly searching the ground for evidence of anyone passing. But despite their caution, the trolags happened upon them without any warning.

Out from behind rocky outcroppings several of them came. They were horrid creatures, standing about eight feet tall. Much of their stooped bodies were covered by dirty brown hair. Their eyes were purple with white pupils. When one of them opened its mouth to snarl at them, black fanged teeth were revealed. They were like animals, primal in their desire to kill them.

The larian screamed and reared in terror. Immediately, Bussi was swinging his battle-axe with Armond and Zorg close behind. Dartanyen sought to get hold of his bow while at the same time trying to keep his larian from fleeing the scene. Adrianna moved herself and Sethanon into the group's center as quickly as possible, mentally reviewing her list of spells. A couple of them she disregarded as soon as they came to mind for she feared that the radius of those spells would encompass her comrades. Ever so briefly, Adrianna became frustrated. How could she cast her stronger spells when her companions were in her way? But by then, Zorg and Armond had engaged the enemy. Amethyst seemed to have disappeared, and Dartanyen had finally decided to let his larian go, and had shot one of the trolags with his bow. To Adrianna's dismay, even Tianna had entered the fray. Adrianna frowned. How could Tianna possibly help anyone with her healing skills if she was busy playing warrior?

Adrianna glanced at Sabian as he finally made it to her side. She saw him assessing the situation with the same disgust as she had. Adrianna shook her head and cursed, focusing upon one of the seven trolags, quieting Sethanon with a pat of her hand on his muzzle. She cast her spell and watched the two missiles of magical energy unerringly strike their target. It startled Bussi, who almost fell back, nearly giving his foe the upper hand. But the halfen was quick to regain himself and struck the massive forearm coming at him with his axe, nearly severing the limb from the body. The trolag howled in pain and lashed out, knocking Bussi away with the other arm. The halfen sailed through the air and landed a few feet away from his angry adversary. For a moment he lay there, stunned, before sitting himself upright. Upon seeing the massive creature coming for him, he was quick to regain his feet and sprinted forwards to meet the trolag once more.

Adrianna turned to see that Zorg had made short work of another of the trolags. Zorg had sheathed his huge, two-handed blade within the belly of the creature. Her eyes widened as she saw the beast fall forwards towards Zorg. The big warrior stood aside to avoid being squashed, but in the process was unable to retrieve his blade from the body. As the trolag fell, Zorg found himself being twisted down with it until he found the pommel being forced from his grip. The creature fell heavily onto its stomach, forcing the blade ever deeper until it emerged out the other side, the once shiny blade now covered with thick, dark blood. Zorg cursed and began to try to turn the creature over, seeking to recover his blade.

Suddenly, Adrianna began to feel the ground rumble. Beside her, Sabian had completed his incantation. The rumbling became more insistent and then, from out of the ground several feet in front of them, five black tentacles emerged. Rope-like, they sprang from the ground, whipping about wildly. In horror, she watched as her companions scattered, hoping to avoid being struck by the waving tentacles. Immediately, one of the tentacles grabbed hold of a nearby tree, tearing it from the ground, and waving it about. Another of the tentacles found one of the trolags. The hairy creature wailed in terror and soon was gasping for breath. Slowly, the trolag was squeezed to death, and when it was finally dead, it swung limply from the tentacle, blood dripping from its open maw.

Meanwhile, two of the other tentacles gripped two more of the trolags. The other found Zorg. While he was busy trying to extricate his sword from the fallen trolag, the whipping tentacle had found him. The tentacle wrapped its massive form around the big warrior. Zorg cried out, clawing at the tentacle with his hands. Adrianna turned to Sabian and shouted, "Stop it! Stop the spell!"

"I can't!" Sabian shouted back over the noise of the battle. "The spell has to wind itself out."

Adrianna glared at the man, angry that he had cast such a dangerous spell that placed her comrades at risk. She saw Bussi rushing towards the tentacle that held Zorg and began to chop at it with his massive battle-axe. She heard the scream of another of the monsters outside the range of the tentacles. She turned to see that it had a dagger protruding from its back. It arched backward, trying in vain to remove the deeply embedded dagger. Two of Dartanyen's arrows protruded from its shoulder and chest and Tianna stood before it with her scimitar, slashing at it in its weakness. The monster fell, as did the one who had confronted Armond.

Adrianna continued to watch as Bussi chopped at the black tentacle holding Zorg. The warrior was quickly losing consciousness. Then suddenly it was done. The severed tentacle fell to the ground, releasing its death grip on Zorg. Bussi dropped the axe and pulled Zorg away from the other four tentacles. The mindless things continued to wave about, three of them holding the limp corpses of trolags. Everyone ran towards Bussi and Zorg. Except for the swooshing noise of the tentacles as they moved and the rapid breathing of the band members, all was silent.

The group made room for Tianna, who knelt beside Zorg. When the tentacle fell, the man had finally been able to take a much-needed breath. However, his breathing was labored. Adrianna suspected that many of his ribs were broken. Tianna gripped her pendant and placed her other hand on Zorg's bared torso. She then began to pray to her goddess.

It was decided that they would set up camp. Sabian and Armond began to work at clearing away what bodies they could. Amethyst went around and collected the weapons that had been used in the fight: Bussi's axe, Zorg's sword, Dartanyen's arrows, and her dagger. After a time, the tentacles slowed their movements and finally lay still upon the ground. Then they disappeared. It was soon discovered that Adrianna was the only one who had been able to keep her mount throughout the battle. All of the other beasts had fled the battle to run back down from whence they had come and were nowhere to be seen. Adrianna sighed heavily. They would just simply have to take the time to round up the beasts. There was no way that they would be able to continue their journey without the supplies those animals carried on their backs.

The group continued to set camp while someone tracked down the larian. Adrianna was finally able to get Sethanon to carry Dartanyen and Tianna, for he was very uneasy about leaving her. It was near sundown when they returned, Tianna riding astride her own larian. Within Dartanyen's palm were the reins of the two lloryk and his larian, while Tianna held those of the other three larian. Adrianna took the reins from Tianna, who held them out to her with a broad smile. Adrianna chuckled to herself as she led the animals to the posting area. She gave them each a few handfuls of grain and then went to go settle down within her sleeping furs. For a while she studied her books and then lay down and wrapped the blankets all about her. She saw the silhouette of Bussi outlined by the light of the moons as she fell into sleep.

***

Sirion and Dramati entered the small wood. They moved silently . . . stealthily. He had bid the rest of the Wildrunners to stay just outside the area. It was up to him to find out what they were up against, where Gaknar was located, as well as his priests. The group would be close by if he got into any trouble, yet far enough away that they would not hinder his reconnaissance mission. It wasn't long before he found the dilapidated temple. Mostly it was a heap of ancient stone that had been scoured by the elements. There was only a hint of where the entrance once stood, but now there was no need for one, time having taken the need away.

Sirion crouched in the shadows. The sun would be setting within the hour. He needed to quickly find out the situation and then get back to the group. There was definite evidence of activity here, but there was no one about. Sirion frowned. Where would everyone be at this time of the day, when most people were settling down to partake of the evening meal-- winding down after the days activities? Sirion slunk around within the trees surrounding the temple. Once he reached the other side he stopped again. He had seen no one. It was then that Dramati raised his head, the muscles in his body stiffening. His ears rotated at the hint of a sound that Sirion could not yet detect. And then he heard it . . . a chanting coming from within the ruined structure.

Sirion felt his frown deepen. Something was going on inside. He began to creep towards the temple, and once amongst the fallen stones he saw a stone staircase leading down beneath the surface. He could hear the chanting emanating from the bowels of the ruins. Slowly he made his way down. He knew that he was placing himself at risk, but he saw no other way. It was best if he found out what was going on now, by himself, instead of getting the rest of the group and taking the risk of being discovered. Once at the bottom of the stairs, Sirion moved in the direction of the chanting. It was dark, the torches few and far apart upon the dank walls. After a few moments he reached a doorway.

The chanting had stopped, but this was where it had been coming from. When Sirion peered through the open doorway, the sight that met his eyes caused a rush of alarm to race through his body. He had to get the Wildrunners right away. The ceremony had begun, and he did not know how much time they had left before Tharizdune was brought into Shandahar.

Riding astride Dramati, Sirion sped back to the group. They were on the alert before he reached them, he having warned them with one of the many calls he used in order to communicate with them while he was scouting. Within moments the group was on the move through the wood, quickly making their way to the fallen temple. Once there, Sirion led them to the staircase. They paused at the entrance. Triath motioned to Dinim and the mage stepped up to the fore. He followed behind Sirion as they made their way down, and once at the bottom, the rest of the group arrayed themselves behind the two at the lead. In pairs they made their way through the corridor. Sorn and Laura walked behind Dinim and Sirion. Triath and Breesa were next, followed up by Anya and Arn. Naemmious brought up the rear.

The group moved within the shadows cast by the flickering torchlight. The place was eerily silent, as though the air itself waited for what would happen next. Dinim felt a charge in the air, knew that magic was being called, being used in some twisted plan devised by one of the most powerful sorcerers in Shandahar. Dinim walked as a leader before the group. For the first time he would be playing a key role as a member of the Wildrunners. He prayed that they were not too late, but Sirion's description of the situation did not give him much hope. Nevertheless, he did not want to show them his fear, he who was supposedly fearless. When they reached the hall that Sirion described, Dinim had to steel himself before looking in upon the scene.

The hall was enormous. Huge pillars were situated about the room, a structural support bastion for the large vaulted ceiling. At the center of the dimly lit room there was a small congregation of about fifty dark-robed priests. They surrounded a circle of what appeared to be five large mirrors. Each one stood at least ten feet in height, and all faced inward towards one another. Within the circle of mirrors sat a boy. He was almost a man, about the age of seventeen. He was bound with his hands behind his back. There was a cloth in his mouth to keep him from speaking. He struggled against his bonds, perspiration wetting his pale blond hair.

Near the periphery of the circle of mirrors stood a dark-robed figure wielding a staff. Dinim recognized the staff as the one belonging to Gaknar. Beside the sorcerer was another robed figure. His clothing was colored a deep crimson, very contrasting to that worn by the other clerics and priests. Dinim knew that this man was not one of the fold, and he wondered why the man was there. However, his questions were very short lived. When the man began the incantation to his spell, Dinim felt the shock race through him.

Dinim cursed under his breath. This man was a Dimensionalist, and the mirrors were not mirrors at all, but portals, portals that would bring Tharizdune into Shandahar. The Dimensionalist became surrounded by an array of floating runes that pulsated with a reddish glow. Apprehension filled Dinim as he saw the man raise his arms to the vaulted ceiling above. "No . . ." he muttered. Dinim made to step forward only to be brought back by the restraining hand of Sirion at his belt.

Then, from out of the darkness before them, came a wind. At first it was light, but it quickly became a gale that whipped the hair from around their faces, seeking to take their breaths away with its onslaught. It careened about them furiously, and with it was the voice of Gaknar raised into a cackling laugh of glee. Dinim shut his eyes tightly, not wanting to believe that they were too late. Damnation! Only a Dimensionalist could open the portals. That was why Gaknar had wanted him. But Aasarak had reached him first, and so Gaknar had been forced to find another. The sorcerer had either bribed or threatened the Dimensionalist in order to get the man to do his bidding.

Suddenly, the stone beneath their feet began to quake. A rumbling filled the air as well as the aura of impending doom. The interior of each of the portals began to glow eerily yellow. Sirion swallowed convulsively, now knowing why Dinim seemed so concerned. He regarded the man beside him, watched Dinim close his eyes. The voice of the crimson spell-caster rose over the sound of the quake. And when a second voice joined that of the first, Sirion looked out upon the scene yet again, and saw that Gaknar was reading from a large tome that was sitting on a pedestal within the circle.

The glow from within the portals became brighter. Suddenly the air was rent with a shrill keening. The group could not help but put their hands over their ears, the wail so piercing that it was painful to hear. Then, from out of the portals emerged a pale mist. Slowly it crept from the portals, whirling and eddying about until it reached the center of the circle. The group became transfixed by the scene, knowing they had come too late, and that they were in terrible danger. But they could not leave now, the power they felt in the air culminating into something the world had never seen before.

The boy at the center of the circle stared wide-eyed at the mist whirling before him. For a moment he was still, but then he began to struggle at his bonds yet again, a desperation to his movements that had not been there before. Sirion felt someone bump into him from behind, and once more found himself restraining one of his group members. Laura had responded to the boy's fear, answering it the best that she knew how. She wanted to go to him, but Sirion's arm around her waist prevented her. And when she almost called out, Sirion put his hand over her mouth just in time, muffling any noise that she would have made.

The whirling mist became dense, veins of blue and grey permeating the mass. The boy knelt before it, wildly struggling against his bonds. The intensity of the gale increased, and Gaknar's voice rose high over the noise. The crimson-robed Dimensionalist stood aside, his work complete. He had opened the portals. That was all he had been bidden to do. Now all that he wished to do was leave this place, escape from this evil daemon cult and its crazy master.

All of a sudden there was a clap of sound, and the energy in the room all seemed to coalesce at the center of the circle. The mist slammed into the young man, rocking him back onto his heels. His head was thrown back on his neck, and his mouth opened. He screamed in agony as he looked up into the darkness of the vaulted ceiling. His body took on a strange glow, as though a light shone from the inside. Then he seemed to grow, his body taking on mass that had not been there before. His legs and arms thickened with muscle, and his height increased. As he continued to scream, the voice began to deepen. The ropes that bound his wrists broke, and his arms rose from his sides and extended upwards.

Dinim stared in awe at what was transpiring before him. The daemon Tharizdune had been released upon the world, and there would be no turning back. Fear coursed through him, followed by hopelessness and despair. What had been done could not be undone . . . unless . . . Dinim's gaze focused on the large ancient tome sitting on its pedestal. If the spell that allowed Tharizdune to enter his host could be reversed . . . No, it would be too risky. But then again, what more had they to lose? With Tharizdune loosed upon the land, the world would be thrust into chaos. Hundreds and thousands of people would become slaves of Tharizdune and his worshippers, the Daemundai.

Dinim turned to Sirion. He found the ranger regarding him intently. It seemed that the usually impassive Hinterlean was hoping that he had some plan, no matter how flimsy, to make right what had just happened. Dinim knew that Sirion did not really care for him all that much, that Sirion felt that he was a charlatan, someone who just wanted to look good. But when Dinim turned to face Sirion, his plan at the fore of his mind, it must have shown through his eyes and translated to Sirion. The faelin's countenance changed, an expression of determination altering his face. Sirion inclined his head to him, almost as though to say, *I am at your service*, a slight grin shaping his mouth.

"I need that book." Dinim spoke softly into the space between them. Dinim focused his eyes onto the tome in the distance and Sirion followed suit. Sirion nodded almost imperceptibly. "I also need time, time enough to re-open those portals."

Sirion's eyes widened, almost as though to say, *"You can do that?"* But the expression was only momentary and he was nodding again. The two men turned back to the rest of the group. They stood there wearing downtrodden expressions on their faces. Even Triath looked defeated. Sirion made his way over to Sorn. The man nodded when he heard what Sirion had to say. Immediately Sorn slipped into the hall and crouched within the shadows cast by the huge columns. "We need a distraction . . ."

Before Sirion could finish his sentence, Arn was at the ready. And then, without warning, he was whipping out his sword and running towards the congregated priests. Sirion shouted at him to stop, but it was to no avail. Naemmious cursed and followed his friend into the hall. Wide-eyed, Anya, Laura, and Breesa watched the men run, pell-mell, towards certain demise.

"Damnation!" Triath bellowed, his face distorted with rage. Sirion felt his own anger begin to build inside of him, but he quelled it. Now was not the time. They would need all of their wits about them if they had any chance of succeeding. He watched Dinim also enter the hall, which was about to become a battle zone.

The surprised priests, their attention now diverted from the ceremony, were preparing to face Arn and Naemmious. Quickly overcoming her disgruntlement, Anya entered the hall and positioned herself behind one of the massive pillars. She readied her longbow, and within moments had shot her first volley of arrows into the crowd of dark priests. Laura remained positioned near the entrance, ready to help any of her comrades if they became injured in the fight. Young Breesa stayed nearby, her skills as an illusionist being virtually worthless in a battle such as the one that was about to erupt. Sirion nodded and Dramati bounded away in pursuit of Naemmious and Arn.

The rest of the Wildrunners entered the hall. Taking advantage of the diversion, Dinim ran towards the circle of portals. He would call upon what he had learned under the guidance of his mentor and re-open the portals. It would take a lot of power, more than he had at his beck. This endeavor was a long shot, but he hadn't wanted to tell Sirion that. Besides, Dinim felt that Sirion knew that their chances of succeeding were low. Stating that fact out loud wouldn't have helped their cause any.

Dinim continued to sprint toward the scene. Tharizdune, within his new host body, still knelt upon the floor, his arms wide in supplication. The portals were closed, but continued to exude a faint glow, testimony of the power that had been present in order to open them and to call forth into this world a being such as this one. Never before had a greater daemon been able to exist upon Shandahar, and now that one had been called and successfully found a host body, the world was in dire peril.

Dinim had almost made it to the circle when a crimson shape collided into him. The two men fell in a tumble of arms, legs, and robes, each one cursing beneath his breath. But when Dinim realized who the man was, he was flooded with newfound purpose. Before the man could get to his feet, Dinim grabbed his arm. The man recoiled, his hood falling back from his face to reveal a Cimmerean. That the man was afraid was apparent, as well as the fact that he regretted what he had done . . . that he had helped the daemon to be brought into their world. "Wait. I am a friend. You and I, we can unmake what has been done here. Help me to make right this horrible wrong." Dinim knew that he must sound terribly desperate, but he could not help it. Together, he and the other Dimensionalist would be able to re-open the portals. Then, with the tome that Gaknar had used to facilitate Tharizdune's seizure of the host body, he would find a way to evict the daemon from his newfound residence.

Dinim heard the sounds of the unfolding conflict: the battle calls of Arn and Naemmious, the angry declarations of the priests, the sickening sound of arrows penetrating flesh and the cries of the wounded. But he ignored all of these, focusing on the man before him. The other mage regarded him in turn, seeking to find out how he came to be here at this moment, to thwart his escape.

"Please, we do not have much time." The desperation in Dinim's voice must have done it, turned the man to his favor. The Cimmerean nodded and helped Dinim to his feet. The men stepped behind the pillar closest to the circle of portals and momentarily discussed their plan. They readied their spell components and then began their incantation.

Pulling Stalker free from its harness, Sirion began to make his way away from his companions. He had no plan, no strategy. All he knew was that he was no help to anyone by staying with them. He feared for Sorn, who had to get extremely close to the enemy in order to retrieve the book. He kept his gaze locked upon Gaknar, hoping that the sorcerer's attention would continue to be diverted by the skirmish erupting a short distance away from him. But the sorcerer's eyes were not on Arn and Naemmious, but on the comrades that Sirion had just left behind. And it was then that Sirion realized . . . saw Gaknar finish an incantation, the sorcerer's eyes riveted upon Triath, Laura, and Breesa. Sirion saw the small red bean fly past him towards his comrades. "Ah Hells," he swore as he quickened his pace. After a few moments he felt the blast at his back, the searing heat sweeping over him from behind, knocking him face first to the hard stone floor. It was hot, so hot. He fought to breathe. His companions suffered worse, much worse. He knew because he had been there before. Those other battles seemed like lifetimes ago, lifetimes belonging to another man, a harsher man. Not to say that he wasn't a harsh man now . . . so very harsh . . . and unforgiving.

The intense wave of heat passed over him, his back aching as though he was sunburned. He slowly stood, inspecting his weapon. Stalker was unscathed, it having been protected beneath Sirion's body. He chanced a look behind him and saw his friends also arising from the ground. Everyone seemed to be functioning, although he did not know the damage that had been sustained by each individual. Resolutely, he turned back to the enemy and moved towards Gaknar again. Laura would help his companions. It was her calling and she was good at it. If anyone could help them it was Laura.

Sirion approached the ceremonial area. The young man within the circle had risen to his feet and was slowly taking in the scene all around him. Sirion knelt into a crouch, Stalker gripped tightly in his palms, ready. Sirion looked about the area, swearing that he remembered having seen Gaknar across the way just moments before. Suddenly he heard movement behind him and he turned, finding himself face to face with Gaknar.

The two Dimensionalists intoned their incantation. Pale red runes circled them, and the yellow glow emanating from the portals was becoming brighter. Dinim marveled at the power they had called. They had pooled their strength and together they had been able to harness the power and use it. He felt buzzed, his body charged with a sensation he had never felt before. He had so much power . . . all at his disposal. He could do anything . . . everything that which he had the skill to do. The mages finished the incantation and once more, a wind was whipping about the room. And then the portals were open. Still ensconced within the circle, the newly arrived Tharizdune regarded the portals with an expression of surprise mixed with alarm. The young man began to make towards the periphery of the area. Dinim quickly realized that he meant to escape. However, before he could move, his Dimensionalist companion had left his side and was dashing into the circle. He grabbed Tharizdune, and threw him to the ground.

Sirion felt his eyes widen, but before he could develop any rational thought, Gaknar had him by the throat. Sirion struggled, but the man was unusually strong, having physical power that no ordinary mortal man could possibly possess. Sirion gasped, finding it increasingly difficult to catch his breath, and he groped ineffectually at the large clawed hand around his neck. Gaknar smiled at him evilly, and then Sirion felt something prick his neck where the sorcerer held him.

Sirion frowned, conjecturing the portent of that scratch, when he suddenly began to feel a rush throughout his body. Following it was pain, the type of agonizing pain he had felt only once before, many years ago when his uncle had shredded his body and left him for dead. Hatred for Sydonnia welled up within him, lending him strength, and despite the pain Sirion swung his staff. Sirion watched Gaknar's smile turn into a rictus of fury as Stalker struck. The sorcerer flew backward and landed on his back, the tome flying from his arms. Gaknar screeched his rage, flopping over onto his belly, scrabbling for the book that had fallen. But Sorn was there, scooping the book into his embrace, and as quickly as he had come, he was gone.

Dinim watched as the Dimensionalist grappled with Tharizdune. But the young man was strong . . . extremely so. The mage didn't have a chance. Yet, he continued to divert the daemon's attention, hoping to buy time for Dinim to begin the incantation that would send Tharizdune back home. Dinim felt his heart go out to the brave Dimensionalist. He could not restrain the realization that this man would be sacrificing himself for the good of the group . . . for the good of all of mankind. His respect for the Cimmerean grew a hundred-fold, and he felt pride for his race. A Cimmerean was doing this thing, something wonderful that would benefit multitudes of people everywhere.

Gaknar quickly returned his focus to Sirion, narrowing blood-red eyes that bore slits for pupils. Sirion tried to increase the distance between them, but his movements were sluggish, the pain from the poison continuing to grip him in its power. Gaknar was quick to recover. The sorcerer struck him, the razor-sharp claws burrowing into the flesh of his cheek. Sirion fell back, heavily falling to the floor. And then Gaknar was upon him. Once again, Sirion found himself with the sorcerer's hand around his throat, squeezing, slowly squeezing, until he could scarcely breathe. Sirion grasped Gaknar's arm, tried desperately to exert enough pressure so that the sorcerer would release him. He began to hear the sound of his heart beating, felt himself begin to slip . . . And suddenly he sensed someone there, another presence beside him. He heard the hiss of magical steel, heard it slice through flesh and bone. The arm in his hand became limp and unresisting, and it dropped to the ground. The air filled with a terrible shriek. Gaknar clutched the stump of his arm in his hand, the other half of his forearm and hand writhing on the ground. Sirion looked up to find Anya standing above them, sword in hand, heaving from the exertion.

Sirion clutched at his sister's pants leg, attempting to stand. Anya gripped his arm to help him, the other hand continuing to hold the sword brandished at Gaknar. The sorcerer's evil gaze returned to him and in that instant, Sirion knew that he was doomed. His instincts shouted at him to run, but his mind and body refused to obey. The sorcerer began to levitate from the ground, the voluminous black robes all around him fluttering in the winds that arose. Then Gaknar began to incant the words to a spell. Sirion's eyes widened as he felt something grip his trousers at the ankle. He looked down to find Gaknar's severed hand and forearm making its way up his body. Sirion grabbed at the hand, trying to dislodge it, but it would not release him, continuing to make its way towards his torso.

Dinim heard a scuffle behind him and turned to find Sorn standing there, the pale flesh of his face beaded in sweat. The other man nodded and held out his arms. Cradled within them was the tome, a huge book with thick leather binding and red runic designs. Dinim clasped Sorn's shoulder as he took the volume. Now it was his turn. He riveted his attention upon the book. He must concentrate, focus his energies and skills upon the tome before him. If the book could set Tharizdune free, it could also re-imprison him. Or so he hoped. Dinim cast a *Detect Magic* spell, hoping there were no locks or traps on the book. He thought not, since Sorn had retrieved it so shortly after Gaknar had used it. Gaknar had not had a chance to re-trap it, but it was possible the book had a spell on it that re-locked it after every use. Much to his dismay, the book was both locked and trapped. This was just great. Nothing ever came easily. Dinim looked up, wracking his brain on how to proceed. He could use a *Dispel Magic* spell, but he was loath to use his energy for it. "Damn," he whispered to himself.

Dinim felt a tap on his shoulder and turned to find Sorn still standing beside him. The half-Cimmerian nodded to the book. "Allow me to try." Dinim silently handed the book back over to the other man, both of them hunkering down to the ground. Sorn swept his hands over the leather binding and then the lock, examining the area closely. He then untied the drawstrings on the pouch at his waist and withdrew the tools of his trade. These were smaller than the usual, the mechanism on the book being much smaller than that upon the doors and chests that Sorn was most accustomed to dismantling. Quickly and efficiently, Sorn worked at the clip, carefully manipulating it so as not to set off the trap.

For a moment, Anyanka just stood there in disbelief. Sirion grappled with the hand and then Anya was attempting to dislodge it as well. But it was to no avail. Sirion cried out as the hand reached his neck, grimacing as it wrapped itself about his throat, his and Anya's efforts to dislodge it fruitless. Gaknar had levitated above and beyond them, his gaze locked upon their companions in the distance, his voice rasping yet another incantation. The hand squeezed and Sirion felt his windpipe begin to crush. The strength in that one hand was immense. He vaguely heard Anya sobbing at his side, her fingers continuing to seek purchase at his throat. The ground rose up to meet him and she fell with him at his side, her tears wetting his face. As the world began to darken at the periphery of his vision, Sirion felt the air above them compress and heard a clap of unseen energy. The hand released his throat abruptly. Sirion drew a strangled breath, the air rushing into his starving lungs.

Sirion panted for breath, opening his eyes to find Gaknar no longer above them. He struggled to sit upright, but felt a restraining hand at his shoulder. He looked into the shining eyes of his sister, noted her tear-streaked face, and placed his hand on top of hers. "I'll be fine now." He smiled at her, but his tone exhorted no argument. She released him and he righted himself. He then labored to rise from the ground, his body protesting at the abuse. Anya was there, and she helped him to his wavering feet. He bent to pick up Stalker and saw that the dismembered forearm and hand lay in several pieces on the ground at his feet. That must have been Anya's doing, but the sorcerer himself was nowhere to be seen.

Time seemed to slow down. Horrified at the events unfolding before his eyes, Dinim watched it all in slow motion, his heart disbelieving . . . it was the fall of the Wildrunners. Dinim watched as Triath released the power of his mind, a force made from the air itself. He watched it strike Gaknar and slam him into the ground. It appeared that Sirion had fallen and Anya hovered over him. He saw that Arn and Naemmious, no longer backed-up by the lady archer, were struggling in their fight with the remaining priests. Dramati seemed to be holding his own for now, but Dinim wondered how long that would last. Laura and Breesa, who had strayed too close to the skirmish, found themselves also fighting for their lives.

Dinim momentarily turned back to Sorn, the faelin continuing his work, sweat beading his pale brow. Inwardly, he urged the other man to make haste, feeling the time slipping away from them. His Dimensionalist companion continued to divert the attention of Tharizdune, but the fight was coming to a close. He was severely beaten and burned. His blood streaked the stone floor and had splattered the front of his robe, but it was almost indistinguishable against the crimson backdrop. One arm was broken and hung limply at his side. Once more, Tharizdune's fist connected with the mage's face. Blood sprayed from his nose and mouth and struck the daemon's face. Tharizdune licked what landed on his lips, the corners of his mouth turning up into a malicious grin.

Dinim heard the soft clink of metal. He looked back to Sorn to find that he had rid the tome of its trap and lock. Hurriedly, Dinim opened the book, flipping to the table of contents. Not finding one, he turned to the prologue and began to speed read. That was one of the many fine skills he had learned from his master. Picking out the information he needed, Dinim began to flip through the pages, quickly finding those he sought. Dinim then attempted to settle himself for a more thorough perusal. Yet, time continued to be of the essence. The Cimmerean would not last much longer, and then there would be nothing to keep Tharizdune within the circle.

Quickly, Sirion took in the scene. The winds in the hall had picked up once again, and despite his ignorance he was aware of the magically charged atmosphere. He saw Triath running across the hall to join Dinim and Sorn, who were situated not too far away from Anya and himself. Sirion felt a wave of relief pass over him. Sorn had been able to get the book to Dinim, and Triath was heading over to him to offer what protection he could. Sirion nodded to his sister and gestured towards their comrades. She nodded in return and the two quickly made their way to the others.

When Sirion and Anya reached their comrades, Triath was in a state of intense concentration, he making some type of attempt at using his powers. Dinim also was focused upon his own work, pouring over the large tome in his lap. Sorn stood over his friends, at the ready in case of any trouble. Sirion frowned, noticing that Laura and Breesa were not with them. Neither were Arn and Naemmious. Sirion was about to focus his energies upon locating them, when he noticed the boy coming towards them from within the circle of portals. His pale body was covered in blood, and Sirion was quick to realize that it was not his own. Momentarily he focused his gaze beyond the boy and saw the fallen form of a man upon the floor. It was the crimson-robed mage who had aided Gaknar in opening the portals. But those portals were open once more, the reason for the winds sweeping through the place.

Sirion stepped forward to meet the boy. Looking into his eyes, Sirion could see the daemon within. The unwavering gaze was murderous as it took in the ranger. As Tharizdune made to step beyond the bounds of the circle, Sirion stepped within, holding Stalker before him. Sirion swung his staff. Without even flinching, the daemon deflected the weapon. Sirion was horrified as his weapon spun out of his grip, landing several feet away. The power behind that parry was enormous. But he knew that he could not allow Tharizdune to leave the circle. He lunged at the boy and they grappled. But the struggle was only momentary. Before he knew it, Sirion was being lifted and thrown from the circle. He felt himself sailing through the air and then he was colliding into someone. They fell together, the hardness of the floor bruising his backside. He lifted himself and found that it was Anya whom he had hit. He then looked back towards Tharizdune. Sirion's heart sank. The daemon had walked beyond the circle. He did not know how they would possibly be able to get him back inside, especially considering that they had been unable to keep him within it to begin with.

"Dinim . . ." Dinim looked up when Sorn called his name, knowing that the man would not disturb him if it were not a matter of dire importance. He regarded Sorn inquiringly, and when he noticed the Cimmerean's attention drawn elsewhere, he looked in the same direction. Dinim felt his heart stop in his chest. Unimpeded, Tharizdune was walking towards him. Time seemed to slow down, and he could hear his last breath exit his chest. The daemon took another step . . . and then another . . . but then he was stopped. Tharizdune frowned. The daemon put his hands out, and they splayed across an invisible surface.

"This area is protected," Triath stated. "I don't know how long I can hold the shell, but for now we are safe." Dinim looked over at the other man. His expression bore traces of continued concentration, but other than that he seemed unaffected by the energy it must be taking him in order to hold the protective shell. Thanking the gods for creatures with strange abilities, he returned his focus to the book. He was close. All he had to do was find the incantation that Gaknar had used to invite Tharizdune into the host body. He had learned many things, skimming through the pages of the book. That boy had been a pure soul . . . unblemished by the harshness of the world. He had been the epitome of all that was good. Dinim balked at the injustice. It was a shame for the world to lose something as wonderful as this boy had been.

Tearing his gaze away from the daemon boy, Sirion looked beyond the immediate vicinity, towards the area where the rest of the group had been fighting the priests. He scanned the area, and saw Dramati sniffing over the fallen priests. Then he saw Laura crouching over a fallen Arn, Naemmious standing over them protectively, and Breesa at his side. "Triath, the others are in trouble."

Triath looked out where Sirion indicated. He then shook his head sadly. "There isn't anything I can do to help them. No one may enter the shell if they were not within the area of effect to begin with. Not only that, but all of my energy and concentration has to remain upon the shell or it will dissipate."

Sirion nodded. He knew what he had to do. He spied Stalker lying a few feet away. He would grab the weapon on his way over to the others. Sirion looked to where Dinim and Sorn sat poring over the book. For now they would be protected by Triath's power.

Before anyone could say anything to try to stop him, Sirion had stepped beyond the boundaries of the shell. He ran over to Stalker and swept up the weapon. He then made his way over to Naemmious, Laura, Breesa, and Arn. "Sirion!" He heard the voice of Anya behind him and grinned to himself. He should have known that she would follow him.

When the twosome approached they heard the agitated protestations of Arn. "Let me up already. I am going to be fine." He swatted at Laura's hands as he rose into a sitting position.

"No, you are not, Arn. That potion has only restored a fraction of your vitality. You are allowing it to give you a false sense of security."

"What do you want me to do? Keep lying here like a dead fish?"

"No. I want you to be careful. We need to get back to the others. We are easy targets out here."

"We came to help you back," Sirion said as he approached Laura and Arn. Dramati had already come over to greet him. Through the link, Sirion could feel Dramati's relief that he was all right. Sirion felt the same, running his hands through the thick fur around the corubis' neck.

Naemmious grinned. "It's good to see another friendly face."

"I bet. How are you holding up?" By the look on the big man's face, Sirion had his answer, but Naemmious wasn't about to let on to Laura about his true condition.

"Better than Arn."

Arn frowned at Naemmious and then rose to his feet. "Shut your gob, Naemmious."

"Both of you be quiet," said Anya. "This isn't the time or the place. Let's just get back to the others."

Sirion was about to mention the situation in which Triath, Sorn, and Dinim had found themselves when he heard something behind him, like a clap of thunder. The sound emanated from where he and Anya had come. *Damn . . . Sirion* turned in place, his fear manifest. He was just in time to see a sheet of flame shroud Triath's protective shell. For a few moments it burned, and then began to die, the fire having nothing to feed it. *Hells, I hope Dinim is ready . . .*

Dinim looked up from the tome, his heart pounding wildly. He felt the urge to flee, to hide with the tome somewhere, removed from his companions. He knew it would mean leaving the sanctuary of the shell, but it would fall to the daemon one way or another, and he did not want to be there to experience it. He had heard the agony in Triath's scream when the last spell had hit the shell, and he did not believe that the man could withstand the onslaught much longer. Dinim stood with the tome, leaned into Sorn, and whispered into his ear. He saw Tharizdune concentrating upon another spell. Now was his chance. Clutching the book tightly beneath his arm, Dinim fled into the darkness beyond the shell, stopping only when he reached the adjacent portal.

Dinim crouched behind the portal, catching his breath. Then he sat, cross-legged, upon the ground. He placed the tome before him, opening it once more to the appropriate page. Dinim reached into his spell components' pouch and pulled out a smaller bag. He opened it and poured the contents into his hand. Dinim muttered the words from the book as he poured the crystal sand from his palm onto the ground, creating a circle around himself. The sand began to glow eerily green and the grains began to melt together into a liquid flowing mass. Dinim held his fore and middle fingers into the molten crystal and then began to inscribe runic symbols into the air before him. Concentrating deeply, he sought to remember the words he had read from the tome. He cringed to think what could happen if he said the wrong word, or even just misspoke a word.

Sirion and his companions quickly made their way back toward the rest of the group. He saw Tharizdune prepare for another assault upon Triath's shell. He could only hope that Triath could hold up for a while longer. Sirion also saw Dinim leave the vicinity of the attack, probably figuring that he would be safer the further away that he got. Tharizdune was not aware of the mage's departure, as he was too busy concentrating upon exacting his revenge. Although, if he had known that the object of his desire was being taken elsewhere, he would definitely have followed it.

Sirion found himself falling back behind the rest of the group, pondering their situation. They could not just walk up to the shell and ask Triath to let them back in. That would give Tharizdune the opening that he needed. Not to mention that they would be fodder to feed his healthy appetite for destruction. Suddenly, Sirion began to feel the hairs on the back of his neck begin to rise. It was then that he remembered . . . he and Anya had never found the body of Gaknar. *Damn* . . . Sirion turned in place, Stalker battle-ready. A few feet away he saw Gaknar, his clawed hand held before him as he began to cast his spell, his few remaining priests arrayed behind him.

"'Ware!" Sirion cried out. But the group was ready. Naemmious and Arn spun around, swords drawn. Anya shot her first volley of arrows at Gaknar. Much to her dismay, the arrows merely struck him and fell to his feet. Sirion heard her curse eloquently in Hinterlic as he joined Naemmious and Arn in their rush towards the priests. It was then that the spell was loosed, the energies coalescing into several small bolts of lightning, arcing outward from Gaknar's fingertips. Sirion made an attempt to dodge the incoming missiles, but it was too late. He found himself being hit, the bolts electrifying him as they passed through his body. Sirion felt his muscles contract spasmodically and then his body hit the ground.

Sirion opened his eyes, blinking them rapidly. He must have blacked out . . . Suddenly he heard another concussive blast and lifted his head from the ground. He saw a shower of fiery meteors striking the protective surface of Triath's shell. From within, Sirion could hear Triath's agonizing screams as he struggled to hold the shell. He scrambled to his feet, wincing in pain. He noticed that Gaknar and his priests were no longer there. Beside him, Anya also rose to her feet, as well as Naemmious and Laura. However, neither Arn nor Breesa moved from their places on the ground.

Laura rushed over to the young woman, turning her over onto her back.

She leaned over, placing her head upon the girl's chest. She then put her fingers to the Breesa's neck. Sirion heard a strangled cry emerge from Laura's mouth as she put her hands to her face and began to sob.

"He's dead." Sirion turned to the sound of Naemmious' voice. The big man knelt at Arn's side, his eyes wide with disbelief. Sirion felt an ache in his chest. His head begin to spin. No, this could not be happening. His friends were dying, and there was nothing that he could do about it. He felt the ache begin to encompass his chest and move up to his throat. He quelled the urge to cry out his grief, his anger at the injustice of what was happening.

Once more Sirion heard a sound. But this time it was different. It was almost inaudible to his ears, but Dramati seemed to hear it with no trouble at all, his head turning once more in the direction of Triath, Sorn, and Dinim. Sirion turned that way as well. The sight that met his eyes almost stilled his heart in his chest. The shell had come down. Triath knelt upon the ground, his head in his hands. Gaknar strode, unimpeded, towards the man. Tharizdune, seeing that the tome was not there, made his way in the direction that Dinim had left.

Dinim heard the shell come down. That meant that Tharizdune would be coming for him. He had very little time left, but that was alright. He was ready. Upon inscribing the fourth rune, the eerie glow turned golden, shedding a greater light. Dinim narrowed his eyes, trying to filter it out. He inscribed the last rune, his voice fading away as he completed it. All nine glowed in the space before him, beautifully golden, shimmering and wavering with energy. He breathed in a deep breath, knowing what he had to do next. It would be difficult. He would have to pronounce what was written in the book in a contrasting fashion, undo what Gaknar had done. He would have to start from the end and make his way to the beginning . . . every word, every gesture, every nuance. Dinim closed his eyes and raised his arms upward as though beseeching the heavens. Others had suffered dire consequences doing what he now attempted . . . casting a spell backwards. He hoped that Sorn would come through and tell Triath the role that he would have to play. He hoped that his companions would reach him before Tharizdune did.

Sirion ran to the scene. Gaknar was about to attack Triath, when Sorn emerged from the shadows cast by the portal. He threw himself at Gaknar, stabbing downward with his dagger. The cult-master screamed, arching backward in an attempt to dislodge Sorn. Triath scrambled out of the way, finally making it to his feet and running in the direction that Tharizdune had taken to find Dinim. Sorn pulled his dagger from Gaknar's back and stabbed again. Once more the sorcerer screamed in agony and then fell. Sorn leapt away before he could be pinned by the body, and landed on his knees a couple of feet away.

Sirion, Anya, Naemmious, and Laura entered the scene. Sorn followed them as they passed through, hoping that they were not too late. Within moments Sirion could see Dinim encircled within a ring of molten gold, his rich voice raised in an incantation. Strange words passed from between his lips, the words of magic . . . ancient magic. The air felt unusually charged, the presence of magic so strong it made his body involuntarily quake. From out of the darkness before Dinim, Sirion saw the form of the daemon boy appear. "No," Sirion called out, arm outstretched as though to stop what was about to happen, his legs carrying him forward, just outside of the glowing circle of portals. Behind him, he heard the labored breathing of his sister, Naemmious, Sorn, and Laura. Everything seemed to happen all at once, everyone acting upon impulse, in desperation, a last attempt at survival.

Dinim finished his incantation. Winds swept through the scene . . . the winds of powerful magic. And then Triath was there, at his side, his eyes glazed with concentration. Suddenly, Tharizdune was thrown back, back, back, until he was once more within the circle of the portals. The daemon boy looked up from the floor where he had been thrown. Upon realizing where he was, he quickly jumped to his feet. But it was too late. The magicks rushed to him, circled him with sparkling light. Faster and faster they spun, and then, from out of the host body began to emerge the mist they had witnessed when they first made it to the hall.

Tharizdune shrieked in rage. The daemon struggled to retain custody of the host body, clinging to it with all of his strength. Then, in retaliation, he began to cast a spell. Dinim realized the imminent danger, but he was in no position to do anything about it. The raw energy being whipped about the place was sure to make the spell misfire. He hoped that it would not have an effect greater than the original spell would have had.

Sirion stared in fascination at the events unfolding before him. He could feel the power eddying all about him. He looked upon Dinim with new eyes, now realizing that he had judged the other man wrongly. Dinim had placed himself at great risk to accomplish what was now being wrought, and at the end of this, Sirion would go to thank him personally. Then, from behind the portal to the right of him, Sirion saw the form of Gaknar. The sorcerer focused upon one of the other portals, and Sirion knew that he meant to destroy it.

Dinim watched, transfixed, as Tharizdune was pulled from the host body. Just before the boy slumped to the ground, his spell was cast. The thick mist that was Tharizdune began to be pulled within the portals leading back to his home world. The spell interacted with the energies eddying about within the circle. Suddenly, Dinim felt the charged atmosphere become activated. He looked in the direction of the new disturbance to find Gaknar at the periphery of the circle, casting his own spell. "Fool!" shouted Dinim as he leaped away from the circle.

Gaknar's spell hit the mass of energy that had formed after Tharizdune's miscast spell. Without warning, a small vortex appeared within the center of the circle. The light emanating from the portals went out, Tharizdune having been pulled back into his world. However, the area became only slightly dimmer, the wild magic spiraling out of control creating a light of its own. The spinning, colliding spells created a cloud that enveloped Gaknar, his body disintegrating within moments. The cloud of un-harnessed magical energy moved towards the vortex, somehow attracted to it. The vortex increased in size and intensity. Instinctively, everyone lowered themselves near the ground, seeking protection.

A loud shriek encompassed the scene and the spiraling cloud of magical energy reacted with the vortex. An arm-like projection emerged from the twisting mass, reaching randomly. The beam caught Sirion full-force, encompassing him within its intense energy. He screamed in agony, the magic washing over him. Every muscle in his body contracted, the pain excruciating. He felt the magic course through him, touch those deepest parts of him that he had kept locked inside himself. It touched the essence of him . . . that untamed, wild part of him that he had developed over the past several decades. It touched his animal nature and let it come forth. He felt himself changing, his physical form altering. The pain ripped through him and his mind could no longer comprehend, could no longer deal with the torment.

CHAPTER 10

It was before dawn when Adrianna awakened. She lay there silently thinking of what it was that had awakened her at such an early hour. She looked all about her without moving. She saw the rest of the group still sleeping with the exception of Armond, who stood watch over them in these early hours of the morning. She regarded him as he stood at the edge of the camp. He seemed to have a tense expectancy about him . . . almost as though he waited for something. Adrianna frowned and crawled out from beneath her blankets. It was then that the world began to shake.

Adrianna cowered upon the ground in fear. *What is this thing that is happening? The world itself is moving . . .* In near panic she looked up to see that Armond, too, had crouched low to the ground. Others of the band were waking, and she heard Tianna call out in a fear-filled voice. Adrianna began to look all about her, and then up into the still-dark sky. The shaking of the world paused. Dartanyen made his way over to Armond. Within the wan light cast by the moons, she saw something swirling about within the darkness of the heavens. She squinted her eyes and could barely see what had, at first, been imperceptible. It was color. Varying waves of color eddied and flowed within the darkness above.

Adrianna clutched at the ground again as it began to tremor anew. She heard Bussi and Amethyst curse as the shaking continued. Unlike the last time, the tremors did not cease. Instead, they became worse with each passing moment. The trees began to shake and all about them the rocks and boulders began to shift due to the power of the movement of the world. Louder and louder the quaking became and she could hear the crashing of the mountains all about them. Fear coursed through Adrianna as she huddled there upon her bedding, feeling the movement of the ground beneath her and thinking that it would be torn asunder. But, through it all, her mind whispered to her of momentous events taking place. She felt the shift of the energies of the world . . . the beginning of a new era. Adrianna heard screaming and realized that it was herself before she blacked out.

Adrianna awoke to find Tianna kneeling above her, the priestess' cool hands upon her face and forehead. In the light of the new dawn she saw Armond and Dartanyen speaking in an excited tone, Amethyst and Zorg standing by in the distance. She looked up into the sky, half expecting it to be bathed in the colors she had seen in the darkness not long ago. She saw nothing but the ordinary colors associated with the dawn, and everything appeared to be normal . . . as though nothing had happened.

"I was worried for you." Tianna's voice interrupted her thoughts. "I heard you screaming one moment, and then suddenly you stopped. I ran over here to find that you had passed out. Are you all right?"

"I think so." Adrianna replied. However, she found that she could not be entirely sure. Before she had blacked out, she had felt a pressure at her temples. It had been a strange sensation accompanied by even stranger perceptions that she could not entirely recall. She had felt something . . . something sinister . . . and it frightened her. Adrianna grunted to herself and began to rise. Tianna sat back on her heels to give her space. As Adrianna rose, she was suddenly assaulted by a horrendous headache that caused her to cry out and put hands to her temples. Adriana lay herself back down rather gingerly, not wanting to disturb her head any more than what she had already. Then Tianna was above her once more, feeling at her skull and whispering the words to a prayer. Adrianna closed her eyes and began to feel a healing magic rush through her.

Only a short time later, Adrianna was loading Sethanon. The next couple of days would be the most difficult, for they were to pass through the portion of the pass that was known to be the rockiest. It was not uncommon for a lloryk or larian to lose his footing and twist his ankle, or even to wrench a knee and fall. They must take care and travel slowly so as to save their animals, and quite possibly even themselves. Adrianna saw that Zorg was moving about with some stiffness, but he seemed to be managing rather well. She glanced over in Sabian's direction and saw him loading his own beast for travel. She continued to be angry with him. The spell that he had cast had been one she had never seen before. It had been powerful and had possibly saved their lives. The trolags had been many, and possibly would have overcome them. With Sabian's spell, the creatures had borne no chance. But Sabian had put the group at risk. He should have thought of some other way to help during the skirmish.

The group traveled up the trail once more, and by the middle of the day, it had changed drastically. The trees had been gradually thinning out as they had journeyed over the days, but now they were all gone. Before them lay a narrow defile upon which only two horses could travel abreast. Along each side of the trail were walls of sheer rock. A long time ago, a mighty river must have cut this pass through the Ratik Mountains, and here at the highest part of the mountain was where the pass was set lowest within it.

The larian picked their way through the large rocks and boulders lying out upon the path. Dartanyen frowned, not remembering the trail to be so onerous as this. He never recalled boulders so large as these, nor so many.

Then it hit him. The shake! The shaking of the ground they had felt that morning had resulted in this! The force of it had caused the steep slopes to let loose these portions of themselves that they now walked amongst. Dartanyen looked about at his comrades and saw Armond looking about as well. Upon capturing his gaze, he saw that he, too, knew what had happened within the pass. The knowledge of whence the boulders had come, however, made him a little jumpy. If these could fall, so could others. He shook his head. He refused to worry about such things. As long as the ground was quiet, the mountains would not fall.

The band traveled onwards. Later in the day they encountered a rather large pile of rocks and boulders over which they had to traverse, for it was so large there was no way around it. It took them a long time to go over it, their mounts having to be careful where they stepped. They were glad once they were over the pile, and they hoped that there were none others like it. They walked for a short while longer and it was then that the world began to shake once more.

It was unlike that which had occurred that morning. It was not nearly as powerful, but it was enough. The ground shook and the mountains responded. Loose rock and debris began to tumble down the steep slopes as people, lloryk, and larian scattered. Adrianna let go of Sethanon's reins, ran towards the left slope, and was able to fit herself within a narrow crevasse before the boulders began to fall. The avalanche was over in moments, the shaking of the ground having stopped. After the dust cleared, Adrianna stepped out of her haven to find the path altered. She was glad to see that Zorg, Dartanyen, and Tianna were unhurt. They found Bussi lying partly beneath a pile of rocks, which they all worked to remove, save Tianna, who was busy mending the hurts of Amethyst and Armond. Upon digging up Bussi, Tianna also used her prayers upon the halfen. However, due to lack of strength and power, she was unable to help him much. She instructed him to lie still until morning, when she would be able to aid him further.

Dartanyen and Armond gathered up those larian that were still about and staked them near the camp. Two of the larian were missing, but no one wanted to stray far from camp in search of them for fear that they could get stuck in an avalanche without the rest of the group. All through the night the ground grumbled and trembled minutely. Fortunately, only small pebbles and dust responded. In the morning the group set off once again, despite their lack of sleep, and traveled as fast as they could. Much to everyone's relief, they caught up to the two missing animals at mid-day. The beasts were pleased to see them and were caught without a fuss. Tianna inspected them and were declared fit.

The rest of the day passed uneventfully although the ground continued to groan and tremor every now and then. It wasn't until near evening that their path crossed with that of a troupe of halfen miners. The group stood before a rocky pile similar to the one they had climbed the day before. They regarded it with trepidation, remembering what had happened after that climb. It was then that they heard voices coming from the other side of the pile. They stood there, waiting, until finally they saw a short man standing upon the top of the hill of rocks. Eight others joined him as he began his descent. Very carefully the man picked his way down the hill, looking warily at them all the while, his comrades following closely behind. Adrianna knew that they must be Morden, the halfen of the mountains. Most probably, they lived nearby, and were being severely affected by the quakes.

Finally, the two groups stood across from one another, each looking upon the other curiously. It was immediately apparent to them that the halfen were miners, for they wore the tools of their trade about their waists and within their overflowing packs. It was a wonder they did not drop everything as they moved. Dartanyen was the first to speak. "Good eve to you all, and how do you go?"

"Our travels are well, although a bit hazardous considering the falling rock and all," replied the Morden leader. The hair on his head was thick and very dark, as was that on his face. His complexion was pale and he had a stocky build, larger than Bussi, who was at least a foot shorter. He spoke politely but continued to be wary, for he had taken note of Bussi and seemed to be taken aback by his presence within the group. Bussi seemed not to care about the others' scrutiny, for he had learned long ago that no others of his race seemed to like him all that much. They seemed to be disturbed by his vocation as well as his violent nature and tendency to rage while in the midst of battle. Bussi just stood there, pretending to pay the others no heed.

"But how goes the trail that which you have recently traveled?" asked Dartanyen, pointing up the hill of rocks and into the direction from whence the halfen had come.

"Ah, the trail . . . it is not good. You would do best to turn back now, for great peril lies upon the path back yonder." The halfen spoke in a knowing voice, raising a dark bushy eyebrow and looking from Dartanyen to the rest of the group.

"Thank you much, stranger. We will ponder upon your words. Good journey, and may the sun shine upon you."

"And to you." With that, the leader motioned to his comrades with a raised hand, and the troupe passed by them, each Morden nodding to Dartanyen and the rest as he passed. The group returned the gesture and watched as the halfen walked from out of their sight.

"Come, let us camp here for the night. We will traverse this hill tomorrow morning," said Dartanyen as he patted his larian heartily upon the neck.

Everyone agreed with him and followed his suggestion. The night passed without incident, although the ground still continued to grouch and grumble. Adrianna tossed and turned in her sleep in response and awoke periodically within the night. In the morning she found that she was virtually un-rested. Her bones and muscles ached and the sockets of her eyes felt gritty. She wrapped her cloak tightly about herself and ate a meager breakfast.

The group led their mounts up the rocky hill, everyone taking care so as not to make a wrong step that would send themselves and anyone following back to the bottom. A few hours later the group stood safely on the other side of the pile of rock debris. Before them lay the downward curving remainder of the Ratik Pass, littered profusely with rocks of varying sizes and shapes. Their spirits began to lift, for the curve meant that this would be the last leg of their journey through the pass. The group resumed their jaunt, Dartanyen taking his customary place at the head of the group, the rest following haphazardly behind.

Adrianna rode in misery. She had become ill. It must have been the change in climate and altitude when they had traveled up the mountain. Despite her ability to endure most environmental changes rather well, it was not unknown for her to suffer from illness as a result every now and then. Not only that, but she was unused to this much physical exertion, and she did not sleep well in the nights. That, too, may have contributed to her body's weakness. So, she was forced to ride astride Sethanon, despite the hardship that it would cause him. She became limp with fatigue, allowing Sethanon the rein to move of his own accord with the rest of the group. Tianna had tried to help her feel better with some herbal tea, but Adrianna continued to feel wretched.

In spite of her weakened state, Adrianna was the first to hear the tremor within the ground. She looked up, listening and hoping it would not increase in magnitude. After a moment, she saw Dartanyen and Armond also respond to the quake, one that, she now knew, would not dwindle away as many of the others had. "Another shake!" Dartanyen shouted. 'Ware and take cover!"

Once again the group scattered as the mountains began to tremble all around them once more. To her dismay, Adrianna saw no refuge for herself, and thus stayed astride Sethanon. She would try her best to dodge any falling rock . . . Then they came, hundreds and thousands of pebbles, rocks, and boulders tumbling down the slopes. Adrianna gave Sethanon free rein so as he may use his animal instincts in order to possibly save them. Adrianna just closed her eyes and lay herself flat upon his back, hoping to reduce her chances of falling off of him, and making sure that he did not become encumbered with her weight, unbalancing him as he worked to dodge the oncoming rock.

Adrianna clutched at Sethanon's mane and pressed her cheek to his sweaty neck. She wrapped her legs tightly about his barrel and could feel his muscles contract and relax as he maneuvered them between the missiles of flying rock. She heard him grunt in pain as the sharp rocks hit him, and she, too, cringed when they happened to hit her as well. Her fear kept her from opening her eyes to see how the others fared, if she could see them at all through the cloud of dust she was sure hung in the air. Suddenly the avalanche stopped. In the resultant near silence she heard her lloryk breathing heavily from his exertion. She opened her eyes to find the cloud of dust she had been expecting. Upon breathing it in, she began to cough and had to bring her cloak to her nose and mouth.

When finally the dust cleared she first saw the altered landscape, and then the forms of Dartanyen and his larian picking among the piles of rock. Adrianna rode her weary lloryk over to him to see him standing over the prone form of one of the larian half-buried in debris. Her eyes widened in fear. It was Tianna's pale beast. The poor animal was dead. Where was Tianna? Dartanyen was already scanning the area and he called out for others of the group, his tone full of fear. They heard a faint reply to their left. They turned to see Amethyst and Armond making their way over to them. A momentary wave of relief washed over Adrianna. Zorg and Bussi, too, were picking their ways towards them. However, Tianna and Sabian did not emerge from the rubble lying all around them. Once more, Adrianna's heart leapt in fear.

They began an all about search, calling out for Tianna and Sabian as they went, receiving no reply from either party as they scanned every square inch of the surrounding area. They found the carcass of Zorg's lloryk not far from that of Tianna's larian and the other animals had been able to keep themselves unharmed with the exception of Armond's bronze larian, who had hurt his leg.

Finally they found Tianna, who had been calling out to them in so soft and weak a voice that they had been unable to hear her. Zorg gently picked her up from the ground and carried her to a place clear of rubble. Adrianna stayed with her as the men and Amethyst went in search of Sabian. Tianna appeared to have a few bruised ribs and her ankle was broken. Adrianna tried her best to bind the ankle under the instruction of Tianna, who spoke in broken sentences. It hurt the woman to breathe, much less speak, and with each movement she cried out in her pain. Adrianna was afraid that a rib may be broken and hurting Tianna's delicate insides, but the healer remained adamant that Adrianna bind her even still.

Adrianna had just finished administering to Tianna when Zorg carried the limp form of Sabian over to them. The young faelin's face was pale and his breathing was very shallow. He bore blood upon his right temple and the area all around it was discolored. "Found him buried beneath several pounds of rock," said Zorg as he lay Sabian gently upon the ground near Tianna.

The young woman rose as though to go to him, but Adrianna pushed her back down. "No, Tianna. You have not the strength."

"But I must. He is severely injured." Tianna protested.

Adrianna looked up at Dartanyen indecisively. After a moment of thought, he nodded his head. Adrianna released Tianna and the other woman crawled over to Sabian. Tianna got to her knees and then settled onto her heels, placing her hands upon Sabian's head. He looked at her out of heavy-lidded eyes full of pain and weariness. She closed her eyes and remained in that position for a long time. Finally, with a deep sigh, the priestess dropped her hands to her sides and slumped her shoulders. "I can't do it. I just can't do it." Adrianna went to Tianna and knelt down to face her.

Seeing the expression upon Tianna's face, Adrianna wrapped her arms about the woman and held her close. "It is all right. You are weak . . ."

"What kind of healer am I if I can not help those who need me?" Tianna continued speaking as though Adrianna had not spoken.

Adrianna looked to Sabian. He seemed a little better than before, but he remained very weak. "Come, follow me over here so that I may give you some tea to help warm you," said Adrianna as she tugged at Tianna's elbow. Adrianna supported a limp Tianna to the small fire that Dartanyen had built with the help of the sticks and twigs he had found lying about. She then returned to Sabian. His eyes were closed in sleep. She helped him onto his bed pallet, laid a thick blanket over him, and wrapped it all around and under him so as to keep out the cold.

For a time they rested there, but then decided that they should move on so as to get themselves out of this corridor of rock as soon as possible. Zorg distributed the loads from Sethanon and the blue lloryk mare equally onto the other larian. Tianna would ride Sethanon while Sabian was strapped to the blue. Despite her illness, Adrianna walked. She refused to ride Sethanon with Tianna, afraid that her weight would cause him to misstep upon the treacherous ground. So, they moved slowly and carefully, hoping to be out of the pass sometime that night without any more mishap. The path began to slope downwards, signaling that their journey was close to an end. They passed a cave as they walked. It appeared that it might have once been hidden before the quakes came. Adrianna's nose picked up a strange and unfamiliar odor as they passed, and the hairs at the back of her neck began to prickle. "Dart . . ."

Before she could complete his name, the oorgs were rushing towards them from the mouth of the cave. They were large creatures, wearing animal hides and pieces of metal that served as armor. Their hair was thick and black, so dirty that the strands stuck together to form ropes. Their greenish brown flesh sported wart-like bumps, and the lower jaws protruded. The largest of the four oorgs pulled his lips back to display gruesome yellowed canines. Then, wielding clubs and battle-axes, they attacked the weary group of riders.

The lloryk pulled at their reins and reared, their precious burdens sliding from their backs. Adrianna struggled to retain a hold on Sethanon as Dartanyen, Armond, Zorg, and Bussi all kicked themselves into action. Zorg drew his massive blade just as the largest of the four oorgs was upon him. Dartanyen drew his bow and was shooting an arrow quicker than Adrianna thought possible. Adrianna was forced to let Sethanon go, unable to soothe him, and he followed the other animals down the path.

Adrianna swallowed heavily as she quickly scanned the scene before her, fighting the fear that arose within her. The creatures were huge, and would be powerful adversaries against the weakened group. She saw Amethyst throw a dagger at the oorg that Dartanyen shot with his arrow, and saw Bussi as he ducked beneath another one, savagely slicing between the creature's legs as he did so. The beast screamed in agony. Armond faced off with another of the oorgs, swinging his blades in an awesome display of skill. Adrianna began to try to concentrate, seeking to rid her mind of the distraction all around her . . . the shouts of her comrades, the scream of the larian, and the raving of the savage monsters that had attacked them without mercy. She brought the magic to her, caressing the strands of energy, manipulating it . . . bending it to do her bidding. It answered her call, flowing to her without hesitation, and then waited for her to use it, to guide it to her will. A stream of fire erupted from her fingertips, striking the beast standing above the prone form of Zorg, who had been weakened from his encounter with the black tentacle and had fallen before the oorg leader. It screamed with pain, clutching at its chest with both hands. Dartanyen put an arrow into it, closely followed by another. The creature fell to the ground and writhed for a moment before it died.

Bussi sought to kill the oorg that he had neutered. He rushed towards the monster, and in slow motion, Adrianna watched as the creature swept a massive forearm towards the halfen and then lift upward as it came into contact with his body. The impact lifted Bussi from the ground. He fell a few feet away from the beast. He did not get up. Adrianna saw that Amethyst had come face-to-face with the oorg she had struck with her dagger. As she faced the creature, her short-sword was pulled from her grasp and turned upon her with a clumsy, but effective, jab in her direction. Her eyes widened in astonishment as she clutched at her side and went to her knees. Adrianna cried out and looked frantically about. She saw Armond, continuing to spar with his enemy. She saw his lips moving, and when she strained to hear, she heard him singing. Then, he was rushing his opponent, his swords glowing a pale red. The creature screamed in agony as the blades cut into him. After a moment the scent of scorched flesh assailed her nostrils. Adrianna couldn't believe what she had just seen. Armond had cast a spell. He was a Talent. Why had he not mentioned his calling before?

Suddenly, as Adrianna stood there watching the fight, the oorg who had been fighting Bussi clubbed Armond in the back. Adrianna screamed as Armond fell from the blow. Fortunately, so did the monster, which he had seared with his blades. It fell on top of him. Adrianna began to concentrate once more, urging the magic to come to her . . . and then the fire was sprouting from her fingertips once more, striking the creature that stood over Armond. The oorg screamed and dropped to the ground. Adrianna wavered and was about to fall when Dartanyen caught her. He had dispatched the oorg who had struck Amethyst and had come to assist Adrianna if she needed his help. Thankfully, he was relatively unharmed, and was able to ease her onto the ground. He could feel her fever as he touched her hands, and wondered how ill she really was.

Dartanyen and Armond set about collecting their comrades from the battlefield. Armond was bruised from his clubbing but was otherwise unscathed. Amethyst was able to make her way over to Adrianna unassisted, her hand at her side. The blood seeped from the wound and was soaking her blouse. Adrianna tried to find some cloth to bind the wound, but found herself too weak to move much. She felt guilty, not having suffered any physical damage from the battle, but unable to help her injured comrades.

The group was forced to make camp for the night. Dartanyen and Armond searched the oorg cave to be sure no others lurked there. Then the two came back to set up camp. During the skirmish, Tianna had been able to pull herself and Sabian out of harm's way after they had been roughly deposited onto the ground when the larian decided to flee. Since then, Sabian had been vomiting. It was very obvious that he was not well. The head wound that he had suffered was making him extremely ill. He was unable to rise and his skin tone was very pale. If they did not find help soon, Adrianna was afraid that he would die.

Tianna was able to tend to the wounds of Amethyst, Zorg and Bussi. However, due to her weakened state, she was still unable to call upon her goddess for magical healing. But at least she could use her skills as an herbalist. She cleaned their wounds and used her medicinal ointments and salves. She made them a medicinal tea that would help ease their pains. She tried to help Sabian once more, and cried when she could not. Adrianna held her as best she could, but found that she was not entirely able. She felt so sick, and so tired that she felt like she would fall over at any moment.

The next day, Adrianna awoke to the sound of hooves on loose rock. She groggily opened her eyes to see Sethanon standing above her. He put his head down and blew gently onto her forehead. Slowly she sat upright. She looked around the camp and noted the late hour of the morning. Many people were still sleeping; weak from the trials they had suffered.

"I got up this morning and decided to have a look down the trail. I found them not far from here."

Adrianna turned towards the sound of Dartanyen's voice. He looked tired, and Adrianna's heart went out to him. Much of the responsibility of setting up camp and keeping watch throughout the night had fallen to him. The person lying on the sleeping roll next to hers stirred and then sat up. "Damnation," said Armond. "I overslept. We had better get going. I don't want to spend any more time than what is necessary in these mountains."

"I agree," said Dartanyen. But I am not sure that the others are able." Dartanyen looked at the rest of the band, sleeping under their blankets. He took in the pale faces, the blood on the cloths that Tianna had used the evening before, the pot of cold tea resting over a pile of ash from the evening fire.

"Well, we should at least make the effort. It would not behoove us to stay here."

Dartanyen nodded. "I know. Let's be sure that the animals are loaded and then wake the rest of the group. Let them rest as long as possible."

Armond nodded and the two of them set to work. Adrianna packed away Tianna's pot and medicines while the men re-distributed the load of the larian. Amethyst awoke with the activity going on around her. She packed her sleeping roll away and then went about rousing the rest of the group. Strangely, no one protested, despite their hurts. Perhaps they had not the energy. Or maybe they saw no point in grumbling; they wanting to be out of the pass just as much as the next person.

With rope from the packs, Armond and Dartanyen worked to tie Sabian onto the back of the blue lloryk mare, and Zorg upon Sethanon, as they were the two weakest members of the group. That done, the weary group set off along the path once more. It was soon that Adrianna began to feel weak and drained. Her head pounded mercilessly, and she was cold, even beneath the thick fabric of her cloak. She was fevered, she knew. She walked beside Sethanon, her hand clutching his dark mane. She leaned against the solidness of the animal and he looked back at her with concerned eyes. It was almost like he understood that she was ill, and that she needed his strength.

In front of her, Tianna walked alongside the lloryk mare carrying Sabian. Her shoulders were slumped and her head down. She walked slowly, her hand across her ribs. Adrianna could see that every step pained her. In front of Tianna walked Amethyst, her hand also across her torso, holding the wound she had sustained during the fight with the oorgs. The girl had her head bowed, her thick black hair hanging in tangles around her face. At the front of the pathetic procession walked Dartanyen and Bussi. Dartanyen held the reins of his larian and those of Sabian's dark-blond beast. Bussi limped beside him, grumbling every so often. Behind Adrianna was Armond, bringing up the rear with his larian. She wondered about him, what powers he possessed. She wanted to know about his Talent, but had not the energy to even turn around to look at him, much less speak to him.

The group walked through the day. Adrianna did not realize the passage of time . . . the concept seemed to have become irrelevant. The only thing upon which she could concentrate was the placement of one foot in front of the other. The rock beneath her feet seemed to impair her every step. As the day progressed, she began to stumble more often and she began to limp. When the group stopped to take a meal, Adrianna would have none of it, waving away Armond's hand when he offered her the bread. Vaguely, she heard Dartanyen telling her that she had to eat, but she did not have the energy to reply.

The day passed uneventfully. Dartanyen pushed the group, knowing that the end of their journey within the pass was close. He worried about Adrianna, who did not seem to even hear him anymore, Sabian, who did not awaken from his comatose sleep, and Zorg, who had sustained a massive injury across his chest by the oorg leader. Bussi, Tianna, and Amethyst suffered in silence as well. Dartanyen was afraid that if they stopped to rest, he would never get them moving again. Not only that, but Sabian and Zorg needed attention as soon as possible. And without medical attention, Amethyst, Adrianna, and all of the others could make a turn for the worse as well. So he kept them moving, albeit slowly.

Dusk approached and, as though it was a creature that had lay in wait, the ground began to shake. Bussi and Dartanyen stopped and turned to look back at the rest of the group. The lloryk and larian pranced about and Dartanyen and Armond sought to quiet them. With wide eyes, Armond looked back at Dartanyen and Bussi. For a split moment they stood there, eyes wide. Then Dartanyen felt the fear course through him, fear for the lives of his comrades. This time, there would be no escape.

Dartanyen hurriedly mounted his larian. "Bussi, give me your hand," he shouted. The halfen shook his head in protest. "Damnit, give me your hand, you stubborn ass." Dartanyen leaned down from the back of the animal and gripped the halfen's arm, pulling him roughly onto the back of his larian. The animal reared and panicked, running down the trail, Dartanyen and Bussi holding on for dear life.

Meanwhile, Armond acted quickly, gripping Adrianna about the waist and swinging her onto the back of Sethanon in front of the slumped form of Zorg. She positioned herself low onto his back and gave him rein, hoping that he would be able to get them through the quake like he had had the last time. With help from Amethyst, Tianna was able to mount the lloryk mare in front of Sabian. Once she was astride, the mare started to run, following the larian who had gone before.

The quake intensified. The mountains began to respond. Armond rushed over to Amethyst, struggling with his larian. He pulled her towards the animal, urging her to mount. She obeyed, her fear of the coming avalanche outweighing the fear of never having ridden astride before. Armond mounted the animal behind the girl, and the beasts began to run. Adrianna gripped Sethanon's dark mane and pressed her face against his neck. She saw Amethyst do the same, Armond pressing his chest against her back.

The ground shook violently, and the mountains answered and began to fall. Adrianna closed her eyes and put her faith in Sethanon. Adrianna could only hope that Zorg would not fall, wondered if the bonds that held him were tight enough. She also hoped that the weight of herself and Zorg would not mean the death of them, that Sethanon would be able to persevere, despite the adversity. And then she had no more inclination to think at all, the roar of the mountains falling filling her mind, her desire to stay astride strengthening her muscles to hold on until the end.

8 Decaren CY593

Adrianna awoke to find herself lying upon a bed with the blankets pulled up beneath her chin. She sat upright in a sudden motion, surveying the stone walls all about her, the fireplace at the far end of the room, the beds lined up against the walls. The room was empty save for herself, although she could tell that others had been resting in the beds nearest to hers.

Adrianna rose from her bed to find that she was wearing a white gown. The fabric was soft and light. She crossed her arms over her chest as though to hide herself and swept about the room looking for her clothes. She did not find her tunic and trousers. However, she did find her pouches and belts lying on a table with everyone else's belongings near the cold fireplace. She also found some robes. She donned one that appeared to be her size and made towards the door. She opened it and left the room, hoping to find her missing comrades, her host and maybe even her clothes.

Adrianna walked the corridors of what appeared to be a temple, realizing almost immediately that, indeed, it was one. Symbols of devotion and worship to the god Tencyndor lined many of the walls, as well as paintings and tapestries depicting the god. Within all of the portraits, Tencyndor was portrayed with curly, chin-length, chestnut-colored hair with a smudge of it also on his chin. His eyes were friendly, and his mouth often bore an upward curve. She stopped before one tapestry, having noted one of the figures out of the corner of her eye. She already knew which one was Tencyndor, having seen him in several other depictions already. But it was not he who had garnered her attentions. It was a woman.

The tapestry was elaborate, portraying four persons. Three of them stood before a throne. Upon the throne was seated a man who exuded an aura of power. The throne itself was carved into the visage of a magnificent dragon. Standing before the throne, the god Tencyndor was flanked by his two companions. One was a man. He had long black hair, tied back within bands made of gold. He was tall for a faelin, and slender. His features were handsome to behold. However, it was the woman who had captured her attention. She was a vision of beauty, her hair the color of spun gold. She wore a sleeveless, shimmering bronze gown that was cut up the length to display shapely pale legs. But there was something else about the woman, something familiar about her. Then Adrianna noticed it . . . the object about the woman's arm. It was a golden serpent. Adrianna felt her eyes widen. She put her hand to her arm and felt the serpent still there, beneath the fabric of the robe. How strange. Adrianna had never seen an object such as this one before, yet now she saw it upon the arm of a woman within a tapestry made for a god.

Finally, Adrianna turned from the tapestry and made her way down the corridor once more, her mind whirling. She turned a corner and just about ran into a man who was turning from the other corridor. Adrianna stumbled back, her hand to her chest. She felt her heart beating rapidly beneath her palm. The priest, also, had a hand to his chest. "By Tencyndor, you sure gave me a fright, young lady." He smiled at her then, making it known that he was in no way offended by her and that he was well. His smile was warm, and it reached into his blue eyes. She smiled back at him, liking the priest already. He was of middle age, wearing beige robes and a symbol of Tencyndor about his neck. His hair was brown and cropped short against his scalp. "You must be Adrianna. Your companions have been wondering when you would awaken. Come. Follow me. I will show you to them. However, two of them are not well, and we are doing all that we can for them. They may not be ready for travel for quite some time." Adrianna nodded and followed the priest.

***

The Tencydorian priests told them about the morning they met the group. It was early, and dawn had barely begun to touch the horizon. When the priests first approached the travelers and their animals, most of the group had not been lucid, many having fallen from the backs of the beasts they had been riding. Sethanon was standing over Adrianna where she had fallen, the body of Zorg slumped over his back. The lloryk female stood next to Sethanon, her head lowered, silently bearing the burden upon her back. Tianna lay beneath the slumped body of Sabian, too weak to move him, but unwilling to fall from the back of the lloryk. Dartanyen, Bussi, Armond, and Amethyst had fallen from their animals after their escape from the pass. The larian had stayed, standing vigil over their fallen riders. The priests had brought them back to the temple and tended them, hoping that they would all survive their ordeal.

The group slowly recuperated from their trials within the mountain pass.

On the fifth day, Adrianna had been one of the last to awaken, her illness having been serious, a fever that the priests said made one weak and delirious. Tianna told her that she had spoken in her delirium, strange things that made no sense. Despite his sound appearance, Bussi had suffered much as well. If not for his iron constitution, he would have fallen long before the last quake. As it was, he had remained bedridden almost as long as Adrianna. Dartanyen, Tianna, Amethyst, and Armond had fared rather well, especially compared to Sabian and Zorg, who had required many medicines and prayers to bring them back from the brink of death. After eight days, Sabian continued to sleep and was monitored by the priests and priestesses of Tencyndor all hours of the day and night. Zorg had finally awoken two days after Adrianna. He was pale and lackluster, but he lived.

The next day Sabian awoke. At first, he did not know who they all were. All they could do was stand there beside his bed, looking at one another, pity for him shining in every set of eyes. But, as the next few days went by, pieces of his memory began to return to him. He recovered rather quickly after that, and once he was up and about, everyone began to prepare for the ride to the city of Celuna, only a day's journey from the temple.

For the past few days, Adrianna had wanted to speak with Armond. His expertise with his blades was phenomenal, and his Talent only increased his skill. Adrianna felt that she and the rest of the group had a right to know about Armond's powers. However, she did not want to pry. Armond seemed to be a secretive type of person, one who did not share information about himself to just anyone. So, it was with a tentative step that Adrianna approached him.

Armond was sitting alone in the general hospice, that place where Adrianna found herself when she first awakened. They had continued to sleep there during the night, the priests not having space for them all elsewhere. He was seated at the big table at the far end of the room, where many of them continued to keep their packs, leathers and weapons. He was examining one of his blades, bringing it close and rubbing a thumb over the edge. Adrianna cleared her throat as she walked across the room, letting him know that she was there. Although, Adrianna was sure that he knew she was there already. She sat down at the table across from Armond and watched him until he looked up from his task. His green eyes were questioning as he regarded her, and for the first time Adrianna realized how beautiful they were.

"Adrianna." He said her name and nodded in greeting.

Adrianna nodded in return. "Armond, I have something to ask you."

Armond placed his sword down on the table before him and then gave her his undivided attention. "What is it?"

Adrianna paused before answering. "During our skirmish with the oorgs, I noticed something."

Armond nodded. "I knew that someone else would notice, sooner or later."

"Why did you not say something to someone before?"

"Well, Zorg knows, but no one asked." Armond shrugged. "I just never brought it up."

Adrianna frowned. "Armond, this is important. You have a rare gift. You could do so much . . ."

Armond interrupted her. "I know that I have some Talent. But I am not like you. My Talent is different. I can only use it to enhance my proficiency with my weapons."

Adrianna regarded him skeptically. However, she could not entirely disbelieve him. She supposed it would only be natural for there to be varying degrees of Talent, just as there were varying degrees of other things, such as ones abiltity to swim. "Tell me about it."

Armond leaned back in his seat, watching her contemplatively. It took him only a moment to decide to tell her about his Talent. "I discovered it when I was but a boy, probably at about the same time that you noticed something different about yourself when you were young. I noticed that there was a particular energy in the world, an energy that existed all around us . . . and that it could be used. My grandfather noticed that I was changing, responding to that energy. He took me aside and began to train me to be what I am today . . . a Bladesinger.

"I do not cast spells the way you do. Instead, I sing to the energy, coax it to me, and channel it into my weapon. For me it is my swords. For others, it may be a hammer, an axe, or a pair of daggers. My grandfather taught me many things, but this was the greatest. Without him, I would not be anything near what I have become."

Adrianna stared fixedly at Armond. His eyes had become piercing and his expression intensely serious. She could see that his grandfather meant very much to him. She wondered what happened to him, but found that she was almost afraid to ask, unwilling to tread where she was not wanted.

Then Armond continued. "The incantation you heard me speak during that battle was *Flameblade*. There are others that I can use, such as *Chillblade*, *Lightblade*, and *Quickblade*. Just like you, I have to practice to learn something new. It takes a lot of skill and patience to get it just right."

Adrianna nodded. "Yes. It takes a lot of studying and practicing to get any new spells that I want to learn just right as well."

Armond nodded and then was quiet. For a moment they sat there, drinking in the silence. Not for the first time, Adrianna found herself wondering about his ancestry. When they first met, she assumed that, much like Dartanyen, Armond must be of Terralean and Savanlean descent. But since then, she had begun to come to another conclusion. His height and eye color came from the part of him that was Savanlean. However, with his black hair and pale complexion, Armond very well carried Cimmerean blood in his veins as well. It was no secret how he felt about Cimmereans, and it was likely that he was unaware of his background. Adrianna wasn't about to say anything about it.

Adrianna rose from her seat. "Armond, I am glad that we talked about this. I meant to ask you before, after I saw your abilities in the temple, but I just never grasped the chance. It will be good for us to know as much as we can about one another. It will allow us to be a better team. Besides, perhaps we can learn something from one another, you and I." Adrianna smiled and began to turn away.

"Yes, maybe you are right. We should practice together some time."

Adrianna turned back to him and nodded. "That would be great."

***

On the dawn of the fifteenth day the group left the sanctuary of the temple. They hoped to reach the city by nightfall. The priests wished them a safe journey and told them to return if ever they needed aid. The group had discussed what they could do to pay the priests back for their generosity. They had little coin left from the work they had done in Sangrilak, but it was all that they had. They offered it to the priests, but they refused. "We will take payment later. When you have coin, and you are nearby, come and visit us. Until then, do not concern yourselves with payment." Dartanyen thanked them profusely, promising that someday they would return and give the priests the gold that they so richly deserved.

The terrain was easy going, especially in comparison to that which they had traveled before. Adrianna, Tianna, Amethyst, Sabian, and Armond rode the five remaining animals while Dartanyen, Zorg and Bussi walked alongside. Sethanon was in good spirits, glad to see his rider again, and happy to be on the open plains. The other animals mimicked his fanciful antics, their heads held high and their tails swishing about behind them wildly. The weather was warm and the countryside exquisite; the northern reaches of the Realm of Monaf were beautiful. The grasses were thick and vibrantly green, and little purple flowers abounded. It was interesting, walking through the lands of another kingdom, for Adrianna had not done so before, had never left the realm of Torimir. It was a good ride, the weather pleasant and the food good. The priests had taken wonderful care of them, supplying them with several days of food and water.

That evening, the group entered the city of Celuna. They spent the night at one of the local inns and awoke at dawn the next morning. They discussed their options as they sat around the morning table, needing to decide in which direction they should go next. They could travel north to the city of Kamden, or they could head east to the city of Dresdyn. Adrianna decided that they should go east, the journey to that city easier and probably closer to the city of Kranton, the place where Vornec had last seen her sister. That city was still very far away, across the Dresnjik River and into the Kingdom of Durnst. However, Dartanyen had no objections to Adria's logic, and so the decision was made.

The group purchased a wagon before leaving the city, spending the last of the coin they had earned in Sangrilak. After only two days of traveling, they adopted a system of shifts, enabling them to travel day and night. They divided themselves into pairs, each pair taking a turn at driving the wagon. Everyone seemed happy with the arrangement, except for Amethyst, who grumbled and groused about being stuck with Sabian. Although, Adrianna was sure that she would have complained about being paired up with *anyone* in the group.

22 Decaren CY593

It was their third evening after leaving the city of Celuna. The group was making good time by moving throughout the night. They traveled at the outskirts of the Vanderess Forest, having just reached it that afternoon. Dartanyen appeared to be in rather good spirits, he having spent most of his early life within this forest. He spoke about those days animatedly, the stories entertaining the group as they traveled. It had been a rather hot day, unseasonably warm for this time of the year. The lloryk pulling the wagon was weary, her head low as she walked. The scattered trees of the forest edge offered some respite from the rays of the sun, but it could not take away the heat. The third shift had recently begun and the sun was beginning to set over the horizon. It was then that they came. They materialized in front of them as though out of a dream, or just simple shedding of the dark cloaks that kept them from being seen. The lloryk pulling the wagon shied at the sudden appearance of the men, and Zorg shouted from his seat next to Armond at the front.

Adrianna started when she heard Zorg's shout. The evening meal suddenly forgotten, Dartanyen jumped to his feet and was out the rear of the wagon before anyone else could react, followed by Bussimot. Adrianna heard the ring of steel rending the early evening air as she, Tianna, Amethyst, and Sabian also slid out the rear of the wagon, which was precariously close to being carried away by the frightened lloryk mare. Adrianna grabbed Sethanon's headpiece and untied him from the wagon so that he would not be injured by it if the mare decided to bolt. Turning around, she saw that Tianna had freed the three larian. Then, from behind the wagon, she viewed the scene.

There were ten of them, most of them spell-casters and dark priests. Three of them were obviously warriors, the metal of their armor shining through the black fabric that covered it. They each also wore a large sword that hung from a belt about their waists. The priests and spellcasters kept a distance from the group, but remained close enough so that their spells and prayers would be effective. However, one of them stood further back than the others. His face remained hidden within the dark recesses of his black hood. His arms were crossed at his chest, and his robes were so long that they pooled at his feet. When Adrianna looked upon him, an icy chill raced up her spine. *Who is he?* But then she had no more time to think about him as the first spell was thrown, the missiles knocking Zorg backwards. He suffered only minimally, however, and was standing once more within but an instant, his blade before him, ready. Bussi was beside him, his battle-axe sitting in his two handed grip. Dartanyen had remained back, close to the side of the wagon, wanting to keep enough distance between himself and the foe so that he would have enough space to use his bow.

Another of the wizards had cast his spell. He pointed his finger and uttered the last of his incantation, releasing a black bolt of crackling energy at Amethyst, who had begun to creep deeper into the forest, hoping to sneak up on the enemy from behind. But she had been carefully watching, and she effortlessly dropped to her knees and rolled, coming to her feet a few moments later, just missing the bolt.

Dartanyen loosed an arrow, striking one of the priests in the right shoulder, interrupting his spell. The priest grimaced in pain, clutching the bolt sticking out of his flesh. Adrianna quickly cast her own spell, a protective spell. If someone were to get close enough, all she had to do was touch that person and a charge of energy would jolt him. Taking a rapid glance about, she could see that Zorg, Bussi, and Armond each had engaged a dark warrior in combat and that Dartanyen had loosed another arrow into the chest of his adversary, killing him. Behind her, Adrianna suddenly heard a gasping sound. She turned to find Sabian clutching his neck. After a moment, she realized that it was a ghostly, eerily glowing hand. Under the pressure of the hand squeezing his neck, Sabian gasped for breath.

Adrianna scanned the battle scene, hoping to be able to find the person who was casting the spell. Suddenly, without warning, Adrianna felt a *whoosh* beside her. She whirled around to find one of the dark spellcasters falling at her feet, a scimitar protruding from his side. At the other end of it was Tianna. He groped at her legs and Adrianna quickly knelt beside him. When he went to clutch at her throat, she placed her hands upon his skull and her spell was discharged. The man jerked spasmodically and cried out in agony, his eyes rolling back in his head. When the energy had passed through him, he lay still upon the ground. Tianna smiled wanly as she drew her blade from the dead body.

Adrianna turned back to Sabian. He continued to struggle with the ghost hand, and he appeared to be losing. His energy was quickly waning. He was pale and he had slumped to the ground. Desperately, Adrianna turned back to the battle scene. She saw that another of the dark mages had cast the *Spectral Hand* spell. The hand had found a target in Zorg, who clutched at his neck. At the same time, Zorg still tried to fight off the warrior with whom he had been in combat before the hand struck.

Bussi and Armond continued to engage the dark warriors, each vying for the winning advantage over their foes. Two well-placed arrows by Dartanyen had caused another one of the priests to fall to his knees. And then, from out of the trees, Amethyst emerged from behind the priest, embracing him within her arms and gracefully sinking her dagger into his back. The priest fell from her arms and slumped to the ground.

Suddenly, Adrianna heard someone cry out. She looked around to find that it was Armond. Somehow, his adversary had gained the upper hand. He retreated from the dark warrior, stepping back, back, back . . . parrying the blows rained upon him. The two continued to get closer to where Adrianna stood near the wagon. It was then that she saw that several lesions had broken out upon Armond's face, neck, and hands. The large, red-rimmed sores oozed blood and pus and appeared to be very painful.

Beside her, Tianna began to make towards the two combatants. Upon reaching the warrior, she swung her scimitar, giving Armond a reprieve. However, the force of the warrior's blow made Tianna stagger under the weight and her weapon was loosed from her grip. Adrianna felt torn, wanting so much to help Tianna, but she knew that Sabian and Zorg were also in mortal danger. Backing away from the warriors, she continued her search for the wizards who were casting the *Spectral Hand* spells. Then she saw them; they were standing at the edge of the battle scene across from her. Adrianna began to incant the words to her spell, closing out the disturbance in the near distance. Then the spell was cast, and the reddish-orange orb was flying towards one of the wizards, striking him in the chest.

His concentration broken, the wizard lost control of the ghostly hand. From where she stood, Adrianna could see that Sabian was breathing more easily. However, he seemed to be inordinately weak, and Adrianna began to wonder if the hand had been stealing his life force. Turning back to the battle scene, Adrianna saw that everything appeared to be spinning out of control. As a result of his struggle with the spectral hand, Zorg had fallen before his opponent. The warrior stood over him, brandishing his gigantic sword. Disarmed, Armond also had fallen before the enemy. He held his left arm close to his chest. The front of his tunic was covered with blood and Adrianna was fairly certain that it was his. Tianna knelt beside him, also having been disarmed. Dartanyen put two bolts into the warrior standing over Zorg and the angry man began to make towards the faelin archer. Amethyst lay unmoving on the ground several feet away.

Then, from the corner of her eye, Adrianna noticed movement near the trees to her right, behind the slumped form of Sabian. It was one of the spell-casters, having slowly made his way in that direction during the course of the battle. It was the one who had stood back and away from the battle from the start, the one wearing the long robes. He pulled the hood back from his face, fixing her with a stare of maliciousness, a slight smile upon his thin bloodless lips. She felt a chill crawl up her spine and she instinctively wanted to run away. It was strange, the way he watched her, and then she felt something, an odd tap, tap, tapping inside her mind . . . a feather-light tickle. Then, just as abruptly, it was gone and Adrianna thought she had just imagined it.

Suddenly, Adrianna heard a battle cry. Momentarily, she tore her gaze away from the spell-caster and focused on Bussimot. The halfen was crazily swinging his battle-axe, his thirst for the blood of his enemies apparent in every move he made. Adrianna remembered another time she had seen Bussi like this, and hoped that he would be able to dispatch as many of the enemy as he did when last he had gone into a rage.

Adrianna turned her focus once more onto the spell-caster. He remained in the same place she had seen him last. Then, unexpectedly, a warrior melted out of the lengthening shadows cast by the trees behind the wizard. Momentarily, Adrianna thought that it was one of the warriors that had been fighting Armond, Zorg, and Bussi. But then she realized that he looked different. He did not wear black fabric over his armor, and his helm was not of the same design as the dark warriors her companions fought. He began to walk towards her, and then, as though in slow motion, the man reached up and pulled off his helm.

Adrianna felt her eyes widen. It was as though time had stopped; she could only vaguely hear the fighting in the background. Upon seeing the face beneath the helm, she gasped in fear, having hoped she would never see that face again, a face that had haunted her since that terrible night almost nine years past. His hair was dark, almost black, and his skin a pale bronze. His eyes were black bottomless pits without a soul. He had followed her. After all of these years he had found her, and he would do to her what he had done so long ago with his comrades alongside the road to Andahye. Adrianna was about to run, when suddenly she was stopped.

Adrianna put a hand to her mouth, stifling a scream. Her legs refused to move, as though they had been paralyzed. Adrianna heard someone laughing and glanced in the direction of the spell-caster. He held her gaze for a moment, an evil smirk upon his face. Fearfully, she regarded the warrior as he approached her. He stopped in front of her, his body uncomfortably close. Her heart felt as though it would burst from her chest, and her breath was labored. She wanted to escape, to run recklessly across the landscape. But, even if she could move, she knew he would catch her. There was no escape, not for her.

The warrior looked down at her, a smug smile upon his lips. He placed his hand upon her right breast and slowly began to massage the nipple. "Mmmm. I remember having had you. I remember the feel of you, the way your flesh yielded to me as I penetrated you. I remember the smell of your fear." He paused and sniffed the air around her face. He then smiled malevolently. "Do not worry, my dear. I shall have you again before all is said and done. I *will* return for you." His eyes gleamed as he removed his hand from her. He turned from her and walked away, melting back into the shadows from which he had come. And then it was as though he had never been, he having disappeared.

Released from the spell, Adrianna felt her legs buckle and she fell to the ground. Wildly, Adrianna looked about. The wizard was gone and the enemy had been dispatched; those who did not flee lay dead upon the ground. Shakily, she stood up and began to make her way towards the rest of the group. Dartanyen and Armond stood over Tianna, who knelt beside Bussimot. No one commented as she walked up to them, and no one asked her about the strange warrior. Everyone's attention was riveted onto Bussi, who was lying on the ground. *It is as though they never saw him.* Adrianna bowed her head, overcome with fear and desperation. *They may never help me, and there is no escape . . .*

CHAPTER 11

It was with heavy hearts that the group left the area the next morning. The smell of smoke continued to permeate the air, and the blackened area they left behind was testimony to what had taken place after the battle the evening before. Despondently, Dartanyen drove the wagon. Armond and Zorg rode inside the wagon, recovering from the injuries they sustained in the fight. Amethyst was doing well, recovering from her magic-induced paralysis soon after the battle was ended. Only one person did not ride away from the battle with them that morning. Bussimot. Only minutes after the battle had ended, so did the halfen's life.

Scared witless after her meeting with the warrior from her past, Adrianna had approached the group, many of whom were standing over Bussi. He looked bad, blood flowing from several deep lacerations on his chest, arms, and back. A small trickle of blood flowed from the corner of his mouth, and his breathing was labored. Tianna looked up from her patient, her eyes shadowed by sorrow. She shook her head and gestured for Dartanyen to take her place beside the halfen.

Dartanyen knelt beside his friend, placing his hand on Bussi's shoulder. The halfen looked up at Dartanyen out of eyes glazed by pain. "Did I get them all?"

Dartanyen smiled a sad smile. "Yes, you did. You saved our backsides yet again. They are lying in a bloody heap over yonder." Dartanyen gestured towards the battlefield.

"Is everyone alright then?"

Dartanyen paused for a moment. "A little bit bruised, but yes, everyone is fine."

"Dartanyen . . ." Bussimot suddenly started to cough. Dartanyen held him in his arms until the fit ended. When he pulled away, flecks of blood spotted his leathers, tunic and trousers.

"Shhhh. Don't talk anymore right now. Rest."

"N . . . no. I need to tell ya . . . I don't think I'm gonna be able to travel with you all anymore." His voice had become low and slightly slurred. Dartanyen leaned closer to him.

"Hist! Don't be silly, Bussi. You will be fine in no time." The tears streamed, unchecked, down Dartanyen's face. "We will just have to keep you tied up the next time . . . make sure that you don't get into trouble like this anymore."

"We've had some good times, haven't we old friend?"

Dartanyen could only nod, unable to speak. He held tight onto Bussimot's hand, as though trying to keep him there. But he knew that it could never be. A few heartbeats later, the brave halfen was gone. Adrianna gasped and put her hand over her mouth. She felt her own hot tears running down the sides of her face. When she glanced at Tianna she saw that the other woman was no better off.

For the next couple of hours, the group worked. Tianna tended to the wounds upon Armond and Zorg. Amethyst's body was sluggish from paralysis, so she was unable to do anything but tend to the fire. Adrianna helped Dartanyen gather the bodies of the dark priests and mages into a pile. They then cleared a circle around the pile, being sure that it was free of tall grasses and shrubs. They collected the coin from the bodies, but left the weapons, Adrianna detecting an evil magical taint upon them.

Dartanyen went to a dead branch he had found earlier and placed one end of it into the campfire. Immediately it caught flame. He then took the fire to the pile of bodies and set it ablaze. It took a while, but when he was finished there was a roaring flame. The group left the vicinity of the fire, moving downwind from it. They tended to themselves and then to their fallen companion. They built a makeshift pyre and placed Bussimot upon it. With him, they placed all of his possessions, including his battle-axe. Tianna said a prayer and then ceremoniously lit the pyre on fire.

Well into the night the funeral pyre blazed. No one slept, everyone keeping a mourning vigil over the pyre. It was a private time, a time in which the living recalled memories of the deceased. It was also their time to say good-bye. The next morning, all that remained was the blackened skeleton of Bussimot on a bed of charred debris. Next to him lay the flame-scorched steel blade of his battle-axe.

***

The group continued to ride towards the city of Dresdyn. Dartanyen's dark mood continued to set upon him like a dark cloak, shadowing him from the rest of the group. Adrianna, also, had fallen into melancholy, thinking about the man who had died while in service to her. She also thought of the pile of blackened skeletal necromancers and priests they had left behind, a group of individuals probably connected to her father in one way or another. Adrianna sighed heavily. Dinim. Where was he? When he was finished with his duty to the Wildrunners, would he be able to find them? She hoped so. No matter how much she tried, she couldn't shake the feeling that he should be there, traveling with them.

It was beginning to get dark when the weary group of travelers entered Dresdyn. Right away they began to search for an inn, looking forward to the luxury of a hot bath and something to eat other than ptarmigan, berries, and tubers. They found one rather easily, the Silver Tankard Inn. They stopped the wagon in front of the establishment, unhitched the blue mare, and led their animals around the building towards the back. Two stable-hands ran out to greet them, first taking Sethanon and the blue. Soon they returned for the larian. Soon after, the group was walking through the side door of the establishment.

The tavern was crowded. The air was filled with pipe smoke that emanated from a large group of halfen in the room's center. Dartanyen led the way between the tables and people, stopping at the bar. He asked for the inn-keep, who was retrieved from the kitchens. Dartanyen spoke to him for a few moments. The brawny, dark-haired inn-keep nodded his head and Dartanyen put some gold coins in his palm. The other man then handed Dartanyen some keys. Dartanyen turned back toward the group and motioned to them. Everyone followed him across the tavern once more, and then up the stairs.

Once at the first landing, Dartanyen stopped to hand out the keys. Adrianna, Tianna, and Amethyst were to share a room, as were Armond and Zorg, and Dartanyen and Sabian. Silently, Adrianna and Armond accepted the keys, everyone knowing that they would not be seeing one another until the morrow. Everyone then went to their respective rooms, thoughts of sleep already filling their minds.

That night Adrianna dreamed. They were those dreams that she had had for so long after her arrival into Andahye, the ones that left her weak and panting for breath. They were almost always the same, with very little variation, something that her mind had devised to torment her. But sometimes they were more than that. There was something about them that made her wake screaming, the reality of them too much for her to handle.

The mists parted before her and *he* was there, waiting for her, that same smile played upon his lips, and the same evil glint in his eyes. As always, she cringed before him, recalling his touch and what she had suffered at his hand. She ran from him through the trees, the sound of his laugh following her, dogging her every footstep . . .

Adrianna awoke, sweat pouring down her face and back. She expelled her breath in ragged gasps, struggling to breathe. Amethyst stirred in her bed and Adrianna shrank away from the sound in fear, thinking *he* was there, watching her from within the shadows cast by the moons. And then she began to cry, knowing it was happening yet again, and that she would surely die this time since she had not the last.

***

Adrianna silently followed Tianna and Amethyst downstairs to the common room. There were few others awake at such an early hour, but Adrianna took note of the Hinterlean faelin seated at some of the other tables. Most hailed from the Vanderess Forest, Dartanyen's homeland to the north, and a few, she was sure, were from Elvandahar and the Sheldomar Forest near Andahye. She knew the realm of Monaf, and possibly this city more than most, to be perhaps the most diverse area this side of the Drujasu Sea. Its population was rich in faelin, humans, and even halfen that hailed from the Tegron Hills and Ratik Mountains. Looking about, she spied Dartanyen, Zorg, Armond, and Sabian sitting at a table against the far wall of the common room. The three women were seating themselves when a serving girl approached the table. The men asked her to bring them some bread, cheese, and eggs to break their fast.

Soon they were eating the food that was brought to them. Adrianna ate little, still tired from the exertions of the previous day and the nightmares of that past night. The front door of the inn was opened and three men strode through. They went to the bar, ordered some food and ale, and then went over to a large table at which were seated five men. They pulled over some chairs and sat down. The two humans and the hinterlean began to talk in excited whispers, their comrades' eyes widening as they continued to speak. As the meal went on, the group began to hear excited mutterings all around, the tale having spread like wildfire through the small tavern. Armond especially was intrigued, having strained to catch parts of the conversation as it ebbed and flowed about them. "Hey, there is something going on around here. Maybe we should find out what it is." His eyes were alight with curiosity.

Dartanyen only shrugged.

Armond looked around the table and when he realized that no one else really seemed to care about gleaning any information concerning the excitement he had been hearing about, he shook his head and stood abruptly from the table. He went to the bar and started talking to a man seated there. While talking with the man, two others came up as well. Soon, Armond was in conversation with five men, each one excitedly adding his own piece of information to the portrait that the blade-singer had drawn in his mind. When Armond finally returned, the interest of the group had been piqued with their own curiosity. At first he said nothing, but when the others continued to silently stare at him, he did not withhold the information.

"There is rumor of a beast lurking about at the outskirts of the Vanderess Forest. It has been hunting the livestock that roam that area." Armond paused,

222

looking from one person to another. "No one has seen a beast quite like this one. It is said that he is at least twice the size of any wemic, and that he wears a thick ruff about his neck like that of a kyrrean. The rangers of Vanderess have been following it for a couple of days, trying to determine exactly what it is and where it has come from. The druids consider the beast an enigma and do not know what to think . . ." Armond stopped speaking, regarding everyone as they pondered his words.

"Perhaps we should go hunting for this creature ourselves," said Dartanyen. Upon hearing this, Adrianna looked up towards Armond. He wore a mask of indifference, but Adrianna knew that he was gratified that everyone seemed to be seeing things his way. It was often that Armond would hide the true extent of his feelings, but if she really looked, Adrianna could see what they were, just as she could with any other person.

Adrianna then looked to the other persons at the table. Zorg also wore an expression of indifference, but in his case, it was the real thing. He truly did not care one way or the other whether or not they went to find the beast. Neither did Sabian. However, both Amethyst and Tianna seemed curious about it, especially Tianna, who was intrigued by anything harking from the natural world. Adrianna herself also did not care much, only that it not take them too far away from their purpose. She thought it silly to waste their time upon the ranting and ravings of a few farmers and livestock breeders.

The group set about preparing to go into the Vanderess Forest. They took the equipment they thought they would need and then walked out of the city in the direction of the forest. It wasn't long before they reached the outskirts of the Vanderess, the city being situated very close to it. They entered the tall trees, and within moments the forest canopy was thick overhead. They walked only a short time before the Vanderess rangers melted out of the trees before them.

The faelin men surrounded them. Many of them carried longbows slung over their shoulders. Their skin tone was slightly browned, almost golden. Most of them had thick brown hair tied back with thin strips of leather. However, some of them did have hair with reddish highlights. The men wore sleeveless tunics and trousers of simple make and their boots reached up to mid-calf. One of the men stepped forward. "Greetings, wanderers. What brings you to our forest?"

Dartanyen stepped forward in response. "Greetings, Tirvorn. I thought that you of all people would have remembered me."

The other man's eyes widened with surprised recognition. "Dartanyen Hildranis. It has been a long time. What brings you here after so long?"

The other rangers relaxed their stance. Looking around at them, Adrianna could see that many of the men knew to whom Tirvorn was speaking. A few of them melted back into the trees from which they had come, but several more stayed. "We have heard rumor that a strange beast has taken up residence near here and we were thinking about tracking it down and having a look at it."

Tirvorn nodded. "Yes. It definitely is a most unusual animal. I have never seen anything quite like him. We have been keeping track of him for a couple of days now, but he is a most elusive creature. He has a way of slipping away from us."

Mentally, Adrianna added another question about Dartanyen to the rather long list she had already. She knew that he was well traveled, but she didn't recall him saying anything to the group about his familiarity with the Hinterlean people who lived in the Vanderess Forest. She supposed that she knew less about Dartanyen than she realized, despite the stories that he told them about his early life in the city of Grondor.

Adrianna sighed, her attention wandering from the men to the environment surrounding her. The forest was beautiful. The leaves on the trees were colored the vibrant green of approaching summer. The vines were beginning to make their climbing ways up many of the trunks. There were several species of flowering bushes, trees and vines, all creating a harmony of color that painted the forest in every shade imaginable.

Adrianna began to slowly wander away from the rest of the group, going over first to one flower and then to another. She saw one vine that had dark green leaves that were outlined by a paler greenish-yellow. One bush sported leaves that were not green at all, but some strange shade of purple. Before she knew it, she was far enough away that she could no longer hear the conversation without straining. She didn't understand what all of the talk was about anyway. They just needed to get on with it. If they would get going, they would see the animal for themselves soon enough. But perhaps it was expected. Dartanyen obviously knew these people and it was probably out of respect that he should stop to make conversation before traipsing around in their lands.

Adrianna continued to walk deeper into the forest. It was a peaceful place, one in which she found she could stay, if given the opportunity. Her thoughts turned inwards and she wondered how her life would be in three or four years. Would she continue to practice magic? Or would she find other things in life with which to occupy her time? Would she even have a future?

Suddenly, Adrianna began to feel a strange sensation. The hairs on the back of her neck began to rise and she knew that she was being watched. No, not just watched, but stalked. Then she felt another sensation. Unhidden feelings and emotions flooded her senses . . . curiosity, caution, and the thrill of the hunt. Confused, Adrianna stopped and looked all about her and into the dense foliage in front of her. She saw nothing, but she knew that something was there. Intriguing scents wafted into the range of her heightened sense of smell.

She felt nervous and edgy; the need to stay concealed consumed her. Then, as suddenly as they came to her, the emotions were gone. She felt bereft as the sensation left her, almost . . . lonely.

Adrianna frowned to herself and started to walk again. She was moving for only a few minutes when she stepped into an open area. In its center was a small lake. The clear blue water lapped lazily at the shore and Adrianna found herself to be awed by the beauty of the place. She looked out across the lake and she saw an island of rock rising from the center. Upon the massive rock was sitting a very large animal.

He was beautiful, with the grace of a feline and conformation of a canine. His copper-colored fur was thick and dappled with dark patches. Upon his head and neck he sported a short, silky mane. For a few moments he watched her, and once again, the strange emotions returned. Adrianna felt the sensation of a mind on hers. She could feel what *he* felt, and she knew that the creature was male; the presence in her mind was definitely masculine. She could tell that he was curious about her and, for a creature that was supposedly wild, he seemed to be no threat to her. Suddenly, Adrianna felt alarm. The creature jumped from the rock and into the waters. He quickly swam to the opposite shore, leapt from the water, and disappeared into the forest.

Adrianna turned to find that the rest of the group had caught up to her, the reason for the alarm she had felt from the creature she had just witnessed. Silently, Zorg motioned to follow the creature. Dartanyen nodded and the two men began to walk around to the other side of the lake, Amethyst and Armond following closely behind. Tianna stepped beside her and took Adrianna's arm in hers. "Isn't this exciting?" she whispered. "He was right there . . . so close. You must have gotten a really good look at him."

Adrianna nodded. Strangely, she felt badly. She was sorry that the animal had been frightened away. He had seemed so content, sitting there watching her.

"Come on. I want to get another glimpse of him."

Adrianna shook her head. "I am just going to sit here for a few minutes. I feel tired, and it would be nice to bathe my feet here for a while."

Tianna nodded. "I suppose it will be safe enough. The Vanderess rangers are close by, and if anything should happen they are only a shout away. I will tell the rest of the group to swing in this direction when we come back through."

Adrianna nodded and sank to the ground. She removed her soft hide boots and dangled her feet into the cool water. Tianna ran off to join the rest of the group. For quite some time Adrianna sat there, pondering what she had experienced in the presence of the strange animal. She reveled in the peacefulness she found in the forest, the beautiful scenery, and the feel of the water on her bare feet. All of a sudden Adrianna heard something behind her.

She became instantly alert, aware to everything around her. And then, without warning, she once more felt the sensation of a mind touching hers. Adrianna whirled around and found herself face to face with the large creature.

Adrianna stiffened. He was so close she could feel the warmth of his breath on her cheek. The emotions whirling around in her mind were ones of surprise and caution. But both held their ground as Adrianna looked up and into his eyes. His gaze was mesmerizing, his eyes the color of molten amber. She could sense that he was intelligent, his emotions so complex they seemed almost human. Adrianna looked deep into his eyes, and she could not shake a strange feeling of familiarity that momentarily washed over her. She was shaken, but unafraid. His mind, somehow so attuned to hers, was also non-threatening. Adrianna found herself beginning to speak to the handsome creature standing over her. It must have been some sight . . . a huge beast poised above the small, supine body of a faelin girl. As she spoke, the animal seemed to relax a little, and when she finally reached out to touch him, he met her halfway and put his jaw into her hand. His fur was soft, softer than that of any other creature, and she continued to croon to the animal lovingly, for already she had formed an attachment to this animal that seemed to have a telepathic link to her. She could feel his emotions, just as he could feel hers. His ears rotated as he listened to her speak, and she had never had someone listen to her so closely before. For a time, it seemed to be just the two of them, as if nothing else in the world existed.

Suddenly, Adrianna felt the animal freeze and she felt a shift in his emotions. He felt defensive and wary. He could smell the others . . . the other members of her 'pack'. They were close, and he knew that they were hunting him. Adrianna heard a low growl emanate from the beast's throat. She placed a hand on his face, soothing him with her mental voice. It seemed to work, for he sat on his haunches next to her, gazing into the forest several feet away.

A few minutes later, Dartanyen, Armond, and the rest of the group slowly emerged from the trees where the animal had been watching. Slowly they began to make their way over to Adrianna and the strange animal at her side. Tianna wore an expression of amazement. Dartanyen and Armond looked at her like she was a dryad, or perhaps a nymph. They looked at her like she wasn't real . . . couldn't possibly be real, especially with a beast such as this one sitting tamely next to her.

The group stopped a few paces away from her. At first she said nothing, silently reading her new companion, gauging him, wondering how he was going to respond to her companions. The animal remained motionless beside her, and it was although he was placing his trust in her, placing the next few moments of his life in her hands. She saw the wary expressions upon the faces of her companions, and she realized that they were apprehensive. They did not know what the animal would do, apparently guarding their young comrade. "Don't worry. He won't hurt anyone."

"How do you know?" asked Amethyst hesitantly. The rest of the group regarded Adrianna inquiringly.

Adrianna paused. "I can sense it." Then, realizing how strange that statement sounded, she continued. "He told me. I can somehow understand him . . . feel what he feels, and sense what he senses. Somehow we are connected. His mind is open to me, and I am certain that mine is open to him. He can understand my thoughts just like I can understand his. I know this sounds crazy, but it is the truth." Adrianna stopped and took in the expressions on her companions' faces. They all wore faces reflecting incredulity and disbelief.

Dartanyen cleared his throat. "So, you know that he will not harm us because he speaks to you with his mind?"

Adrianna nodded, stopped, and then shook her head. "Yes. I mean . . . no. It isn't like that. He doesn't communicate with speech. It is his emotions that I sense. And right now, I sense no aggression."

Dartanyen nodded. "I see."

Adrianna stood up. "So, are we ready to go?"

Dartanyen nodded again. "If you are. Although, I have a feeling that the Vanderess rangers are going to find this . . . situation, a bit interesting."

Once more, Adrianna felt the animal on the alert. His body and mind had become tense and expectant. His mind was drawn to some others, people like herself. It was those who had been following him for days now, hunting him but not stopping him from continuing with his activities. He did not feel threatened by them but he was cautious, wondering about them. Adrianna stood next to the animal, sending him soothing thoughts. She knew that he sensed the approaching rangers and had become guarded. Within moments the rangers emerged from the forest on the other side of the lake. Slowly, they made their way over to Adrianna and her group.

Once the small group of rangers reached the area, they stopped. The leader, Tirvorn, wore an expression of skeptical bewilderment. Adrianna remained silent as the rangers regarded her. "You know, we have been trying to get close to this animal for days now. It seems that he has chosen you," said Tirvorn.

Adrianna frowned slightly. "What do you mean, 'chosen?'" Adrianna was confused and her thoughts translated to the creature. His ears pricked forward with his awareness, alert to any change in the situation playing out before him.

"When a corubis cub is old enough, he is introduced to several pre-pubescent boys and girls who will endeavor to learn the skills of a ranger. Out of them he will choose as his companion that person with which he will share his life's experiences. This very moment, my own corubis companion roams this forest, hunting for her next meal."

Adrianna pursed her lips. "That is very interesting. However, you are forgetting two very important things. This animal is not a corubis, and I am not a young girl with hopes of becoming a ranger." Adrianna was surprised by her petulant response to the man. Perplexed, she looked to the animal sitting quietly beside her, wondering how much of her emotion was really hers. From him, she could sense a growing apprehensiveness tinged with agitation and she wondered how much longer he would sit idly by.

Tirvorn grinned. "Fiery, are we not? I suppose I deserved that. I sometimes forget that outsiders are not accustomed to our ways." He paused. "But I would really like to know . . . what is it that you have done then? How did you bring him to you? Is it some type of spell? I have never encountered one like it before."

Adrianna narrowed her eyes slightly. She looked towards Dartanyen and she saw him discreetly shrug his shoulders and shake his head. For a moment she had thought that Dartanyen must have said something to this man about her Talent. However, the response had indicated to her that he had said nothing. Tirvorn was merely making a stab in the dark, not really knowing what she was about, but determined to find out. Nevertheless, it was quite an accusation for him to make, spell-casters being few and far apart. And they were not a very popular group of people either.

Adrianna regarded Tirvorn intently, assessing him before she spoke. "I assure you, I could do no such thing." She would not admit to her profession, but she would not deny it either. Instead she chose a way around it, taking care with her response. "Does such a thing even exist?" Adrianna schooled her expression into one of ignorance. "He simply approached me while I was bathing my feet in the lake. Then I noticed that I could understand what he was thinking. It is like we are sharing some type of telepathic link."

Dartanyen glanced at Tirvorn. The man remained thoughtful. Dartanyen could hear the excitement in the voices of the five men that Tirvorn had with him. Dartanyen could not help but feel the same excitement. Tirvorn was right. For some reason, the animal had chosen Adrianna, linking himself to her the way in which a corubis pup does when he first impresses upon a young faelin ranger. He smiled to himself. The young woman would no longer be in need of protection. This animal would do the job nicely all by himself. Somehow, Dartanyen knew that the animal would wish to stay with Adrianna. The creature had bound himself to her . . . had shared himself with her. And, inadvertently, Adrianna had opened up to him and shared a part of herself as well.

"I think it is about time that we took our leave. We only have a few hours of the daylight left in which to travel," said Dartanyen.

"Yes," said Adrianna. "We have spent enough time here." She turned back to the Vanderess rangers. "Thank you for allowing us to spend the morning here. It has been a wonderful experience." She glanced back at the creature wistfully as she rejoined her comrades.

Meanwhile, the animal stood. He looked after Adrianna for a moment and then slowly began to approach the group. Adrianna heard a sharp intake of breath at her right. She glanced beside herself to see that Amethyst's eyes were wide and focused in front of her. Adrianna turned to find that the animal was following her. She sent him an inquiry through their link, and to her amazement, she realized that he wanted to stay with her, to go with her wherever she wished to go.

Adrianna walked back to the animal. Through their link, she told him how happy that he had made her. His reply was one of delight, his joy paramount in his thoughts. He was glad that she wanted him. When she reached him, Adrianna reached up and stroked his face. He placed his cheek in her palm and regarded her with his warm amber gaze. She could not help but feel that she had just found her best friend.

***

The group traveled east from the city of Dresdyn. From the back of her new companion, Adrianna watched as the miles sped beneath them. She had come to call him Cortath, a name she had chosen for him a couple of days into their journey. He seemed to like it, and responded to the name as though he had always borne it. Alongside of them rode the rest of the group. The lloryk and larian grudgingly allowed the beast within their ranks, but continued to be wary of him, a predator walking amongst them. Tianna rode astride Sethanon; Adrianna was glad to see that they seemed to have taken to one another rather well. Sabian rode beside her upon a newcomer to the group, a larian purchased with some of the coin found upon the necromancers. The group no longer traveled with the wagon, Amethyst learning how to ride rather quickly. Everyone carried their belongings with them on their respective mounts. Armond and Zorg brought up the rear of the procession as usual, and Dartanyen rode at the fore.

After leaving the Vanderess Forest, the group had needed to go back to the city to get the larian and the lloryk. They also needed to collect the belongings that they had left behind at the inn. They knew that they could not take Cortath within the city walls, so Dartanyen, Armond, Sabian, and Amethyst went back into the city, while Adrianna stayed outside the city walls with the beast. Tianna wanted to stay with Adrianna, and Zorg was asked to stay with the two women for protection.

It was well past mid-day by the time they returned with the animals and travel packs. Adrianna took Sethanon's reins and quickly looked through her packs to be sure that everything was there. The larian and lloryk were nervous around the large carnivore, and it took them the larger part of an hour to get them to cooperate. The new larian was the most nervous, he never having had time to become accustomed to a new rider before being plunged into a group with a predator. Adrianna took note of the missing wagon. Dartanyen caught her gaze and then told her that he had sold it, knowing that they would need the coin. Adrianna nodded, knowing the other reason why Dartanyen had sold the wagon. No longer did they travel in the presence of a halfen that refused to ride astride a larian.

The days passed very quickly for Adrianna. To her, the world had suddenly become a brighter place. That first day, when she had mounted Sethanon, Cortath had looked at her strangely. He sent an inquiry to her through their link. She was surprised by his perplexity. Mystified, she sent a query back to him and he responded by crouching upon the ground. Her interest piqued, she dismounted and went up to the animal. She placed her hand upon his face, and stroked the soft fur of his silky mane. With his head, he nudged her to his side, and with his mind he urged her to sit upon his back.

Adrianna was surprised. She had never even considered such a thing . . . to ride upon the back of this beast. But when she finally placed herself comfortably behind his withers, it seemed so right, and Cortath seemed happy to have her there. The ride was nothing like she had ever felt before. He was fast . . . so fast that the air took her breath away, tugged at her clothing, and whipped her hair behind her as they ran. Suddenly, the world was new to her again, so wonderfully alive. She remembered what it felt like to have the soil beneath her bare feet, to inhale the scent of it after a storm, to realize that everything depended upon it for life. She remembered the sound of the wind through the trees, the feel of a summer rain upon her bare shoulders, and the thrill of rising above it all.

At night, when everyone settled down to rest, Cortath would come to her. He would settle himself down beside her, his head on his paws. Adrianna would lean against his warm side. He would sigh and feelings of contentment would filter to her through their link. She would take a moment to realize what he had brought to her, the joy he had given her after only a few days of knowing him. He had given her a piece of herself, a piece she had thought to be lost. And with him she felt safe, safer than she had ever felt before. When she would finally fall asleep, the dreams from her past would come to haunt her, as they were wont to do. But now, instead of succumbing to them, she did not have to face them at all, for her friend was there to chase them all away.

2 Finoren CY593

Slowly they rode towards the group. It had taken some time, but finally Thane had been able to track them down. For a time, it had seemed that his daughter and her rag-tag band of friends had dropped off the face of the world. But then he had picked up her trail once again in the city of Celuna. By then it was a bit old, but he and his minions had ridden hard, and here they were, so close that he could smell her.

Thane looked to the sky. Dawn was not far away. With the approach of daylight, his powers would diminish. However, he was not concerned. He and his men would have the group destroyed for quite some time before the first rays of the sun lit the night-darkened sky. Thane dismounted and motioned for his men to do the same. Their mounts followed behind them as they crept closer to the camp. Then it was before them. A small fire flickered weakly in the center of the camp. Before it was the slumped form of a girl. Thane felt his mouth turn up in to a smile. Fools. They were fools to leave a mere wisp of a girl in charge of the nighttime watch. However, the fact that they were fools would be to his advantage, so he was not too upset by that fact. Thane motioned for his men to circle the camp, and once they were ready, they began to close in upon the sleeping band.

Adrianna turned on her bedroll and pulled her blankets up to her chin. She had suddenly felt a chill and she momentarily thought about retrieving another cover out of her pack. But then she realized that it was summer, and she should not need to use another blanket. Not only that, but the warmth of Cortath's body should have kept away any chills. Drowsily she opened her eyes, and at that moment she heard something at the edge of the camp.

Adrianna's mind lurched into a state of wakefulness. Beside her she heard Tianna stir in her bedroll. Adrianna sat up and looked in the direction that she had heard the noise. The sight that met her eyes numbed her mind to anything else. In the center of the camp, outlined by the pale light of the dying fire, was the tall form of a man. His shoulders were wide; she could tell despite his armor, which was all black. He wore a horned helmet, and the only thing not concealed by it was the man's eyes. They stared at her where she lay, piercingly blue as they seemed to reach into the very depths of her soul. Without having seen him for almost a decade, she knew the identity of this man, knew without a shadow of a doubt. "By the gods." Adrianna spoke without meaning to, the words tumbling from her lips of their own accord.

Beside Adrianna, Tianna responded, still half asleep. "What is it? Go back to . . ." Then she stopped, that part of her that was so attuned to the natural world immediately sensing that something was terribly amiss. Tianna sat up suddenly, and when her eyes focused upon the man standing within the circle of their camp, she cried, "Ware! Intruder in the camp!"

There was a momentary flurry of activity, the men grabbing at their nearest weapons. But then they suddenly realized that they were surrounded, the dark figures emerging from the darkness around the camp. There came a lull, almost like the calm before a storm. The man standing in the center of the camp raised his hands to his helmet and pulled it off. The face behind the helm was ghastly, only a grotesque shadow of the man that Thane used to be. He bore an appearance of emaciation, the skin shrunken around the bones of his face. His thin hair hung in lank tangles down to his shoulders. The only part of him that remained unchanged was his eyes, and they continued to stare at Adrianna.

Adrianna stared back at her father. She rose from her bedroll, never taking her eyes off of him. Fear began to course through her, terror clutching her heart in a vice-like grip. He had become an abomination, an undead thing that walked the world. Why was it that no one had thought to tell her what she would face? Thane raised a hand yet again, reaching towards her. He began to step forward and Adrianna felt herself freeze, like the way a rabbit freezes when it is being hunted by a fox. "Gemma. My dear, beloved Gemma. How long I have waited to set my eyes upon you once more."

Adrianna felt her heart thump in her chest. He was mistaken . . . had mistaken her for her dead mother. Did they really look so much alike? Then he was closer, and closer. Suddenly he stopped. His eyes narrowed into slits, and the expression of benevolence was wiped away from his face, replaced by loathing. He bared his teeth into a grimace of disgust. "Ah, it is you. Adrianna, for a moment, you had me fooled. It is wrong, so wrong that you should bear so many of her features. But your eyes, they are different. Yes, my Gemma had eyes the color of a crystal blue lake in winter."

Thane paused for a moment and then continued. "You know why I am here, do you not? For a long time now I have waited for this moment. I should have killed you when you were but an infant, having just emerged from your dead mother's belly. But I was too soft then . . . too *human*. But now, I am not so encumbered. Come, why don't you accept the inevitable. Give yourself up easily, and I will make your death a painless one."

Adrianna shook her head. Suddenly finding herself mobile once again, she stumbled back from her father, widening the distance. "Ah, such a pity. I don't understand why you cannot make this one thing easy for me. Always you have been nothing but a burden." Thane raised his arm, glancing at his minions as they stood around her comrades. Everyone was silent, watching the scene unfolding before them. "Kill them." Thane lowered his arm and the activity began anew. The ring of steel rang through the air and Adrianna found her attention momentarily diverted, her fear for her companions manifesting itself.

Thane lunged at Adrianna, seeing her distraction as his chance. At the last moment, Adrianna saw what he was about and was able to lurch away from him. Adrianna began to run, but it was no use. Thane captured her around the waist and flung her to the ground. The impact jarred her body, causing her to bite her lip. Adrianna looked up at him, saw the hatred in his eyes as he loomed over her. She just shook her head, so much wanting him to go away, to be only a dream gone seriously awry. Maybe Cortath would have been able to chase this one away, just as he had the others.

***

It was late eventide, that time of the night that was close to the dawn. The third moon, Meriliam, was beginning to lower in the sky, following her sisters, Steralion and Hestim. She was the smallest of the three moons, but the most beautiful. Her pale lavender glow illuminated the large form of an animal sitting in the tall grasses of the Monaf steppe-lands.

Cortath sat alone. He had slipped away from the group, the watch not having noticed him quietly lope away from Adrianna's sleeping side. That particular individual was not a good watch anyway, she being too young, as well as too desirous of her sleep. Despite her methods used to induce wakefulness, the girl had a tendency of nodding in and out during her watch. Many times, Cortath kept one eye open, alert to any change in the environment around camp. But not tonight. This night, he had too many questions on his mind, keeping him wakeful and restless.

Since his decision to journey with this group of individuals, in particular the girl they called Adrianna, Cortath could not shake an unwavering sense of familiarity that he had for the group. There were things about them, things that struck a chord somewhere deep within the recesses of his mind. Especially when it came to Adrianna. She had become important to him, but he could not help but feel that she always had been. This knowledge preyed upon his mind, and he wondered, *who am I? Where am I from? Why am I here?* If he knew the answers to these questions, he was sure that the other things would become clear to him as well. Cortath felt something stir somewhere deep within his mind. He sought to capture it, but it slithered out of his reach and was gone.

Cortath sighed heavily. Such as it was for him, and had been since he had awakened upon the plains several days past. How many nights had come and gone since then he was not sure, but he knew that it was more than he had toes on two paws. Once more he looked up into the night sky and gazed upon the purple moon. Yes, it felt so right, being here at this moment. He tasted the freedom on the air, freedom he had heretofore always longed. It felt good, and he knew that much of his feeling of euphoria came from his connection with the faelin girl. They had a connection, this ability to share their emotions with one another. When she was happy, sad, disappointed, elated, surprised, worried, and all of the feelings in between, he knew it. And for her, it was the same. She knew when he was on the alert, when he was content, hungry, angry, excited, or anxious. With her, this connection was a wonderful thing.

Cortath lowered himself to the ground, the tall grasses tickling his belly. He rolled around, kicking the thick fronds with his hind feet, snapping at them with his powerful jaws. All of a sudden, he began to feel a deluge of emotion. Through the link that he had with Adrianna, he began to sense a terrible fear. Immediately Cortath was on his feet, sprinting through the grasses in the direction of the camp. He had left her, and wished that he had not. She was in danger, and whatever it was that was causing it would feel his teeth and claws.

Within moments Cortath was upon the scene. He lowered himself into the grasses and brush, knowing that he needed to remain hidden. He surveyed the situation, taking in the details before rushing in. Six individuals surrounded the group. The area reeked of death and Cortath knew that these were not ordinary people. A battle had broken out, and the sounds of metal clashing against metal could be heard all around. Opposite of him, on the other side of the camp, stood six steeds. They appeared to be one with the night, and if they were not wearing barding, he may never have taken notice of them. They were the size of lloryk and the color of the night itself. A layer of fog outlined them, and when they moved it swirled about them. It seemed to rise from the ground upon which their hooves trod, and with each stamp of a foot more mist arose.

Cortath looked away from the shadow-lloryk and focused on the battle. First he noticed Dartanyen. There was something reminiscent of the way he knocked his arrow and sent it aloft. It struck one of the dark knights in the neck. The undead creature turned and trained its gaze upon Dartanyen. The archer then let loose a volley of arrows that struck the knight in the chest, arms, and legs. The knight began to make towards Dartanyen. However, before he could reach his adversary, the tall form of Zorg blocked his way. Zorg dodged the knight's shield punch and countered it with a sweeping broadsword attack that took the knight off of his feet. Zorg followed up with a mighty swing, but the knight was too quick. All Zorg hit was the metal of a shield that the felled knight employed at the last moment. Seeing an opening, the death-knight kicked at Zorg's legs, causing them to buckle. The big man fell to the ground. The two combatants both rushed to their feet, but it was the knight who won the initiative. His sword being one-handed and lighter, he was able to ground himself more quickly. The dark knight swung and sliced at Zorg, the blade catching him in the arm.

Beside the two warriors, Amethyst and a shrouded figure had faced off. Each had drawn a short-sword. Amethyst reared away from a sweep from her opponent, the bone sword just narrowly missing her face. She swung in retaliation, just to find her blade being pulled from her grip by a vein-like whip. Stunned, Amethyst fell back. The whip cracked through the air once more and it wrapped around one of her legs. She squealed as the shrouded figure pulled her to the ground. Thinking quickly, Amethyst pulled her dagger from her boot and plunged it into the whip, pinning it to the ground. The shrouded figure hissed angrily, pulled something from its belt, and lunged at the girl on the ground, punching her in the stomach. An agonizing scream rent the air. When the enemy pulled its hand back, it held a bloody claw in its hand.

Seemingly from out of nowhere, Tianna emerged into the fray. She ran past Armond, who seemed to be holding his own against another dark knight. His blades glowed an eerie yellow before his movements began to increase in speed. Within half the time, he was able to parry the enemy's thrust and make one of his own. Tianna also ran past Sabian, who had thrown a spell at the death mage. His eyes were wide, discovering that the spell had borne no effect upon his opponent. Much to his horror, he found his own spell being thrown back at him. He staggered under the effect of the spell, the magical bolts hitting him mercilessly in the chest.

Tianna stopped her headlong rush when she reached Amethyst. She had drawn her scimitar and was able to block the shrouded figure's next attack upon the fallen girl. The figure hissed once more and turned its focus onto the young healer. It rose from the ground, the freed whip in hand. It arched back and was about to crack the whip, when five bolts of magical energy hit it in the chest. Angrily, it turned to its new attacker. It was Sabian. Having seen the plight of his comrades, he had cast the spell. However, he had left his own adversary with the upper hand. The mage had approached him, and upon doing so, laid a hand upon him. Sabian stiffened, crying out in pain. He then collapsed to the ground.

Meanwhile, Tianna pulled Amethyst away from the enemy. Once she was far enough away, she knelt over the young girl. Groaning, Amethyst held her hands to her belly, the blood seeping between her fingers. Tianna moved the girl's hands away and placed her own hands upon the horrible wound. She began to pray, her voice lifting above the noises of battle. Within a few moments, the prayer was complete, and the healing begun. Amethyst began to breathe easier and looked up at Tianna, gratitude shining from her eyes. Suddenly, a dagger whizzed past Amethyst's face and embedded itself into Tianna's leg. She cried out, wrapping her hands around the hilt of the dagger. She looked up to see the shrouded figure staring at her. With a heave, Tianna pulled the dagger from her leg, biting her lower lip to keep from crying out yet again. The blood flowed quickly from the wound and she quickly stuffed her skirt into the deep laceration.

Cortath desperately searched the area for his companion. As of yet, he had not seen her. He remained unseen among the tall grasses and short bushes. Then he saw her, at the far side of the battle scene. He saw her on the ground, holding her side. She was looking up at the large figure standing above her. Cortath growled savagely and burst from his hiding place, racing towards Adrianna and her attacker. As he sped through, he noticed that a fog had begun to permeate the area. It seemed to emanate from the death mage. When the fog touched him, Cortath began to feel slightly weakened. But then he was past it, and speeding toward Adrianna. He could feel her fear, and it coursed through him, giving him strength. As Cortath approached, he saw the large knight raising his sword. But then he was there, leaping into the air towards the knight.

Cortath's body slammed into Thane. They fell, Cortath maneuvering himself so that he landed in between Adrianna and Thane. He would be the wall that Thane had to break down in order to reach Adrianna. Thane quickly rose from his knees and glared menacingly at Cortath. He glared back, unruffled by the challenge. Then Thane was rushing towards him. Cortath responded and met Thane halfway. Cortath rolled at the last moment as Thane brought his broadsword into a downward arc. Cortath sank his teeth into Thane's leg and his weight caused the knight to slam into the ground. Cortath almost gagged when he tasted the rotten flesh and brought himself on top of his adversary, pinning him to the ground. However, Thane had been able to reach his dagger. The knight reached up and took a fistful of Cortath's mane. Thane then plunged the dagger into his chest.

Cortath stiffened in pain and then felt the impact of Thane's feet kicking him away. The knight rose from the ground and was able to retrieve his sword before facing Cortath once more. Cortath felt his life-blood pouring from the wound in his chest. But he would not back down. Never. He would die before he let this abomination touch Adrianna again. All of a sudden he heard the shrill sound of a whistle. Thane responded by looking to the sky. Noticing that the first rays of dawn were about to emerge, he nodded his head in acknowledgement. He returned his attention to Adrianna. He spoke some words to her and then turned away.

Cortath was not able to understand everything that was spoken, but he did understand that Thane had made a threat. Cortath lunged at Thane once more. Somehow, the knight shrugged him off. The last of his strength spent, Thane mounted the shadow-lloryk that seemed to have appeared out of nowhere. He raised his arm and then he was cantering away, his minions behind. Cortath thought about pursuing the knight, but then stopped. Adrianna needed him there with her, needed his comfort. He turned back to her, seeing the healer Tianna at her side. He approached her and she put her hand to his face. He rubbed his jaw against her hand, his affection for her pouring to her across their link. He then lay down next to her, giving her all of the comfort that she needed.

***

The group rode under the cover of the night. Despite their weariness they rode, keeping as much distance between themselves and the enemy as possible. That day, the group had crossed the mighty Dresnjik River. With the coin they had scavenged off of the unfortunate priests and necromancers they had met en-route to Dresdyn, they bought their way across. It took the ferry all day to cross the river, and the group was happy to be on dry land once more as the sun began to set on the horizon.

Since their meeting with Thane and his minions they had gotten very little sleep. After the battle they had fled, riding hard until they reached the river. Once upon the ferry they tried to rest, knowing that they would not be able to do so once the ride was over. But peace of mind was hard to find, and thus sleep was a hard-won commodity.

Throughout the day, Adrianna had remained withdrawn. She ate little and spoke to no one. Cortath was her shadow, silently staying by her side as she fought her daemons. Tianna took advantage of the downtime and dressed the wounds that the band members had acquired during the skirmish. She had been able to see to Amethyst and Adrianna right after the battle, but Zorg and Sabian had not had the chance to be tended. Sabian seemed to be in the worst condition, but Tianna felt that with adequate sleep, he would be able to regain his energy and be well again. Amethyst's wounds were definitely the most profound. The claw that her opponent had plunged into her belly had been wickedly curved, ripping through her abdominal wall, causing perforation of the bowel and severe blood loss. Tianna spent most of her time with the girl, praying arduously to her goddess for the power to heal Amethyst. Finally, Tianna stopped her ministrations and slept, needing to regain her strength after the use of so much energy.

Dartanyen also had been preoccupied and withdrawn. Every so often, he would swing his gaze in Amethyst's direction, a frown on his face. The only thing that kept him from her was the gravity of her wounds. Because she had fallen asleep at the watch, Thane had almost killed Adrianna. Without Cortath's intervention, he surely would have. His disappointment was profound, and Dartanyen knew that he would never be able to trust her again.

237

This worried and saddened him both at the same time. It was difficult to travel with someone to whom you could not even depend for the nightly watch.

Throughout the night the group rode. Finally, in the wee hours of the morning, the group arrived at the city of Torrich. Dartanyen considered passing the city, but when he saw Sabian, Tianna, and Amethyst all slumped over the backs of their larian, he chose to stop. Sabian looked rather ashen, and Dartanyen knew that the man seriously needed some good sleep. Adrianna looked a trifle pale as well, but he could understand why she would be putout. Dartanyen nodded to Armond and Zorg and the two men dismounted. They woke the rest of the group and then led their animals around the side of the inn to the stable and placed them in the paddock, giving them grain and water. Meanwhile, Dartanyen rang the bell at the entrance to the inn. After a few moments the owner appeared at the door and bade Dartanyen enter. He told the innkeeper that he had six companions that also needed lodging, and the man assured him that there was room for everyone.

Adrianna had bid Cortath stay outside the city walls, warning him to not let anyone see him, for it would cause trouble for the group. She was loath to leave him, but she saw no other alternative. She was afraid that he would cause too much of a stir if she brought him into the city, and she did not want to bring any untoward attention to them. Thane would be coming for them, but she did not want to lead him to the very inn at which they hoped to find a least a few hours rest.

Once everyone was inside the inn, the owner handed them the keys to their rooms. Once again, Adrianna would be sharing a room with Tianna and Amethyst. Zorg and Armond would share another room, while Dartanyen and Sabian shared the third. They all bade one another goodnight as they all headed for their respective quarters. Dartanyen supported a weak Sabian down the hall and Adrianna and Tianna helped a still-sore Amethyst. Once within the room, Adrianna fell onto her side of the bed she knew that she would be sharing with Tianna, and before she knew it she was asleep.

***

Adrianna awoke, stretching her arms above her head and arching her back, seeking to rid herself of the stiffness that deep sleep brings. She sat up, scratching her scalp. She frowned in disgust. Her hair was nasty with dirt and oils. She would go to the bathing room that the innkeeper had described when they arrived. Gently she eased herself out of the bed, not wanting to awaken Tianna, who was still soundly asleep. She then tip-toed across the room to a small table upon which rested a towel, a bar of soap, and a flask filled with a pale amber liquid. She grabbed all three items, including her bag and the key to their room, and left, locking the door behind her.

Adrianna walked about the establishment for a while searching, until she found the women's communal bathing chamber. She walked inside, pausing at the entrance to collect another towel, and went to the large pool in the center of the room. She shucked her clothing and sighed deeply as she stepped into the steaming pool. Since she was the only one there, she used the entirety of the pool for herself, submerging herself beneath the water's surface. She drank from the flask and discovered it was a fruity wine. She took up the floral scented soap and washed all of her body and her hair. When finally she was satisfied that she was clean, she got out of the pool, dried herself, stepped back into some fresh clothing, and combed her hair. She wadded up her dirty clothes and stuffed them into her bag. She then left the room, taking the half-emptied wine flask with her.

Adrianna made her way to the tavern, suddenly very hungry. She had not even bothered to eat an evening meal the night before, as she had been so tired. Upon entering the tavern, she looked about and noted only a few patrons present, none of them her comrades. One man sat alone at a large table, some parchments strewn about before him. Adrianna went to the bar and asked the barkeep to bring her a fresh breakfast of nuts, berries and leafy greens. She then walked across the room to a corner table, passing the man sitting alone at the large table. He looked up at her as she passed and smiled.

Startled, Adrianna's step faltered, but she smiled back at him. "Good morn to you milady. Would you care to join me?" The handsome faelin swept his hand towards the empty chair beside him. His thick hair was blond and curled at the nape of his neck. His complexion was golden, and his eyes the color of palest blue. Adrianna determined that he must be of Savanlean descent. Adrianna paused, not sure whether she should accept his invitation or not. But there was something about him, something slightly familiar.

"Yes, that would be nice," she replied. She did not hesitate as she sat herself down beside him, placing her bag on the chair beside her and a half-emptied flask on the table, her gaze locked to his.

The young man smiled a winning smile. "It is such a pleasure to be graced by the presence of one so lovely as you." He held her gaze with his own, plucked her hand from the tabletop, and kissed the top of it. A warm tingle traveled down her spine and into her belly.

Adrianna flushed and smiled at him, taking him in. He was more intoxicating than the wine she had partaken in the pool. Her heart beat rapidly in her chest and her flesh buzzed with his nearness. Momentarily, she wondered how much of her reaction to this man was a result of the drink. "Who are you?" she breathed, moving her face closer to his.

"My name is Dimitri," he replied huskily, bringing his own face close to hers.

"Dimitri." She whispered his name, rolling it over her tongue. She wet her lips as she gazed into his eyes, her hand still caught within his.

"Yes," he whispered back, moving ever closer to her.

"Good morning, Adrianna." The sound of Armond's voice broke the spell. Startled, both she and Dimitri snapped out of their shared reverie, turning toward the tall faelin. He regarded Adrianna oddly.

"Hello, Armond. How was your rest?" asked Adrianna.

"Good. Thank-you." Armond then turned to her table companion. "Who is your friend?"

Dimitri swept his hand towards the other chairs situated around the table. "The lady just settled down to break her fast. Please, join us. My name is Dimitri."

Armond regarded the other man intensely. Adrianna turned from Armond to look at Dimitri. *He is so familiar.* Then it struck her. *Dinim.* Her eyes widened involuntarily and her heart skipped a beat. Without turning his head from Armond, Dinim looked back at her and caught her surprised, but delighted, expression. His disguise had hidden his identity from her for long enough. Adrianna shook her head as one corner of his mouth turned up in the crooked grin typical of Dinim.

Meanwhile, Armond looked from Dinim to Adrianna, scowling minutely. Then he, too, knew with whom he spoke. Adrianna watched as it dawned upon him that it was Dinim who sat before them. Ever so slowly, Armond began to smile. Then he was sitting down at the table with them. "How in the world did you know we were here?"

"Oh, I asked around here and there." With that statement, Dinim idly looked about the room, making sure that no one was listening in to the conversation. Adrianna and Armond also looked about, finding that the remainder of the group had raised themselves from their beds. Tianna, Amethyst, Zorg, Dartanyen, and Sabian were making their way down the stairs.

Adrianna looked at Dinim once more. She was glad to see him and that he was well. She caught him glancing in her direction and saw his smile widen. Drat the man! He had tricked her . . . and so well, too. What was it that had passed between them before Armond happened upon them? It had been something she had never felt before, and she knew that if Armond had not come along, *something* would have happened. Even still, she could feel the warmth rushing through her body, the racing of her heart and the waves in her guts.

Dinim glanced sidelong at Adrianna. She had a half-smile upon her lips. Her cheeks were flushed, and her eyes sparkled. Had he done that? Or had it just been as a result of an excess of wine? He had been so close to her, he could smell it on her breath. She had responded to him like no woman ever had before. His flirtatious remark had been answered in kind. He remembered her eyes widening innocently . . . her lips parting . . . saying his name so seductively. Dinim shook himself out of the memory. Now was not the time. He had much to tell the group, and unfortunately most of it was bad news.

One by one the rest of the group joined the trio at the table; there were just enough chairs. It took a few moments, but soon everyone knew that the faelin Dimitri was Dinim in disguise. Sabian clapped him on the back in greeting, and Dartanyen shook his hand. Everyone was curious, and wanted to know about the Wildrunners, Tianna in particular. "Dinim, what news do you have of the Wildrunners? How is Sirion?"

Dinim paused to regard Tianna. She looked back at him, leaning forward in her seat. He felt so sorry, having to tell her in this manner, but he did not see any other way to do it. He had to give her the facts, and one of them was that Sirion was dead.

The Wildrunners had been devastated after the battle. They had started out as nine, but in the end, all that remained were five. Laura, Arn, and Breesa had died in the fight, and Sirion had been sucked into a magical vortex, one into which he never returned. For a couple of days they had stayed together, more for protection than anything else, while everyone was given a chance to recover from the wounds they received in the battle. Then everyone had gone their separate ways. Triath and Sorn headed back to Sangrilak, and Anya to Elvandahar. With her, she took Sirion's personal effects. Naemmious headed north, and Dinim went to try to find Adrianna.

When Dinim did not answer her right away, Tianna's face paled. Dinim shook his head, looking her in the eyes as he spoke. "Gaknar was successful in bringing Tharizdune into our world, but we were able to reverse the spell and send him back. It was a horrible battle, and not everyone was able to escape."

Dinim stopped speaking. Tianna's hands gripped the edge of the table and she shook her head. "What are you trying to say?"

Dinim sighed. "There is nothing we could do. At the end of the battle Sirion was caught in a magical crossfire. The energies of several spells being cast at the same time caused the creation of a vortex. Sirion was sucked into it. There is no way that he could have survived." Dinim said it in a matter-of-fact tone, his gaze never leaving Tianna's face.

Adrianna couldn't believe what she was hearing. She looked back and forth from Dinim to Tianna. His expression was one of intense sorrow, his eyes full of sympathy for the woman sitting before him. Upon Tianna's face she only saw denial. The young woman continued to shake her head, slowly rising from her seat. "No. It just can't be. You are wrong. I don't believe you!" The last she screamed at him, her voice high pitched, tears streaming down her flushed cheeks.

Dinim stood as well, holding out his hands to her, palms up in supplication. "Tianna, I am so sorry. I wish there were something I could do. I know that this is difficult for you . . ."

Tianna spun on her heels and ran from the table. She ran up the stairs and the sound of a door slamming could vaguely be heard. But Adrianna paid it no heed, her mind reeling from the shock. Sirion was dead? Tianna was right; how could that be? Adrianna began to struggle with her own feelings of loss, not entirely understanding them. Why would she feel like she had just lost something intensely important to her? She had hardly known Sirion, yet they had made a connection. That day seemed so long ago now, but in reality, only a period of weeks had passed.

Adrianna shook her head and knit her brows in confusion. Her chest and throat ached as she felt the need to cry without knowing why. She raised her face and focused upon the ceiling, perhaps hoping she would find the answers to her emotions written there. She struggled to keep her tears at bay, but a few escaped to travel down her temples and into her hairline. She sighed deeply and began to compose herself. Tianna needed her. She would go to Tianna and comfort her. Perhaps she herself would find solace within the embrace of one who had known Sirion so well. Perhaps the mere presence of Tianna would heal this inexplicable rift in her soul.

***

Dinim sat alone in his room. He tapped his fingers on the desk, brooding. What had started out as a wonderful day had suddenly turned very bad. Tianna's reaction to his announcement had been unfavorable to say the least. After she had fled from the table, the rest of the group sat around for a few moments, absorbing what had just transpired. Everyone offered him their condolences, knowing that he had known Sirion better than any of them, with the exception of Tianna. Their food was brought out to them and they ate the meal in silence. Afterwards, Adrianna left the table, probably to offer some consolation to Tianna. Amethyst left as well, mentioning that she was going to take a quick look around the city. Dartanyen asked that she keep herself relatively close by, and the girl nodded her head before striding away.

"So, really. How did you know where to find us? How did you even know that we were still together?" Armond asked. His voice was low as he spoke, remembering Dinim's reaction when he had asked the question before.

Dinim was glad for the conversation. The silence had probably been a gesture of respect, but it had bothered him. He hated to be the bearer of bad tidings, and felt that somehow he would be placed at blame. He hoped that

that was not the case, and began to relax a little when the conversation began anew. "Actually, it was more difficult than I had let on," he began.

The four men leaned forward in their seats, all bearing expressions of curiosity. "After the battle, we left the Ubekwe Valley, a place outside of Grondor. We made our way back to the city and then, after a couple days of rest, we said our farewells and went our own ways. I had no idea that you all were still together . . . all I knew was that I needed to find Adrianna, for I had promised her that I would return to help her against Thane.

"Grondor is a large city. A person can find anything his heart desires, if only he knows how to look. And look I did. I needed to find some way to locate Adrianna. I knew that she was probably somewhere within the central portion of the continent, but that narrowed my search only marginally. I knew that I needed something . . . something that was beyond my realm of expertise.

"I decided that I needed a scrying device. It would be the perfect way to find Adrianna. I went to several shops, but none of them carried such a device. The shop owners told me that such items were difficult to obtain, not to mention extremely expensive. I began to lose hope . . . but that is when I noticed the gypsies. I thought to myself . . . perhaps one of them would be able to help me. I had heard stories about gypsy magic, that many of the women have certain Talents. So, I went up to one of the men. I asked him if he knew someone who could help me. At first he laughed and called some of his friends over. For a while, they all laughed. Then I decided that I needed to take a chance. I needed to show these men what I really was, so they wouldn't think me a mere charlatan."

Dinim paused. The men were engrossed in his tale. They watched him from wide eyes, taking in every word of his story. "So what did ya do?" asked Zorg.

Dinim smiled. "I cast a spell."

"An' then what happened?"

Dinim's smile widened. "They stopped laughing at me."

Dartanyen, Zorg, Armond and Sabian grinned, imagining the shock value of that act . . . an act that had become so commonplace to them, but to others was a rarity. Dinim continued. "I showed the man that I had money, and that I would pay for any help that they could offer me. They looked at one another, and then back at me. They then led me along a line of wagons that comprised a large caravan. At one of the covered wagons they stopped. One of the men entered the rear of the wagon for a few moments and then returned. He told me that I could go inside, and that is when I met an old woman."

Dinim stopped once more and regarded the men around the table. "Go on. Tell us what happened next," urged Zorg.

"In return for my services, she was able to scry for Adrianna. In doing so,

I discovered that you all still traveled together. I also knew where you were located."

"What type of services?" asked Dartanyen.

"I traveled with the caravan to this city, functioning as a guardsman. If anything untoward were to happen on the road, I would use my Talent to aid the caravan."

Dartanyen nodded. "Well, I must say, I am glad that you have joined us. We have a lot to discuss."

Dinim nodded, noticing the pensive tone of Dartanyen's voice. "I figured as much. Let's go up to one of our rooms. I don't want anyone to overhear."

Dartanyen agreed and the group rose from the table. They made their way up the stairs and into the room that Dartanyen shared with Sabian. The men settled themselves about the room. For a moment there was silence. Then Dartanyen began to speak, telling Dinim about their journey from Sangrilak through the Ratik Pass. He spoke of the animal, Cortath, and of their first meeting with Lord Thane. Dinim took it all in quietly, not interrupting.

Once more silence reigned. Then Dinim stood up from his position on the floor and went to the door. "Let me think about this for a few hours. I will see you all for the evening meal."

Dartanyen and the other men nodded. Dinim left the room, only to return to his own. Here he sat, pensively considering the actions that they should take next. The group was in terrible danger. Thane was not far away, and probably knew exactly where they had gone. Somehow, they had to find a way to lead Thane off of their trail, to find a way to escape him. Tonight they would be especially vulnerable . . .

Dinim stood and went over to the window. He looked out over the city street, watched the passersby as they went about their business. Somehow, Thane had been able to track the group this far. Dinim knew that the man had spies, but he did not feel that they were the only means with which he tracked the group. Thane and his minions were able to travel with supernatural speed, and Thane's powers of 'persuasion' were great. He had probably been able to find out where they had been by checking the registry logs at the inns, and by asking the locals about any groups of wanderers that had passed through recently. The group had to find a place to hide . . . and they had to find one fast.

CHAPTER 12

Adrianna sat on the steps to the inn. She paid no heed to the people that walked by, her melancholy making her withdrawn and introspective. She had been able to offer comfort to Tianna, but had been unable to find any for herself. The other woman had clung to her desperately as she sobbed, and Adrianna knew that Tianna's heart was breaking. Tianna spoke to her in broken sentences, professing her love for Sirion and her wish to see him just one last time. Adrianna had felt her throat close up, and fought to keep the tears at bay. She had never loved anyone like that, except for her sister. But she had not cried when her sister left, not once had she shed a tear. When finally the woman quieted down and was able to fall into sleep, Adrianna had crept out of the room and gone downstairs. None of the group was in the common room, so she came out here to sit and to reflect.

Adrianna's joy upon seeing Dinim had come to a quick close. It was unfortunate, especially since she had missed him these past weeks and wondered how he fared. Sirion's loss had come as a shock to everyone, and Adrianna felt herself feeling it more than she thought she would, but the fact still remained that they were being hunted. The group was in grave danger, and the longer they stayed in Torrich, the closer her father came to achieving his goal. She didn't know if she would be able to handle it if another group member was lost to her cause. Bussi's death weighed heavily on her mind, and she felt that another death would break her.

Through their link, Adrianna could feel Cortath probe gently at her mind. He was worried about her, and wanted to come to her. Adrianna refused him, reminding him of the mayhem that his presence may cause in the city. Adrianna insisted that he remain where he was, hidden in the tall grasses at the outskirts of the city. She could feel Cortath's hunger, for he had forgone hunting while in the vicinity of the city, and she promised that she would bring him meat when she was able.

Adrianna began to hear a commotion down the street. At first she ignored it, but then, as it seemed to be getting closer, she looked in the direction from which the noise came. After another moment she saw Amethyst running towards the inn. The girl called out, "Adrianna, hurry and get Tianna. Tell her to bring her medicines."

Adrianna jumped up and went back into the inn, running up the stairs to the room she shared with Tianna and Amethyst. "Tianna, wake up. Something is going on outside. I think someone is hurt."

Tianna leapt from the bed and grabbed her medicine pouches on her way out of the room. The women ran down the stairs, and when they reached the veranda the disturbance had reached the inn. Dinim had responded to the commotion and had arrived upon the scene just before the women. He was helping a man down from a lathered larian. The beast looked like it might fall at any moment. Adrianna scanned the group that had formed around the man and his mount, and noticed one of the stable hands. "Hey, stable boy," Adrianna called to him over the hubbub. "Get that animal back to the stable and give it some water." The boy nodded and went to the larian, taking the animal's reins and leading the beast away from the small crowd.

Meanwhile, Tianna began to help Dinim bring the man up the veranda stairs. He had been badly beaten, and could hardly support his own weight. The innkeeper held the door open for them as they brought him inside. He then took Tianna's place and lifted the man, helping Dinim get him up the stairs and into a room. The two men deposited the beaten man onto the bed of the first room they came to. Tianna entered with all of her bags and medicines. Adrianna told the innkeeper to get some hot water and clean cloths. Amethyst stood out of the way, near the far wall, silently watching Tianna use her skills on the dying man. Once Adrianna had the water and cloths, she began to attempt to clean the man's wounds. He groaned when she touched his broken body, and Adrianna wondered how he had ever ridden as far as he did.

Tianna and Adrianna worked on the man for many hours. Finally the man achieved some level of comfort and Tianna was able to take a step back. Tiredly, she looked at Adrianna and thanked her for her help. "Tianna, we should get something to eat. You haven't had food all day," said Adrianna.

Tianna was about to shake her head, but when she noticed the expression on her friend's face, she altered her response. She knew that Adrianna would badger her until she had eaten. Tianna nodded and the two women went down to the common room. The rest of the group was there eating their evening meal. They made space for the two of them at the table and placed some food onto some extra plates. "How is the man? Will he live?" asked Dartanyen.

Tianna nodded. "I think so. His wounds were extensive, but I think I was able to see to most of them before my energy ran out. I will need to rest after this."

Adrianna noticed Dartanyen and Dinim share a glance. She knew what they were thinking. The group could ill afford to stay here any longer. Dusk was not far away, and Thane would come for them. Suddenly she felt her appetite diminish and she placed her fork onto the table beside her plate. Zorg noticed her actions. "Eat up, little lady. You need to eat more. Yer too thin as it is."

Adrianna grinned and Zorg smiled back at her. He was a quiet man, but little escaped his notice. That he cared about everyone in the group was apparent by his actions. He had a very protective nature, and that made him endearing to her. She picked up the fork and forced herself to eat a little bit more just to satisfy Zorg, who nodded when he saw her eating again.

After the meal, Tianna and Adrianna went back to see their patient. To their surprise he had awakened. He slowly turned his head when they entered the room. Tianna sat down beside him. "How do you feel?"

The man spoke slowly. "I've been . . . better." His speech was broken and it was apparent that his mouth was dry. Adrianna took up a cup and filled it with water. She brought it to Tianna and she placed it to the man's lips. Slowly he drank the water, some of it leaking out of the corners of his mouth to trickle down his chin and onto his neck. When he was finished, he lay his head back onto the pillow.

Tianna patted his shoulder. "Do you think you have the strength to tell me what happened to you?"

The man nodded. "I was traveling with a merchant caravan towards this city. We were attacked . . ." The man paused, fear in his eyes. "They were hideous to behold . . . creatures that are the stuff of nightmares. They were dead . . . dead . . ." The man's voice trailed off and Tianna and Adrianna looked at one another from across the bed. They knew that it was Thane. He was coming for them.

"Can you tell us anything more?" Adrianna asked the question, afraid of what she would hear, but needing to know.

The man turned his head towards her. "They began to slaughter . . . everyone. Even the children." The man's eyes filled with tears. "Despite the pleas of the women and the cries of the children, they would not stop until everyone was dead. Except for me. I was finally able to hide myself. It was after they began to burn the wagons that the other people came."

Adrianna frowned. "What other people? Can you describe them to me?"

"They were men, at least twenty of them, all wearing black robes. They were evil warlocks and dread priests. I do not even want to contemplate for whom they answered. They surrounded the undead abominations that destroyed the caravan. There were two of them that began to speak, one from each side. I don't understand what they said, the language being unfamiliar to me. Then the fighting broke out. I huddled in the grass, far enough away to keep from getting killed in the crossfire, but close enough to know how the fight ended. When the dust finally cleared, the dark priests and warlocks were dead. All that remained were the undead knights . . ."

The man stopped and shuddered. Adrianna's mind whirled. Her father and his minions had massacred a band of priests and sorcerers more than three times their size. She felt the icy grip of fear begin to close around her heart. They had to leave this city as quickly as possible. Tianna put a hand on the man's forehead, smoothing back his damp hair. "Shhh. Rest now."

But the man continued, determined to finish imparting what information he knew. "But they were weak . . . had suffered damage in the fight. They mounted their dark steeds and cantered away, in the opposite direction of the city."

Adrianna's eyes widened and she took the man's hand in her own. "Are you sure?"

The man nodded. "I was able to drag myself to my larian and get onto his back. I rode in the opposite direction of the . . . creatures."

Adrianna let loose an explosive breath, relief washing over her. Thane and his followers had been severely damaged in the battle. They had gone somewhere to recuperate. Inadvertently, someone had given them the time that they needed to escape. She squeezed the man's hand, grateful for the information he had imparted to them despite the discomfort it must have caused him. "Rest now. You will be safe here." She rose from the bedside. "I will go inform the group."

Tianna nodded to her as she turned and left the room. Adrianna went to Dartanyen's room. She knocked on the door and within moments he had opened it and was ushering her within. He closed the door behind her and she saw that Sabian and Dinim were there as well. Their packs had been arranged and were sitting on the bed, ready to go. Adrianna went over the bed and seated herself on it. She watched Dartanyen as he began to don his studded leather. "You won't be needing that tonight."

Dartanyen looked up from his task to give her a look of disbelief. "Are you crazy? You know that Thane is hot on our trail. We have to leave the city tonight."

Adrianna smiled and shook her head. "No, we don't. Thane will not be coming for us tonight. He is currently . . . preoccupied."

Dartanyen frowned and stopped fastening the belts. "What do you know that the rest of us don't know?"

Adrianna's smile widened. "That Thane has been detained and will not be traveling anywhere this evening."

"Well, fill us in. Tell us what you know", said Sabian.

When Adrianna finished telling Dartanyen, Dinim, and Sabian about what the man had imparted to her and Tianna, they too were wearing smiles. "That's a relief," said Dartanyen.

"Another night of sleep will do us good," said Sabian, taking his pack off of the bed.

Dinim nodded. "This gives us some time to rest and put some extra distance between us. I am thinking that he will be incapacitated for at least two nights. However, we still need a plan."

"I agree," said Dartanyen. "But let's get some rest and talk about it tomorrow. I am going to tell Armond, Zorg, and Amethyst the good news."

Adrianna nodded. She cast Dinim a quick smile as she turned to leave the room. He returned the gesture. Dinim regarded her as she left, watched the sway of her hips as she walked away. When she disappeared around the corner he turned to the bed and took up his pack. He had an idea and wanted to talk to Dartanyen about it after he informed the others about their new situation. The gypsy caravan with which he had traveled to this city had left just this morning for the city of Risset. If the group rode quickly in the morning, they should be able to catch up with it a little past mid-day on the morrow. He thought it would be a good idea for the group to travel with the gypsies, there being safety in numbers. Not only that, but there was the possibility that the old gypsy woman might know some way that would keep Thane off of their trail.

***

Early the next day, the group left the city of Torrich. Cortath was glad to see his companion once again, expressing his happiness by running around the group, rubbing his head on Adrianna's back and torso and yelping with glee. Adrianna had brought him a large haunch of leschera meat and the group waited patiently while he ate it. After he was finished they began to move. At first Cortath was slightly sluggish from his meal, but after a while his pace picked up. At that time Adrianna agreed to get on his back. He caught up with Dartanyen and was happy to share the lead with him as they traveled.

All morning the group rode fast. By mid-day Dartanyen could tell that the caravan was not too far up ahead. Adrianna had agreed that it would be a good idea to travel with a larger group of people. They were traveling in the direction that she wished to go, and the possibility that the gypsy woman could help them to escape Thane's detection was motive enough for her. A couple of hours later they could see the caravan in the distance. The entourage seemed larger than Adrianna had originally thought, consisting of several wagons. When finally they were beginning to approach the caravan, they were met with the caravan guard. It consisted of ten men and two women. The guards eyed the group warily as they approached, especially Cortath and the woman who rode on his back.

Upon reaching the guards, Dinim felt the tension in the air. Most of them stared at the animal he had come to know as Cortath. He could understand how they could be afraid. The animal was huge and fierce-looking. At second glance, Dinim noticed that one of the men was familiar to him. It was one who had taken him to meet the old gypsy woman several days past. The man recognized Dinim as well and Dinim could see the other man visibly relax. Dinim rode up to the guards. "Greetings. I apologize if we caused you any unnecessary alarm. We have ridden hard to catch up with you, hoping that you would be willing to have us in your midst. We have a skilled archer and two swordsmen to help out with the guard as well as the nightly watches. What do you say?"

The men looked at one another and then back to Dinim and the rest of the group. "What about yon animal?" asked one of the men.

"He will not hurt anyone. This animal is a friend. The woman who rides him is his companion and she will take care of him. He will not be a burden."

Most of the men remembered Dinim from when he traveled with them before. They nodded. The man that Dinim knew more personally spoke. "You all are welcome to travel with us. It is always good to have some extra warriors to take the watch. However, I have forgotten your name."

"I am Dinim, and this is Dartanyen, Adrianna, Tianna, Amethyst, Sabian, Armond, and Zorgandar." Dinim gestured towards each of the group members as he spoke.

The man nodded. "I am Thalen. Come. Let us catch up to the caravan. We must let Ami Rayhana know of your return. She likes you and would be upset if I did not tell her you were riding with us again." The man smiled as he turned his larian. The other guards followed suit and soon all of them were galloping into the vicinity of the caravan. The populace stared at them as they rode through, the children watching them from the wagons and the men from atop their larian. Most of the women rode in the wagons, but a few rode with the men.

Finally they arrived at the large covered wagon at the head of the procession. Thalen spoke to the driver, telling him that some wanderers had joined them. They spoke for a few moments longer and then Thalen returned to them. "Maroch has given his permission. I will inform Ami of your presence. Make yourselves at home amongst us. An hour before dusk we will stop for the night. We will talk some more then."

Dartanyen nodded. "Thank you so much for your benevolence. It is good of you to take us on. We look forward to speaking with you tonight."

Thalen nodded and waved as he rode away. Adrianna looked around her, taking in the new environment. The people were obviously Denedrians, a nomadic people that originated from the west. Their features were much like Amethyst's. Their skin tone was bronzed, appearing as though they spent all of their time in the sun. Their hair was dark, ranging from medium brown to jet-black, and their eyes also were dark, all varying shades of rich brown.

The gypsy women, especially, were creatures of beauty. Their dark, almond-shaped eyes and full lips gave them an exotic appearance. They tended to be full-figured, having all of the right curves in all of the right places. More than once Adrianna caught Zorg and Armond glancing at one woman or another with expressions of appreciation. However, it was more than just the color of their eyes and the shapes of their bodies. It was the way they dressed, and the aura that surrounded them. These women seemed to have no modesty as they stared at the male newcomers, casting them seductive glances, and positioning their bodies just so . . . the low necklines of their blouses showing off ample cleavage.

These gypsies were a proud people, and this quality manifested itself in the way the people lived their lives. They led a nomadic life, traveling from one end of the continent to the other, trading their wares for those items that they did not make themselves, and performing in entertaining escapades that left their audiences clamoring for more. The gypsies were a colorful people. The women wore long pleated skirts with multihued patterns and billowy-sleeved blouses of red, blue, green and yellow. They wore their hair long, often with nets of shiny multi-colored stones within, as well as long, dangly earrings. About their waists they wore belts made of silver or gold bedecked with a variety of chimes that tinkled as they moved, and upon their arms they wore decorative bracelets of all shapes and sizes. The men wore billowy trousers with brightly colored sashes, often with cloth bands about their foreheads of yet another color. They, too, had body piercings, and wore thick, decorative armbands made of silver or gold.

After a few more hours of traveling, the caravan slowly came to a halt. The order to stop started from the front wagon and by word of mouth the order trickled down the line of wagons until it finally reached the end. Some of the riders helped, calling out as they galloped down the line, "Stopping for the night! Everyone halt your wagons; we are stopping for the night!" The wagons that were at the end drove until they reached the front of the line, and within the hour the wagons had all formed a circle around a central location. Meanwhile, the women bustled to life, setting up the campfires and starting the evening meals. The women worked together, having partitioned themselves into groups, each group performing a different task. Before long, the tantalizing aroma of cooking meat and vegetables was wafting through the air.

The group had found a place of their own within the protective circle of wagons. They prepared their own fire, and began to prepare a meal. Cortath left the area to hunt, but after only a short while he had returned with a large fowl in his mouth. He presented the bird to Tianna, who took the offering and thanked him profusely. He wagged his tail happily, glad that he could be of use. Amethyst came over, took the bird, and began to pluck the feathers. Tianna continued to cook the grain. Adrianna set out her own bedroll as well as those of Tianna and Amethyst. The men laid out their own rolls and began to settle down to tend to their weapons.

Before long, Thalen approached the group. With him was another man and two women. Each of the women carried platters full of food. Dartanyen stood up and greeted the group. The women went over to the fire and set the platters down beside it. "We have brought you some food. While you are with us you need not prepare your own. We will be more than happy to share what we have."

Dartanyen nodded. "Thank you. This is very generous of you. The food looks delicious." The women beamed when they heard Dartanyen's remark. "But next time we will bring some meat for the stew pot. We have a very good hunter in our midst." Dartanyen indicated Cortath.

Thalen nodded. "We would appreciate any offerings you care to give us."

Dartanyen gestured towards the fire and the food. "Would you care to join us? It appears that there is plenty of food, and Tianna makes wonderful tea."

Thalen nodded. "That would be good. We can discuss the night watch and the daily guard duties."

Everyone sat about the fire and passed the platters all around. The food tasted wonderful, and was seasoned with spices that were unfamiliar to Adrianna. The men talked about which shifts that they would take while they traveled with the caravan. Dinim was the first to rise after finishing his meal. Thalen looked up at him as he rose. "Could you direct me to Ami's wagon? If it is not too much of a bother, I would like to speak with her for a few moments."

"It should be no problem at all. Hers is the red covered wagon across the way," said Thalen, pointing across the central campfire.

Dinim nodded and thanked the man. Adrianna watched him walk across the camp. Many of the young men and women had begun to gather at the central fire. Their talk was animated, and many people had begun to play some music. It was a festive environment, and the people free-spirited. "Would you like to join us at the bonfire? I am sure that you would enjoy the stories and the camaraderie. Not only that, but we would like to hear some of your stories as well," said Thalen.

Dartanyen, Armond, Zorg, Tianna, and Amethyst all went to the bonfire. Sabian settled down on his bedroll with a book. Adrianna lay upon her bedroll as well. She was in no mood to join in any festivities this night. She felt uptight and broody, her experiences with her father too recent in her mind. It would take her a while to wind down from the stress of being pursued, and so nearly caught. She still bore the dark bruise under her rib cage, testament of Thane's hatred for her. He had hurt her with that well-aimed kick, and without Tianna, she would not have fared well at all. Actually, without Cortath there to save her, she would not be alive at all. Adrianna put her hand into the animal's thick mane. She did not know what she would ever do without him, did not even want to contemplate such an existence. Already, it seemed like she had known him all of her life and that he had always been by her side. Cortath put his massive head in her lap, his emotions responding to her own, telling her that he loved her too.

Love. Yes, Adrianna loved this creature. She loved him more than she had loved anyone in a long time. She stroked his face and Cortath closed his amber eyes. Somehow, he had filled a rift in her life that she never knew existed until now. He had made her complete, and she knew that she had done the same for him. It was like they were meant to be . . . that it had been fate that brought them together, knowing that they were meant to be in each other's lives.

Adrianna lay herself down. Cortath re-adjusted himself until they were both comfortable. As they lay there, Cortath curled protectively around her, Adrianna looked out upon the bonfire. She spied her comrades, noticing that Dinim had joined them. As of yet, she had not been able to get a chance to speak with him. Despite having only known him a short time before his departure to rejoin the Wildrunners, she had missed his company the last several weeks. Somehow, she preferred his over that of any other person. And what had transpired between them yesterday morning at the inn . . . she could not even begin to explain her reaction to him, the emotions that had surged through her. And yet, her feelings of profound loss when he had told them of Sirion's death had confused her as well. Even still the ache remained in her chest, and she felt lost somehow . . . forlorn. Only the presence of Cortath had been able to alleviate some of that, and had made her able to be a functioning member of the group.

Adrianna continued to watch Dinim across the camp. She noticed the gracefulness of his movements, the way he tilted his head when he smiled, and the way he carried himself with self-assurance and confidence. He was an incredibly handsome man, and the gypsy women's reaction to him was testament to that fact. Adrianna rolled her eyes. These women . . . would they ever let up? They had accosted Armond and Zorg as well, sitting next to them at the fire, leaning into them as they spoke, batting their lashes and smiling seductively. One woman who sat next to Zorg was leaning so close that her breasts touched his arm. He didn't seem to mind, and laughed at whatever it was that she said.

However, it wasn't just the gypsy women who were having a good time. Adrianna noticed Tianna also sitting at the fire, and next to her was a gypsy man. Adrianna could hear her melodious voice float through the air, followed by her laughter. Adrianna sighed, her eyes beginning to close. Tianna needed something . . . someone to take her mind off of Sirion's death. Adrianna did not necessarily agree with the methods she was using in order to do so, but she supposed it was favorable to other things. Although at the moment, Adrianna could not really think of anything less favorable. She yawned and noticed that Dinim had rid himself of the women that had affixed themselves to him and was walking back towards their fire. She thought of getting up, perhaps now would be a good time to talk with him. But somehow she could not find the energy to do any such thing; she was so comfortable and sleepy here, beside Cortath. Adrianna slept.

***

Adrianna estimated that there were close to one hundred and twenty people in the caravan. Many of the gypsies rode within the wagons, but some of them did not, choosing instead to travel on the backs of their larian, making conversation with themselves and the group as they traveled. They journeyed north, keeping the Dresnjik River to the west. The caravan traveled a little bit slower than what the group was accustomed to moving, but the company was good. Dartanyen, Zorg, and Armond were part of the caravan guard with the other warriors. However, she, Tianna, Amethyst, Sabian, and Dinim were left to their own devices.

Upon waking at the break of dawn, Adrianna was surprised at how loud it was as the caravan broke camp. Everyone was talking as they took down the tents and loaded the wagons. Tianna seemed in good spirits as they packed away their bedrolls. Amethyst grumbled about the early hour. Since it took the caravan more time to get started in the mornings, they broke camp early so as to make maximum use of the daylight hours. Adrianna caught Dinim glancing in her direction a couple of times. She looked down at her tunic and then at her trousers, seeing if there was anything amiss. Finally she asked Tianna if there was something about her that needed fixing. Tianna shook her head and gave Adrianna an odd look.

Adrianna rode astride Cortath. She smiled as she sunk her fingers into his thick, soft fur. He was ever her good friend and companion, staying with her even though he really wanted to travel at the front of the caravan, scouting ahead to see what lay before them. When they realized that he was no threat, most of the populace accepted Cortath without any reservations. The children especially liked him. From within their wagons, they stared at Cortath and his rider. They were engaging, and asked Adrianna multitudes of questions. She just smiled, and answered them all, telling them the story of how they met.

Late in the morning Dinim rode up next to Adrianna. For a while he just rode beside her, saying nothing. Finally he turned to her. "Dartanyen told me about your meeting with Thane."

Adrianna nodded. She knew that this topic would arise sooner or later.

She preferred that it had been later, but it seemed that Dinim wanted . . . maybe needed to address it. "The circumstances were bad, and may have been made better had I known that the man was undead." Her voice held a slightly accusatory tone and she flinched inwardly. She had not meant to say it that way, but she must have been more upset than she had thought. She felt that Dinim should have told her what she was up against.

Dinim was silent for a moment. "I know . . . and I am sorry. It's just that I didn't know how to tell you. You were going through so much, that I was afraid of bringing more burden down upon you."

"But it could have cost me my life and the lives of my friends."

Dinim nodded. "I know that now."

"In the future, no matter what happens, never keep anything like this from me again. I need to know what to expect."

"I will. You have my word." Dinim paused. "Will you forgive me?"

Adrianna looked over at Dinim. He wore a despondent expression on his face, but his eyes were bright. He was funning her, and he knew that she knew it. "I suppose I should consider it," she said, keeping herself from smiling at him.

"Please do, Lady, for I do not think that I can live another day without the warmth of your lovely smile upon me."

"Oh, hush. You are such a scoundrel!"

Dinim grinned and Adrianna could not help but break out into a smile of her own. She fell into a fit of giggles and then composed herself. "So, have you any information that can help us?"

"I am not sure. However, I have been able to find some background information. Tonight let's sit and talk about it. I have a couple of books that I can show you."

"Where did you get them?"

"The library in Grondor."

"They let you borrow them?"

"No. I . . . took them."

Adrianna glared at Dinim. "You *stole* them?"

"Shhh. Lower your voice. I don't want the whole caravan to know that I am not just a scoundrel, but a thief too." Dinim's eyes twinkled.

"You are unbearable."

"Yes, but you like me."

Adrianna turned away from him in mock dislike. "I'm not too sure about that now. I had no idea that you were a scoundrel *and* a thief."

"But you liked me when you still knew that I was a scoundrel."

Adrianna narrowed her eyes into slits, knowing that she had been trapped. She turned back to him. "You are also an impossible rake."

Dinim only chuckled.

***

Near the end of the day the trackers discovered grang spoor. The caravan became instantly alert of any possible threat about them. However, nothing approached the caravan. Even the groups of dumb grang were not so foolish as to attack a retinue so large. Finally the signal was given and the caravan began to stop for the day. Before long the evening fires were made and the meals prepared. Adrianna shook her head as she watched the women at the fires with the men. They were temptresses, with their low-cut blouses, and the slits up the sides of their long skirts, revealing golden flesh browned by the sun. They had definitely captivated Zorg and Armond with their dark beauty. However Sabian and Dartanyen seemed unaffected, Sabian reading his books, and Dartanyen either observing those about him, or conversing with the other men in the caravan.

After the evening meal had been eaten, and everyone was settling down to some camaraderie before turning in for the night, Thalen approached the group. "Ami Rayhana wishes to see you all. She wanted to meet you sooner, but she has been very busy with other things. She offers her apologies."

Dartanyen nodded and everyone stood and followed Thalen. They walked across the center of the camp, passing many wagons before coming to one of the largest ones. As they approached it, the brightly colored flap was pulled aside and a woman gestured for them to enter. Adrianna saw the woman smile at Armond as he passed by her on the way into the wagon.

Once inside, the group was ushered toward the front of the wagon, and there, sitting at a round table, was an old woman. Beneath the deep age lines, the silvering hair, and the blemishes to her complexion, Adrianna could tell that she had once been very beautiful. Her long hair was pulled back from a delicately featured face, and her eyes were a rich chestnut brown. The old woman regarded them intently for a moment and then spoke. "Welcome. Everyone calls me Ami Rayhana. You may call me Ami as well. Please have a seat." She gestured towards the other eight seats around the table. The woman who bade them enter stood at her left side, watching the group. Everyone silently seated themselves as Cortath settled himself on the floor near Adrianna. Adrianna found herself sitting with Dinim on her left and Armond on her right. At Dinim's other side was Dartanyen and Tianna. At Armond's right side were Zorg, Sabian, and Amethyst.

Ami regarded the group intently out of dark eyes. She looked at each person in turn. "I know that you are in danger," she stated ominously.

Adrianna started. She then narrowed her eyes imperceptibly. What did this woman know that would cause her to believe they were in danger?

"I have seen what follows you. He is a powerful adversary, but is nothing compared to what will come after. You must all come together to overcome your enemies. You must realize one others' strengths and weaknesses, accept them, and work together to fulfill the destiny set before you."

The old woman stopped speaking and looked around the table. Adrianna shook her head. "What are you talking about? How did you know all of this?"

"I see many things. That is my Gift."

"Well, you are wrong. There is no 'destiny'. After Thane is dead we will all go back to our normal lives. So much for your 'Gift'." Adrianna spoke in anger, and realized that she had stood from her seat. The rest of the group was staring at her, as well as Ami and her daughter.

The old woman shook her head. "You have much hurt and anger within you. Your family can help you, if you let them . . ."

"No. You know nothing about me. I don't have any family. My mother is dead, my father wants to kill me, I haven't seen my brother in over a score, and my sister has been gone for at least eight years. Stop talking as though you know what I am feeling . . ."

The old woman's voice rose over that of Adrianna. "The undead lord will not stop until he sees you dead. For now his vision is clouded, but he will find you again. You cannot run from him forever. And after him there is another, one so dark and so foul that he will raise an army like no other that has been seen on the face of this world. If he succeeds, another cycle of the world will end, and the future will never come to pass."

Adrianna shook her head. "What are you . . ." She paused and then started again. "No. What you are talking about is craziness." Adrianna turned to her comrades. "Come on. I am ready to go . . ."

Dinim stood up next to Adrianna and took her arm. "Adrianna, please just calm down. Maybe you could listen for just a moment longer . . ."

"Dinim, you have got to be joking. This is a farce, and I want to leave."

"Adrianna, sit down," said Dartanyen.

Adrianna stopped and looked around at her comrades, tears in her eyes. "What have I done? I have dragged you all here, into this hell that my life has become. Already, one of us has died. And for what . . . just to face even more trials? After Thane, there will be more of this . . . nightmare? I am so sorry . . . so sorry for everything."

Adrianna turned from the table. Dinim grabbed the sleeve of her tunic, but it slid out of his grip as Adrianna ran back through the wagon and into the night, Cortath following behind her. Dartanyen rose and made as though to follow her, but Dinim's hand on his arm stayed the other man. "Let her be. She needs some time to herself."

Dartanyen nodded. Then he turned to the old gypsy woman. "Thank you for seeing us tonight. I apologize for my comrade. She has had a difficult time as of late."

"There is no need to apologize. She is hurting, and found me an easy target at which to lash out. She carries the terror of her past deep inside of her. One night, it must come out."

Dartanyen frowned. He was about to question the woman, but then noticed her leaning back on a cushion that was situated behind her. The woman who had ushered them into the wagon stepped forward. "Please, my mother is tired. She needs her rest."

"Of course. We will go now."

The group rose and left the wagon. Everyone was introspective as they made their way through the middle of the camp. Suddenly there was a shout. They turned towards the noise and saw several people gesturing them over to the bonfire. The group changed course and moved in that direction. It would be a good diversion from the harsh reality they knew they would soon be facing.

***

Adrianna ran back to the group's campfire, her thoughts too jumbled to be coherent, even to herself. Her hot tears stung her eyes and ran down her face, the air cooling her cheeks as she ran. After a few moments she began to take notice of her surroundings. All around her there was laughter and music. She slowed her headlong flight and looked all about herself. The camp looked like a festival. Off to one side there was a group of entertainers. Currently, the music was lively and upbeat. Near them were some dancers, their hips gyrating with the beat of the music. It was the music of gypsies; so different than any she had heard before. And the dancing seemed to have been made for just this type of music; they went together so well. She saw some of the men handing out mugs of some kind of drink and before she knew it she was making her way over to them and receiving a mug of her own. The man smiled affably at her as he handed her the mug of warm liquid. Adrianna took a long swallow of the drink. It was alcoholic, just as she knew it would be.

Adrianna walked over to their fire. None of the other group members were there. They must have gone to enjoy the festivities, even Sabian, who had been spending most of his time with a book in front of his face. Adrianna looked towards the bonfire where most people tended to be gathering. None of her comrades were to be seen. Cortath went over to her bedroll and lay down next to it. Adrianna drained the contents of her mug, the liquid sliding effortlessly down her throat. Then she looked down into the mug. Yes. The warm ale was definitely gone. She sighed heavily. She would have to get more.

Adrianna drank two more such drinks, unashamedly watching the enthralling actions of the gypsy women. The dancing, and the music that went with it, was surely seductive to say the least. It definitely caught the attention of many a man, including Armond and Zorg, whom she saw with one woman or another. She turned away from the scenes, feeling the loneliness creep up upon her. How many more nights like this would they have . . . nights where the sky was clear and one could see every star in the heavens? How many more good times would they have before their enemies struck them down? She had placed the group in more danger than she had realized. She thought that once she found her sister, everything would somehow be all right. But in reality, that could not possibly be. Thane would still be hunting her, and then Sheri would be in danger too. Adrianna let the thoughts take her, and she sat down on her bedroll before the small fire.

How long she sat there staring into the flames she did not know, but after a time she roused herself, allowing the effects of the alcohol to carry her towards the festivities. She bade Cortath to stay and continue resting. She sang to herself . . . a children's song she used to sing when she was young and watching her sister learn the use of a sword. She had wished that she, too, could learn to be a warrior, to be able to protect herself from anything that came to hurt her. But even then she had realized that no sword could protect her from the hurt that her father inflicted upon her heart.

As Adrianna had grown older, the wish remained, deep within her. Mairi's husband was an embittered man, and used her as someone upon which to take out his anger at the world. The mental abuse was bad enough, but when she went to school and she refused the sexual advances of the head master, she found herself being punished physically. When the master then lied to Hafgan about her academic performance, she was beaten yet again when she got home in the afternoon. She remembered carrying bruises on her legs and buttocks for weeks. The master tried on many occasions to persuade her to touch him, and when she continued to refuse, he continued to cane her. When he finally realized that she would not give in to him, his hatred for her became set, and even when he stopped pulling her aside after school; he found any and every excuse to lash out at her.

The memories swirled around sluggishly in her mind as Adrianna got another refill of the intoxicating beverage. As she walked around the circle of wagons, she began to dance to the sound of the music, mimicking many of the movements that the gypsy women made. After a while, she found herself ensconced within the shadows cast by some of the larger covered wagons. She began to hear some noises nearby and slowly began to creep closer to one of the wagons. As she got closer, the noises became more distinctive. There was moaning, and the sound of labored breathing. Adrianna noted some movement between two of the wagons. She crept alongside the larger wagon, and when she reached the juncture, she peered around the corner. The scene that she discovered was unanticipated.

It was a man and a woman. They strained at one another in a tumble of bare arms and legs. The man lay partially on top of the woman, her skin tone a sharp contrast to his. That was when Adrianna began to suspect . . . and then she caught a glimpse of the woman's face, saw the chestnut hair fanned out upon the ground beneath her, heard the timbre of the moans that escaped her parted lips. Adrianna backed away from the scene, startled by what she had seen, yet also strangely stirred. She didn't notice that she was not alone in her eavesdropping until she felt herself bumping into someone behind her.

Adrianna spun around. It was a man. He smiled at her, and she saw that he was very handsome. His black hair swept back from his forehead, and his light brown eyes regarded her appraisingly. His gaze then briefly settled onto Tianna and her lover. "Captivating, are they not," he said quietly.

Adrianna stepped back. "I . . . I really wouldn't know . . ."

The man looked back to her and grinned. "Come now. I have been watching you . . . watching them." He spoke softly, almost seductively. "You have a beauty of motion. I saw you dancing."

The man was suddenly close, so close . . . and he caught up her hand and pulled her next to him. He put one arm about her waist and continued to hold her hand captive within his. He then began to lead her in a dance, moving his body to the sound of the music in the distance. "By the way, my name is Errow."

"I am . . ."

"Adrianna. I know who you are." Errow said huskily, continuing to lead her in the dance. Adrianna's mind whirled. He had been watching her . . . had seen her spying on two people in the act of making love. He even knew her name . . . And he was close, his body pressing into hers as he danced to the gypsy music. She felt her body respond to him, and she began to feel an ache in the lowest portion of her belly. Adrianna brought her face close to Errow's chest, inhaling the intoxicating scent of him, and she gripped his sleeveless tunic in her hand and allowed herself to be swayed by the music and the man who held her in his arms.

Adrianna felt as though she could float away, forget the rest of the world and soar. Instinctively, Adrianna knew that this man wanted her, could feel it in the way he held her, the response of his body to her nearness. He had sought her out, wanting her before he had ever formally met her. And somehow, a part of her wanted him too. Perhaps it was the alcohol, or maybe the scene she had witnessed between Tianna and her lover. It confused her, frightened her, and excited her, all at the same time.

Finally the music ended. They swayed for a few moments longer and then Adrianna looked up at him, into his eyes. Errow's gaze was smoldering as he looked down at her, his eyes sweeping over her face, and his hands doing the same over her back and then down to her buttocks. He was close, ever so close, and she could feel his breath on her face, on her lips. Her hands kneaded the fabric of his tunic, feeling the contours of his muscular chest. Errow's hands slid from her backside to her waist, and then up her sides to her breasts.

Suddenly a wave of fear washed over Adrianna. The memories rose to the surface of her mind, another man . . . his dirty hands, his rank mouth, his dagger on her naked flesh. Adrianna stiffened and found herself pushing away from the man before her. "Please, stop." Her heart beat rapidly in her chest, her fear causing her to back away. She looked into the man's face, saw his expression of surprise, and then reluctant acceptance. "I . . . I'm sorry. I didn't mean to lead you on this way."

"No apologies are needed, Lady." Errow's eyes searched her face, and she saw that he appeared to be concerned.

"I need to go. Good night." Adrianna turned from the man and ran back towards her campfire. Her head swam with the effects of the alcohol, but she at least had enough of her wits about her to make it back to her camp without needing to ask someone for directions. As she neared the camp, she saw that Dartanyen, Sabian, and Amethyst were already there. Cortath was sitting up next to her bedroll, looking out in the direction from which she was coming. She felt a questing at her mind, but she blocked him out. This was something that she could not share, even with him. She slowed her pace to a jog and then to a walk. Nonchalantly she strode into camp and seated herself on her bedroll. She prepared herself for sleep and then lay down, pulling the light blanket over her.

Cortath curled next to her bedroll. Through the link she felt his hurt, the sting of her rejection echoing in his mind. She felt sorry for the hurt she had caused him, but she refused to let him know about those dark aspects of her past. No one would ever know about those things, things so horrible that she was afraid even just to recall them. Yet she could not help but remember, and she slipped her hand into the front of her tunic and traced the scar than ran between her breasts. No man would ever want her, not after what had happened to her. But that was fine. No one would see her for what she really was, and for all of the many things she was not.

***

The next morning the camp was sluggish to awaken, everyone's physical state reflecting what had been enjoyed the night before. Adrianna had a slight headache from her reckless imbibing of large quantities of alcohol. Dinim seemed to be suffering from one as well, his eyes narrowed within the light of the sun. Dartanyen appeared to be just simply tired, but Sabian appeared not to have suffered at all. Neither did Zorg or Armond, whom Adrianna spied emerging from another camp. Their clothes were a little wrinkled and hair a bit tousled, but they definitely looked well from the wear.

As the caravan began to move off, Adrianna mounted Cortath and found herself riding alone. That was fine with her, she being too tired to even contemplate making conversation. Cortath was quiet as well, very little filtering to her through the link. Adrianna continued to feel badly about hurting his feelings, and sent him loving sentiments. After a while Adrianna began to be more alert to her surroundings. She broke her fast, eating some roasted nuts she found in her pack. Feeling better, she urged Cortath to walk a little bit faster, spying some of her comrades in the line ahead. Cortath obliged her, having recovered from his dejection.

As they made their way up the line, Adrianna spied some the gypsy women glaring at her from their wagons. Their expressions of contempt were difficult to miss, and Adrianna wondered what she had done to warrant such animosity. After a while, when Adrianna had almost caught up to the group, Armond rode up on his larian. He nodded to her in greeting and then fell in beside her. "How are you faring this morning?"

"I'm all right I guess. I think I may have drank a little too much ale." Adrianna replied, grinning lopsidedly.

Armond smiled back at her. "I think we all drank a little too much last night." He then regarded her intently, his gaze ponderous. The warm wind blew some errant strands of pale hair across her face, and she impatiently brushed them aside. She was a very lovely woman, possibly more beautiful than any he had ever met before. Her beauty was entrancing and had captured the attention of many of the men in the caravan. Armond knew that she was unaware of her effect on the men, and it probably made her all the more fascinating.

Last night, as he sat around the bonfire, Armond had heard some of the men talking about Adrianna, many of them expressing their attraction to her. Some of them expressed more than just that, and a few of them became downright lewd. He felt himself becoming protective over her, knowing that she was not deserving of the treatment about which the men fantasized. And now, as he looked down upon her face, he knew that he could not tell her what he had heard, despite the fact that she should know to stay alert and to be careful. He sighed inwardly. He would just have to be vigilant, protect her himself. And perhaps he would tell Dartanyen and Dinim, so that they would watch over her too.

Adrianna watched Armond, trying to figure out the myriad of expressions that passed over his usually stoic countenance. Then he was smiling at her once more and her bewilderment passed. She shrugged and replied to his efforts at conversation. When Tianna rode up a few moments later, Adrianna tried not to look at her too intensely, not wanting to alert her to any knowledge that she had of the previous night's activities. But the other woman was in such good spirits, she didn't even begin to notice Adrianna's strange behavior.

Dinim rode unobtrusively behind the rest of the group. He was glad to see that Adrianna did not seem to carry any ill sentiments from the evening before. He had been worried about her when she left Ami's wagon so precipitously, but had not wanted to interfere. It had been obvious that she was very upset, and that she needed time to think to herself. And now, seeing her speaking so freely with Armond and Tianna, he was glad that he had given that to her.

After the small group had parted to go their separate ways, Dinim increased his pace to ride beside her. Adrianna smiled at him as he moved up next to her. "Adrianna, I was thinking that perhaps we could take a look at some of my notes today. There is a wagon not to far away where we can sit and look over the books that I 'borrowed' as well."

Adrianna's smile widened. "Actually, that would be great. I was just thinking about it. Are you sure that no one will mind?"

"Positive," he replied. Dinim lead her to the wagon that Thalen said they could use for the day. He tied his larian to the back, collected his bags and then helped Adrianna to jump from Cortath's back and into the wagon beside him. They then sat down and began to pull the books and parchments out of the largest bag.

Adrianna pulled one of the books onto her lap and opened it. She flipped through the pages until she came to one that had the hideous picture of some type of half-eaten corpse. With a look of disgust, she turned to Dinim to find him watching her. He grinned when he saw her expression and then passed her another book. "Here, this is what you are looking for."

Adrianna took the book and regarded the open pages. Scrawled across the top, in large letters, was the word *Azmathion* and below it *The Box of Death*. Adrianna frowned. "I think that your father is Azmathous," said Dinim. "That is why I confiscated this book for our use. It tells all about the Azmathion, and how it can be used to create monstrosities such as Thane."

"But how did you even know where to start looking? I mean, I would never have thought to look for something . . . like this." Adrianna gestured to the page.

"When I was captured by Gaknar's priests, I was taken to the temple beneath Sangrilak. Only a mere one day later, priests of Aasarak overran the temple. I was taken, and my identity given to the doppelganger Ixitchitl so that it could act as a spy for Aasarak. I escaped the guards, but not my prison. I was forced to live in the temple for several weeks, waiting for one Lord Thane to come for me. It was during that time that I heard of the Azmathous, that Aasarak had begun to master the power of the Box of Death, and that he had been able to begin amassing his minions."

Adrianna shook her head, Ami's words running through her mind. Oh gods, is this what the old woman was talking about . . . this sorcerer, Aasarak? Oh gods . . .

"Thane is a follower of Aasarak, and it seems that he was the first of the Azmathous that Aasarak created. Others have obviously been created since then. This book describes the Azmathous, including their desire for revenge against those whom they perceive to have done them wrong in the world. At first, the Death Master can create only warriors, but as he gains in strength, he can make sorcerers as well. Aasarak has become very powerful very quickly if he has been able to harness a sorcerer already."

Adrianna fought to steady herself. She would not even think about Aasarak right now. She needed to focus on her more immediate problem; Thane. Even now he was coming for them. "So what exactly do you know about Thane? Does this book tell us what powers he and his followers may possess?"

Dinim shook his head. "No. Each of the Azmathous is different. The abilities of each one will depend upon the skills each possessed in life. If the warrior was a swordsman in life, then he will be a master with that weapon in death. Of course they all have some powers in common, such as the ability to cause uncontrollable fear, a supernatural strength, and an immunity to unenchanted weapons."

"Well, at least that is a start."

"Indeed."

Adrianna frowned again, and Dinim questioned her. "I am afraid, Dinim. Even now we are being hunted. He will find us, traveling with this caravan, and he will kill everyone . . ."

Dinim interrupted her. "No, he won't."

"How can you say that? You know what my father is capable of."

"He will not find us here. The caravan is protected. I spoke to Ami, and she told me that the caravan carries something that will make it impossible for Thane to see us. When he tries to scry for you, he will find only cloudiness. The power of the device that is contained within the caravan will keep him from seeing us for as long as we are with them. Once we part ways, we will not longer be within the area of effect, and Thane will be able to track us once more."

Adrianna sighed in relief. "So you were the one that told Ami that we were in danger."

Dinim shook his head. "No. I told her nothing about Thane. I just told her that a debt collector was following us, and that he owned a seeing orb. That was when she told me about the anti-scrying device."

Adrianna grinned. "You're funning me. You did not tell her . . ."

Dinim raised an eyebrow. "You want to bet?"

Adrianna pouted her lower lip. "No . . ."

"Then hush. You should know better than to think that I would let anyone know about our business."

Adrianna nodded. *But how in Shandahar had Ami known about Thane?*

***

The caravan continued to travel north alongside the Dresnjik River, across the Kingdom of Durnst toward the city of Risset. The days turned into a week. The gypsy women continued to watch her disdainfully. They never made outward displays of hostility, but Adrianna could feel it nonetheless, lurking behind their frigid stares. She saw the man, Errow, only once. He smiled at her as he passed by her on his larian, but that was all. Tianna continued her lustful affair, taking nightly jaunts across the camp to meet her lover. Her spirit seemed to be recovering from Sirion's loss, and Adrianna was glad to hear her tinkling laughter once again.

However, Adrianna was finding it difficult to find happiness for herself. She found solace and some measure of joy in her companionship with Cortath, but that did not take away her pervasive feelings of guilt and fear: guilt for Bussimot's death and the possibility of continuing danger for her comrades, and fear that they may all meet a similar fate. Not to mention that she was constantly looking over her shoulder, afraid of whom she may find standing there, watching her . . . waiting. She also felt sorry about the way she had treated the gypsy matriarch. The old woman had not deserved her wrath, and Adrianna knew that she needed to offer her apologies. The woman had shown herself and her friends nothing but kindness, and Adrianna had repaid her by throwing her Gift in her face.

Cortath carried her over to Ami's wagon. The cover over the rear entrance was closed. Adrianna was wondering how she should alert the occupants of her presence, when Ami's daughter pulled aside the cover. The woman smiled at her kindly and gestured her within. Cortath moved close to the wagon, and when she made it off of his back and into the wagon, he fell back at an easier pace. He would wait for her until she needed him, and then he would take her back to her comrades. All she had to do was call to him with her mind and he would come for her. "Ami has been waiting for you."

Adrianna nodded and followed the woman into the recesses of the wagon. The cover closed behind them and the area dimmed considerably. "Ami has been resting. That is why it is so dark, but when she wishes it we will pull back the cover and let the light in."

Adrianna only nodded once more. Looking ahead, Adrianna could see a soft glow of light. It got larger, and then she could see the withered countenance of Ami Rayhana. The old woman smiled. "Sit, child." Ami gestured toward the pile of pillows situated opposite her. "Would you care for a refreshment? Some tea perhaps?"

Adrianna smiled. "That would be nice, Ami." Ami's daughter turned to a small pot, poured the tea into a cup, and handed it to Adrianna. "Thank-you."

There were a few moments of silence while the two women drank their tea. Adrianna found that it was quite good, almost as good as the tea that Tianna made for the group in the mornings. "You have come to ask me about what I have seen" stated Ami bluntly.

Adrianna looked up at the old woman, and regarded her intently. "I have come to apologize to you for my wretched behavior a few nights past."

Ami chuckled. "An excuse for everything, have you?"

Adrianna contained the sigh that threatened to emerge. The old woman was perceptive. Indeed, there was a part of her that wanted to hear what Ami had seen in her visions, but there was an even larger part of her that did not. Yet, here she was, sitting in front of the seer, sharing a cup of tea. She supposed that there could be more to her visit than a simple apology. "Is there something more that you would like to tell me?"

"To *share* with you, yes." Ami paused. "There is more to you than meets the eye, my dear. I have seen your dreams. Through the years, I have learned that dreams can be changed . . . altered to fit the needs of the world . . . altered through space and time to be a mold for one place . . . one warrior."

"You speak in riddles, Ami. Please be plain with me."

The old woman pursed her lips. "The world will need a hero, and the prophecy has foretold the coming of one who will open the way to a new place. Inadvertently, she will save the world from becoming lost forever."

Adrianna shook her head. "I don't know what you are talking about. Perhaps I should not have come . . ."

Ami Rayhana got a distant look in her eyes, and her voice began to rise. "There will be born a child, and she will be a beacon of light within this world of approaching darkness. With her a new era will begin, and the dragons will call her sister. When the Balance tips, the angels will fall. Her actions will cause the ascendancy of a new power. She will open the way, and when all seems lost, a new people will answer the call."

Adrianna stared at the seer. She could feel her heart racing in her chest. She had never heard the words of prophecy spoken before, yet knew that she had heard them uttered from this woman's mouth. The old woman closed her eyes, and her body slumped. Ami's daughter came over to the woman, and situated the woman more comfortably upon her pillows. Adrianna stood. She was more than a little rattled, and felt the need to escape.

"Thank you for the tea. I have to go now."

Ami's daughter turned to her and nodded. "It is always disarming when Ami has a vision."

Adrianna nodded in return, and then walked to the rear of the wagon, calling Cortath to her. He was waiting for her when she pulled back the cover, and she slipped onto his back. She urged him away from the wagon, as far away as they could go. She mulled over Ami's words, and her hands would not stop shaking. The words of the prophecy had bore no meaning to her, yet she felt the power of them. All she could do was wait, for she was sure that the prophecy would come about, and she would begin to understand, whether she wanted to or not.

***

Sheridana looked out across the plains from the back of her larian. It was morning, and the caravan was breaking camp. Five days ago they had left the small city of Kranton behind. It was about time. She had found herself tiring of the city after having been there only a couple of days. However, there were no caravans leaving the city and she and her family were forced to stay in Kranton for over four days. One evening, when Sheridana found out that the visiting gypsies were planning on leaving the next morning, she went to them and asked where they were planning on going next. When they told her that they were going to the city of Risset, she asked if she could join them. Clan Mustafa readily welcomed her into their ranks.

Traveling with a caravan this large, it was easy for Sheridana to keep herself occupied. She made herself useful by helping with daily guard duties and contributing her share to the evening stewpot. The gypsies were a vociferous people, and there was never a dull moment. She and Carli had captured the attention of many of the young men right away. Sheri spurned their advances with ease, not interested in the purely physical relationships that these men were offering. However, Sheri saw that Carli was entranced by them, never having had much interaction with men before. She was a pretty girl, and vibrant in her youth. Sheridana felt that it was good for her to find a connection with a member of the opposite sex. However, Sheri was quick to warn the girl of what the gypsy men were about. Despite her assurances to Sheri that she understood, Sheri was concerned about the girl possibly getting in over her head. Without ever having had a relationship with a man before, the girl was vulnerable to peer pressure, as well as the mixed signals that her body would convey to her when she found herself in a situation in which sex was involved. Sheri found herself keeping an ever-watchful eye on her young charge as Carli interacted with the male population, being sure that no one would pressure Carli into doing anything that she would regret later.

In another three days they would be reaching Risset. She, Carli, and Fitanni would rest there for a couple of days and then travel to the Dresnjik River. It would be only a couple hours' ride there, and then they would hire the ferry to take them across. They would have to leave the city very early in the morning to make it to the ferry before it departed. It would take most of the day to cross the river, and at the end of the ride they would be in the Kingdom of Monaf. They would ride to the closest village and stay there until they could find a means in which to travel to the city of Kamden safely.

When Sheri and her family finally reached the city of Raxel, she decided the route that they needed take. It was the safest one, she being unwilling to take the shorter, riskier route through Orocish territory. They departed Raxel after spending only a single day there, and rode to the Trinsek River. Once there, they found themselves boarding the ferry with another group of people. It wasn't long before Sheri discovered that they were traveling to Kranton. After making it across the river, Sheri and her family journeyed with the group for the two days that it took them to get to Kranton.

Sheri sighed. They had been lucky to find those people. With them, she had felt safe enough to make the trip to Kranton. However, she knew that she would not be able to count on her luck a second time. It was unlikely that they would find another group of people who would be crossing the river and going to the same place as she. So, they would have to stay at a village until someone passed through, someone who was willing to have her and her family travel with them to Kamden. Once they reached Kamden, they would stock up on their supplies and then go to Celuna. From there they would traverse the Ratik Mountain Pass that would take them home. Sheri couldn't wait to be in Torimir once again, and she would be able to find out where she might find her sister.

CHAPTER 13

On the eighth evening with the caravan, Adrianna sat alone near the evening fire, reading. Cortath had gone hunting. She did not like for him to go alone, but there seemed to be no other way. He seemed never to go very far, however, and this assuaged her fears a bit. Dartanyen had joined some of the other men in a hunt of their own. It was hoped that they would bring back fresh meat. Dinim and Sabian had wandered off together, deep in conversation, and Zorg and Armond had gone over to another fire to converse with the men and women sitting there.

They had only one more day of travel before they reached Risset. Once at the outskirts of the city, the caravan would camp for the night. The next morning the men would enter the city and see if there were any business ventures for them there. If they found some, the Firasat Clan would stay. If they did not, the men would stock up on supplies and the caravan would move on towards the next city.

Adrianna found herself unable to concentrate. They had traveled so far and now they were getting close. Once they reached Risset, Adrianna would begin asking around about Sheridana. Hopefully she would meet someone who had heard of her, or possibly the group she had been traveling with . . . Thritean's Pride. Cortath seemed to have picked up on her excitement, bounding up to her with a fresh kill in his jaws, and then dropping the hare at her feet. Adrianna picked up the offering and praised him for his fine efforts. Happily, Cortath accepted the praise, and then lay down next to her. Dartanyen collected the kill from her on his way by, taking the meat to Tianna, who would prepare it for the evening meal.

All that night and the next day Adrianna lived in a state of mild anticipation, so much hoping that the journey would not be in vain. Late in the afternoon they reached the outskirts of Risset. In the distance, another line of wagons could be seen, situated closer to the city. Some of the men rode out to meet the owners of the other caravan. After only an hour they returned. It was another gypsy caravan, Clan Mustafa. It was an excuse for a celebration, it being far and few that they received the opportunity to spend time with another family. The caravans moved closer together, and once they met, the wagons were situated in a huge circle. Camped at the outskirts of Risset, the city lights became a beautiful backdrop to the festivities. It would be an especially safe camp with the city being so close, and it was the last night that the group would spend with the gypsies.

Soon, the camp became a place much like the one from a few evenings before, with musicians, dancers, games, drink, and food. The people were lively and upbeat, excited to have a reason to celebrate. A few people had relatives with the other clan, and families were reunited for the evening. Travelers passing on their way through towards the city stopped and mingled with the crowd for a while, making the scene larger than ever.

Adrianna stayed near the camp, watching the goings-on. She tended the fire and stirred the contents of the pot that Tianna had over it. Suddenly the other woman was sweeping into the camp. She was quite a vision, wearing a blue and yellow skirt and a green blouse. Adrianna found herself being hauled away from the fire and swept away behind some of the wagons. She was then ordered to remove her clothing. When she looked at Tianna with an expression she was sure bordered on shock, she found some clothing being pressed into her hands with orders to put them on. She looked down to see a red and yellow gold-embroidered skirt with a gold-colored sash in her arms, as well as an orange blouse with gold embroidery. She just stood there for a moment, staring at the clothes. "You will look beautiful in this," Tianna reassured her excitedly. "Now take off that tunic and your trousers and put it on."

Adrianna obeyed, taking off her clothes and donning the blouse Tianna had brought for her. Tianna helped her step into the skirt, and then fastened the golden sash about her waist. Tianna then began to examine Adrianna's ears. Adrianna struggled with the blouse, which seemed too small. When Tianna noticed her attempts to pull the blouse down over her belly, she slapped away Adrianna's hands and fastened the blouse beneath her breasts. "It is meant to be worn as such . . . like mine." Tianna then displayed herself.

Adrianna frowned and shook her head, glancing down at her chest and belly. "No way. I will look like a harlot." She felt naked, and felt the cool air hitting her flesh. She blushed to discover that it was quite low-cut, something she would never wear had she the choice. She began to pluck at it once more, trying to adjust it to cover her cleavage, but she found her hands being slapped away from it once more.

Tianna chuckled. "You look very fine, Adrianna Darnesse. And you do not look like a . . . harlot. Anyway, you deserve to have a good time. I bought the clothes for you so that you could have a new experience . . . let yourself go for a change."

Adrianna looked down at the ground. She had not told Tianna about the other night, when she had drunk so much alcohol that she had nearly been swept away by a dark, handsome stranger. Then Tianna was taking her by the shoulders and leading her back to the fire. She bade Adrianna to sit, and then took something out of her belt pouch. She placed the small object in the flame, turning it this way and that for a few moments before turning back to Adrianna. "Now, don't move. This will only hurt for a moment."

"Tianna, what are you . . . ouch!" Adrianna screamed the last and put a hand up to her ear. Tianna quickly took the hand away from the area, removed the pin from the lobe, wiped the wound with alcohol, and then placed a decoration there. Tianna then repeated the procedure with the other ear. At the finish, Adrianna had pierced ears.

"You could have told me first."

"If I had, you would never have let me do it."

"You are probably right."

Tianna smiled. "Come on. Let's get something to drink." Then she stopped. "Wait, these are for you too." Tianna took a pair of gold-colored slippers from her bag and handed them to Adrianna. She placed them on her feet, thinking *Gods, what will the rest of the group say? I can't let them see me this way.* But then it was too late. When she was finished lacing the slippers, she looked up to see Dinim striding into the camp.

Adrianna's mind whirled. She thought about hiding behind one of the wagons, and was about to dart away when she saw him notice her. Adrianna saw his eyes widen as he saw her. Dinim slowed his pace as he walked towards her. Finally he stood before her, his lavender gaze drinking her in from head to foot. "Wow," he exclaimed. "You look so . . ."

"Different," she supplied in a monotone voice, not really wanting to know what he was going to say.

"Yes, definitely that," he replied almost breathlessly. Tianna stepped up to them. "We were just about to get something to drink. Do you want to come with us?"

In the distance Adrianna heard the music begin. She walked toward it with Dinim on one side and Tianna on the other. When they reached the bonfire, someone offered them each a drink. They graciously accepted the mugs. Adrianna took a few swallows from the mug, having felt thirst since late mid-day but not having stopped to take a drink of water. The drink was a strong one, the liquid racing like a warm river down her throat. Beside her, she heard Dinim reacting to the drink as well, clearing his throat.

Before she knew it, they had joined many others near the entertainers. Excitedly Tianna tapped her shoulder and then pranced away, going over to the musicians in order to join them. Tianna began to sing, lifting her beautiful voice in accompaniment to the other singers. For a while Dinim and Adrianna watched the performers, the instruments being played, the people singing, and the women dancing. Adrianna continued to drink from her mug and, after a while, realized it was almost empty. The music began to infiltrate into her thoughts, and she began to sway slightly with the music. Someone refilled her mug and she continued to drink from it.

Dinim and Adrianna walked around the bonfire a few times, laughing at some the antics of the children, as well as the adults. They walked slowly, side-by-side, enjoying one another's company, their sides bumping every now and again. Adrianna noticed the way many of the people looked at her, especially the women, not even trying to hide their contempt anymore. Adrianna mentioned this phenomenon to Dinim, and he told her that they were merely jealous. She shook her head, telling him that he must be wrong, for there was nothing about which to be jealous. Dinim then stopped and turned to her.

"Don't you realize . . . there is something about you . . . an aura to which people find themselves being drawn. You are an exceptionally beautiful woman. Hasn't anyone ever told you that?"

Adrianna shook her head. "Not really. And Dinim, I know that you are just saying that."

He shook his head. "No, I'm not . . ."

In the distance Adrianna heard another round of music being struck up by the musicians. "Come on. I want to go back over near the entertainers. I want to hear Tianna sing. She has such a wonderful voice, don't you think?" Adrianna took Dinim's hand and began to lead him towards the music. He allowed himself to be taken away, only shaking his head and smiling at her. She was like a little girl at her first carnival. She was an entrancing creature, to say the least, and he so much wanted to find out more about her. What was her childhood like, or her years studying in Andahye? What were her goals in life, her dreams and aspirations?

Finally Adrianna stopped and they stood there for a few moments, listening to the music. Dinim noticed that his mug had been filled again, as well as Adrianna's. Indeed they had partaken of much of the wine, and the color of Adrianna's cheeks and the sparkle of her eyes told him that she was under the influence. He was as well, without meaning to be. It was getting later in the evening, and many other people had partaken of the wine and ale as well. Emotions were on the rise, especially those of the lustful type. From where he was standing, he could count at least three couples who were well on their way to finding a bedroll soon. Or maybe not. The ground would do just as well. But he would not think of these things. It was enough that Adrianna was standing right next to him, the delicate planes of her face accented by the light cast by the fires.

Adrianna listened to the music, content to just stand there and sway. It was nice to have Dinim beside her, a strong, comforting presence. Besides, she had drunk too much . . . again, and she could feel the sense of euphoria that one gets when one has had too much to drink. But she felt good, and could not possibly regret it. She felt warm and tingly, and was glad, for the first time that evening, of the lightness of the dress she wore.

"Dance with me, Adrianna."

She turned her head to see Dinim holding out his hand. She smiled as she accepted. "Don't mind if I do, kind sir." Adrianna felt herself being pulled in towards him, his other hand at her waist. Suddenly she remembered the last time she had been so close to him. It was when she had discovered that Mairi had been killed. He had held her while she cried those bitter tears of loss, his arms wrapped tightly around her protectively. She had felt safe in his embrace, just as she did now. She allowed herself to relax, her body melting into his. She felt the attraction for him rise within her, the excitement of being alive, at this time and this place . . . with this man. And then she was a part of the music, the beat moving all about and within her. She was a part of the rhythm, and her body moved as it dictated.

Adrianna let the music carry her away, allowed the rhythm to take over. Her body moved with the music and suddenly she was no longer in Dinim's arms but dancing in front of him . . . for him. She raised her arms and let her body move to its seductive cadence, circled Dinim as she danced, her hips bumping him lightly as she moved around him. She felt the feather-soft touch of his fingertips upon the bare flesh of her arms and waist. His movements accompanied her own, and then his hands were on her waist, at the small of her back, bringing her into him. Her body moved against his and they began to move in synchrony to the music, each moment that passed making her yearning increase. Her senses began to spiral out of control, and all that existed was Dinim and the tempo of the music.

When finally the music paused, Adrianna regained some of her senses. From her place within the circle of Dinim's arms, she looked up into his face, ever so close to her own. His breath came in rapid bursts from his slightly parted mouth, and she could feel the warmth of it on her cheek. His eyes were dark with passion, and how she knew that fact she did not know. She could feel the beating of his heart beneath the palm of her hand, which rested upon his chest. Her other hand was circled around his bare upper arm. She felt somehow that she had never been this close to a man, not physically, but spiritually.

"That was wonderful," Dinim whispered to her. His voice was deep and his breath tickled her ear when he spoke. Adrianna found herself smiling and she pulled back slightly to see the expression on his face. His desire was manifest as she regarded him, and she felt herself responding, her body becoming energized. Suddenly there was a hand on her arm, and it wasn't Dinim's. She turned to see Armond standing next to them, smiling appreciatively.

"Adrianna, that was great. Where did you learn to dance like that?"

Adrianna flushed and pulled away from Dinim. She suddenly felt self-conscious. Dinim seemed to be feeling the same way, running a hand through his black hair.

"I learned while I was studying in Andahye. Master Tallek felt that it would be a good outlet for me, so he hired someone to teach me how to dance." Feeling strangely disturbed, Adrianna wrapped her arms about her mid-riff and backed away. "I'll be back in a few minutes. I need to take a walk to cool off."

Adrianna fled the scene, looking about as she walked away. She did not see any of the rest of the group. It was just as well that they had not seen her wanton display of affection for Dinim. She would not have known how to explain it, and mere drunkenness would never have been believed. She shook her head. This was the second time that Armond had interrupted them, inadvertently stopping something from happening between herself and Dinim. She wondered about that fact as she allowed her body to recover from the thrill of being so close to Dinim. But she could not help but think . . . what would have happened between them? How far could it have gone? Perhaps she would never know.

15 Finoren CY593

The next morning the group rose early. They assembled the lloryk and larian, loading the animals with the travel packs. They then said their goodbyes to the new friends they had made. It was a sad parting, but Adrianna was so glad that they had almost reached the city. Once there, she would begin to ask around about her sister. An hour later they were riding away from the caravan, and a few hours after that they were riding through the city outskirts. Through the link, Adrianna bade Cortath to lie low until they left the city. He just lay down in the tall grasses, the link unusually silent. Adrianna had noticed that throughout the day, Cortath had seemed rather lackluster. Perhaps he was not feeling well. She wondered about him as they rode into Risset. The group made their way to the first reputable inn, The Golden Tankard. They paid for their accommodations and then went to deposit their belongings within their rooms.

Upon settling down into the inn, Adrianna felt the immediate urge to take a look around the city. She wanted to get a feel for the place before she started questioning the residents about the whereabouts of her sister. She needed to judge the mood of the place, and the best way to do that would be to just keep her ears open and her mouth closed. However, the need for a bath screamed at her, and the first thing that she did when she reached the room was order one. Tianna, Amethyst, and Adrianna shared the hot bath that was brought to the room. It was good to feel clean again, and it put everyone in better spirits. The women then piled their dirty clothing into the lukewarm water and left it to soak.

When the threesome finally made it back down to the common room, the rest of the group was already partaking in an evening meal. Adrianna seated herself next to a freshly bathed Dinim. Upon receiving her meal, she heartily consumed it, and she even accepted a mug of warm mead after her meal. Adrianna leaned back in her chair and glanced around the inn, taking in the diversity of the crowd. She had become spoiled by the easy-going lifestyle of the gypsies. Everyone had. They had become accustomed to the lazy days and the sultry nights. The ale had flowed easily into them while they had traveled with the gypsies, and now they were continuing the habit. But this night Adrianna did not mind. Upon the morrow she would continue the process of finding her sister.

Late afternoon melted into early evening. The crowd in the tavern became larger. The ale and mead having loosened their tongues, the group spoke animatedly amongst one another, simply enjoying one another's company. Every now and then Adrianna would look around the room, taking in all of the people that had entered the establishment. Adrianna heard the sound of a woman's laughter coming from the direction of the bar. Somehow, it bore a familiar element, but Adrianna was not sure what it was. Her interest piqued, she turned in that direction and saw from whom the laughter must have come.

The woman sat upon a barstool, talking with a man seated next to her. Her back was turned to the rest of the room, so Adrianna was unable to see the woman's face. Her hair was dark, and was plaited into a long rope that hung down her back. Adrianna focused upon hearing the woman's voice, and when she finally made a reply to a statement that the man made, Adrianna felt a rush of familiarity sweep over her. Adrianna found herself leaning forward in her chair, staring fixedly at the woman. She felt Dinim beside her, nudging her in the ribs. Once again the young woman laughed at something the man said, and suddenly Adrianna knew why the voice was so familiar.

"Sheridana . . ." Adrianna whispered the name to herself as she rose from her chair. The group hardly noticed as Adrianna left the table. She slowly made her way over to the woman seated at the bar, scrutinizing her, wishing that she knew for certain that it was her sister. When Adrianna finally stood behind the woman, she reached out to touch her shoulder. "Excuse me . . ."

The woman turned around in her stool, her blue eyes regarding Adrianna questioningly. And then the woman's expression changed . . . altered into one of disbelief. "Adrianna?"

Adrianna felt a widening of her own eyes, felt a wave of relief pass through her. "Sheridana, is that you?"

"By the gods, Adrianna what are you doing here?" Sheridana got down from the barstool and it was then that Adrianna noticed the tears in her eyes.

"I came here looking for you." The words were so simple, yet had a profound effect. The tears spilled from Sheridana's eyes and trickled down her cheeks.

"I can't believe that you are truly here. By the gods, I have missed you, Adria!"

Adrianna suddenly felt Sheridana's arms around her. For a moment she just stood there, dumbfounded. And then the memories came flooding back to her. Adrianna closed her eyes, feeling her own tears beginning to well up within them. It seemed like forever had passed since she had seen Sheridana last. And now, here she was, standing within her sister's embrace.

"I missed you, too." Adrianna returned the embrace and the sisters clung to one another for a few moments longer, reveling in one another's presence.

Dinim silently watched Adrianna and the other woman. The rest of the group had noticed as well and had all turned in their seats. They watched as the two women finally parted, and Dinim wondered what Adrianna was saying to the dark-haired stranger. All of a sudden, he knew. He could see the similarities . . . the way they smiled, the shape of their eyes, and the way that they made similar gestures when they spoke. This woman was Adrianna's sister. A strange emotion came upon him then, one that he could not fully understand, and one somewhat akin to jealousy. But why he would suddenly feel that type of emotion now, he could not conceive.

Dinim watched as Adrianna beckoned her blue-eyed, dark-haired sister over to their table. She was a beautiful woman, almost as lovely as Adrianna. Her features were slightly hardened by the elements, and her body moved as that of a seasoned warrior. She wore only simple tunic and trousers, but as she approached the table, he could see the muscle that rippled upon her legs as she moved, the thickened muscle at the juncture of her neck and shoulders, and the roughness of her hands. She was a swordsman. Dinim's gaze flicked back to Adrianna. He had never seen her so radiant. Her face was flushed with excitement, and her eyes sparkled with a light he had never before seen within their depths. He swallowed, his throat having become suddenly dry. The strange, inexplicable emotion continued to surge through him.

"Sheridana, these are my companions, the group I have been traveling with for the past several months." Adrianna gestured around the table, introducing her to everyone. At last she introduced Sheridana to Dinim. Very suavely, he placed a smile onto his face and nodded. Sheridana pulled up another chair and seated herself beside Adrianna at the table. Dartanyen beckoned to a serving girl, and when she approached the table he asked her for a loaf of bread and another flask of wine.

"It is so good to meet you. Adrianna has told us a lot about you," said Tianna. Adrianna cast her a questioning look. Tianna nodded her head imperceptibly. Actually, Adrianna had told the group very little about her sister. Tianna was trying to make Sheri feel comfortable and was being friendly. With her small gesture, Tianna had told Adrianna that she would say nothing to Sheri about their search for her, or the reasons behind it. Adrianna could only hope that the rest of the group would be just as thoughtful, realizing that Adrianna had not yet had the chance to tell Sheridana about their situation.

Sheridana felt a little uncomfortable sitting at a table full of people whom she had never met before, alongside a sister she hadn't seen for several years. For a moment she thought of her daughter and realized that she would need to tell Adrianna about Fitanni. She dreaded Adria's reaction to the child, but she knew that she could not keep it a secret. Not only was the child bastard-born, but also the daughter of their father's brother. It was important for Adrianna to know; especially when she would find out sooner or later, by her mouth or not. Sheridana forced herself to set these thoughts aside for the time being. Everyone seemed friendly toward her, and they were even willing to incorporate her into their talk. Suddenly, Sheridana looked down to find a small, folded bit of parchment near her right elbow. She picked it up, unfolded it and read what had been written upon it. In fine precise handwriting she saw, *"Congratulations upon the birth of your daughter."*

Sheridana stiffened. She read the note again and her heart skipped a beat. She looked up as she crumpled the parchment in her fist. She looked about the table until her gaze rested upon that of the Cimmerean man. His eyes told her everything. Momentarily, she thought about saying nothing, merely letting it slide by. But she knew that she could not. She had to know how he knew about her and her child. He had suddenly become a threat to her, and the need to protect her family swept over her.

Sheridana rose from her seat, her hands balling into fists at her sides. "What is the meaning of this?" she demanded, her voice harsh even to her own ears. "How do you know about this? Who are you?" Sheridana began to tremble with fear and anger. She knew that her reaction would cause a stir with the rest of the group, but she could not sit passively by and allow this man to bully her. She vaguely noticed her sister stand up beside her. For some reason, the Cimmerean was mocking her . . . baiting her. He looked up at her out of knowing eyes. He had intended to get her attention, and to hurt her.

Dinim remained seated as he looked up at Sheridana, unconcerned. "My name is Dinim Dimitri Coabra. All it means it what it says."

Sheridana waved the fist containing the paper at him. "How is it that you know about my life? Are you some kind of spy? How dare you do this to me!"

With a single fluid motion, Dinim stood from his chair. He smirked at her. "It means nothing more than what it says. Why can I not congratulate you on such a joyous thing as that? Were I mocking you, I may have announced it to the entire room." With that statement, Dinim raised his arms into the air. Sheridana gaped at him, her eyes full of the horror of what he was about to do. "Attention everyone." Dinim waited until just about everyone in the room was looking toward the group. "I just want to congratulate this young lady upon the birth of her daughter. Such a joyous thing should not go unheeded." Dinim looked at Sheridana as he spoke his last words. Everyone in the room began to applaud. The man seated upon Dinim's other side began to chuckle, as though he had just heard a joke, and jabbed Dinim in the ribs with his elbow.

Beneath her pale golden complexion, Sheridana had visibly paled. Her eyes were glassy with suppressed tears, and she swallowed convulsively. Once more he smiled at her, the smile that a snake would give her as it wrapped her within its coils. The group stared openly at her, and Adrianna's body had stiffened beside her. Dinim's last words reverberated through Sheridana's mind, *". . . should not go unheeded."* He had definitely noticed, and he had wanted her to know that he had noticed, that her life was not a secret to him. She looked into his smiling face, and realized that she had made a big mistake. She had hoped to fit in with these people, but he had just proved to her that she could not.

"I can't believe this . . ."

"Well, you had better believe it. We know a lot about you, my dear." Sabian smiled and chuckled. Dinim seated himself and turned to stare at his companion for a moment before refocusing upon Sheridana. Damn. He wished that Sabian had said nothing. He had shared his knowledge concerning Sheridana with the other man when he had met back up with the group. Now he regretted having said anything at all. The person that he should have told was Adrianna. But, for some reason, he had not, and now his actions were about to turn around to bite him in the backside.

Sheridana stared at Sabian out of wide eyes. *What did he know? How did he know . . . ?* She looked back to Dinim to find him regarding Sabian with a strange expression on his face. *Escape. She had to escape.* With only that thought in mind, Sheridana spun upon her heel and ran from the table.

Adrianna was shocked. How could he do this? *Why* would he do this? Sheridana had done nothing to him, yet he had humiliated her in front of an entire inn full of evening customers, not to mention in front of the group. She exploded. "Dinim, what have you done? Why . . . I can hardly believe that you would be so rude, and so callous as to hurt someone like this." She had wanted everything to go so smoothly, and to be so right. She had wanted Sheridana to be accepted into the group, and now she was certain that it was Sheridana who would not accept *them*. It hurt her to see that Dinim had so little regard for her that he would hurt someone whom she cared about so much. "Mere words cannot begin to describe how disappointed you have made me." Adrianna almost choked on the words as she said them. She turned away and made her way towards the front of the inn.

Adrianna decided that she needed some fresh air, and she opened the door and walked out onto the veranda. It was a nice night, the wind blowing gently across her face. It was the coolest weather she had felt in days. The tears that had threatened to fall when she confronted Dinim would no longer be held back. She leaned her back against the wall and began to cry in earnest. By the gods . . . what was happening? She suddenly felt like she was in a dream; this could not possibly be real. Dinim would never do such a heinous thing. She wanted to wake up . . . will herself out of the dream.

Adrianna looked up at the clear night sky, the bright orb that was Steralion dominating. No, this was real, and Dinim really was a pile of lloryk dung. Her sister was upstairs, within this very inn, probably wishing that she had never seen her this night. A part of Adrianna had wanted to go to Sheridana, but the rational side of her would not allow it. What if Sheri didn't want her? They had not seen one another for almost a decade. What connection they had once shared was long gone. Sheri probably wanted to be alone . . . but no, wait. That was not possible. Sheridana had a child. The tears ran anew down her cheeks. A baby . . . her sister had a baby, and Dinim somehow had known about it. He had known that her sister had a child and he had not shared that information with her. Instead, he had told Sabian. She had trusted Dinim, put all of her faith in him, for what? Just to have her heart crushed beneath his heel. She remembered the evening before, how she had behaved so wantonly. He must have loved it, seeing her act like such a fool . . . all for him. But no. At least she could give herself a little credit. She would never have behaved that way if she had not imbibed so much of the gypsies' wine. *Damn it all . . .*

Adrianna pulled herself away from the wall. She needed to leave, walk off the excess energy that now seemed to burn through her. She knew that it was just her anger, but she absolutely did not want to go back into the inn, possibly have to face Dinim and lay awake all night thinking about what she had done, or not done. Adrianna leapt from the veranda and ran into the street. She knew where she would go. She would spend the night out under the stars, with Cortath. He could always make her feel better. Already she could imagine herself pillowing her head upon the softness of his fur, feel the warmth of his body curl around her as she slept. Yes, this would be the most therapeutic thing for her.

Into the darkness of the night she ran . . . away from Dinim, away from her sister, away from the hurt that she knew would follow her anyway. Once she was out of the city, Adrianna was running through farmland. This place, it was so similar to Sangrilak. She felt herself beginning to tire and she began to slow. Her mind began to rationalize her situation, and she began to realize that she was a fool . . . again. It was dangerous for a lone woman to be out at night. Adrianna opened her mind, hoping that Cortath would be there. As always, he was. And he was closer than she had realized. He materialized in front of her, his shape appearing even larger in the light cast by Steralion and the newly emerging Hestim.

Adrianna rushed up to Cortath, placing her arms about his neck. He brought his head down over her shoulder and she could feel the warmth of his breath on her back. She was so glad that he was there. She had almost started to become afraid, out there all alone in the dark. After a few moments more, Adrianna got onto Cortath's back and bade him to take her where he had been keeping himself. For a short while they walked, Adrianna resting herself upon his back, lulled by his easy lope. When he stopped, Adrianna slid off of his back and found that he had found himself a small copse of trees under which to rest himself. Beneath the largest one, Adrianna saw the indentation in the grasses where he had been laying. Cortath took himself over to that spot, and then lay down within the indentation.

Adrianna followed Cortath over to the spot. Suddenly she found that she was tired, and she was more than willing to join her friend in his nest. She settled down next to him in the flattened grass. Cortath placed his head on his paws and closed his eyes. For a few moments Adrianna sat there and stared at him. His communication with her through the link had been barely minimal. She was accustomed to feeling and experiencing so much more with him. She did not receive any negative emotions from him, so she knew that he was not upset with her about anything. Deep within her gut, she knew that something was wrong, but she could not figure out what it was.

Adrianna lay her head upon Cortath's side. He did not curl around her as he usually did, nor did he adjust himself to make her more comfortable. He merely lay there, his eyes closed. His breathed deeply and slowly, as though he had fallen asleep already. Adrianna gently caressed his face, and ran her fingers through his silky soft mane. Cortath did not stir. Finally she curled up into a ball next to him, pressing her back into his side. Shortly, she was fast asleep.

***

Dinim walked down the stairs. His head ached from drinking too much the night before. Not only that, but his sleep had been restless. After Adrianna had left the table, Dinim had partaken of more of the ale. After a couple hours of drinking heavily, he had stumbled up the stairs to the room he shared with

Sabian. He fell into bed just to find himself replaying the whole horrible scene in his mind, over and over again.

Dinim heard the voices of Tianna and Dartanyen when he reached the bottom of the stairs. "Are you sure that she never came back?" said Dartanyen.

Tianna put her hands on her hips. "What do you mean, 'are you sure'? We share a room. For the love of Beory, you men . . ."

"What's going on here?" Dinim joined Tianna, Dartanyen, Amethyst and Armond.

Armond turned to glare at him. "Adrianna did not return to the inn. Tianna has been waiting up for her for half of the night." Armond's tone was accusatory, and his glare bordering on menacing. Dinim felt a chill of fear sweep through him. Because of him, she had left the tavern. Because of him, she had wandered into the night. What had happened to her? It was not like her to not let them know of her whereabouts. Something had happened to her, and it was all his fault.

Tianna must have seen the myriad of expressions passing over his face. "Okay, let's not jump to any conclusions. Just because she did not come back to the inn last night does not mean that something has happened to her."

After that statement there was silence. No one knew what to say, all realizing that, most likely, something had indeed happened to Adrianna. Why else would she not have returned? "Gather the rest of the group, Tianna. We need to start looking for her," said Dartanyen quietly.

Tianna nodded and went up the stairs to do Dartanyen's bidding. Armond followed her, casting one last nasty glance at Dinim as he left. Silently, Dinim stood before Dartanyen. Finally the other man spoke. "I don't know why you did what you did last night, nor do I want to know. All I want to say is that it was wrong of you, but I think that you know that already. Adrianna has shown you more kindness and given you more friendship than anyone else in this group, yet you betrayed her trust in the worst way." Dartanyen paused and shook his head.

"I don't know why I did it. I have wished, a million times over, that I had told her about the child . . ."

Dartanyen put a hand on Dinim's shoulder. "We all make mistakes. But it is the way that we rectify them that makes us good men."

Dinim nodded. "I know. But I don't think that Adrianna will ever forgive me."

"Then you don't give her enough credit."

"Perhaps."

Dartanyen and Dinim looked towards the stairs, hearing the rest of the group making their way down. Dartanyen raised his voice. "Let's split up into twos. I want to have the whole city scoured by the mid-day hour."

***

Adrianna walked slowly back into the city. She was worried. There was something definitely wrong with Cortath. She could tell that he was ill, but she could not get anything from him. Through the link, all she could feel was his lethargy, as well as the sensation of heat, which she had come to believe was a fever. Adrianna walked down the street, back to the inn. She hoped that her comrades had not worried about her. And if they had begun to wonder about her, she hoped that they would realize that she would be with Cortath.

Adrianna walked up the stairs to the inn. She found that she was still tired, and was looking forward to going back to sleep. But no. She had to find a meal for Cortath. It had quickly become apparent to her that he had not fed himself. His stomach had rumbled to her all throughout the night. Yet, despite his belly's indications, Cortath had not roused himself to obtain a meal. Adrianna was about to open the door when someone from within opened it for her. Startled, Adrianna jumped back, her hand to her chest. From the entryway, Dartanyen stood there staring at her, and behind him was the rest of the group.

Tianna rushed out of the inn and grabbed her by the arms. "Adrianna, where in the Hells have you been? We have been worried sick about you."

Adrianna felt her eyes widen. "I went to spend the night with Cortath. I did not think you would worry about me. I'm sorry . . ."

"Don't ever do that again," Tianna said angrily. "You are no different than anyone else in the group. You let us know when you are going somewhere. How dare you . . ."

Dartanyen put a hand on Tianna's shoulder. "I think she gets the point."

Adrianna regarded her companions standing at the doorway. She realized that they had been about to go out looking for her. She must have been wearing an expression of chagrin on her face, because Dartanyen gave her an, 'Its okay' look. Adrianna saw Dinim standing with all of the rest of them. Why he even bothered she could not begin to fathom. He obviously did not care about her. Perhaps he was just doing it because Dartanyen asked him for the favor.

All of a sudden Tianna was rushing at her. Adrianna steeled herself, but soon realized that the other woman was merely embracing her. "I was so worried about you. I'm sorry. I didn't mean to yell at you. It's just that . . . I love you so."

Adrianna patted her friend's back. She was touched by Tianna's words. She had not known how much she had come to mean to Tianna. Adrianna felt the same. She had become close to the other woman, and they shared a special connection. It was almost like Tianna had become a sister to her. *Sister.* Damn. Sheridana . . . where was Sheridana? Adrianna hoped that she had not left. She had so much to say, and had not been given the chance. Perhaps she should have followed Sheri last night after all, despite her fear of rejection. Her sister deserved at least that much, especially having been attacked by one of her best friends. Adrianna realized that perhaps she still carried some measure of resentment inside of her, despite the love she had for Sheridana, because it was Sheri who had been the one to leave all of those years ago.

Adrianna sighed, her mind returning to Cortath's plight. If she had gone to see Sheri, she may never have found out about him. "Tianna, Cortath is ill. I don't know what is wrong with him. You have to come with me, and help me find out what is making him sick."

Tianna pulled away from Adrianna, a frown furrowing her brow. "Okay. I will go and get my bags." Tianna then turned and went back into the inn. Zorg and Amethyst also went back inside. Armond came over to her and put a hand on her shoulder. "I am glad to see that you are all right." He smiled at her and then followed the other two back into the inn.

Dartanyen then stepped up to her. "I will accompany you and Tianna to Cortath."

Adrianna nodded. Tianna re-emerged from the inn. "I'm ready."

"Let me go and get a couple of the larian," said Dartanyen. Adrianna only nodded again, her mind questing at Cortath once more. She could only hope that Tianna would be able to help him.

* * *

Adrianna sat at the dinner table, picking at the remnants of her meal. Tianna had been unable to discover what was wrong with Cortath. She had noticed the mild fever and his lethargy, but she could not find any seeping or open wounds that would be the cause of any infection. She had prayed to her goddess to heal him, but when Tianna placed her hands on Cortath, she had felt nothing festering inside of his body that would cause his illness. Tianna told Adrianna that perhaps Cortath was just simply worn out . . . that perhaps he needed a rest. To Adrianna that didn't seem right. The time they had spent traveling with the gypsy caravan had been relatively stress-free. Nothing had been expected of Cortath, and he had been able to rest as often as he wished. No, it was not lack of rest that was wrong with her friend. But at least he ate the food that Adrianna brought for him. Perhaps he just had a common ailment, like the flu, and needed to be taken care of for a few days. She supposed that everyone got sick, even animals.

Adrianna dropped her fork. She just wasn't hungry anymore. She pushed the plate away from her and leaned back in the chair. She was alone, the rest of the group having left the table quite some time ago. She knew that she had some decisions to make now. She knew that she needed to go to Sheri, to explain away the damage that Dinim had wrought the night before. Then Adrianna had to tell Sheri about Thane . . . that their father had been hunting her down so that he could kill her. Adrianna sighed heavily. She knew that Sheri had not left the city. Upon asking the tavern owner, he had told Adrianna that the young woman was still renting one of his rooms.

Adrianna leaned into the table and put her head in her hands. She had so many things on her mind . . . so many decisions to make. What was she going to do about Thane? He would continue to come after her until she was dead. She could not run from him forever. One of these days, she had to face him. He would be able to dispose of her easily. With Adrianna dead, it was a good possibility that the rest of the group would be saved from his wrath. But then, what of Sheridana and her child? Did their father want her to die as well?

Adrianna knew that it was silly to think this way, especially about her own death, but she did not really know what else to consider. She was stuck between a rock and a hard place. Not only that, but Ami Rayhana had warned the group that Thane was not their only enemy, that it was their destiny to be the bringer of his downfall. Gods, it was too much to contemplate, especially when she didn't even know where she should go when she left this city. Back to Sangrilak, she supposed.

Suddenly, Adrianna felt a hand on her shoulder. Startled, Adrianna's body jumped. She brought her head up to see Sheridana standing beside her. The other woman removed her hand from Adrianna's shoulder. "I'm sorry. I didn't mean to startle you."

Adrianna shook her head. "No. It's okay. Have a seat." Adrianna gestured to the chair next to her.

Sheridana took the proffered seat and sat down. For a few moments there was silence, but then Sheridana spoke. "Your friend, Tianna . . . she came to my room."

Adrianna raised an eyebrow. "Really? When was this?" She was surprised to hear that Tianna had gone to speak to Sheri. Tianna had not said anything to her about doing any such thing.

"She came just about an hour ago."

Adrianna nodded. "What did she come to say?"

For a moment, Sheridana continued to look down on her clasped hands, and did not reply. Adrianna regarded her intently, and when Sheri finally looked up once more, her eyes shone with unshed tears. "She said that you have been moping about all day."

Adrianna nodded once more, feeling her own tears begin to threaten. "I suppose I have."

Silence reigned once more. Adrianna found herself struggling with her emotions, wondering what she should say. Maybe she should say, *Oh, Dinim usually isn't such a bastard. He didn't mean to hurt your feelings.* Or maybe, *Dinim is such an oaf. He doesn't realize the way he comes off sometimes . . .* But Adrianna didn't want to say either of those things. She didn't want to stick up for him. Perhaps she should say*, That man, he is such a lloryk's ass. I don't really know him very well.* Damn, she didn't really want to lie either. But, she had to say something. "Sheridana, I am so sorry about last night. I . . ."

Sheri put her hand on top of Adrianna's. "Don't be. It's okay." Sheri looked into the eyes of her twin sister. It had been so long and she had missed Adria so much. The years had been good to Adria. She was more beautiful than Sheri ever remembered her being. When she had seen Adrianna standing there in the midst of the bustling tavern, her heart had stilled, and then it had swelled so large that she thought it would burst from within her chest.

Adrianna caught Sheridana's gaze. She saw her hurt, but it seemed to be merely a surface thing. Most of all, she saw love reflected there. Love for her. Adrianna rose from her seat and Sheridana followed suit. The two women embraced one another. Sheridana sighed. It felt so good to have Adrianna hold her, to embrace her as she had when they were children. Sheridana was so glad to have her sister back, and now she was afraid that she would see Adrianna walk out of her life the way she had walked out of Adrianna's all of those years ago. "Adrianna . . . it is so good to be with you again."

Adrianna pulled away and smiled at Sheridana warmly. "I feel the same. Come. Let's go take a walk. It seems to be a nice evening."

Sheridana nodded. "Yes, that would be nice. Just let me run upstairs for a moment." Sheridana needed to let Carli know that she would be leaving the inn for a while. Sheridana turned and began to make her way to the stairs when Adrianna's voice from behind stopped her.

"Sheridana, aren't you going to introduce me to your baby?" Her sister's voice sounded sad and more than a little hurt. Sheri turned around and saw the emotion written across Adrianna's face. Suddenly she felt badly. It would be natural for her sister to want to meet her niece. But Sheri had been so wrapped up in her own feelings, she had not bothered to stop and consider Adria's.

Sheri nodded and smiled. "Of course. Please, come upstairs with me. You can meet both Carli and Fitanni." Sheridana reached down, took Adrianna's hand, and began to lead her up the stairs.

Adrianna followed Sheridana up the stairs and to the door of the third room on the right, not far from her own room down the hall. Sheri opened the door and stepped into the room. Adrianna followed her sister inside. The room was just like the one that she shared with Tianna and Amethyst. Against the far wall was a wash-stand, and against the right wall there was a desk. In the center of the room there were two beds. Upon one bed there was a young woman with dark-brown hair. She was reading a book. She looked up from the book and smiled when they entered the room. On the other bed was the small form of Sheridana's daughter. The child was asleep, her thumb in her tiny mouth. Her golden curls were damp with sweat. Tears sat on her plump cheeks below her eyes, testimony of her cries. "She has been crying for you, Sheri. I think that she wanted you to rock her to sleep," said the young woman.

Adrianna watched as Sheri gently seated herself upon the bed. She swept a finger down one rosy cheek and then stroked the hair from the child's forehead. "This is Fitanni." Sheridana smiled tenderly at the baby. She then looked up at Adrianna solemnly. "She is everything to me."

Adrianna also sat upon the bed. She leaned over the sleeping child. "She is beautiful Sheridana." Adrianna was surprised to see that most of the child's features appeared to be human. Her ears were rounded instead of arched and pointed and her face was not so angular. But she was a lovely child, nonetheless.

"She is the greatest thing I have ever done."

Mildly surprised, Adrianna quickly looked up to find Sheridana regarding her solemnly. She saw the sadness etched upon Sheridana's features, the pain of loss still evident. She wondered what had happened to her sister, where the father of the child was. She also wondered about her uncle, if he fared well. "Someday you, too, will know what I feel. When you look at your children, you will see a miracle, a gift from the gods, and you will treasure them with every breath you take."

Adrianna stared at Sheridana, taken aback by the passion that emanated from her. She had never thought about having children. She did not know with whom she could possibly consider having them. But now that she thought about it, she assumed she would feel about her children the way Sheridana felt about hers. Yes, if the future allowed it, perhaps one day she would know what it felt like to bear a child and to love it. Then Ami Rayhana's words echoed through her mind and Adrianna felt her own moment of sadness. For her, the future seemed nothing but bleak. It seemed that this kind of happiness would not be something that she would be able to have.

***

Late into the night Adrianna and Sheri stayed in one another's company. Once the ice was broken, the women discovered the ease with which conversation came to them. In this way, it was as though they had never been apart. But then again, it was because they had spent so many years away from one another that they had so much to talk about. The conversation was light-spirited, and easy-going. They bantered back and forth like schoolgirls, and the topics that they chose to speak about had the same quality. With each other, they were able to recapture a small portion of their youth, which somehow seemed to have escaped them long ago despite their tender years.

For women with faelin blood, Adria and Sheri were indeed young. In spite of the multitude of similarities, the faelin and human races still had their differences. In general, faelin tended to live longer than humans. Inasmuch, faelin young tended to develop at a slower rate than human children. At twenty-three years, they were barely out of adolescence. If they had been brought up within faelin society, they would still be receiving formal education. Leaving their father's house would have been out of the question.

At the age of twenty-one, Sheri had become pregnant. For a woman with faelin blood, this was extremely uncommon. For eleven months Sheridana carried her child. Any human woman would have carried for only nine months, and a true-blooded faelin woman almost fourteen. Because of her young age, Sheri had difficulty during labor, and when the child was finally born, she lost a lot of blood. The infant had been small, as faelin babies tend to be. And just like any other humanoid infant, she was completely dependent upon her mother for survival.

Into the wee hours of the morning the sisters talked. They spoke of Gareth, the brother they hadn't seen in so long. When the girls were but twelve years of age, he had left the household and had never returned. Sheridana claimed that he left because he had been unable to get along with their father. Adrianna found herself not responding to that statement, unable to bring up the subject of Thane, and unwilling to ruin this moment of camaraderie with Sheri. Likewise, Sheri did not mention Fitanni's father to Adria. It would be a shock when her sister found out that Ian was her niece's father, in addition to finding out that he was dead. Instead they spoke about their hopes and dreams, the interesting things they had learned in one another's absence. Upon many occasions the talk became so animated that the baby woke and Sheri had to soothe Fitanni back into sleep. Adrianna found that she had fallen in love with the child already, and the baby seemed to have taken to her as well.

Finally, the women decided that they should both get some rest. Adrianna was about to get up to go to her own chamber when they heard a commotion in the hallway outside the room. Sheri sprang from her bed, and, on her way to the door, grabbed her bow that hung upon the bedpost as well as a couple of arrows that lay on the little table she had placed by the door just in case a situation arose. She and Adrianna burst out of the room to find a naked woman running through the hallway. It took Sheridana a moment to realize who it was: the woman Tianna.

"You get back here with my belongings, you son of an umberhulk!" Tianna screamed.

Sheridana's gaze flickered down the hall to see the retreating back of a man. She quickly turned to look in the other direction and saw Dartanyen knocking an arrow in his bow. He let it fly at the man down the corridor. Just before the arrow was about to hit the man, he careened around the corner and disappeared. For a few moments everyone just stood there. Dartanyen made his way over to Sheri and Adrianna. Unmindful of her state of undress, Tianna had followed the man down the hall and had disappeared around the corner as well. Then from the direction that the man and Tianna had gone, they heard a shout, a series of curses, and then another shout. Dartanyen grunted with satisfaction. The thief had met up with Armond in the rear stairway.

The man came running back around the corner. Sheridana knocked her arrow and let it fly. It hit the thief in the right shoulder and was joined soon after by an arrow from Dartanyen in his left leg. The man cried out in pain, wrenched the arrow from his thigh, and continued towards them down the hall. When he saw Sheri and Dartanyen prepare their bows yet again, he staggered to a stop. The man turned about in desperation, and was about to go back down the hall when Armond emerged from around the corner. Tianna followed him, now wearing Armond's cloak. "You rancid maggot! How dare you . . ."

The man turned and tried to turn the knob on the door closest to him. He shook his head as he wrestled with it for a moment and then moved on to the next one. He opened the door and entered the room. Dartanyen, Sheri, and Adrianna rushed to it to find the man escaping through the window within.

"He's going down!" Dartanyen bellowed as the three of them rushed into the room, alerting those still in the hallway to make their way to the place where the man would be landing . . . or not. The man disappeared from the windowsill. Sheridana ran to it to see him land upon the ground below. She aimed at him once more and her arrow was true. It struck him in the shoulder blade, catching him off balance. He staggered, but continued to run. Sheridana turned from the window to find herself the sole occupant of the room. She rushed out, trailing the others by an arrow shot.

Adrianna followed Dartanyen down the front stairway and out the one-way door leading from that corridor to the outside. Dartanyen was fast, much faster than herself, and she had to strain to keep up with him. Once outside they turned the corner of the building to see that Zorg and Armond had intercepted the man's flight and were herding him back into their general direction. Dartanyen raised his bow and shot another arrow. It hit the man in the chest and he pitched backward onto the grass. Sheridana ran up to Dartanyen's side, breathing heavily due to her mad dash down the staircase. The two then walked towards the downed man. They did not hurry; there was no need. He was theirs. Adrianna took in the similar expressions they wore upon their faces: the look of a predator closing in on the kill, and their body movements reflected as such . . . the slow methodical pace of ones who know the blow that will be delivered.

Finally, Sheridana and Dartanyen stood over the man. Even Tianna had stepped aside at their approach, she too having seen the intensity etched upon their features. Zorg and Armond stood behind him, closing off any chance of escape. Sheridana nudged him with her bare foot. "Have you anything to say for yourself?"

The man had rolled over onto his stomach, and lay heaving on the ground. Armond knelt at the man's side, attempting to see if he was all right. Suddenly the man lunged from the ground, a dagger in his hand. He stabbed Armond in the chest, and the Bladesinger fell back. The thief began to run once more, bowling past Zorg in his desperation. Tianna knelt beside Armond, who was cursing profusely. "I guess not," Sheridana murmured as she let loose her last arrow. It hit the thief in the back, and he fell once more to the ground. Adrianna knew he was dead when he did not arise. She glanced around at the rest of the group. Adrianna saw that Dartanyen was regarding Sheridana with surprise, interest, and something more. He looked upon her the way a man looks upon an equal in battle. Adrianna smiled to herself.

***

The wind whispered through the trees. The silver leaves rustled, creating a melody of sound that could soothe and heal the soul. It was a summer wind, full of warmth and the scents that could only be assimilated at this time of the year. Soon, the warmth would dissipate, and the air would become cooler. The leaves of most trees would begin to turn color. Shades of crimson, orange, and golden yellow would suffuse the forests. But not this glen. The leaves from the silver oak trees never changed color.

Very few silver oak forests existed. The largest, most extensive forest in Shandahar, Elvandahar, was a silver oak forest. All of the other large forests in Shandahar were comprised of maple, birch, oak, and ash. Elvandahar was also home to the largest population of Hinterlean faelin. It was a beautiful place, and many people went there just for the experience that it offered. This glen was one of the only other areas where the silver oak tree grew. Very few other types of trees could grow near the silver oak, and so, in areas where it grew, it was predominant.

Dremathian walked among the tall trees. He was home here in the glen. His people called it Krathil-lon, or "silver creation". It was a place of power, a sinkhole for magic. Wondrous things could be done or undone here, and Dremathian presided over it. However, only for the past several years had he been the arch-druid of Krathil-lon. His predecessor had presided for over eighty years. Like himself, Mesendric had been half-faelin, and Dremathian hoped that he would live just as long.

Introspectively, Dremathian continued to walk. For the past few days he had not been feeling well. For several nights now, his sleep had been disturbed by strange images. During the day he functioned in a state of fatigue, and his appetite was severely diminished. His mind had begun to focus upon events from the past, and no matter how hard he tried to tune the memories out, they continued to clutter his mind. But for the most part they were good memories of times spent with one of his dearest friends. Dremathian supposed it could have been worse; he could think of no one else about whom he would prefer to reminisce. So, he had been spending the last three days thinking about Sirion Timberlyn and virtually nothing else.

For the past two decades, Dremathian had borne the honor of calling Sirion one of his finest friends. During the time when their friendship was new, Sirion had defended Dremathian and his Order on several occasions. Historically, rangers and druids worked within the natural world as a team. The druids functioned as guardians of the wilderness, and the rangers as protectors of the druids. But something happened; a fight broke out between the two peoples. Druids, with all of their rules and restrictions, tried to impose their lifestyle upon their freer and more liberated ranger counterparts. The rangers rebelled and eventually left the druids alone to their own devices. Now there were very few rangers left, and most of them hired themselves out to the Kingdom of Elvandahar, or to anyone who needed safe passage through the larger forests. They continued to be protectors, focusing instead upon the flora and fauna of the forest within which they resided. But no more did any ranger endeavor to protect any druid. Until Sirion.

Dremathian remembered those days like they had happened only yesterday. Sirion had defied his fellow rangers, and had ventured to help Dremathian and his Order with a lycanthrope problem. Sirion had dispatched the shirwemic with deadly aptitude. The druids of his Order had been shocked by the quick efficiency of Sirion's work, his single-mindedness, and his strength. After the threat had been dissipated, Dremathian had taken Sirion to his home, where he bandaged the man and bade him rest. For several days Sirion had stayed in Dremathian's home, healing from the wounds he had suffered from the shirwemic leader. When Sirion had recovered enough to leave, he chose not to do so, instead taking Dremathian up on his offer to show him the life of the druids within his Order.

For over a third of a year Sirion stayed with the Order of Krathil-lon. Dremathian taught him many things, and Sirion was always eager to learn. A few nights before Sirion left the glen, Dremathian engaged Sirion in a bonding ceremony. It was one in which he participated with all of his fellow druids. It made them brothers, and he wished for Sirion to be that to him as well. Once their blood had mixed and the ceremony was drawing to a close, the men sat across the fire from one another. There was something that Dremathian had wanted to discuss with Sirion for quite some time, but he had never been able to broach the subject.

Within the time that Sirion had spent with him, Dremathian had begun to notice something about his friend. Anger. Sirion had a lot of anger, anger that was just biding its time, waiting to be unleashed. Within Sirion it crouched like an animal, becoming stronger and stronger. Dremathian knew that Sirion had had a difficult childhood: had been raised by his father to be a fighter, had almost been murdered by his uncle and had been through several brutal battles. Sirion had not come away unscathed by these experiences, and Dremathian felt that the crouching animal within him was a culmination of all of these experiences. Dremathian had no doubt that the animal within would come leaping out of Sirion one day, and Sirion would not be able to control it.

That night after the ceremony, Dremathian spoke with Sirion about the anger. Sirion did not say much about it, but did not deny Dremathian either. Dremathian offered Sirion his best advice, told his friend that he should learn to accept his past, to not trap the anger inside of himself, and to come to terms with the beast that lived within his soul. When Dremathian warned Sirion about the consequences of allowing the creature within to gain strength, Sirion asked him what could happen. Dremathian did not have the answer to that question. A few days later, Sirion left the glen. Over the years, Dremathian saw Sirion every now and again. Whenever that happened, they spoke to one another like no time had passed at all. Dremathian was glad to call Sirion 'brother', and cherished the few months they had spent together in Krathil-lon.

Dremathian suddenly stopped walking. He felt ill, the sickness rushing through him like a wave. He doubled over and vomited. When finally he was able to straighten himself, he began to make back towards home. He just needed some rest. Suddenly, Dremathian found himself beset by images: a corubis with a mane, a wagon, a group of people Dremathian did not know. The druid clutched his skull and fell to his knees. He called out, hoping that one of his brothers would come to help him. The images continued: Sirion, the Wildrunners, a vortex of lightning . . . and then pain so intense that Dremathian cried out in agony.

Dremathian awoke to find two of his brothers kneeling over him. "Wha . . . what has happened to me?"

"We heard your screams. We arrived to find you convulsing on the ground. We thought we had lost you for a moment," said Brother Verdec.

"Indeed," said Dremathian. He felt cold, and his hands were sweaty. He ran a hand through his short silvering hair, to find that it was damp as well.

And then it all came rushing back to him . . . the images of Sirion. Dremathian rose unsteadily from the ground, Brothers Verdec and Matthias helping him. "Please, let's get to the council hall as quickly as possible."

"Why, Father? Is something amiss?"

Dremathian nodded. "My friend is in great danger. We need to reach him as soon as possible. When we get to the hall, sound the claxon. A group of us will be leaving in the morning."

CHAPTER 14

The group followed the Dresnjik River southward. Upon the morrow, they would cross the river and head to the city of Kamden. It was a different route then the one they had taken to Risset, but they did not want to retrace their steps in case Thane was still following them. Adrianna was relieved yet disquieted by the fact that they had not heard from him since the day that they heard about the skirmish in which he had taken part outside the city of Torrich. She remembered the words spoken by Ami Rayhana; that Thane's vision had been clouded for a time, but that when his sight returned he would renew his search for her. She still had not told her sister about Thane, and she was not sure when she would find the time to do so. She knew that Sheri would be greatly upset when she learned about their father, and Adrianna was not ready to dump that pail of sludge on her just yet.

Two days ago, the group left the city of Risset. Their numbers had grown by three. Now, not only had Sheridana joined them, but Carli and baby Fitanni as well. The men had been leery about the idea of traveling with a child, but the women had quickly been able to convince them that it was for the best. They really had no other option. When Adria finally got the chance to take Dartanyen aside, she told him her fears that the child would be at risk if she and Carli were left behind in Risset. If Thane were following them, he would probably track them there. Carli and the baby would be there alone, unprotected, and would be easy targets for an angry Thane. Dartanyen agreed with her rationale, and the next morning the group stocked up on supplies, collected the lloryk and larian, and left.

When the group reached the farmlands, Cortath was there to greet them. He looked better than he had the day before, and even seemed to have regained some of his vibrancy. When Sheri saw him for the first time, she was shocked to see how large he was. But when she saw how gentle Cortath was with her sister, and saw how much Adrianna loved him, Sheri could not help but accept him. Adrianna studied her friend for a time, and only when she was sure that he was strong enough did she finally give in and ride astride him for a while. She was glad that he was getting better, and her worries began to fade.

For the first day there was more than a little tension between certain members of the group. For the most part, Adrianna ignored Dinim, and could barely stand to be within a few feet of his proximity. The few times that he had addressed her, Adrianna had either responded to him with the minimal amount of interaction, or she had not deigned to respond at all. Sheri also avoided him, and Sabian as well. Although her avoidance tactics were not needed, since much of the time Sheri was inside the wagon tending to her daughter. However, she made a nightly contribution to the stewpot, more than making up for any delinquency. She also helped in the nightly watch, tending to take the last one since the baby woke her up early in the morning anyway. It worked out well, and neither Adrianna, Sabian, Dinim, nor Tianna needed to take any watches, their time instead spent upon their studies.

On the second day of their journey, Adrianna noticed that Cortath appeared to be getting sickly once again. He was lethargic, and when she touched his nose, she could feel that it was warm and dry. Once more, the emotions that were transmitted to her via the link were vague. As the day wore on, Cortath became more listless and he refused to eat. Adrianna began to fret anew, and she wondered what was wrong with him. At the end of the day, he merely lay down on the ground next to her bedroll and closed his eyes. After the evening meal, Adrianna lay down next to him and fell asleep as she stroked the soft fur around his face.

The next morning Adrianna found herself unable to rouse Cortath. He was either unwilling or unable to wake himself sufficiently to travel. This day they were to cross the Dresnjik River. Once upon the ferry, Cortath would be able to rest all that he needed, but that was not the real issue. Through the link, Adrianna could sense that he was becoming very ill. Adrianna called Tianna over to them in order to assess the situation. Tianna frowned when she placed her hands upon Cortath. She shook her head and said, "Adria, Cortath is very sick . . . I can feel it inside of him. But I just can't figure out why. He does not have an infection, and he has not been poisoned. The only thing I can think of is that this may be a magic-induced illness."

Adrianna was silent for a moment. "Can you help him?"

Tianna shook her head once more. "I can do nothing for him. Whomever, or whatever, is doing this to him has taken a strong hold." Tianna paused. "I am sorry, Adria."

Adrianna knew what Tianna was implying by that statement. If Cortath continued to get worse, he would surely die. Dartanyen approached the scene and stood over them for a moment. "Come on. Let's get him into the wagon. We have to leave soon if we are to take the ferry across the river today."

Adrianna nodded. Dartanyen and Tianna left to finish packing their bags. Adrianna continued to kneel next to her friend, her tears falling onto the thick mane of fur around his neck. She buried her fingers deep into the fur until finally she reached the soft skin beneath. Suddenly she felt something. She traced it with her forefinger. It felt like a cord. She hooked her finger under the cord, and slowly began to pull it up through the thick fur. It took her a few moments, it having been trapped beneath the layers of fur. But finally she could see the cord.

It was black, appearing to be made out of leather. She continued to struggle with it, trying to get it out of the hair. Finally she took her dagger and cut it. She pulled on one end of the cord and it slipped through the fur. For a moment it caught, and she tugged on it until it came free. When she finally beheld the entire length of it, she found that the reason why it had been so difficult to remove was because of the leather pouch that was suspended from it.

Adrianna took the pouch, finding it to be about the size of her hand. Feeling around on it, she felt something inside of it. She paused for a moment before she opened it. What was a leather pouch doing around the neck of an animal? Had Cortath once been a companion to someone else? Had he been a message carrier, and this was his last undelivered message? He had never let on to her about having known someone else before her. But then again, she had never inquired either. Slowly, Adrianna opened the pouch, dumping the contents of it into her lap.

The first thing that Adrianna picked up was the ring. She was surprised to find that it was a signet ring, bearing a crest carved within the gold. The crest was a depiction of a hawk carrying leafy sprigs within its talons. Looking closely at the depiction, Adria could see that the leaves appeared to be from some type of oak tree. It was a beautiful ring, inlaid with tiny silver gems. It was definitely worth a small fortune. Next she picked up a long sharp tooth, appearing to be from some type of canine. She turned it this way and that, and then set it down next to the ring. She then picked up the tiny whistle. It was made from a dark wood, and had a tiny carving of a corubis upon it. Adrianna put the whistle to her lips and blew on it. Nothing emerged. She frowned, shaking her head and placing it next to the tooth.

Finally, Adrianna picked up the last item that she found within the pouch. It was a piece of folded parchment, appearing like it may have been some kind of message. "Adrianna, I have your things packed and in the wagon. Let's get Cortath in there now." Adrianna looked up from the contents of the pouch. Tianna was striding over to her, Dartanyen and Zorg following behind. The wagon was being backed up, closer and closer to where Cortath lay. "What do you have there?" Tianna crouched next to her.

"It's strange actually. I found this pouch around Cortath's neck. It had these things in it." Adrianna held up the pouch and gestured to the four items.

"Humpf." Tianna picked up the signet ring and examined it. Suddenly her eyes widened. "Adrianna, did you say that you got this ring from that pouch?"

Adrianna nodded. "Yes. Along with these other things."

Tianna put the ring closer to her eyes, narrowing them. "I can't believe this, but it's true . . ."

"What . . ."

"This ring bears Sirion's house crest upon it. Only two were made just like this one. Anya wears one and Sirion had the other. Adria, I think this is Sirion's ring!"

Adrianna was taken aback. How could this possibly be Sirion's ring? Sirion was dead. Not only that, but why would this animal have been carrying it around his neck? Adrianna watched Tianna pick up the pouch and the whistle. "By the gods, can it truly be? Adria, these are Sirion's belongings."

"Are you sure?"

"I have no doubt. I have seen Sirion call Dramati with this whistle on more than one occasion."

"But it doesn't work."

"How do you know?"

"I tried it, and nothing came out."

"I am sure that it did. Only wemic and corubis can hear the frequency emitted from this whistle. Sirion made it. I can tell, because he carved Dramati into it. See?"

Adrianna looked to where Tianna pointed. Indeed, there was the carving of the animal she had seen before. Tianna was so excited, and seemed so sure that this was Sirion's pouch. But that did not explain why it happened to have been found around the neck of her friend. Adrianna looked up to find Dartanyen, Zorg, and Armond coming over to them. "Come on. Let's get Cortath into the wagon and get going," said Dartanyen.

"Take a look at this," said Tianna elatedly. "Adrianna found this pouch around Cortath's neck, and I think that it belongs to Sirion."

The three men came over and listened to what Tianna was saying. Dinim climbed down from the back of the wagon and joined them. He caught the last portion of her description when he made it over to them. When he looked down at the pouch, and heard Sirion's name, he began to frown. "I have seen a pouch similar to that one around Sirion's neck."

"See . . . I told you. This is Sirion's pouch."

Dinim shook his head. "Tianna, you know that is not possible. I told you . . ."

Tianna narrowed her eyes. "Dinim, I know what you told me, but I am telling you that this pouch belongs to him. This is his ring, his whistle, and Dramati's first tooth. I would know. I have seen these things several times before."

"But Tianna, what was it doing around Cortath's neck?" asked Adrianna.

Tianna stopped and looked down at Cortath. She looked at his face, into his eyes. Cortath regarded her in turn, slowly lifting his head from the ground. Through the link, Adrianna could sense his awareness that they were talking about him. Once more, Adrianna watched as Tianna's eyes widened. "Cor . . . Cortath . . . he is Sirion." She said the words almost breathlessly, like she could hardly believe them herself.

"What . . . are you crazy?" asked Dartanyen.

"No, I am serious. His eyes . . . now I know why they have always been so familiar to me. They are *his* eyes . . . *Sirion's* eyes."

"You *are* crazy," said Zorg.

"Maybe not," said Armond. "She could be right."

"No way," said Dinim. "I saw him get sucked into that vortex. No one could have survived it."

"Sirion did." Tianna said it plainly. Adrianna just looked at her, wordless. Could it really be true? Could Cortath really be Sirion?

An hour later the wagon rumbled to a stop. Adrianna heard a series of expletives from the driver's seat. She pulled back the cover and saw the angry expression on Dartanyen's face. "Dartanyen, what is it?"

"We missed the damned ferry." Dartanyen proceeded to climb down from the wagon. Adrianna walked through the wagon to the rear. She pulled aside the cover and saw the ferry. It had only recently pulled away from the shore and was beginning the journey across the river.

Adrianna sighed and turned back to Cortath. His large body took up most of the wagon. His eyes were closed and his body shook every now and again as he slept. She crawled over to his head, lifted it gingerly, and placed it in her lap. She hummed softly beneath her breath, rocking herself back and forth. They would have to camp here for the day and take another ferry across the river tomorrow morning.

The day wore on. The group was grouchy. Dartanyen and Sheridana went hunting and came back with several peafowl. Adrianna offered one to Cortath, but he only lifted his head to sniff it. He then turned away. Through the link, Adrianna could sense the raging fever, the weakening of his body, and the turmoil in his soul. She didn't understand what it all meant, but eventually it would cause his death. She sobbed piteously over him, her tears wetting his fur. Tianna was there much of the time as well, and her eyes were red and puffy from her own crying. Amethyst, Sheri, and the men would enter the wagon every once in a while to see how Cortath was doing. But they always went away with bad news. Cortath was only getting worse.

The fact that her companion could be Sirion did not affect Adrianna. To her, he would always be Cortath, the one who understood her the best, who always kept her nightmares at bay, and who loved her the way no one else ever had before. She could not bear to think of her life without him. She was afraid, and she plead with Tianna to ask her goddess for help once more.

The tears spilled down Tianna's cheeks. "Adria, I have tried everything. I cannot help him; his illness is beyond even Beory. Dear gods, I can't stand to lose him again!" Tianna broke down, her body shuddering convulsively with the force of her sobs. Adrianna could only hold her, her heart breaking. Adrianna knew what Tianna was referring to. To her, Cortath was Sirion, her friend and childhood protector. Tianna had lost Sirion once, and now would have to lose him again.

The day moved into the early evening. The camp was somber. There was very little interaction, everyone mostly keeping to themselves. They had moved Cortath out of the wagon, hoping to give him some fresh air. He lay stretched out upon the ground. Suddenly his body started to convulse. Adrianna felt herself being thrown back by the force of the muscular contractions. The rest of the group rushed over, everyone trying to reach Cortath amidst the twitching legs. The animal made strange sounds deep in this throat, and his eyes began to roll back in his head.

Adrianna stood there watching her friend. Was he dying? Would he leave her now, to live her life without him? Then she sensed that someone else was there, people other than members of the group. She turned to find several brown-robed figures rushing up to the scene. One of them gently put his hands on her shoulders and moved her aside as he made towards Cortath. When Dartanyen noticed the people who had come, he ordered everyone to step away from Cortath. One of the men, the one who had moved her aside, knelt next to Cortath. He placed his hands on both sides of the animal's head, and leaned in close. "I am here my friend. I will help you. You are not alone."

***

Everyone hurriedly made their way down the passageway. Armond, Zorg, and two of the druids carried the litter that held Cortath. After several moments they found themselves in a corridor that widened into a large chamber. Adrianna took in the scene as they entered. In the center of the chamber there was a raised platform. It contained a pedestal upon which rested an open book as well as an object that appeared to be a fifteen-foot-high oval mirror. The druids walked up onto the raised dais, beckoning the group to follow.

The druid leader, Dremathian, walked over to the pedestal and the open book resting upon it. Strangely drawn, Adrianna made her way over to the book as well, Dramati at her side. Dremathian turned to her as she approached. Once she was beside him he spoke. "This will take us to Krathil-lon. Only there will I be able to help Sirion."

Standing beside the druid leader, Adrianna looked upon the book. There on the page she saw a wooded glen. The winds moved through the treetops, the silver leaves rustling gently. Below the life-like scene was a phrase written in the words of magic. Adrianna knew instinctively that upon reading the words, the portal before them would open to take them to the place represented upon the page in the book.

Dinim stepped up and stood behind Adrianna. He was awed by the book, never having seen its like ever before, even in his master's citadel. Adrianna looked over her shoulder, glancing at him for a moment before turning back to the book. Dremathian began to recite the words below the scene on the bottom of the page. What had appeared to be a mirror was no longer, as swirls of color began to move through the center of the oval space before them. The swirling reached a plateau and then began to stabilize into a shimmering wall of blue.

The druids picked up the litter and began to move towards the portal. Dremathian turned back to Adrianna. "Come. It is not painful . . . merely disorienting for a moment or two."

Adrianna nodded and began to follow him. Upon seeing her moving towards the portal, Dartanyen, Armond, and the rest of the group began to follow suit. Zorg helped the druids with the litter carrying Cortath. Once she was standing in front of the portal, Adrianna paused. She knew that her life was about to change once more. The group all stood behind her, waiting. Adrianna watched as Father Dremathian stepped through the shimmering wall. *Put your faith into what you most believe* . . . Adrianna stepped into the portal.

***

The group found themselves being shown to the place where they would be living during their stay in Krathil-lon. Upon arriving, they had found themselves within a large structure that the druids referred to as the Apoptos. It was the place where the library was kept, as well as the Brothers' chambers and the meditation and meeting halls. A short time later, as the group followed Brother Henning to the cabin, they walked along the paths of the forest. It was a place full of the beauty and tranquility of nature in its purest form. And there was magic; Adrianna could feel it the moment they stepped through the shimmering blue portal. Once they arrived, Dremathian and several other druids had swept Cortath away. She never got the chance to tell him how much she loved him, or to say good-bye.

When the druids found them at the river, Cortath had been in the midst of a seizure. The leader knelt over him and began to speak in a strange tongue. After a few moments, Cortath's convulsions ceased. Adrianna could only assume that something the man had done had helped her friend. Once the episode was over and Cortath's breathing was unlabored, Adrianna approached the man. Dartanyen had already engaged the man in conversation, and she learned that these people were of the Order of Krathil-lon, druids that lived in a small forest located in the southern reaches of the Sartingel Mountains. The leader was known as Father Dremathian, and was an old friend to Sirion. His dreams had revealed to him that Sirion was in trouble and so he had come to help Sirion to the best of his ability.

Adrianna was overcome with emotion. Tianna was right; indeed Cortath and Sirion were one and the same. Vaguely, she heard the healer in the background. Her voice was full of excitement as she told the druids of her suspicions prior to their precipitous arrival. Meanwhile, a couple of the druids were erecting what appeared to be a litter, one that they had brought with them. Adrianna wondered how they had carried it so far, and it was then that Adrianna realized that it was not just people that had joined them by the river, but several large creatures as well.

The beasts were huge, their bodies resembling a combination of a muscular feline and a great bird of prey. Their heads were largely feline, adorned with ruddy/gold feathers. The paws bore the talons of an eagle and a pair of large golden wings was folded against their furred sides. Adrianna stared at them wide-eyed, awed by their majesty and predatory beauty. She had never seen a griffon before, much less a cohort of them. They seemed to be friendly, their mannerisms un-aggressive. Upon their backs there were strange saddles, and many of them carried bags full of things about which Adrianna could only imagine.

Standing amongst the griffons was another animal as well. He was familiar to her: a corubis. She recognized him as Sirion's companion, Dramati. He seemed lost and forlorn, so different from the creature she had met in Sangrilak so many months ago. When he finally noticed her, Dramati seemed to brighten a little and loped over to her. She reached for him, and placed her hand into his soft fur. He leaned into her caress, and almost seemed to sigh. He missed the gentle rubbing that he used to receive from his comrade.

Once the litter was ready, Armond and Zorg loaded Cortath onto it. Adrianna and Dramati watched as the druids then rigged the litter onto the back of the largest of the griffons. The ruddy creature turned his feathered head to watch as the druids adjusted the litter with varying straps and other apparatus. It would be a heavy load for the beast to carry, but he seemed prepared to take on the job.

The group watched as the druids prepared to leave. Tianna had approached Dremathian, and was speaking to him in a low voice. She then went to the wagon, taking her belongings from inside of it. Adrianna stared at her, wondering. Was Tianna leaving with the druids? Well, Adrianna supposed she could not blame her. Sirion was her childhood friend after all. It would be natural for her to want to accompany him. Adrianna felt the pain of loss sweep through her for the hundredth time that day. Cortath was leaving her. Upon the backs of the griffons, these druids would take him away and Adrianna would never see her dear friend ever again.

Adrianna turned away from her thoughts when she felt a presence in front of her. She looked up into the kind face of Father Dremathian. His blue eyes were piercing as they looked at her. "Lady, you would do well to consider coming with us to Krathil-lon. I have felt something in the winds . . . something that is coming in this direction. I have never felt anything like it before, but I know that it is evil and that it could do you harm."

Adrianna stared at him, startled. Dremathian's expression was one of extreme seriousness. Fear rushed through her, and she suddenly knew who it was that was coming. Lord Thane had found them, and he was closing in for the kill. Dremathian seemed to know when she came to the realization. He nodded his head minutely. Adrianna nodded as well. It was the only indication Dartanyen needed to start unloading the wagon.

Everyone flew into a flurry of activity, loading the griffons with the group's belongings. Finally they were done. Adrianna felt a moment of sadness, hating to leave her lloryk, Sethanon, behind. Dartanyen and Armond released the animals, slapping them on the hindquarters. They galloped off into the distance, away from the incoming menace. Then everyone mounted the griffon to which he or she had been assigned. The creatures were carrying loads that were heavier than usual, but they seemed to have no problems as they began to run. They ran faster and faster, their wings unfurling from their sides. The wind whipped at the tendrils of hair about Adrianna's face, and she found herself leaning low over the back of the griffon. She saw everyone else doing the same. Suddenly she felt a strange feeling in the pit of her stomach, and then they were rising into the air. Higher and higher they rose. A feeling of exhilaration gripped her, and Adrianna felt like crying out. Never had she felt something so awesome, so breathtaking. She looked down from the back of the griffon, and saw the river winding, snakelike, through the land. She saw their abandoned wagon, as well as the lloryk and larian they had set free. And then she saw something else, something that made a chill rise up her spine. It was Thane. He had almost reached the place where they had been camping.

With him were his six minions, all of them riding steeds that seemed to have been made of darkness itself. She closed her eyes, thankful to the fates that had afforded them this escape. For surely she and her companions would not have escaped from Thane alive this time.

***

Thane stared up at the sky, watching the griffons carry her away from him. Angrily, he clenched his hands into fists, and then inhaled deeply. When he exhaled, he opened his mouth wide and a hideous wail was brought forth. Damn! Once again she had escaped him, and once again he would have to track her down.

The evening after their last meeting, Thane had started to track Adrianna and her group towards the city of Torrich. On the way, they encountered a caravan and easily destroyed it. However, they had been so focused on the caravan that they did not notice the approach of Grimwell and several more of Lord Aasarak's priests and sorcerers. Before they knew it they had found themselves surrounded. Words were exchanged, and then a battle was ensued. They were able to defeat the priests, but not without a cost. Weakened and unable to continue tracking Adrianna, Thane and his band rode back to the place they had rested the evening before. It took them two nights to fully recover from the battle, but by then Adrianna was gone. When he tried to scry for her the gem was clouded, as though she was being protected.

Thane went to Torrich anyway, but when he couldn't find Adrianna, he began to scour the countryside. It wasn't until almost two weeks later that Thane was able to detect her again, and he immediately began to track her down once more. Today they had been so close . . . and to see her flying away from him to gods knew where only made him angry in the extreme.

What had started out as simple desire to see the girl dead had become a fiery obsession. He had been angry when he lost her in the temple, infuriated when he lost her outside of Torrich, and now consumed with such rage he could barely see two feet in front of him. After losing her in the temple, he had not placed half as much effort into finding her as he did this time. Somehow, his obsession had become all encompassing, even to the exclusion of doing his master's bidding.

Thane glanced around the area in which he found himself. There was a wagon, as well as the remains of a campfire. Hells, if only he had not decided to leave the night of their last meeting, if only he had decided to stay and finish her off despite the arrival of the dawn. But the large canine had been an element that he had not considered, and his band had been weakened. But now she had managed to thwart him yet again, and he would be forced to take even more time to find her once more.

Next time he would show no mercy. As each day passed, he and his minions grew in power. When next he met his daughter, he would crush her as he should have done that night only two weeks past. Thane gestured to his mage, and the dark warlock cast his spell. The flames surrounded the wagon, and Thane watched as it burned to the ground. Yes, he would watch her die, and he would enjoy every moment.

***

Sirion slowly awoke. Somehow, he knew he had been asleep for a long time. Yet, someone had awoken him.

"Sirion . . ."

There it was again, the familiar voice that had awakened him from his deep slumber. He opened his eyes and found himself surrounded by darkness. The darkness was familiar. He knew it to be the prison of his mind, the place to which he had been deposited when his body changed from that of a man into that of a beast. It was that last vestige of him that was a man, that part that had been slowly dwindling away as the weeks passed. As the place became ever smaller, he had less and less contact with his senses outside. His animal nature had become predominant and Sirion had begun to forget who he was. He had begun to sleep for longer periods, escaping from the depression and loneliness and letting the inevitability of death have its way with him. But someone had awakened him.

"Sirion, my old friend . . . are you there?"

There was the familiar voice again. He tried to place it. It came from his past, this voice. He tried to speak, but nothing came out but a whine, his animal form unable to speak. He then tried to project a reply with his mind, as he had done with the Lady Adrianna. But he had quickly realized that his connection with her was different, that he could not communicate thusly with just anyone. Yet, he had nearly forgotten that fact, his influence over the body declining as his humanity faded away.

"Sirion, I know you are there. But I can not help you if you do not help yourself."

The voice stopped. Sirion waited, pensive. Help himself? How many times within the past weeks had he tried to do just that, just to meet complete and utter failure? How could he help himself if he did not know how to go about doing it? In angry frustration, Sirion began to struggle, pushing at the darkness. He pushed harder and harder, harder than he had since he first discovered what he had become.

Sirion opened his eyes. He saw through the eyes of an animal, the vision distorted, different than the sight of a man. Crouched before him there was a human . . . no, a half-faelin. The man was familiar to him, wearing a non-descript brown robe. The man looked deeply into Sirion's eyes and then began to smile. His graying dark hair was tied back and it hung over one shoulder. His blue eyes reflected happiness. Sirion, too, felt happy. He had not seen Father Dremathian for many years. He began to lift his head, but then lowered it again. It was too much of an effort. It was then that he realized that his body was dying.

"Sirion! It is so good to see you after so many years," said Dremathian. "I am going to help you as much as I can, but in the end, you will have to help yourself. Only you can get your life back again, and then only if you want it badly enough. But your time is limited. Hurry, Sirion. Fight your jailors, climb your barriers, and overcome your insufficiencies! Be stronger than you ever have before."

Sirion began to fade out, not having the strength to retain contact with the outside. He struggled to regain his hold to no avail. He found himself in darkness once more.

It was silent . . . noiseless. It was familiar to him now, having withstood it for so long. But Dremathian had made him remember, and a host of memories had come flooding back to him. He especially recalled those years he had spent with his father. It was with Servial that he had met Zandibar, Baltheros, Chans, and the other individuals who had taught him all he knew about hand-to-hand combat, weapon usage, meditation and a host of other skills he learned as a boy. Servial himself had taught Sirion the finer arts of being a ranger, including archery and swordplay. Memories of his father's brother, Sydonnia, also arose, and he was filled with hatred. The man was the bane of Sirion's existence. Sirion would kill him one day . . .

Sirion felt himself beginning to slip. The familiar tiredness overcame him. He felt compelled to give into it, but Dremathian had told him that he needed to be strong. Sirion let the memories fade as he struggled against the oppressive darkness and fatigue. It was difficult, more so than ever, but he persevered.

Dremathian stood over his friend. The animal lay dying at his feet. It was his doing. Dremathian had given Sirion an herb to ingest. Sprinkling it within some water, he had offered it to Sirion. Dremathian watched as the beast drank all of the water. The animal then lay down. Dremathian had given the potent herb in hopes to release Sirion from his internal prison, to give him another chance to win himself free of his self-imposed bonds. Where Sirion had failed before, Dremathian hoped Sirion would now conquer.

Dremathian knew that Sirion had suffered much in his life, including tragic loss and betrayal by his own family members. He had been primed by his father to become nothing short of an assassin, a rugged killing machine that would someday be capable of destroying that which Servial could not . . . his own brother, Sydonnia. Dremathian had heard it all as told by Sirion so long ago, during the months Sirion had stayed in Krathil-lon. Dremathian had come to know Servial as a self-serving bastard. The man had taught his son many things, especially the purpose for fighting. But Servial never taught his son the most important lesson . . . the purpose for living. In that way, Servial had done his child the worst injustice, and Sirion would never be free until he learned the meaning of life.

The darkness pressed close to Sirion. He disliked its proximity to him but tolerated it. He had not much of a choice. But the floodgate had been opened and memories returned. They coursed all about him like a maelstrom. In the center of the vortex, Sirion heard all of the voices and saw all of the faces of the many people he had known in his life. They circled and eddied about him and he became sucked into the recesses of his mind.

Without form, Sirion raced through time. He sped past scenes in his life: people and events that had been important to him. His mother and father arguing as he and Anya looked on . . . his mother crying softly to herself, her hands over her face, her body shaking with the force of her sobbing . . . his father speaking with another ranger . . . *"Servial, don't concern yourself with Lilandria. She is just a woman, and you are the best ranger in these parts. Don't let her spoil that for you."* The scenes shifted. He and Anya playing amongst the tall forest trees at home in Elvandahar, his father holding his hands in the proper position on a small bow made just for him, his mother kissing his forehead, her beautiful face radiant with love, Father Dremathian sitting across the ceremonial fire, Sirion having grown into a man . . .*"Sirion, family is the most important thing a man has. Without family, a man is nothing."*

Sirion's journey through his life continued. The scenes made him remember how he thought and felt at those times. Pensively, Sirion considered the scenes. He felt sadness upon seeing his mother's loving face. He had not seen her for several years. He felt good when he saw Dremathian. He had learned more from him than he had from any other person, with the exception of his father, of course. But Sirion's feelings concerning Servial were mixed. Servial had never taken Sirion back home. Sirion had returned there only after his father had been killed by Sydonnia.

Sirion watching, helpless, as his uncle tore out his father's throat, Sirion grasping Nora's arm tightly, he having recognized Sydonnia's scent on her, saying, *"No matter where you go, I will track you down and I will kill you."*. . . Sirion and his father sitting with the rest of the fighters . . . one of the men leaning into Sirion, *"Show your opponent no mercy. Be strong, give him all you've got, and utterly defeat him.* The scenes shifted. Sirion sitting across from his father at the evening fire, smiling as the older man told him stories of his youth . . . facing Zandibar in the ring, the fighter showing him how to evade an opponent's grasp . . . Baltheros, his large hand on Sirion's shoulder saying, *"When a man is down, and unable to rise, always consider showing him mercy. It portrays strength of character."*

Sirion became angry. The scene of his father's death by Sydonnia's hand brought back all of the old fears. He hated Sydonnia for what he had done. No matter what Servial had done to Sydonnia in the past, he did not deserve to die for it, even if it was Servial's fault that Sydonnia was cursed with lycanthropy. Sirion let his rage consume him. When they finally met, he would show Sydonnia no leniency. The man had not only killed Sirion's father, but others he cared about as well. He had even threatened his mother, although Sirion knew it was only to goad him. Sirion knew that Sydonnia loved his mother too much to ever kill her. Sirion moaned in anguish. Sydonnia had loved Lilandria more than his father ever did. She had deserved so much more than what Servial had given her. Yet, Sirion had forsaken her as well . . . her own son.

The darkness pressed upon him once more, the scenes from his life slowing down. Through the rage and guilt, the pressure was crushing and he gasped. He felt his life slipping, the voices from his life in accompaniment.

His own voice. *"Do I love myself? That's a silly question. I've never really thought about it. I suppose I do . . ."*

His father's voice. *"Your life is worthless Sydonnia! You have accomplished nothing and no one cares about you."*

Anya's voice. *"When I got old enough, and confident enough, I thought about finding you, tracking you down. I knew I could have succeeded. I wanted so much to see my brother again, despite my anger."*

His mother's voice. *"Life is a wondrous thing, Sirion. It is a miracle, nature's gift to us all."*

Chans' voice. *"Don't judge something upon the words of someone else. Experience it for yourself and, only then, lay judgment."*

Sorn's voice. *"Sometimes I wish my life was different, that I could be a normal man, with a home and a family. I often tire of the constant traveling, of not knowing where I will end up next, who I will kill on the morrow, or if I will find myself killed instead. What of you, Sirion? Don't you want something different sometimes . . . something real?"*

Dremathian's voice. *"The world . . . it is all around us, speaking to us. If we open our hearts, we can hear all that it has to say, in all of its many voices."*

Sirion clung to the edge of the precipice, clawing at the substance of his mind, feeling it slip beneath his fingers. And then, with nothing at his feet, he fell, his hands reaching for the ledge that was no longer there. He plummeted through the nothingness, the voices fading away, the scenes from his life having left him. His last thought was what a shame it was that he never got to know the Lady Adrianna as a man, that he wouldn't be the one . . . the one who would make all her sorrows undone.

Dremathian regarded the beast on the ground, watching for him to take his next breath. He waited. Time slipped by in slow motion, Dremathian refusing to believe what lay before his very eyes. The tears flowed, unchecked down his cheeks. The breath did not come. The old man went to his knees before Sirion, lifting the head of the animal into his arms. Dremathian rocked his body, silently weeping, his tears wetting the soft fur. He had failed. Dremathian had failed his student, failed to teach him properly. Dremathian did not deserve to be called Father of Krathil-lon.

***

Sensing someone was watching him, Sirion turned around. He saw her standing across the street . . . the woman with moon-colored hair, Lady Gemma Darnesse. His interest piqued, Sirion made his way over to her, stopping only when he was a couple of paces away. She was heavy with child, her belly stretching the fabric of her dress. Yet her beauty was something to behold, her pale blue eyes regarding him intently.

"Is there something you wish of me, Lady?"

She hesitated for a moment before answering, almost as though considering if she should say anything at all. The indecision however, was only momentary. Her voice was almost musical in quality, like the burbling of a mountain stream. And much to his surprise, she spoke in the language of Hinterlean faelin.

"You are Sirion Timberlyn, are you not?"

"Indeed I am, Lady."

"I have seen you in and about the city many times within the past couple of years. Since I have become with child, I have had dreams about you. Yet, we have never met before. Does this not seem strange to you?" Gemma's delicate eyebrows pulled together, her forehead creasing in a frown. Her confusion was apparent in her demeanor, and her desire to have the solution to her strange predicament.

Sirion nodded. "Yes, Lady. That must be quite disturbing for you. But what can I possibly do to help you?"

"I have a Talent, a Gift if you will . . . of seeing what Destiny holds in store for us. Perhaps if I speak to you of the dreams, I will cease to have them. Allow me to speak the words of your destiny, and perhaps I can be freed. Maybe you will become freed as well."

Sirion frowned. He did not hold much stock in the ranting of seers and fortune-tellers. Yet, this woman did not seem to be just another fortune-teller, and she did seem to be concerned about her dreams. "As you wish, Lady."

"You are meant for more than what you have become. When your destiny calls out to you, it will not be with the voice of the wilderness. You must make a choice, and only in making the right one will you ever know true happiness. In this you must find your inner strength. I have seen a woman in my dreams. She is meant for you, and you for

her. With her at your side, you are more than just the warrior, the dreamer, or the hero. Always remember."

Lady Gemma smiled at him then, one that reminded him of the mother he had left behind so long ago when his father had taken him out on his first Run. Sirion felt an upwelling in his chest, the sensation of hope being born. This woman had come to him and given him something he had never known before. He wanted to say something to her, but she was moving away from him down the street. He thought about calling after her, but he did not know what to say.

Sirion called out to Dramati once more, following the direction in which the faint replies emanated. He wondered why the corbubis would not come to him, Dramati always having come at his call before. Through their link, Sirion could not sense anything amiss with the animal, so he was not worried that Dramati was sick or injured. When Sirion crested the top of the hill he stopped. Dramati lay there within the grass, his body curled around the form of a small child. Sirion's eyes widened with surprise as he approached. It was unlike Dramati to take to another person so well. Although he was more tolerant of children, and was always gentle with them, he was never one to run off with them.

Sirion stood over Dramati and the girl. She was a beautiful child, her hair the color of pale silver gold. She wore tunic and trousers like a boy, but her small, delicate feet were bare. She had one small fist curled tightly around a tuft of Dramati's neck fur. She was a fair child, but when she opened them, Sirion looked into eyes so dark, he could almost become lost in them.

The child slowly sat upright and then stood, watching him intently. Her features were familiar to him, and Sirion suddenly knew her to be the late Lady Gemma's daughter. He remembered when he had learned of the woman's death several years ago. He had been sad to hear that she had died in childbed. This must be that child that she had given her life to bear.

Finding that he was staring, Sirion stumbled out a greeting. He liked children, and even seemed to have a connection with them, but this one was different. It was as though this one could see into his very soul. The child greeted him in return, and slowly began to walk over to him. Once she was standing before him, she reached out and touched his hand. He grasped the small hand within his larger one, and he could not help but smile. The girl smiled in response. She was a beautiful creature, so much like her mother.

Sirion smelled the young woman before he saw her. That was simply the way it had become. He was so attuned to her scent, and he would know it anywhere. Then he saw her . . . a graceful step here, a shy glance there, a glimpse of her soft throat, her pale hair plaited in a long rope hung down her back. Her long dark cloak streamed behind her as she moved down the street. Once more, Sirion considered stepping up to her, speaking to her, letting her take notice of him. But then he remembered his physical state: his tousled hair, dirty hands, and grimy clothes. He reeked of the wilderness, and of his own body odor, not to mention the odor of some of the trolags he had slaughtered the day before.

So Sirion just watched her, as he did every time he saw her. Her beauty took his breath away, and her fragrance had become like opium to him. He remained an aspect of the shadows across the street from her, and she never knew it was he who observed. She just looked around from time to time, knowing only that someone watched.

Sirion walked across the street to Volstagg's inn. The night seemed to be a busy one, the patrons staying a bit longer than usual. They knew that the Wildrunners were back in town, and the rumors preceding them were interesting ones. Upon entering the establishment, he smelled a fragrance he hadn't encountered for a long time. He felt his brows draw together. It couldn't be . . . she had gone to the city of Andahye almost a decade ago. But there she was, sitting at the bar, speaking with Volstagg. His heart hammering in his chest, Sirion began to make his way to the bar. Volstagg saw him and grinned. Sirion approached and took the seat next to the woman he knew as Adrianna. Her scent was overwhelming; he had never allowed himself to get this close to her in the past.

Tiredly, Sirion placed the large sack he had been carrying on the counter. It contained much of what he and the rest of the Wildrunners had earned within the past few months. It would go towards the expansion of the inn. Volstagg picked it up appreciatively and placed it beneath the counter. Then they began to speak in earnest, using his native tongue. He felt her watching him then, her dark gaze searching him. At a break in the conversation he turned toward her. He caught her gaze, her dark eyes widening in surprise. He heard a quick intake of breath, raised an eyebrow, and turned away. Gods! She was more beautiful than he remembered!

Sirion struggled. He was drowning, but he wanted so much to make it to the surface. He felt a sudden rush and, fueled by determination, he began his ascent. He felt the muscles working in his arms and legs and he felt his heart pumping fiercely in his chest. He wanted to live! He wanted to see the world again . . . to run bare-footed through the forests of home . . . to hear the song of the wind in the trees, to feel the cool waters of Lake Tashinade upon him after a refreshing rain. He wanted to have something real, something for which to come back after a Run. He wanted to live his own life . . . not just simply accomplish those tasks set out for him by others. He wanted to be more than just the best there was at what he did. He wanted to be more than what he had been primed by his father to be. He wanted to be more than just a warrior, and more than just a hero. He wanted to be a son, a husband, and a father.

Sirion pushed aside the darkness and the oppression. He kicked with his legs and he continued to move ever upwards. He felt the blood rushing through his veins and an exhilaration he had felt only as a boy learning the ways of a ranger in the forest of Elvandahar. He thought of all of the things he wanted to see again, and all of the things he had never seen but wanted to see. He thought of his mother and his sister, of Volstagg, Sorn, and Dremathian. He thought of all of the people who had loved him in his life and who had given him the will to endure, to face his daemons, to accept what he had become, and to realize what he could be. He thought of Adrianna, and hope for the future surged through him. He wanted to live, and at the end he wanted to look back on it all and be complete.

***

The group spent several days in the silver glen of Krathil-lon. Adrianna filled the days by walking the forest paths, spending time with her sister and niece and studying in the library. She had been able to find a book that contained the ingredients and incantations to some spells that she had never seen before. She copied those into her own book and pored over them. They were spells that were difficult to read, much less learn, but she knew that it would only be a matter of time before she would master them. Master Tallek had always admired her motivation, and it had served her well in her ability to learn the skills of a magic-user.

But Adrianna knew that she could not yet put forth all of her efforts into spell casting. Her mind was distracted with her need to speak to Sheridana about Thane. It was wrong of her to keep the information from Sheri, despite her good intentions. Adrianna had also been considering telling Sheri about the men that had attacked her upon her journey to Andahye so long ago. She sincerely did not know how, or even if, she was going to tell Sheri about it, but a part of her knew that she should, at least for her own sake. She didn't like thinking about it, much less speaking about it. She had told no one about the incident, although the medicine man she had been forced to see upon her entrance into Andahye had a good guess as to what had happened to her. However, Adrianna was not focused upon these things that she knew she needed to tell her sister. Instead, her mind found itself preoccupied with the absence of Cortath.

Adrianna spent her nights sleeping alone, without the warm and comforting presence of Cortath curled around her. She had grown rather accustomed to his warm body, the rise and fall of his breaths, the long tail laid protectively over her. She missed his large presence beside her, walking through the paths of the forest. She remembered the feeling of the soft fur of his mane pressed against her face as she laid across his back for a good run, and she remembered looking into pools of molten amber. Adrianna smiled wistfully and tried to smother her feelings of loneliness. It was difficult, for she knew she might never see Cortath again. However, she knew that Dremathian would do his best to help Sirion to break free from his bestial prison so he may walk Shandahar as a man once more.

Time crept by, and for quite some while there was seen no sign of either Cortath or Dremathian. The group asked several members of the order about Sirion, but the answer was always the same. No one had heard anything. Tianna was in a state of constant agitation and was difficult to be around. Dramati seemed to be similarly afflicted, although his temperament was much better. But the rest of the group just bided their time, Zorg and Armond developing their techniques in sparring practice, Amethyst snooping around the place like a shadow, and Dartanyen helping Sheri to hone her skills with the bow. Dinim and Sabian could be found many a time within the library, and when they arrived when Adrianna was there, she made it a point to leave shortly after.

But finally Dinim approached her. He stepped into the hallway ahead of her as she was making her way to her chamber for a brief rest before dinner. She attempted to step around him, but Dinim blocked her way with his body and a well-placed hand onto the opposite wall of the corridor. With a heavy sigh, Adrianna glanced up at him balefully. "Dinim, please remove yourself from my path."

"No. I just want you to listen to what I have to say. Then you can order me to leave if you still wish it."

Adrianna crossed her arms beneath her chest. "Fine. I am waiting."

"First, I want to apologize to you for my behavior several nights ago. Honestly, I don't know what came over me. Whatever sickness it was, it is gone now, and will never return. I have already offered my apology to your sister, and she accepted it as gracefully as I could have expected. She still continues to ignore me, but I don't really blame her. Second, I want to tell you that since that night I have wished a hundred times over that I had told you about your sister before I left to rejoin the Wildrunners. A part of me thought that Volstagg would tell you, but that night when everything spun out of control I realized, too late, that he had not. I am so sorry that you had to find out like that, and it was never my intention to hurt you. You have to believe me when I say that I would never intentionally do anything to harm you . . . ever."

Adrianna raised her chin. "I don't have to believe anything you say."

Dinim hesitated. He could see the wounded expression on her face. She wanted to believe him, but she was afraid. "Adrianna, I will not betray your trust again. Please give me another chance."

Dinim regarded her beseechingly. She so much wanted to believe in him again. The fact that he had come to her and was practically begging her for forgiveness weighed heavily with her. It meant that he cared about her after all, and that was the part that had been bothering her the most. She had allowed herself to care for him, and when it seemed that he did not feel the same affection for her, her pride had been sorely shaken.

Watching her, Dinim could see her resolve crack. A wave of relief rushed through him. He had missed Adria's companionship so much, and the last few days he had come to realize how much he had come to depend upon it. It was she who kept the boredom and monotony out of his days, and she whom he had begun to dream about at night. Especially since the last night they had spent with the gypsies. Images of her dancing before him: the bare flesh of her waist, her mesmerizing dark eyes, and her captivating movements, had aroused him like no woman ever had before. Many a night he lay awake, unable to sleep as a result of the effect she had on his body. And that had made him feel all the worse for his treatment of her and of the person she held most dear to her.

Dinim reached out and put his hands on her shoulders. "Adrianna, I care about you. I will never keep anything like that from you again, no matter what. I consider you my equal, and whatever I do, I always have you and the rest of this group in my thoughts. Please . . ."

"All right."

Dinim frowned. "All right, what?" Inwardly he smiled. He finally had been able to break through to her.

"All right, I forgive you already. Now, will you please get out of my way? I am tired, and I want to get some sleep before the evening meal is served."

Dinim stepped aside, sweeping his arm down the corridor. "As you wish, Lady."

Adrianna just shook her head. "Humph. Whatever."

***

On the seventh night of their reprieve in Krathil-lon, Father Dremathian finally came to them. The group was at the Apoptos, sitting around the dinner table and enjoying some camaraderie after a good meal. Tianna was the first to notice him, and when everyone else turned to look in the direction in which her attention had been drawn, all talk ceased. Everyone's attention was focused upon the druid as he approached the table. "A couple of nights ago, Master Sirion finally returned to us. Only today has he been strong enough to accept visitors. He is presently in the meditation chamber if you would like to see him."

Everyone rose from the table. Tianna was the first to reach Dremathian, and when she embraced him, she said, "Thank you so much. You have worked a miracle."

"No," replied Dremathian. "Only gods perform miracles. I am merely a man. Sirion did most of the healing himself. I just guided him along the way."

The group followed Dremathian through the halls to the meditation chamber. Adrianna could feel Tianna's excitement as she walked beside her down the corridor. At the end of the hallway Dremathian opened a set of doors. The group walked into the large room. It was virtually unfurnished, with the exception of the extremely large ornate rug on the floor. Lying upon it was Dramati. He regarded the group intently as they entered, but did not move from his spot. At the far end of the room there was a large window. Leaning beside it and looking out, was a man.

His skin was the color of pale bronze. He wore no tunic, only a pair of tawny trousers. His back and shoulders were muscular, and his shoulder-length hair a fiery chestnut. He moved his body away from the wall upon which he had been leaning, and then slowly turned around.

For a moment no one said anything. Sirion slowly appraised them, his amber gaze traveling from one face to the next. Standing back behind the rest of the group, Adrianna watched him. She could feel her heart thumping in her chest as she looked upon his eyes. They were so familiar to her, those eyes. They were the eyes of the creature who had become her best friend, her companion Cortath, whom she would never see again. That is, unless she looked into the face of Sirion and saw his eyes.

"Sirion . . ." Tianna launched herself towards Sirion, her arms outstretched. Adrianna could see him steeling himself for the impact before she was upon him, nearly knocking him off of his feet. She wrapped her arms around his neck. "By the gods I have missed you."

Sirion's voice was deep, deeper than Adrianna remembered. She could hear the hint of amusement in his tone. "Hello, Tianna." He chuckled and embraced her heartily, the muscles of his arms flexing as he lifted her slightly from the floor. Finally Sirion was able to pull himself gently away from Tianna. She had been crying, and her tears wet her cheeks. He spoke to her in a soothing voice, placing his forefinger upon her trembling lips. "Shhhh, everything is all right now. Calm down."

Tianna shook her head. "I thought I had lost you."

Sirion put his hands on the sides of Tianna's face, wiping her tears away with his thumbs. "I know, I know. We'll get a chance to talk later." He patted Tianna's shoulder reassuringly and she stepped away. Sirion then turned to the group and grinned. "So how are you all doing?" Sirion picked up his tunic, which was lying on the windowsill, and pulled it over his head as he made his way towards the group. "It's good to see you all again."

Dartanyen stepped forward to meet him. "And even better to see that you are well again, Sirion." Dartanyen took Sirion's hand and shook it. Behind Dartanyen were Armond, and Zorg. Each of the men greeted Sirion, patting him on the back and expressing their delight to see him hale and whole once more. Dartanyen then introduced Sirion to Amethyst, Sabian, and Sheridana. They had never met Sirion prior to his, rather miraculous, transformation.

Finally, after all of the introductions were made and greetings exchanged, there was a momentary lull. Adrianna stepped forward from the back wall of the room and began to approach the scene. Sirion glanced around at the group of people before him. Where was she? Why hadn't she come? Perhaps she did not really care, after all. Sirion focused beyond the rest of the group and suddenly she was there, walking towards them from the rear of the room. He let out the breath of air he had not realized he had been holding and he felt himself begin to smile.

Adrianna saw when Sirion realized her presence. He caught her gaze and began to smile. She couldn't help but smile in return. He was a handsome man. She could hardly believe her eyes. He looked so different from the individual she had met at the Hapless Cenloryan several months ago. So much had changed since then, and she wondered what he saw when he looked at her.

Sirion had to keep himself from staring at her; she was radiant, just as she had been that evening in Sangrilak so many moons ago, when the group with which she had allied herself had first met one another. He had treated her coldly that night, aloof and a little standoffish. He had regretted it later, berating himself for letting an opportunity to get to know her pass by. Letting the memories fade into the back of his mind, Sirion stepped up to the woman approaching him.

Sirion reached out and took Adrianna's hands into his own. He inclined his head to her. "Hello, Adrianna."

Adrianna responded in kind. "Hello, Sirion."

"I am glad to see you are well."

Adrianna nodded. "Likewise."

His gaze was intense as he regarded her, and Adrianna felt herself becoming slightly uncomfortable. She was about to look away, when, to her surprise, Sirion moved closer to her, placed his face alongside hers, and put his mouth near her ear. "And I want to thank you . . ."

At that moment the doors to the chamber opened abruptly. Adrianna and Sirion parted and turned to find Dinim striding across the room towards them. He had a huge grin on his face.

"By the gods, Sirion, it is so good to see you."

Glancing at Sirion, Adrianna could see a strained expression pass over his features. But then he was smiling back at Dinim, walking forward to greet him.

"I thought you had been lost. It has been so difficult . . ."

With a slight shake of Sirion's head, Dinim ceased speaking, and merely placed his hands upon Sirion's shoulders. "Hells, we have to feed you. You are thin as an oak sapling."

Sirion chuckled and then began to laugh. It was infectious and soon everyone was laughing. Then everyone began to talk all at once. Adrianna could only vaguely hear or understand anything that was being said, but she was glad that everyone was coming together. She heard expressions of gratitude from Sirion and questions concerning Sirion's well-being from the group. She heard Dartanyen suggest that they all go somewhere where they could all sit down. On their way out of the meditation chamber, Sirion grabbed a wooden cane that had been resting against the far wall. He was a bit wobbly on his legs, but kept up with the others as they returned to the dining hall. The group sat down for a while over some food and ale, Dinim letting Sirion know what had happened to the rest of the Wildrunners after their final battle. After a short time, Adrianna excused herself from the table, patting Dartanyen on the shoulder as she left to let him know not to say anything to Sirion about Thane. He nodded, and without looking back, she left.

Adrianna left the Apoptos and walked back to the cabin in the semi-darkness, the sun having just set upon the horizon. Upon reaching the place, she went up to her room. She closed the door behind her as she entered and then sighed and seated herself on the bed. It was good to see Sirion strong and robust after his ordeal, but she missed Cortath still, even knowing that that beast resided within the man she had seen today. She leaned herself back upon the pillows at the head of the bed, letting her body melt into them as she pondered the reunion. She closed her eyes, envisioning Sirion once more, the color of his eyes, the ripple of muscle across his chest as he moved, the shape of his mouth when he smiled . . .

Adrianna started when there was a knock on her door. She fought to collect her scattered intellect. She must have drifted to sleep for a moment. She rose from the bed, her heart beating rapidly in her chest. She wondered who was at her door, but knew the answer before the words left her lips. "Wh-who is it?"

"It's me." There was a pause. "Sirion."

Adrianna swallowed convulsively, and the muscles in her stomach began to tighten up. She went to the door and opened it.

"Good evening. I haven't disturbed you have I?" Sirion's brows came together in the beginning of a concerned frown as his gaze swept over her face.

"No . . . not at all. Come in." Adrianna stood aside. She caught the floral/musky scent of his bath soap as he entered. Once Sirion was inside the room she shut the door. For a moment Adrianna just stood there, not knowing what to say. "How have you been?" The words came simultaneously from two throats. It seemed to lessen the tension and they both grinned.

"I am well, thank you. Here, sit." Adrianna removed her travel pack from the nearest cushioned chair and motioned him over to it.

"Thank you." He seated himself in the chair as she sat upon the bed. "So how have you found it here?"

Adrianna smiled. "This is a wonderful place. I have never been anywhere quite like it. I feel restful here, at peace, able to think more clearly. Despite the circumstances of our arrival, I don't think I've ever felt more relaxed." Adrianna stopped and looked down at the floor fretfully. She hadn't meant to put it like that. She hadn't meant to imply that it had been burdensome for her to come.

"Yes, Krathil-lon is indeed a wonderful place. I first came here several years ago, when I was a much younger man. I met Dremathian, and we became good friends." Sirion smiled. "This place has become a sanctuary for those who know of its existence. The order takes care of this place so that it may continue to serve those who need it most. It is a place of power, and magic abides here, un-harnessed."

Upon seeing that he did not seem to have taken offense to her statement, Adrianna relaxed, listening to Sirion's voice. It was a soothing one, deep and gentle. She could get accustomed to it rather quickly, she thought. "The journey here wasn't a difficult one I hope. Unfortunately, I do not remember most of it," he said.

"No, it wasn't bad at all. It was exhilarating actually, to ride upon the back of a griffon. It was one of the most awesome experiences of my life. The beasts were wondrous, and the one I rode even seemed to take to me . . ." Adrianna let her words die out as her thoughts turned inwards. Then, after a moment, she remembered who was seated across from her and she came to. It was Sirion, a member of the Wildrunners, someone who had become a hero in the eyes of all who knew his story. Her eyes refocused to find him studying her nonchalantly. He seemed so self-assured and confident sitting there, while her belly was working itself into knots and her palms were becoming sweaty with nervousness.

For a few moments, the silence stretched out, neither saying anything. Adrianna knew not what to say at all, feeling strange all of a sudden. What was she to say? A virtual stranger sat before her, although he was not, for Cortath had known her in ways that no one else had ever known her. Then Sirion broke the uncomfortable silence.

"You know, there are some things that I remember, and some that I do not. But one thing I know for certain is that you were there for me, a companion to me when I needed someone the most, and I appreciate that." Sirion looked away and he stirred in his chair, exhibiting signs of uncertainty for the first time. Only then did he seem so normal, like any other man. "The animal . . . Cortath . . . is something that existed inside of me. When he emerged, his dominant animal nature began to take over. I began to lose that part of me that made me a man. But when you were there, the transformation could never be wholly completed. You kept me from the brink, and I am indebted to you."

Sirion looked at her once more. His eyes were shadowed, and Adrianna could see how hard it was for him to speak to her about how dire his circumstances had been. She shook her head and reached out to him, placing her hand atop of his. "No. You owe me nothing. What I shared with you while you were in that form, it was good for me. Cortath healed me in ways that I cannot begin to explain. I am glad that I was able to help you just as much as you helped me."

Sirion nodded and then smiled at her. "Thank you. That means a lot to me."

Adrianna looked at him, and then down at her hand. When she realized that it continued to clasp Sirion's hand, she pulled it away, flushing slightly.

"Well, I suppose I had better get some sleep. I feel like I haven't slept for about a year." Sirion said as he rose from the chair. Adrianna rose from the bed and they made their way to the door.

"I am glad you came. It was good to talk," she said.

"Indeed it was. Have a good night."

"You have one as well." Adrianna opened the door and Sirion walked through. "And Sirion . . ." She paused until he turned to face her once more. "Welcome home."

Sirion smiled a wide smile, his eyes sparkling warmly in the torchlight. "I am home, aren't I?" He paused. "Thank-you."

Sirion regarded her for a moment, longing to embrace her, but he dared not. Her words had touched him like no others could, and it was all that he had dreamed of and more. It was what he had hoped for all his life . . . and he hadn't even known it. With her, he felt he truly could be home, for it was because of her that he had returned. He would be the one. Finally he left her bedchamber to return to his own. There was always tomorrow.

CHAPTER 15

Adrianna and Sheri walked through the silver woods. They would not be spending many more days in Krathil-lon, so they decided to take advantage of the fair weather. The air was cool, much more so than it was when they were traveling through Durnst. It had been quite a dramatic change for them when they arrived at the glen. They had been experiencing the heat of mid-summer: very little winds and hardly any rain. But since arriving here, they had experienced a sharp decrease in temperature as well as days where rain was the chief event in the forecast. The glen was situated within the Sartingels, the mountain range north of Tusbir. The climate here was different, probably not quite as temperate as one would find in the area east of the Ratik Range, but definitely milder here at this time of the year. Adrianna did not want to think about what the area would be like during the winter months.

Companionably, the two women walked in silence, merely enjoying the ambiance. It was peaceful here, and Adrianna found that she was loath to leave. Once they were away from this place, the real world would rear up to slap her in the face once again and the serenity of Krathil-lon would quickly become a distant memory. Sirion was recovering nicely from his ordeal and Dremathian had given them the go-ahead to leave in a few days.

Within the trees ahead of them Adria and Sheri began to hear someone speaking. As they got closer, they realized that it was a voice raised in anger. A younger voice replied and an argument ensued. The two women glanced at one another and then nodded, agreeing to eavesdrop. Quietly they crept towards the scene.

"You are a disgrace, Lucien. Your actions have proven to me that you are not ready for the Tabanakh ceremony. You are not ready to become a part of the Brotherhood."

Adrianna and Sheri peered through a break in the foliage. They lay in a depression made by the roots of a large silver oak tree, watching the man and his tyro. The boy was on the verge of manhood, about the age of seventeen.

"I think you are being too harsh on me, Brother Donavan. I wasn't the only one. The other boys were there too."

"That is the key word, is it not? Boys. You, Lucien, are no longer a boy, but one who is supposed to become a man this very evening. All of the others are younger than you by at least a year or more. You fell in with them, following them like a pup. I repeat . . . you are not ready for the ceremony."

The young man looked away from his mentor, crimson coloring his cheeks. He was angry and shamed, his teacher having brought him down low. Adrianna's heart went out to the boy. He had made a mistake and now he would pay the consequences.

Brother Donavan held out an earthenware jug. "This drink is very powerful, meant only for those who are ready. Those who drink it will experience visions of the past, present, and future. Only those who are strong enough will be able to understand the visions and use them in order to meet their destiny one day. I will tell the others that we will not be having a ceremony tonight. You will have to wait until you have grown a bit more."

Brother Donavan turned away, placing the jug near the small fire that was situated within a ring of large stones.

"But Brother . . . I am ready. I know that I am."

The older man held up a hand, palm facing the boy. Lucien was immediately quiet. "I have made my decision. There will be no ceremony. You are dismissed."

Once more, anger flashed across Lucien's face, but the emotion was short-lived. Shame quickly returned to set upon his features and he turned and left the scene. Adrianna and Sheri waited patiently, not wanting to move within the quiet and be discovered. Finally Brother Donavan stood. His shoulders were slumped and his face bore an expression of sadness. Adrianna realized that it had been a difficult decision for him to make. The man left the clearing, probably to tell his brothers and sisters about his decision.

Adrianna and Sheri lay there for a few moments more, just to be sure that he would not return. Then they got up and entered the clearing. Beside the fire-pit, the earthen jug still sat. Sheri turned to Adria. Right away, Adrianna could tell what was in her sister's mind. Pensively she regarded the jug. They did not know what type of drink it was, only that it made one have strange visions. It could have other side effects, and could even make them ill. Then she shrugged and nodded to Sheri. A smile lit up her sister's face. Adrianna could not help but smile in return.

Adrianna and Sheri went over to the fire pit. Lying upon the ground next to it was a pile of wood. Sheridana broke some of the larger sticks in half and then placed them onto the small fire. Soon the flame was becoming larger, gaining strength. Adrianna pulled the cork from the jug and passed her nose over the lip. The drink had an unfamiliar scent. Looking at Sheri, she slowly placed her mouth to the opening and then took a swallow. The drink flowed down her throat, making a warm path to her belly. It tasted like nothing she had ever drunk before. Then she handed the jug to Sheri, who also took a swallow. The two women smiled conspiratorially, knowing that what they were doing would be considered naughty.

The sisters sat opposite one another, the fire between them. The red, orange, and gold flames were nearly hypnotizing. Adrianna realized that the drink was beginning to influence her already. It seemed that the flames could put her into a trance within moments if she would only allow it. She knew that after a while it would happen whether she wanted it or not. As the effects of the drink took hold of them, they began to feel warm. Tunics came off first, followed by trousers. All that remained was small-clothes and ornamentation: the serpent coiled about Adria's upper arm, a golden torc about Sheri's throat, a delicate platinum bangle around Adrianna's ankle, and gold armbands on Sheri's upper arms. Long pale and dark tresses were bound upon the tops of their heads and sweat ran down slender bodies.

The women continued to feed the fire, and the fire blazed hotter. Perspiration began to appear, and impurities flowed from the pores of their skin. Late afternoon had darkened into night, and the pale form of Steralion rose above them. The women continued to regard one another from across the fire. Adrianna saw scars across Sheridana's left side and thigh. They looked to have been made by a large predator. It must have been won in battle. Belatedly, Adria realized that Sheridana would be noticing similar things about herself. Adrianna returned her eyes to those of her twin and saw that Sheri had indeed noticed the marks upon her and that she was wondering about them, just as she was wondering about those upon Sheri.

The sisters continued to say nothing. The fire burned on, and the sweat poured down their bodies. How long they had been seated in front of the fire, they did not know. The fire danced before their eyes, the tendrils twisting together lovingly, caressing one another with a soft touch here, another touch there, until Adrianna could see a form within the depths of the flame. She saw two people dancing. The couple swirled about in the fire, the woman's gown flowing behind her. Or was it her cloak? Adrianna leaned forward, hoping to see the figures in more detail. As she did so, the scene changed. She saw what appeared to be a dragon in flight. Upon its back was a person, an arm raised in victory. Adrianna frowned. She had never heard of a man flying upon the back of a dragon. It would be a wonderful experience, she mused to herself. Suddenly, Adrianna jumped out of her trance. She saw that she had been very close to the fire, too close in fact. She saw that Sheridana was in her own trance, but that she was also aware of Adrianna. Sheri began to speak.

"I remember a time before I left Sangrilak. I spent much of my time in training. Father taught me the sword while Ian taught me the bow. Father also taught others who wished to learn the art of swordplay. Thus it was that I often sparred against others, my

skills pitted against those of the others. All too often I wasn't good enough and Father would be angry with me, wanting me to work even more. He wanted me to work harder despite the fact that I also trained in things other than the blade and that by the end of each day I was so tired I sometimes did not eat my evening meal. I became distraught with my lot in life, and it was our uncle who came to ease me. Despite the strands of silver in his curly golden hair, he was as he had been twenty years before. With his wise words, he could always take my thoughts from myself and turn them to those of lesser fortune, those who lived their lives with much less than what I received every day. He told me tales from his young adventuring days, and that Father had not always been such a harsh man, and that he had once loved a woman so much that a part of him went with her when she died.

I remember a time soon after our departure from Sangrilak. We began to travel with a group called the Dawn Treaders. With them was a man who taught me hand-to-hand combat. By that time, I had become rather skilled with the long sword and the longbow. Even Father appreciated my skill. Very often, Ian and I would hunt for food, and thus it was that we spent much of our time together. With time, we came to know each other so well, we could almost finish one another's thoughts. We spent two years with the Dawn Treaders and then met up with Thritean's Pride. With this group we spent the next four years. Within the third year, Father left the group to pursue other interests, and after another several months, Ian and I refused to deny ourselves what we had known for over two years. We were lovers up until that fateful night that would take him away from me forever.

Ian and I had been hunting. We were on the trail of a leschera. It would feed us for several days. Suddenly, I had the feeling that we were being watched, but before I could issue a warning, a man had leapt from the bushes near us. I never saw his face as the man hurled himself into me, knocking the breath from my lungs and my feet out from under me. My face in the dirt and his knee between my shoulder blades, I could feel his hot, fetid breath upon the back of my neck as he loomed over me. I felt something rake across the left side of my body and my blood flowed thick and warm from the terrible wounds. He then released me, unsheathed my long sword as he stood and plunged it into the flesh just below my shoulder, pinning me to the ground.

Then the man turned upon Ian. I could see two of Ian's arrows sticking out of the man's back as he turned around. His armor was black, and he wore a horned helmet upon his head. With one massive blow the dark warrior swept the bow out of Ian's hands and with the other he backhanded him across the jaw. Ian stepped back with the impact, his hand to his face. Ian then drew his long sword. The ring of metal rang through the air as he pulled it from its scabbard and the magical weapon glowed softly in the night. The man laughed, the sound of it eerily familiar. Ian swung the sword. With his clawed gauntlets, the warrior took the weapon, leaving deep wounds in Ian's forearm and hand. The man then took Ian by the tunic and raised him up off of the ground. He threw Ian into a nearby tree and I heard the sickening crack of bone as Ian's body struck it. Ian moaned in agony, but tried to rise once more. The warrior's voice was deeply hoarse, yet strangely familiar. "You will watch him die an agonizing death, and his screams will haunt your dreams . . ."

I knew that he was speaking to me. I struggled to remove the sword from my shoulder. I felt the flesh of my chest tear and then the warm blood gush out of the wound to soak my tunic. Tears streamed down my cheeks as I watched the dark warrior walk over to Ian and proceed to disembowel him. Ian's cries echoed into the darkness. I desperately sought to remove the sword, crying with frustration. It slowly began to move, and I began to hope that, when I got there, Ian would still be alive. The dark warrior made quick work of Ian, glanced once more at me, and I could feel him smiling at me behind the metal of his helm. He said something to me in a strange tongue and then left. Finally, with a massive pull, I was able to remove the sword and move to my beloved Ian's side. He was dead. I kissed him one last time upon lips that were still warm with the life that had once flowed through his veins. Then I put my head upon his chest and cried myself to sleep, his entrails strewn all about us and my blood taking my life with it as it poured onto the ground."

Adrianna's gaze was locked upon the dancing flames of their fire. She felt the vision begin to take shape. She was afraid, so afraid of what she would see. But Sheri had enfolded her within her nightmare, weaving it tightly about the both of them, sharing it as only she could share it with her twin. Adrianna could see what Sheridana saw, as well as that which Sheridana could not.

The dark warrior had made Ian suffer before killing him, raking his wickedly clawed gauntlets down Ian's chest to his belly, and then began to slowly pull out the entrails. Adrianna could see the suffering in Ian's eyes and she cried out to him. She so much wanted to go to him, to ease his pain. But she could not. She was trapped within the future. But to some, time was no boundary. The dark warrior looked up . . . and into her eyes. In shock, Adrianna recoiled. She could feel Sheridana struggle within the link. Her father looked at her out of dark-brown eyes that were so familiar to her. Thane grinned evilly at her and then savagely thrust his hand deep into Ian's body. Her uncle cried out briefly in a voice full of such agony that Adrianna almost fell to her knees. Then he died. Thane's gaze flicked to Adrianna, but then turned back to Sheri. *"I will return for you . . . in time. We will meet again and I will kill you as I have killed him."* As he spoke he turned back to Adria. Her heart pounded hard within her chest. The all-too-familiar eyes burned into her . . . and then he was gone. Adrianna returned to reality to find Sheridana emerging from the memory of her nightmare.

Sheridana stopped. Her eyes refocused onto the face of her sister. Adria regarded her silently, the expression in her eyes echoing what she had heard. Her breasts rose and fell rapidly with her breaths. Sheridana shook herself, the nightmare falling away from her. It felt good to have it melt away from her, her mind cleansing itself of the pain and horror of that night. She knew she would never forget, but now she would finally begin to heal, and maybe one day she would be able to live a normal life.

Adrianna shifted herself across the fire from her. Dear Adrianna. How she had missed her when she had gone away with her father and uncle! Every day of their absence from one another Sheri had thought of her twin sister with whom she had shared everything. She had desperately wished for Thane to miraculously accept his second daughter and bid her come with them. But their father did no such thing. Sheridana had left Sangrilak, never to see Adrianna again until that fateful day just a couple of weeks ago. So many years had passed by, and Adria was not quite the same person Sheri had known so long ago. Adrianna had changed somehow. Sheri couldn't put her finger on it, but the change had not been a small one. She had noticed it right from the start. Her sister's eyes had given it away.

Adria looked back at Sheridana. The other woman appeared to be refreshed, as if a great weight had been lifted from her shoulders. Looking into the eyes of her sister, Adrianna knew that Sheridana did not know. She did not know that Adrianna had been there in the past with her as she had told her story. Adrianna could barely believe it herself. She would have never known if the man had not looked at her. He had seen her! How could he have possibly seen her? Or perhaps he had merely sensed her somehow? Adrianna shook herself. Goosebumps had risen upon her arms; the absolute strangeness of the situation unnerved her.

Sheridana waited. She could see that her sister was wrestling with something. Finally Adria looked up at her. Her dark eyes were haunted, full of fear. Tendrils of her silver/gold hair had freed themselves from their prison and streamed about her face, glowing in the firelight. Her pale skin shimmered with a thin film of sweat. She had become a beautiful woman within the years they had spent apart. The awkward skinny girl had become a lovely young woman. Sheridana assumed that she had as well, but with one big difference. Pregnancy and childbirth had changed her forever. Sheridana absently rubbed her hands over her hips and the slight, hardly noticeable roundness of her belly. She sighed deeply, tears coming to her eyes. She suddenly hungered to hold her baby close to her, to breathe in the scent of her. Her child . . . Ian's child. *Gods, even now, I still ache for him . . .*

"Thritean's Pride found me at Ian's side. Joshua was able to tend to me before I would have died. For many days he worked over me, praying to his goddess for the power that would make me well. Finally my wounds healed and I was able to run with the Pride once more. But I became reckless and withdrawn. I became more a liability than

an asset and when I realized this I decided to leave the group. Damar tried to stop me, but my mind was set. Almost immediately I got a job as part of the personal guard for the Crown Prince of Durnst. Thus I became a mercenary, a sword for hire. It was soon after that I began to notice the changes in my body. For quite some time longer I continued to deny what I had already known for many weeks. I was with child. The time came when I could hide the fact no longer, and it was then that I resigned my position. Soon after that I became ill. I was weakening and losing blood. It was fortunate for me that Joshua had a friend in the city of Tragesser. He and his wife allowed me to stay with them and live with them as a part of their family. For fear of losing the child I remained bedridden until the birth. For many weeks postpartum I stayed with them. Their eldest daughter helped me to care for Fitanni when I continued to be ill after my difficult labor. I had no strength but to nurse the child and to think of Ian. As I slept, Carli watched over my tiny daughter, who was the one for whom I found the will to live after my ordeal. When I finally became well again I took over most of her care and began to make preparations for my departure. The need to return home had come upon me. Carli and I had become rather close and she begged me to bring her with me back to Sangrilak. I spoke with her father, and he finally gave Carli his consent for her to leave with me. I was glad, for the road is a dangerous one for a woman traveling alone, for two women as well. She would care for the child while I remained ready in case something went amiss. Many weeks later I entered the gates of Risset and I found my twin sister after several long years of being apart . . ."

Adrianna regarded Sheri across the fire. Her sister had shared with her the secret of Fitanni's parentage. Adrianna was bewildered by the new knowledge, but accepting of it as well. Ian was Fitanni's father, but now he was dead. The child would grow up without a father, the way she had. Adria's heart ached for that fact as she turned her focus to the fire.

Suddenly, from out of the flames before her danced a woman. She wore layers of multi-colored diaphanous material about her shapely figure. She also wore bangles of gold about her arms and ankles, necklaces and belts of platinum, and earrings and veils bedecked with semiprecious stones. The young woman was very beautiful, more so than any woman Adria had ever seen. Her long, dark, plaited hair lay over her shoulder and her dark-brown eyes shimmered with freshly shed tears that ran down the golden flesh of her face. The woman danced sensuously for a richly attired audience. With the grace of a feline she moved, her hips swaying provocatively as she circled her arms above her head. One could almost see her breasts through the filmy fabric of her attire, and every curve and contour of her small, lithe form. The audience clapped and murmured in approval after her dance was done. At the finale, she placed her kneeling form before a large man dressed in the finery of a king. He wore a crown beset with rubies, sapphires, emeralds, topaz, and diamonds.

He motioned the girl closer to him. Upon trembling legs the young woman moved nearer, prostrating herself before him. Adrianna could see a shimmering tear as it fell onto the ground beneath her. The man reached out his hands and touched the girl, fondling her breasts. He nodded his approval and then motioned her away, gesturing for her to wait for him in his tent. Without a word, the young woman left him to the laughter of the other men, and the smiles of the women. After leaving the circle of light, she ran towards the tents and into the largest one.

Adrianna suddenly found herself staring at a fire once again. The vision had been so real: the colors so vibrant, the sounds and the sensations so explicit. She saw her sister sitting across from her. Sheridana's eyes were half closed, her long dark lashes a smudge against her cheeks. For a moment, Adrianna was reminded of the young woman of her vision. Adrianna added another piece of wood to the fire and the flames licked at it hungrily. Sheri refocused her attention onto Adria, waiting for her to speak.

Sheridana knew that Adria had something to share with her. It hung about her shoulders like a dark cloak, waiting. She could see it in her eyes . . . the sadness was always there. She could see the scars not only upon her flesh, but her soul as well. Then Adrianna began to speak. She spoke of their father, saying that he had gone mad and that he was hunting her down. She told her that he had already killed Mairi in his search for her and that she and the group continued to be in danger . . . that he would not stop until Adrianna was dead. Sheridana listened to her sister in shock, not truly understanding what was being said to her . . . not wanting to believe that Thane had gone that far. She had not seen him for several months, probably not for over two years now. What had become of him? Why was he doing this? How could he hate his daughter that much?

Adrianna saw the shock on her sister's face, the pain of the knowledge that she imparted to her. But Adria found that she could only tell her sister half of the story. She could not find the courage to tell Sheri that Thane had killed the father of her child, that it had been her father who had tortured the man she loved, and then left her out in the forest to die. She could not find the heart to tell Sheri that Thane was probably hunting for her too, seeking to kill his brother's child just like he sought to kill his own daughter. It was enough that she had told Sheri about Mairi, the woman who had raised them as her own daughters.

Sheridana collected herself. She could see that it had taken a lot for Adrianna to tell her about their father. But somehow she knew her sister continued to keep something from her. Sheri watched Adria from across the fire, waiting for her sister to shuck her cloak of pain and loneliness, to share her secrets the way Sheri had shared hers with Adria.

Adrianna began to have another vision. She saw a man with dark hair staring into an orb. The mists within the orb swirled and eddied to form a scene. A woman lay upon a bed pallet. It was clear that she was dying. The woman seemed familiar, and upon closer examination, Adrianna saw that it was the beautiful woman she had seen from her earlier vision . . . the dancer. "Stupid woman, get off of your deathbed while you still can and come to me." The man spoke angrily into the orb. He then rose from his seated position and began to pace the room. He was handsome, his black hair cropped short, his eyes the color of palest blue. His robes whirled around his ankles as he spun about on his heel and began to pace in the opposite direction. He was tall and lean. His face appeared to be young, but his eyes bore a timeless expression that gave one the impression that he had lived for years beyond his time. The room was obviously a laboratory. Bookshelves lined the walls and contained within them were books and multitudes of vials, bottles, and flasks of varying sizes and contents. "Damn! If only . . ." He sputtered to himself in anger and self-recrimination. "If only I had known sooner." The man put his head in his hands. "Alejandra . . ."

Adrianna continued to stare into the flames. Within the fire she saw a woman. In her arms she held an infant. A man stepped close to her, smiled, and put a hand upon the child's head. The scene changed. Adria saw a dragon winging across the sky. It then began to fall. It plummeted to the ground. A swarm of men rushed over to it and began to stab it with their swords and lances. The dragon died upon the open plain. After the men left, a lone figure wandered over to the dead creature. It was a woman. She knelt before the massive head and put her hands upon it. She then began to cry. Her tears fell upon the scales of the dead beast. The scene changed once more. Adrianna saw a creature, one she had never seen the likes of ever before. It was humanoid, yet bore a feline countenance. Its eyes were canted, and startling green. It sported a spotted mane around its face and neck, and it wore a strangely colored armament. The scene shifted again. Adrianna turned her gaze away from the fire. What in the Nine Hells was this? What manner of fire was this that it showed her such things? Or, what was wrong with her that she would see such things within a mere fire? But then she remembered. The strange drink was showing her these things.

Adrianna's head began to spin and she had to remain still for a few moments in order for it to clear. Sheridana still continued to watch her. Instinctively, Adrianna knew it was time to return to the real world. She rose to her feet. The fire had been reduced to a smaller flame. It was dark, but she knew that dawn would soon be approaching. Sheridana just continued to watch her. Adria walked over to stand over her sister. Sheri had a strange look upon her face. The other woman rose from her sitting position to stand in front of Adria. She sighed and frowned. "Adrianna, I know that you are keeping something from me. I can see it in your eyes. I have laid my very soul open to you, yet you still continue to shut me out."

Adrianna shook her head. "I don't know what you are talking about . . ."

Sheri's frown deepened. "Eventually it will begin to haunt you, this thing you hide inside of yourself. It will whittle away at your soul until nothing is left but the pain and emptiness. I don't want to see that happen to you. Adria. Why won't you just tell me . . ."

Adrianna just continued to shake her head, not knowing what to say. She was surprised that her sister had become so perceptive, had never known her to be that way before. Perhaps motherhood had changed her.

Sheridana felt hurt. She thought that they could tell each other anything. She stepped closer to Adrianna, grasped her upper arms and shook her for a moment, and shouted, "It will eat at you until nothing is left. But you won't listen to me . . . what does Sheri know? Just remember, you are the one who has placed this barrier between us, and it will keep us apart until you tear it down."

Sheridana released her sister. The woman weaved upon her feet for a moment before crumpling to the ground. Guiltily, Sheridana knelt at Adria's side for a moment, being sure that her pulse was still strong. Satisfied that Adrianna would be all right, Sheri doused the fire, retrieved their clothes, and began to try to rouse Adrianna. Partially successful, Adrianna was able to at least support herself as they made their way back towards the cabin. Adrianna's weight was heavy against her side, and Sheridana stumbled several times along the path. Sheri soon found herself becoming exhausted and she struggled to hold her sister upright as Adrianna became unconscious. She began to worry. What was in that drink? Just as Sheri was about to let her sister fall to the ground, a man grabbed Adrianna's other side. "Sirion," Sheridana said, surprised. "What are you doing here?"

3 Brinaren CY593

Adrianna awoke but made no effort to rise from her bed. She could tell that it was still early, the golden rays of dawn not having yet adorned the morning sky. She was not eager to rise this morning, knowing that she would be leaving Krathil-lon. So she just continued to lie there, thinking back upon the last couple of days.

After arriving at the cabin the morning after she and Sheridana had imbibed the Tabanakh drink, Adrianna continued to feel its effects. Worried for her welfare, Sirion demanded Sheridana tell him what had happened to her. Sheri told him about the drink of which they had partaken, and Sirion then proceeded to call Dremathian. The druid leader came to assess her. He was mystified by her condition, knowing that the drink had a more severe effect upon those who had a propensity for such encumbrances. Most of the group did not understand to what Dremathian referred, but Sirion, knowing the properties of the drink, knew exactly what Dremathian was trying to say. Adrianna had been affected so strongly by the drink because she had the Gift of Seeing. Many persons who were drawn to the druidical orders also tended to have a slight inclination for this Gift, but most other people had not even an inkling of it. It was surprising for Dremathian to find one who was so strongly Gifted outside of the druidical sphere.

It wasn't until well into the day that Adrianna was recovered enough from the drink that she could begin to function normally again. When she awoke, she found Father Dremathian sitting beside her bed keeping vigil over her. It was then that he explained to her what had happened, as well as the truth about her Gift. Adrianna told him that he must have made some mistake, for she was not a Seer. But Dremathian was adamant, telling her that he was certain of her Gift, and that she should stay with him here in Krathil-lon to join the Order.

Adrianna found herself in a state of shock. Stay here . . . in Krathil-lon? There was a part of her that wanted that so much . . . to stay in this wonderful place. But there was an even larger part of her that knew that she could not. She had unresolved problems in her life that she had to deal with, things that she found herself describing to Dremathian, things that she had found difficult to tell anyone else. Dremathian told her that the Order would be able to help her against Thane, that violence was not the only way to defeat one's enemies. But Adrianna had made up her mind. She knew, in the case of her father, that violence was the only way. She sadly turned down Dremathian's offer, and he left her then, telling her that she should consider it more fully before making her final decision.

Adrianna sat up and let the blankets fall to her waist. The coolness of the room shocked her naked flesh and it rose into goose pimples. Adrianna climbed out of the bed, wrapping the blankets around her. She slowly made her way to the clothing folded in the cushioned chair and began to don the tunic and trousers. She quickly re-braided the long mass of her hair and looped it about itself to form a bundle at the back of her head. She then took up her travel pack and belt pouches, looked about the place to be sure she was leaving nothing behind, and then left the room.

Adrianna walked the path that would take her to the Apoptos. At least she and Sheridana had not received too much grief from their poor decision to imbibe the drink. Their transgression seemed to have been overlooked in light of the discovery of Adrianna's Gift. Yet, she continued to feel badly for having alarmed everyone.

Just the day before, Sirion was given Dremathian's permission to travel once again. The group began to make plans, and it was decided that they would leave the next day. Sirion told the group that he needed to go to Elvandahar to let his family know that he had survived the battle against Gaknar and Tharizdune. His sister had gone home to tell his family about his death, and he felt the intense need to go there to rectify the tale. Having been apprised of their situation with Thane, Sirion invited the group to accompany him, telling Sheri that it would be a good place for her to keep the baby, at least for now. He explained that the place was very well protected, and that the baby would be safer there than most other places. Adrianna and Sheri discussed this option, and they agreed that it was their best plan.

Adrianna walked up the steps leading into the Apoptos. She then passed through the halls leading to the dining area. Upon reaching it she found Sirion, Sheridana, Tianna, and Dinim already there. They rose from their seats at the nearest table. Sheridana wore tight-fitting, pale blue tunic and trousers on top of which she wore navy studded leather and her long swords carried cross-wise across her back. She reminded Adrianna of Armond, but he wore his swords differently, one at each hip. Sirion wore a sleeveless brown tunic, trousers, and studded leather. His hair was tied back at the nape of his neck, and he wore the signet ring that Adrianna had found in the pouch about Cortath's neck. Adrianna went over to the table and picked up a honey bun from the platter. She then poured herself a mug of milk and sat down.

Sirion's gaze flicked from her hand holding the honey bun back to her face. He knew of her rejection of Dremathian's offer to stay in Krathil-lon, and he also knew why she had made that particular decision. Her life's calling lay somewhere that was not Krathil-lon and the order of druids that resided there. Dremathian had a lot that he could teach her and she would probably learn to be a powerful druid, but her destiny called her elsewhere. Yet he knew that Dremathian would make one last attempt to get her to stay. With her Gift, she would be an excellent addition to the Order and would quickly advance in their ranks.

Sirion's gaze went to Dinim as the man seated himself next to Adrianna. He began to speak with her in an easy-going tone, teasing her about her slightly disheveled appearance, her decision to fall in with her sister to drink the Tabanakh brew and her condition the morning after. Of course Dinim got her to smile. Sirion could not help but stare at her for a moment. Her beauty seemed to still his heart in his chest and an ache lodged there. She seemed to have a good rapport with Dinim, and Sirion could easily see that the Cimmerean was attracted to her.

Sirion turned away from the scene when he felt someone sitting down next to him. He turned to see that it was only Tianna. The young woman smiled at him as she placed a plate on the table in front of him. "Here. Eat this. Dinim is right. You are thin."

Sirion regarded her dolefully. He felt discomfited by the almost maternal attitude that Tianna had begun to adopt towards him. He already had a mother, and thus did not need another. Yet, she had been acting strangely in other ways as well. On several occasions he had found her staring at him, an almost forlorn expression on her face. She seemed much more preoccupied with her appearance than he remembered, but perhaps he should attribute that to the fact that she was a woman now . . . no longer a child. Although to him she would always be the little girl who had chosen to follow him around during the time she was but an orphan with the Order of Reshik-na in Elvandahar.

It seemed that Tianna sought him out rather often, and when she spoke to him, the conversations tended to lean towards the future . . . sometimes his and sometimes hers. What would he be doing five years from now? She hoped to be married, but had yet to find the right person. Had he thought of settling down and having a family? Sirion found himself shying away from these conversation topics, not knowing how to respond to her, wondering if she needed someone to talk to . . . perhaps another woman who could help her to ease her way into her emergent womanhood.

Sirion regarded the plate set before him. He was not hungry, but would humor Tianna and eat at least a small portion. He picked up one of the figs and popped it into his mouth. The rest of the group finally filtered into the hall. Amethyst was the last to enter, her tousled appearance giving one the impression that she had just awoken and had donned her clothing on the way over. The petulant expression on her face also spoke that she hated the fact that she had been wakened this early in the day. Dartanyen and Armond seemed well prepared and were already discussing the length of their journey.

By the time Dremathian entered the hall, everyone had broken their fast. The platter of honey buns had been emptied of its sweet contents, and the milk had disappeared as well. Water flasks had been filled and food packets divided among all. Everyone turned their attention to the druid as he approached the table. "I see that you are all ready to embark upon your journey to Elvandahar. I wish you the best of luck."

"We will need all of the luck we can get. It is going to be a very long trip, especially without the lloryk and larian with which we are accustomed to traveling," said Dartanyen. "I am thinking that we will reach the northern tip of Elvandahar in about three weeks. After that, the going will be slower as we move through the forest."

Dremathian nodded. "I have another way. If you choose, you can utilize the portal that was used to bring you here. It will not be a problem for me to take you to it."

Dartanyen shook his head. "No, that will only take us further away from out destination. It will be best if we just leave on foot from here and go south across the plains of Cortubro. It is a relatively safe journey, and will only cost us some time."

Dremathian smiled. "You don't understand. The portal had more than one destination. It actually has several that are scattered about Shandahar. One of those destinations is here, and obviously the Vanderess Forest. Another destination is the junction of the Selmist Forest and the Bryton Hills in the Kingdom of Karlisle."

Pensively, Dartanyen regarded Dremathian. "That would save us almost two weeks."

Dremathian nodded once again. "Come, I will take you to the portal."

The group walked through the halls of the Apoptos. Adrianna followed behind Sirion. His pack hung crazily from only one shoulder as he walked briskly among them. It was difficult to believe that he was there, a member of the legendary Wildrunners, and that he had found her in a compromised state the morning after her rendezvous with the Tabanakh drink. It was embarrassing to say the least, and she could only hope that his opinion of her had not been too altered by that event.

Several corridors and a staircase later, they reached the portal room. Dremathian walked over to the pedestal holding the open book. Adrianna followed him, intrigued by it as she was with most items that bore magic. She watched as Dremathian turned to the next page of the book. Upon it she saw the image of a large citadel. Its highest towers seemed to reach up to the sky. Adrianna found herself narrowing her eyes. It seemed familiar to her somehow . . . yet she knew that she had never seen a place like it before. Then Dremathian was turning to the next page. She saw the image of a cave situated within a deep wood. This would be their destination. She looked up to find the rest of the group standing near the platform before the portal.

Dremathian began to read the words at the bottom of the page. A slight breeze wafted through the room, pushing the errant tendrils of hair from Adrianna's face, a whisper of magic and power from the creators of the portal. The current within the portal began to move, and once more Adrianna watched until it turned into a wall of shimmering blue. Zorg and Armond were the first to walk through, followed by Tianna, Amethyst, Sabian, and Dartanyen. Sirion, Dramati and Sheridana turned from the portal to look back at Adrianna. She found that she had not moved from her place beside Dremathian. Realizing this, she looked up at the man, and into his face.

"You know that my offer still stands. You are welcome to stay here. There is much I can teach you."

Adrianna shook her head. "You know that I can not."

Dremathian smiled. "Go in peace, then. And may the sun shine upon you."

Adrianna walked away from the pedestal and stepped up onto the platform. Sirion and Sheridana turned and stepped through the portal. Adrianna paused only to hike her pack onto her shoulder, and then she and Dramati followed. She felt a slight wrenching as she was sucked within, very unlike the first time she had traveled in this fashion. She momentarily wondered if she had done something wrong. But then she was stumbling into a cool place. Before she could fall, she felt a hand at her elbow. Adrianna saw a flare of light and focused upon the face of Sirion beside her. Zorg held the torch aloft and the walls of the cave were all around them. "Well, I hope this is the place," he said.

***

"Good evening."

Startled, Adrianna looked beside her to see that Sirion had come upon her unawares. Adrianna inhaled and smiled nervously, it being strange to her that he had been able to move up beside her with not even a whisper of sound. Her sharp sense of hearing usually detected those things.

Sirion crouched down beside her, knowing she had been startled. She had a book in her hands, one that she had been meticulously poring over. It was something that he remembered seeing Dinim doing a few times when they had been with the Wildrunners. "I am sorry if I startled you. It is difficult to remember that I need not step so lightly with friends, that I need not think of stealth when I am not busy scouting. It seems I have fallen into my old habits rather quickly." He gave her a warm reassuring smile, hoping to dispel the tension he had inadvertently created.

"That's all right. I must remember with whom I am traveling." Adrianna glanced at him and then to the ground next to her. *Yes indeed*, she thought to herself. She had to remember that he was Sirion of the Wildrunners. How could she, or anyone, expect any less? He was known to be the best ranger in this area, possibly even in all of Shandahar.

Sirion frowned momentarily. He knew what she was thinking. It felt good to be known by many, to be called a paragon within his chosen profession. Some even called him a hero. But he disliked it when it got in the way of his relationships. He wanted Adrianna to see him as something other than a warrior or a hero. He wanted her to see him as Sirion the man.

Sirion did not understand that it would be difficult for her to see him as anything different than what she had heard about him for almost her entire life. Sirion had been especially well known in the city of Sangrilak, for it was there that he had begun his career as a tracker. It was also there that he had met the Wildrunners, and that group had become so well known over the past decade, they had become a favorite conversation topic to the native people of the area. The people had begun to take pride in the group that had originated within their city, and even felt as though the city was the 'home' of the Wildrunners. Adrianna could not help but remember these things as she spoke to him, and especially when she began to feel stirrings for him in the pit of her stomach. She would then recall that he was so much her senior in years and experiences both.

They sat there for a few moments, taking in the scene around them . . . the darkening sky, the shadows of the maple, oak, and birch trees scattered about the area, a nice breeze upon the bare flesh of their arms and legs. It had been a warm day, warmer than any they had experienced in Krathil-lon. But they had come south, further south than they had started out. The climate here was definitely warmer and by mid-day, many clothes had found themselves inside travel-packs.

Sirion looked across the way, where the evening camp had been situated. Adrianna had taken herself away from the bustle, probably hoping that she would not be bothered. And here he was, sitting here next to her, offering her a distraction that she did not need. "The meal is ready. Tianna seems rather proud of it this time."

Adrianna nodded. Tianna had been taking extra measures of late, hoping to please Sirion. It was plain to see that she loved him. Adrianna felt a twinge of envy. Sirion was a good man, and Tianna could not do much better. She would be fortunate to have him at her side. However, sitting here looking into his eyes, Adrianna was not so sure that he loved Tianna in return. He seemed to think of her only as his little sister. Adrianna was worried about her friend, afraid that Sirion would inadvertently break her heart.

Adrianna shut her book and stood from her place beneath the tree. She rubbed her backside, it having become sore from sitting for so long. Sirion stood as well, fighting to keep a grin off of his face. She was funny, standing there . . . He suddenly noticed that she was looking at him, and he then knew that he had not been successful in his attempts to keep the smile off of his face. She narrowed her eyes for a moment, but then began to grin as well. She began to chuckle, and Sirion found it to be contagious.

They walked over to the camp and took their plates. The meal was delicious, as usual. But Tianna had definitely outdone herself this time. Soon after, Adrianna found herself quite tired. She lay herself down upon her bedroll and watched the cooking fire die out. The rest of the group also began to prepare for sleep, they being unused to the pace at which they had been moving. At mid-day tomorrow they would reach the Denegal River. They would find a place at which they would be able to cross and would camp there for the night. Adrianna closed her eyes and soon was falling into sleep.

She slipped silently within the low-lying brush. She remained alert, ever vigilant for any sight, scent, or sound that may herald a danger to her. She could indeed smell them. Their scent was all around her. This time she would escape; she could already savor the taste of her freedom. Carefully she continued to slip away from the camp. Each moment that passed took her farther away, and made her success more palpable. Suddenly in the trees to her right she heard the snap of a branch. She stopped, rotated her ears toward the sound, and sought to detect any more movement. After a few moments she moved forward once more. It must have been another animal. She took one step, then two. With the third step, she heard the harsh snap of metal, and felt the sharp teeth sink into her right hind leg. Then she was suddenly being swung up from the ground. She felt the muscles in her hindquarters tear and the bone become removed from its socket. She screamed in agony, the pain shooting up her leg and into her dislocated hip.

Wildly the copper/gold fox vixen writhed within the hang-trap, and struggled to free herself. She heard their laughter, and saw them step from out of the trees and bushes around her. Limply she hung within the cruel trap they had set for her. The blood flowed thick and warm up her leg and into the thick soft fur of her belly. One of the men took the other of her rear legs and swung her. The movement brought renewed agony and she mewed piteously. She had failed. She would never have her escape, and they would have their way with her, as always.

Sirion suddenly found himself awake. He waited for a moment and then heard the noise again. From across the banked fire, Adrianna moaned low in her throat. Silently, Sirion continued to lie there. He heard her moan again, the tone of it from one who was in pain. He heard a shuffling noise and knew that she was seeking to escape something. Sirion sat up on his bedroll and looked to the place next to him. He saw her thrashing about. Her moans intensified and began to take on an edge of fear.

Sirion rose from his bed. He quickly padded over to Adrianna and kneeled beside her. "Adrianna . . . Adrianna wake up. It is naught but a dream."

She continued to thrash about, her movements seeming to become more desperate. "No . . . no . . . please stop," she mumbled and then groaned once more.

Sirion leaned in closer to her, placed his hand upon her face. She was wet. He rubbed his thumb beneath her eye and knew that she had been crying. His heart went out to her. He would end this dream for her. He cupped her jaw in his hand. "*Shendori*, wake up." Sirion paused for only a moment, the term of endearment having slipped from his lips before he had even known it was there. It had come naturally to him, even though he had never used it before.

Pretty girl, it meant in Hinterlic . . . something he had heard his father call his mother during a time when the fighting had been at a low. "Adrianna . . . it is only a dream."

The woman called out in desperation. It was in a language that he did not recognize, and he wondered how many languages she knew how to speak. Her thrashing intensified and Sirion found himself straddling her, seeking to gently restrain her. He held one of her hands and continued to hold her face in the other hand. Soothingly he spoke to her again, "Adrianna, wake up. I am here to help you."

Adrianna suddenly awoke. Her eyes snapped open. She began to sit upright when suddenly she found Sirion there. Her face almost smacked into his, but she was able to stop the collision. He was close, so close, that his lips almost touched hers. Her heart raced in her chest not only from the surprise at finding a man hovering over her in the middle of the night, but also from the fact that the man happened to be Sirion Timberlyn.

Sirion looked into her wide eyes, saw her profound surprise. He felt her breath against his mouth, so close to his. For a moment, neither one of them said anything. But then he broke the silence. "You were dreaming. I tried to awaken you, but you sleep deeply."

"Yes, my master used to tell me that. He said that it was one of my only shortcomings." Adrianna hoped that she did not sound too breathless.

"Are you all right? Do you need me to get anything?" Sirion slowly began to retreat. He found himself reluctant to do so, his body unwilling to move away from her.

Adrianna smiled slightly. "No, I will be all right now." Adrianna paused. "Thank you."

Sirion returned to his bedroll. Adrianna re-adjusted herself upon her own bed. She felt badly that she had awaked him. But the dream had been so intense, the pain so real. Her leg ached as though it had been twisted and broken. Her dreams had not been that intense for years. Perhaps it had been because of the drink she had imbibed in Krathil-lon. It had brought about so many strange visions, and may have been the cause of some resurfacing of her bad memories. She sighed heavily. She had the feeling that this time, they may not go away.

***

Adrianna stood from her bedroll. She looked around the camp, noticing that everyone else was asleep. Everyone, of course, except for Zorg, who was keeping the watch. She sighed heavily. It had been an unbearably hot day, and she felt dirty. She knew that she should have bathed earlier, but her books had called to her. Now she knew that she wouldn't be able to fall into a much-needed sleep, not until she had bathed. Adrianna caught Zorg's attention, passing him as she went to the lake next to which they had set their camp. She nodded in the direction of the water and he raised a hand in acknowledgement as she passed. She walked among the trees, beginning to remove her clothes as she moved, impatient to feel the waters envelope her. Tianna, Amethyst, and Sheridana had bathed earlier, having taken advantage of the water right away. It would have been nice to join them, but it was even nicer to bathe now, in the light of the pale moons. The waters shimmered silver as she stopped at the edge of the lake. She slipped her loosened tunic over her head and then stepped out of her trousers. First one bare foot and then the other stepped into the cool waters. Smiling at the soothing feel of the water, she removed her small clothes, depositing them in a heap on top of her tunic and trousers.

Adrianna walked deeper into the lake, luxuriating in the feel of the water encasing her body. She immediately began to feel cleaner, the sweat and dust from her travels washing away from her. The ground beneath her feet dropped precipitously and before she knew it she was up to her shoulders in the cool waters. Adrianna tipped her head back, closing her eyes and allowing the top of her head to be submerged. She them sank beneath the surface and began to swim to the center of the lake.

From his place across the fire, Sirion watched as Adrianna left her bedroll. He followed her with his eyes, saw her nod to Zorg as she passed into the copse of trees in which the lake was secluded. Then he rose himself, motioning for Dramati to stay. Sirion also nodded to Zorg as he passed by, catching the slightly surprised expression on the big man's face as he passed in the same direction that Adrianna had gone only moments before. But the warrior said nothing, returning to polishing his sword.

Cloak in hand, Sirion shook his head. Despite having made Zorg aware of her whereabouts, Adrianna should have known better than to leave the safety of the encampment alone at night. As usual, he would watch out for her, be sure that no harm came to her, just as he would for anyone else in the company. He told himself this as he followed Adrianna to the lake. Her faelin senses would have noticed him, but he moved silently behind her, not making a sound as he passed. He remained concealed among the trees as she reached the edge of the water and began to remove her clothing. He did not wishing to disturb her.

Sirion told himself that he should look away, that he should afford her at least some measure of privacy. But he did not, and continued to keep his eyes on her as she removed first her tunic and then her trousers. She was beautiful, her hair shining in the light of the moons. Her pale gold flesh was radiant as she stepped into the pool. He watched as she removed her underclothes and submerged her body gracefully into the water.

Adrianna waded in the lake and rinsed the dirt and grime from her hair.

She bathed herself until she began to notice the coolness of the water, her body being leached of its heat. She then made her way towards shore, dreading the exposure she would have to endure in the cool night air.

Sirion began to step from the concealment of the trees. His eyes remained riveted upon the woman before him. She was quite possibly the most beautiful creature he had ever seen. Water droplets glistened upon her as she emerged from the pool. Her small, slender body was magnificent in every perfect detail. He made towards her as she stepped from the lake.

Adrianna stepped out of the water. As she emerged, she immediately realized that she was not alone. She looked up to see Sirion standing a short distance away. Surprised, she stopped. Involuntarily, she brought her arms to her chest, making an effort to conceal herself from his intense gaze. Her heart began to thud wildly in her chest and her breath seemed to explode from her lungs. It was then that she realized that she had been holding it. She remained still as he strode towards her, his cloak extended to her.

Sirion reached her and wrapped his cloak around her shoulders. He felt suddenly ashamed . . . she had tried to hide herself from him when she had seen him. Guiltily, he had quickly made his way over to her and wrapped her chilled body in his cloak. He should have made his presence known to her while her body had been concealed within the water. But the vision of her beauty had been burned into his mind. He felt her tremble beneath his touch and then realized how fast his breath came from his nostrils. His body had responded to her and he, too, trembled, although not from the night air.

Adrianna felt her body tremble. It was not a chill she felt, but something more than that. It was the way her body had responded to him before. And it was the way he had looked at her, the intensity of his gaze as he had taken her in . . . her nakedness unveiled for him to see. And she was ashamed. She clutched the cloak closely about her, afraid of what she was feeling, never having felt it before.

Sirion gripped her shoulders. "You should have bathed earlier, when the air was warmer."

Adrianna nodded as she looked up at him. He rubbed her shoulders and arms, attempting to bring warmth back to her body. She trembled anew, his proximity twisting her belly into knots. She said nothing, not knowing what to say. He must have been awake and seen her leave the encampment. He must have felt that it was his duty to look after her. But why had he not warned her of his presence?

"And you should have brought a cloak. You would have made your clothes damp if you were to have donned them so soon after bathing." Sirion stopped rubbing her shoulders and back. "And you should have told me you meant to leave the safety of the camp. It is my duty to protect you." Sirion chastised her gently, not wishing her to think he was truly angry with her.

"I will remember next time." Adrianna looked up at him, her dark eyes wide. "I am sorry, Sirion."

It was then that Sirion saw that he still held her upper arms. She stood before him, seeming so small. He so much wanted to bring her in to his embrace, to hold her close to him, but instead he released her. He smiled slightly. "Don't. There is no need. Come, let us get you back to camp."

Sirion turned as she bent to pick up her clothes. She dressed herself hurriedly, she not wanting to keep him waiting longer than he already had. He walked beside her as they made their way through the trees back to camp. Zorg raised a single eyebrow at them as they passed him by on their way to their own bedrolls. Adrianna felt slightly embarrassed. She knew what it must look like to him, she with wet hair and he with a damp cloak. After combing and plaiting her hair, Adrianna settled herself upon her bedroll. She cast a glance in Sirion's direction and saw that he was still awake, staring silently into the glowing embers of the banked fire.

CHAPTER 16

At the end of the third day the group sat quietly around the evening fire. A half-day's ride to the north lay before them, the forest of Elvandahar awaited. The journey across the river had been an uneventful one, as ferry trips tended to be. Adrianna's sleep had been very restless the night before, and in the morning she was slightly fatigued from lack of sleep. Thus, for much of the day, Adrianna kept to herself. Her dreams disturbed her, and her thoughts kept sifting through them. Sometimes Adrianna was no longer sure what was fact and what was fiction. Her dreams about the original event had become so diverse and she had had so many that it was difficult to keep dreams and reality separate.

But why had they returned to her now, after all of this time? She had a few when she first left Andahye, but they had been nothing like the night terrors that she experienced the first several months after the event, or the ones that she had begun to experience the past couple of nights. It was like a flood gate had been opened, and all of the dreams that had been waiting were now drowning her within a deluge. When she had started her apprenticeship under Master Tallek, the dreams had miraculously faded away and Adrianna now found herself wondering if her master had made it so. When Cortath had come into her life the few dreams that she had been having had disappeared as well. Perhaps through the link that they had shared, Cortath had been able to keep them from her. But now . . . now there was nothing to hold them back.

That night Adrianna once again slept fitfully. In her mind's eye, the darkness of the nightmare loomed over her, threatening to engulf her. It spoke to her with the voice of despair, and her dream-self shrank away from it in fear and loathing. But once again she was thrown into yet another aspect of her most fearsome dream, and her greatest failure.

The fronds parted as she slithered through them. Slowly she moved, the muscles of her body contracting together to push her through the tall grass. She felt the cool ground beneath her belly, and she found herself yearning for warmth. But then, there was something else that she wanted more than a meal or the sun. Freedom. She wished to escape from those who sought her . . . those that would brutalize her and then kill her.

Suddenly, she felt a vibration of the ground. Someone was close, and becoming nearer. She increased her pace, no longer worried about stealth. But then they were upon her. She dodged one blow, and then another. The clubs only narrowly missed her as she slithered first on one direction and then another. She increased her pace even more, fear coursing through her. But it was not enough. The third blow did not miss. She felt the hammer fall upon her, crushing her body beneath its hideous weight. When the weapon lifted, she tried desperately to continue to flee, but her body was slowed by the massive wound that flattened it. She could feel the blood flowing out of her, coating the blades of grass as she coiled over them.

The hammer fell again, and she felt the agony of her body being crushed once more. There would be no escape for her. She would suffer the tortures that would be inflicted upon her body. Then she would die. Death would be preferable to living and remembering what had been done.

Adrianna sat upright upon her bed. Her breaths came in harsh gasps from her raw throat, her heart beat wildly in her chest, and her body shook uncontrollably. Getting her bearings, her gaze raked through the camp, hoping, praying that *they* would not be there. Once she realized where she was and who she was with, she began to calm herself. The dream had been so real . . . and the pain so agonizing. She hoped that she had not cried out too loudly, and she looked about the camp once again. She had begun sleeping further away from the others in hopes that she would not awaken them with her cries. But her plan had not worked. From across the way, she saw Sirion looking at her from his own bedroll. He gazed at her fixedly, and she could see the questions lurking there in his eyes. It was not the first time that she had awakened him.

"Adrianna, are you all right?"

It was the voice of her sister. Adrianna turned towards Sheri's bedroll and nodded. "I'm fine. It was just a bad dream. Go back to sleep."

Sheri tuned over, wrapping an arm around Fitanni. On the baby's other side slept Carli. The girl was still sleeping and Adria was glad that not everyone had been awakened. She lay back down upon her bedroll and curled onto her side. There was no indication from anyone else that they had awoken. She wanted to close her eyes, so much wanted to sleep, but now she was afraid. She knew that if she slept that the dreams would only return. So she lay there with her eyes open, staring into the night.

***

The group walked through the silver trees of Elvandahar. It was a beautiful place, very much like the glen from which they had come. But it was hot, the canopy overhead keeping much heat and moisture trapped beneath. Adrianna hoped that there would not be many more days like this one, where the humidity was so thick it was suffocating. But it was more than the heat that made Adrianna sick and weary. Her lack of sleep was weighing upon her, and her dreams were no longer a thing of the night, but had become an element of the day as well. No matter where she turned they would not leave her, and she feared that her sanity would soon become forfeit.

After a few moments, Adrianna noticed that someone had come to walk beside her. She turned to find Sheridana. Her sister smiled and Adrianna had to struggle to return the smile. "Adria, are you okay? You don't seem to be doing very well. You are falling behind, and we have begun to slow down."

Adrianna turned away and gazed at the ground. "Sorry. I'm just a little tired. I will try harder to keep up."

Sheri frowned and then put a palm to Adria's forehead. "Are you sick? You feel a bit warm."

"No. I will be fine. I just need some rest."

Sheri nodded. "I'll let Dartanyen and Sirion know. Maybe we can stop early today."

"No. Don't do that. I don't want to hold everyone up. I'll just be sure to keep up."

Sheri frowned again. "Well, if you say. But just remember, we are your friends, and no one will mind if we have to stop because you are ill."

Adrianna smiled slightly. "I know."

Sheridana left Adria to go back nearer the front of the line. Adrianna increased her pace, and by the end of the day she found herself in a state of exhaustion. But when she crawled upon her bedroll for the night, she found herself afraid once more. She did not want to fall asleep. The dreams were so real, and she suffered in them the way she suffered that horrible night eight years ago. She felt the tears flow unchecked down her cheeks and she angrily wiped them away. Why was she so weak? She tried to be strong like Sheri, yet she continued to be a weakling. For quite some time she lay there, but her body finally gave in to the fatigue, and Adrianna slept.

In a haze, Adrianna saw the three men. She began to run through the trees. The branches tore at her clothes, face, and arms. Faster and faster she moved, and abruptly she found herself beginning to change. Before she knew it she was a golden hawk, and she felt her arm muscles unfurling expansive wings. She felt the wind lift her from the ground and she was airborne. High above the trees she flew, screeching her defiance at the men below. She felt the sun's rays upon her glorious feathers and her heart soared with the victory of her escape.

Suddenly, a pain blossomed in her chest and she faltered. She felt a second arrow rip through her right wing. Her body began to plummet from the sky and by the time she hit the ground she was a woman again. The men were there, waiting. They beat her until she could hardly breathe, pummeling her ribs, slapping her face and putting their hands around her neck . . . squeezing her windpipe until she was expiring from lack of air. Then they would release her only to watch her fall to the ground so they could kick her. It was her punishment for trying to escape them yet again. And it was a warning that they would kill her next time.

From far away, Adrianna heard her name. It was Sheridana, her sister. Desperately, Adrianna tried to awaken from the dream. But she could not awaken. The haze grew thicker, as if enveloping her soul, trapping it within the fabric of the nightmare. From without, Adrianna felt her body being shaken. The thick mist tore and her soul was released. As if in a deep pool of water, Adrianna struggled to the surface and finally broke free. Her body trembled from the effort, her breathing was labored and she was covered in wetness. "I was a hawk . . . I was a hawk and I still couldn't get away. I tried so hard to . . . to escape." Her body convulsed with the force of her sobs. Sheri held Adrianna tightly, telling her it was all right and other such nonsense phrases. Nonsense because Adrianna knew better. The nightmare meant to have her one way or another and she had to sleep sometime.

Sirion was there as well, kneeling next to her bedroll. He regarded her out of large, concerned amber eyes. Adrianna watched his lips as he mouthed reassurances to her. She finally stopped crying and attempted to collect herself.

"Are you all right?" Adrianna looked into her sister's eyes and nodded. "You had me frightened. You sounded like someone was torturing you."

"I'm fine and I am sorry that I woke everyone up. It was just a bad dream."

"It sounded like more than that. Do you want to talk about it?"

"No." Adrianna almost shouted the word. "Just . . . just go back to bed. I'll be fine. I just need some good rest, that's all."

Sheri sighed heavily. She felt slightly put out. She wished that she knew what was wrong with her sister. These dreams, they seemed to be haunting her. It seemed that she was trying to escape from something . . . or someone, but was unsuccessful. Sheridana rose from her place beside Adrianna, saying nothing as she went back to her own bed. From his place beside her, Armond asked Sheri if Adrianna was all right. She found herself nodding to him, and telling him that Adria had just had a nightmare. But it had definitely more than that . . . much more.

***

Adrianna walked behind the rest of the group, her summer cloak wrapped about her slender body, the hood pulled over her silver/gold hair. She was already having difficulty keeping up with the group, and they had been walking for only about an hour. Once again she stumbled, and she just barely caught herself against Dramati's side. Continuing onward, she shivered within her cloak despite the warm weather. She knew that she was indeed becoming ill. But she did not want to stop. What good would it do? She would continue to sicken, for the nightmares would not leave her. Perhaps she would finally die, even though it was so long after the event. Her attackers will have won after all.

Sheridana looked back at her sister once more. She looked like a walking cloak, shadowed as she was within it. The face that peered at them from within the hood frightened her. Adria's eyes were large and dark within sunken sockets. Her color was a pale gray, and her lips were bloodless. She seemed so small and frail within the cloak, and Sheridana saw a look of fear pass over Dinim's usually confident features. He was afraid for her, just as Sheridana was afraid that the thing within Adria would finally succeed in killing her.

The day passed on, Sirion leading them through the forest of his childhood home. The group was unusually quiet as they continued through the trees. Thankfully the weather had cooled, but the sky had become grey, a herald to the approaching storm. Adrianna continued to be quiet and withdrawn. Her thoughts were focused inwards, on a battle that she knew would come with the fall of dusk and end with the rise of a new dawn.

That evening the group sat around the evening fire. Sheridana looked behind her to the form of her sister. Adrianna had lain her bedroll in a place removed from the rest of the group and she sat upon it, her knees drawn up beneath her chin. Her head rested wearily upon the hands she had folded upon her knees. She looked so weak, and so tired. Food had been offered to Adrianna but she refused it, stating that she was not hungry. When Sheri tried to argue the issue, Adrianna only became angry, snapping at her to go away. So here she sat with the rest of the group, when all she really wanted to do was make her sister well again.

"Sheridana, something is seriously amiss with her. Has she not told you anything?"

Sheridana looked back to Dartanyen. He regarded her with a concerned expression on his face. All she could do was shake her head. Adrianna would tell her nothing. Every one of her inquiries had ended in rejection.

"Do you know anything at all?" Dartanyen asked.

Sheri scowled darkly. "At this point, you know her better than I do. You figure her out. She won't tell me anything."

"Sheridana, we are just trying to find out what could be wrong. This is so unlike her," said Tianna.

"I know. I'm sorry. It's just that I don't like to see her this way."

"None of us do," said Armond.

"All we can do is wait. We will decide whether she is fit enough for travel tomorrow. If she isn't, either we can stay here or we can build a makeshift litter," said Dartanyen.

Adrianna sat on her bedroll, her head lowered with fatigue as she watched the group settle in for the night. Unwilling to lie down for fear of what the night would bring, Adrianna continued to stay awake. But after a while, she didn't have a choice and her body began to sway. Adrianna only knew enough to put her hands beside herself to steady her body as it lowered onto the bed.

The darkness enveloped her within its cold embrace. Adrianna floated in the void, waiting. As always, the mist came, as well as the scene that had dominated her dreams for eight years. But then the trees seemed to become smaller as her form shifted into that of a large feline, a kyerrean, larger than life in all her majesty. She roared her defiance. This time, she would not attempt to escape. She would not flee. For the first time she would face her enemies. She had come to realize that she had been stripped of everything she had held dear: her happiness, her pride, and her sanity. She had nothing to lose anymore, and had everything to gain.

The kyerrean eyed the men that came at her out of the trees. They drew their swords and began to slash at her. She felt the massive muscles of her hindquarters coil as she leapt at the men. Valiantly she fought, using teeth, claws, and brute strength against her enemies. But the men were skilled, and she finally she fell to the sword blows. She lay in a pool of her blood, panting her life away. And then she was a woman once again, and the men began to beat her mercilessly. They meant to kill her. They would not leave her for dead this time.

Adrianna screamed in her sleep. Her body convulsed and her legs kicked out, as if trying to escape something. Sheridana and Sirion ran to her, shaking her so as to awaken her. Adrianna screamed again, recoiling from their hands upon her. Adrianna struggled to awaken from the nightmare and finally succeeded in opening her eyes.

Adrianna was awake, yet not. She existed somewhere in between. Her eyes focused upon Sheridana and Sirion hovering above her. Behind them she saw the rest of the group. Adrianna gripped her sister's arm, pulled Sheri down toward her. She whispered, "They killed him, Sheri. They killed Nahum. Now I have no one, no one to keep them from me." Blood poured from a cut in her lip, probably inflicted by her teeth as she struggled. Adrianna's eyes filled with tears and then lost focus. Once more she entered her world of pain and misery, wishing that it all would end, thinking that it would have been so much easier if they had just been more thorough and killed her after they had used her body for their cruel pleasures.

Beside him, Sirion felt Sheridana's body spasm with shock. Adrianna's eyes closed and she released Sheridana's arm, her body becoming limp. The woman took Adrianna's shoulders, lifted her from the bedroll, and cradled her in her arms. "Adria . . . Adrianna. Please wake up. I am here for you now . . . this time."

Sirion put his hand on Sheridana's shoulder. Her tear-filled eyes riveted on him, and upon seeing his expression, she let Adrianna fall back onto the blankets. Sheri covered her face with her hands and began to cry. She cried for her sister, now having an idea of what had befallen her. She wished that Gareth were there to punish her for having left their sister behind all of those years ago. But she had not seen her brother for a long time, and did not even know if he still lived.

Sirion knelt next to Adrianna. He noticed the flushed color of her cheeks and he placed his palm upon her brow. He felt the heat and knew her to be fevered. Hells, the woman was delusional, speaking in half-sentences that could not be properly understood. Sirion scooped her up from the blankets and carried her across the encampment to his own bedding. Tianna's own bedroll lay close by and he knew that it would be easier for Adrianna to be brought to her than for Tianna to have to move all of her things across the fire. He lay her upon his blankets and Tianna was at his side the next instant. She knelt next to Adrianna and placed her wrist upon Adria's forehead. "She is burning with fever," she exclaimed.

Adrianna moaned and shook once more, consumed by her dream . . . consumed by her past. She was trapped, and feared that this time she would not awaken. It was a hell she had created for herself, trying for so long to flee from those who she thought pursued her. But the dreams continued to come and there was no escape. One time she was a wily fox, hoping to sly herself free. They set a trap from which there was no escape and crippled her. Another time she was a slithery snake in the grass, hoping to slide past those who watched. But they saw the parting fronds and smashed her with their clubs. Yet another time she was a hawk, hoping to fly away so high they would never reach her. But they took their bows and arrows and shot her out of the sky. The last time she was a fierce kyerrean. They battled her with their swords. They cut her, and when she finally fell they tied her up and stripped the pride away from her. They tried to break her spirit so that she would never try to escape again.

Now, it is too late for her. She was tired now . . . so tired. All she could do was turn around and fight the final battle. But she was happy; she had already won. Her death would release her, or if she returned victorious, their deaths would give her the same release.

For the third time she turned around to look behind her, and once again saw no one there. Dusk was falling and it was time to find a place to camp for the night. The road to Andahye seemed empty save for herself and Nahum, but Adrianna was nervous and fidgety nevertheless. Her mentor noticed, and sought to calm her with small talk, but it helped little. After a while they broke off from the main road, entering the protective covering of the trees. It was then that they were attacked.

Nahum's eyes widened just as a large form barreled into Adrianna from behind. She fell forward onto her stomach and face, the breath knocked out of her. She bit her lip as her jaw hit the ground and the grit in her mouth told her she had chipped a tooth or two. For only a fraction of a moment Adrianna was stunned, but she quickly regained her wits and began to struggle for the dagger she had tucked into her knee-high boot. The man pinning her down tried to get a proper grip, and for a while she was successful at evading his thick-fingered hands. Finally, she was able to reach the boot and she pulled out the dagger. But, she wasn't quick enough. He gathered her intentions before she could do him some real harm. He moved his forearm just in time to intercept her backward plunge into his otherwise unprotected ribs. She ended up cutting into his arm, which only served to make him angry. He clouted her in the head, thus successful in immobilizing his victim, and it was then that Adrianna saw Nahum and the other two men. It was the end, and he looked at her as he crumpled to the ground, lifeless. One of the men went and kicked the inert form, and then put his sword through Nahum's chest. Adrianna cried out. She heard an angry curse, and then felt something hit her upside the head.

She awoke to find herself hanging upside down. There was pressure at her abdomen, and she quickly realized that she was slung over someone's shoulder. Her hands were bound behind her back, and her braid hung beside her face, hitting her jaw with each step the man took deeper into the forest. Fear coursed through her. She had never felt fear this strong in her whole life, even when Hafgan had raised his hand to her in anger. The men were large. Their clothes were dirty, their faces were hairy, and they stank of their own filth. Her heart beat fast within her chest and her head ached with every step the man took. The warm wetness running down the side of her face told her she had been hit with more than just a fist. Yet she dared not scream. She had the dreadful feeling that no one would hear.

Eventually they reached an encampment. The man holding her over his shoulder deposited her roughly onto the ground. The force of the impact made her head throb, but once on the ground she tried to scramble away. The three men laughed. "You aren't going anywhere sweetie; not before we are finished with you." They made a few more lewd comments, bound her ankles, kicked her a few times in the ribs, and then sat around what would become their evening fire. As they sat there and talked for a while, she had a horrible thought of what the men had in store for her that night. Adrianna tried desperately to get her wrists free of the bindings, but served only to make the skin so raw that the cord bit through the flesh of her wrists. She began to feel the stickiness of blood on her palms. She then tried to loosen the bindings at her ankles to no avail.

Time crept past. By the time the men stood up from their fire, Adrianna's desperation had reached new heights. The rope at her wrists was so wet and her flesh so swollen that she could no longer move her hands. Shocks of pain swept up her arms when she was defiant enough to move and her skull ached with awesome ferocity. She felt like she was going to die, and she would soon come to wish she had.

The largest of the men approached her. His hair was long, dark, and stringy and his skin was brown and hairy. He bent down, cut the bindings at her feet, grabbed her arm, and hauled her up. Adrianna gasped with the sickening pain, and when he noticed the bloodied bindings he laughed mockingly. He dragged her nearer the fire and the other two human men. Once there, he cut the bindings at her wrists. Pain surged through her hands at the sudden rush of blood. She held them out in front of her as she realized she was free. Her heart leapt, and in fear and panic she began to run. But they were prepared for that. The hairy brown man was behind her faster than lightening. He caught a fist-full of hair and jerked her backward. Her neck whipped back from the force, succeeding in stopping her. He hauled her around to face him, and put his long, wicked dagger at her throat.

He taunted Adrianna with the long-knife. He put the cold metal to her flesh; watched her flinch when it drew blood. For quite some time he toyed with her . . . enjoyed seeing her fear and pain. The pounding in her skull was so loud, it drowned out most of his words. Finally, he mumbled something about "preserving her pretty hide" and pulled her against his person. Instinctively she struggled, and for her efforts she was backhanded in the side of her head. As Adrianna fought to regain her senses, he savagely cut the clothes from her body. She felt the long-knife cut through the flesh between her breasts before she was shoved to the ground onto her backside. The man went down with her, tearing at the remains of the tunic.

As Adrianna began to struggle once again, one huge hand wrapped itself around her throat. The man held her there while he touched her. Ineffectually she tried to disengage the fingers from her throat but the more she struggled, the tighter his grip became. Then he began to work at her trousers. She was afraid to move too much; his grip was stifling and it was difficult to breathe. She concentrated on that activity, and when he had the trousers away and she was about to expire from lack of oxygen, the man pinned her thighs to the ground with his knees and released her throat.

As Adrianna gasped for air, he put the tip of his long-knife to the deep cut between her breasts. She hissed involuntarily as the fresh blood welled from the wound and dripped down her sides. "Yer blood is the same color as mine, faelin bitch. I've been waitin' a long time fer this. Think yer better than us do ye?" The knife continued its way down her torso, but he didn't apply pressure until he was below her navel. Her body trembled from exertion and fear. She began to struggle again as the tip of the knife went into her flesh. The man put his large hand on her chest and held her there as he cut downward into the delicate skin. Again he laughed, mocking her, enjoying himself at her expense. His eyes were filled with what she had come to realize as lust, and he dropped the knife and began probing between her legs. He handled her roughly, but the pain was nothing compared to what would come. He continued to hold her down with one hand *while he untied the fastenings on his trousers. The renewal of her efforts to escape him seemed to increase his excitement. He grinned maliciously and growled as he bent over her, touching her, salivating on her. His hands were rough over her skin, and his breath against her neck was rank.*

Finally the man tired of his game. He was tired of restraining her and he hit Adrianna once more. But she had reached a state of exhaustion. Her senses reeled from the blow, and she wished that he had succeeded in knocking her witless. When he parted her legs, lifted her hips, and slammed his manhood into her, she felt the breath exit her lungs. If she had entertained thoughts of dying before, she definitely wanted to die at that moment. Adrianna screamed as the searing pain tore through her body. Every thrust was torture, and her agony only seemed to enhance his pleasure.

It seemed like forever and a day passed by before he was finished with her. Adrianna could no longer understand his words, and she found that it had become difficult for her to see as well. When the pale-haired, pale-skinned man came to take the first man's place, she quickly realized that the agony would not cease for many hours to come. Thus, they took their turns with her and their faces became burned into her memory forever. She finally passed out when the third man took her, her mind whirling away into sweet oblivion where she felt only nothingness.

Adrianna awoke sometime in the middle of the night. Her movements must have caught the men's attention, because they were looming above her almost immediately. Once again they took her, and once again her mind did not pull away until the pain was unbearable and she felt as though the insides of her body were being torn apart. After they finished, they hit and kicked her body, muttering vile phrases. A swift kick to the temple and she was plunged into darkness once more.

The next time Adrianna awoke it was daylight. Her broken body refused to move at first, but with agonizing slowness, she rolled herself onto her belly. She felt the blood begin to flow anew and she struggled for a moment just to breathe. The men were gone, the fire put out. They had left her there to die . . . to bleed to death in the middle of the woods. She recalled the previous night with vivid clarity and she began to tremble. Even this small activity was painful, and she blacked out.

Adrianna did not know how long she lay there, coming in and out of consciousness. But she knew that she was dying. She remembered thinking to herself that only something magical would be able to save her.

Adrianna slowly awoke. She felt the bedding beneath her, turned her head and saw her sister sitting next to her, her chin on her chest. She felt her hand encased within Sheri's. She tried to move her body and moaned involuntarily. Sheridana looked up at her and then placed a hand at her brow. The hand was cold and Adria shivered. Her body ached, and she felt as though she had been raped all over again. "Adrianna . . . please speak to me." Sheri implored, her eyes wet with unshed tears.

Adrianna shook her head. She found that she could not speak. She had to conserve every iota of energy within her. She knew now what she had to do, what she had always had to do. And if she failed at least she would die trying, and she would die a warrior's death even though she did not wield a sword. Adrianna saw Sirion come to kneel behind her sister. It was so good to see him. His eyes were full of concern for her. She suddenly wished she had known him when she was younger. Somehow, she knew that he would have let no harm come to her.

Once again, Adrianna's mind began to spiral away. Images passed before her, images of her father, of Hafgan, and of the men who had used her so brutally. She hated them, yet hated herself even more for her fear of them. That fear had dominated her life for almost nine years and now it would come to an end. She would attempt to defeat them in her dreams. If she succeeded, she knew that she would have to face them once more in the world she knew as reality. But she would be ready. She refused to be weak anymore. She would begin to take the place that Master Tallek had helped her to create for herself.

Then she was there. The scenario was the same as always. The forest trees surrounded her. She knew that they were there watching her, waiting for the right time to ambush her. She was alone. Nahum was not with her. Her mentor had died many years ago. She walked along her ordained path. She made no attempt to protect herself from what was to come, not like she had before. She did not shift into a hawk, a kyerrean, or a fox. She did not draw her dagger or attempt to use a sword. She had tried all of those things before, all of those and more over the passage of the years. This time, she would be herself.

Adrianna began to concentrate. She cast an Armor *spell. It would help to protect her against the men when they came at her. Then she cast a* Shocking Grasp *spell. Just as she completed the casting, the first man surprised her, jumped out of the bushes and knocked her to the ground. But she did not suffer as she always had before. Her body felt less vulnerable, as though a layer of thick leather covered her. She felt the man on top of her convulse with the electric shock that passed through his body. He fell away from her, gripping his sides.*

Adrianna stood up. The other two men regarded her for a moment, wondered what had happened to their comrade. Then they advanced toward her. Adrianna reached into the pouch at her hip, found the coil of rope within it. She began to back away from her adversaries. They smirked maliciously. The blond man drew his dagger and the other took a garrote from his satchel. Adrianna began to cast her Bind *spell, hoped that she would remain out of their grasp until the spell was complete. But the men were in no hurry. They advanced upon her slowly, grinning more and more widely as they got closer. Then the spell was complete. The blond man caught up to her and grasped her arm. She cast the rope at him, commanding it to bind him within its coils. The rope obeyed her, unfurling to encase the man. The man stared at the rope, fascinated, as it bound his arms to his body. When he realized what had happened, he looked at her in surprise. She plucked the dagger from his hand as the other man stepped up to her. He reached around her and placed the garrote at her neck.*

Adrianna felt the pressure of the garrote biting into her flesh. She began to choke and desperately she reached back and shoved the dagger into the man behind her. He yelled into her ear, nearly deafening her. She felt the garrote loosen from about her neck and she pushed back into her adversary. He fell away from her, his hand upon his thigh. He then snarled and leapt at her. Adrianna dodged out of his way and he careened past her. She ran past the bound man and then past the one she had shocked earlier. He had recovered, but allowed her to pass him by. He dared not touch her again, afraid of what would happen to him if he did.

Adrianna ran up the path and into the trees. She hid under a fallen oak and waited for the men to come for her. She had not long to wait. The men came looking for her, the others having untied the one who had been bound. A strip of cloth had been tied around the leg of the one whom had been cut by the dagger. Adrianna completed her spell. She waited, hoping it would work. She had never summoned anything before and wondered if it truly would happen. And then she heard it. The sound of a swarm of insects could be heard in the distance. It got closer, and closer. And then it was there. The shimmering whirigs converged upon the men. They began to swing their arms, and then to yell. The yells began to heighten in pitch as the insects began to sting them. Adrianna crawled from beneath the fallen tree and ran in the direction of Andahye. She would place as much distance between herself and the mercenaries as possible.

Adrianna felt lucky to have been able to summon the whirigs. She heard that the creature summoned each time was different. She could not have asked for a better ally. Adrianna ran for as long as she could and then slowed to a walk. Her heart was light as she continued her journey. The darkness upon her soul began to fall away and was left upon the road behind her. Nahum was not with her, but she was unharmed. He had died protecting her, and she would always remember him for that.

Adrianna awoke. It was daylight. The sunlight shone through the leaves of the trees above her. She slowly moved her head, glancing about the camp. Sabian sat a few yards away, his back to a large tree. He was reading a book, as always. Adrianna sat up, slowly beginning to remember her dreams from the night before. But the after-effects of the dreams were not so bad this time. This time she had won, and the oppression she had been feeling since her stay in Krathil-lon had finally begun to retreat.

Nervously, she looked around the camp once more. But what exactly *had* happened? Had she spoken out loud in her dream-state? Did everyone know what had happened to her . . . that she was a lunatic? Where was Sheridana? Tianna saw her and walked slowly over to her. "Adrianna, how do you feel?"

By the look on Tianna's face, Adrianna knew that the other woman had some idea what had gone on the night before, knew that she had been raped all of those years ago. That probably meant that the rest of the group knew as well. Adrianna shamefully turned her gaze to the blankets that she rested upon. She studied them for a moment and suddenly realized that they were not hers. She frowned.

Tianna knelt next to her and placed a cool palm upon her brow. "Your fever has broken. This is a good sign. You were gone for two days."

Adrianna shook her head. "Tianna, what is going on? What happened to me? Whose bedding is this?" Adrianna lifted the corner of one of the blankets.

Tianna regarded her intensely for a moment before replying. "It is Sirion's. He brought you over to his bedroll the night you went into your delirium. You have been resting upon it ever since."

Adrianna's breath almost caught in her throat. Sirion. He knew about her as well. Hells, she felt sick to her stomach, wished she could sink into the ground. She put her arms around her belly, felt the tears spring to her eyes. She felt like such a whore, even more so now that she knew that her comrades knew how she had been used.

Tianna watched Adrianna fold into herself, saw the self-recrimination pass over the young woman's face. Once more Tianna felt a surge of sympathy. She wanted so much to reach out to her, to help her. But Tianna felt so hurt herself; she had watched while Sirion had taken Adrianna to his bedroll and tended to her, even slept next to her, as though his presence would somehow help her. Mayhap it did; Tianna was sure it would have helped her had she been as sick as Adrianna had been.

Tianna reached out and put her hand on the woman's shoulder. "Adrianna, you have been ill. Here, let me get you some tea . . ."

"No. I don't want anything. Please, just leave me."

Tianna shrank back from her, from the despair she heard in Adrianna's voice. She saw the tears slide down Adrianna's pale cheeks, the slump to her shoulders. Then she saw Dinim coming back from his bath. Seeing that Adrianna was awake, he quickly made his way over to them, a look of relief upon his handsome face. But once he saw Tianna's expression and Adrianna's pallor, his expression changed. His eyes were full of questions as he knelt beside Tianna in front of Adrianna. Then, turning to Adrianna, he found that she was crying. Instinctively, he wrapped his arms around her and pulled her to him.

Adrianna found herself being pulled into someone's embrace. By the scent of him, she knew it to be Dinim. She buried her face into his shoulder. Her body began to quake and her sobs intensified. He knew. They all knew. She felt so vulnerable. It was almost as though the mercenaries had won after all, having beaten her even though she had finally won the physical fight. She beat her fists against Dinim's chest, felt his muscles tighten against her onslaught. "I am so lost, so lost. Please help me, I beg you."

"Adrianna, I know how you feel. You are not alone. I am here for you."

Adrianna lifted her face from his chest, looked into his eyes. She expected to see a face full of pity, eyes that wanted to understand her plight, but did not . . . could not. Instead, she found sympathy and understanding so deep that she wanted to cry out.

Adrianna put her arms around his neck, clutched him to her. He responded in kind, embracing her tightly, kissing her face and hair. They had hurt her. She had almost died, and Dinim knew that she sometimes wished that she had. He continued to hold her, knowing that she needed him and knowing that he needed her too.

Tianna stepped back from Dinim and Adrianna, not really understanding what was transpiring between them. But it seemed that Dinim could help her friend in a way that she could not. Tianna did not truly understand Adrianna's plight; and she was glad of that. She did not want to even contemplate how she would have been able to deal with the terrible abuse that Adrianna had suffered.

Tianna noticed some movement at the periphery of the camp. The hunting party had returned. Sheridana and Dartanyen carried a leshera between them and Sirion carried a brace of hares. It wasn't until the hunters had lay down their kills before they realized that Adrianna had awoken. Sirion was the first to see them. Tianna watched the multitude of unreadable expressions pass over his face. He just stood there for a moment, taking in the scene across the encampment. Then he slowly began to make his way over to them.

Sheridana saw Sirion moving away from them. She turned in the direction in which he was moving. She saw her sister and Dinim in an embrace. She was surprised and wondered what had happened, but she was also happy, so happy to see Adrianna awake after two days of fever and sporadic ramblings in languages she did not understand.

Sheri ran past Sirion and reached her sister and Dinim. "Adrianna, I am so glad to see you well!"

Adrianna and Dinim parted and Adria went to embrace Sheridana. Adrianna closed her eyes, hugging Sheri close. Adrianna was happy to see her sister, pleased to note that her knowledge did not make Sheri treat her any differently. "Adria, we brought down a leshera. We will eat well tonight."

Adrianna opened her eyes and was about to respond when she saw Dartanyen and then Sirion standing a few feet away behind Sheridana. She felt her breath lodge in her throat. Sirion carried his longbow in his right hand and a quiver of arrows over his left shoulder. His face was expressionless, but his eyes seemed to beckon to her. She resisted, her feelings of inadequacy and vulnerability surfacing once more.

Sheri stepped away from her and took her hand. "Here, Adrianna. Sit close to the fire that we are going to build. You have been sick. This fresh meat will be good for you."

Adrianna allowed herself to be lead away by her sister. Her eyes remained on Sirion as she was pulled toward the beginnings of the evening fire. She saw his gaze follow her for a moment before looking away and making his way to his bedroll and packs.

***

The group moved deeper into the faelin realm of Elvandahar. After getting adequate rest, Adrianna was feeling much better and her fever had abated. While she had suffered in her delirium, the group had constructed a litter upon which they had carried her. Zorg and Armond joked about how heavy she had been, and made a big rumpus about how happy they were to leave the litter behind. Adrianna could not help but smile at their antics, knowing that they only teased her, for she knew that her weight had been nothing for them to carry. They made light of the situation, and Adrianna felt better that they did not feel that they had to treat her any differently than they had before.

As they traveled, Adrianna had begun to feel a change in the air: an aura of protection surrounding the place. There was magic here, great magic. They moved slowly, everyone seeming to feel a strangeness about the forest, a sense of not belonging. Everyone felt it except for Sirion, who continued to walk confidently through the trees of his home. Even Tianna seemed to appear a little out of place. The forest was magnificent, the silver oaks towering over them. The bark was a dark grey, but the color of the leaves on the trees was what gave the forest its nickname, Silverwood. They were the color of shimmering silver. Beneath the silver, one could see a hint of green. Looking up, it was almost blinding, each leaf reflecting the light of the sun off of its surface. Finally Sirion stopped, holding a hand up as he did so. Adrianna and Tianna stopped. Behind her, everyone else halted in unison. Suddenly, from out of the shadows of the trees all around them, emerged a retinue of faelin. Each carried a cocked crossbow and a quiver of arrows at his or her shoulder.

"Greetings, wanderers. Please state your house and your business." The speaker was a young Hinterlean male. He had light-brown, curly hair. His eyes were a dark-brown and his skin tone bronzed. Adrianna could see that he was skeptical and nervous about them, although he seemed to regard Sirion with more than a little interest. Within moments, Adrianna realized that nearly the entire troupe of them was composed of young individuals, each barely out of adolescence.

"Greetings to you as well. I hail from the house of Timberlyn." Sirion stepped forward as he spoke, displaying his signet ring. "My business is my own. However, I do wish to know the whereabouts of my mother, whom I have not seen for several years."

The young man's eyes widened. He swallowed nervously and turned to look at his comrade, who had stepped up next to him. The second young man shook his head and shrugged his shoulders. He also seemed to be agitated. The first man looked back to Sirion. "Did you say the House of Timberlyn?"

Adrianna saw Sirion's eyebrows come together in a frown. "Yes, I did. What is it to you? Listen, we really don't have the time for this. Just by looking at me you should be able to see that I hail from this realm." Sirion gestured behind him to the rest of the group. "And they are with me. We have urgent business, but I need to know the whereabouts of Lady Lilandria Sariansee Timberlyn."

Once more the young man glanced at his companion and then replied. "My Lord, the Lady resides at the center of Elvandahar, in the Sherkari Fortress."

Sirion frowned at the title with which the young man addressed him but said nothing about it. "Thank you. I am sure I know the way there. I visited the fortress as a child. It is about a six days journey from here is it not?"

"Yes, my Lord," replied the man. "You know that we are in dangerous times. I apologize for my having to interrupt your journey. Travel in peace." With that said, the young Hinterlean and his retinue began to melt back amongst the trees.

Frowning, Sirion put up a hand and stopped them. "Wait. What is this you speak of? What danger?"

"We have been having trouble with some lycanthropes. Their leader is powerful, and they have begun to infiltrate the communities surrounding Alcrostat."

Sirion narrowed his eyes. "Who is this leader? What do they call him?"

"They call him Sydonnia. He is an evil man, and cruel. He has no mercy."

Sirion nodded. Adrianna could see the muscles in his jaws clenching. He was angry. "Take care and keep safe."

The young man nodded and he and his archers left. Adrianna pondered the man's behavior. He had seemed to change his attitude towards Sirion when he had affirmed his affiliation with the House of Timberlyn. He had also begun to use a title of respect when answering Sirion. Adrianna glanced back at Sirion just to find him and the rest of the group moving away from her. She began to walk as well. She glanced at Tianna to find the young woman staring at Sirion. Adrianna had noticed a lot of that as of late. She shrugged. Maybe she was reading more into it than what was really there.

The group walked ever deeper into the Silverwood, Sirion and Dramati at the lead, Tianna remaining just behind. For three days the group continued to travel unhindered through the forest. The trees became larger and older as they passed. They sheltered the group when it rained, the thickening canopy above a shimmering kaleidoscope of silver. They encountered no one. If anyone lived in the areas through which they passed, the individuals did not make themselves known.

Adrianna quickly regained her energy and youthful vibrancy. Her dreams had become a thing of the past, and they no longer haunted her. But the memory was still fresh in her mind, and she thought of it every now and then as she walked. But her friends and family were there with her this time, and she was not so afraid. She knew that she still had some obstacles to overcome, but she knew that she would be able to make it through. Dinim spent much of his time with her, and they talked. In him she had found someone who truly seemed to understand her. She was happy about this fact, yet sad as well. Dinim had to have suffered his own trials in order for him to commiserate with her. She wondered what had happened to him, but dared not ask. She knew how difficult it was to remember.

The evening after the group encountered the Hinterlean scouts, they came upon a small clearing within the trees. Everyone happily set up camp, glad to have a place to sleep where they would not have tree roots digging into their backs, or spiders falling from the bushes into their faces as they slept. Soon they had a happy fire going, and Tianna was preparing the evening meal. The men busied themselves by tending to their weapons. It would be foolhardy for them to ignore them when they knew that they may be encountering some trouble. Sheridana and Dartanyen soon joined Zorg and Armond. Sirion took his own weapon and went to the far side of the clearing where he started to do some exercises. He caught the attention of the others and after a few moments everyone had joined Sirion and had begun a friendly sparring competition.

With avid interest Adrianna watched as Dartanyen and Sirion squared off with some staves, and Sheri and Armond with their swords. Adrianna was especially interested in the quarterstaff spar, for she had received some formal training with that weapon while she was an apprentice to Master Tallek. Sirion was excellent with the weapon, and it was obvious that he far outranked Dartanyen with his ability. Dartanyen took his defeat in good stride, and soon Tianna was taking his place to face Sirion. Adrianna looked towards the fire to see that the meal had been completed, and that it awaited their attention. However, she had no inclination to take herself over to the pot to obtain a meal, as she was too interested in the sparring match.

Sirion made quick work of Tianna, offering her some pointers as he soundly defeated her. Adrianna noticed Tianna's sloe-eyed expression, and she wore a low-cut blouse that displayed her ample cleavage. Sirion seemed oblivious to Tianna's efforts, but as of yet she had not become deterred. Amethyst, Sabian, and Dinim came to sit next to Adrianna, bowls of steaming stew in their hands. Dinim offered one to Adrianna and she gratefully took it.

Sirion had noticed Adrianna sitting at the periphery of the match, and when she was still sitting there after his spar with Tianna, he began to walk over to her. She seemed interested in the game, and he thought he would ask her if she cared to learn how to use the quarterstaff. He saw Dinim offer her a bowl of stew, and he quickened his pace. It would be ill advised for her to spar on a full stomach, and he would not get the chance to build this common ground upon which he could begin to get to know her better. "Wait. Adrianna, I noticed that you have been interested in watching us spar with the quarterstaff. Would you like me to show you a few moves?"

Adrianna was surprised. She did not think that Sirion would be interested in showing her how to use the staff. She nodded and placed her bowl back into Dinim's hand. "Yes. It will be good for me to get back into practice again."

Sirion felt his own measure of surprise. He had never thought that the reason why she would be interested in his sparring matches because she was familiar with the weapon. "You have had some training, then?"

"Yes, back when I was an apprentice in Andahye. It is customary for the students to have some type of training with a weapon, usually a quarterstaff or a dagger. I chose the quarterstaff because my master preferred it."

Adrianna glanced at Tianna as she and Sirion stepped into the circle that had been drawn for the matches. The other woman had a hurt expression on her face, and Adrianna wondered if she had wanted Sirion to participate with her in another match. Or perhaps it was just that she hoped that she would be able to keep his attention for a while longer. Nevertheless, Adrianna became slightly worried about her friend. Tianna so much wanted Sirion to notice her and to see her as his equal. Adrianna saw Dinim hand Tianna the bowl of stew that he had previously offered to her. Tianna sat down next to him with the bowl and began to eat. Adrianna began to feel a little better. If Tianna had been too depressed, she would not have taken her meal.

Sirion handed Adrianna one of the makeshift staves that he and Dartanyen had found in the forest. Adrianna took it and assessed its weight and feel. It was not completely balanced, but it would be acceptable for the match. It was slightly heavier than she would have preferred, but she would adjust to the weight quickly enough. Sirion took a place opposite her and she made herself ready for his attack. Within moments the spar was ensued.

After only a few minutes, Adrianna knew that she was severely outmatched. Sirion was a master with the weapon, his skill outranking even the master with which she had learned the basics of the art. But Sirion did not compete with her the way he had with Dartanyen and Tianna. Instead he acted as a teacher, giving her suggestions on how she should hold her weapon, how she should place her feet, and how she should position her hips and spine. After a while she began to tire. He pressed her for only a short time longer before he called a halt to her training. He smiled at her as he came over to take the staff from her. "You did well. Perhaps we can make a habit of practicing in the evenings before dinner."

"I would like that. Thank you, Sirion." She smiled at him in return. He seemed so different from the man she had met in Sangrilak a few months ago, so different than the man he had been portrayed by others to be. There was something about him . . . a sincerity when he looked at her. It reminded her of the way that Cortath used to look at her and she felt a twinge of sadness, as well as something else. In a way, it seemed that Cortath had returned to her, and she would have some measure of his companionship again after all.

CHAPTER 17

The group walked through their sixth day within Elvandahar. It was warm, yet cooler than it had been recently. Autumn would arrive soon. Halfway through the morning, Sirion stopped the group. He put up a hand, motioning them into silence. There was danger afoot. Sirion closed his eyes and raised his face. Adrianna could see his nostrils flare as he sniffed the air. His body stiffened and Adrianna braced her own body in response.

Sirion's eyes snapped open. He looked into the trees, the path upon which they had chosen to take into the Hinterlean city of Alcrostat. Adrianna followed his gaze. In the distance from out of the shadows of the trees emerged a man. He stood in the path and waited. Sirion bade Dramati forward and the rest of the group silently followed.

As the group approached, seven other individuals stepped out of the forest. Sirion kept his eyes fixed on the first man, his father's brother, Sydonnia. Sirion knew that the others were his followers. He would not be surprised if another score of them lay in wait within the forest trees, watching to see if an attack should be made.

It had been many years since Sirion had seen Sydonnia last. And within those years, Sirion had finally found the means with which he could cure his uncle of the curse that bound him. Upon discovering that Sydonnia had been causing havoc within his homeland, he was not surprised. For a long time Sydonnia had been trying to get a foothold in Elvandahar and he had finally succeeded. Not only that, but it was his way of bringing Sirion to him. But little did Sydonnia know that his nephew had been ill, unable to answer the call of the Silverwood . . . the call of home.

Sirion approached his uncle, a staying hand upon Dramati's withers. Sydonnia smiled, a smile of self-fulfillment and victory. Sirion stopped a few feet from the other man. He had changed very much, although age was not an issue. Sydonnia showed no signs of aging at all. Stricken as he was with lycanthropy, he would never age, would technically live forever . . . unless he was killed.

Sirion looked the other man over. He was a little bigger, and his curly brown hair a little longer. He wore old, disheveled clothing. There was a time that he would never have done so, he who was so particular of his appearance and how he was perceived by others. Sirion looked into his eyes. They were feral . . . wild. He had gone mad. Sirion didn't want to believe it, and struck the thought from his mind.

"Sirion, I knew that you would come . . . eventually." Sydonnia smiled, an evil smile full of hate and malice.

"Yes, Uncle. I am full aware of the goings on here, the panic you have probably created. The people are afraid. In this you have found power. I suppose it is the only way you could have attained it."

Sydonnia's smile was immediately wiped away, followed by a hideous frown. "Just like your father, you are. So full of yourself. Didn't you learn anything, Sirion? Didn't you learn what it was like to be more than just a tool, a thing to be used to kill?"

Adrianna saw the hands at Sirion's sides clench in anger. She, also, was incensed. She remembered this man. He was the faelin who had given her the message at Volstagg's inn, a message to Sirion, threatening . . . no, promising his death. She had then met him again in an alleyway deep within the city of Sangrilak. She and her companions had watched him kill a man in cold blood, and they had left the scene feeling fortunate that they had been able to escape with their lives. But what was this? Sirion was an assassin? No, that was impossible. Sirion was above that . . . very much above the mere role of an assassin. Sydonnia had to be lying.

But Sirion did not repudiate Sydonnia's words. Adrianna felt her throat begin to constrict. Sydonnia spoke again. "I could have had power once, perhaps. Had I wanted or needed power I could have had it. Your mother . . . . she comes from a very influential family. Had she chosen to stay with me, I would have married into that family." Sydonnia got a faraway look in his eyes. "But with Lilandria, I would not have needed anything . . ."

Sydonnia snapped his eyes back to Sirion. "You know that I hate you, hate you for what you represent. You are a symbol of my ultimate failure, a remembrance of what I could not be. I loved her more than life itself, yet he took her from me, charmed her into loving him even though he did not love her in return. He only wanted Lilandria because I did. You should not even exist."

Sirion flinched inwardly. He now knew what he had always suspected. Damn his father. Sydonnia was right. Had things gone the way that they should have, Sirion would never have lived. Sirion felt a momentary pang of pity for the man standing before him, the man that was no longer a man. Now he was a monster, killing wantonly for his own selfish pleasure.

Sydonnia cocked his head to the side and began to smile once more. Sirion was instantly on guard, wondering what his uncle had in store for him. He knew that Sydonnia had known the moment they had entered Elvandahar. He had chosen this time for them to meet, had set his plan into motion days ago.

"Oh Sirion, my dear boy. Too many things you have left behind for others to find . . . to pick up." Sydonnia's smile widened. And those things, they will betray you, have betrayed you."

Adrianna saw a paling of Sirion's bronzed complexion, saw his nostrils flare once more. With vivid clarity, she knew that he was afraid. The emotion put her on edge and she shifted her weight onto her other foot. She caught the attention of Sydonnia. He pierced her with his feral gaze. She held her breath; felt like an animal caught in a hunter's sights. He regarded her intensely. Then he looked back to Sirion.

Sydonnia made a gesture with one hand, continuing to hold Sirion's gaze. From out of the trees emerged a beautiful woman. Right away, Adrianna could tell that she was half-faelin. Her hair was light brown, shining golden in the light of the sun. Her complexion was pale and her ears rounded. But her body was slender, her face slightly angular. Her eyes were a pale shade of blue, mesmerizing in their quality. The woman walked with the grace of a leshera, softly and quietly over the vines littering the forest floor.

Adrianna watched Sirion, the widening of his eyes, the exhalation of his breath, the slump of his shoulders. She saw him swallow heavily, saw the tic in his lower jaw. Sirion stared at the woman. It was obvious he knew her, that they had shared something together.

Involuntarily, Sirion's gaze left Sydonnia to focus on the woman that emerged from the forest trees. It was Joselyn. He had not seen her for almost twenty years. She was as beautiful and alluring as always, gracefully stepping up to Sydonnia's side. Sirion knew that he must look like a fool. He had been taken off-guard, although he knew that he should have come to expect anything from his uncle.

"Hello, Sirion." Her voice was musical in quality. She wore pale robes and a silver circlet at her brow. The talisman she wore at her throat designated her as a druid, one who lived in and for the wilderness. Adrianna saw the tension around her mouth. The woman wondered what Sirion would do, how he would react to seeing her after so long.

Sirion quickly composed himself. So, Joselyn had given in to his uncle. She had given in to Sydonnia when she had refused to give in to him those many years ago. What had drawn her to him, Sirion could only wonder. In general, druids had no taste for power, finding fulfillment in the natural world around them.

"Hello, Joselyn." Sirion nodded to her. He struggled to keep his face expressionless. "Time has treated you well, I see."

Adrianna watched as Sirion struggled to remain lighthearted. But beneath it all she saw the hurt. Adrianna felt someone watching her and turned back to see Sydonnia staring at her. A chill crept up her spine. She knew that he wanted to hurt her. Did he know that Sirion had come to mean something to her? Had he been able to see that through the mirror of her eyes? Would he use her as a weapon against his nephew thinking that perhaps Sirion may have come to care for her as well?

Adrianna turned away and looked down at her feet. She was afraid, afraid that she may have set the stage for what was to come. Adrianna heard the tinkle of Joselyn's laugh. "Oh Sirion, charming as always."

Sirion cocked his head. What game was she playing, flaunting herself before him as his uncle's consort . . . for he knew that was what she had become. "But not half as charming as my uncle, I see," replied Sirion.

Joselyn flushed and averted her gaze. Sydonnia continued to smirk. "My dear nephew, don't be so hard on her. She did not know if you would return for her. She wanted . . . *needed* a man in her life." Sydonnia grinned, gripping Joselyn about the waist.

"I didn't," said Sirion, regarding Joselyn intently. "I didn't return for her. I came to end the evil that has overrun my homeland. Joselyn and I said our good-byes a long time ago." Sirion raised an eyebrow at her pointedly as he said the last. Once more the other woman averted her gaze.

"Well, then you won't mind to discover that she has been my lover for over three years." Sydonnia pulled Joselyn to him, put a handful of her hair to his nose, inhaled her scent. "She is a feisty little thing. She says that I am the best she has ever had." Sydonnia kissed Joselyn's neck and glared at Sirion triumphantly.

Sirion returned his gaze to Sydonnia. "It's just like you to want another man's leftovers," he said pointedly.

Sydonnia glared at Sirion maliciously. "I will kill you," he growled menacingly. "It is only but a matter of time."

"You can try," said Sirion in retaliation. "We will see who is left standing."

Sydonnia grunted. "I will come for you. Then I will kill you, finally be rid of you after all of this time. I wish I had finished the job all of those years ago." Sydonnia said the last in introspect, almost as though to himself.

That's your problem, now isn't it," stated Sirion, stepping away from his nemesis and turning back to the group.

"No, it's my *promise*." Sirion glanced back to his uncle to find him gone. So were Joselyn and Sydonnia's followers. Sirion sighed deeply. He would prepare for what was to come.

***

The morning of their tenth day in the Silverwood, the group walked up to the Sherkari Fortress. It was magnificent to behold, a palace in the trees.

Adrianna could feel the magic surrounding the place and knew that wards protected it. Other magic had bent and shaped the trees in order to form a place within which people could live. High within the canopy the structures could be seen, each one connected to the others by elaborate bridges constructed of living wood and vines. A series of platforms and pulleys existed for the purpose of lifting people from one level to the next. Two isterian, or palace guards, stood before the platform that would take them to the first level. "State your name and business," said the one on the left.

"I am Sirion Timberlyn. I am here to see my mother, Lady Lilandria." Sirion revealed his signet ring to the guards. They both glanced at one another before saluting him. "Welcome home, my Lord," said the one on the right.

"Thank you, but the name is Sirion," he said, walking through the door that had been opened to him.

"The solar is this way, my Lord," said the left.

"Come, follow me this way," said the guard on the right to the rest of the group. "I will show you to your alcoves." The group glanced at Sirion. He nodded at them and they followed the guard down another bridge.

Sirion trailed Adrianna with his eyes, watching her follow the rest of the group. She turned and saw him, meeting his gaze. He hoped that he would be seeing her and the rest of the group again soon, for this must be a strange place for them. He wondered why the guards were being so formal with him, for the son of a duchess did not require this much ceremony. It was irritating to say the least, and he hated having to correct people all the time.

They walked quickly through the interconnecting bridges of the fortress. He had never been within its protection before, but he did not bother to look about as the others had. He was too nervous, intent upon seeing his mother after more than twenty years. Finally they arrived at a door. The guards pulled it open and Sirion entered. "Lady Lilandria . . . your son is here to see you." The guard then bowed and exited the solar.

Sirion regarded the profile of the small, slender woman upon the terrace. Her copper-gold hair was plaited in a thick rope that hung down her back to her hips. Emeralds glistened from within the plait and hung from delicate ears. Sirion suddenly knew why his father had favored her. Not only had Lilandria been chosen by another man, she was very beautiful. She wore an exquisitely embroidered gown in varying shades of green. When she turned to face him, he was met with a pair of light-brown eyes and a face that seemed to light up the alcove.

Sirion swallowed heavily. He had not seen her in so long. His mother looked so much like she had all of those years ago, when he had seen her last. She regarded him solemnly at first, but then he saw a tiny tear escape from the corner of her right eye. Sirion strode up to the woman and put his arms around her.

"Mother, I have come to tell you that I am well. I know that Anya has been here to tell you otherwise, but she does not yet know that I survived our battle," he said softly.

Sirion felt her tremble in his arms. "When the scouts came to me two days ago, bearing the tale that you yet lived, I refused to let myself believe them, afraid that I would get my hopes up for nothing. But here you are, standing before me . . . holding me in your arms like I dreamed you would."

Sirion then clutched her firmly to him. He had missed her so much, had not realized exactly how much he had. "I will never leave you again," Sirion whispered to her.

"I believe you," she replied. She wrapped her arms around his neck and kissed his cheek. Sirion closed his eyes, remembering his mother's closeness when he was yet but a child, before his father had taken him away from her.

Finally they stepped apart. Sirion continued to hold her hands, knowing that she did not want him to let her go. "I am also here to serve the realm. I am here to aid in the removal of the lycanthrope threat."

Lilandria looked deep into his eyes. "My son, you are the realm," she replied.

***

Sirion prepared himself for his meeting with the king. That morning he and his mother had spoken for quite some time. He had told her about his time with the Wildrunners, their entanglement with Gaknar, his transformation and subsequent liberation. Sirion told her of Sydonnia, his curse, and his affiliation with the other lycanthropes in the area. He saw that she was disturbed about what he had shared with her, and he wondered if he had done the right thing. He asked her about Anya and she told him that his sister had left several days ago upon a mission about which she would not tell Lilandria. However, his sister had left his personal effects behind, and with them was Stalker. This fact pleased him immensely, for he had missed the feel of the weapon in his hands.

Sirion pulled a clean tunic over his head. It matched the trousers that were buckled about his waist. Both were colored a deep red, with bronze embroidery at the shortened sleeves and the v-neckline. He had decided to make himself presentable, had been much better at doing so since his ordeal. He had bathed his body and his hair, and then had the mass cut by one of his attendants. Instead of halfway down his back, his dark copper hair rested at his shoulders. It felt strange to have the weight of it gone. Not only that, but he did not have to pull it back anymore. It feathered away from his face and curled slightly behind his ears and at his shoulders.

Sirion wondered about the rest of the group, hoped they found their alcoves satisfactory. His own was quite extravagant. The moment the house attendants had realized his position with the Lady, his quarters had been prepared. When he had come to the rooms after speaking with his mother, he had found three of the hralen waiting to take him to the hot spring. Once there, Sirion bathed himself and then relaxed for a few moments. It was a beautiful place, the pool heated from somewhere under the ground. He knew that the group would enjoy it when they got the chance to come.

Once back within his quarters, Sirion went to the chest where he found clothes that fit his size, as well as several cloaks, belts, brooches, torcs, and other adornments. The sleeping place had been made out of the bough of the tree within which the main structure of the alcove had been made. The canopy of the bed was made of sheer silk and the pallet out of the softest furs. The floor was littered with luxuriant rugs and the 'walls' with magnificent tapestries. The ceiling was nothing but the canopy of the silver oak trees, all thickly fitting over and under one another to keep out the elements.

Sirion tied the bronze silk sash about his waist. It was a nice accent to the tunic. Two platinum griffons pinned his cloak to his shoulders. They had eyes made of shimmering rubies. He fingered one of the pieces in his palm. It was of excellent quality, perfect in every detail. He knew from personal experience. The pieces must have cost a fortune. And then he was thinking about it again, what his mother had told him. He was the heir to the Hinterlean throne.

After Servial left her, Lilandria had finally remarried. Servial had taken her son away, but her daughter, Anya, remained. For several years they lived alone in the daladin that Servial had made for his family. Then Lilandria left it, too proud to stay there when her husband had obviously abandoned her and their child. Despite the indignity, Lilandria returned home to her father, and for a while, she and Anya lived within the Hamzin of Kleyshes' daladin. Then, once again, Lilandria left, having procured an establishment of her own. For another several years they resided alone together. Anya chose the vocation of an archer, not quite the solitary life of a ranger, but close enough. Lilandria lamented upon her daughter's behalf, praying that Anya would not answer the call of the wild that Lilandria knew beckoned to her child.

But Anya remained true, and she never left her mother's side, at least, not for long. When she met up with a group called the Wildrunners, Lilandria feared yet again, wondered if her last child would be taken from her. But Anya always returned to her, recounted her adventures to her, took away the loneliness she knew when her child was gone from her.

But then Lilandria came under the scrutiny of the king. Upon noticing her at her father's side once more, he asked his advisor about her. The man told the king about her unfortunate circumstances, and Thalios felt his heart go out to her. He wished to know her, and so planned festivities to which she and her father would be obligated to attend. So, in this way, the Hinterlean king fell in love with the Samshae of Kleyshes.

When Lilandria learned that Servial had met his demise . . . that he had died in the line of duty, she was released from her marriage bond to her husband. The next year, she married the King of Elvandahar. Despite her hurt, she had come to care for Thalios, had learned to trust another man. She believed that he would care for her, and that she would give him an heir. But as time went by, she knew that was not possible, that she was not fertile any longer. Despondent, she withdrew from her husband. But Thalios came to her, told her that he loved her; that she had brought to him something he had never had before, true happiness. He told her that her son by Servial would be the heir to his throne.

***

Adrianna viewed herself in the looking glass. The gown was gorgeous. She honestly did not believe that she had ever worn anything this exquisite. The fabric was a soft pale brown, like the color of rich cream. At the sash and neckline the dress was adorned with swaths of medium-brown velvet and the bodice and hem artfully decorated with dark-brown embroidery. The excess material at the waist was gathered at her back and fell in a thick wave. Around her throat she wore a ribbon of dark-brown lace, and from it hung a golden drop containing an exquisite ruby. Similar drops hung from her pierced earlobes. Golden clasps pinned a similarly colored brown cloak to her shoulders. The fabric was wonderful to touch; it was the softest she had ever felt. Behind her, one of the hralen was binding her pale hair onto the crown of her head with golden combs beset with rubies. A few tendrils of her hair hung in loose ringlets at the sides of her face. Looking at her image, Adrianna could hardly believe it was she, so different did she appear. She wondered if the rest of the group was being transformed in the same fashion as herself, and wondered how Sirion was accepting the ministrations of the hralen.

Sirion. After their encounter with Sydonnia, he had become slightly withdrawn, and very intent upon their destination. Just as he said he would, he took the time every evening to give Adrianna lessons with the quarterstaff. It was at these times that Sirion seemed to open himself, and he endeavored to teach her all that he knew. Over the past few days Adrianna had found herself looking forward to sparring with Sirion at the end of the day. Although she did not want to admit it, she had missed his company last night. After spending the evening with her sister and niece, Adrianna had gone to bed, only to think about Sirion. This fact had begun to worry her, and she did not quite know what to make of it.

Adrianna was suddenly startled by a knock at her door. One of the hralen opened it and in danced Sheridana. "Oh Adria, can you believe how wonderful this gown is?"

Adrianna took in the image of her sister. Gone was the hardened, muscular warrior. In her place was a radiantly beautiful woman. The sides of Sheri's long dark hair were pulled away from her face and pinned at the back of her head. The rest of her hair cascaded down her back. Adrianna had not seen her sister's hair down from its customary plait in several years, since before they had parted company in Sangrilak so long ago.

Adrianna glanced over the pale blue dress that Sheri wore, the dark-blue lace at the hem and waist, the same colored lace collar at her throat. The gown dipped at the neckline revealingly, although not overly so. A dark-blue cloak flowed behind her as she moved to the looking glass before which Adrianna was seated.

Sheridana came to stand before her sister. Truth be told, Adrianna was quite possibly the most beautiful woman she had ever seen. Every plane, every angle of Adria's face was perfect in every detail. Her features were small, delicate. Her brown eyes were large in her face, framed by pale lashes so long, they touched her cheeks when she closed them. The lace ribbon she wore accented her long graceful neck. Her chest was small, but pushed up by the support of the gown, decorously concealed by the velvet swaths. She was slender, but had all of the curves in all of the right places. Adrianna was wondrous to behold, and Sheri wondered how Sirion would react.

Sheridana was a perceptive individual. She knew that the handsome ranger watched her sister, watched her more than he did any other member of the group. His insistence that he watched over the group merely to protect them was moot with Adrianna. Not only did he look after her wellbeing, but in Sheri's estimation, he looked at Adrianna the way a man looks at an attractive woman, one that he would like to know better. Sheri grinned. Much better.

Sheridana bent to kiss her sister at the lips. They had become close again, like they had been before she had left with their father. That was something she would never do again. She would never leave her family like she had all of those years ago. Sheridana found Adria taking her hands. "You are beautiful."

Sheri kissed the tops of Adrianna's hands. "So are you."

Sheridana sighed. Actually, she envied her sister. Sirion was a good man. That he had begun to care about Adrianna was more than apparent to Sheri. He treated her like a precious jewel, and Sheri had the conception that he would always treat her thusly. Sheridana wished that she had that, the type of love she had shared with Ian. Sheri flinched inwardly. Ian, she missed him still

. . . so very much. And she so much wished that he were there with her now, by her side.

Adrianna stood from her seat. "Come Sheri. The hralen have told me that dinnertime is near. We will be escorted there by the isterian."

Adrianna nodded to the hralen that had worked so hard to make her presentable to the queen of the Hinterlean people. Why Sirion had not told them about his mother's status before was an enigma to her. Adrianna shook her head. It was almost as though he hadn't known. But how could that be? His mother had been queen for several years now.

The hralen bowed to her and left. They were a friendly people, dressed in simple beige tunic and trousers. Upon their left hand was a mark, one that Adrianna had been wary to ask about. She had no wish to be intrusive; or to ask personal questions of people she hardly knew. But perhaps it was a mark of their position within the royal house. She had noticed that the isterian, or palace guard, sported their own mark upon the upper right arm.

"Sheri, I feel so . . . so out of place."

Sheridana felt her eyes widen. "Why, whatever for? You look wonderful."

Adrianna smiled. "Yes, but you are biased," she stated, running her hands over the bodice of her gown.

"No, I am one woman looking at another and telling her that she is beautiful."

Adrianna lost her smile, gazed at Sheridana intensely. "I love you, Sheri."

Sheridana touched her sister's face gently with her palm. "I love you more," she whispered.

Both women startled when another knock sounded at the door. Adrianna opened it to find one of the isterian standing there. He paused for a moment, staring, and then finally found his voice. "The Lady Queen wishes your company for dinner." Sheridana joined her sister at the door. "Please follow me," said the man as he turned on his heel.

The guard led them through the interconnecting conduits of the fortress. Each bridge was connected to another, and then another, until there was a large network of them high above the ground. Along the way, they stopped to pick up the other members of the group. First was Armond, and then Dartanyen and Amethyst. Looking at the girl, Adrianna had never seen someone so transformed; or so out of place. She was stunning, her red gown accenting her bronzed complexion and dark hair. She looked like a woman instead of a girl, and even Armond had to look at her twice. Amethyst was extremely uncomfortable, and she kept bringing her hands to the shortly cropped hair that feathered away from her pretty face.

They collected Zorg next. His hralen answered the door, and finally he stepped through, obviously put out. His gray tunic and trousers matched the color of his eyes. His vest and cloak were a dark green and his sash a dark blue. "You don't know how long it took for them to find something to fit me. They finally had to go to the former isterian captain, who happens to be human . . . and big, like me." Zorg's gaze took in the rest of the group, contemplative. "I hope they didn't have this problem with you."

Sheri smiled widely. "I am glad to say that they did not."

Zorgandar seemed to relax. "Of course not. You would be easy to find clothes for."

The group went to Sabian's alcove, and then Tianna's. The healer wore a gown colored a pale purple, trimmed in a darker shade of the same hue. As usual, Tianna was the epitome of beauty, and she would portray herself as such throughout the evening, especially to one Sirion Timberlyn, for whom she felt passionate emotions. Sheri was sure of it. She had been watching the other woman, saw her playing upon Sirion's masculine side. Much to Sirion's credit, he did not respond to Tianna's sexuality, and seemed to see Tianna only as a younger sister.

Finally they reached Dinim's quarters. When she saw him, Adrianna could not help but glance at him appreciatively. He was handsome, as he was always wont to be, dressed almost entirely in black. The only color was the maroon sash at his waist and the matching embroidery at the hem of his tunic. A black cloak trailed behind him.

The group finally made it to the dining room. When they reached the dining area, the two guards standing at the entrance stepped aside. They entered and paused to look at the magnificence of the large alcove. Adrianna only momentarily took in the opulence all around her as she began to look for Sirion. Much to her dismay, she did not see him. Slowly, everyone made their way to the dinner table. At its center was an excellent array of breads. They seated themselves, four isterean holding chairs for Amethyst, Tianna, Sheridana, and Adrianna. For only but a moment did they wait before the Lady Lilandria entered. Upon her right arm was Sirion. Behind them strode the king of the Hinterlean people.

The hralen and isterian bowed upon the entrance of the Lady and her King. The group followed suit. When Lilandria, Sirion, and the king were seated, the rest of the group sat down in their own chairs. Adrianna looked around at the confused faces of her companions. Not many others had chosen to ask the questions that she had. Most of the group had no idea that Sirion's mother was married to the Hinterlean king, making her the Queen of Elvandahar.

Adrianna watched Sirion discreetly. His thick hair had been cut and it curled at his neck. It was one of the features he had inherited from his mother. Sirion escorted his mother to her seat, pulling out the chair for her. The woman gracefully seated herself and he helped to re-adjust her chair closer to the table.

She wore a beautiful gown made of varying shades of green. At her brow was a platinum circlet. Beside her, the king seated himself. At his brow was a splendid crown. Embedded within the platinum were five jewels: a ruby, a sapphire, a diamond, an emerald, and a golden topaz. Adrianna had once heard it said that that each jewel represented the five domains of Elavandahar.

Sirion looked around the table and when his eyes came to rest upon Adrianna, they widened. By the gods, she was a beautiful woman. The dress she wore accented her complexion. Her moonlight hair was piled on top of her head like a crown. He had never seen her look so beautiful. She sat like she belonged there, like she knew what her destiny held for her.

"Welcome to the realm of Elvandahar."

Sirion tore his gaze from Adrianna to look towards the head of the table . . . at the man who had become his stepfather. He watched as the group nodded solemnly to the king. Sirion shivered involuntarily. He did not want to be the heir to a realm, did not want the responsibility. He wasn't cut out for it . . . the call of the wilderness was too strong within him. Sirion did not crave power, felt he had no use for it. He felt that someone else could rule his people better than himself, someone with more patience, truth, and compassion.

But who would reign after Thalios? Not just anyone. If Sirion rejected the throne, it would be offered to Anya. But he doubted that she would accept it, based upon the same premise that he rejected it himself. Other powerful influential families would attempt to claim the throne. There would be political strife until the most powerful candidate took over. So, after much deliberation, Sirion had come up with the solution to his predicament.

The evening before, after his reunion with his mother, Lilandria took Sirion to meet her husband. The king had greeted him and welcomed him into his house. Thalios was friendly yet wary, wondering why Sirion had returned after so many years away from his family and loved ones. Sirion knew what the other man was wondering, knew that he would wonder the same things were he in the king's position. So Sirion got straight to the point.

"My Lord, my decisions surrounding my family have not always been the best ones. However, due to some recent experiences, I have come to realize the error of my ways and I have finally come home. Once within Elvandahar, I came across someone who has been causing a great amount of trouble for you. Upon deep contemplation pertaining to this threat, I have decided that I can be of aid in helping you to eradicate it. I implore you to accept my services to your realm."

Thalios regarded Sirion solemnly. He weighed his options, knew there to be precious few. They lived in dangerous times. But it was more than just Sydonnia and his bands of lycanthropes. The magical Balance of the world had been tipped. Daemon-kind found more and more ways to infiltrate the world upon which people lived. They became ever more powerful while sorcerers and scholars were hunted and killed. Anyone with any knowledge of the world upon which they lived was a threat to the evil powers-that-be, and targets for annihilation.

Sirion waited. Impassively, the Hinterlean king continued to look at him. Sirion continued to stand his ground. Finally the king turned from him and began to pace the room. Then Thalios spoke. "I thank you for your desire to help our cause. To be truthful, we have had very little impact upon the threat. And with each passing day it grows, out of control, like a plague . . ."

Thalios stopped, looked Sirion in the eye. "I do not know how you could possibly help us. They are out of control, unstoppable. They are strong, extremely so, more than any normal men. They change their shape at will into kyrrean, wemic, or alothere."

Silently, Sirion listened as the king spoke, taking in the enormity of the situation. Villages had been burned to the ground, entire domains overpowered, women raped, and children killed for sport. The lycanthropy was a disease, plague-like, taking some while sparing others. Members of the king's own personal guard had succumbed to the illness already.

Finally, Thalios stopped speaking. He stood before the young ranger, Sirion, his wife's son. "So, how could you possibly help us?" Thalios asked the question not out of speculation, but as an end to his tirade. There was an air of desperation about him, and it almost seemed that he had given up. The king of Elvandahar was at a loss, felt that he had failed his people. But that was all about to change.

Sirion regarded the other man intently. He felt the corners of his mouth turn up into a malicious grin. "My Lord, I have spent the last ten years of my life in pursuit of lycanthropes. For many of those years I have tried to find a cure, and for even more I have discovered the weapons that will harm them. I have learned their strengths and their weaknesses. I have hunted them down and killed them without mercy, taken from them what they so wantonly took from others. You ask me how I can possibly help you. I tell you that today is the best day of your life."

Sirion returned his attention to the present. "Sirion has told me all about you, and that you wish to help us to rid ourselves of the threat that has begun to overtake us. For this I thank you." The king raised his wine glass and the rest of the table followed suit. "You will be richly awarded for your efforts. A toast . . . a toast to the end of the lycanthrope menace."

Everyone put their glasses to their lips in a toast to the end of the threat overtaking Elvandahar. Dinner was then served to them. The meal was delicious, roasted fowl accented by mildly seasoned vegetables and legumes, fresh grains, and pale wine. Adrianna relished the food; thought it to be the best she had ever tasted. She could very quickly become accustomed to this type of lifestyle.

As they ate, lively conversation ensued around the table. King Thalios seemed to let down his guard. Adrianna did not join in any, but was content to listen to the conversations of everyone else all around her. The king seemed to be a good man. He cared strongly for his people. Sirion's mother also seemed to be very genuine, her smile true. She was different from her son, a social creature in contrast to his solitary nature. Adrianna felt herself being watched. She turned to find Sirion watching her from across the table. He sat at his mother's right, and she next to Thalios at the head of the table. Dartanyen sat at the king's other side and next to him was Sheridana. Adria sat between her sister and Tianna, who had been staring at Sirion the moment he had entered the room.

Adrianna met Sirion's gaze. His amber eyes did not waver from hers, but continued to watch her. She felt her cheeks begin to flush and she noticed a slight smile playing at one corner of his expressive mouth. She turned away, self-conscious. She wondered what he thought about the gown she wore. Then she felt like a silly schoolgirl, entranced with an older man. She did not see his smile widen, or see him look at her in appreciation. She felt embarrassed, wishing she were not there at all.

Finally the meal was over. The dishes were cleared away and bottles of wine set upon the table. The men drank and began to tell tales of their adventures. Soon after, Thalios and Lilandria retired for the night. After a while, Sirion retired as well. Adrianna also felt fatigued. It had been a long journey. She excused herself from the table and was escorted back to her alcove by one of the isterian. Later, she lay in her bed and thought about Sirion. She thought about Sirion and the woman Joselyn. What had they shared together? Did he love her? It was apparent that the woman still loved Sirion, despite the years that separated them.

***

Adrianna walked the path that led from her quarters to the thermal pool. It was a place that she came to visit at the beginning and end of every day she had come to spend at the fortress. She knew that she would not always have this luxury, and so she took every advantage of it. She had almost made it to the pool when she heard movement coming from the path behind her. She turned and saw Tianna making her way to her, walking quickly so as to catch up.

Adrianna smiled as her friend approached. As of late, she and Tianna had not been able to spend much time together, circumstances having begun to take the opportunities away from them. She had come to miss Tianna's company, her carefree nature and spirited personality. But Adrianna knew it was more than the lack of free time or the arrival of Adrianna's sister. It was Sirion. Tianna had begun to place all of her energies into him, and had allowed her friendship with Adrianna to fall into a lull. But it was not just Tianna's fault, she knew. It was hers as well. She spent much of her time with her sister and niece, and had also begun to continue her training with Sirion.

Tianna smiled back at her as she caught up to Adrianna. But Adrianna saw the hesitancy and the slight strain around her mouth. She wondered what it was that was bothering Tianna so much. But she had an idea what it may be, and Adria wished that she could do something that would help Tianna.

The two women made it to the pool and removed their clothing. They then stepped into the warm waters, sighing as they sank up to their necks. They waded there in the center of the pool for a few moments, neither one saying anything. But finally Tianna spoke, unable to hold back any longer, her questions needing to be answered.

"Adrianna, what is Sirion to you?"

Adrianna turned towards her friend, her eyebrows pulling together into a frown. "What do you mean?"

Tianna regarded her for a moment. "I mean . . . what does Sirion mean to you?"

Adrianna felt a moment of surprise. She stared at Tianna, noted the tension around her mouth and the seriousness of her gaze. Contemplatively, she considered Tianna's question. Honestly, she had not thought much about it. There was a part of her that still connected him with the individual she had known as Cortath, the companion she had come to love before he had become transformed into a man. She supposed that she was attracted to Sirion, but who wouldn't be? He was a very handsome man. He was also intelligent, worldly, and a paragon within his field of expertise. He was nothing short of a legend, and that fact only served to make him all that much more appealing. However, despite those things, she supposed that all that she truly wanted from Sirion was his friendship, especially knowing that Tianna was obviously in love with him. Aside from a few twinges of envy, Adrianna supposed that she was fine with the concept of Tianna and Sirion as a couple. Although she knew that once that concept became a reality, her attraction to him would become a liability.

"Tianna, you know that I hardly know Sirion. What could he have possibly come to mean to me within the past three weeks that I have known him? Really, what is going on, Tianna?"

Tianna sighed heavily. "Oh Adrianna, I know that you are right, but I had to ask, just to be sure. I know that he sees me as just a child, but I so much want him to see the woman that I have become. I love him so much and I know that I can please him, if only he would give me the chance."

Adrianna smiled. "He will, Tianna. You'll see. He just needs some time. He has been through a lot and needs all of your support right now."

Tianna nodded. "I feel so much better. I should have spoken to you sooner. You always know what to say." Tianna smiled and wiped a tear from her cheek.

Adrianna began to wade out of the water, to the towel she left at the side of the pool. "Come on. Let's get some breakfast. I'm famished." As she dried herself, Adrianna continued to think about Tianna's question. What did Sirion mean to her? She did not really know, but she now knew that she needed to find out.

***

The talisman glowed red in the darkness of the alcove. Although the communication link had been severed, the object continued to bear the residual effect and would not diminish for another few moments. He placed the talisman deep within his travel pack far from any prying eyes. He would be a fool to keep it near the top, where someone might catch a glimpse of it. It was not something that he wanted others to see, for fear that they may recognize it and discover the true reason why he traveled with the group.

The fold continued to be in a state of dissention. Since Gaknar's destruction in his fight against the Wildrunners, the priesthood had begun to disseminate. Gaknar had been powerful and had borne the ability to guide the fold into a new era. Since his loss, a nebulous void had replaced goals for a future of prosperity and power. When Gaknar had failed in his attempt to bring Tharizdune into Shandahar, all of the hard work that had gone into that endeavor was swept away. And without a leader, the priests began to bicker and no one knew what the fold was destined to become.

Without the light cast by the talisman, the alcove was plunged into darkness. Since arriving here it had been easier for him to communicate to his allies in the fold. He did not have to be constantly on guard, afraid of someone happening upon him while he was working with the talisman. Despite Gaknar's loss, he still had his orders. He would stay with the group, monitor them, and report their activities to the fold.

Gaknar himself had brought him into the fold. Most of Gaknar's followers were priests. However, there were a few necromancers who had allied themselves with him as well. As one of the only spell-casters within the fold, he was a valuable asset. He was well rewarded for his efforts, and he felt the cause to be a good one. Currently, his efforts seemed to coincide with those of the group and he was in little danger. He hoped that it would last, but knew that it would be unrealistic to think that it would. He knew that it would only be a matter of time before their interests began to conflict with his. Then, there would be problems, and he would have to deal with those issues when they arose.

***

Adrianna stood upon the terrace. The gentle wind caressed her face, lifted her hair from her cheeks. Breathing deeply, she inhaled the smell of the forest, heard the wind in the leaves, felt the sway of the trees all around, beneath, and above her. The treetop fortress was like none she had ever seen before, awesome in its immensity and its proportions, exceptional in its beauty and majesty. Her lodgings were magnificent. The bed was blanketed in luxurious furs: blue foxes, silver hares, and black mink. The pillows were made of the finest material and stuffed with knapseed-pod silk. The canopied bed arched high overhead, silver tassels hanging from the four posts at the corners. Beautifully woven rugs adorned the wood flooring and colorful tapestries hung upon the walls. Only a thin curtain separated the interior of the room from the exterior balcony. She felt the light fabric sweep about behind her as the winds blew.

Adrianna sighed. For several days now the group had been staying in the fortress. Every afternoon, with the exception of the first two, Sirion had continued her quarterstaff training. Just today they had sparred, an exceptionally good match. The training had become intense, much more so than it had ever before. Adrianna remembered feeling energized. Perhaps she was getting better! Sirion seemed to be working up a sweat this time, and his expression was that of one who had become focused upon a task. Then it happened. Sirion swept at her with his weapon. He bore into her, and then savagely disarmed her with a twist of his staff. Adrianna fell back, and Sirion followed her onto the ground. With her weight and his applied to her backside, Adrianna found herself crying out. Sirion quickly disengaged himself from her and knelt over her. He asked if he had hurt her, an expression of concern on his face. Then he was helping her to sit upright, a hand behind her back. He wiped her hair back from her face, his hands brushing against her cheeks, his face moving close to hers, ever so close.

But then it was over. Dartanyen came upon the scene and Sirion stepped away from her. Adrianna picked herself up from the ground and wiped off her trousers. Breathless, she vacated the area, leaving the two men to their discussion. She went in search of a bath, but continued to think about Sirion, unable to get him out of her mind. With him, she had begun to let down her guard. She realized he had become something special to her, more than just a hero and more than just a legend. He had become a man.

Adrianna closed her eyes, felt the warmth of her tears at the corners of her eyes. She placed her hands upon the balustrade in order to steady herself. By the gods, she was falling in love with him. She could not deny it anymore, even

377

though she wanted to. She knew that she had been attracted to him for quite some time, greatly enjoyed his company, and looked forward to spending time with him at the close of every day when he sparred with her. But she had been loath to admit to herself that she cared deeply for him. Especially when she knew that he loved another woman.

The tears escaped from behind her closed lids. Adrianna bowed her head, felt the wetness become cold on her cheeks as the wind touched it, felt the tears fall from her face to the wood beneath her. Joselyn. He hated what the druid had become, but Sirion continued to love the woman that she had once been. However, Adrianna found herself confused. It was the way he looked at her, the way he respected her, and the way that he spoke to her that made Adrianna think that he may care for her too. She remembered the heat of his gaze, the feel of his hands at her back and on her face. But she did not know if he truly cared about her, if he could find it in his heart to truly love her. She liked to think that perhaps he could. But the expression in his eyes a few days past had told her everything. He had loved the woman Joselyn, and Adrianna could only believe that he loved her still, even though she had broken his heart.

Sirion stood at the entrance to Adrianna's alcove. He watched her as she stood upon the terrace, her moon-colored hair playing about her shoulders and back, her robe a dark contrast to the pale gauzy fabric of the curtain, her hair, and her complexion. He had only been able to see her during their training sessions. His mother had asked him about her, knowing with her mother's intuition that there was something about her that captivated him. However, he had told her nothing except that she was a sorceress, someone who had the Talent to manipulate the magic of the world. He knew that his mother was not satisfied with this response, yet she wisely said nothing.

And here the woman in question stood, her head bowed as she leaned against the railing of the terrace. He was tired, so very tired, but he so much wanted to see her, to ask her how she fared after their spar. But, in actuality, he wanted to know if she missed him when they were not in one another's company . . . the way he missed her. Over the past two weeks, he had finally begun to get the feeling that he had reached her, broken through that barrier that she had erected around herself. He had found a common ground upon which to access her, but he wanted more than that. During the day, when they were apart, he found that he had come to miss her and he craved her company as more than just someone to whom he could teach how to use the quarterstaff.

But Sirion's fatigue was more than just the hours of deliberation and strategic planning. It was the half-faelin druidess Joselyn. Thoughts of her kept him awake at night and haunted him during the day. It had pained him immensely to see her standing at Sydonnia's side as his consort, to know that she had chosen the path of evil . . . for druids were much immune to the disease of lycanthropy. He remembered how much he had cared for her and the times they had shared. But despite everything, they both had known that something was missing, for they knew that neither one of them would ever give up his or her profession for the other if the need arose. So they had parted ways, speaking sweet words and promises to treasure one another always. But that had been a long time ago, and things changed in almost ten years.

Sirion had faced his true self and had found it lacking. He had embarked upon a journey of discovery to find that every man needs other men, and that those of faelin and human kind were not meant to walk alone. He had broken the mold set forth for him by his father and become the man he had always dreamed he would be. He had set new standards for himself and began to live by the rule that life was what one made of it. And he had finally found that thing for which he had been searching all of his adult years. Sirion refocused his thoughts upon the woman on the balcony. Silently, he moved himself from the doorway and into the room. He felt the breeze as he neared the balcony, breathed in the sweet scent of her as the winds carried it to him. Finally he stood behind her in the shadows, aching to reach for her, to bring her into him, and feel her body pressed close to him.

Adrianna sensed that Sirion was there just before she felt his hand on her shoulder. Her heart lurched in her chest, not in fear, but in anguish. It cried out for him, aching to be heard. A lump came to her throat and the tears burned there, waiting to be unleashed. His hand was gentle as he moved it down her arm and his other hand brushed her other shoulder. She could feel the warmth of him behind her, close. She knew that she should turn around, but she could not bring herself to do so. She did not wish for him to see the unshed tears in her eyes and to ask about them.

"Adrianna . . ." He gently spoke her name, hoping she would turn toward him. He so much wanted to see her face, to see her expression upon meeting him after their spar. After speaking with Dartanyen, he had thought to go searching for her, but had been accosted by yet another isterian about another issue in need of his attention. So he had not been able to come until now. He touched her shoulder but Adrianna did not turn. He sensed the sadness emanating from her and felt her body tremble beneath the light touch of his palm. "I just wanted to see if you were all right after our spar." He ran his fingers gently through her hair and brushed her neck ever so softly. She sighed and seemed to lean towards his touch. As always, he felt intoxicated by her presence, and his fatigue kept him from keeping himself in check.

Her heart lurched again as Adrianna felt the feather-light touch of his fingertips at her neck, his hand brushing her hair away. She could feel the warmth of his body as he stepped even closer, and then his breath on her as he unexpectedly placed his lips at the curve of her neck. Her body quaked and her belly tightened. She felt the softness of his lips on her skin and a myriad of thoughts raced through her mind. Within moments she was muddled, all coherent thoughts having been swept away by emotion.

Sirion heard her sharp intake of breath, felt her body tremble. Momentarily he hesitated, and thought that perhaps he was going too far. She did not turn around, but continued to lean back into him. He placed his hands at her shoulders and finally turned her around to face him. He felt slight resistance but continued anyway, needing to look at her face-to-face. When he looked upon her, he saw her tears and spoke her name once more, deep in his throat. He didn't know why she had been crying, but with one hand in her hair and the other at her shoulder, he brought her into him. He felt her body melt against him and she rested her head against his shoulder.

Adrianna pressed herself against Sirion's lean body. It was the way he had spoken her name, his intense gaze, and the deep color of his amber eyes. It was the way he touched her, his gentleness as he turned her around to face him, and his kiss upon the sensitive flesh of her neck. Sirion wrapped his arms around her and she felt safe, more protected than she had ever felt in her entire life. Within his embrace, she knew that nothing could ever harm her. But she remembered the way he had looked upon the woman Joselyn, and her grief was renewed. She didn't want just a part of Sirion, she wanted, needed, all of him, especially if he was to have all of her. So the tears sprang anew, and they ran, warm, down her face and onto the fabric of his tunic.

Sirion held Adrianna close to him, her proximity making him feel reckless. He brought his face to the curve of her neck once more and kissed her. Her skin was soft and he could feel her pulse at his lips. He moved his hands down her arms to ever-so-gently rest at her waist. He inhaled her scent, floral from the bath oils. For so long he had wanted this moment, especially since the night he had eavesdropped on her at the lake. It almost seemed like he was in a dream; he felt exhilarated and he felt his body tingling from her closeness.

Adrianna felt him place his hands at her hips. Her breath caught in her throat, and she felt the power of her emotions begin to overtake her reason. Hesitantly, she placed her palms upon his chest. She felt his muscles ripple at her light touch. He tightened his hands about her waist and he pressed her hips into him. She felt something rise from deep within her, felt it stir within the lower depths of her belly. She slid her hands up his chest, onto his neck and into his thick hair.

Sirion kissed her neck once more, her response to his passion fueling the fire burning within him. But he remembered that she had been crying . . . was obviously upset about something. He struggled to tear himself from her. He separated his body from hers, his lips making a trail from her neck to her jaw. Then he looked at her once more, and saw that she looked not at him but down at the floor. "Adrianna." His voice sounded deep and husky, even to his own ears. "What is wrong, *Shendori?*" He spoke to her in Hinterlic, recalling that she had used that tongue to speak to him when first they had met. Suddenly he realized what her efforts had been and he regretted his rather coarse treatment of her.

Adrianna felt him disengage from her, felt the effort it cost him. He spoke to her then, his voice low and tender. She yearned to look up at him, to look into his eyes. But she was so afraid . . . afraid of Sirion, afraid of herself . . . afraid of what she would find there. Then she felt his hand at her chin, bringing her head up. And he urged her to look at him. "Please tell me," she heard him whisper to her. The emotion she saw written upon his handsome features almost stilled her heart in her chest.

"Did I hurt you today?" Sirion was suddenly afraid. Indeed, perhaps he had hurt her, and she was in pain. Perhaps she did not want to tell him, afraid of how he would respond.

Adrianna shook her head. "No. You did not injure me in the spar today."

"Then what is it?"

"Please, I can not . . ." Her voice cracked and she looked away from him once more, fresh tears shimmering at the corners of her eyes.

Sirion felt his heart go out to her. With a forefinger he touched her cheek, captured a tear, and rubbed it against his thumb. He closed his eyes. He hated to see her so unhappy, disliked it even more that she could not share her feelings with him. Her lower lip trembled. He moaned deep within his throat and he felt his passion for her envelop him. His hands were at her waist once more, gently pulling her into him. Then he lowered his head and took her lips with his.

Adrianna hesitated for only a moment before she felt the passion sweep through her. Her emotion was so strong that she felt that she would collapse against him. She gripped the front of Sirion's tunic in her fists, her mind whirling with a kaleidoscope of thoughts. What was happening . . . how . . . why . . . Was this a dream from which she would find herself awakening in the morn? She returned his kiss, matching him in his intensity. Her fears began to take a back seat to her emotions, and she found herself living in the moment. Just to have this one moment in time, right now with Sirion, was something that she would never have imagined could be.

With Adrianna in his arms, Sirion began to make his way off of the terrace and into the alcove. He slid his hands from her waist to her back, and then down to her backside. She was soft and pliable against him, responding to him with a passion that he never dreamed would exist within her. He felt her hands at his chest, his throat, his hair. And then she was touching his face, ever so softly caressing him with her fingertips. Sirion felt his passion soar, felt

his body respond to her touch. He backed her into the room until they reached the canopied bed. He gently laid Adrianna down, following her with his body. He wrapped his arms tightly around her as he continued to kiss her mouth, her nose, and her eyes. She moaned as he moved over her, and she ardently returned his embrace. She moved her lips from his mouth to the tender flesh of his throat, her hands kneading the fabric of his tunic, her hips and legs moving against his own. Her movements were beginning to drive him wild, and he knew that he should stop . . . knew that he needed to stop. But he did not want to stop . . . wanted to have her so much that it hurt.

Adrianna put her lips to his throat, using her tongue to give Sirion the pleasure that he had given to her. She felt his response, felt him clutch her to him, felt the beating of his heart against her hand at his chest. Adrianna felt herself spiraling out of control, and knew that the same thing was happening to Sirion. Instinctively, she knew that he wanted her, could feel it in the way that he held her, the way he kissed her. And she wanted him as well, wanted him in a way that was unfamiliar to her, never having felt the need to have a man before. There was something about it that frightened her, but it invigorated her at the same time. She knew that they should stop, that they were involved in something that was quickly becoming a thing over which they would soon have no influence.

Suddenly there was a knock at the door. It took Sirion a moment to realize that fact, his body and mind so focused upon the woman beneath him. Sirion dragged his mouth from hers, hovering above her for a moment. By the gods, she was the most beautiful woman he had ever seen. Her lips were red from the ferocity of his kisses and her eyes were bright with passion, passion for him. The frequency of his breaths matched hers, and he was about to resume their activity when he heard the knock once more. Reason began to return to him, and when he glanced at Adrianna he could see the same thing happening to her. He felt her shift beneath him and he moved off of her. They both stood up from the bed, smoothing their clothes and their hair. "Adrianna, are you awake in there? It's me, Sheri."

"I'm awake now," Adrianna growled. "What do you want?"

"Dartanyen wants to see us all in his room . . . something about . . ."

"Right now?" Adrianna interrupted.

"Yeah. I'll meet you there."

"Fine. Just give me a few minutes." Adrianna turned back to Sirion, finding that he was watching her intently. Suddenly she felt embarrassed, the images of the activity they had been sharing coming to her mind. How that had come about, she could not remember, could scarcely fathom. The man that stood before her was distant, and seemed slightly ill at ease.

Sirion nodded to her and cleared his throat. "I will see you tomorrow then. I am glad to see that you were not harmed from our spar earlier this afternoon."

"No. I am fine. Thank you for the concern."

Once again Sirion nodded and then went to the door. He opened it cautiously, looked about down the hallway, and then left her room, closing the door quietly behind him. Adrianna stared at the closed door for a moment, confusion sweeping over her. He had become so detached, and it was like nothing had happened between them. She had been afraid of this, but had let things spiral out of control anyway. She thought that perhaps she should regret it, but then realized that she could not. She loved Sirion, and she could regret nothing that they had done together this night.

CHAPTER 18

Sirion paced the length of the alcove, paused, turned around, and paced back towards Lilandria and Thalios. Already he had told them about lycanthropy, the way the disease was contracted, the duration of the disease, the way in which infected individuals could be disposed. He was allowing the information he had imparted to them time to sink in, knew they had to be disturbed about his revelation. He stopped to glance at his mother. He could see her putting two and two together, knew that she was figuring out the past, why things had worked out the way they had. She would begin to know the role that Servial had played in the eventual decline of the realm. And Sirion knew that she would blame herself.

Sirion sighed and began to speak again. "Tomorrow we will leave the safety of the fortress. I will have to hunt Sydonnia down. He will not make this easy for me, despite his desire to see the end of me." *Or for me to see an end to him.* But Sirion would not speak it out loud. For many years now, Sydonnia had been waiting for this, knowing that the only person who ever had a chance to end his hated existence was Sirion.

"Are you ready? Do you have all that you will need?" Thalios asked.

Sirion nodded. "With just a few more supplies, we will be prepared."

The king nodded. "Anything you need, you have only to ask for it. What about manpower? How many of my men will you require?"

"None. It will be just me and the people I have brought with me. I trust them, know them to be free of any influence from Sydonnia. They have had no contact with the disease."

Thalios nodded again in understanding. He knew that some of his own men had already been stricken with the disease. He also now knew why some yielded while others had not. It was proclivity. Those who bore a tendency towards evil succumbed to the illness after being bitten, while those who had only good intentions were spared. "I wish I could help you more. I want to do so much more for the son of my queen."

Sirion stopped, mid-stride. He turned his full attention to the man before him. Thalios looked back at him solemnly. Sirion knew what he had to say. He had made his decision the night before. He would not accept the throne. It was not for him, but meant for someone who had the inclination to rule a realm, to live for the people. Sirion then glanced at his mother. He knew that she would be disappointed. But when she heard what he had to offer in return, he felt she would be satisfied. He just hoped that Thalios would be as well.

"King Thalios . . . " Sirion knew that it would be difficult for him to say, and that the king may take his rejection as an insult. So he chose his words carefully. "My mother has told me much about your family. You are the only son of the late King Renault who also had no siblings. She told me that you remained unmarried until you met her, and that you have no children . . . no heir to the throne. She told me that you had no qualms about making one of her children your designated heir, that you would show us the ways of a ruler."

"That is correct. I have no natural heirs. There is no one who could rule after I stepped down. Other influential families would vie for the throne, and the realm could be thrown into internal conflict and chaos. In order to alleviate that possibility, I asked Lilandria if one of her children would take the throne after me . . . agree to be my heir. I see that she has done that already. "I must admit, I have been watching you, Sirion, watching you from the first moment you stepped into my home. I have seen nothing from you but goodness, honesty, and fairness. These are the qualities that make someone a good ruler. I would be honored to have you as my successor."

Sirion found himself swallowing heavily. This was not going to be easy for him, for he liked the man Thalios already. "My Lord, that is just it. I wish I could say that I would be accepting your proposal . . . that I would agree to be your heir. But I cannot. I do not feel that I am the man you are looking for. I am not cut out to be a king. The wild calls out to me so powerfully that I would feel trapped by my status and rank within the realm." Sirion paused, felt the disappointment emanating from his mother. "I am sorry, my Lord."

King Thalios was silent for a moment, his eyes downcast. But when Thalios looked back to Sirion, he could not discern any emotion on the king's stolid features. "Don't be sorry. It shows me that you have integrity and goodness of character. I would much rather have it that you were honest and forthright with me. However, I cannot deny that I am troubled by your decision. I am rather at a loss about what to do about this situation. I fear that there will be so much internal strife, and that if we were to be invaded, our enemies would not be hard pressed to claim this realm as their prize."

There was only momentary silence before Sirion spoke again. "However, my decision to not accept your proposal does not mean that you will be left without a successor." Sirion glanced at his mother and noticed that he had her attention, much as he had Thalios'. "In my stead, I offer you another heir, a younger one . . . one that you can train right from the start. One who will grow up knowing that he will be the King of Elvandahar one day."

"And please, pray tell us, who is this young person?" Lilandria stared at

Sirion pointedly, already assuming that there was something he had not told her about himself.

"In my place, I offer you my first-born child. My son will be your heir."

King Thalios could not keep the smile off of his face. "And you have this child already at your disposal?"

"No. But within the next few years, I am sure that I will."

"You are so sure that you will have this son, and that he will be your first-born child? You are so sure that you will soon have a woman with which you will produce this son?"

Sirion regarded the king solemnly. "There is no doubt in my mind."

"I can see that."

Lilandria had made her way to his side. "And do you at least know the woman . . . this woman who will bear you this son?"

Sirion smiled, knowing the ways of women . . . that they always had a way of finding things out, things that men sought to keep from them. But he answered her anyway, despite knowing that she sought to manipulate him, because he knew it would make her happy. "Yes, Mother. I know her."

Sirion said nothing else, but excused himself from the alcove. Yes, he knew her, the woman that he hoped would give him a son. She was not his yet. But he wanted her to be. He wanted her like he had wanted nothing else in his whole life. Sirion sighed heavily as he quickly made his way down the passageway. He had appeared confident before his mother and her husband, but he could not say for certain that she would want him the way he wanted her. Only time would tell.

21 Brinaren CY593

Sirion walked silently among the trees. The group had set out that morning. He scouted ahead of them, hoping that he would catch some sign, somewhere, that Sydonnia was near. He knew that he was being watched . . . followed. He knew that it was Joselyn. The first thing that had given her away was her scent. It had always been her scent; he knew it just as he knew Adrianna's scent. Suddenly he was engulfed by his memories of Joselyn, the times they had shared. He remembered the feel of her against him . . . Sirion put his hands at his hips and slowly turned around. From behind one of the gigantic trees, Joselyn emerged. Sirion felt any ire that he had been feeling begin to melt away. He stood motionless as she walked gracefully up to him. He studied her, saw the shape of her supple body beneath the silk of her gown. Her long light-brown hair spiraled down to her hips. It was threaded with tiny white chamdaroc flowers, their scent thought to have intoxicating qualities. Then Joselyn was standing before him, close. Sirion quickly discovered that her scent was indeed intoxicating to him, much as it always had been before.

"Sirion?" Joselyn laid a tentative hand upon his chest.

Her voice was low, seductive. He remembered that voice. She had used it on him when she had been unsure of his mood, or when she sought to placate him. He looked down at her, took in the slight pout of her lips, the rise and fall of her breasts beneath the fabric of her gown. White . . . he could see her breasts beneath the thin fabric. She wore it, he knew, on purpose, to thaw his resolve against her.

"What do you want, Joselyn?" He stepped back from her. Joselyn let her hand drop to her side.

Joselyn continued to pout. "Why didn't you return for me, Sirion?"

The question surprised him, but then again, it did not. Nothing surprised him anymore.

Sirion sighed heavily. "You know why. We had an agreement. Neither of us was willing to give up our profession for the other. Either that, or we were unwilling to compromise. Each of us wanted to be the best at our chosen vocations. We had no future together."

Joselyn regarded him intently. "You really believe that?"

Sirion frowned. "Yes, it was spoken between us." Sirion sighed again, lowered his head. "You left the Order, then." For a moment there was silence. Then he heard her voice crack.

"Yes."

"Why, Joselyn? Why did you do it?"

She looked up at him, her blue eyes beseeching him. "I did it because I yearned for you, longed for you to return for me. Over the years the Order became a constant reminder that I had chosen it over you. And then, several months ago, Sydonnia came. I knew that you would seek him out. Only, I did not know it would take this long. I thought maybe you would come for me if you knew that he had taken me. But you never came."

Joselyn stopped speaking, her head lowered. Sirion looked at her, the pale chestnut tresses framing her lovely face. "Joselyn, it is over. You knew that I would never accept you . . . not under these circumstances."

She looked up at him, tears at the corners of her blue eyes. "I hoped you would. I prayed that you would have me back at your side." She paused and then continued. "There is someone else, isn't there?"

Sirion paused. Thoughts of Adrianna raced through his mind, thoughts of what she had come to mean to him, the warmth of her smile, the way she looked at him . . . like he was the best thing that had ever happened to her. He remembered what they had shared the other night, the passion, and he knew that he had never felt that way before. Sirion shook his head and then nodded. "Perhaps . . . but what is it to you?"

"I thought so. I saw her the other day, watching you. And Sirion . . . it means everything to me. Please, have me back; have me by your side once more."

"No, you have chosen the path of corruption. Despite your claim to have been in wait for me, you have shared my uncle's bed, become his consort. You have chosen the path he has offered you."

"Do you love her?"

Once more, Sirion paused. But he already knew the answer, felt he had always known it. But he did not wish her to know, afraid that she would use her knowledge against him, she who had chosen the easy path.

"Perhaps. But it is not really any of your business."

"But I care about you so very much." Once again she was standing close to him . . . too close. "She can not possibly mean to you what I once did. I want you, abundantly so. Do not make me ask you again."

Once more, her hand was at his chest, her body pressed close. Then she was putting her arms around his neck, placing her lips upon his. Sirion responded to her kiss, much as he always had before. But this time it was different . . . it was wrong. He pulled away from her then, placing distance between them once again.

"Go back to my uncle, Joselyn. You can no longer manipulate me the way you did before. Once, I may have loved you, but no more. You have defiled my memory of you and I feel shame."

"Sirion, please."

"No. You have chosen your path." Sirion turned from her and walked away.

***

Tianna silently looked up at the sky. Evening was approaching. Already she could discern the pale shape of Steralion above. She sighed and then began to help prepare the evening camp. Slowly she unpacked the cooking pot and silently accepted the dry tinder that had been collected by Amethyst. She poured some water into the pot and set it over the fire that Dartanyen prepared. Feeling disheartened, Tianna then sat down next to the pot and poked at the small fire with a stick.

For two days now the group had been attempting to track down Sydonnia. Upon the first morning, Tianna had been quick to perceive the change in the relationship between Sirion and Adrianna. There was a tension between them that had not been there before, and she caught them glancing at one another when they thought that no one else was watching. Yet they did not speak to one another very much, and their conversations were limited to the business at hand. Tianna knew that something had happened, but could not come to a decision about what it might be. She could only hope that it was not one of the more disturbing thoughts going through her mind.

However, the situation with Sirion was not the only thing weighing upon Tianna's mind. It was her family. While passing through the domain, the group had seen the effect that the lycanthrope menace was having upon the people. They lived in fear, largely keeping to themselves and staying inside their tree-top homes, hoping that any lycan that came by would leave them alone. Many places had been destroyed, and families murdered. They learned that two of the domains, Filopar and Mirpur, had been similarly affected and the closest one was where the druids of Reshik-na resided.

Reshik-na was a place situated within the domain of Filopar. Several years ago, a mission to the farthest reaches of the domain of Mirpur had found the child Tianna at the site of a village demolished by an unknown threat. The mission had taken Tianna back to Reshik-na, and she came to live in the house of Father Domick. Withdrawn and constantly wary of others, Tianna did not thrive. She became sickly and was somewhat frail . . . until the day that the young ranger Sirion arrived at Reshik-na. He became the medicine that soon made Tianna well again. She began to blossom under Sirion's protective wing, and she started to show an inclination for a desire to learn about the art of healing.

However, when Tianna began to approach puberty, she realized that she was not prepared to live the life of a druid. She left the Order and journeyed to the city of Sangrilak. There, she entered into the priesthood of Beory, and began to study herbal medicine in earnest. Within a few years she had advanced within the ranks of the priesthood and had become a qualified healer. Within that period of time, Sirion had come to visit her in Sangrilak, but she never forgot the times they had shared together in Reshik-na. As she developed to maturity, she began to realize her true feelings for him, and had begun to endeavor to settle Sirion to her mantle.

Tianna continued to poke at the growing fire, her thoughts turned inwards. She was worried about Father Domick and the rest of the druids in Reshik-na. She loved them like they were her family, and she could not help but think that they needed her.

"Is something bothering you, Tianna?"

She looked up from the fire to find Sirion standing over her. Her heart quickened momentarily upon seeing him. She regarded him for a moment and them exclaimed, "I feel so torn. I want to help you find your uncle, but I also know that I should go to my family and see if they are all right."

"Then go, Tianna. Nothing is holding you back," Sirion replied, crouching next to her.

"But you need me. Who will be there if you, or anyone, gets hurt?" Tianna stopped, glancing in Adrianna's direction.

Sirion took Tianna by the shoulders. "I will be fine. Go. Your people need you more than I do."

Tianna turned back to Sirion, questions in her eyes, but she asked none of them, afraid of the answers. "But what I really want is to be with you," she whispered.

But Sirion did not hear her as he rose and turned from her, making his way back to the unsheathed short-swords lying on his bedroll. "When you go, just be sure that you take someone with you. You should not be traveling alone."

Tianna remained silent. Her loyalty to the people who had taken her in as an orphan was strong. But her desire to be with the man she loved was stronger. She felt an overpowering urge to stay, hoping that her presence would keep the inevitable from occurring. But something was happening whether she wanted it to or not, with or without her presence there. She could see the connection between Sirion and Adrianna, and knew that they hardly perceived it themselves. She felt the tension between them, and knew it to be the attraction that they attempted to ignore.

She knew that she had to go. It was not right of her to stay for the wrong reasons. If her only reason for staying was to try to keep Sirion and Adrianna apart then she would be doing herself, her people, and possibly Sirion and Adrianna a disservice. Of course, it wasn't her only reason for staying. She knew that her help would be greatly welcomed, but she also knew with every fiber of her being that her people needed her more.

"I will be leaving in the morning then."

Sirion looked back at her. "Who will be going with you?"

"I don't know. Perhaps the king can spare some men."

Sirion put his hand beneath his chin, stroked it for a moment, and then replied, "Perhaps, but I don't trust them. At least one of us should go with you." Sirion looked around at the rest of the group. They were all preparing for the night, laying out bedrolls and blankets. Sheridana was busy preparing the evening meal, and Zorg was conducting a perimeter check.

After a few moments Armond spoke up. "I will go with you."

"Excellent," replied Sirion. "I will send Dramati back to the palace with the message that we need three of the king's best men to accompany you. I am sure they will be here by morning." Sirion removed a parchment from his pack and began to write. He called Dramati to him and the corubis came, allowing the message to be tied around his neck. Sirion held the animal's face in his hands and gazed into Dramati's eyes. Then the animal was gone, bounding into the forest they had trekked through that day.

Sirion looked up to find Tianna still watching him. He smiled. "You had better get some rest then. You have a big day ahead of you tomorrow."

"Will you return for me when your task is through?"

Sirion chuckled. "Of course. We can't remain too long without our medic now, can we?"

Sirion's good humor was infectious, and Tianna felt herself smiling in return. It was one of the reasons why she cared for him so much. Despite his often stoic demeanor, he was able to make her smile when nothing, or no one else could.

She went over to Armond and they began to make plans for the next morning. Then she took Sirion's advice and went to bed. Whatever was meant to happen would happen. She knew that she could not stop it; it was beyond her manipulations. No matter how much Sirion had come to mean to her, she could not make him see her as anything more than the little girl he had met over twelve years ago. But she could always hope.

***

Once more, the group made camp for the night. Sirion dropped his pack and looked out into the forest contemplatively. Just that morning, Tianna and Armond departed for the farther reaches of the domain of Filopar in the company of three of Thalios' men. Dramati and the warriors had arrived early in the morning, and before the entire group was awake for the day, they had left again. Tianna had embraced him before leaving, kissing him on the mouth and then quickly turning away. He had been surprised by her actions, for she had never done it before. He had contemplated it for a few moments after she left but then let it rest. Perhaps she was just distraught about her journey to Reshik-na.

Sirion frowned, felt the tension in his body beginning to build. He knew they were close. He had seen signs that Sydonnia was close . . . and Sirion could feel his nearness. Sirion glanced cursorily about the encampment, told Dramati to stay there, and then began to walk into the forest. He would just take a quick look. Perhaps that is all that Sydonnia wanted . . . to catch him alone.

Sirion made his way into the forest, his footfalls nearly silent as he moved. He allowed his senses to extend outwards, to encompass the world around him. Then, not only did he hear the wind in the trees, he heard the movement of the animal life in the leaf litter, saw the scat of a leshera, followed the tracks of an alothere, and smelled the scent of rain on the wind. Suddenly he knew he was being followed, but before he could turn around he heard his name.

"Sirion?"

It was Adrianna. He heard the fear in her voice, the unspoken questions. She had followed him, probably wanting to be sure that he was well. Sirion turned around to face her. She stopped a couple of feet before she reached him. He saw the worry in her dark brown eyes, in the creases at the corners of her mouth.

"Sirion, where are you going? Is something out here?"

He pulled his hand through his hair. He probably shouldn't have left like that, without telling anyone. But his thoughts were so full of Sydonnia that he could not think to remember anything, or anyone else. "No, I don't think so. I just wanted to be sure before we camped for the night."

Adrianna nodded. He was just doing a perimeter check, like the one Zorg tended to do in the evenings as they set up camp. But this night Sirion was doing it, probably hoping to be alone, needing some time to think to himself, despite the fact that he had been doing it all day. "Do you want me to leave you alone then?"

Sirion regarded her solemnly. She seemed to have aged within the past few days, the stress of her situation weighing on her. Yet he had been so engrossed with his own worries, he had forgotten about hers. "No," he heard himself say. "You know that I always enjoy your company." He smiled at her then, sincerely happy that she had sought him out.

Adrianna felt surprise when Sirion took her hand in his, and felt a weight lift from her chest as they walked together in silence. For the first time since the passionate embrace they had shared the other night at the fortress she began to feel that everything just might be all right. He had continued her training, but had otherwise not spoken to her very much. In light of the situation into which they would soon be walking, it bothered her that he had become so distanced towards her. She was afraid that something would happen to him, and he would never know how she felt. But at the same time, she did not know how, or even if, she should divulge this information to him, afraid that it would push him away from her even more. "Sirion, what is going to happen?"

He turned towards Adrianna; saw her eyebrows pulled together in a frown. "I don't know," he responded, wishing that he could give her more than that. But he had no more to give. He had an idea of what would happen . . . that he might not return to the group, alive. That, and if he lost against his uncle, Sydonnia and his minions would come for the rest of the group and attempt to defeat them. Suddenly Sirion was afraid. He was afraid of just that, and that Adrianna's life would be forfeit, even if it did not need to be. Then he was suddenly angry, angry with his uncle, with himself, and with the world.

Sirion fiercely ran his fingers through his hair and then clenched his hands into fists. "Why? Why me? Of all of the people of Shandahar, why me? I can help him . . . I told him that I could. But he would have nothing of it. Why does my life have to be the dung-pit that it is?" Sirion paused and then continued. "He is out there waiting for me, uncaring of the position in which he has placed me . . . the position for which my father trained me. You never asked me, but I know that you have wondered. You have wondered what Sydonnia meant when he said that I was a killer."

Adrianna regarded him impassively, listening intently. She knew that that is what he needed, someone to which he could vent his frustration.

"My father. For years he trained me to be a fighter, a damn good one. It was all done for one purpose . . . to kill his brother. He knew that I was the only one who could do it, he being too weak to do it himself." Sirion chuckled to himself. "My father, he was so selfish, training me to do something that he was unwilling to do himself."

Adrianna listened, sickened that a man could care so little for his own son. Yet, she had suffered in much the same way and, even now, was being hunted by her own father. Adrianna stopped and Sirion followed suit. They turned to look at one another, saying nothing. Adrianna saw the pain in his eyes, the years of grief. She wished that she could take it all away, ease the hurt in his heart.

Sirion saw the compassion in Adrianna's eyes, and was glad that she had come after him. He needed someone to listen, and she had proved that she was good at it. Then she was standing in front of him, and before he knew it she was embracing him. Instinctively he wrapped his arms about her and she put her head on his shoulder. He felt better that he had spoken to her about his problems, and that she offered him comfort. It made him feel better about what he had done to her a few nights ago, almost having taken advantage of her in a weakened state. They held one another for a few moments and then stepped apart.

"Come on, let's head back. The others will wonder about us."

"You go ahead. I will follow you in a moment. I just need to figure some things out." Sirion nodded to her to go on without him. She nodded in reply and then turned back the way they had come. Sirion watched her walk slowly back towards the camp. He stood there for quite some time, deep in thought. Memories of his father and his uncle raced through his mind. What exactly had happened all of those years ago? Why would Servial betray his own brother? But he would never know. Servial was dead, and soon Sydonnia would be as well.

Once more, Sirion knew that he was being watched. He began to move in the direction that Adrianna had taken back to camp. Then from out of the darkening shadows, two forms stepped out from among the trees. "Your day of reckoning has come," said one of the men.

Sirion's mind reeled. Adrianna. He had told her to go back to camp, alone. He could have hit himself. She was in danger, much danger. He was about to call out to her when one of the men stepped up to him and took his arm. Sirion felt the point of a sword against his back and knew there to be others behind him. "I wouldn't do that if I were you. Besides, it is too late. Sydonnia already has her."

Damn . . . Sirion shut his eyes tightly and hung his head. It was his fault. He should have escorted her back to camp. But he had not, and she was in

Sydonnia's grasp because of him. Sirion gritted his teeth as he was led away by Sydonnia's men. He would kill his uncle and end this threat. If Sirion did not kill Sydonnia, then Sydonnia would almost surely kill Adrianna.

***

"Where is Sirion?" Dartanyen looked around the camp. "Where is Adrianna?"

Sheridana looked up from her plate. She looked around the camp. Both Sirion's and Adrianna's packs lay on the ground, at opposite sides of the fire. Neither one had unfurled their bedrolls, which told Sheri that they had been gone for a while. Dramati lay next to Sirion's pack, his head on his paws. Sirion must have told him to stay there.

Sheri's eyes darted about camp once again, hoping that they would miraculously be there. A bad feeling began to suffuse through her. She saw Dinim looking around the camp as well, and then back at her. Almost as one, they stood. "I don't know," said Sheri, walking over to Dartanyen.

"I think I remember seeing Sirion head off in that direction when we first got here," said Zorg, pointing into the trees to the right of the camp.

"But that was almost an hour ago," said Dartanyen.

"But what about Adrianna? Did anyone see her leave?" asked Dinim.

"I can only assume that she must have followed Sirion," said Sheridana.

Dinim frowned. "Why would she do that?" His voice sounded a little odd . . . strained.

Sheri glanced at Dinim. She wasn't going to spell it out for him. Besides, he knew just as well as she what had begun to transpire between Sirion and her sister, whether he liked it or not.

Dartanyen put his hands up. "It doesn't matter," he said. "Let's just find them before *all* of our light is gone."

Sheridana shivered involuntarily. Dartanyen was right. They had precious little light left. The sun was beginning to set and the air was becoming slightly chilly. She slipped on her cloak and couldn't help but wonder if Adrianna had hers.

"Well, we may as well all go," said Zorg. "If they are in some kind of trouble, they are going to need as many of us as possible."

"This is ridiculous," mumbled Amethyst. "Sirion is a big boy. I am sure that he can take care of himself."

"And what about Adrianna? What about *her*? She doesn't know how to protect herself against a lycanthrope," Dinim snarled.

"I am sure that the ever-so-brave Sirion would come to her rescue," Amethyst spat nastily.

"Amethyst," shouted Dartanyen. "Cut the crap. We don't need your censure right now. Just get your pack and let's go."

Amethyst stomped over to her pack and slung it over her shoulder, silently shaking her head. Sheri rolled her eyes. Sometimes Amethyst could be a great person to have around, but when she was sick or just simply tired, she was best left alone. Sheri wondered which one it was, and then thought that it may be neither. Human women tended to be rather nasty during their menses as well. Perhaps it was Amethyst's moon-time.

The group filed out of the camp, Dramati following behind. Sheri found herself wishing that Tianna and Armond were with them, despite any problems that she and Armond seemed to have with one another. Even though they were starting to get at one another's throats, she respected Armond as a fellow warrior. She was glad that they were on the same side.

Sheri continued to become more and more nervous as the time passed by. And the longer they walked, the longer the shadows became. Suddenly she heard a whine behind her. She swung around to find Dramati standing on the trail through which they had just passed. His head and tail were held high and she knew that he was sensing something from Sirion.

The snap of a branch to Sheri's right warned her of approaching danger. She drew her swords from their sheaths at her back just as an arrow came slicing through the air, landing in Dramati's left side. He snarled viciously as he fell, the arrow embedded deep. He began to bleed profusely as he sought to tear the arrow free of his flesh. Sheri began to run to him. She heard shouts from the others behind her and then suddenly found her way blocked by a large form. She jumped out of the way as it lunged for her. It barreled past her and she did a quick turnaround, smacking the broadside of her right sword onto the person's back.

Quick as lightening the person turned to face her. She was met with a terrible visage. The person was not quite human, having features that were also like that of an alothere. The flesh was greyish and short wiry hairs sprouted from the exposed flesh on the arms. The eyeteeth in the lower jaw were elongated, coming up over the upper lip. His muscles were hyper-developed, and she was sure that he would be able to overpower her very quickly. But the most frightening thing about him was his eyes. They were black as pitch, seemingly without emotion.

The alothere-man was about to move towards her when a shrill scream pierced the air. It was Adrianna. Sheri's heart skipped a beat and her flesh turned cold. But it was the distraction that she needed. She ran past the creature and back towards the group. She saw Dinim running towards her, and in the distance, past Dinim, she could see five other lycanthropes that had Zorg, Dartanyen, Amethyst, and Sabian surrounded. As Dinim flew by her, he grabbed her hand and they sprinted in the direction from whence they had heard Adrianna's scream.

***

Adrianna screamed. She didn't mean to . . . it just happened. But perhaps it would turn out to be a good thing. The group may have heard her. Or maybe even Sirion. But when she saw the expression on Sydonnia's hideous face, she changed her mind. He grabbed her roughly by the arm and hauled her to him. His breath stank and she couldn't keep herself from averting her face and squeezing her eyes tightly shut. He was terrible to behold, not quite man, not quite wemic. And he was strong, so strong that she was sure she would sport bruises for weeks. That is, if she lived. He chuckled maliciously in her left ear, sending chills down her spine. What would he do to her?

"Little whore," he spat, his spittle drizzling her face. "My nephew, the womanizer. He always has a woman hanging around."

Adrianna stiffened. Sydonnia laughed again, feeling her reaction. "But don't worry, my dear. I will have you. I am beginning to sicken of Joselyn. She is a weak woman, not worthy of the powerful individual I soon will become."

Adrianna began to tremble, the situation in which she had found herself reminiscent of one she had endured several years before. Desperately, just as she had then, she began to struggle. Sydonnia only tightened his grip about her arms, and she cried out in pain. Once more he laughed, watching her try in vain to escape him. But suddenly he stopped . . . roughly taking her face in his large hand and holding it still. He studied her intently, his feral eyes narrowing into slits.

"I know you. We have met before."

Adrianna nodded her head, her eyes wide.

"When? Where?" Sydonnia demanded.

"At the Inn of the Hapless Cenloryan, several months ago."

Sydonnia shook his head. "No. It was some other time, some other place."

Adrianna shook her head, knowing that if she had met him before then she would have remembered.

Sydonnia shook his head as well. "I know I have met you before. But it doesn't matter now. My nephew will be here any moment. I will kill him and I will reign supreme in this realm forever."

The last Sydonnia said disdainfully, a smirk on his ugly face. For, indeed it truly was. His teeth were yellow, his canines slightly elongated and sharp. His eyebrows had thickened, as had the hair over all of his body. His body had also increased in size, and his muscle mass had nearly doubled. He was in his transitional form, the one he assumed before reaching animal-state. He was very powerful in this form, having the best of both humanoid and animal worlds.

Adrianna said nothing, barely able to tolerate his proximity to her. He was an abomination, a freak of nature. He was a monster created by parents to scare their children into obedience. He was an anathema to her, and she would escape him at her first opportunity. And then she would help Sirion kill him, if needed, just to be sure that the world was ridded of an abhorrence such as he.

Suddenly, Adrianna heard a commotion in the near distance. Sydonnia barked an order to one of his men to have it checked out. He gripped her tightly once more and began to drag her down the trail with him. Adrianna struggled. He snarled and raised his hand to her. Then, from out of the trees before them, Adrianna heard Sirion's voice. "Don't you dare touch her. I swear I will cut your hand off and shove it down your throat."

Sydonnia lowered his hand, an evil smile suffusing across his hideous face. "Sirion, it is so good of you to join us."

The commotion behind them got closer, and before they knew it, Sheridana and Dinim emerged upon the scene, three shirwemic following close behind them. Sirion and his own captors emerged out of the trees to the right of her and Sydonnia. His hands had been bound behind his back. Two shirkyerrean followed, each holding one of his arms. In the other hand, each held a sword to Sirion's back.

Recklessly, Sheridana continued to sprint towards Adrianna and Sydonnia. Sydonnia barely had time to position himself for the attack before Sheri was upon him. She slashed out at him with her long-sword, slicing his forearm and driving him back. Involuntarily, Sydonnia released his grip upon the struggling Adrianna. He snarled in anger and retaliated. With one of his massive claws, he reached out and gouged Sheri's shoulder and upper arm, sending her spinning to the ground.

Dinim watched the scenario unfold before him. He called out to Sheridana as she ran to her sister. The largest shirwemic he had ever seen held Adrianna captive, his large hands imprisoning her arms to her sides. The young woman struggled in futility. Dinim saw a captive Sirion emerge out of the forest to the right, two shirkyerrean at his back. If looks could kill, Sydonnia would have been dead, Sirion was so angry.

Dinim began the incantation to his spell, began to weave the magic between his hands. Suddenly a large weight slammed itself into his back and he found himself on the ground. Damn, he had conveniently forgotten the two shirwemic that had been trailing himself and Sheri. Dinim removed his face from the dirt. One continued to sit astride his back while the other ran towards Sheri, who had injured the shirwemic that had held Adrianna. Adrianna had gotten herself free of her captor, and was sprinting into the forest at their left.

With lightening reflexes, the large shirwemic struck out at Sheri, sending her to the ground. Then he bellowed a command, and Sirion and the two shirkyerean followed him back into the forest to their right.

Dinim watched, helpless, as the other shirwemic who had been following them stooped to pick up Sheri from the ground. His hybrid form had progressed. His face was more lupine, as were his legs and hands. Sheri lunged for her sword, but was snatched roughly up from the ground. She struggled until the creature wrapped his massive, clawed hand around her throat and began to squeeze. Dinim himself began to struggle as the shirwemic leered evilly at her. Somehow her studded leather had been torn, and it hung in a flap down to her midriff. The creature sank his teeth into the flesh of her chest above her left breast.

Sheridana shrieked. She was able to extract the dagger from its sheath around her upper thigh just as she felt the teeth sink into her flesh. She raised the silver dagger above her head and slammed it down into the creature's neck. Sheridana felt herself being sprayed with thick, warm blood. The shirwemic screamed, the sound of his voice like that of a wemic . . . a long drawn-out howl. Her throat released, she began to fall. Sheri caught herself, scrambled against the shirwemic, struggling to keep the dagger in his neck. She felt it ripping through his flesh, and sought to maintain a hold on the now blood-slicked weapon.

Dinim felt the weight of the shirwemic leave his back. He jumped up in hot pursuit of the creature, drawing his sword as he ran. The shirwemic reached his injured companion and Sheridana. He reached out with his claws, sought to disengage the woman from his companion. Dinim called out a warning to Sheri just as a crackling black bolt of energy passed before him, striking the creature about to attack Sheridana. Dinim jumped back and cast a glance into the trees to his left to see Adrianna standing there. Her expression was one he had never seen on her before, one of intense hatred.

Dinim heard a pathetic wail from in front of him and he turned back to the scene to find the shirwemic that had been hit by Adria's spell somewhat reduced. Surprised, Dinim regarded the creature for a moment before closing in on it. He knew what spell Adrianna had cast. It was an *Enervation* spell, one that reduced the energy, or life force, of its victim. Usually, it seemed to act to reduce the overall constitution of a person, taking away their ability to resist attack or to attack others. In this case, with the lycanthrope, it also seemed to affect them in their hybrid state, making them temporarily vulnerable and weak. Not knowing how long these effects of the spell would last, Dinim jumped at the opportunity to attack.

Sheridana continued to hold on to her weapon, resisting the creature's attempts to be rid of her. She knew that she was at risk, not only because she had already suffered a bite from the creature, but because she knew that he would finally use his clawed hands upon her to disengage himself from her. But she knew that she must not let go. Her weight pulled the weapon down, tearing the flesh of his neck, cutting into the blood vessels located there. Each moment that went by made him more and more weak, more vulnerable to future attacks.

And then it happened, just as Sheri knew it would. She felt the claws of the shirwemic scrape against her studded leather vest, across her back and side, felt the prickle of the sharp nails as they tore the fabric and her flesh between the studs. She felt her grip on the dagger begin to slip, and she knew that she could hold on only a short while longer. All of a sudden she felt something topple into them, and down they went in a tangle of arms and legs.

Sheri struggled to disengage herself from the mess. She felt a hand grasp her upper arm and she looked up to see Dinim trying to help her up. When she was free of the tangle, she found her sword being thrust into her hand by Adrianna. Then she looked back down at the two shirwemic, both of them kneeling on the ground. One of them was holding his hand to his bloodied neck, and the other was trying to cover a gaping hole in his lower abdomen. Sheridana wasted no more time. She swung her sword back, and then forward again. It whistled past the first one's face and struck the other one. His head rolled off of his neck and onto the bloodied ground, the body slumping to rest beside it.

Sheridana then saw a sword going into the chest of the other shirwemic. Blood gargled out of his mouth and the gaping wound in his neck. His eyes bulged in his hideous face as Dinim pushed the sword in deeper, the tip coming through his back. Then the body slid off of the sword, crumpling to the ground next to his comrade. Sheri then finished the job, cutting his head off as well.

Adrianna, Sheri, and Dinim looked down at what they had wrought. The creatures slowly began to revert to their humanoid state. Adrianna smiled to herself, pleased that the creatures were dead. They all nodded to one another and headed back in the direction in which they knew the rest of the group to be. They knew what the others were up against and knew that any help from them would be sincerely appreciated.

***

Darkness had fallen. The area was lit by tall standing torches set into the ground. Sydonnia circled Sirion, his brother's son. In so many ways the young man reminded Sydonnia of Servial. It was the way he was built: slender and lithe, but with an undertone of physical power that was much more enhanced in Sirion than it ever had been in his brother. It was the way he held himself: self-assured and confident. It was his eyes: the same color as Servial's had been.

Had been. Sydonnia had killed him, had killed his own brother. He had killed him when the rage took over, at a time when he could not bear the curse that had befallen him . . . to live forever as a monstrosity, to never know the true joys of life, to never hold Lilandria in his arms like he had so long ago.

But Sirion looked like his mother as well. He had her hair color, her charisma, and her heart. Sirion had honor and nobility of spirit that Servial never possessed. But Lilandria had possessed both of those qualities, somehow having passed them to her son before Servial had taken him from her. Taken him to turn him into an assassin.

"My brother's whelp. So long have I dreamed of this moment, dreamt it in every detail, down to the feel of you expiring in my hands, the feel of your blood washing over me. I hear your pleas for mercy in my ears, even now." Sydonnia stopped in front of Sirion, a slight smile on his face.

"Your dreams are nothing more than that . . . dreams. I would never plead to you, not for my life."

"Oh, I know you would not plea for your life . . . it was for Joselyn's, and even more recently, for the life of the young woman you call Adrianna."

Sirion felt himself stiffen. Sydonnia continued. "It was such a shame she got away. I so much would have loved to see her scream, and to see you beg me for her life."

"You are lucky that she got away, Uncle. I would have tormented you for all of the days of forever had you harmed her."

"Ah, so Joselyn was right. You do love the Savanlean woman."

Sirion did not dignify Sydonnia with a reply. It figured that Joselyn would open her big mouth. In every way now she had betrayed him, betrayed him to one of the only men who could possibly kill him. But he would not think of her now. To do so would be folly, and she would end up being the death of him.

"Joselyn, that bitch. I'm glad that I left her when I did. She is nothing to me. Does she service you as well as she did me? I do remember you saying that she was 'feisty'."

Sydonnia's smile never reached his eyes. He must have thought that she would have been more useful to him against Sirion. Sydonnia merely shrugged. "She serves me well enough." Sydonnia began to circle Sirion once more. Sirion refused to turn his head to follow his movements. Sydonnia sought only to make him nervous, to lose his focus. He was not succeeding.

Sirion sighed. Once more he would ask this question, once more offer his uncle the gift of freedom from his affliction. "Uncle, over the years I have spoken to people, learned things. I have discovered the thing that will make you into a man once more. I can save you, if you would only let me."

Suddenly, Sydonnia was standing before him again. Sirion could feel the anger emanating from him. "Save me. You speak of saving me. You are such a fool. What if you were to cure me? What then? What life would I live? I would be an outlaw. Do you know how much blood is on my hands? Not only that, but all of the people I have ever cared for are gone . . . even your mother, who I hear hates me. Do you think I would give this up now? All that I have worked for? I will rule this place, rule it on a throne of pain on top of a mountain of bones." Sydonnia grasped the front of Sirion's tunic, brought his face close. "No, I do not want liberation, not now. All I want from you is the battle which I have craved for over twenty years."

With that, Sydonnia let out an ear-splitting howl. Sirion felt the hairs on his scalp begin to rise, his body responding to the eminent danger in which it now found itself. Sydonnia walked around Sirion again, his hand on Sirion's left shoulder. Sydonnia paused behind him. "That battle begins now, Nephew." Sirion felt a tug at the bonds around his wrists, and then felt them fall away. Then Sirion heard his uncle speak once more, his mouth at his right ear. He spoke in a low, anticipatory voice. "Run, Sirion. Run."

Sirion needed no urging. He ran from the clearing, away from the light and into the darkness of the forest. He knew that Sydonnia would be close behind, knew that he would not give him that much of a head start: only enough to make it a game for him. Sirion ran as fast as he could, his thoughts only on his survival.

***

Adrianna, Dinim, and Sheridana made their way quickly through the trees. Darkness had fallen, but the moon above them, Steralion, offered at least some light and it would be even lighter when the second moon, Hestim, rose to join her sister. They moved in silence, each with their own thoughts. Dinim knew that they were not far from the others, as they had not traveled far to locate Adrianna. Thank the gods. Who knew what would have happened had they not reached her when they did. He did not even want to consider what might have befallen her in the captivity of that man. But she had begun to become rather powerful. The spell she had cast had been executed coolly and concisely. She hadn't known what effect the spell would have on the creature, but she had tried it anyway. It was a wonderful strike of luck that she had. Or was it skill speaking now? Was it becoming more than just luck with her?

Walking alongside Dinim, Sheridana stumbled. Instinctively, he put out a hand to steady her. He felt the heat of her flesh beneath his hand, and suddenly realized that she was fevered. He stopped in mid-stride. She stopped with him, placing a warm hand on his shoulder to steady herself.

"What is it?" asked Adrianna, stepping up to them.

Dinim put the back of his hand to Sheri's brow. She was burning up. And then he remembered. The creature had bitten her. "Damn," he cursed. "The fever has begun to set in. Sirion always said it was quick, but I didn't know it was this quick."

Adrianna put a hand on her sister's arm. "What do you mean?" She looked up at Dinim, her eyes wide.

Dinim sighed heavily. "She will soon begin the ordeal of fighting the disease. The creature bit her. Now she will have to fight against the illness. That, or succumb to it."

Dinim watched the fear play across Adrianna's face. But then she turned to Sheridana. "Sheri, come on. We have to hurry and get you back to the group. You need to rest."

"Rest," mumbled Sheridana. Dinim caught her as she began to collapse. He picked her up in his arms and he and Adrianna again moved in the direction of the group. Within only a few minutes they found themselves at the battle scene. Dinim lay Sheridana down at the periphery of the battle. He looked to Adrianna.

"You go," she said. "I will stay with Sheri." He nodded and sprinted in the direction of the fighting. Adrianna placed her palm on her sister's forehead. Tears sprang to her eyes. Sheri was so hot. She sat down and put Sheridana's head on her lap. She stroked her dark hair back from her face, crooned a song under her breath, and rocked her body back and forth.

Dinim passed the bodies of two lycanthropes on his way to the fighting. One was covered with a plethora of boils, lesions, and seeping abscesses. He knew how that one had met his demise. Both were also headless. They had reverted to their human states after death, just as the ones that they had killed earlier had done. A few feet away from the two bodies, he stopped at the still form of Amethyst. He knelt next to her, felt her neck for a pulse. It was there, but she bled profusely from a claw wound to her back and right side. Dinim tried to staunch the flow, but felt hurried. He knew that the others needed him. He could not afford the time it would take for a field dressing. It would have to wait.

Dinim wrapped the girl in his cloak and ran to the fight just in time to see Dartanyen go down. Sabian finished casting a spell. The electricity slammed into the shirkyerrean standing over Dartanyen, knocking him several feet through the air. He landed heavily and was still. Dinim quickly made his way over to the creature and cut off the head just as the shirkyerrean began to stir. Zorg continued his battle with the last of the shirkyerrean, sweat pouring off of his forehead. He was quickly tiring. Dinim began the incantation to his *Enervation* spell, grinning. He already knew the effect it would have on the creature. When the black bolt of energy struck the lycanthrope, the creature began to diminish. It seemed like it was a painful process, for the beast clutched himself about the midriff as the spell took effect. While he was distracted, Zorg used the opportunity to run the creature through with his broadsword. The creature fell to his knees. Zorg withdrew the sword from the shirkyerean's belly and lopped his head off, disposing of the threat in the same manner as all the others.

Dinim, Sabian, and Zorg gathered together at the center of the makeshift battlefield. Zorg looked around. "Where are Sheridana and Adrianna?"

"Back there," replied Dinim, pointing behind him. "Sheridana has been bitten, and the fever has taken hold. If the wound gets infected, she may die. But she will need to fight the disease no matter if the wound goes septic or not. I passed Amethyst on the way over here. She also has been injured, but I think it is just a claw wound."

Zorg headed in the direction in which Dinim pointed, while Sabian went to get Dartanyen. Finally everyone was gathered at one location, the injured having been carried or dragged there. Adrianna had begun to cleanse Sheri's wound. She poured some water onto one of the soft cloths that Tianna had given to her before she left. She then took a pouch from her pack and rubbed a green powder onto the wet cloth. She applied it to Sheri's wound and kept it there.

Dinim hunkered down beside her. "What is that?"

"I'm not really sure. All I know is that Tianna told me to apply it in this fashion to any wound that anyone sustained."

Dinim nodded. "Then you will want to see to Amethyst and Dartanyen as well. Amethyst has already lost a lot of blood from her injury, but Dartanyen sustained several deep lacerations before he fell."

Adrianna nodded in reply. "I will see to it then."

She made to move away when Dinim took her arm. "Adrianna, I am glad that you are well."

Adrianna made eye contact. His expression showed gratitude and relief, but underneath there was something else that Adria could not quite place. Seeking to comfort him, Adrianna placed her hand on his face. "I am too. I was so happy to see that you had come for me."

Dinim covered her hand with his for a moment, then took it and kissed her palm. He smiled at her and then rose. He walked over to Zorg, who was having trouble wrapping his arm. Adrianna watched him for a moment before moving to Amethyst's side to tend her injuries. She had been overjoyed to see Dinim and her sister running out of the trees. She had been so afraid, knowing that Sydonnia would kill her to get at Sirion. Sirion. Where was he? Was he alive? Somehow Adrianna knew that he was, felt that she would know if he were not. She so much wanted to go to him, just to be by his side.

Adrianna tended to the wounds of Amethyst and Dartanyen. They would be extremely sore when they awoke. There was a drink that they could take, one that Tianna had shown her how to make, but that was all that Adrianna could do for them. While the rest of the group slept, Adrianna put the pot over the fire, filled it with water, and began to add the herbs that Tianna had provided. She prepared the drink and sat, staring at the dancing flames of the fire.

At the appropriate time, she went over to awaken Dinim for his turn at the watch. She then crept to her bedroll. She was tired, exhausted actually. She lay there, wide-eyed, while Dinim shuffled around the camp. Finally he settled against the trunk of a tree, his sword across his knees. She watched Dinim try valiantly to stay awake at his watch, but his eyelids drooped every now and then. She hoped Sabian's turn was up soon. Then, out of the corner of her eye she saw movement. She focused into the trees and finally made out the form of a large animal.

Her heart leapt in her chest, but then subsided. Dramati! It was poor Dramati. Where had he been? What had happened to him? Adrianna crept out of her blankets and slipped over to him, keeping an eye on Dinim. The man did not move, did not even look in her direction. Dramati had settled onto the ground. Adrianna ran her hands over his body, felt the matted fur, the caked blood. He snuffled her hair as she inspected him the best she could in the pale light of the moons. The night would be over in a few hours. Then she would be able to tend his cuts. But why was he here? Why wasn't he with Sirion?

Adrianna spoke Sirion's name to the animal and Dramati quickly stood up, his tail waving rapidly. It was apparent to her that he wished to go to his companion. Then Adrianna had a thought. She crept back over to her bedroll and picked up her pack. She slung it over her shoulder. Dinim continued to remain motionless. She passed Sheri on her way back to Dramati, placed her hand on her sister's face, kissed her fevered brow. Adrianna hated leaving her, but her desire to be with Sirion had taken away her reason.

Adrianna approached Dramati. He crouched to the ground once more. She took his fur in her hands and pulled herself onto his back. Memories of riding astride Cortath tumbled through her mind. Sirion. It had been upon Sirion's back that she had ridden. "Dramati, take me to Sirion." Then he was up and running through the forest.

CHAPTER 19

S irion continued through the forest. It was almost light, the sun beginning to crest the horizon. Between runs, he had been able to rest for small spurts of time, just enough to get his wind back and to give his body a chance to reclaim some stamina. Sydonnia had studied up on him thoroughly. Sydonnia had known that Sirion had been endurance trained. He sought to strip Sirion's endurance from him by beginning their battle with a chase. Sirion had considered turning around and facing his uncle when this first started over two hours ago. But then he had thought better of it. He knew of an abandoned outpost not much further away. He felt that he might be able to use it to his own advantage.

So Sirion had given his uncle the chase that he wanted. He continued to run, the shirwemic not far behind. The sun began to rise and twenty minutes later he reached the massive outpost. One there, he circled around to the rear. He entered the main bunker through a concealed door. Once inside he took stock of his situation.

In essence, the building was an absolute wreck . . . if one would even call it a building anymore. The walls were beginning to crumble and stones littered the floor. Much of the ceiling had begun to cave in, allowing the outside world to encroach upon the inside of the structure. The main room consisted of broken tables and chairs, some old candelabra, shards of broken pottery and glass, and some old musty piles of fabric. Outside, Sirion heard a series of howls, followed by one long drawn-out one. They were near. Sirion unsheathed Stalker from his back harness. Now it was only a matter of time.

Sirion waited in the center of the dilapidated room. Stalker thrummed in his grasp. They were right outside; the weapon could feel their nearness. Sirion placed both of his hands, side by side, on the cool dark metal weapon. He visualized his will to the weapon and it began to glow. A moment later, it was two blades. He pulled them away from one another just as the front door splintered open. In strode Sydonnia.

"My, my what a place we have found here. It is interesting that you would choose this to be the place of your downfall. It was once a vast military base, one of the last to be re-taken in the Krish-Alneez. It is also where I used to meet your mother. It is funny how things meet fullcircle, is it not?" Sydonnia's lips turned up into a bittersweet smile, his eyes taking on a far-away cast. "It is always such a shame when life brings you down to nothing." His expression became greatly saddened and his shoulders seemed to slump.

But then Sydonnia snapped out of his contemplation. He took in Sirion's stance, his battle-ready countenance. Sydonnia smiled once more. "I have been waiting a long time for this moment."

"So have I," Sirion replied. "But killing you will bring me no pleasure."

Sydonnia drew his massive blade. He was big enough and strong enough, to wield it single-handedly. "Let us begin, shall we? I am just *dying* to know how powerful a fighter my brother created to be my nemesis."

"Well, pay close attention. You will see it only once."

All of a sudden, Sydonnia leapt at Sirion, swinging his broad-sword over his head in an arc. Sirion quickly rolled to his right, forced into a backflip over a broken table. Sirion quickly found that his balance was slightly off, and Sydonnia quicker than Sirion had given him credit. Sirion found the pommel of his uncle's sword in his gut and he fell back, back in between two more tables. He landed and rolled underneath one, disappearing into the shadows. It was easy, for the building was largely unlit, despite the morning light outside streaming through the cracks in the ceiling.

Sydonnia began searching around, toppling the tables as he went. When his back was turned, Sirion leapt at him. Sydonnia managed to block his first attack, but Sirion's second blade cut deeply into Sydonnia's left thigh. But Sydonnia was quick, ever so fast as he crossed his blade back over and made a slice across Sirion's belly.

The studs had taken away much of the impact, but the sword had still been able to pass through some of the armor. Sirion sought to control his expression as they began to circle one another. The wound burned horrifically. Sirion schooled his features into nonchalance, not wanting to give anything away to his opponent. Sirion tried to predict what Sydonnia would do next. Sirion feigned a thrust, resulting in a similar attack. Sirion spun into him, parrying the attack. But with his other blade, Sirion sliced into Sydonnia's arm. Sirion continued to spin past Sydonnia, and placed the blades together once more. Stalker glowed briefly and became a quarterstaff once again. Sirion followed through with his spin, dropping to the ground and swiping at Sydonnia's feet with the staff.

Sydonnia began to fall to the ground but turned it into a roll, attempting to alleviate much of the impact of hitting the ground. By then Sirion had risen and begun to take advantage of Sydonnia's grounded state. Sirion swung in an upward arc, and Stalker connecting with the side of Sydonnia's head. Sydonnia growled menacingly as Sirion backed away.

Sydonnia slowly rose to his feet. "You are better than I have given you credit. Servial taught you well. It's a shame he can't be here to see the fruit of his labors." Sydonnia sneered. "But this is when I begin to really have fun." Sydonnia spoke a word under his breath and a pair of hooks sprang from the crossbar of his sword. The pommel and blade of the weapon lengthened. It was possibly the largest sword Sirion had ever seen. Then, without warning, Sydonnia sprang at him. Sirion blocked his swing, but as the weapons met, Sydonnia twisted his blade alongside Stalker, capturing the staff within one of the hooks upon the crossbar. Before Sirion realized it, the staff had left his hands and was spinning across the floor with Sydonnia's own sword. Suddenly, they both disappeared into a hole in the floor.

Sirion cursed under his breath. Sydonnia definitely had the upper hand now. Then Sydonnia was upon him. Sydonnia punched Sirion in the abdomen, and Sirion felt the air exit his lungs. Next Sydonnia delivered a harsh uppercut, one that Sirion knew he would be feeling for days; that is, if he survived this encounter. The swing sent him flying backwards. Sirion's backside hit the floor and he was sure that his butt was broken. Sydonnia followed him and as Sydonnia began to kick at him, Sirion picked up a candelabrum from the floor and swung it at Sydonnia's face. Sydonnia tried to block the blow and it ended up striking his arm and glancing off the side of his head. Blood began to well out of the wound and run down the side of his face.

As Sydonnia dropped to one knee holding his face, Sirion scrambled to his feet and ran across the room to the nearest stone pillar. He untied the chandelier still posted to it and let it go. He watched it descend upon his uncle. It fell upon Sydonnia with a massive crash, shards of pottery scattering in all directions. Sirion slowly walked towards the downed chandelier, one arm around his middle. Blood from his cut had begun to soak through his tunic and studded leather vest. He was sure that the blows to his abdomen had not helped his situation any.

Suddenly, Sirion felt the floor beneath his feet begin to crumble and give way. Down, down he plummeted, into the basement of the bunker. A few minutes later, Sirion was able to pick his bruised and battered body up off of the floor. In the distance, Sirion could see the glint of Stalker lying in a pile of debris. Sydonnia had already succeeded in digging himself out from beneath the debris and had made his way over to Sirion. Sirion was unable to escape as Sydonnia picked him up by his throat and slammed him into the nearest wall.

Sirion gasped for breath as Sydonnia bent to grab his leg. Then, holding him by the throat and one leg, Sydonnia hurled Sirion from him, throwing him through a wooden door. Sirion went through it and slammed into a stone staircase. Sydonnia stepped through the shards of the door and came at Sirion, his mouth open wide. Sydonnia's hybrid form had progressed, and he began to appear more and more beast-like. Barely having time to react, Sirion picked up a large wood shard from the floor near him and shoved it into Sydonnia's maw. As Sydonnia screamed in agony, Sirion crawled between his legs, scrambling towards the weapon he knew to be Stalker lying in the distance.

Sirion reached the weapon and opened it once more, the blades separating from one another in a fluid hiss. Then Sirion turned around. He saw Sydonnia remove the stake from his jaw and throw it away from him. Then he was charging at Sirion once again, and Sirion towards him. Sydonnia swung at Sirion, but the other man ducked underneath and swung Stalker upward, striking Sydonnia in his jaw once more. There was a crunching of bone and an ear-piercing wail that reverberated throughout the basement.

Once more the two circled one another, each one sporting a multitude of battle wounds. However, as Sirion continued to look at Sydonnia, he noticed the other man beginning to heal. By the gods, Sydonnia was regenerating. He had seen it in other lycanthropes, but had not expected to see it from Sydonnia so soon. He definitely was in a class by himself, far exceeding the abilities of the other individuals with the same curse. Then, before Sirion's eyes, Sydonnia disappeared into some shadows. Sirion cursed and panicked. He did what an amateur would have done . . . he stepped into the light.

Sirion saw Sydonnia too late. Sydonnia emerged out of the shadows, grabbed Sirion by the tunic, and threw him into a pillar. It was a supporting structure, and it cracked under the force of Sirion's body being applied to it. Sirion then fell heavily to the floor, holding his ribs. He knew some of them were broken. He could feel them pressing against his lungs with every breath he took.

Sirion continued to lie there as Sydonnia came at him once more, picking him up from the floor and slamming him into yet another supporting pillar. Time seemed to pass in slow motion. Somehow, Sirion had been able to retain his grip on one of his blades. He found the energy to raise it and strike. The blade passed up through Sydonnia's ribs and into his chest, piercing his heart. Sydonnia slumped upon the blade and the cracked pillars holding up the ceiling above began to crumble. Sirion also fell to the ground, the pillar he had been slammed against falling on top of him. It protected him from the rest of the ceiling as it came tumbling down upon him. Sirion's last thoughts were of Adrianna as he was stuck by a large stone and knocked unconscious. He hoped she was well and he was sorry that he would be unable to return to her.

***

Dramati began to slow his pace, until finally he was at a slow walk. Stealthily, he moved through the trees, his eyes and ears alert for any signs of danger. They were close; Adrianna could feel it. Dawn had begun to break and light was beginning to suffuse the landscape. Adrianna signed for Dramati to stop. He crouched to the ground to allow her to slide off of his back. Then she stepped in front of him. He regarded her steadily from amber eyes. She took his face in her hands and spoke to him. "Dramati, stay here. Wait for Sirion and I to return for you." Adrianna knew that a corubis could be a great companion to have at one's side in dangerous circumstances, but she knew that his fight with the shirwemic had wounded him and she had a feeling that he did not have the strength to endure another such encounter.

Adrianna continued alone through the trees. After only walking a few feet, she reached a clearing. Before her was a series of dilapidated buildings. Once, it may have been some type of fort or outpost, but now it was just an old ruin. Adrianna continued to move with caution. She could see that the place was occupied, there being several men moving about the area in and about the ruins. Some of them were in humanoid form while others were in hybrid form. She knew that there were probably even more of the lycanthropes moving around in the forest surrounding the outpost.

Adrianna stopped for a moment, pondering what move she should make next. She knew that Sirion was inside the ruins, probably in the largest building. There was a rather large clearing between her and the ruins now, but perhaps if she kept to the trees until she reached the rear of the building, she would be able to get inside undetected. That would be a trial all in itself, she knew. The forest was probably swarming with lycanthropes.

Adrianna moved as quietly as she could through the trees. The world continued to become lighter with the rising of the sun. It was a longer walk than she thought it would be and she began to make haste. She had to stop a few times to avoid detection, hoping each time that the slight breeze carried her scent away from the lycanthropes. Then she was there, at the rear of the largest building. No one appeared to be in the vicinity. She cursorily glanced around, but upon first inspection she did not see a way of gaining entry. Then she stepped up to the building and began to walk slowly along its length. Maybe there was a concealed door somewhere. Using her faelin-sight, she carefully searched the stone wall until finally her labors paid off. Grinning to herself in satisfaction, she stepped behind the flora growing in front of the hidden doorway and then slipped into the narrow space between two walls of stone. It was the fortification for a military fort.

Adrianna quickly made her way into the fortress proper. As she stepped into the main chamber she heard a huge crash, and the floor beneath her feet vibrated. She hurried into the room and then stopped to look at what lay before her. The place was in absolute chaos. All around there were shards of pottery, glass, and wood. Tables and chairs lay overturned. In the center of the room there was a large hole in the floor. It was the culprit of the thunderous sound that she had heard. Beginning to cast her spell, Adrianna began to walk slowly towards the collapsed flooring. Dust rose from the open maw. She completed her casting and ate a dried spider from her pouch. She felt the change in her body immediately. She would be at least a little safer, now that she had the ability to climb the walls, floors and ceilings with the agility of one of the creatures she had eaten. It was a *Spider Climb* spell, and she thought that it just might serve her well in a situation such as this.

Adrianna removed her boots, tied the laces together, and slung them over her right shoulder. She carefully walked up near the rift and then crouched, steadying herself with her hands. She continued thusly to the edge and then looked into the opening. Through the dust and darkness she could see nothing. Suddenly, she heard movement to her right. Her head snapped up. In the near distance a woman walked towards her. It was the woman Joselyn.

Adrianna remained crouched at the large cavity. She tensed, wanting so much to hurry down into the basement, knowing that Sirion was down there and that he needed her. She did not want to deal with this woman, but dared not take her eyes off of her in order to make her way down into the hole. The woman finally stopped a few feet from Adrianna, regarding her intensely. Then she looked down into the cavern herself. Adrianna took the opportunity to get her bearings and then began to carefully make her way over the edge and down into the hole.

"Please wait." Joselyn rushed over to her. "Please take me with you. I can help."

Adrianna paused, regarded Joselyn briefly. She didn't have time for this. How Joselyn would be able to help was beyond her, unless she had some healing skills. Adrianna suddenly wished that she were a mindreader, so that she knew if the other woman was sincere. "I don't know how far the drop is."

"Can you carry me?"

Adrianna raised an eyebrow. "As far as I can see it, you are larger than I. You might take me right off of the wall."

"Couldn't you just try? Please?"

Adrianna sighed heavily. She was so gullible. Joselyn just looked so desperate and pitiful, she couldn't help but want to aid her. But Adrianna was nervous. She could very well fall with the added weight of Joselyn on her back. "Fine. Come on."

Joselyn climbed onto Adrianna's back and Adrianna slowly began her descent. Adrianna stifled a moan as she progressed, wishing she had never agreed to this insanity. A couple of times she almost slipped. Joselyn at least had mind enough to put her own hand onto the wall to steady them. About three-quarters of the way down however, Adrianna could hold them no longer. She wished that she had cast her *Featherweight* spell as she fell. Within moments, both of them hit the floor. Unfortunately, Adrianna caught the brunt of the impact. Joselyn rolled away from her when they landed, helping at least to remove the possibility of crushing Adrianna under her weight.

Adrianna stood slowly. She kicked at the rocks she had landed on, cursing to herself. Her head throbbed, and when she brought her hand away, it was covered in blood. Joselyn rushed passed her and Adrianna followed. The two women made their way over to a pile of rubble a short distance away. They searched among the debris, but much of it was large, much too large for women of their stature to lift. Adrianna heard a low moan. She turned toward it and caught a glimpse of shining metal between two large stone fragments. "Sirion!" Adrianna cried his name as she knelt at the rocks, scrabbling to move them. She only succeeded in moving a couple of the small ones, before she lashed out at one of the larger ones, cracking her knuckles against it.

Adrianna put her face in her hands. She breathed heavily and began to feel the wetness of her tears in her palms. Sirion would die beneath these rocks; they were much too heavy for him to be able to survive for long. She attempted to calm herself, tried to think rationally. She wished only that the stones were lighter. Then she stopped. Lighter. She had the means with which to do just that, make the stones lighter. Adrianna calmed herself, relaxed her body. She beckoned the magic to come to her as she cast the *Featherweight* spell. She was so glad that she had not used it before; this was a much better use to which she was putting the spell.

Adrianna placed her hands above the rocks and debris. Briefly they glowed pale amber. Then she began to remove the rocks. Before she knew it, Joselyn was at her side. Adrianna looked up at her briefly before turning her attention back to the rocks before her. Joselyn worked on some a few inches away. Finally she reached him, removing the rock from atop the remains of a pillar. Beneath the pillar lay Sirion. "Sirion." She spoke his name as she leaned over the pillar, putting her hand in the hollow beneath it where Sirion lay, touching his hand.

He stirred and moaned. His eyelids fluttered open. "Adria . . . Adrianna. You . . . must go . . . dangerous here." He struggled to speak and she knew that it must be painful for him.

"Sirion," her voice cracked. "I am here to help you."

"Adria . . . please . . ." Sirion stopped, his eyes focusing on something behind her. Adrianna turned to find Joselyn there beside her.

Joselyn shouldered past Adrianna and knelt at the fallen pillar. "Sirion, let me help you. You know that I can. Here, let me just move this last stone . . ."

Adrianna looked from Joselyn to Sirion, and then back to Joselyn again. Sirion raised no objection. Adrianna realized what was beginning to transpire. Joselyn had used Adrianna to get to Sirion, and now she would attempt to take advantage of the situation, to have things the way she wanted them: in particular, Sirion by her side. That possible reality bothered her, but now was not the time to be concerned about such things. She started to help Joselyn get Sirion out of the hollow, when she felt someone watching her.

A chill crept up Adrianna's spine. She looked down at the debris all around her, at the disturbed area over Sirion and another one not even a foot away, at his feet right next to her. She saw the shiny dark metal of one of Stalker's blades, and then the hilt of the other, buried into a leather vest. Her eyes traveled up the vest and into the hideous leering face of Sydonnia. Quick as lightening, before she could even think about moving out of his way, one of his massive hands grabbed her wrist.

Adrianna screamed as she found herself pulled down on top of Sydonnia. The stench of blood was overpowering. She struggled against him, hit at him with her free hand. Sydonnia slowly brought himself into an upright position. He twisted her arm, ending her assault against him. He pulled her back against his chest, put his face to the crook of her neck, and inhaled the scent of her. Adrianna squeezed her eyes shut, blocking out the unfolding scenario.

Sirion heard Adrianna shout, saw her disappear within the pile of rubble all around him. He begged his body to move as he pulled himself from beneath the pillar. His sides screamed in protest, and his head felt as though it would fall off of his neck. Then Joselyn was there beside him, helping him out of the hollow the pillar had created for him when it fell. He crouched there for a moment, watching Sydonnia. The man held Adrianna next to him and he was laughing, saying something to her. She was limp in his arms and Sirion felt a rush of fear course through him. What had he done? Then he saw movement, saw her sides ripple, as though she held back her emotion.

Sirion saw the hilt of one of his blades protruding from Sydonnia's upper abdomen. How the man was able to move and function so well after a blow such as the one Sirion had delivered was a mystery to him. Such a strike would have been fatal to any other man, maybe even any other lycanthrope. But Sydonnia was different, his will to live strong. Or perhaps it was the will of the curse, seeking to keep his body alive? Sirion did not know, did not wish to contemplate it as he searched for his other blade in the debris. Locating it, he struggled into a standing position with Joselyn at his side, supporting him. His eyes riveted upon his weapon, he pushed her from him and began to make his way over to it.

Joselyn grunted as she lost her footing and fell. Cursing under his breath, Sirion quickly turned towards Sydonnia to find his uncle's gaze now riveted upon him. "Ah, Sirion. You have proven to be tougher than I thought you were. But now I have something you may want." Sydonnia took a fistful of Adrianna's hair and jerked her head back on her neck. She made no sound, but he saw her dig her nails into the leather of Sydonnia's vest. Her eyes were tightly closed.

Sirion heard Joselyn regain her feet. Damn her. Damn them both. What had possessed them to come down here, and how did Adrianna get to the bunker in the first place? Before any of this had ever started he had told the group to stay out of his fight with his uncle. But here she was, being used against him as a pawn in this game that Sydonnia was playing with him.

Sirion thought quickly. Adrianna's life would depend on it. He began to speak, sought to keep Sydonnia occupied while he slowly continued to make his way to his blade. Sirion was banking on the thought that Sydonnia did not know that the other blade lay in a shallow depression in the rocks not far from Sirion. Sirion kept his body moving, swaying back and forth, making it appear that he was weak, that it was difficult to keep his position in one place. Much to his disgruntlement, it was not too far from the truth.

"Sydonnia, why don't you let her go? She has nothing to do with this."

"She has everything to do with this," Sydonnia spat. "I will make you suffer the way Servial has made me suffer all of these years."

"But I am not Servial. Servial is dead. You killed him. If you wanted to torment someone, why did you not torture my father when you had the chance?"

"I was too angry to toy with Servial then. All I wanted was his blood. And now, you are the closest thing to Servial that I have left. His blood runs through your veins. I wish to take that away from him, even in death. He will have left nothing of himself behind in the world to show that he ever existed."

"But what about Anya? I do have a sister, you know."

"I will hunt her down and kill her. It will be effortless. She will be easy to dispatch."

Sirion shook his head. He was close to the blade now, so close. "It seems you have everything figured out."

"I have had many years to think about it."

"But you have forgotten one thing."

"I much doubt that, Nephew. I rarely leave anything out."

"My son. I have a son. Servial will live on through him."

Sydonnia's eyes narrowed. His grip on Adrianna tightened. "You lie. You have no offspring."

"No, Sydonnia. You are wrong. There is a period in time in which you did not know of my whereabouts. Is that not true?"

Sydonnia grimaced disdainfully. "That may be true, but I happen to know that you have no son."

Sirion cocked his head to the side. "So sure of yourself. There was a woman. I did not know her long. I lay with her, and recently I discovered that she has borne me a son. Too bad you do not know where she is. Your plans are moot, Sydonnia. I do have a successor to my bloodline. Servial will live forever."

Sydonnia's face suffused with anger. "Liar . . . liar! I will kill you once and for all . . . kill her." Sydonnia lifted Adrianna from the ground, much as he had picked up Sirion earlier, by one arm and one leg. Sirion swiftly crouched to retrieve his weapon. The hilt vibrated in his hand, the weapon wanting to taste Sydonnia's blood as much as Sirion wanted to spill it. Sydonnia lifted Adrianna above his head. With sickening clarity, Sirion knew that Sydonnia meant to crush her against the rocks strewn all around them. Sirion sprinted towards his uncle, and when he reached him, Sirion barreled into the other man. His right shoulder bore most of the impact, and his already bruised and battered body screamed at the abuse. His blade entered Sydonnia's lower gut and Sirion twisted it inside of him as they fell.

Sydonnia screamed in agony as he fell onto his back. Adrianna was flung backwards. She hit the floor heavily, fortunately avoiding most of the rocks. She sought to right herself and hissed when she put her weight onto her left hand. The wrist was broken, she was sure. She returned her attention to Sirion and Sydonnia. They lay in a heap on the rocks. They seemed to move in slow motion, their bodies straining after so much illtreatment.

Sirion pulled his blade free of Sydonnia as he struggled to rise from the rocks. Sydonnia brought himself into an upright position and before Sirion knew to react, Sydonnia had lobbed a sharp rock towards Sirion's head. Joselyn screamed as the stone fragment struck Sirion in the upper arm. Sirion went down once more.

Adrianna began to stumble towards the scene when she heard shouts from above. She looked up at the breach in the ceiling, noticing dust and small rocks falling from above. Nervously, she glanced all around her. The ceiling was going to collapse, the whole ceiling. The structural integrity of the place had been violated when the supporting pillars had been destroyed. Adrianna cupped her hands around her mouth. "Get out. Get out of the building. The ceiling is going to cave in!"

Sydonnia stumbled towards the fallen Sirion. Joselyn followed him, desperately pleading with him to spare Sirion's life. Sydonnia swung at her angrily and she fell. She stay where she landed, moaning and sobbing piteously. Sydonnia stood over Sirion and then crouched. His nephew appeared to be dead. His skin was pale and he could not see the breaths that indicated life. Sydonnia opened his mouth and lunged for Sirion's throat.

Sirion waited. He felt the rocks beneath him shift as Sydonnia crouched over him. Sirion tightened his grip on the hilt of Stalker, biding his time, waiting for just the right moment. And then it came. As Sydonnia lowered his head, Sirion mustered what strength was left in him and swung Stalker up from the ground in an arc. The blade swiped across Sydonnia's neck, beneath his head. Sydonnia continued to come at his throat, his mouth open wide. Sirion had just enough energy to move his head to the side as Sydonnia's landed on top of him. As the head rolled away, the blood of the severed neck poured over Sirion, onto his face, neck, and chest. Sirion strained to breathe with the weight of Sydonnia's body on top of him, and weakly tried to push the body off.

Sirion's consciousness began to waver. In the near distance, Sirion heard Adrianna's voice . . . something about the building collapsing. And then she was there, tugging at Sydonnia's headless corpse. In vain she attempted to move the body . . . to no avail. Tears began to stream down her cheeks, and her face grimaced in pain. Suddenly, others were there, and Dinim and Sabian removed the body of Sydonnia. Sabian knelt to help Sirion up, while Dinim led Adrianna away. Joselyn threw herself over Sydonnia's corpse, wailing uncontrollably.

Sirion tried to clear his head, attempted to focus. He thought he saw dust and grit falling from above. He shook his head, sought to clear his vision, but it was still there. Sirion saw several rangers, saw one retrieve his blades and another try to get a hold of Joselyn. She lashed out at him and he retreated, shaking his head. He left her at the body, rushing ahead with the others. Sabian urged Sirion to follow him, his voice urgently insistent. The two made their way through the main chamber and into a passageway. After a few moments, Sirion began to hear a low rumble in the distance behind them and Sabian began to move even faster, urging Sirion onward.

Sirion and Sabian entered another chamber. They saw the exit passageway in the wall of the basement and saw the others enter. Sirion struggled to move himself, his body being dragged in part by Sabian. A ranger up ahead saw them struggling and ran back to them. He took Sirion's other side and the two men levitated him from the ground and carried him towards the passage. All of a sudden, in the distance behind them, there was a shout. Sirion's heart skipped a beat. It was Joselyn. "Wait . . . wait. It's Joselyn." Sirion struggled to be set down.

Sabian and the other man fought against him. "Sirion . . . no. The building is coming down. We can't stop now." The rumble intensified and the rocks rained hard on them. The dust began to clog their nostrils and they began to cough. Despite Sirion's protestations, the men carried him into the waiting passage, away from Joselyn's shouts for them to wait for her. Just as they entered it, the ceiling in the chamber came crashing down. The impact knocked them down and the rocks and debris blocked the entrance to the passageway. The torches went out and the passage was thrown into darkness.

Sirion lay in the dark passage, his breath labored. Joselyn was gone . . . gone forever, buried beneath the ruins of the old outpost. She had called out for him to help her and he had not come. His chest constricted with emotion. She was dead. She had failed him in every way imaginable to him. But he had failed her as well. Sirion's mind began to spiral away and he lost consciousness.

***

Adrianna looked down at the form of Sheridana beneath the covers. Finally she slept peacefully, the fever and fits of frenzy having passed. She had not succumbed to the disease, and would now begin to recover. Tiredly, Adrianna stood from her bedside vigil, sweeping the damp hair from Sheri's brow. She needed her own rest, having stayed at Sheri's side for almost two nights now. She had been so worried that the fever would kill her sister, but the warrior within her had persevered. She had also been worried about another warrior, one who lay several bridges away within his own chamber. Sirion had suffered many injuries from his battle with Sydonnia. Adrianna had gone to him to be sure that all was well with him, but he had not seemed to care for her company. So she had left him alone and had not returned to him since.

Adrianna left Sheri's alcove and began to walk across the bridges that lead to her own. Halfway there, Dinim stepped from an adjoining conduit onto the pass that she was taking. She smiled wanly as he fell into step beside her. "I assume Sheridana is doing well. Otherwise I would not be seeing you here," he said.

Adrianna nodded. "She is doing much better. They say that she will recover quickly now that the fever and convulsions have ended."

Dinim regarded Adrianna intently. He could easily see that she was exhausted. He had offered to sit with her sister so that she could rest, but she had refused. He had tried to help her in other ways, by bringing her hot meals and companionship. But she had eaten little and had spoken even less. He knew that something was wrong . . . more than just worry over her sister. He could only guess as to what the problem might be, and his mind kept returning to one person. "Have you been to see Sirion?"

"Not since yesterday morning. How is he doing?"

"Good. The healer says that he should be ready to travel in no time."

Adrianna nodded. Dinim noticed the tension around her mouth and frowned. So Sirion was the cause of her distress. This fact bothered him, but he tried not to let it get to him too much. What possibly could have happened between them that would cause her to be upset? Actually, they hardly knew one another, aside from the time that Sirion was Cortath . . . But he did know that there was definitely something between them, some type of attraction that he could not really understand. Perhaps it was only this that was bothering Adrianna, but somehow he knew that it was definitely more.

Adrianna arrived at the entrance to her alcove and pushed open the small door. She turned to Dinim as she entered. "Let me know if Sheri needs me?"

Dinim nodded. "Don't worry. She will be fine."

Adrianna backed into the alcove and closed the door behind her. She went over to the bed and lay down. For quite some time she lay there, re-thinking the confrontation with Sydonnia. What would have happened if she had not been there? Would Sirion have died beneath the pile of debris under which he had been trapped before she freed him? Or would he have somehow found a way to escape? She knew that she should never have taken Joselyn with her beneath the fort; the woman would still be alive if Adrianna had refused her.

Tears sprang to her eyes. She knew that Joselyn's death weighed heavily upon Sirion, and he was probably blaming himself. A part of her wished that she had never interfered, but the other more rational part of her knew that he probably would have perished beneath the stones if she had not intervened. She could not help but be afraid that a part of Sirion was holding her accountable for Joselyn's death, and wished that she knew how to make things better. But she knew that the only thing that could heal Sirion's heart was to turn back time, and that was a power beyond her ability to perform.

4 Cisceren CY593

The group traveled east through the realm of Elvandahar in the direction of the domain of Filopar. Tomorrow they would reach Reshik-na, and they would meet up with Tianna and Armond. The day before, a message had been sent to them via Dramati, and the corubis had returned this morning with a reply that everything was fine and that Tianna and Armond would be ready to meet them the next day.

Sheridana lagged disconsolately behind the rest of the group, her thoughts upon the child she had left behind over three days ago. After the fever passed, Sheridana had recovered from her illness rather quickly, and had spent as much time with Carli and Fitanni as possible. But she knew that it wouldn't be enough . . . knew that no matter how much time she spent it would never be enough. Sheri could still hear the cries of her daughter as Fitanni cried out for her, wanting her Ama to stay with her. Her heart ached to hold her baby close to her and never let her go, and she could feel her tears as they swept down her face. She had promised Carli to return as soon as her duty was done, and bid the young woman to care for Fitanni like she was her own daughter. Sobbing piteously, Carli had embraced her. Sheri held the young woman close to her, the baby between them, fighting the rush of emotion that surged through her own body. She kissed Carli and Fitanni, then turned and walked away.

Sheridana sniffed again, wiping the back of her hand across her face for the hundredth time since she had left the Sherkari Fortress. She hadn't wanted to leave, but knew that Adrianna needed her. They needed to face their father together, and put an end to the abomination that he had become. Already so many innocent people had been killed, and Sheri knew that she would not be able to live with the deaths of countless others over her head if she did nothing to stop Thane. Sheri turned her head to regard her sister. Adrianna also appeared to be in a state of melancholy. Sheri knew that part of that was for the same reason as her own depression, but also knew that there was something more. Sheri knew who that 'more' concerned, yet said nothing. That was for Adrianna and Sirion to work out in their own time.

Walking beside Sheri, Adrianna noticed her sister watching her out of the corner of her eye. Adria sighed to herself. She knew that she most look a bit on the pathetic side, yet she could not snap herself out of the despondency that was weighing upon her. Sirion was constantly in her thoughts, and she wished that her mind would stop pondering him so intently. She tried not to let his disinterest in her bother her, yet she seemed unable to shake her disappointment. She had hoped that, given a few days, he would begin to recover from his loss and begin interacting with her normally again, but as of yet, that had not happened. He had not re-started their sparring sessions, rarely spoke to her, and could hardly seem to even look at her. To his credit, Sirion did not speak much to anyone, and spent much of his time scouting ahead of the group, thus minimizing his contact with everyone in general. However, his avoidance of Adrianna had been noted, although not yet commented upon.

That evening the group sat around the fire, silently partaking of their meal. The evenings had begun to get a bit cooler and Adrianna found that she was glad that the heat of summer was beginning to abate. By mid-day tomorrow they would reach Reshik-na and the group would be complete once more. Adrianna was looking forward to seeing her friend again, yet not. She felt more than just a little guilty about her feelings concerning Sirion, especially since she had led Tianna to believe that there was nothing for her to worry about. Adrianna could not entirely blame herself because at the time, she had not known her feelings herself. However, she had not hurried to let Tianna know the truth either. The few days following that passionate interlude with Sirion had left her slightly dazed and very confused. She had been in no state to tell Tianna anything, and by the time she had gathered her wits, Tianna was gone.

Now several days had passed by, and so many things had changed. Sirion could hardly stand to be near her, and she found herself fighting to keep him out of her mind. Despite their attraction for one another and the camaraderie that they had shared before the battle with Sydonnia, any relationship between them seemed to be misbegotten. They couldn't even seem to sustain the tenuous friendship that had begun to form between them, their more primitive emotions getting in the way of that and making it uncomfortable for them to be near one another. And now, it seemed that Sirion felt nothing but dislike, his attitude towards her aloof and maybe even cold. It reminded Adria of the man she had met in Sangrilak all of those months ago, when she had first arrived home after her apprenticeship in Andahye.

Adrianna lay down on her bedroll and stared across the fire. On the other side she could see Sirion, his back turned towards the fire. Unheeded, the tears found their way down her cheek to wet the blankets beneath. Despite the turn of events, her feelings for him remained unchanged. After a while Tianna would be able to see that. Adrianna could only hope that Tianna would not ask Adrianna what Sirion meant to her again. Perhaps Tianna would finally be able to win Sirion to her side, and he would become the husband that she wanted him to be. Adrianna could not begin to contemplate how that would make her feel, how it break her heart. But she would try not to let it interfere with her responsibilities, and when the time came, she would leave, and hopefully never see Sirion Timberlyn again.

***

Just as planned, the group reached Reshik-na by mid-day. Armond and Tianna had their travel packs ready when they arrived, prepared to leave as soon as possible. But Father Domick, the man Tianna called 'father', had other plans, inviting the group into his home for supper. Not wanting to pass up a freshly cooked meal, Dartanyen accepted the invitation on their behalf, and the group heartily ate fowl, beans, fruits, and sweetmeats. Afterwards, they talked for a short time over some mead while the remainder of the meal was packed away for them to eat on the rest of their journey through Elvandahar.

Tianna and Armond had arrived in Reshik-na several days after the druids had been attacked by a contingent of lycan. Many of the Order had been severely injured. None had succumbed to the disease, but a few had perished. When Tianna arrived, she was able to offer many skills that the druids did not have at their disposal. She was able to save many that could have suffered permanent disability or even death. Some she was unable to save from permanent impairment, but none died beneath her tender ministrations. After she healed the wounds of Father Domick he bade her stay with them, telling her that someone with her skill would be especially appreciated in the Order. But Tianna refused him, telling him that her destiny lay elsewhere.

So Tianna left the domain of Filopar with the ranger Sirion and the group with which he traveled. Father Domick had pled with Sirion to change Tianna's mind, he knowing that it was for the young handsome ranger that she left. But Sirion told Father Domick that the decision was wholly up to Tianna, and that he would say nothing to try to alter her intentions. In his heart Sirion knew that Tianna could never stay with the druids, knew that it was not the life for her. The restrictive nature of the Order would eventually be too much for the young woman, and her spirit would stagnate.

For two more days the group traveled east through Elvandahar. Once they reached the outskirts of the realm, they knew that the Terrestra River would only be a single day's journey more to the east. It was strange to be out in the open, without the protective canopy of the trees above them. Adrianna found that she missed it, and wondered if she would ever find a reason to return to Elvandahar one day. Once they crossed the river, the group would journey north to the city of Entsy. There they would be able to stock up on food and supplies, and maybe even purchase some larian with the gold that Thalios and Lilandria had given them for their efforts concerning the lycanthrope menace.

Happy to be back with the group, Tianna gaily spoke of her accomplishments healing her family and friends, and mildly boasted of how far she had come in her skills since she had seen them last. Dartanyen congratulated her on a job well done, and she beamed with the praise. It took her almost into the evening of the first day to realize that Sirion was not walking with the rest of the group. She looked around for him, and then realized that he was probably scouting ahead. It was only when they finally found a place to set up the evening camp that Sirion returned to the group. It took Tianna very little time to realize Sirion's withdrawn state, and she began to wonder what had happened during her time away from the group.

As the group sat around the evening fire, Tianna heard about Adrianna and Sirion's capture by Sydonnia, the battle with the lycan, and Adrianna's subsequent escape with the help of Dinim and Sheridana. Dinim told the story as well as any bard, leaving out none of the details. He told of Adrianna leaving the safety of the group in the middle of the night upon the back of Dramati, and Sirion's rescue by her and Joselyn. He left nothing out, ending the story with the battle with the lycan outside of the bunker and the final collapse of the structure, with Sirion and Sabian just barely making it into the escape tunnel before the ceiling caved in on them.

Avidly, Tianna listened to the tale. Adrianna's actions did not go unnoticed by her, and she even saw Dinim casting her friend a glance or two as he recounted the story. His expression had been one borne of mixed emotions, and Tianna was unable to understand the meaning behind the glances. However, Adrianna's expression was unreadable, she barely even seeming to take notice of the story being told. Sirion's face also bore an unreadable expression, his attention apparently absorbed by the weapon he was busy cleaning in his lap. Tianna felt theirs to be strange reactions to an account that was being told primarily about them, and she wondered what else was going on, what had not been said in the tale . . . unknown by the storyteller.

After crossing the Terrestra River, the group traveled north. Day by day the climate became cooler, the need for long sleeved tunics and thicker cloaks becoming quickly apparent. The nights were becoming all the more difficult, they having not the thicker blankets they would need in order to travel at this time of the year. Blankets and clothes would be only a couple of the things that they would need to purchase once they reached Entsy. They passed villages along the way, but the people tended to be wary of travelers in general, especially those in mixed company such as themselves. The sight of humans and faelin traveling together was a rare sight, one that many people never got the opportunity to see. So the group simply passed the villages by, not even bothering to ask if there was an inn.

The group only had to travel another two days before they reached the city of Entsy. Along the way Tianna silently watched Sirion and Adrianna. There seemed to be no indication of anything at all forming between them like she had thought there might be before she left to go to Reshik-na. This discovery heartened her. Perhaps she would make one last play for Sirion after all. She would forget her innuendos and feminine enticements and finally be straightforward with him, finally tell Sirion how she felt about him.

Once in the city the group immediately sought out an inn and paid for their rooms. They made sure that they chose a decent one, knowing that they would be spending at least two or three nights there. Having arrived at midday, they situated themselves in their respective rooms, ate a small meal, and then left the Golden Griffon Inn and went out in search of supplies. Adrianna followed obligingly behind the rest of the group. She did not have a particular destination in mind, and thus went where everyone else led her. As they made their way through the streets, Adrianna felt the strange sensation of someone watching her. Satisfying the urge, she glanced about for a moment. Seeing no one out of the ordinary, she returned her attention to the group and hurried to catch up with them.

***

The small group of travelers walked through the streets of Entsy. They knew that the other group was here, for Anya had tracked them all the way from the Terrestra River. Until now, they had been unable to catch up with them and all they needed to do now was find a way of catching them unawares. They knew that the city was not the best place to have a fight, but they did not want to wait until the group wrecked another inn, killed another man, or laid waste to another field.

Triath looked around at his companions. They all looked weary, too weary. Once more, he caught himself looking around for the others, others that were no longer there. Seeing none of them, he mentally berated himself. Arn, Laura, Breesa and Sirion were all dead, and Dinim had been untraceable. They really could have used the sorcerer's help, but Triath had not been able to locate him. Actually, he had been loathe to contact the others, knowing that they all wanted, no *needed* to get on with their lives. But they had unfinished business that Triath could not manage alone. The acts of their doubles had become more and more deadly, and were beginning to cause extensive damages to the cities and villages of the realm.

Triath had sent messages to his last remaining companions: Anya, Sorn, Naemmious, and Dinim. All had responded except for Dinim. Anya had been the farthest away, she having gone back to Elvandahar as soon as the battle with Gaknar and Tharizdune was over. Sorn and Triath had returned to Sangrilak, their city of origin, and Naemmious had gone into the hills west of the southern tip of the Ratik Mountain Range. All agreed that they needed to do something about the 'evil' Wildrunners, and so, for one last time, they found themselves in one another's company.

And now here they were, making their way through Entsy, wondering how they were going to defeat their enemy. They had barely survived the encounters before, and that was when they still had Sirion, Arn, and Laura with them. This weighed heavily on everyone's minds, but they sought to keep light hearted. They had always persevered before, and this time would be no different.

"Hey, how about this one?" said Sorn, stopping in front of the Silver Serpent Inn and Tavern.

"It looks good to me," said Anya, pulling her pack up on her shoulder and turning towards the establishment.

The foursome entered the building and procured two rooms for the night. They then settled down to discussing how they would find the group without being noticed themselves, and then how they would go about defeating their doubles. As the conversation wore on, Triath became more and more despondent. Perhaps they would have to wait for the group to leave the city and then try to catch them unawares in the middle of the night. But that sounded like a stupid idea, and he knew it. If only they had been able to find Dinim. If only they had Sirion.

CHAPTER 20

Tianna regarded Sirion across the table from her. He leaned back in his seat, his meal, barely touched, sitting in front of him. As usual, his expression was unreadable, but she got the impression that he was bored. For the past two days now she had been contemplating the moment she would approach him. However, Sirion had made it difficult, continuing to be distant and withdrawn. She knew that she could not approach him in his present state, and wondered how she could break the ice with him. Something was amiss with him, seriously so, and she was determined to find out what it was. She just had to find the right time . . .

Tianna allowed her gaze to travel from Sirion's face down to his chest. He had taken off his studded leather before dinner and she thus had a good view of his lean muscular shape beneath the light fabric of the sleeveless tunic. Tianna could not suppress the sigh that escaped her lips, imagining the feel of his arms around her, the contours of his chest beneath her palms, and the sensation of his mouth on hers. Tianna's gaze continued downwards until the table blocked her view. But she knew what was beneath it: his finely shaped legs encased within tight fitting trousers. Suddenly, the image before her eyes shifted. Tianna swung her gaze back up to Sirion's face to find him watching her. He raised a questioning eyebrow and Tianna felt her cheeks flush with embarrassment. Damn! She could only hope that her expression had given nothing of her thoughts away to him.

Suddenly, Armond sat bolt upright in his seat. He placed his hands on the table and sat there for a moment, saying nothing, an intent expression on his face. Then he turned around in his chair, facing the table behind him and the three human men that sat there. "Hey, what was that you just said?"

The man sitting immediately behind Armond turned around in his own seat. He looked at Armond questioningly before answering. "Just a rumor . . . I heard a tale about a horned warrior who has been wreaking havoc in the realm of Monaf."

The other conversations at their table stopped. Beside her, Tianna noticed Adrianna leaning forward in her seat. Sirion, also, had abandoned his relaxed position, and he too sat straight in his chair. Everyone's attention was riveted upon Armond and the man with which he spoke.

"Have you learned any details about this warrior?" asked Armond.

"They say that he is an abomination . . . no longer human . . . and that he travels with a group of men who are abominations themselves. The dark warrior and his band have leveled villages and ransacked towns. They have no mercy, killing indiscriminately."

"Does this warrior have a name?"

"Lord Thane." The man paused and then continued. "Rumor has it that he is searching for someone, and that he will not stop until he has found her."

Adrianna felt her breath catch in her throat. She knew whom the man was speaking about. Her father continued his search for her, killing anyone who was in his path. He was cutting a swathe of destruction as he made his way across the continent for her. She felt a pair of eyes on her and turned to find Sheri looking at her. Her sister's eyes were wide, a multitude of emotions manifesting themselves there: sadness, loathing, and fear.

"Where did you hear these rumors?" asked Armond.

"I started hearing the tales in the city of Driscol before I left to come here. The two towns that I passed through had also heard the rumors. They say that the dark warrior and his band have been making their way through Monaf."

Armond nodded. "Thanks for the information. We were thinking of going that way ourselves. Now we know to be careful."

The other man nodded and turned back around in his seat. Armond did the same, his expression serious as he focused on the group. His gaze sought out Adrianna and he regarded her intently for a moment before speaking. "It seems that we should not stay here overly long." He spoke quietly, his voice barely perceptible over the background noise of the inn.

"It seems that he has gone on a rampage," said Dartanyen. "Remember, he lost our trail south of Torrich. He probably was not very happy about that."

Adrianna saw Sheri's hands clench into fists. "We need to put an end to this."

"Don't worry, we will," said Dinim. "But we shouldn't rush into something that we don't have enough information about. Let's just focus on getting our supplies, and then on finding out as much as we can about Thane: his strengths, his weaknesses, where he gets his power, and how he formed his band. All of these answers will be integral in his defeat. If we don't know anything about Thane, he will surely kill us all."

Sirion nodded. "Dinim is right. We need to gather as much information on Thane as we can. But in the meantime, let's get some rest. In the morning we will restock our supplies and decide where we will go from here."

Almost in unison the group rose from their table. Everyone, with the exception of Armond and Dartanyen, left the common area and went up the stairs to their rooms. Adrianna looked all around her as they walked through the hall leading to the room she would be sharing with Sheri. This was a really nice inn. Instead of a tavern, the common area downstairs was referred to as a dining room. The hallways were wide, the floors clean, and the bedchambers spacious. On the way to their room she and Sheri passed a sitting room. It contained a fireplace, two tall shelves full of books, several cushioned chairs, and a large sofa. People could sit in front of the fire with a book before retiring to their beds for the night.

Once in their room, Adria and Sheridana were quick to get into their beds. Adrianna felt good to be able to have a bed to herself, and not have to share one with Tianna anymore. She was sure that her friend felt the same. Although, Adrianna was still a bit sorry that Tianna had to share her room with the grouchy Amethyst. Tiredly, Adrianna shook her head, turned onto her side, and closed her eyes.

***

Tianna slowly walked down the hall to the room she knew to be Sirion's. This was the only time that she would have to speak with him. She knew that, starting tomorrow, everyone would have all of their energies focused on Thane. She needed to know what was going on with Sirion before then, knew that she needed to get him out from behind the barrier of ice he had erected about himself.

Tianna knocked on the door, and immediately received a response. ""Who is it?"

"It's Tianna." Within moments the door was opened.

"What is it? Is something wrong?" Sirion's face bore an expression of mild concern, his eyes searching the hallway behind her.

"No, nothing is wrong."

Sirion furrowed his eyebrows. "What is it, then?"

"I just wanted to talk to you for a few minutes."

Sirion sighed. "Can't it wait until tomorrow?"

"Please?"

Sirion sighed again and opened the door wider. Tianna stepped into the room and he closed the door behind her. Sirion removed his travel pack from a red cushioned chair and gestured for her to sit. Tianna did so, and watched Sirion as he seated himself across from her on the bed.

For a moment there was silence. Tianna fought to collect her thoughts, suddenly forgetting how she had decided to angle the conversation. Patiently, Sirion waited, watching the woman in front of him. When he saw that she was not going to say anything, he sighed for a third time. "Tianna, what is this about? What do you need to talk about that can't wait until tomorrow?"

"It can't wait until tomorrow because you will be busy tomorrow."

"Tianna, I am always busy."

"You aren't right now."

"That is because I was about to go to bed."

Tianna made a sigh of her own. "Sirion, I need you to talk to me."

Sirion slapped his hands down on his thighs. "I am talking . . ."

"No. I mean really talk. You are holding something back and I want to know what it is. Since I have been back with the group I have noticed a change in you. You have become so distant . . . so withdrawn from everyone. I know that something happened during your battle with Sydonnia, and I want you to share it with me."

Sirion regarded Tianna intently, noticed the obstinate expression on her face, the rigid set of her shoulders. She meant to get him to talk to her, even if it meant a fight. If he still wasn't so upset about the events that had taken place during and after his fight with Sydonnia, he may have even cracked a small smile. She was a tough one, his Tianna, and he was glad to have her on his side.

"It was a bad fight," he said. Sirion saw Tianna relax her body and he continued. "I wanted to help my uncle but he would have none of it. We met in an abandoned fort and we fought there until the floor collapsed beneath us. I became trapped beneath the rubble. Joselyn and Adrianna dug me out."

Sirion paused in his recitation. Tianna waited patiently, knowing that it was hard for him to tell her the story. She knew that Adria had used a spell to release Sirion from his rocky prison, and could not help but feel grateful that her friend had been there.

"Somehow, Sydonnia gathered enough of his strength and he grabbed Adrianna. I had to focus whatever energy I had left on getting her away from him. Finally, he lay dead on top of me. I heard Adrianna shout something about the ceiling coming down. The rest of the group came, and we all ran to escape from the collapse. But somehow Joselyn got left behind. She called for me, and I wanted to go to her. But I didn't have the strength. We barely made it into the tunnel before the bunker collapsed."

Tianna looked at Sirion. His shoulders were slumped and he stared dejectedly at the floor. She moved herself from the chair to the spot beside Sirion on the bed. She put her arms around him and just held him for a moment. Sirion took her hand and held it, expressing his gratitude. When she finally pulled away from him she was glad to see that he had recovered from the painful memories the story had evoked.

"I can understand why you have been so upset, but Sirion, it wasn't your fault."

Sirion shook his head. "I failed her. She called for me, and I did not come."

"You were unable to come. You were severely injured, Sirion. I heard about the extent of your wounds. You cannot blame yourself."

"But I do, and I always will." Sirion looked up and into her eyes. "Somehow, I feel responsible for her death. Because of me, she lies beneath a pile of rock and debris."

Tianna shook her head. "No. That is not true."

"She came to me a few days before my confrontation with Sydonnia. She bade me to have her back by my side. I refused her. If only I had taken her back, this would have never happened."

"You don't know that. Perhaps fate would have taken her from you anyway."

Sirion shook his head. "Perhaps . . ."

"Besides, she made choices in her life, choices that did not involve you. Why would you drop everything in your life for her when you know that she would not have done the same for you?"

Sirion stared at Tianna for a moment before replying. "It seems you have become wise in your advanced years."

Tianna pressed her lips into a thin line. "Don't make fun of me, Sirion. I am serious."

"So am I."

Tianna sat back for a moment, contemplating the man before her speculatively. Perhaps he wasn't funning with her after all. Maybe he was finally realizing that she was not a child anymore, and he could begin to see her as a grown woman. Perhaps now was the time, the time to finally tell Sirion how she felt about him, had been feeling about him for so many years now. "Sirion, there is something that I must tell you."

Sirion continued to look at Tianna, noticed her expression change. She was different somehow, her eyes having taken on a new quality. Her hand still encased within his, Sirion felt her pulse increase, and noticed a glow begin to suffuse her. He heard her breaths begin to accelerate as well and Sirion wondered what it was that she needed to say that would make her react like this. "I am listening."

Tianna opened her mouth as though to speak, but then changed her mind. She would show him how she felt. Simple words would not be able to describe it. Suffused with passion and her desire to show Sirion how much she cared about him in the best way she knew how, Tianna felt her heart begin to race in her chest. She leaned into Sirion and she placed her lips to his.

Tianna felt Sirion begin to fall back and she followed him down onto the bed. The feel of his lips ignited a fire that swept through her body and down into her pelvis. The feel of him beneath her was euphoric, and she never wanted this moment to end. For so long she had longed for this moment; his response had been better than anything she ever could have dreamed.

Sirion lay beneath Tianna on the bed upon which they had been sitting just a moment before. His mind reeling with surprise, and no small amount of shock, he was slow to respond. It took a moment, but he finally got his mouth to move. Only a small sound made it out, something that may have sounded like a groan. Sirion started to move his arms into a position that would allow him the leverage to hoist his and Tianna's weight off of the bed when he noticed that someone else was in the room. It was Adrianna.

His arms around Tianna, Sirion sat upright on the bed. Noticing a change in Sirion's behavior, Tianna moved back. Questioningly, she turned in the direction in which he was staring and saw Adrianna and Dartanyen at the entrance to the room. Adrianna's face was pale, too pale. The other woman was shaking her head back and forth, and then was apologizing, "I'm sorry . . . didn't mean to intrude . . ." Then she was sweeping past Dartanyen and out of the room.

For a split moment silence reigned. "Sorry, Sirion. I didn't mean to interrupt. I didn't know that you two . . . well, you know . . ." Then Dartanyen just shook his head, turned, and left the room, closing the door behind him.

Sirion jumped off of the bed and turned towards the woman sitting on it. "Tianna, what has come over you? What possessed you to do that?"

Tianna shook her head. "I . . . I just wanted to tell you . . . to show you how I feel about you."

For a moment, all Sirion could do was stare at her. It suddenly all began to make sense . . . the way she watched him when she thought he wasn't looking, the conversations about the future, the change in the way she dressed, and even the way she had begun to move around him. Sirion swept his hands through his hair. "By the gods Tianna . . ." Then he stopped and just shook his head. "Just go."

Tianna stood slowly from the bed, tears in her eyes. Once more Sirion ran his fingers through his hair. Damn! He had made her cry. She slowly walked to the door, opened it, and left. Sirion just stood there, in the center of the room. He could not get the image of Adrianna's face out of his mind. The hurt . . . the pain he had seen reflected in her eyes. He had to find her, explain to her that there was nothing between himself and Tianna.

Sirion opened the door to the room and swept out into the hallway. He found himself being brought up short by the presence of Dartanyen. "Where did she go?"

Dartanyen pointed down the hall. "Tianna went to her room."

"No. I mean Adrianna. Where did Adrianna go?"

Dartanyen frowned. "I think she may have gone outside. I hope she comes back soon; within the hour it will begin to get dark."

Sirion nodded and then turned and went back into his room. If she had left the inn then he would need to get his leather and Stalker . . . just in case. By the time Sirion had made it out of the room again, Dartanyen was no longer standing outside. Sirion rushed down the hall and then down the stairs. At the bottom he met Dartanyen and Armond. "Do you want us to go with you?" asked Dartanyen.

"No, just leave it to me. I will bring her back in. Get some rest. We will have a long day tomorrow."

Dartanyen nodded as Sirion made his way to the front of the inn and out the door. He stopped once he was out on the veranda, wondering which way Adria may have gone. Frustrated, he sighed heavily, and finally chose to go right. He skipped down the steps and out into the street. He knew that he needed to hurry. The shadows would soon be lengthening with the approach of the dark.

***

Hearing the door to the room open, Amethyst turned from the window. She had just opened it so that she could get some fresh air, knowing that it would make her feel better, not to mention that she would have the perfect opportunity to spy on the two men talking out in the street below. Tianna swept into the room and fell onto one of the beds, sobbing hysterically. Surprised, all Amethyst could do was stand there for a moment, wondering what in the Nine Hells had happened to make Tianna so upset.

Amethyst walked across the room to the door, opened it, and looked up and down the corridor. A few doors down she saw Dartanyen and Sirion talking in the hall. She pulled herself back into the room but continued to keep the door open, hoping on being able to hear what they were saying. To her dismay, she heard a door close and thought that the men had probably gone back into their room. Then, unexpectedly, she heard footsteps coming in her direction. Amethyst quickly closed the door, being careful not to make any noise as she did so. She then waited for a few moments with her ear to the door, waiting for the person to pass by. Amethyst glanced over her shoulder at Tianna, who was still lying on the bed. The woman continued to cry with her face in a pillow, unnoticing of Amethyst standing at the door. After another couple of moments had passed by, Amethyst very slowly opened the door once more.

Amethyst poked her head out the door, looking back down the hall where she had seen Sirion and Dartanyen talking. She saw no one. She sighed almost imperceptibly, wishing that she knew what was going on. Suddenly, she heard a door open and she quickly pulled herself back into the room and closed the door until just a crack remained. She put her face to the crack and peered out. She saw Sirion rush by. Right after he passed, Amethyst opened the door slightly wider, just enough to see that he was going down the stairs. She darted out of the room and to the stairway. She pressed herself against the wall at the top of the stairs and listened. She heard Dartanyen's voice, and then Sirion's in reply, stating that he would bring someone back to the inn.

Amethyst heard the front door of the inn opening and she rushed back to her room. She swept into the chamber and over to the open window. Looking outside, she saw Sirion standing on the veranda, looking pensively up and down the road. She then saw him jump off of the veranda, heading east down the street. Glancing behind her at the woman on the bed, Amethyst saw that Tianna was turned away from her, her body and head covered by the blanket from the bed. Amethyst then slipped out of the window and onto the roof. Quickly getting her bearings, she crouched and swung herself off of the roof. For a moment she hung from the gutter and then dropped to the ground below.

Amethyst cushioned her fall, immediately going into a crouch when her feet touched the ground. Then she was up and running in the direction that Sirion had taken down the street. For a few minutes she sprinted to catch up, and it did not take her long to see him walking briskly down the street in front of her. Concerned that he may notice that he was being followed, she began to follow him more discreetly, widening the distance between them, and keeping herself close to the buildings.

For quite some time, Amethyst followed Sirion. It became less and less difficult for her to stick to the shadows as they grew with the coming night. But this was her element, and she felt at home in these darkening places, not feeling the reticence that most other people would be starting to feel at about this time in the evening. And Sirion was the same as most other people. She had noticed a hastening to his pace, and an increased focus upon his objective. She continued to wonder what that objective may be, and also what her curiosity was taking her towards. Only time would tell.

***

Adrianna walked briskly down the street. Night would be falling soon, but she did not care. She felt sick to her stomach, the muscles there tensing into knots. Her breath came in ragged gasps, her chest and throat so tight that it hurt. She had not realized how strongly she would react to seeing Tianna and Sirion together. It had come as a shock to her, not thinking that it would happen so soon. But now that the two had come together, Adrianna would have to find a way to deal with her feelings, at least until their work together was done. Once Thane was stopped, Sirion would go his own way, taking Tianna with him. Adrianna and Sheri would collect Fitanni and Carli from Elvandahar and make a new life together, as a family.

In the distance behind her Adrianna began to hear someone calling. She quickened her pace, not wanting anyone to catch up to her. She needed to be alone.

"Adrianna . . . Adrianna, please stop. We have to talk."

Damn. It was Sirion. He was the last person she wanted to see. There was nothing that he could say that would ease the hurt. Besides, she didn't want him to see her cry. Adrianna found herself quickening her pace even more, almost into a slow run. She glanced behind her and saw that he was rapidly closing the distance between them. She thought about trying to lose him in the alleyways, but then thought better of it. He would still find her. It would only prolong the inevitable. He would stop her and make her listen to him whether she wanted it or not.

Adrianna stopped and turned around in the street. It took Sirion only a few moments longer to catch up to her. She kept her face impassive, hoping to give nothing of her inner turmoil away to Sirion. "Adrianna . . . what you saw back at the inn . . . it isn't what you think."

Adrianna regarded him intently for a moment, fighting to keep her blank expression. He must surely think her a fool if he thought that she would believe that. She should not have bothered to stop. Adrianna turned away from him and continued down the street.

"Adrianna, you have to listen to me." Sirion matched his stride with hers. "Tianna came to me, claiming that she just wanted to talk. Before I knew it, she was on top of me. I swear . . . I had no idea that she had those types of feelings for me."

Adrianna continued to walk, taking in Sirion's words. Was it true? Maybe, but he had seemed so involved in his actions with Tianna. It was hard for her to believe that he had not been participating with equal intensity. Suddenly she felt his hand on her arm, urging her to stop.

"Adrianna, you have to know that I don't feel that way about her. I only have feelings for you."

Adrianna stopped and turned back to Sirion. She searched his face, finding only sincerity there. Ever since his battle with Sydonnia, she had been hoping that he would begin to talk to her again, continue the friendship they had started. Only in her dreams had she imagined that he would tell her that he cared about her. She felt the tears begin to pool in her eyes. Then he was closing the distance between them and wrapping his arms around her. Adrianna lay her head on his shoulder and allowed him to hold her, never wanting him to let her go.

For several moments Sirion and Adrianna remained in their embrace. She took in the feel of him, the scent of him. His smell was different than she remembered having sensed it before, and she thought that he must have used a different type of soap for his bath. He was silent as he held her, and she longed to hear his voice in her ear, murmuring to her the way he had that night at the fortress. His arms around her were warm and strong, yet they seemed unyielding somehow.

All of a sudden, Adrianna felt a prick in her upper arm. "Ahhh," she spoke as she pulled away from Sirion. "Something pinched me . . ." She put her hand to her arm and began to rub the area.

Sirion looked at her, a concerned expression on his face. "Are you all right?"

Unexpectedly, Adrianna felt herself begin to sway. She put her arms out to steady herself. Sirion gripped her shoulders and she put a palm to her forehead. "I . . . I feel so strange . . ." Sirion's face began to blur before her eyes. "Wha . . . what's happening to me?" She felt herself begin to fall, and then there was only blackness.

***

Sirion caught the woman as she fell into his arms. Grinning, he looked down into her face, her beauty almost taking his breath away. Then he looked back up at Sorn, who continued to hold the small dagger in his hand. He saw his friend smiling too, the import of what they were doing making them giddy. Picking her up, Sirion carried Adrianna into the nearest alleyway. Although the streets were nearly deserted, he did not want to take the chance of anyone seeing them. He was glad that the woman had chosen this path, it being in the Old Quarter and made up mostly of buildings dedicated to business and storage. As most of the tradesmen had gone to their homes for the evening, the place was virtually empty.

Sirion could still hardly believe what the day had brought him. He and Sorn had been rather shocked to see Sirion's double walking through the streets of Entsy. Rumor had led them to believe that he was dead. When they recovered from the initial surprise, they followed him and the group with which he was walking. Sirion experienced his second shock when he saw the woman Adrianna with the group. Remembering that his double had an inexplicable attraction to her, Sirion knew that he had to have her.

While Sirion returned to the rest of their group to tell them that his double was still alive and in the city, Sorn followed the group until they returned to the inn at which they were staying, The Golden Griffon. Via telepathic communication with Triath he was able to let Sirion know where he was, and after bathing and cropping his hair shorter to match that of his double, Sirion had rejoined his companion. Sorn had been able to discover the rooms in which the group was staying, and was spying on Adrianna and her sister as they prepared for the evening meal.

After that it was merely a waiting game. The plan was to wait until the women fell asleep for the night, and then to take Adrianna from her bed. However, Sirion received his third shock when Sorn reported to him that Adrianna had caught his double in a compromising situation with a woman that Sirion remembered was called Tianna. Sirion could not believe his good luck. Sorn beckoned him to hurry, telling him that the woman had fled the establishment. The two men followed Adrianna from a distance, waiting for the right time to approach her. When she entered the Old Quarter the men began to close the space between themselves and Adrianna.

When Sirion decided that he would begin to call out to her, he knew that she would probably increase her pace. This was not an issue for him, yet he was glad when the woman finally decided to stop and wait for him. She was making it so easy for him to approach her, and probably even easier for Sorn, who was keeping to the shadows behind him. When he began to speak to her, he chose his phrases carefully, but he was the most proud of himself when he told her that he 'had feelings only for her'. That was the defining moment, and Sorn had the perfect opportunity to prick Adrianna with his poison -tipped dagger when she allowed him to embrace her.

Sorn sheathed the dagger and gestured to Sirion that he would take Adrianna's other side. Together, the two of them carried Adrianna between them towards the inn at which they had been staying the past couple of nights. It would be easy for them to stick to the side streets, the inn not being very far away. As they walked, Sirion could not keep from smiling to himself. If he knew his double, the man would come searching for this woman as soon as he realized she was missing. He didn't know what the man was doing with the other woman, nor did he care, but he was a fool to let this one get away. With just one glance at her, he had found himself smitten by her beauty and knew that he would endeavor to keep her.

It wasn't long before the two men were approaching the Snorting Gorgon Inn. It was easy for them to get Adrianna to Sirion's room, the inn being only a single level. They passed her through the open window of Sirion's room, which happened to be located at the back of the establishment. Naemmious lay Adrianna down upon Sirion's bed and then left the room to find Triath.

Sirion silently stood over the bed, staring at the woman they had brought to it. He wanted her . . . could feel the tightening in his loins already. He had seen the effect she had on the other men in his company, and this insight only made him feel possessive. Even Sorn had looked upon her with ill-concealed lust. Upon hearing the door open, Sirion turned to see Triath, Anya, and Laura enter the room. Triath wore an expression of malicious glee on his face, even his black, soul-less eye appearing to have emotion. Laura grinned at him conspiratorially, and Anya just looked like she was bored.

"I had to come and see her for myself," said Triath. "It will only be a matter of time before your double realizes that we are here. When he comes for her, we will be ready. Without his companions to back him up, he will be easy to dispatch."

"But what of the sorcerer, Dinim? I saw him with this new group with which my double has aligned himself. The Dimensionalist is powerful . . ."

Triath's grin widened. "Don't worry about the magic-user. I will take care of him. Now, I will leave you to your . . . business. I am sure that you have much to orchestrate." Anya rolled her eyes in Sirion's direction and then glared at Triath. Then Laura stepped up to Sirion, pulling something out from within her robes. She handed him a bundle of sheer fabric, a brazen expression in her eyes, her lips curved up in a seductive smile. He immediately knew what it was and he felt his own mouth curve upwards.

"Tsk tsk. He will probably molest her before he gets it on her," said Anya scathingly.

Sirion heard Triath begin to snicker as he swung a contemptuous glance at his sister. "Fine, bitch. Why don't you put it on her?" he said, throwing the cloth at her.

Anya caught it and then tossed it to Laura. "Sorry, that is more like a chore for Laura. I might just kill her before I get it on her." Anya then turned and left the room, followed by a chortling Triath and a solemn Sorn. Once the door was closed behind them, Sirion turned to Laura. Comprehending the demand in his eyes, she began to make towards the bed.

***

Sirion walked down the darkening streets of Entsy, his mind a maelstrom of concern and confusion. Blast! Where was that woman? It was so hard to believe that things had worked out this way. And now she had gone and run off, to gods knew where . . . But Sirion knew it was his fault. If only he had paid more attention to Tianna, he would have realized her feelings for him. He then would have put a stop to things before they went too far. And now, here he was, tracking down Adrianna in the middle of the night. Well, not quite the middle of the night . . .

Sirion noticed a small group of people coming towards him from down the street. Quickly getting his thoughts under control, Sirion focused on the group. He thought about turning down one of the alleyways just in case they wanted trouble, but then thought better of it. The chances of that were slim, and not only that, he would be able to ask them if they had seen a woman fitting Adrianna's description this evening.

Sirion slowed down as the group came closer. There was something familiar about them . . . the way they walked, the way the woman wore her clothes, and the patch over one of the men's eyes. And then it hit him, and

Sirion almost felt his heart stop in his chest. These people were what remained of the Wildrunners. Sirion stopped in the street, watching them as they continued to approach. And then he saw Sorn take notice of him, and he put a hand on Triath's arm.

The Wildrunners stopped walking. Sorn said something, and Anya shook her head. Naemmious said something as well, and once more Anya shook her head. She then started to walk towards him. Sirion could not help but smile to himself. She knew it was him. Even though she knew he was dead, she also knew that it was him standing here in the middle of the street.

A few feet away from him, Anya stopped. Her eyes were wide as she said, "Sirion, is that you?"

Sirion closed the distance between them, and when he reached her, he took Anya in his arms, embracing her tightly. "It's me, Anya. It's really me. I survived the vortex . . ."

"By the gods!" Sirion heard the shaking in her voice. "I can't believe this is true! There have been so many times that I wished that this was so, and here you are . . ." Anya pulled back from him, tears running down her face. "Sirion, where in the Hells have you been?"

"It is a long story, and I would like to tell you about it, but I am looking for a friend of mine."

"Sirion, can it really be you?" Hearing Sorn's voice, Sirion turned towards the rest of his friends. The men embraced one another, each one expressing his joy upon seeing his comrade hale and whole. Everyone wanted to know how he had survived, and where he had been all of this time. Sirion only shook his head.

"Listen, I can talk all you want when I have found my friend. She is out here somewhere, and I need to find her before it gets too much later."

"Who is this woman and why is she roaming the streets alone at night?" asked Triath, raising an eyebrow.

Sirion sighed. "Her name is Adrianna. She is one of the members of the group I have been traveling with. She is of half-faelin descent, and has long blonde hair. She was wearing a green long-tunic and trousers when she left. Have you seen her?"

Everyone shook their heads. "Damn! Where could she be? I have been searching for at least two hours. I have a bad feeling . . ." Sirion stopped speaking when he noticed Sorn casting a pointed glance at Triath. "What? What is going on?" Sirion put his hands on his hips.

Triath sighed. "Steel yourself, Sirion. You are not going to like it. For several weeks now we have been on our last mission together. We have been tracking our doubles and we followed them into this city."

Sirion felt his eyes widen. "Are you telling me that our doubles are here? Now?"

"That is exactly what I am telling you."

Sirion shook his head. "This is bad. Upon first examination, Adrianna may not know the difference between my double and I. That would give him enough time to hurt her . . . or worse, take her somewhere. Do you know where they are staying?"

Sorn grinned maliciously. "Hmph . . . do we know where . . . of course we know where they are staying! Courtesy of my skills, of course." Sorn sniffed emphatically. "They are holed up at the Snorting Gorgon Inn. It will take us a while to get there, but it isn't too terribly far."

"Then what are we waiting for?" asked Sirion. "Lead the way."

"What about the group you have been traveling with? Couldn't they help us?" asked Anya. "You know how powerful our doubles are . . ."

"We don't have time. If my double has taken Adrianna to the Snorting Gorgon, she is in great danger."

"How do you know?" asked Sorn.

Sirion regarded his friend intently. "Trust me. Her well-being is imperiled every moment she stays with that damn bastard."

***

Adrianna felt herself beginning to awaken. Her mind felt sluggish, like it did not want to bother with coming to awareness. After another moment or two, she began to experience sensations, exotic ones that were both wonderful and bothersome at the same time: wonderful because they felt good, and bothersome because she did not know who was creating them. Waves of passion swept through her, and she felt a mouth on hers, a pair of arms encircling her and hands that seemed to be everywhere at once. Adrianna heard moans, and as she started to embrace alertness, discovered that they were coming from her.

"Sirion . . ." Adrianna moaned his name, struggling to move her apathetic limbs. She heard an answering reply deep within Sirion's throat, felt his hands kneading the flesh of her thighs and buttocks, his fingers precariously close to her femininity. This realization made her nervous, yet the sensations that his fingers invoked made her arch towards him for more. Confused, Adrianna spoke his name again, hoping that he would stop.

Adrianna began to feel herself being swept away by the power of her lust. Sirion moved his body over her and she felt a pressure parting her thighs. Suddenly, her awareness sparked. Adrianna felt as though she was rising up from within a deep well. Her senses began to respond to her mind and her body began to protest beneath him. "Sirion . . . please . . . stop."

She found that it was difficult for her to speak, and that it was even harder for her to move her body. She was finally able to turn her head. Just a few feet away, on the wall nearest the bed, Adrianna saw herself in a mirror. She was wearing a sheer gown of shimmering gold. On top of her was a shirtless Sirion, his head between her bared breasts. Her eyes began to widen. How . . . she didn't remember receiving a gown like this, much less putting it on.

"Sirion . . ." Adrianna began to struggle against him, her mind finally beginning to have control over her limbs. She felt the passion begin to drain away from her, fear beginning to roll into its place. "Sirion, please stop." Adrianna heaved at Sirion and he finally looked up at her. The expression on his face nearly unnerved her. It didn't look like the man she had come to know. His eyes seemed wild somehow, almost fanatical.

"Mmmm. I want you . . ." He bent his head to kiss her and she found herself jerking away.

"Sirion, no. I feel sick . . . don't remember . . ."

Sirion's brows pulled together in a frown. "I'm not stopping now. You brought me this far, and I mean to have you."

Shocked, all Adrianna could do was stare at him, into his eyes. Looking there, she could see no real emotion. Frightened, she began to struggle. Sirion pinned her onto the bed, his weight bearing down on her. She kicked her legs and arched her body, hoping to dislodge him. Suddenly he reared back, pulled back his hand and slapped her hard across the face.

For a moment she was still. Adrianna could hear the beating of her heart, could feel the warmth of her tears falling into her hairline. But she so much did not want to feel at all. She wanted to feel nothing of what was about to happen to her. Detaching herself, Adrianna turned her face away from Sirion and her body went limp on the bed. Once more she began to feel the pressure between her legs, but it was as though it was from a distance, like it was happening to someone else.

All of a sudden, something changed. Adrianna felt the weight of Sirion leaving her. She looked up to find him standing in the middle of the room. Then there was a flurry of activity as he refastened the ties of his trousers. Sirion quickly donned his tunic, and then his leather. Then she heard it; a commotion outside the room, somewhere down the hall. He snatched Stalker from its position near the desk, and then looked towards the bed. Narrowing his eyes, he grabbed the rope that was lying on top of the desk. Adrianna quickly sat upright as he approached her. Viciously, he seized first one wrist and then the other, binding them together and then to the headboard of the bed.

"We will continue this when I come back . . . and believe me . . . I *will* be back." Sirion took a fistful of her hair and pulled her face to him. He kissed her brutally, his teeth cutting into her lower lip. When he released her, he pushed her back onto the bed. She saw her blood on his mouth as he turned away from her. When he was gone, her tears began anew. She knew that the man was not Sirion, yet he looked so much like the man with whom she had fallen in love.

The fact that he was about to rape her weighed on her mind and she could not get rid of the image of him assaulting her.

With a cry, Adrianna pulled savagely at the rope that tied her to the bed. The rope bit into the flesh of her wrists, but she did not care. Like an animal, Adrianna writhed upon the bed that was her prison. She pulled so hard at the rope that she felt the tendons in her wrists begin to pop. She struggled until she had no energy left, and finally she just lay there, her body bathed in sweat, her breaths laboring to come forth. She put her tongue to her lips and still tasted her blood there, where he had cut her with his cruel kiss. Now all she could do was wait . . . wait for Sirion to come back and take her.

***

Keeping to the walls, especially those places in which she could also hide behind tables, Amethyst slowly circumvented the melee. The Wildrunners had hoped to keep their presence unknown for a while longer, but Anya had not expected to run into anti-Sorn on the rooftop. Their scuffle alerted the others inside the inn and the battle was ensued. The Wildrunners still did not know that they had been followed; Amethyst had taken pains to make it thus. She did not want to hear Sirion order her to stay behind. Besides, she knew that she could be of help.

Amethyst entered the hallway from which she had seen anti-Sirion emerge. She knew that Adrianna had to be back here somewhere in one of these rooms. There was a part of her that wanted to stay and help in the fighting, but she knew that Adrianna needed her more. The woman was probably trapped, and was feeling utterly helpless. Not only that, but there was always the possibility that she was hurt. But Amethyst hoped that she wasn't, and that Adrianna would be able to help the Wildrunners if she was freed.

Amethyst walked slowly down the hall, trying each of the doors as she came to them. Many of them were locked and she continued past them, but some were not. These doors she opened, having a quick look abut the rooms to be sure that no one was within. Finally her efforts paid off. At the end of the hall she came to a room of which the door was unlocked. She opened it and poked her head inside. There, lying upon the bed, was Adrianna.

Despite her clothing, or lack thereof, Amethyst knew right away that the woman on the bed was Adrianna. Her hair gave her away, Amethyst never having seen hair the color of the moon upon any other person. Amethyst quietly entered the room and went into a crouch, noiselessly shutting the door behind her. Adrianna's eyes were closed and she breathed heavily, as though she had been struggling against the bonds that imprisoned her. And upon closer examination, Amethyst could see that that was indeed the case. As Amethyst approached the bed, she saw the perspiration that bathed her body, as well as the wounds at her wrists where she had desperately tried to free herself. Remembering that Adrianna had suffered at the hands of men in the past, a surge of pity suffused her.

On the way over to the bed, Amethyst saw Adrianna's belt containing her pouches and grabbed it. Once she reached the bed, Amethyst stopped and went up to her knees beside it. The sheer gown that Adrianna wore was twisted about her hips. Her chest heaved from her exertion, and the tears continued to flow from beneath her closed eyelids. It had been impossible for the woman to lay comfortably on the bed; the rope that bound her was too short, making it so that Adria's head and shoulders remained off of the pallet. Her heart having somehow become stuck in her throat, Amethyst suddenly found it difficult to speak.

"Adrianna . . ."

Adrianna's eyes sprang open and she lurched back on the bed.

"Adria, please don't be frightened. It is only I, Amethyst. I have come to free you."

"Free me?" Adrianna's brows came together in confusion. Her words were slurred, almost as though she was drunk.

Amethyst nodded. "Yes. I even retrieved your belt for you." Amethyst slowly placed her hand on the bed. "I am going to climb up here and I am going to cut that rope, all right?"

Adrianna stared at Amethyst for a moment, processing what had been said. Then Adria nodded her head. Amethyst climbed onto the bed and crawled to the headboard. When she took the rope in her hands, Adrianna hissed. Amethyst turned back to Adrianna and saw the expression of pain on her face. "Oh, gods. I'm sorry, Adria. I will try to be more careful."

When the rope was finally cut, Adrianna lay back on the bed for a moment, cradling her wrists to her chest. Amethyst glanced about the room, hoping to see Adrianna's clothes. "Thank you."

Amethyst turned back towards Adrianna. "You are welcome."

The women stood from the bed. Adrianna began to fasten the belt about her waist. Once more, Amethyst took in Adria's state of undress. "Damn, Adria. I wish I had something for you to wear." Amethyst then looked down at her own clothing, a smoky gray blouse and a pair of snug, coal black trousers. Adrianna didn't even have small clothes beneath the filmy gown that she wore. The material left nothing to the imagination.

Adrianna sighed. "That's all right. No one will even notice. They are too busy trying to kill one another."

Amethyst glanced over at Adrianna to find her grinning slightly. Amethyst smiled in return, but somehow she knew that that wouldn't be the case, no matter how much she wanted to believe otherwise. Suddenly, the sounds of battle no longer seemed to be contained within the tavern. There was shouting, as well as the clash of steel. Then there was the sound of footsteps approaching the room.

Amethyst felt Adrianna tense beside her. Someone fumbled at the door, and then it opened. A huge man burst into the room. However, only a fraction of a moment passed before Amethyst felt the surge of power, and then the spell was being cast. The bolt left Adrianna's hands, the electrical power rushing towards the giant man. The energy struck him in the chest and he was cast back, back through the doorway and into the wall within the corridor outside of the room. Amethyst heard the sound of bone breaking, and the stench of charred flesh. When the smoke cleared from around the man, Amethyst could see a blackened hole in his chest. His head had hit the wall upon impact, and blood ran down his temple and face. His eyes were open, but there was no longer any life there, it having been expired by the spell-caster.

Amethyst turned back to Adrianna, her mind suffused with awe. Adrianna walked out of the room. She did not even pause at the body as she walked by it. Amethyst followed behind. "Damn, that was so awesome . . ."

***

Once more, Sirion swung his sword at his double, grimacing with the pain in his forearm. The bastard had clipped him there at the beginning of the fight, and the damn wound bled profusely. But finally he had obtained the upper hand. Sirion bore into his opponent, his sword straining against its counter-part, his face only inches away from that of his double. The man still had blood on his lips, blood that had been there when the fight began. Sirion looked down the hall from which he had seen his double come when the fight broke out. Somewhere, in one of those rooms, was Adrianna.

Sirion pushed his double back, and with a massive shove, knocked the man to the floor. However, instead of following up with another blow, Sirion took the opportunity to glance around at the scene. The friend closest to him was Sorn, who was having the unfortunate experience of skirmishing with anti-Anya. Across the room, he saw Naemmious at combat with anti-Arn, and Triath and anti-Triath seemed to be locked into a battle of minds, their mental struggle apparent by their expressions of deep concentration. As his double lurched up from the floor, Sirion saw Sorn get a good kick in at anti-Anya. The woman flew backwards and hit the wall behind her.

Sirion saw his chance. "Sorn, go find Adrianna." Sirion deflected anti-Sirion's blow and then ducked and rolled. He came up behind his double, blocking any chance the man would have to give chase. Sirion saw that Sorn had entered the hall and was quickly checking the doors.

"Naemmious, to my chamber," anti-Sirion yelled down the hall. He then turned back to Sirion, a grimace spreading across his face. He licked his lips, tasting of the blood that was there. "She tastes sweet, and feels even sweeter. You were a fool to let her get away from you."

"You bastard; what have you done to her?" Just then, Sirion heard a scuffle in the hallway. He glanced over to find anti-Naemmious standing over the fallen form of Sorn. *Damnation . . .* Sirion blocked a blow from his nemesis just in time, staggering under the power of it. He heard anti-Sirion's laugh, and then the sound of him making his way down the hall. Sirion rushed after him, and as anti-Naemmious reached a door at the end of hall and fumbled at it, Sirion had caught up to his double and knocked him into another chamber.

The two men grappled on the floor, beating one another with their fists, and issuing malicious epithets. Suddenly they heard a crash, followed by a large thud. The two men looked towards the sounds, and knew them to be coming from the room that anti-Naemmious had sought access. Then anti-Sirion acquired the upper hand, straddling his opponent upon the floor, a dagger to Sirion's throat. Anti-Sirion grinned and Sirion narrowed his eyes. "It is a shame that you never had her. She is good . . . very good . . ."

Suddenly freeing his arm from beneath the weight of his opponent, Sirion knocked the dagger from out of anti-Sirion's hand, sending it across the room. "I am going to kill you." Sirion wrapped his hands around the throat of his double, and anti-Sirion followed suit. Once more they rolled about on the floor, each one seeking to end the other. They hit a table, sending it falling on top of them. The lamp that had been standing on it rolled across the floor and over to the window.

Sirion removed one of his hands from around his double's neck and took up the splintered leg of the table. He hit anti-Sirion across the face, and the other man reared back, holding his face and screaming. Sirion scrambled up off of the floor, only to be brought down again by his opponent. He squirmed and kicked against the other man, hoping to get him away. All of a sudden, Sirion inhaled the scent of smoke. Anti-Sirion noticed it too and they both glanced at the flames that had climbed up the draperies that outlined the window.

Sirion snatched the chance and kicked anti-Sirion in the face. He got up from the floor, looking about wildly for the dagger he knew to be in this vicinity. He felt his eyes widen, the realization striking him just as anti-Sirion lurched up from the floor. The dagger gleamed within the light cast by the growing flames as it arced towards him. Sirion dodged the lunge, and anti-Sirion stumbled. Sirion snaked out his hand, hoping to capture the dagger, but anti-Sirion refused to release it. As the two men fell, Sirion attempted to manipulate the weapon. The two men fell to the floor.

For a moment no one moved. Finally Sirion lifted himself from off of his double. He quickly turned the man over and found the dagger deeply embedded in the man's chest. Noticing the increasing warmth, Sirion looked at the inferno that had begun to encompass the room. The cheap tapestries that hung on the walls had all caught flame. Disoriented for a moment, Sirion glanced wildly about the room, and then saw the doorway. On the other side of it was Adrianna.

Sirion ran out of the burning room. Once out in the hallway, he knelt before Adrianna. "Adrianna, are you all right?" Without waiting for answer he continued. "Come on. We have to move away from here, let someone know that the building is on fire." Sirion took her arm, urging her to her feet. He did not notice that she seemed unusually complacent, and somewhat lackluster.

"Adrianna . . . Sirion. Are you two all right?" Amethyst rushed down the hall, calling out to them.

"Get back . . . get back Amethyst. The room is on fire." Sirion began to lead Adrianna away from the room towards Amethyst just as the flames began to emerge from the room behind them.

Behind Amethyst, the rest of the Wildrunners had gathered. Sirion saw Triath take Amethyst's arm, urging her back down the hall. Resisting, she continued to wait until Adrianna and Sirion had nearly reached them before she allowed Triath to take her through the tavern and out of the building.

By that time, others had arrived, men carrying large buckets of water to put out the fire. Sirion led Adrianna down the steps of the establishment into the chilly evening air. Immediately feeling the cold, Adrianna shivered and she wrapped her arms around herself. *Damn this gown . . . and what had that man done with her clothes?* She noticed that Sirion had stepped back from her and she looked up at him to find him staring at her. Suddenly feeling the need to hide herself, Adrianna sat down on the steps and pulled her legs up nearer her chest.

Despite the darkness, it was easy for Sirion to see Adrianna. The multitude of torches cast a light in the area that made it almost seem like it was day. He could not help but stare at her, the sheer quality of the dress she wore demanding his eyes to rest upon her. Through the diaphanous material, he could see the contours of her breasts, the shape of her waist and her thighs. He watched her as she sat down on the steps of the Snorting Gorgon Inn, wrapping her arms around herself. By the gods, what had that man done to her? Sirion could only imagine, and could hardly stand the thought of him touching her . . . removing her clothes to make her wear this piece of material that showed more than it covered.

Seeking to offer comfort and shield her from prying eyes, Sirion began to approach her. The moment he began to move in her direction, Adrianna focused her attention on him. Sirion knelt down before her. "Adrianna, are you all right? Is there any thing I can do to . . ."

Sirion reached out a hand to touch her, and suddenly Adrianna reared back. Awkwardly she stood up, backing away from Sirion, her hands out in front of her. He saw the fear in her eyes, and he wondered once more what had happened to her. "Adrianna, I just want to help you. Come here, let me . . ." Sirion stepped up next to her, putting an arm around her shoulders, hoping to keep some of the chill away from her.

Adrianna pushed away from Sirion. "Don't touch me!" she screamed. The tears began to roll down her cheeks and she continued to step farther away. "Just . . . just stay away from me. Haven't you done enough?"

Dumbfounded, Sirion stared at Adrianna. Her fear and pain were manifest. Her body shook with emotion, and she seemed to have folded into herself, her arms wrapped around her midriff. Sirion glanced at his comrades, the Wildrunners and Amethyst. They were silent as they watched the scenario before them. When Adrianna turned and rushed down the street, Amethyst broke away from the rest and went after her.

Sirion stared after them, his mind encompassed within an envelope of disbelief. After a few moments, Triath stepped up next to him, placing a hand on his shoulder. "Let's go back to the inn. I am sure that your young comrade will bring Adrianna back there." Sirion nodded, turned, and followed Triath and the rest of the Wildrunners.

CHAPTER 21

Through the remainder of the night and well into the next day, Adrianna slept. When she finally found the desire to get her body out of bed, it was almost mid-day. When she discovered herself still wearing the gossamer gown, she stripped it off of her, throwing it into a shimmering heap on the floor. Then, her body shaking, she stood in the middle of the room. For a few moments she felt disoriented, but then reason returned to her. Once she found some clothes to wear, she dressed herself and then sat on the chair next to the window.

Adrianna did not know how long she sat looking out of the window. The time just seemed to slip by, without her even taking notice. Vaguely, she wondered if there was something wrong with her, but then discarded that idea. When she finally returned to the inn last night, everyone in the group was awake. Sheridana had noticed that Adrianna had not retired for the night, and once waking Dartanyen, he realized that Sirion had not returned either. It wasn't until Sheri and Dartanyen decided to go look for them that they realized that Amethyst was also not in her room.

Sheri, Dartanyen, Dinim, and Armond were about to leave the inn to search for their missing comrades when Amethyst returned with Adrianna. Adria was immediately taken up to her room and laid into her bed. Sheri tucked the blankets securely about her, and then went back downstairs to find out what had happened. In the middle of Amethyst's account, Sirion and the Wildrunners arrived at the inn. There was very little talk as the Wildrunners procured accommodations and went to their respective rooms to get some sleep. Sirion, Dartanyen, and the others followed suit, all realizing the advantage to some rest. They would figure out what to do about the mess at the Snorting Gorgon on the morrow, as well as make a recount of exactly what had happened.

Throughout the morning and afternoon, Sheri checked on Adrianna. The second time that she went to the room, she found her sister sitting next to the window. Sheri asked Adria about her wellbeing, if she could get anything for her, or if she needed to talk. Adrianna had told her that she was fine, and refused offers of food, drink, and companionship. As per the opinion of the rest of the group, Sheri left Adrianna alone after that, giving her sister as much time as she needed to recover from her ordeal. Telling the group about Adrianna's sluggish motions and decreased awareness, Tianna and Triath agreed that she must have been drugged. Called Esfexanar, the poison could be administered in many ways, but one of the quickest ways was to place it directly into the blood stream via a cut. If too much of the poison were to be administered, a person could easily die, but used properly, the poison would have effects upon the recipient that they saw in Adrianna.

Finally, as afternoon began to darken into early evening, Adrianna left her chamber and made her way down to the common room. She found her companions seated at a large table. Others had joined them . . . those that were left of the group that had once been the Wildrunners. Food and drink had just been brought to the table, and everyone was beginning to serve themselves from the large platters. Sheridana was the first to notice Adria's presence, and she made room for her at the table between herself and Amethyst, quickly snagging a nearby chair and sliding it into place.

Adrianna took the seat and looked about the table. There were greetings all around, and then inquiries regarding her welfare from Dartanyen and Armond. Sitting directly across from her was Sirion, and one of his Wildrunner companions, one who she remembered went by the name of Triath. She noticed that Sirion looked at her, but stayed silent. It was just as well, he being the last person with whom she wanted to share conversation. Tianna also seemed unusually quiet, but Adrianna found that she could barely look in the other woman's direction, much less determine her condition.

The food disappeared quickly, and the drink even more so. Even Sirion participated in the imbibing of large quantities of mead. The companionship was good, the two groups getting along with one another rather well. The Wildrunners told stories of their earlier days, and the ones about Sirion tended to be the most humorous. Even Adrianna could not keep a grin off of her face a time or two. However, inevitably the conversation shifted to traveling plans.

Once the 'evil' Wildrunners were destroyed, the Wildrunners had agreed that they would disband. "It is about time that we returned to our homes," said Triath. "Not only that, but we have dedicated so much to the cause, not to mention the lives of our friends." Triath lowered his head for a moment. Seated next to him, Sorn clapped Triath on the back and nodded his agreement.

There were a few moments of silence and then Dartanyen spoke. "We should probably be leaving the city soon. The faster we meet up with Thane, the better."

"Have we decided where we should go next?" asked Armond.

"I think that we should head in the direction of Driscol. It is a larger city than Entsy, and more likely to have a bigger library. There, we will more likely find the information that we are seeking about our enemy. Not only that, but

Driscol is in the direction from which I have been hearing about Thane's recent activity."

Sheridana nodded. "It sounds like a good plan. In the morning we should probably invest in a few larian. They will be able to get us to Driscol quicker than we could on foot."

"We can spend the rest of the day gathering our supplies and resting. We will be able to leave Entsy the next morning," said Armond.

From his seat between Dartanyen and Sirion, Dinim took in the conversation. It seemed like a good plan, but he doubted they would find much information at the library. He would have to see if he could find Paxil. That crazy old mage knew everything, and just happened to keep his abode in the foothills east of Driscol.

What seemed like for the hundredth time, Dinim glanced at Adrianna. She looked a bit pale and tired. But she remained beautiful nonetheless. This thing between her and Sirion bothered him greatly, but as of yet, he had not found a solution to his dilemma. He cared about Adrianna a great deal, maybe even loved her. He knew that at one time she may have felt the same for him. But since Sirion had become a part of the picture, things had changed. A mutual attraction had sprung up between the ranger and the sorceress, one that was not easily explained. At first, Dinim refused to see it, but now he had no choice. The recent turn of events could not be ignored, and because of this *thing* that was going on between the two of them, Adrianna's life had become endangered more than once.

Dinim glanced away, knowing that he could not let his feelings become known. His heart ached and he so much wished that things could be as they were, before Sirion joined their ranks. He wanted to make this hurt go away, and he had even begun to try to come up with some things that were not so good about Adrianna. Still, even under this scrutiny, there was very little that was wrong with the young woman, and Dinim found it difficult to find anything negative about her upon which he could focus. However, there was one thing; she was weak.

It was something that Dinim had noticed right away about her. It was the way she carried herself, the way she let others make decisions for her, and the way she went about life in general. Her confidence in her skills and abilities was meager and her self-esteem laughable. She contributed very little to the decision-making process, although she may have spoke up once or twice. For someone of her Talent, Dinim would have expected something . . . well . . . more. Instead of making her stronger, her experiences in life seemed to have made her weaker, and her inability to truly apply herself was depriving her of the power that lay just below the surface.

Yet, despite this key flaw in Adrianna's personality, he had fallen in love with her. Deep inside of himself, he knew that this flaw could be overcome, and he fancied himself the one who would break down those walls. But, then again, he knew that he would not be that person. It would be someone else, and the fact that this person may be Sirion Timberlyn rankled him to no end. But in spite of his hurt, he could still be her friend, and he would make a play for her affections anyway.

"Adrianna, I was wondering if you wanted to get some studying in tonight. I have a book that you might be interested in. It may have a spell in it that you haven't seen yet."

Adrianna looked up at Dinim and smiled. "That would be great. Whenever you are ready just let me know."

"Are you sure that is a good idea? Maybe you should focus on getting some rest," said Sirion. "You have been through a lot."

"No, I'm fine. It will be good for me to get my mind off of things."

"Adria, are you sure? Maybe Sirion is right. You do look rather tired," said Sheri thoughtfully.

Adrianna swung her gaze to Sheridana and frowned. "Actually, I don't recall asking Sirion for his opinion, and as much as I value yours, you are just going to have to trust me when I tell you that I am fine." Adrianna raised an eyebrow, and then looked at Sirion pointedly.

Sirion's eyes darkened. "You didn't ask me for help with this Thane-thing either, but here I am."

"Perhaps you shouldn't be here then."

"Maybe I will just return to Elvandahar with Anya. I can see now that my help is not appreciated here."

"Be my guest; go to Elvandahar. Actually, that would be great. Then I wouldn't have to deal with watching my friends groping one another for the next few weeks."

Sirion's voice began to rise. "Why are you acting like a child?"

Adrianna's eyes widened with mock astonishment. "Me, acting like a child? What about you, Sirion? Moping about after your encounter with Sydonnia, constantly scouting ahead of the group, not talking with anyone, and growling when you do?"

"I was going through a hard time!"

"Well, now *I* am going through a hard time." Adrianna rose from her seat. "Excuse me, everyone. Perhaps I am tired after all." Her voice sounded shaky, and she could not think of anything but escape. Adrianna ran from the common room. Her chest felt heavy and the sobs caught in her throat. Damn Sirion! Because of him, she was crying yet again. Within the short time she had known him, she had cried more than she had the previous twenty years of her life. Adrianna swept into her chamber, slamming the door behind her.

Her breath came in ragged gasps and she felt sick to her stomach. She wrapped her arms around her belly and leaned against the door. She had treated Sirion badly, very badly. But the words had just slipped out. And now, when they needed him the most, he was going to leave, and it was all her fault.

The group silently watched as Sirion stood from the table and followed Adrianna out of the room. For a moment there was silence, and then a voice spoke up. "I am going to bet that Sirion wins this one. Damn, was he *angry*," said Sorn. He turned back to the people sitting around the table. He had a glint in his lavender eyes, and his mouth was pulled up slightly into a grin.

Triath smiled. "Yeah, he was pretty mad, but the Lady was too."

Sorn reached into his belt pouch and pulled out a gold piece. "I am betting that Sirion wins the argument."

"No way," said Sheri with mock indignation. "Adria will surely win this one." Smiling, Sheri pulled two gold out of her own pouch and set it on the table.

"I agree with Sorn. Sirion will take this fight. He isn't one to lose, not even to a lady," said Naemmious, putting his pouch onto the table.

"Wha . . . what in the Hells are you doing?" said Armond. "You are going to take *bets*?"

Amethyst grinned widely. "Why not? This is as good a reason as any."

Armond frowned. "This isn't right. There are two people up there who are obviously very hurt and confused right now. I can't believe that you people are going to exploit that."

Zorg clapped Armond on the back. "Come on, Armond. Loosen up a bit. It's jus' a bit of friendly gamblin'. I vote that Adrianna wins the fight. She has more spunk in 'er than people realize."

Naemmious shook his head. "Well, you obviously don't know Sirion very well."

"Don' have to. I know Adrianna."

"Well, I know my brother, he won't back down. I say that Sirion will win this one," said Anya, bringing her own pouch to the table.

Sabian cackled with glee. "I'm with Anya. Sirion will win the argument. I don't think Adrianna is up for the fight."

"Come on, Triath, what do you think?" asked Sorn.

Triath narrowed his eyes for a moment. "I don't know. Maybe no one will win."

Naemmious guffawed. "You know better than that, Triath. You and Sirion have had your fair share of scuffles. I suppose even more than your fair share."

"I suppose I should lay my own wager," said Dartanyen, interrupting with a sigh. Sheri cast him a sidelong glance. He made it seem like he was slightly put out, but she knew better. She could see the sparkle of amusement in his eyes. "I say that Adria will win the argument. Zorg is right. She has fire in her. What say you, Dinim? Who do you think will persevere?"

Dinim frowned slightly. He felt out of sorts, angry that Sirion had butt in where he was unwanted. He had upset Adrianna . . . again . . . and that made him even angrier. But he wasn't just mad at Sirion, but at Adria as well. Her ability to win a fight was up for debate, and that went too much along the lines of his opinion of her faults. He could not help but feel very upset, and it swayed his decision in favor of Sirion. "Sirion will win the argument. I agree with Sabian that Adria is not up for the fight."

The moment the words were out of his mouth, Dinim regretted saying them. He saw Sheri's eyes widen with surprise, she knowing that he was one of her sister's strongest advocates and friends. Dinim sighed to himself and began to tap his fingertips on the table. Damn . . . he could never win.

"And what about you, Tianna? What do you think?" asked Sorn. Everyone swung their eyes in her direction and she felt like she would melt under their scrutiny. Many of them had an idea of what had happened between herself and Sirion . . . it being the cause of Adria's flight from the inn and subsequent capture by the 'evil' Wildrunners. She regretted what had happened, and was angry with herself for having misread Sirion. Yet, she knew him still, and Adrianna as well. She could not accurately determine which of them would be the 'winner' of their argument. "Perhaps Triath is right. Maybe they will both win."

Sorn put his hands on his hips. "Now why would you think that? We all know that Triath is a freak and that he would believe something like that, but not an intelligent creature like yourself. Now come on, be honest."

"Hey friend, don't push it," growled Armond. "This is a stupid bet anyway. Let the lady be. She has been through too much lately to be bullied around by the likes of you."

Sorn narrowed his eyes. "And what do you mean by that?"

"Hey, hey, hey," said Dartanyen. "Cut it out. We aren't here to fight. I thought this was just for fun."

Sorn held up his hands. "Yes, you are right. This is all just for a bit of friendly gambling. So, we have Dinim, Sabian, Naemmious, Anya, and myself in favor of Sirion. And we have Sheridana, Amethyst, Zorg, and Dartanyen in favor of the lady. Let's put our money where our mouths are." Sorn then flung his bag in the center of the table. The others began to follow suit.

"Wait a minute," said Armond. "Put me in favor of Adrianna."

Sheri smiled. "I knew you would come around."

All Armond did was frown and grumble incoherently as he threw his own money pouch onto the table.

***

Once she was able to catch her breath, Adrianna walked over to the bed and fell onto it. She pulled the blankets over her, placed the pillow beneath her face, and continued her pathetic sobbing. Her chest ached and the muscles in her abdomen contracted spasmodically. Damn Sirion . . . but she loved him so much. She shook her head against the pillow. She refused to even think about that! She would have to go and apologize to him, get him to stay with them until the fight with Thane was over. She would pretend that nothing had happened between them. She would continue to exist as a part of the group, and keep her distance from him as he had been doing with her. She knew she could do it; it would just take a little bit of time . . . just a few days. Yes, then she would be just fine, as if it had never happened.

Adrianna's faelin senses picked up movement out in the hallway just as the door to her room was quietly opened. She couldn't see who it was, since she was facing the wall, but thought that it was probably just Sheridana. Adria pulled the blankets all around her, not wanting Sheri to even think about bothering her.

Sirion slowly opened the door to Adrianna's room. Within the wan light cast by the lamp, he saw her pull the covers up all around her as he entered. He paused at the doorway, not really knowing what to say, not knowing how to breach the distance that had grown between them. He knew that the separation was his own doing, for it was she who had sought to comfort him the morning after that fateful night.

He had bid her stay away from the battle scene, but Adrianna had come anyway. It had irked him that she had so flagrantly dismissed his wishes, but another part of him had also been touched, pleased that she had wished to remain by his side, even in the face of such danger. But he had chosen to push her away, despite her attempts to soothe him. And he had remained cool towards her, almost as though he sought to punish her for her disobeying him.

Sirion slowly walked across the room towards the bed. He felt remorseful, sorry that he had treated her so coldly. It wasn't her fault that Sydonnia had not wanted his help, and not her fault that Joselyn had died with him. Sirion hated himself for bickering with her, he who was jealous over her companionship with Dinim, wishing that he shared something like that with her himself.

"Adria . . . Adrianna I am sorry." His voice came hoarsely out of a dry throat. He sat himself next to the blanketed hump on the bed, placing a hand where he knew a shoulder to be. Leaning over her, Sirion slowly turned her towards him, brushing wisps of her pale hair from her face. She resisted him, and when he felt wetness on his fingertips, his chest constricted.

"*Shendori,*" he whispered, and without another thought he took her shoulders and pulled her up towards him. Tucking her head beneath his chin, Sirion held her tightly, felt her body tremble within his embrace. He rocked his body back and forth; stroking her hair as he murmured into her ear. "I am so sorry, Adrianna. It was wrong of me to shut you out. But I hurt so much . . . and now I have hurt you."

Adrianna found herself in Sirion's arms, her head on his leathered chest. He whispered to her in Hinterlic, his voice tight with suppressed emotion. She allowed herself to be rocked within his embrace but said nothing, not knowing what to say, or if she really wanted to say anything at all. And then he was stroking her hair, caressing her back, running his hands over her soothingly. Her tears stopped and she began to relax, despite not knowing what to think, not knowing whether she should allow herself the luxury of his touch.

Sirion felt her ease against him, felt her barriers crack. He felt a type of elation, invigorated that he had been able to ease her hostility towards him. He felt himself responding to her already, his body reacting to her nearness. He ran his hands over her back and arms, hoping to further relax and soothe her. He wanted to make it all up to her, wanted to show her that he cared for her, cared for her very deeply. He wanted to show her that his harsh nature was just a part of him, that there was so much more to him, if she were to just give him the chance to show it to her.

Adrianna closed her eyes, Sirion's rhythmic rocking a comfort to her. She was aware of him, aware of his body so close to hers. She could feel each breath that he took and heard each beat of his heart. Once again, she could feel the warmth of her tears as they ran down her cheeks. She loved him; she could not deny it. Despite her resolve to forget about him and what they had shared together that night in the Sherkari Fortress, the memories came rushing back to her. She had to stop this, had to pull away from him, protect herself from the heartache she knew she would suffer. Just as she was about to do that, Adrianna felt him put his face in the hair at her neck, felt him tighten his grip around her waist. She felt a slight shift in the aura that surrounded him, and felt the answering response in her own body.

Adrianna felt the emotion begin to gently eddy around them. She felt the stirrings of passion within her, an answer to what she was beginning to feel from the man before her. This was a mistake, and she knew that she should pull back, to escape from him. She struggled within herself, and just as she felt that she might win her battle with desire, he kissed her.

Sirion pushed the hair away from Adrianna's neck, felt the smooth silkiness of her skin beneath his fingertips. Unable to resist, he gently kissed her neck. He felt a tensing of her body, but then it subsided. He continued to kiss her, his tongue flicking out to taste her. He felt her respiration increase; felt his own breaths beginning to accelerate as well.

Adrianna felt his lips at her neck. She felt a slight stirring in her belly and suppressed a moan of dismay. Her body would react to him of its own volition, whether she wanted it to or not. She found this disturbing but did not pull away, unable to do so even if she had wanted it. Adrianna placed her hands on his chest, feeling the stiffness of the leather. He had not removed it after he and the Wildrunners had gone back to the Snorting Gorgon to help clean up their mess and pay for the extensive damages.

Adrianna ran her hands over the leather, felt the studs of metal encased within it. The studded leather was the maximum amount of protection he would use. He once told her that anything heavier impeded his ability to move and to be an effective ranger. She moved her hands up to his shoulders, over the ornate clasps that bound his cloak, and then ran her fingers through the hair that rested at his neck. Adrianna felt Sirion's lips move from her neck to her jaw, felt the warmth of his breath She felt her heart flutter in her chest and she moved her face so that her lips barely brushed his.

Sirion felt her hands move to his shoulders, and cursed the leather armor he had not cared to remove earlier. He so much wanted to feel her body against him, to feel her touch him. Sirion brought his lips to her jaw, and she turned her face to brush her lips against his. Passion surged through him, and he could barely control his trembling as he lowered himself onto the bed, pulling her down with him. Adrianna wrapped her arms around his neck, her warm breath continuing to brush over his face. Sirion ran his hands over her back and hips, seeking to bring her closer to him. Gods, she was driving him crazy.

Sirion took her face in his hands and put his mouth to hers. He kissed her deeply, his tongue darting between her slightly parted lips. She trembled within his embrace, and he could feel her reaction to him. Sirion gently rolled Adrianna onto her back, careful not to hurt her with the studded leather he continued to wear. He regarded her out of narrowed eyes as he kissed her. Her eyes were closed, her long golden lashes resting upon tear-dampened cheeks. He took his mouth from her lips and gently kissed each of her eyelids, tasting the saltiness there. Huskily he whispered to her, "I love you, Adrianna. You are the only one for me."

Adrianna opened her eyes and found herself looking into pools of molten amber. His words brought to her a pleasure she had never known before. Lovingly, she placed her hands on Sirion's face, tracing the contours with her thumbs. She put her lips on his mouth and kissed him tenderly. He responded and the passion between them began to grow with each passing breath. She felt his hands on her, at her waist, her hips, and then her buttocks. She pressed into him and he groaned into her lips. He imprisoned her with his hands, pressing her into his hardening groin. A slight tingle of fear passed through her, but then it was gone. She knew that Sirion would never hurt her. Despite what had recently happened to her, she trusted this man. Once again she brought her hands to his chest, wishing that the leather were gone. She wanted . . . needed to feel the warmth of his body against her.

As though he read her mind, Sirion reached for the buckles that bound the leather armor. With one hand he quickly unfastened them. He tore himself away from Adrianna just long enough to slip the leather over his head. He tossed the armor aside and then brought himself back to her, finally reveling in the warmth of her body next to him. He moved his lips from her mouth to her throat, and when she rolled her head back, he made a path from her throat to her neckline. With one hand he held her at the small of her back, and with the other slowly began to unfasten the laces of her tunic.

Sirion watched her as he slowly pulled the tunic down over her shoulders. Adrianna kept her eyes fixed on his, the emotion she saw there bidding her stay. Despite the fire of the passion they shared, Sirion was ever so gentle as he brushed his hands down her arms, his eyes searching her for any hint of uncertainty or fear. His kisses were fervently tender, and his motions ardently mild. He had become something other than the hardened warrior. He had become the hesitant, tender lover. And before Adrianna began to spiral away into a vortex of pure joy, she felt the brush of Destiny . . . a feather-light touch from Fate telling her that this was right.

15 Cisceren CY593

The group left the city of Entsy on the backs of their lloryk and larian. Between themselves and the Wildrunners, they had just enough gold to purchase an animal for everyone. Except, of course, for Sirion, who rode astride Dramati. Adrianna left the city behind without even a backward glance. She hoped that she would never have the pleasure of visiting Entsy again. The city held more than just one bad memory for her, it being the last city within which she and Nahum had stayed before he was killed, not to mention her most recent ordeal. However, she had to accede that it was there that she and Sirion had finally come together, and there that he told her that he loved her. She had to give Entsy at least that much.

Adrianna glanced about her as she rode, her heart lighter than it had been in months. Their numbers had grown, for Anya, Triath, Sorn, and Naemmious had decided to join them in their efforts against Thane. The decision was made the morning of the day before, when Triath had requested to know the details of their mission. Once hearing an account of what they had been through the last few months, including Sirion's personal ordeal, Triath had stated that he would like to join their cause. Anya whole-heartedly agreed to lend them her sword as well.

Dartanyen couldn't help but grin, thankful for their willingness to help. But then he turned them down. "Your expertise and skill would be a great help to us, but you would be placing yourselves at risk. Once you align yourselves with us there is no turning back. Thane will hunt you down until you have been destroyed. I am sorry, but I just can't accept the responsibility for something like that, not knowing what I know now."

Triath leaned back in his seat and regarded Dartanyen thoughtfully. He then shook his head. "I am not asking for your permission, Dartanyen, I am telling you that I am joining your company in order to put an end to a mutual threat. Thane is not only hunting you, but he is murdering countless others. You need me to help you in this fight, and I am going to stand by you."

Dartanyen reached across the table, his palm open. "Welcome to the team."

Triath smiled and took the hand. Anya placed her hand on top of Triath's. Then the hands of Sorn and Naemmious joined the pile, followed by those of Armond, Sheridana, Sirion, Dinim, and Adrianna. Tianna and Amethyst came down the stairs. "What is going on here?" Tianna asked with a slight frown.

Sheri smiled. "The Wildrunners have decided to help us with our fight against Thane. Our numbers have grown, as well as our power."

Amethyst glanced around at the group. "And him, too?" she said, pointing at Naemmious.

Sheridana looked from the large man to the young girl. Amethyst had a doubtful expression on her face. Sheri nodded. "Naemmious has joined us as well."

"Don't worry," Triath said. "He is a good fighter, and loyal to his comrades. I know that he looks a bit intimidating, but he is a good protector."

Amethyst continued to look doubtful. "Whatever." She turned and began to make her way to the front door. Then, in afterthought, she said over her shoulder, "I'm going out. I will be back at mid-day."

Sheri watched the girl as she walked out the door. "She will come around. She just needs some time," she said, turning to Triath and Naemmious.

"Naemmious takes a lot of getting used to. I wouldn't worry about Amethyst. As you said, she will come around," said Triath.

Sheri nodded and then glanced at her sister. Adrianna was happier than Sheri had ever seen her before. The night of the bet, Sheri had finally gone back up to the room she shared with Adrianna. Hearing something going on inside, Sheri had paused at the door, putting her ear to it. She heard the sound of Sirion's voice coming from within, and she stepped back. She had then gone down the hall to Dartanyen's room. Sheridana knocked on the door and asked Dartanyen if she could have the other bed for the night. Grinning, Dartanyen opened the door wider, and Sheri went inside. Sheri didn't have to say anything, the words written all over her face. The only ones to win the bet were Triath and Tianna, and they had not wagered at all.

After the two groups had decided upon a merger, everyone went out in search of clothing and other supplies. With gold given to them by the King of Elvandahar, Sheridana bought herself a suit of partial plate mail to replace the studded leather she had lost in her fight with the lycanthropes. Armond and Zorg purchased similar suits, knowing that, as the first line of defense, it would behoove them to have more than the simple studded leather that they had been wearing. The group met back at the inn for the mid-day meal, and then went out in search of some larian that they could purchase. They did not make it back to the inn until near sunset, and once they had taken their meal, everyone went off to their beds. Earlier in the day, Sheridana had removed her bags from Adrianna's room and moved them all into Dartanyen's room. She piled Sirion's belongings into a heap and put them at the foot of the bed. She figured that he would get the hint when he came later. That evening Sheri was happy to see that Sirion's things were gone. She wouldn't have to worry about taking them to Adria's room herself.

As the group rode to Driscol, they set up a pattern of activity. They rode hard all day, letting the larian rest for an hour at mid-day. They had deliberately chosen animals that were hardy, and that would be able to endure long distances at a fairly rapid pace. They had also chosen animals that would be able to tolerate the company of a corubis. Although Dramati was often scouting ahead with Sirion, the animals still had to deal with the presence of a predator in their midst. The group also had another scout, Anya. She would often check their perimeter as they moved, being sure that they were not being followed or that they would not be caught unawares in an ambush.

In the late afternoon, Sirion would begin to look for a suitable campsite, and by the time the sun was beginning to set, one had been located and the group was busy setting camp. The evening shifts were split up into four, maximizing everyone's sleep. The shifts were taken in pairs, first by Triath and Amethyst, then Sorn and Naemmious, next Armond and Zorg, and finally by Dartanyen and Sheridana. The spellcasters were relieved of watch duty so that they could obtain adequate rest, and the scouts were not included either, they having worked hard all day.

It seemed to be a good system, working well for everyone. The merged groups also seemed to be getting along rather well, with very few problems. The first night they were on the road, Sirion resumed Adrianna's sparring sessions, and they continued every evening thereafter. Some nights many of the others would participate as well, and Adrianna found herself pitted against them. It was a good time, and it increased group cohesion and companionship. Sheridana found herself discussing it with Dartanyen a time or two during their turn at the watch, and she was pleased to realize that he agreed with her on many aspects of group unity, the way battles should be fought, and the ways they could pull the group together.

So, it wasn't long before Sheri and Dartanyen's discussions were brought before the group members. They had developed a plan that they would begin to utilize in battle, one that could maximize everyone's skills. Everyone quickly saw the logic in their words, and within a few nights, everyone was adjusting well to the strategy sessions. Dartanyen and Sheridana came up with the scenarios, and the group would decide the best way to deal with that situation while using everyone in the group. At first they allowed the group to discuss the strategy among themselves, but then Sheridana and Dartanyen decided to make it more realistic, and to have each member state his or her intent within their pre-specified order. This was problematic at first, but within a few more nights, everyone was becoming accustomed to this test as well.

It took them almost two weeks to reach the city of Driscol. Along the way, they passed through several towns and villages. All had heard of Lord Thane and the waste he was leaving behind as he swept through Monaf. By the time the group was at the outskirts of Driscol, they had learned that Thane was near the city of Celuna. It was apparent that they had been traveling towards one another, like an unseen power was seeing to it that they meet sooner than later.

**

The group set camp inside a small cave situated within a small copse of trees. As the nights grew chillier they took the extra measures to find a campsite that had some barrier to the winds. Tianna walked among the trees, foraging about in the vegetation. Some wild onions would go well in the stewpot this evening, and she needed to restock her clover supply as well. By mid-day tomorrow they would enter the city and would be able to replenish much of their stores, but she did not mind finding many of the herbs herself. Tianna pulled back a xinthafroz bush and murmured with delight. Beneath the leaves of the large shrub, she had found the vine of a hybanthis flower.

Tianna carefully picked up the vine, following it with her eyes until they beheld one of the tiny flowers. The bloom was gorgeous, emerging only at the end of summer. This vine was carrying its last blooms of the year, and soon they would be falling to the ground. Tianna plucked the beautiful pink flower and placed it into her pouch. This plant had special properties, ones that were not entirely understood. However, the flowers were needed for a drink that she knew how to make, one that could be blessed by the goddess to help the person who drank the brew the ability to see into his inner being, to realize his true feelings. However, if the drink were made too strong, the person would suffer a distorted perception of his feelings, and could become ill.

As Tianna continued to pick the flowers, she was sure not to touch the blue thorns adorning the vine. They were known to produce the same effects as a hybanthis drink, and could make the person ill. It could take days for the poison to leave the person's body, and during that time the person would have a fever, would feel his emotions very strongly and possibly be unable to deal with those emotions. Each person reacted differently, so one could never tell how one would react until they had been poisoned, but Tianna wasn't about to find that out for herself. As soon as she acquired enough flowers, she left the area and returned to the rest of the group.

Tianna walked into the small cave and seated herself in front of the stewpot, suddenly remembering why she had gone foraging in the first place. She sighed heavily and then shrugged to herself. Oh well. The stew would have to go without this evening. Tianna stirred the contents of the large pot, and then removed a ladle-full and sampled it. She nodded to herself. It was good, but definitely could have used the wild onion. Hearing a shout, Tianna glanced up from the stew and looked in the direction of the spar. Sirion had disarmed Adrianna and had grabbed her from behind. He picked her up and she shouted again, kicking her legs and telling him to put her down. Smiling, Sirion acquiesced, and then spun her around to face him. For a moment, he just stared at her, and then he was placing his face alongside hers, like he was whispering something into her ear.

Tianna tore her gaze away from them, returning her attention to the stewpot. In all of the years she had known him, she had never seen Sirion so happy. Everyone had gotten a chance to see a side of Sirion that they never knew existed. Adrianna had brought that side of him into being, and it seemed that he was finally complete. Tianna was happy for Sirion, but only wished that it had been her who had been able to make him whole.

As the sun set upon the horizon, the group prepared their bedrolls for the night. Triath and Amethyst situated themselves near the mouth of the cave for their watch. Lying on her bedroll next to Sirion, Adrianna was situated the farthest back into the small cave. She was glad that Sirion had found it, for it was rare that they got the chance to sleep unhindered by the elements. Adrianna was about to drift off to sleep when she heard a noise. It was a dry, raspy sound that seemed to be coming from the cave interior behind her. For a few moments it stopped, and she began to think that it was nothing. But then she heard it again. A long deep hiss followed the rasping.

Adrianna put her hand on Sirion's chest. "Sirion, I think I hear something."

Suddenly Adrianna felt Sirion's arms wrap around her, and they were rolling towards the cave entrance. Sirion stopped once they hit another of their companions, and quickly got to his feet. Stalker in hand, Sirion faced the interior of the cave. Adrianna and a disturbed Dartanyen stood up and then turned. The thing emerging from the depths of the cave was frightening to behold. It was long and reptilian, its head a hideous cross between a lizard and a bird of prey. Two thick black horns sprouted from the ridges over the yellow eyes. Its jaws were huge, sporting long sharp teeth.

The red-brown wyvern slithered towards the group. Out of the corner of her eye, Adrianna saw Dartanyen rise to stand beside her. "By the gods . . ." Amethyst's voice trailed away, almost as though it had been silenced. Sirion slowly began to back away from the creature and Adrianna followed suit, his body pushing her back. Beside her, Dartanyen moved back with her, and she noticed that most everyone else was trying to make it to the front of the cave as well.

The wyvern hissed again and raised its head, narrowing its yellow eyes. The full length of its body had become visible. It had four legs, too small to be of much use to the creature, which was why it used its belly upon which to slither like a snake. Its leathery wings, too, were undersized, and were folded up along its back. More than half of the creature was made up of its tail, which Adrianna noticed had a thick knot at the tip. From it protruded a sharp stinger.

"Adrianna," Sirion whispered, "Get behind me . . ." Just then the wyvern charged. Sirion separated Stalker into two blades, and she heard the ring of steel as Sheridana, Zorg, and Armond drew their blades. She saw one arrow, and then two, as Anya and Dartanyen fired at the creature with their bows. Adrianna darted out of the way of the charging wyvern, narrowly missing its sharply clawed feet as it lurched past her.

From within the depths of his concentration, Dinim saw Adrianna just narrowly miss being crushed by the wyvern. He felt concern, yet continued weaving the magic of his spell. He was about to cast it when he felt something strong hit his upper legs. Dinim flew back, finally striking the ground just outside of the cave. He lay there for a moment, slightly dazed, and then realized the pain in his legs. He reached down to feel if they were both still in one piece, and once finding them to be so, began to move his body into a seated position. It was then that he noticed the pain in his hand. He lifted his hand off of the ground to find a thorny vine lying beneath it. Cursing, he ripped the vine up off of the ground and threw it away from him. He then clutched at the bloody hand, the blue thorns of the vine having cut deep into the palm. As he sat upright, Dinim suddenly felt a slight sense of vertigo, and attributed it to the fact that he had just been knocked several feet through the air.

Slowly Dinim stood up, turning back towards the battle. From his spot just outside of the cave, he saw the wyvern lash its tail at Zorg. The big warrior jumped over the barbed tip and brought his sword down onto the thick flesh just above it. The creature shrieked in pain, taking its attention away from a cornered Sheridana. But it was too late for the wyvern. Armond struck at the beast with his strangely glowing blades. As he struck, visible shocks of electricity coursed through the creature. Already weakened by the missile spell that Adrianna had cast, the deep wounds caused by Naemmious's wicked flail and Sirion's attacks, the wyvern expired quickly. Holding himself up against the cave wall, Dinim watched as the creature fell over onto its side and took its last breath.

For several moments there was silence as everyone caught his or her breath, looking at the downed wyvern. Then Anya looked up at Sirion, a deep frown on her face. "I thought you told us that this cave was safe."

Sirion's expression became one of chagrin and he shook his head. "I'm sorry. I scouted the place out before I brought you here, but I obviously missed something."

"Yeah, a really big something."

"I know. I'm sorry . . ."

"Hey, everyone makes mistakes," said Dartanyen. "Let's just clean up this mess." Naemmious, Zorg, Armond, Dartanyen, Sirion, and Sheri began to move the large carcass out of the cave. Tianna busied herself with the wounds of the group, Sabian, and Dinim needing the most work. Sirion went back into the depths of the cave, just to be sure that nothing remained that could cause harm to them. Once he was satisfied that the place was clear, he returned to the group.

Once more, everyone settled themselves down for sleep. Sorn and Naemmious sat down for their watch, taking the last hour of Triath and Amethyst's shift. Dinim watched with narrowed eyes as Adrianna lay down next to Sirion. His bound hand throbbed, despite the cream and fresh wrapping that Tianna had applied to it. He had been curt towards her as he gave clipped answers to her inquiries about the wound, but he could not seem to control his behavior. Maybe he was just tired and needed to get some extra rest. Dinim lay down on his bedroll and stared into the darkness.

29 Cisceren CY593

Dinim and Adrianna rode towards the area where he knew their destination to be. They had left the rest of the group behind over thirty minutes ago and were close to the abode of the crazy mage known as Paxil. Two days ago the group had ridden into the city of Driscol. Once they had found a suitable inn, Armond decided that he would make a visit to the closest local smithy, Sorn and Amethyst went off to find some type of weird rogue's equipment, and Dinim left in search of someone who could tell him the whereabouts of Master Paxil. The information was not difficult to obtain; all he had to do was find a shop that dealt in the magical arts. In a way, it was harder to find the shop than it was to find out where the mage resided.

Once he returned to the inn, the rest of the group was just settling down for the evening meal. Dinim listened to the talk as he picked at his food. He had not been feeling well since the skirmish with the wyvern; he had a mild fever and his appetite was seriously diminished. Once the meal was cleared away, Dartanyen asked Dinim what he had discovered about Paxil. Dinim told him what he had learned, and that he would be a greater resource than any library. The old man possessed a power, a power that gave him the ability to know things without having to be told them.

Dartanyen nodded in agreement. "In the morning we will restock our supplies and any equipment that we will need. This is the last city we will see before heading into the Ratik Pass. Armond, are you and Zorg ready to travel?"

"Yes," replied Armond. "We had only minor adjustments to make to our weapons. We will be ready when everyone is prepared to leave."

Dartanyen nodded. "Good. Let's all get some rest then."

Early the next afternoon the group left the city. They traveled northeast into the foothills. When Dinim knew that they were getting close to the location about which he had learned, he bade the group stop for the night. "Tomorrow morning I will go to the mage. He is old, and more than just a little insane. Too many people will make him nervous. I don't want us to get too close and then find him gone when I get to his cabin."

"I am not about to let you go alone," said Dartanyen. "You need to bring someone with you."

Dinim frowned.

"I will go with you," Adrianna piped up. Dinim continued to frown and she shrugged her shoulders. "Maybe I can be of help . . . you know, he being crazy and all."

"Fine," said Dinim. "We will leave at daybreak. Be ready."

And here they were, riding towards uncertainty. Dinim hated that almost as much as the hand that Dartanyen had forced him to play. He would much preferred to have gone alone, but truth be told, he would have wanted none other than Adrianna to accompany him. He had missed her companionship, her sweet voice, her gentle ways. She probably could be of help in this type of situation, her feminine appeal enough to charm the boots off of any man . . . at least any man with eyes or ears. Yet she was blind to that, unaware of the effect she had on people.

Dinim suddenly held up a hand. They had reached the home of Master Paxil. The house was old and dilapidated, hardly a fit structure in which to take up residence. But Dinim could sense the power surrounding the place, and he knew that magic was keeping the small cabin from falling to the ground. Dinim and Adria dismounted, and then bound their larian to a scrawny tree.

Slowly they approached the cabin, and when they reached the door, Dinim put out a hand and rapped on it.

For several moments they stood at the door, straining to hear any sounds from within the cabin. They heard none. Dinim knocked again at the door, and once again, there was nothing. He pressed his lips into a thin line. "Damn," he exclaimed. "He must have known that we were coming . . ."

"I sure did know that you were comin' to pay me a visit."

Adrianna had to put her hand over her mouth to keep herself from crying out as she turned to face the white-haired, squinty old man standing behind her. She couldn't believe that she had not heard him approaching. Beside her, Dinim also swung around, his expression a mixture of consternation and relief. "Are you Master Paxil?" asked Dinim.

"In the flesh," replied the old man, regarding them critically from his good eye. "Please, come inside . . . and don't worry, the place will not fall down upon you." Paxil cackled and clapped his hands together, stepping between them to open the door.

Once inside, Adrianna had to give her eyes a few moments to adjust to the lack of light. The windows emitted very little, they being grimy beyond belief. Paxil lit another candle, setting it upon one of several cluttered tables. He also had shelves along the walls, ones that were just as disorganized and cluttered as the tables. As she walked further into the room, Adrianna tripped over something on the floor. She looked down to realize that there was precious little walking space, the floors having books, parchments, and various baubles lying everywhere.

"I know why you have come here."

Adrianna felt herself beginning to frown. She had heard words similar to those before, spoken by one Ami Rayhana. She did not like their portent, nor the fact that others seemed to know more about her than she knew herself. However, Adria held her tongue, glancing at Dinim as he spoke.

"Indeed. We have a powerful enemy, one we wish to know more about."

"Lord Thane is the least of your problems," Paxil hissed, narrowing his eyes. "He is merely a pawn, one created by a power far greater than the world has experienced before. Aasarak has the Box of Death, and has used it . . ."

Adrianna felt a chill crawl up her spine. She glanced at Dinim to find that his expression had turned stony. The mage came closer, squinting and scrutinizing them with his rheumy eye. He examined Dinim only cursorily, but stopped in front of Adrianna. He opened his good eye then, and he looked eerie, one eye clear and the other clouded by cataract.

"Ahhhh," the old man exclaimed. "I know you. How did you come to be so far from home, my dear? I am sure that your mother misses you."

Adrianna stiffened. This man, he was indeed crazy. How could he possibly know her? She had never met him before. And he obviously did not know her mother, otherwise he would know that she was dead. For a man that knew 'everything' he seemed not to know much at all. Perhaps all of his powers of knowing could just simply be attributed to mere insanity.

"My mother is dead, Master."

"Ah yes, such a shame it was. So much potential wasted."

Adrianna suppressed a sigh. They had only been there a few minutes, but already she was prepared to leave. There was nothing that this man could tell them. He was a joke.

"Please, Master. Have you any information that can help us against our enemy? Even now he hunts us, and he is close," said Dinim.

"I know how close he is!" snarled Paxil. "And yes, I suppose I could help you . . ." Paxil turned away from Adrianna, making his way over to one of the messy shelves. He shuffled some things around a bit. "While the master has been busy, the creation has been in pursuit of a personal vendetta. Such is the way of Azmathous. Revenge is their priority. Aasarak should have known that, the fool." Paxil withdrew a small box from the clutter. He then walked over to Dinim and handed it to him.

Dinim slowly opened the box. Inside, nestled upon a bed of dark velvet, was a ring. Dinim picked up the ring and examined it closely. Then his eyes widened in wonderment. "Is this what I think it is?"

Paxil smiled. "Probably. But I am not a mind reader, you know." The old man chortled for a moment, and then continued. "What do you think it is?"

"This is the Ring of Aboleth."

Paxil cackled again. "Right you are. You are a smart one . . . well-read."

Dinim frowned. "Are you sure that you want to give this up?"

Paxil shrugged his skinny shoulders. "It is for a good cause, eh?"

All Dinim could do was nod his head. Adrianna remained silent. She wondered what was so great about this ring. And why did Dinim seem so hesitant? If the ring could help them, he should take it.

"But Master, it is the only one in existence. How did you come about it?"

Once more the old man shrugged. "I don't even remember any more. I have so many things, and so many tales to go with them, they all seem to mesh together now. You know, old age and all."

Dinim nodded. "Thank you. This . . . this is a great gift. You must think us to be trustworthy."

"We all must put our faith in something. I am old. I do not have a future. But countless others do have one. You and your comrades have the power to make possible the beginning of a new era. That is worth fighting for . . . worth believing in . . . worth trusting someone to make the right decisions."

"But what if we are not strong enough?"

"Then the world as we hope it to be will never exist," said Paxil sadly. "Strength comes not only from the body . . . or from the mind . . . but from the heart."

Adrianna found herself staring at Paxil. Suddenly he did not seem so crazy anymore. He spoke with a wisdom that he had learned through the ages. Who knew how long this man had lived? And he was so old, it was difficult to even tell his race. Was he faelin, human, or something in between? But her mind quickly returned to the business at hand. "But how do we fight someone who is already dead? We know that he has great powers: unfathomable strength, the ability to instill mindless fear, and not to mention the attributes he possessed as a mortal man."

Paxil turned to her. "Just because he is dead does not mean that he cannot be killed again. Thane is not a god. He is a construct, one created by an even greater evil. As a creature of the night, he will gather most of his strength and powers at that time. However, even then he can be destroyed."

Adrianna nodded.

"Come, your companions await you. I have helped you all I can." Paxil walked towards the door and Dinim and Adria followed. When he opened it, the light from outside almost blinded them for a moment. Dinim turned. "Thank you, Master. I hope that we will be able to meet your expectations."

"I have no doubt," replied the old man, glancing at Adrianna. Then he was waving them away. "Come again sometime . . . when you don't need me to give you anything. I like companionship every now and again, you know."

Adrianna and Dinim waved back to the man, and then walked towards their larian. They untied the beasts and began to lead them away. They turned back to the cabin to have one last look, but the house was gone, as though it had never been.

CHAPTER 22

Adrianna and Dinim walked side-by-side, their larian trailing behind them. It would take them some good thirty or forty minutes to make it back to the rest of the group, but they were not in any hurry. It would be a mild day, the air a bit warmer than it had been as of late, and it would be good to take it easy. Besides, it had been a while since she and Dinim had shared meaningful conversation. Adrianna missed the comraderie they had once had together, and she hoped to recapture that.

"What a strange old man. Now I know why he lives so far removed from the rest of civilization."

Dinim nodded in agreement. "Not to mention that he probably doesn't want to be robbed. Did you see all of those books? They were probably originals! And all of those artifacts . . . who knows what he had hidden in that house." Dinim stroked his chin thoughtfully. "Well, on second thought, Paxil probably isn't concerned with being robbed. It would be effortless for him to keep others out, especially with that *Cloaking* spell he has on the house."

"He said he was expecting us. He probably disengaged the spell so that we would be able to find the place."

"Most likely."

For a few moments they walked in silence, and then she remembered. "Hey Dinim, tell me about the ring that Paxil gave us. What can it do? Do you really think it can help us?"

Dinim frowned and turned to her. "We aren't going to use that ring."

Adrianna frowned in return. "Why not? Paxil seemed to think that it could be of use to us."

Dinim sighed heavily. "Paxil is old and crazy. He doesn't realize that none of us is strong enough to wield the ring."

"Tell me, Dinim. What does the ring do? How do you know so much about it?"

Dinim looked away from her and stared at the ground in front of him. "It is called the Ring of Aboleth. I learned about it several years ago while I was studying under Master TC. It is an object of great power, and no one seems to know exactly where it comes from or how it was created. I think that TC has some ideas, but he would never share them with me."

"But what does it do?"

Dinim turned his head to look at her again. "They say that the ring has been infused with the power of life itself."

Adrianna raised an eyebrow. "The ring is alive?"

"No, but it has the power to bring life forth."

"You say that as though it is a bad thing."

"Well, it can be. As mortals, it should not be up to us to decide upon the emergence of life."

Adrianna smirked. "But Dinim, we do that every day. We have killed men, caused the life to leave their bodies. And every day, somewhere there is a woman giving birth, bringing new life into the world."

Dinim began to frown again and stopped. "No, Adria. This is different."

Adrianna stopped as well and turned towards him. "Well explain it to me, then."

"Just imagine, Adrianna, if a bad man had this ring in his possession. What might he do with it? He could perhaps use it to bring back the lives of his companions lost in battle, or perhaps countless others and make himself an army of warriors who are beholden to him. Perhaps he would bring to life things that were never meant to have it, such as a sword or a cloak." Dinim paused and then continued. "The point is, the ring can be used to do great evil, and even one with the best intentions can do wrong. Great power like that can be enticing, and can make one thirst for more. Once started, one may never be able to stop, the temptation too difficult to ignore."

"But the ring can do great good as well, Dinim. Our mission is not just about us. It is about all of those other people that Thane will not hesitate to kill if we do not destroy him. If the ring can help us do that, then isn't it worth the risk?"

"No."

"Why not?"

"Because the temptation may take us over the edge. We would then be a liability. We could put countless others in danger, and then what purpose would the ring have served? None. We would be right back where we started."

Adrianna crossed her arms over her chest and stuck out her lower lip. "I do not share your opinion."

Dinim sighed with exasperation and then put his hands in the air. "So what? What do you know, anyway? You are but a girl, thinking that everything is black and white. Well, Adrianna, let me break it to you. The world is in color! This is not a child's game. The ring is dangerous, and not intended for ones like us."

"Why did you take it from Paxil then?" Adrianna spat. "You think that you are so high and mighty, and that you will be able to use it yourself one day. Do you think that you will not succumb to the same temptation as others?"

"No," Dinim shouted in return. "I took it because it was a gift. When next I see Master TC, I will give the ring to him."

Adrianna stepped up to Dinim, putting her face near his. "And so, in the meantime, you are going to allow us to risk our lives? You know what we are up against. So does Paxil, and that is why he entrusted the ring to us. How many of us will die in this fight?"

Dinim stepped back from her. "Shut your face. You have no idea what could happen. Whoever wields the ring . . . they could become like another Thane, making the decision of who lives and who dies. That kind of power could turn a good person into one who does only evil things."

"You are a fool, Dinim," said Adrianna, stepping up to him again. "If you never take a chance in life, how do you ever expect to win? The ring is not inherently evil, it is just that it is possible to do evil things with it. We could anchor the wielder, give him the support that he needs to return to us."

Dinim shook his head. "No, I will not allow it. I understand your argument, but it just isn't worth it. We will fight Thane as though we knew nothing about the ring."

"I am not asking your permission, Dinim. This is my mission and I say that we use the ring."

Dinim smirked malevolently. "This isn't your mission anymore, Adrianna. It has become everyone's mission. And *I* say that we will never use this ring."

Adrianna felt herself seething. She couldn't believe that Dinim could not see past his own faulty reasoning. "Damn, you are a coward. I should have seen it from the start. I can't believe . . ."

Dinim stepped back from her. "I am a coward? That's a joke. You are the weak link, Adria. You are just a little girl playing in an adult's world. You are always afraid, hoping that the rest of the group will step up for you. I have yet to see you make your own decisions. You have no confidence, and even the rest of the group has wondered if you are up for a fight."

Adrianna found herself shaking her head, taking in Dinim's scathing words. She stepped back, seeing the expression on Dinim's face, the rictus of rage that had taken over his features. She could still feel her anger, but the slight ring of truth she heard in Dinim's words tempered it.

"You are a little idiot, Adrianna. You have no idea of the gamble that you would be taking to use that ring. But do you care? No. You can barely see past your nose. You would take one threat and exchange it for another possibly more malignant one, just so that you can rid yourself of the one that you consider to be your responsibility. Well, this is what I think about you and your dung-eaten plan."

Adrianna began to hear the murmuring of a spell being cast. She felt the shift in the air around her, the answer of magic to one who could summon it. She stared at Dinim, saw his hands as they made the symbols in the space before him, saw him put one hand into his pouch of components. What was he doing? Adrianna looked around her, trying to find that for which he would cast a spell. She saw nothing out of the ordinary and then began to get a sensation of unease, one of eminent danger.

Adrianna looked back at Dinim. The look on his face was terrible, all reason appearing to have left him. He looked like a crazy man . . . Suddenly Adrianna felt a burning sensation on her upper arm. She gripped it, feeling the golden serpent beneath the fabric of her blouse. And then the spell was cast. Adrianna watched the energy as it raced towards her, her mind recoiling in shock. *He was casting the spell at her.* And then the spell struck her. Adrianna felt herself being thrown back, back, back, and then she was hitting the ground. All around her there was a sphere of vibrant color. Adrianna closed her eyes, the impact taking her breath away. She was dead, and her friend had killed her.

"Adria! Adrianna!" The shout was coming from behind her. She stirred and felt the grass beneath her fingertips. That was strange. If she were dead, why would she be lying on the ground? "Adrianna?" The voice was louder now, more insistent. She opened her eyes and her vision swam, the sky above her swirling about crazily. And then the face of Anya was there too, tilting this way and that. "Adrianna, are you all right?"

"I . . . I think so," she replied, sitting upright.

"I saw the eruption. What in the Hells was that?"

Adrianna's eyes widened and she pushed Anya to the side, searching desperately for Dinim. He was standing where she remembered seeing him last. He was staring at his hands, an expression of bewilderment on his face. Anya turned to look where Adrianna was staring. "Is he all right? What happened here?"

Adrianna stood up and gestured to Anya. "Come on, we have to get back to the others."

Frowning, Anya contemplated her solemnly. "Where are your larian? You left with two of them this morning."

"They must have been frightened away by the spell." Adrianna turned and began to walk.

"The spell? Adrianna, what is going on here?" Anya grabbed Adrianna's arm.

Adrianna tore herself out of the other woman's grasp. "Anya, I don't want to take the time to explain this all to you right now. Let's just get back to the group."

Anya held up her hands. "All right, fine. But what about Dinim?"

Adrianna cast Anya an intense glance, one that brooked no argument. "Leave him."

Anya stared at her for a moment and then began to walk. "The group is this way."

Adrianna fell in behind Anya, her mind in a state of confusion and turmoil. He had meant to kill her. Dinim hadn't just cast a light spell to merely frighten her. He had smitten her with an upper level incantation. Adrianna rubbed at her upper arm, the pain still there. Whatever was there, the serpent was resting right over it, abrading it. She still couldn't believe what had happened. Maybe it wasn't Dinim back there. Maybe it was another doppelganger and the real Dinim was trapped somewhere, needing their help.

After only another ten minutes of walking, Anya and Adrianna had reached the group. The larian were loaded and ready for travel. Dartanyen stood up and approached them when they walked into camp. "So, did you find out anything useful?" Dartanyen looked beyond her and Anya. "Where is Dinim?"

"He is still back there," Adrianna said in a low voice.

Dartanyen looked back to her and frowned. "Back where?"

Adrianna took her thumb and gestured behind her. Anya put her hands on her hips and began to tap her foot on the ground. Dartanyen glanced from one woman to the next. "What in the Nine Hells is going on?"

"That's what I want to know," said Anya.

"What's up? Did we find out anything that can help us?" asked Sirion as he walked up to them.

"I saw an eruption of . . . of some kind of energy," said Anya. "I ran towards it, afraid that perhaps someone was in trouble. I saw Adrianna lying on the ground. I thought that she was hurt . . ."

Dartanyen turned back to Adrianna. "Did something happen?"

Adrianna nodded. "Dinim attacked me. He cast a spell at me. I don't know why I'm still alive. I left Dinim back there, where it happened."

Dartanyen and Sirion looked at one another and then began to make in the direction that Adrianna indicated. "Armond . . . Zorg. Grab your weapons. We have trouble," shouted Dartanyen. The two men jumped up with their weapons in hand, running to catch up with Dartanyen and Sirion.

Adrianna turned to Anya. "I'm sorry. I just wanted to get far away from him as soon as I could."

"It's all right. I would have felt the same way," Anya replied, patting Adrianna on the shoulder.

Adrianna nodded. "What is going on?" asked Triath as he approached them. "Where are they going?"

Suddenly they heard a commotion coming from the direction that the men had taken. They heard a few shouts, and then, "No, don't touch me. I am fine." Dinim stumbled into the camp, his hands in the air before him. Behind him were Sirion and Dartanyen, followed by Armond and Zorg.

Sirion glanced quickly about the camp and his eyes alighted upon Tianna. "I think that he is ill."

Tianna frowned and rushed over to Dinim. "I tell you, I'm fine." She put her hand upon Dinim's brow, and then began to frown.

"Sirion, you are right. His skin is damp and he has a fever."

"Bring him over here," said Sorn, lying out his bedroll. Tianna and Sirion helped Dinim to the bedroll, and then urged him to sit on it. Tianna then went to her larian, where she removed her medicine bag and water pouch. Returning to Dinim, she poured some water into a cup, and then sprinkled some greenish powder into it. She swirled it about until the contents were mixed, and then handed it to Dinim.

Dinim took the cup and drank from it thirstily, not even bothering to ask her what she had put in it. He then gave the emptied cup back to her. Tianna set it aside and took up his injured hand. Dinim jerked the hand back. "I'm fine, Tianna. Let's just go. We have a lot of ground to cover today."

"Dinim, I need to see your hand. It might be infected. That could be the cause of your fever."

Dinim rolled his eyes at her and then held out the hand. Tianna slowly removed the bandages, and then inspected the wounds. The deep lacerations were red, but not infected. She looked closer at the wounds, seeing exactly how deep they went. The muscle had been deeply penetrated, almost as though he had fallen upon something very sharp. "Dinim, tell me again how you got these cuts."

"I got hit by the wyvern, and I fell. You know that."

"But what did you fall on?"

"Some type of wretched bush." Dinim frowned. "Or maybe it was a vine. I don't remember."

A thought popped into Tianna's mind, one that made her begin to feel nervous. "Did the vine have thorns?"

Dinim's eyes widened. "Yes, as a matter of fact, I think it did. I could swear that they were blue, but I know that can't be right. I have never heard of a plant with blue thorns." Dinim chuckled to himself.

Tianna frowned. "Dinim, I think you have been poisoned."

"What?"

"You have been poisoned. Don't tell me that you haven't been feeling a general malaise for the last couple of days."

"You're right. I haven't been feeling well. Actually, I have been having a lot of strange thoughts lately too . . ."

"That is what I mean. You were poisoned by a hybanthis vine. The secretions are toxic, and have brain-based effects on their victims. It can cause fever, a feeling of illness, and can cause the person to experience heightened emotion. Even that night, after the skirmish with the wyvern, I noticed that you were a bit testy. I attributed it to the fact that you were probably in some amount of pain, and that you were unhappy that you had been unable to participate in the defeat of the creature. I had no idea that you had been poisoned."

Dinim frowned and looked at the ground, his mind reeling. He then cleared his throat and asked the question lurking in his mind. "Could this be why I cast a spell at Adrianna today?"

"What?" Tianna looked up at him in shock.

Dinim looked up and into her eyes. "Yes. I cast a spell at her. I didn't mean to. Well, actually I did, but it was almost like I couldn't control myself . . ."

"Dinim, what kind of spell was it? It was just a minor one, right?" Tianna looked at him, her eyes pleading with him to tell her that it was a lesser incantation.

"No. It was one of the most powerful spells I know."

Tianna put a hand over her mouth. "Oh gods."

Dinim took her other hand. "Tianna, you have got to help me. Please cure me of my affliction."

"It will have to work its way through your system. It can take several days."

"I implore you, tell me that it was only because of the poison that I attacked my friend."

Tianna shook her head. "I can't. The effects of the poison only act upon what is already there. Whatever you were feeling towards Adrianna was of your construct. The anger that was there was purely yours. The poison only magnified this emotion, making it so that you were unable to deal with the intensity of it. Then you reacted in the best way that you knew how."

Dinim stared off into the space before him, his eyes wide with the horror of what he had done. "I can't believe that she is still alive. All I remember is that I wanted to kill her . . ."

***

For one more day, the group traveled through the foothills, and then camped that night at the entrance into the Ratik Pass. The attitude pervading the group the first day in the pass was solemn, many of them remembering the last time they had been there. They had barely escaped alive, and now here they were, plodding through it once more.

Adrianna rode behind Sheri on her larian. Since two of the animals had been lost, courtesy of Dinim and his spell, she found herself having to share with her sister and Sirion. Dramati did not mind carrying her weight in addition to that of Sirion, but she did not want to overtire him. So, the first half of her day she would ride with Sirion, and the second half she would ride with Sheri. Dinim had to do the same, riding with Tianna or Sorn the first half of the day and then with Sabian the second half.

For the past couple of days after the argument with Dinim, Adrianna had remained withdrawn and introspective. His words continued to echo through her mind. She found herself dwelling on the way that her comrades perceived her, hoping that Dinim had only said those things to hurt her. Yet, she could not be sure. She knew that they liked her, but that was not what worried her. She wanted them to see her as an equal in battle, and she just didn't have the answer to that question.

Adrianna scratched at the burn that circled her upper arm, a burn that coiled around it in exactly the same place that the golden serpent rested. That afternoon, after Dinim had hit her with his spell, Adrianna had removed her blouse to find the burn festering there beneath the ornament. Adrianna bit her lip as she moved the serpent further up her arm to uncover the wound. The metal easily gave way, and readjusted itself upon her arm. The serpent watched her from sparkling eyes, and Adrianna could not help but stroke the smooth scales. She then focused upon the burn. It was an angry red, and the skin had begun to peel from it. Noticing her state of undress, Sheri had approached her, and upon seeing the wound, had called Tianna. The healer came and examined it, and then rubbed a stinky salve on it.

"I know it smells bad, but it will heal the burn in next to no time." Then Tianna frowned. "Did this object give the burn to you?" she asked, pointing to the serpent.

Adrianna nodded. "When Dinim began to cast his spell, I felt a burning sensation on my arm. Somehow, it must have protected me from the spell because I became surrounded by a protective shell." Then she frowned. "But I really don't understand it because I have been hit with other spells before, and the serpent did not react to them that way."

"Perhaps it is simply the particular spell that Dinim cast. Maybe it protects the wearer from spells of a certain type or caliber," said Tianna.

"Yes, perhaps," Adrianna conceded softly.

Tianna contemplated her speculatively for a moment. "You know that he was poisoned."

Adrianna nodded. "I know."

"He is not entirely to blame. The effects of the hybanthis make one feel overwhelmed and unable to deal with their emotions."

Adrianna sighed. "I know what you are trying to say, but I cannot absolve him of his transgression. He cast a lethal spell at me, Tianna. Without this talisman, I would have died. Despite the poison, there was a part of Dinim that was still there, a reasoning part of him. Yet, he cast the spell anyway. I cannot just forget that."

Tianna nodded. "You are right. I understand what you are trying to say, and I would probably feel the same, but I know that Dinim deeply regrets what he did."

Adrianna shook her head. Feeling the tears beginning to build, she lowered her eyes to the ground. "It is not enough." Tianna patted her shoulder, and then walked away.

Adrianna rode silently for the rest of the day, and that evening she sat on her bedroll, a volume on her lap. She read the words, but she understood nothing of what they were trying to say as her mind continued to be preoccupied with the ring that Dinim continued to carry on his person. No one knew about the Ring of Aboleth, save for herself and Dinim. When asked questions about their meeting with Paxil, its existence was never mentioned. Neither she nor Dinim spoke about the ring, and it continued to lie waiting somewhere within Dinim's leather belt-pouch. Until tonight.

Earlier in the day, during their mid-day break, Adrianna had pulled Amethyst aside. She told the girl that she needed to speak with her later that evening, and that it was important. Amethyst nodded, and agreed to come to her after the evening meal. Later, when the group began to set up camp for the night, Amethyst had made it so that her bedroll was situated closer to Adrianna's than usual. However, as the group members tended to make their beds in the same places every night, she did not place it so close so as to bring attention to herself.

As everyone began to situate themselves for the night, Amethyst went to see Adrianna. Sirion continued to sit at the fire with Dramati, talking to Sorn and Triath, so he was not there to overhear the conversation. Amethyst and Triath were usually the first to take watch, so it was not unusual to see her still awake and walking about camp. No one paid her any heed when she seated herself next to Adrianna on the bedroll.

"Amethyst, there is something that I was hoping that you could do for me. It is something that I would never ask you to do unless I felt it to be of utmost importance," said Adrianna, a somber expression on her face.

"What is it?" asked Amethyst, leaning slightly forward.

"The other morning, when Dinim and I went to see Paxil, the old man gave him something. It is a ring, a magical ring. It has a power that we may be able to use against Thane."

Amethyst frowned. "Why didn't you tell us about this before?"

Adrianna lowered her voice even more. "Because the ring is the reason why Dinim and I started to argue. He feels that the ring is too powerful to use, and that it may cause more harm than good. However, I feel that it is worth the risk, if it will save the lives of people in this group."

Amethyst nodded. "You want me to get the ring from him, don't you?"

Adrianna nodded. "Yes. Dinim is not willing to use the ring. He didn't even tell Dartanyen or Triath about it. I am afraid that if we don't at least try, and people die in the battle against Thane, that I will never be able to forgive myself."

Amethyst nodded again. "I will get the ring for you, Adria."

Adrianna regarded her intently. "Are you sure? You feel the same way I do, then?"

"I trust you, Adrianna. I know that you would never do something to bring harm to us. I believe that you will make the right decision."

A lump began to form in her throat as Adrianna stared at Amethyst. "Thank you. That means a lot to me."

Amethyst grinned. "Give me a couple of days, and I will have the ring for you."

"All right," said Adrianna. "Let me tell you where I think it might be."

***

The next evening Adrianna sat on her bedroll, removed from the activity of the rest of the group. Once again she had her book open and in her lap, and once again she pretended to read the words on the pages. But this time, Adrianna did not even attempt to look at the words, instead focusing on something else. Within the crook of the book rested the Ring of Aboleth.

Adrianna touched the golden ring with the tip of her forefinger. Even with that slight caress she could feel the power of the object. Dinim had been right to be wary of it, for even she, with her relatively narrow scope, could sense that she could be sucked within the power of the ring and never return from it. She was more than just a bit scared, but she felt she had little choice. Thane's power was great, and she . . . they . . . needed something to counter-act it.

Adrianna looked up from the ring and caught Amethyst's gaze as the girl regarded her from across the encampment. Only an hour ago, Amethyst had solemnly presented the ring to her. It was then that Adrianna had seen how much it had taken for Amethyst to steal the ring from Dinim. Both of them knew that it was wrong to use one's skills against another member of one's company, yet they had done it anyway. Amethyst was feeling the weight of her transgression, and Adrianna felt guilt at having placed Amethyst in that position. However, she could not entirely blame herself. Of her own free will, Amethyst had chosen to steal the ring and to give it to Adrianna.

With a slight nod, Adrianna sought to dissipate Amethyst's disquiet. She then took in the rest of the group: Sabian studying his books, Tianna concocting another strange potion for them to drink, Anya and Dartanyen plucking the feathers of the meal they had procured. Dinim was busy as well.

That morning, he had announced that he might have figured out a spell that would enable him to enchant a weapon.

"Hey, that's great, Dinim," said Dartanyen.

"Maybe you can try out your spell on Zorg's sword," said Armond.

Dinim nodded. "Everyone will need at least one magic-infused weapon to use against the Azmathous. Normal weapons will not even touch them."

That evening the group set up camp early. Zorg handed his blade over to Dinim, who then began to work on the enchantment. Adrianna regarded him for a moment as he worked, her hand wrapping around the ring. At the mid-day break, he had approached her for the first time since their argument. He had seated himself next to her on the ground, and when she couldn't ignore him any longer, Adrianna turned to him. She found him watching her out of eyes shadowed by the pain of what he had done. He had dark smudges beneath his eyelids and the lines of his face were deeper than she remembered.

Adrianna stood and Dinim followed. "Adrianna, I will not ask you to forget what I have done to you, but please consider . . ."

Adrianna held up a hand and stopped him. In a very quiet voice she said, "Dinim, please don't do this. Just . . . just stay away from me." She then walked to the larian she rode with Sheri. Dinim did not follow her, and she was glad of it. His nearness made her stomach turn, the hurt of what he had done to her too strong for her mind to accept.

Adrianna opened her hand, continuing to contemplate the ring. Now that it was in her possession, she needed to tell the rest of the group about it. They deserved to know, and they needed to have a say in the decision to use it against Thane. Adrianna sighed to herself. But she was afraid of their reaction towards the fact that she and Dinim had kept the existence of the ring a secret. Not only that, but the decision of whether or not to use the ring may cause a rift in their ranks. Dinim had shared some very good points with her during their argument, and she could see others sharing his views. However, she knew that some people would share her opinions as well, as Amethyst already did.

Adrianna knew that the group could ill afford to be divided now. They were close to their confrontation with Thane, and the rift could cause the group to lose cohesion in battle. Perhaps this should be a decision she made by herself. Adrianna frowned. She did not like that idea, but she was beginning to wonder if there was any other way. Besides, wasn't it Dinim who said that she needed to step forward and make her own decisions? But was she letting her anger with Dinim cloud her reason? She could not allow herself to do that. She would be doing herself and her comrades all the greatest of disservice.

"Adrianna, are you all right?"

Adrianna closed her hand over the ring once more as Sirion sat down beside her. She glanced up at him, noting the expression of concern on his face. Adrianna nodded and looked back down at her book. "Yes, I am fine," she lied.

Sirion's frown deepened. "You don't look 'fine'."

"I think I'm just tired."

Sirion nodded and took her hand in his. She looked back up at him and he said, "I know you are going through a hard time. If you need me, I am here for you." Sirion brushed her face with his fingertips.

Adrianna felt a tingle race up her body, an answer to his caress. She smiled at him and then put her head on his shoulder. "I know. Thank you, Sirion." Sirion put an arm around her and held her next to him. As he held her, his embrace slowly began to settle the turmoil in her mind. She had a difficult decision to make, but it did not have to be at this very moment. Sirion was a strong and solid warmth against her, and she felt safe. She threaded her fingers through his, and she felt his hand tighten in response. She would think about it tomorrow.

***

Adrianna wrapped her winter cloak more tightly about herself. It was getting colder each day that they spent in the pass. Not only were they going higher, but they were getting closer to the cold season as well. Soon they would encounter cold rains, and possibly even snow as they continued upward. Adrianna pressed herself closer to Sheri's back, seeking the warmth of another warm body. Her sister passed her a pair of gloves and Adrianna took them gratefully and then pulled up the hood of the fur-lined cloak.

Upon waking that morning, the weight of the decision that she needed to make descended upon her. For most of the day it weighed on her mind, but she kept returning to the same series of thoughts. She needed to tell the group about the ring, and she needed to do it soon. However, she would insist upon its use. She knew that Dinim would repudiate her, but she would consider her next course of action when she obtained an idea about how the rest of the group felt about it. If everyone was entirely against it, she would most definitely not use it. But if there was a split . . . well, she would have another decision to make.

Late afternoon turned into early evening. A suitable site was found and the group stopped to prepare camp. Dinim settled himself down to studying his books, he having decided to enchant some of Dartanyen's arrows. His work with Zorg's blade had taken virtually all of the previous night, but with the break of dawn it had been complete. He only got a couple of hours' sleep before the group started to move for the day. Now he seemed utterly drained, the energy it had taken out of him to harness the magic to enchant the weapon taking everything out of him, not to mention the lack of sleep. But Zorg had been pleased with his blade, and Sabian had congratulated him on a job well done. Dartanyen and Triath had agreed, clapping him heartily on the back. Dinim smiled and took it all in good stride, pleased by his accomplishment.

Once again, Adrianna sat on her bedroll, removed from the group. The rest sat around the fire, just having taken their evening meal. Adrianna held the Ring of Aboleth in her hand, the chain from which she had suspended it twined between her fingers. Now was the time. She had told Amethyst earlier in the day what she planned to do, and the girl had agreed. Her transgression would be revealed, but she disliked keeping the secret as much as Adrianna.

Adrianna stood up, and Amethyst's gaze swung to her. The girl knew what was about to happen, and Adria saw her square her shoulders for the events about to unfurl. She then squared her own, steeling herself for the possible battle and subsequent decision she would have to make. Adrianna stepped up to the circle of her comrades about the fire. There was a space made for her but she ignored it, continuing to stand. People started looking up at her, wondering, and after a moment she had everyone's attention, the expression on her face having told them that she had something to say.

"I have a confession to make." Adrianna paused. Everyone continued to watch her. She noticed some puzzled expressions on a couple of faces, but then continued. "There was something that Dinim and I did not tell you about our visit with Master Paxil."

Adrianna saw Dinim's expression turn into a bewildered frown. She noticed his body tense, as well as that of Dartanyen, Armond, and Triath. "Master Paxil gave us something, an object that may be able to help us in our fight against Thane."

"Why didn't you tell us about this before?" Dartanyen's question echoed that of Amethyst just a couple of nights ago. Adrianna looked from Dartanyen to Dinim, and then back to Dartanyen. "Because it is the reason why Dinim and I began to argue after our visit with Paxil. It is the reason why he cast a spell at me."

For a moment there was silence. Then Dartanyen spoke again, "Well, what is it?"

Once again Adrianna glanced at Dinim. She saw him starting to put his hand to his leather pouch. She opened her hand to reveal the ring lying in her palm. "It is the Ring of Aboleth." Dinim had reached into his pouch and pulled out the small box. His gaze was icy as he realized the ring wasn't inside.

Dinim stood up. "Adrianna, I can't believe you have done this," said Dinim. "I can't believe you stole the ring from me."

Dartanyen also stood, his frown deepening. "You *stole* this ring from Dinim?"

"No, I stole it," said Amethyst, also rising.

Dartanyen glanced from Dinim to Amethyst, and then to Adrianna. "I asked her to steal it for me," she said. "Master Paxil gave the ring to us so that we could win our fight against Thane. Dinim feels that we should not use it, its power being too great for any of us to wield safely. However, I have a differing opinion."

"Adrianna, you don't know what you are doing. Give the ring back to me," said Dinim, holding out his hand.

Adrianna shook her head. "No, Dinim. No matter what the risk, I think that we should still use it. It is not a decision for you to make alone."

"Well, it's not a decision for you to make either," said Sabian.

Adrianna nodded her head. "I know."

"Then why did you have it stolen?"

"Because I was afraid that, upon asking, Dinim still would not relinquish it."

"All right," said Dartanyen. "Let's get down to the point. What does the ring do?"

"It infuses the wielder with the ability to bring forth life," said Dinim roughly. "I know that it sounds like a good thing, but it's not necessarily that. The power is addictive, and can take away the wielder's ability to reason properly. The person could go mad, using the ring to perform acts that seem right in their twisted mind, but are actually of the greatest evil." Dinim turned back to Adria. "Please, give me back the ring. It isn't worth it," said Dinim desperately, stepping towards her.

Adrianna stepped back from the circle. "It is worth it, Dinim," she said, her voice rising in pitch. "This ring could save lives . . . all of our lives. Doesn't that mean anything to you?"

"Of course it does, but that may not be all that happens . . ."

Sirion stood up. "Adrianna . . . Dinim, let's talk about this."

"No!" spat Dinim. "You don't understand. The wielder could become lost, lost in the power of the ring. There may be no turning back . . ."

"But what if you are wrong?" Tears began to fall down Adrianna's face. "What if there is a way to come back? What if . . ."

"Just give me the ring!" Dinim lunged towards Adrianna, only to be caught by Armond. Frantically, Adrianna scrambled away, fear etched upon her face. Her ankle twisted, and with a cry she fell. Vaguely, she heard Sirion shouting at Dinim. Dinim continued to curse, and Armond strained to hold him back. She noticed Triath slowly making his way towards her, his hands outstretched. "It's all right. We will talk about this. Why don't you let me have the ring . . .?"

Adrianna shook her head, her eyes widening as she scooted further away. Triath would take the ring, and there would be nothing left . . . nothing that would save them from the doom that awaited them. They had very little chance against Thane, and she did not know how much more the ring offered, but it had to be better than nothing.

Adrianna unfurled the fist clenched around the ring. She stared at it for a moment, and then back up at Triath. Behind him, she could see that everyone was up in arms, upset about what had just been revealed. Arguments ensued. Adrianna could hear none of what was being said, despite the loudness of the voices. Adrianna took the ring between her thumb and forefinger, making her decision within that moment. "Adrianna, no . . ."

Adrianna heard Triath calling out to her as she slipped the Ring of Aboleth over her finger. Suddenly she heard no sound at all as she felt the rush of power surge through her body. It was all-encompassing, sweeping through her veins and touching every part of her within a single burst of fire. She felt energized, the sensation one like she had never felt before. She felt the magic all around her, migrating to her without her even having to call it.

Then she began to hear again, to see, and to touch. She felt the ground beneath her body, saw her comrades as they stood, staring, a few feet away from her. "Oh gods, what have you done?"

Adrianna heard Dinim's voice and turned towards it. The expression on his face was one of fear and disbelief. She picked herself up from the ground, dusting off her cloak and trousers. She felt her heart pounding in her chest, the accelerated rate of her breaths. "I feel so . . . so strange." She looked down at her hands, saw the ring circling her middle finger.

"Adria, are you all right?" Adrianna turned to Sirion. His brow was creased with worry.

"Yes, I think so." He put his arm around her and she leaned into him. It was done. She wielded the Ring of Aboleth. She may have made a grave mistake, made the wrong decision, but she hoped she hadn't. Their future rested on it.

***

The group rode silently through the next day, everyone keeping to his or her own thoughts. The events of the previous evening weighed on everyone's mind, and the sacrifice that may have been made an uncertainty. Dartanyen rode at the head, waiting for the scouts to return for the evening. He was worried about Adrianna and what exactly she had done when she put that ring on her finger. He allowed himself to fall back, until finally he was riding beside Dinim and Tianna. Both turned to him as he reined in beside. Knowing what he was about, Dinim sighed, pressing his lips into a thin line.

Dartanyen finally spoke. "What is going to happen?"

Dinim shook his head. "I honestly don't know."

"Then what *could* happen?"

Once more Dinim shook his head. "Adrianna has placed herself at great risk, and possibly all of the rest of us as well. She may not be strong enough to withstand the power of the ring, and we will have a situation on our hands when the battle with Thane is through."

"Situation. What type of situation? Speak plainly with me, Dinim."

"Adrianna may become so wrapped up in the power she will discover in the ring, she may not be able to return from it. She may begin to make the decisions of life and death herself, and consequently become a threat even greater than Thane."

"How do we stop that from happening?"

"We can't."

Dartanyen frowned and regarded Dinim intensely. "There must be a way."

"If there is, I don't know what it is."

"Damn!" Dartanyen hissed.

"I'm sorry, Dartanyen. I wish there was something . . ."

Dartanyen shook his head angrily. "If you are going to feel sorry, feel sorry for Adrianna. If this 'situation' comes about, we may be seeing her last days."

Dinim stared at Dartanyen as he galloped back to the front of the group. He hadn't wanted to contemplate it. Adrianna's death was not something he could think about easily. He saw Sirion approaching, he coming to give them the word on where they would camp for the night. They rode for another forty minutes before they came to a place where the pass began to widen. Then they reached a type of clearing. The place was not as rocky as most of the rest of the pass, and even a few trees had been able to take root and grow. Everyone dismounted and prepared to make camp.

Adrianna helped Sheri and Tianna with the fire. It was difficult to start, the wind having picked up. It didn't smell like rain, but the dark was fast approaching, and it was getting colder. Nearby, Dartanyen, Triath, Armond, and Sorn were attempting to pitch the two tents that they had purchased before leaving Driscol. Beyond them, Zorg and Naemmious were tending to the lloryk and larian while Amethyst was looking through the bags for the tools needed to pick the rocks from the animals' cloven feet.

Adrianna and Tianna hovered over Sheri, hoping that she would be able to get the fire lit. The wind began to blow even harder, hitting them with a chilly blast. Adrianna looked into the direction from which it was coming. The air . . . it had a strange feeling about it, one that she couldn't quite describe. And then she began to hear a keening sound being carried in the wind. The others began to hear it as well, and everyone began to look in the same direction. The wail became louder, chilling them to the bone, causing an unnatural fear to suffuse them. But Adrianna knew what it was without ever having heard it before. From the depths of her being, she knew that it was her father, and that he knew that she was here.

Dinim spoke loudly over the noise of the winds and the wail. "It is the Azmathous. Thane is in the pass, and he knows that we are here as well." Dinim paused, his eyes wide with the effects of the death-wail. "He will be coming for us."

"How much time do we have?" asked Armond.

Dinim shook his head. "It is hard to say. I don't know how far he is. It could be as soon as a couple of hours from now, or maybe even sometime tomorrow. However, I can at least say this with certainty: Thane will not attack us during the day because his power is greatest at night. If we get through the night without encountering him, then we will be safe until the next night."

"If we make it through the night, then I think we should stay here. It is a good location, and it would be best if we made Thane come to us instead of meeting him in another, possibly less desirous, location," said Sirion.

Dinim nodded in agreement. "Yes, that would definitely be best. I will be able to finish the enchantments on Dartanyen and Anya's arrows tonight, but then I will need to rest tomorrow. I will need all of the sleep I can get before the encounter."

Dartanyen nodded his head. "Will do, Dinim. We will stay here tomorrow then. I guess all we can do is wait."

"Yes, wait and pray that he doesn't reach us tonight," said Triath.

***

The night passed, and then the following day. The only person to really get any rest was Dinim, he being so drained of energy that he had no choice but to sleep. But even that would not be enough for him. Everyone knew that the strength it had taken for him to cast the enchantments was not going to be returned with just a single day's worth of sleep, and that he would be weakened before their battle. But everyone else had made preparations as well. The warriors tended to their weapons, and the magic-users to their books and spell components. Everyone tried to rest as much as they could, and ate as heartily as possible. Of course, before a battle that was nigh impossible there was much turning in bedrolls, and a lot of picking at meals.

When the afternoon began to darken into early evening, they cleared the area. Travel packs, bedrolls, and other equipment were put aside. The lloryk and larian were tightly tethered a distance behind them down the pass. Sirion bade Dramati to stay with them, and told him that he was not to enter the fray, no matter what. Armor was donned, and weapons strapped to hips and backs. And then they waited. All day they had felt them, felt the nearness of Thane and his undead minions. With the lowering of the sun, the Azmathous would come, and with them the fight that had been too long in coming.

The cold wind swept through the small clearing in the Ratik Pass. Darkness slowly descended, and just as they predicted, with it came the Azmathous. They sat upon steeds made out of the darkness one finds in the deepest of shadows. Mist swirled from their nostrils and from beneath their cloven feet. Over the winds, the phantom jingling of bit and rein could be perceived. The Azmathous had them surrounded within the blink of an eye. Steadfast, the group held their ground.

There were seven of them, including Thane. Most of them were obviously warriors, they wearing the accoutrements of the profession. Armor, helm and gauntlet were all black. However, two of them were different, wearing black robes and cloaks. They could only be the mage and the rogue. From the circle around them, Thane rode forward, removing his horned helm. Adrianna could only imagine what Sheri was thinking at that moment, beholding the face of their father in all of its hideousness.

"At last we meet," spoke Thane, his voice redolent of the wail they had heard the night before. He looked from one daughter to the next. "And you two have found one another as well. How lovely. You have cost me a lot of time, Adrianna, but perhaps it will be worth it now that I don't have to track down your sister. You did all the work for me."

Adrianna felt herself stiffening, despite knowing that Thane sought only to goad her, to make her lose her concentration. Adrianna began the incantation to her protective spell, knowing that Dinim and Sabian were doing the same. Thane narrowed his eyes, placing the helm back over his head. Dartanyen and Anya saw the cue, and readied their bows. "Fine, no more talk. I will crush you as I had intended when last we met. This time there will be no escape."

Then the shadow lloryk were charging towards them. Dartanyen and Anya fired their first round of arrows. As the missiles raced through the air, they suddenly multiplied into four times the original number. First one, and then another of the death warriors was struck by the magical arrows. Many of the arrows bounced off of the black armor, but a few were able to penetrate. The warriors fell back from their mounts, clutching at the arrows that pierced their armor. The steeds galloped away from their fallen riders, but the knights were fast to rise from the ground, pulling the arrows free of their undead flesh. But by then the other warriors were upon them, and the battle was officially ensued.

Zorg leapt into action, swinging his mighty broadsword at the legs of an approaching shadow lloryk. The dark steed screamed and faltered, the knight upon its back thrusting himself away from the falling beast. Zorg took the advantage, springing towards his enemy, slashing at the warrior, but the other was quick, blocking Zorg's attack with his shield, and then following with a massive swing of his mace. The weapon slammed into Zorg, knocking him to the ground.

From the protective circle of the warriors, Adrianna cast her second spell. Her first had been a protective one, so that she may be more impervious to any hand-held or missile attacks. This next one was a simple missile spell, but she had become strong enough that she could send at least five missiles at a time. The magic sprung from her fingertips and arched towards the last knight that had not lost his mount. To her discouragement, the missiles fell away from him, demonstrating his immunity to such spells.

Adrianna's attention was drawn to Dinim as he cast his spell. She watched the sphere of fire roll towards the two death-knights who had been the first to lose their mounts. The fire encompassed the warriors, and Adrianna waited to see if it would have an effect on them, deciding that she would cast her own *Flamesphere* spell if it did. But then she found herself focusing on something else. Walking just outside the effect of the spell, she saw Thane. She felt a creepy, cold sensation traveling up her spine, and she knew that his eyes were riveted on her, and that he was coming to kill her, just as he had promised.

Sheridana rushed past Dartanyen and made her way to Zorg, placing herself between him and the hovering knight. Just as he was about to strike her fallen companion, Sheri blocked his mace with Destroyer. Angrily, the knight turned to her and swung his mace again. Sheri stepped past him, swinging her own blade. She felt it cut into his side. The death-knight howled, sending a chill of fear coursing through her. She felt the effect of the wail tap-tapping at her, seeking to paralyze her in fear, but she refused to let it in. But overcoming the power of the death-wail was the least of her problems. The knight was fast, much too fast, spinning back to face her, and hitting her hard in the side with his mace. Sheri heard herself cry out as she fell, and then vaguely saw that Zorg had risen, and that he was standing over her, protecting her with the barricade of his broadsword.

The flames of Dinim's spell dissipated, revealing the two knights caught within the conflagration. It was obvious that they had suffered from the fire, but not as much as Adrianna had hoped. Thane continued towards her, and she found herself beginning to incant the words to her own *Flamesphere* spell. Behind Thane, she saw the dark-robed figure of the death-mage. Even from this distance she could feel the Talent he possessed, a master of necromancy in death, just as the knights were masters of their own weapons in their death. Adrianna saw Dartanyen and Anya cast another volley of arrows just as she cast her spell. The fire swathed Thane and the death-mage, but before it could burn to its full intensity, she saw the energy gravitate to the mage, swirling into him.

Taking the magic of the spell into him, the mage spoke only a single word as he then cast the *Flamesphere* back at her.

Adrianna felt her eyes widen, and heard the shouted exclamations of her companions. She felt a familiar burning sensation on her upper arm as the flames encompassed them. Once more the prismatic shell was surrounding her. The fire burned around her, yet she did not even feel the heat. And then the flames were gone. In front of her, Dinim and Dartanyen lay huddled on the ground, scorched from the fire. Oh gods, it was her fault . . .

Then Tianna was there, kneeling before them, laying her hands upon them. Adrianna looked away, back up to where she remembered having seen Thane last. Adrianna felt her heart begin to hammer in her chest and she stepped back, back, back. Thane advanced towards her, and she could see the malicious excitement reflected in his blue eyes. But suddenly someone was standing between Adrianna and her advancing father. He gripped his quarterstaff in its center, his hands touching, and then he held two blades, one in each hand. Sirion stood, battle-ready.

"A champion; how sweet. I will enjoy destroying you almost as much as my daughter" rumbled Thane.

Sirion said nothing, continuing to hold his stance. Adrianna shook her head, the words refusing to come from her mouth. *No, Sirion . . .*

Armond advanced towards the death-mage. He knew that the dark sorcerer would be largely immune to their weapons, despite their enchantments, and was obviously able to take the energy of the spells cast at him and to throw it back. But maybe, just maybe, Armond would have a chance against this foe. Because of his particular Talent, his ability to harness it into the structure of his weapons, perhaps he would be able to strike the creature when nothing else would be able. It would be raw Talent flowing through his blades, not the effect that Talent had upon the energy of the world.

Amethyst threw the dagger at the dark warrior wielding the battle-axe, the one fighting Naemmious. It was the dagger that Sorn had given to her, telling her that it was infused with magic so that she would be able to damage the undead enemy they would be facing. The dagger struck true, piercing the warrior's throat. The knight staggered back, and Naemmious saw his chance. He struck the knight with his flail, splitting the skull. As he fell, the knight disintegrated into dust, leaving behind only the black armor he was wearing, and the battle-axe he had been wielding. Suddenly, Amethyst found something wrapping around her throat, felt it tighten into a stranglehold. She then felt herself being jerked backward, and she fell to the ground, clutching at the vein-like whip around her throat. She looked up to find herself staring into the hood of the death-rogue. She felt her eyes widen as the fear coursed through her. She wanted to scream, but no sound could come out.

In the close distance, Armond saw the mage take notice of him. Narrowing his eyes, the dark sorcerer began to encant the words to a spell. Armond felt himself falter, knowing that the mage would probably be able to squash him like a bug. But suddenly he found Sabian at his side. "Here, eat this," he commanded over the sounds of the battle, thrusting something towards Armond's mouth.

Armond turned his face away, yet continued to watch the death-mage as he spoke the words to his spell. "What the Hells is it?"

"Just do it!" Sabian yelled. "You don't have time!"

Armond opened his mouth and Sabian thrust the substance inside. Armond almost gagged and his eyes watered. Just then, the dark mage cast his spell. Beside him, Armond felt Sabian tense his body, and Armond did the same. The spell slammed into them, and the force of it nearly sent Armond to the ground. However, nothing else happened to him. After recovering from the initial shock, Armond looked around. Sabian lay unmoving on the ground at his feet, blood seeping from the corner of his mouth. *Oh gods, Sabian had cast a protection spell on him, but had left himself vulnerable . . .* But then Armond had no more time to think about Sabian. The death-mage was upon him.

Thane lunged at Sirion, swinging his massive sword. Sirion parried the attack, following up with a thrust of his own. Thane blocked the attack, and then pushed forward, sending Sirion flying through the air to land several feet away. Instantly, Thane's gaze sought her out and he began advancing towards Adrianna once again. Sirion scrambled up from the ground, and flung himself towards Thane. Once more, the attack was blocked, and Sirion was thrown back. Adrianna had the powerful urge to run, but she knew that it would do her no good. Thane would find her and kill her one way or the other.

Sheridana watched as the knight lunged for Zorg yet again, he barely having a chance to recover from the previous blows before another was inflicted. The death warrior was powerful, very powerful, and fast, too fast for a single mortal man. Sheri lifted herself slowly off of the ground, the pain in her side excruciating. She made it up just in time to see Zorg get hit with the mace once again, the wicked weapon sending him heavily to the ground. And then there was another knight, one wielding a long-sword. He stood over Zorg for a moment, and then plunged his blade downwards. "Nooooo . . ." Sheridana screamed, running towards the dark knights, her pain forgotten. One slash, and then two, and the head of the knight wielding the mace came toppling off of his neck.

Tianna looked up when she heard the scream. She saw Sheridana remove the head from one of the knights, and a moment later she was engaged in a swordfight with another. The still form of Zorg lay a few paces away. Tianna looked back down at Dartanyen and Dinim. She had helped them all she could. Their burns had been extensive, but not too much for her to handle. There would be some scarring, but very minimal compared to what it would have been had they been hit by a *Flamesphere* a mere couple of months ago. Her skills and her powers both had grown, and her companions would reap the benefits.

Tianna rose from her charges and darted into the melee. She had been able to move Dartanyen and Dinim a bit to the side, where there was less chance of them getting killed. She hoped to bring Zorg there as well, although she was rather nervous about the prospect of moving him by herself, for he was quite a large man. But when Tianna made it to Zorg's side, she knew something was terribly wrong. His face had become ashen, and when she checked for his breaths, she found none. She saw the pool of blood seeping from beneath him, and knew he had suffered a fatal hit.

Tianna shook him, hoping that he would stir. "Zorg, Zorg please wake up." She put her lips over his, hoping to share her breaths with him, but it was no use. Zorg was beyond her ability to mend, and there was nothing that she could do to save him. She glanced up from Zorg, knowing that she could not stay by him much longer. She would become a target, and then she would not be able to help anyone. Tianna moved out of the way just as Sheridana lurched past her. Damn! She had to get out of there.

Amethyst struggled weakly against the death-rogue, her life seeping away from her. Her vision was dimming, and her head swam from lack of air. On her knees, she clawed at the garrote as it continued to cut, ever deeper, into her neck. But suddenly it loosened. Amethyst found herself pitching forward to fall on her face. She gasped with the rush of air into her lungs, and she lay there on the rocky ground, unable to truly comprehend what had happened.

Sorn threw his dagger and it struck the undead rogue in the back. Behind him, Triath focused his psionic energy, and as the rogue loosened his grip on the whip, Triath let loose a mental blast. The rogue flew several feet through the air to finally hit a large boulder. Sorn rushed the enemy, and before the rogue could even begin to stir, Sorn was upon him. Sorn stood over the rogue, gripped his short-sword with both hands, and then sheathed it into his chest. Writhing, the creature let loose a hideous wail, and Sorn was forced to step back, his hands clutched over his ears.

Kneeling beside Amethyst, Triath slammed his hands over his ears, the death-wail causing him to shake with uncontrollable fear. He had unwrapped the whip from about the girl's neck, and he grimaced with the strangeness of it. It had a rubbery consistency, and was colored a deep red with shocks of purple. It seemed to have a life of its own as it slipped through his hands and writhed upon the ground. But just as suddenly as the wail began, it stopped. Triath got control over himself, and then looked to where Sorn stood. He was looking down at the black-hooded cloak that had been worn by the rogue.

Adrianna watched as Sirion was thrown to the ground for the third time, the wound in his side beginning to bleed profusely. She felt the warmth of her tears on her cheeks, and fear for Sirion suffused her body. Once again, Thane had her in his sights and was coming towards her. Oh gods, this was it. She couldn't . . . wouldn't let Sirion die for her. Suddenly remembering the ring, Adrianna looked down at her hand. Damnation! She knew nothing about it, save that it infused the wielder with the ability to give life. But what would it do against someone who not only was dead, but had used the vilest of means to make himself one of the undead?

Then Thane was upon her. Her father grabbed her by the front of her tunic and lifted her up from the ground. She clutched at the gauntleted hand, the spikes at the knuckles biting into the soft flesh of her neck. High enough that she could see over his shoulder, Adrianna saw Sirion struggling to rise off the ground. Then she felt herself being shaken like a rag doll, and she refocused on the face of her father. "I will break you with my very hands," he rumbled. "You are so small, and so weak, just like a newborn babe. I have hated you it seems like forever. Just as I was a contributor to your beginning, now I will be your ending."

Adrianna felt her tears continuing to fall. She turned her face away from that of her father, unable to stand the reek of him. Her throat burned with the power of her emotion, and her mind could scarcely believe what her life had come to . . . and how it would now end. She saw her pale hand resting upon Thane's black gauntleted hand; saw the golden ring around her finger. Adrianna closed her eyes, focusing on the Ring of Aboleth. Gods, she had no idea how to tap the power of the ring, or how to . . . but then it was there, as though it had merely been awaiting her signal.

The power flowed through Adrianna, and she suddenly felt charged, just like she had the evening she had put it on her finger for the first time. She opened her eyes once again, and turned back to her father. He was speaking to her, but she could not hear his voice . . . could not hear anything over the deafening surge coursing through her. Adrianna took her hand from Thane's hand and slowly reached out to him. In that moment, she heard every beat of her heart, and every breath her lungs took. She felt the pain of the burn around her upper arm, the prick of Thane's gauntlet beneath her chin, and the strange feeling of lightening flooding her veins.

Adrianna reached out to her father, and for the first time in her life, she touched his face. Once, it could have been a loving gesture, one that a daughter would bestow upon her father. But now it was only instinct that told her to touch him there, one of the few places upon his body that was not covered by metal armor. Thane's eyes widened with shock and his mouth stopped moving. Adrianna began to feel another sensation, minimal at first, but then quickly became something monstrously terrible. They became frozen in place, the magic of the Ring of Aboleth circling them in its power. The unnatural life force began to leave Thane's body, a pale ghostly light that seeped from his face and into the hand that touched it. When Thane was able to let her go, Adrianna dropped to the ground. But as she sat there, with her hand outstretched to Thane, the blue glow continued to flow into her. The sensation was horrific, and the pain intense, as it swept through Adrianna like a storm. And when she felt like she would no longer be able to handle the torment, she cried out in agony.

Then it was over. The blue glow dissipated, and Adrianna slumped to the ground. Thane stood over her, his arms held out to his sides. His expression was one of incredulous anger. "What have you done?" Weakly, Adrianna lifted her head off of the rocky ground. Her vision swam, and she found it difficult to focus. She could barely move, her body feeling as though several pounds of rock rested upon it. As though in slow motion, Adrianna watched as Thane unsheathed his sword. His face contorted with rage, he swung the blade over his head in an arc, and then began to bring it down. Suddenly his expression changed, his eyes widened as though in shock, and his body shuddered. Then Adrianna saw the tip of a sword poking through the black armor covering his chest.

Adrianna just managed to roll out of the way as Thane's body crashed to the ground. She looked up to find her sister standing where Thane had just been, holding a bloody blade in her grip. Adrianna moved Thane's arm off of her as she stood. Sheri stumbled over to her, dropping her blade. The women embraced one other, each one leaning into the other for support. Finally, they pulled apart and then looked all around at the destruction that had been wrought.

As though in a haze, Adrianna embraced her sister. When they parted, she took in the scene all around her, Tianna tending to the fallen, Naemmious supporting Anya as they made their way over to Sorn, and Triath carrying Amethyst over to the place where Sabian lay. Adrianna felt strangely energized, and despite what she had suffered when she made Thane mortal once again, she felt somehow larger than life itself. Her pains seemed to have melted away, and she felt a sense of invulnerability that invigorated her to a height she had never experienced before.

Adrianna walked among her comrades, saw the healing burns on Dinim and Dartanyen, the laceration around Amethyst's throat, the series of cuts that marred the flesh of Naemmious' arms and chest, and the deep wounds in the side of her sister. She felt pity for them all, wishing they had come through the fight as unscathed as she. Obviously they were weak, pathetically frail in comparison to the fortress she had become.

Adrianna heard her friends speaking to her . . . calling out, but she merely passed them by, somehow drawn to a place removed from them. And then she saw him lying there, alone upon the cold rocky ground. Adrianna walked over to Zorg and then crouched over his lifeless body. His flesh was ashen, and his pupils fixed and dilated. When she put her hand on him, she felt that the warmth had already begun to leave his body. But she also felt something else . . . the rush of power flooding her mind, telling her that it need not be this way, and that she could bring her companion back to life.

Adrianna placed her palms onto Zorg's chest. His heart was no longer beating, and his lungs no longer filled with the breath of life. But she could change that, make it so that death had never come to him. Behind her, Adrianna heard the voices of her other companions, but for some reason, she could not hear them. Adrianna shook her head, dissipating all of the voices save for one. It was the one she had heard before, in an argument. Ah yes, it was Dinim. "No . . . please . . . don't know . . . wrong . . ." She could hear only snatches of what he was trying to say to her, but his voice had a pleading quality to it. She struggled to understand what he was saying to her, but then his words from their argument came flooding back to her: *The ring can be used to do great evil, and even one with the best intentions can do wrong. Great power like that can be enticing, and can make one thirst for more. Once started, one may never be able to stop, the temptation too difficult to ignore.*

Suddenly, Adrianna found her mind clearing, as though a thin veil had covered it. She found herself with her hands resting upon Zorg, her desire to bring him back to life manifest in her mind. Adrianna shook her head, and then removed her hands from Zorg's body. No, she would not bring him back. His time had come, and he had died for their cause. She did not want his efforts to be in vain, and she did not want to do him a disservice by bringing him life, when he had died so valiantly for the lives of others. Sadly, Adrianna rose from Zorg's side. The others would see to his funeral pyre. She would not bring back Zorg, but there were other places to go, places that needed her power, places that needed the life that the Ring of Aboleth could bring. And she had become the master of that power, above the puny efforts of other mortals. Adrianna felt the power, allowed it to suffuse her. She reveled in the sensations, the intoxicating vibrations that it brought to her. "I will go . . . leave this place and find another."

Sirion stood by as the glow encompassed Adrianna. He was afraid, and when he glanced around at the others, he found that they were as well.

Adrianna had left Zorg, somehow having overcome the temptation to use the power of the ring to bring him back to life. But she had decided upon another course of action, and that was to leave . . . to do gods only knew what. But he had hope. If she could master the power of the ring to make the decision not to bring life back to Zorg, her friend, then he believed that she could do it again, and resist the temptation to leave.

Sirion stepped towards Adrianna. He could feel the raw power that encompassed her, the unharnessed magic. He was afraid for her, as well as for himself. But he knew that he could not stand by and watch her leave. He would not lose her, not this way. He had faith in her that, with his support, she would be able to break away from the temptation of the ring. "Adrianna, Adria please listen to me. I need you to stay with me. These other places, they don't need you the way I have come to need you."

Once again, Adrianna heard the voices of the people behind her. But they were so difficult to understand, and Adrianna felt the need to make haste. But this time, another voice rang out to her, one that she could not ignore. It had a quality to it, one that she remembered hearing not only in her daily life, but one that she heard in her passionate nights. It was Sirion. Adrianna struggled to listen to his words, but ultimately found herself unable to do so.

Sirion continued to speak to her, his fear mounting. He wasn't getting through to her. "Adrianna, I have come to love you, love you in a way that this power never will, despite the emotions it imparts to you. You have opened up a part of me that I never thought existed, and without you, I will never feel this complete ever again." Sirion stepped closer to Adrianna, despite the heat of the energy surrounding her. "I cannot let you leave this way, for I will be unable to live without you. Adrianna, you have to fight this, be strong, stronger than you have ever been before. I will be here by your side, just as you have been by mine. I will not let you go . . ."

Sirion took a deep breath, and then launched himself into the glow that enveloped Adrianna. It was hot, so hot, but when he reached her, he took her by the arms. He put his face next to hers, so that his mouth was by her ear. "I know that there is a part of you that hears me, Adrianna. I need you, want you, and love you with every fiber of my being." He then clutched Adrianna to him, embracing her within the sweltering inferno surrounding them. And then he was putting his mouth onto hers, kissing her with a passion he demonstrated only when they were alone, in the deepest part of the night.

Adrianna felt Sirion's kiss, felt the ferocity of it despite the intensity of the power surging through her. And then she felt herself responding, her passion an answer to his call. She felt the magic around her begin to temper, and then she felt herself beginning to break through the shroud that covered her. Her vision began to clear, she began to hear again, and she felt the sensation of Sirion's studded leather beneath her palms. Then she began to fall, and Sirion was there, catching her in his arms, and resting her gently on the ground. Adrianna found herself staring into his amber eyes, saw the love reflected there, and knew that he had been her bastion and her anchor at a time when she needed it the most. She caressed his face with her fingertips, and then his lips were at her mouth once again, and he was wrapping his arms tightly around her, as though he never wanted to let her go.

EPILOGUE

24 Thaliren CY593

Only a day's ride outside of Sangrilak, the group set up an early evening camp upon the plains of the realm of Torimir. Despite the long days of travel, spirits were high, the prospect of reaching home on the morrow giving everyone yet another reason to feel happiness. Tianna roasted the ptarmigan that Dramati had caught over the open flame of the campfire, the tantalizing aroma of the seasoned meat wafting through the chilly air. The sounds of Sirion and Adrianna practicing the quarterstaff echoed all around, Sorn and Amethyst were deeply immured within their lessons, and Dartanyen and Anya were practicing with their bows.

After the battle with the Azmathous, and Sirion's subsequent success at bringing Adrianna back from the brink of magic-induced insanity, the group had been forced to stay in the Ratik Pass for two days. Sabian's wounds had been extensive, the spell cast by the death-mage having caught him full force. If not for the protection spell he had cast upon himself at the beginning of the storm, he surely would have died. Physically, Amethyst had been able to recover rather quickly. However, mentally was another story. Her experience with the death-rogue had been one that she could not easily forget, and her dreams were testimony to that fact. Sorn had offered to teach her some of his skills, and Amethyst had been quick to accept the offer. It was something that she could do to counteract the dreams and fears of something like that happening to her again.

Dinim and Dartanyen had recovered very well from their collision with the *Flamesphere*. It was those two whom Tianna had been able to treat first, her skills being the most powerful at that time. Their burns were almost gone, and there would be minimal scarring from the fire. Dartanyen had a dark weal across the left side of his face, which was one of the places where the flames had scorched him the most. But the scar was not disfiguring, and his sight had not been affected by the burns. Naemmious had also recovered well from his extensive wounds. He was a big man, extremely hearty and easy to heal. He was still able to keep the nightly watch after he had been treated.

After her encounter with the addictive nature of the Ring of Aboleth,

Adrianna had fallen into a state of extreme fatigue. Sirion also suffered the same tiredness, he having given to her some of his strength so that she would be able to persevere. Wrapped in one another's embrace, they had slept a healing sleep that returned color to the unnatural pallor that had pervaded after the glow of magic had subsided. Once they had awakened, the passion they had shared while fighting the temptation of the magic swiftly returned, and their absence from the immediate area briefly noted. But no one said anything, everyone knowing how much love it must have taken for the grip of magic that strong to be broken. They deserved to be together, even for if only a short while.

The ones that seemed to have escaped relatively unscathed from the battle were Triath and Tianna. Armond had suffered only minimal wounds from his fight with the death-mage, thanks to Sabian's spell. Sorn also carried only trivial injuries. Sheridana and Anya had suffered more, but with adequate rest were able to ride back down the pass two days later. Sabian had to be tied to his larian, and Dinim and Dartanyen had to rest often. Despite the delays, they made it out of the Pass only a week after the battle. Once they reached the city of Driscol, they were able to rest for a couple of nights in the comfort of an inn. But then they were moving again, crossing the Tangir River, and then resting for a night in the city of Ferent. Since then they had been making towards Sangrilak as swiftly as possible, thoughts of home paramount in everyone's mind. Sheri had sent a message to Carli, telling her to bring Fitanni and to meet her in Sangrilak. Sirion had enclosed a message to his mother as well, telling her that Carli and Fitanni should travel in the proper company, and that he and Anya would be to Elvandahar to see her as soon as possible.

However, there was something that was definitely missing. Despite the relief of having finally defeated Thane, and the happiness of arriving home after so long, thoughts of a lost comrade weighed on everyone's mind. The memory of that dark sword coming down to skewer her friend dominated Sheri's dreams, and no matter how many versions of the battle that her mind created, Zorg's life always ended the same way. The group had held a ceremony, and made a funeral pyre. It took the rest of that night and into the dawn for the fire to consume the pyre. Then it smoked for the rest of the day, and by the time the evening rolled around again, all that remained was a scorched heap. On top of it rested Zorg's enchanted broadsword.

The next day the group rode into the city of Sangrilak, up to the Inn of the Hapless Cenloryan. Volstagg was there to greet them, as well as Carli and Fitanni. Volstagg swept Adrianna up into his massive embrace, while Sheridana took her baby into her arms after so long being apart. Then there were greetings all around, and the sounds of laughter could be heard echoing down the streets. The Wildrunners had come home, and with them a new generation of heroes.

***

Tallachienan sat at his desk, poring over the message that Dinim had left for him in the Travel Notebook. The device had turned out to be ingenious, and one of the best things he had invented to use in order to communicate with his journeymen after they left him for other pursuits. They all carried Notebooks similar to the one that sat before him, and when they wrote a message upon the pages of their own Notebooks, he would see the words written upon the pages in his own. He would then be able to write a message in return, and thus an open line of communication established. He had a Notebook for each one of his journeymen.

When Dinim had been imprisioned by Aasarak, it had driven him crazy. Not only would the man reply to him via the Notebook, but whatever magic had been used to incarcerate him also kept TC from seeing him in his Vision Orb. TC knew that something foul had happened to his journeyman, but was forced to wait until Dinim was finally able to free himself.

TC shook his head. Now was not the time to reminisce about such things. However, he knew that it was largely due to the training that he had bestowed upon Dinim that made the young man able to escape from Aasarak's priests, and to eventully defeat the wielder of his prison. And this was what he was supposed to be focusing on . . . Adrianna's training. It was nearly time, and final preparations needed to be made.

TC had completed his mission to bring the other students that he had been tracking into the citadel. Two of them were women, a first in his program. The other was a man. All of his other students were Cimmerean, but the man and one of the women were not, instead being another race of faelin. He knew that it would take a lot of time from his older students to get accustomed to the changes that he was making in the program, but he had faith that they would all learn to accept one another. And then there would be Adrianna. She would be like a star that had fallen into the citadel, lighting up the darkness like a beacon in the deepest part of the night. In the past, she had out-ranked everyone with her Talent, and he could not help but assume that it would be the same this time as well.

TC closed the Notebook just as he heard the door to his chamber open. In strode Pylar. In every way, Pylar was TC's right hand, and without him, the citadel would probably fall apart. Pylar kept order in a place which would otherwise thrive upon chaos, and the students found him a comforting presence that kept many of their fears at bay. "Master TC, you called for me?"

Tallachienan nodded. "Yes. Adrianna and her companions have completed their mission, and have returned home victorious. It is time for us to make the final preparations for her arrival."

Pylar nodded in return, a lock of his thick red hair falling across his face to hide his left eye. TC could have swore he saw semothing lurking there, an expression that he had been unable to read. But then Pylar was speaking again, and TC let it be. "Of course. Most of the preparations have been made, but the final stages of the move have not yet been implemented. When we make the time shift, some of the students may have the power to perceive it, so I think that we should put them to *Sleep* before we begin.

"Very well. You know the students better than I do. We will plan for the move two weeks from now; that will give us plenty of time to be sure that nothing goes wrong. Once the move is complete, we will have to be careful that we do not enter the places that we spoke about. Do you remember?"

"Yes TC, and I have told Coaxtl as well. It should not be a problem."

"Good. In only a few more weeks, Adrianna will come, and her training will begin anew. This time I will see to it that she succeeds." Tallachienan rose from the desk, placing the Notebook back in its spot on the shelf with the others. His gaze drifted to another Notebook, an old one, removed from the others. He had not had the heart to take it away, and so it had stayed here throughtout the centuries. TC stopped to caress the binding thoughtfully before turning away.

Pylar watched TC, keeping his expression hidden. His heart went out to the master, remembering what had transpired the last Cycle. However, his heart also went out to Adrianna, a girl he knew very well, but whom he had never met. Her training would be harsh, and the master could be so unforgiving, especially when it came to himself. This time, Adrianna may succeed, but at what cost would the victory be won?

GLOSSARY OF TERMS

Alcrostat (al-kro-stat) – the largest city within the realm of Elvandahar – residence of the Sherkari Fortress, home to the King

Alothere (al-o-thayr) – large porcines that are cousins to the wild boar – they live in the forests and steppes of the temperate regions of Shandahar

Andahye (an-duh-high) – mystical city located at the northern edge of the Sheldomar Forest – it is the place where many mages receive their arcane training

Azmathion (az-math-ee-on) – the arcane artifact that gives Aasarak much of his power – it is a geometrical work of art, and one must work the puzzles contained within it in order to divine its secrets

Azmathous (az-math-us) – the most powerful of Aasarak's undead creations – with the power of the Azmathion, they are reborn and are able to retain the skills and abilities they possessed in life

Baalor (bay-loor) – the largest of the greater daemons, their skin is deep red, and massive black horns come out of the sides of their heads – they are one of the most powerful in the Nine Hells

Burbana (bur-ban-uh) – a small ermine-like animal with exquisitely soft fur

Calotebas (kal-o-tee-bas) – a foul-tempered creature that lives near swamps – the taste of their flesh is equally as repugnant as their personality

Cenloryan (sen-lor-yan) – a creature made of magic, it has the lower body of a lloryk and the upper torso, arms, and head of a faelin

Chamdaroc flowers – small white flowers that grow within Elvandahar and other forested regions of northwestern Shandahar – it is said to have intoxicating qualities

Cimmerean (sim-ur-ee-an) – one of the sub-races of faelin – also known as 'dark' faelin, they live in vast labyrinths below the surface of the world

Common (com-mun) – the universal language across most of the main continent of Shandahar

Corubis (kor-oo-bis) – large canines that have tawny fur with dark dappling – they live in packs headed by an alpha male, but many of them find companionship with faelin, especially hinterlean rangers

Daemundai (day-mun-die) – an organization of those who strive to give daemon-kind influence and power in Shandahar

Daladin (dal-a-din) – a hinterlean house

Degethozak (deg-eth-o-zak) – the smallest and most numerous of the dragon sub-races – at maturity their color ranges from black to varying shades of green with darker backs and feet – their alignment tends towards evil and chaos

Denedrian (den-ed-ree-an) – one of the human sub-races – they are largely nomadic, originating from the western plains and deserts

Doppleganger (dop-pel-gang-er) – a bipedal being made of magic, it has the ability to shift its shape into any humanoid between four and eight feet tall – it is a master of trickery and disguise that works for the most powerful of sorcerers

Elvandahar (el-van-da-har) – large forested region in the vee of the Terrestra and Denegal Rivers – it is ruled by Hinterlean faelin, and bears the largest population of these people

Faelin (fay-lin) – one of the native races of Shandahar – they are slightly shorter than humans, and more slender – they are the long-lived and tend to live life to the fullest

Farlo (far-low) – the equivalent of several feet

Filopar (fil-o-par) – one of the five domains of Elvandahar

Fistantillus bush (fist-an-til-lus) – a bush that has poisonous thorns that can make a person violently ill for several days

Garbatezu (gar-bat-eh-zoo) – a greater daemon that appears to be a large oroc with the hind legs of a lloryk – they tend to be the most treacherous and intelligent, rallying other daemons to their cause

Grang (grang) – slightly shorter than halfen, these small, bony humanoids live primarily on the steppes - they are primitive and voracious, but not very smart, their greed often getting in the way of thieving strategies

Gremlin (grem-lin) – an intermediate daemon that has the ability to scale walls and manipulate metals with supernatural ease – they are often the stolid followers of the baalor and garbatezu

Griffon (grif-fon) – large animals that have both feline and avian features – they are friendly and intelligent, and can often be found in the company of druids

Haldorr (hal-door) – one of the worlds of the Seven Heavens – it is the place where dragons reside

Halfen (hal-fen) – one of the native races of Shandahar – shorter and more stout than humans, they have a preference for mining and metal-working

Hamzin/Hamza (ham-zin/ham-zuh) – the title given by the King to the one who rules within one of the five domains in Elvandahar

Helzethryn (hel-zeth-rin) – one of the dragon sub-races – at maturity their color ranges from pale gold, to deep bronze, to fiery red – they have the highest propensity towards Bonding with other species

Hestim (hes-tim) – one of the three moons of Shandahar

Hinterlean (hin-ter-lee-an) – one of the faelin subraces – they live in treetop villages within temperate forests

Human (hue-man) – a race of people that is not native to Shandahar – they are slightly taller and more robust than faelin and easily adapt to any climate or terrain

Humanoid (hue-man-oyd) – any creature that walks upright on two legs (bipedal)

Hybanthis (hie-ban-this) – a vine that has poisonous blue thorns – poison has brain-based affects that heighten a person's emotional state, making emotions difficult to handle

Imp (imp) – the least of the lesser daemons, these small creatures are the pests of the Nine Hells – they make themselves present whenever there is any type of activity

Karlisle (kar-lyle) – the realm neighboring Elvandahar on the other side of the Denegal River

Kleyshes (klie-shays) – one of the five domains of Elvandahar

Krathil-lon (kruh-thil-lon) – a forested glen located within the southern reaches of the Sartingel Mountains – it is where Father Dremathian and his druidical Order resides

Kyrrean (kie-reen) – large blond felines with dark brown dappling and oversized paws – they make their existence on the warm temperate plains and borderlands

Larian (layr-ee-an) – with only minor differences, these are smaller cousins to the lloryk – they are able to carry faelin and most humans

Leschera (lesh-er-uh) – very gentle, larian-sized, deer-like creatures that grace the temperate woodlands

Lloryk (loor-ik) – large muscular equine-like creatures that are able to carry humans and small orocs – they are omnivorous and beneath the top coat of silky fur, have modified hair shafts that appear similar to scales one would see on a reptile

Lycanthrope (lie-kan-thrope) – one afflicted with the disease of lycanthropy – they are humans, faelin, or hafen that can transform into animals (usually wemic, althothere, or kyrrean) – the disease is spread by the bite, and only those who have no tendencies towards evil can resist it

Mane (main) – a lesser daemon – they stand only about 2 ft. tall and have vulture-like features - tend to go wherever there is the opportunity to wreak any kind of havoc or chaos

Mehta (may-tuh) – the title given to the leader of the Daemundai

Meriliam (mer-il-lee-am) – one of the three moons of Shandahar

Merzillith (mir-zil-lith) – otherwise known as a mind flayer, this intermediate daemon is from one of the Nine Hells – it has psionic power, the ability to use the energy of the world in a way that is different than the magic that is used by mages

Mirpur (mir-poor) – one of the five domains of Elvandahar

Monaf (mon-af) – the realm neighboring Torimir on the other side of the Ratik Mountains

Morden (mor-den) – one of the halfen sub-races – they live in deep caverns within the mountains

Oorg (oorg) – one of the humanoid races of Shandahar, they are even larger than orocs and are often called giants – they often fight with brute strength alone, but are not good with any type of real strategy

Oroc (or-ok) – one of the native races of Shandahar – they are muscular and broad, standing at least six to seven feet tall – faelin are their greatest enemies, and the two races find any excuse to maim and kill one another

Pact of Bakharas (bak-hair-us) – an agreement between daemon and dragon kind that does not allow one or the other too much influence over Shandahar

Papas fruit (pay-pas) – a small pink orb about the size of a nectarine – it grows on the papas tree, which is prevalent throughout the temperate borderlands of Shandahar

Recondian (re-con-dee-an) – one of the sub-races of humans – they live in the central region of the continent

Reshik-na (resh-ik-na) – an Order of druids that lives within the Elvandaharian domain of Filopar

Rezwithrys (rez-with-ris) – the largest of the dragon sub-races – at maturity their color ranges from silver to steel blue to metallic violet – they have a propensity for magic

Samshin/Samshae (sam-shin/sam-shay) – the son/daughter of the hamzin or hamza

Sangrilak (sang-ri-lak) – city located within the northwestern quadrant of the realm of Torimir – it is the place of Adrianna and Sheridana's birth

Savanlean (sav-an-lee-an) – one of the sub-races of faelin – they live in majestic cities built into mountainsides located in the more northern regions of the continent

Serenitee (sir-en-i-tee) – one of the worlds of the Seven Heavens

Shagendra (shuh-gen-dra) – the root from this plant can be used to make a person's mind vulnerable to suggestions – also causes general lethargy, dulls the senses, and slows reflexes

Steralion (stir-a-lee-an) – one of the three moons of Shandahar

Tabanakh drink (ta-ban-ak) – a drink prepared by the druid elders as a right of initiation for their tyros – it has properties that exaggerate the visions of those who are so Gifted

Terralean (ter-a-lee-an) – one of the faelin sub-races – they inhabit many of the borderlands between the forests and steppes and are the most widespread

Thalden (thal-den) – one of the halfen sub-races – they live within the temperate hills

Thritean (thrye-teen) – very large silver felines with black striping and six legs – they live in cold northern forests

Torimir (tor-eh-meer) – the realm neighboring Elvandahar on the other side of the Terrestra River

Tremidian (tre-mid-ee-an) – one of the human sub-races – they live on the eastern side of the continent

Trolag (trol-ag) – one of the humanoid races of Shandahar, they are tall and stooped, their long, gangly bodies covered with dark brown wiry hair – they have the ability to heal quickly

Umberhulk (um-ber-hulk) – large, stout beasts of burden with thick umber colored skin that is virtually devoid of hair – used to pull carts in the towns and villages and many times even in the caravan trains

Varanghelie Vault (vair-an-gay-lee) – a highly protected storage facility located within Andahye – it is where many people keep their most valuable possessions

Wemic (wee-mik) – in some places better known as wolves, these animals appear to be distant cousins to the corubis – they run in temperate to sub-arctic forests and have never been tamed

Wraith (rayth) – a corpse that has been re-animated – they are mindless, following the commands of their necromantic masters – their bodies are ravaged by the effects of decay and they wield only the simplest of weapons

Wyvern (why vern)   a large snake like creature with four stubby legs and a poisonous barbed tip on its long sinuous tail – it lives in shallow caverns in temperate climes

Zacrol (zak-rol) – the equivalent of about a mile